Chronicle of the Murdered House

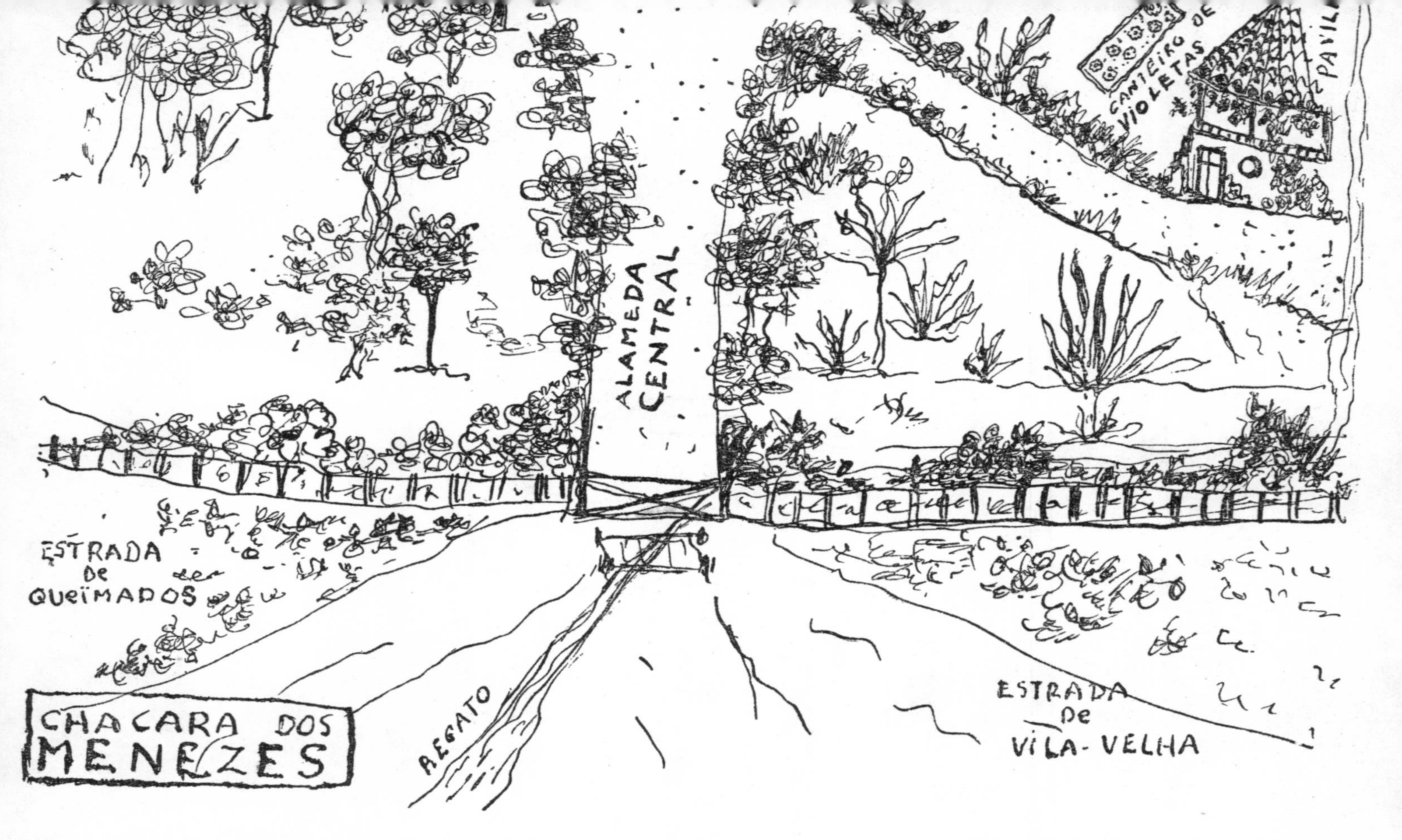
CHACARA DOS
MENEZES
ESTRADA
DE
QUEIMADOS
REGATO
ALAMEDA
CENTRAL
CANTEIRO DE
VIOLETAS
PAVIL
ESTRADA
DE
VILA-VELHA

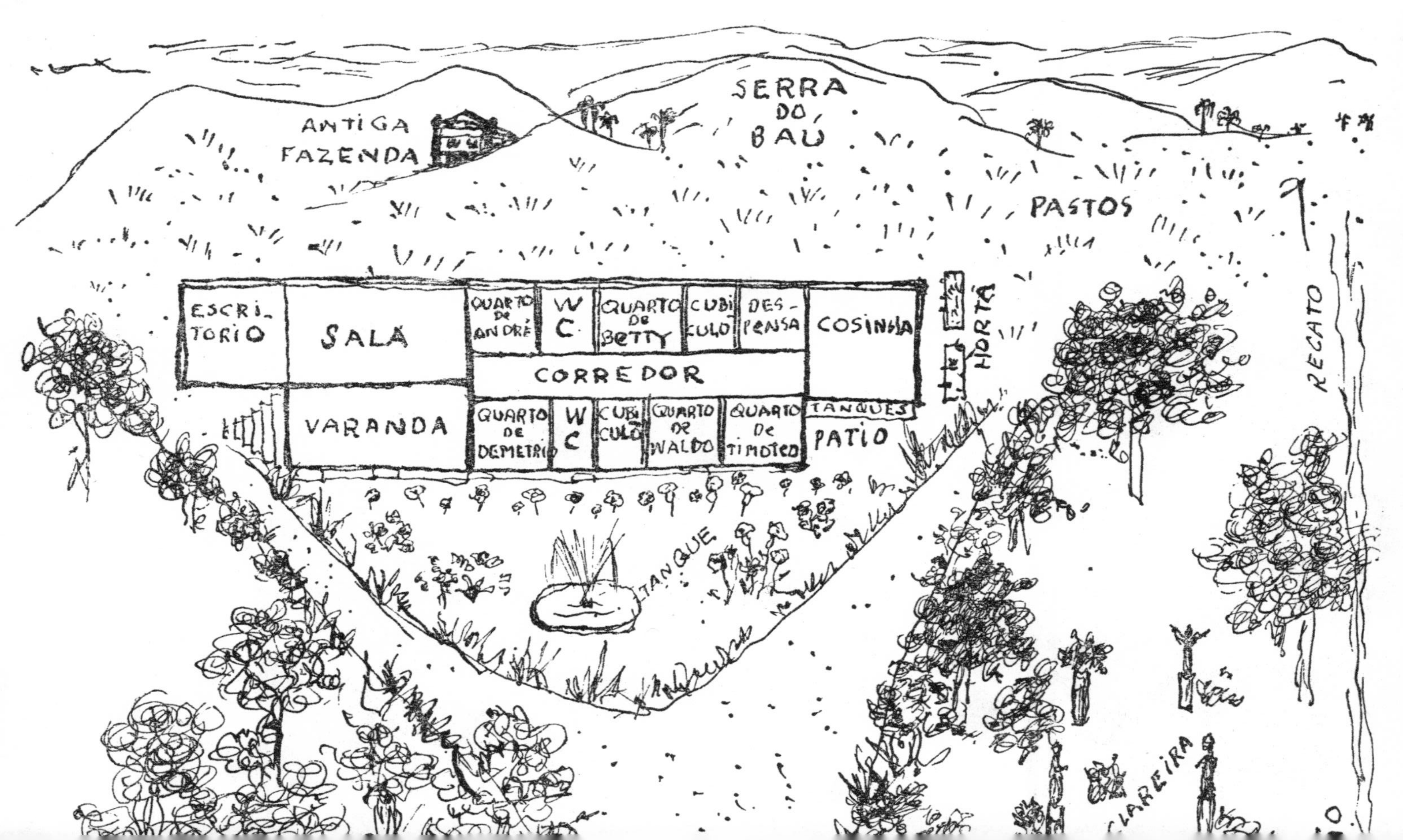
SERRA DO BAÚ
ANTIGA FAZENDA
PASTOS
ESCRI-TORIO
SALA
QUARTO DE ANDRÉ
WC
QUARTO DE BETTY
CUBÍCULO
DES-PENSA
COSINHA
CORREDOR
VARANDA
QUARTO DE DEMETRIO
WC
CUBÍCULO
QUARTO DE WALDO
QUARTO DE TIMOTEO
TANQUES
PATIO
HORTÃ
RECATO
TANQUE
CLAREIRA

Translated from the Portuguese
by Margaret Jull Costa & Robin Patterson

Chronicle of the Murdered House

Lúcio Cardoso

Biographical Note by Benjamin Moser

First published in Brazil as *Crônica da casa assassinada*

First edition, 2016

Map (pp. ii-iii) is from the 1st ed. of the original 1959 publication in Portuguese.
Painting (p. viii) is from Benjamin Moser's personal collection.

Library of Congress Cataloging-in-Publication Data:

Names: Cardoso, Lúcio, 1912-1968, author. | Moser, Benjamin, writer of introduction. | Costa, Margaret Jull, translator.
Title: Chronicle of the murdered house / Lúcio Cardoso ; translated by Margaret Jull Costa and Robin Patterson ; introduction by Benjamin Moser.
Other titles: Crônica de casa assassinada. English
Description: Rochester, NY : Open Letter, 2016.
Identifiers: LCCN 2016020063 (print) | LCCN 2016024405 (ebook) | ISBN 9781940953502 (paperback) | ISBN 1940953502 (paperback) | ISBN 9781940953519 (e-book) | ISBN 1940953510 (e-book)
Subjects: LCSH: Families—Brazil—Minas Gerais—Fiction. | Gay men—Brazil—Minas Gerais—Fiction. | Psychological fiction. | BISAC: FICTION / Literary. | FICTION / Classics. | FICTION / Gay. | HISTORY / Latin America / South America.
Classification: LCC PQ9697.C256 C713 2016 (print) | LCC PQ9697.C256 (ebook) | DDC 869.3/42—dc23
LC record available at https://lccn.loc.gov/2016020063

Work published with the support of the Brazilian Ministry of Culture / National Library Foundation
Obra publicada com o apoio do Ministério da Cultura do Brasil / Fundação Biblioteca Nacional

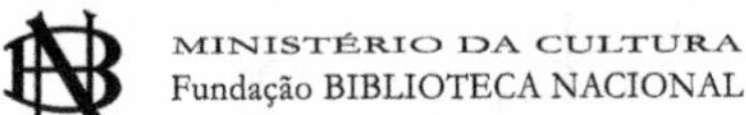

This project is supported in part by an award from the National Endowment for the Arts

Printed on acid-free paper in the United States of America.

Text set in Caslon, a family of serif typefaces based on the designs of William Caslon (1692–1766).

Design by N. J. Furl

Open Letter is the University of Rochester's nonprofit, literary translation press:
Lattimore Hall 411, Box 270082, Rochester, NY 14627

www.openletterbooks.org

For Vito Pentagna

LÚCIO-62

Biographical Note: Bette Davis in Yoknapatawpha

by Benjamin Moser

I keep a tiny watercolor on a bookshelf in my house. It is only a few inches square, slightly larger than a playing card. To all appearances, it is the work of a child: some dabs of color transversed by two black slashes. It looks like something an encouraging parent might have stuck to the refrigerator—but it may be the most poignant thing I own.

In the bottom right corner, in tiny script, someone—not the artist—has written LÚCIO 62. Those characters let it be dated to within a few weeks. It was made in the last days of 1962 by the Brazilian writer Lúcio Cardoso, fifty years old and at the height of his powers when he suffered a stroke on December 7. He would linger another six years, paralyzed, unable to speak or write, devoting his remaining time to making paintings like these. This smear is what remained of one of the most prodigiously gifted artists of twentieth-century Brazil.

It is tempting to read symbols into these blotches. Are those black lines a sign of despair? Is that yellow half-circle a setting sun?

•

Today, Lúcio Cardoso is primarily remembered for two things: being gay, and being loved by Clarice Lispector, from whose great name his is inseparable. While still a student, the eighteen-year-old Clarice took a job at a government propaganda outfit called the Agência Nacional. There, among the bored young staff, was Lúcio, a twenty-six-year-old from a small town who was already hailed as one of the most talented writers of his generation.

His father, Joaquim Lúcio Cardoso, had studied engineering but left university without a degree, due to the death of his own father. He then headed into the backlands of the interior state of Minas Gerais, where he enjoyed a period of great prosperity, at one time accumulating eight thousand head of cattle, only to be forced to hand over his fortune to a textile factory owner to whom he was indebted. After the death of his wife, he created a soap factory; but his volatile personality brought him trouble with the local merchants, who boycotted his products. His business ventures failed, Joaquim and his second wife, Dona Nhanhá, raised their six children in relative poverty.

Their town of Curvelo was typical of the backwoods of Minas Gerais, a state said to imprint a special character on its inhabitants, and one whose personality occupies a prominent place in Brazilian mythology. The *mineiros,* the stereotype goes, are tight-fisted, wary, and religious; there is a joke that Minas dining tables have drawers built into them, the better, at the first approach of a visitor, to hide food from potential guests. It is a place where mannered elocutions play an important role in the local language. Nobody in Minas is crazy, or *louco*; the preferred euphemism is "systematic." There is a taboo against overt descriptions of medical procedures: "They opened him, and closed him back up" is the most that can be conceded of a surgery. A *mineiro,* above all, does not draw attention to himself. One native, returning home from São Paulo, recalls his puzzlement at being the object of amazed stares. He finally realized that it was because he was wearing a red shirt.

That was in the capital, Belo Horizonte, one of Brazil's largest and most modern cities, in the 1960s. Four decades earlier, in the no-name village of Curvelo, it was presumably even easier to provoke a scandal. And nobody did it quite as well as Joaquin and Nhanhá Cardoso's youngest son, Lúcio, who refused to go to school, was obsessed with movie stars, and played with dolls. This last point especially galled his father, who fought with his wife about it. "It's your fault," he would charge, "you brought him up clinging to your skirts, and the result is this queer. Where did you ever hear of a boy playing with dolls? Why doesn't he like playing with the other boys? He's a nervous child who's never going to amount to anything."

It was impossible to keep him in school, but he was curious about everything, and his older sister, Maria Helena, who became the best chronicler of his life, oriented his reading. This ranged from Dostoyevsky to the romantic novels serialized in the newspapers, which Lúcio and Maria Helena followed avidly. In his teens, the family moved to Rio de Janeiro, and he was sent to boarding school, where he was predictably miserable, and he eventually ended up working at an insurance company, A Equitativa, run by his uncle. "I was always a terrible employee," he said. "All I did was write poetry."

But he was finally free and in the capital. He was twenty-two when, in 1934, with the help of the Catholic poet and industrialist Augusto Frederico Schmidt, he published his first novel, *Maleita*. By the time he published his third novel, *The Light in the Basement,* two years later, he had attracted the attention of Brazil's ultimate cultural arbiter, Mário de Andrade, who dispatched a typically colorful letter from São Paulo. "Artistically it is terrible," Andrade thundered. "Socially it is detestable. But I understood its point . . . to return the spiritual dimension to the materialistic literature that is now being made in Brazil. God has returned to stir the face of the waters. Finally."

•

One reason for Mário de Andrade's enthusiasm, no matter how grudgingly expressed, was that Lúcio Cardoso's early books represented a real revolution in Brazilian literature. This literature had been nationalistic, consumed with questions of Brazil and Brazilianness: "Whoever examines the Brazilian literature of the present day immediately recognizes its primary trait, a certain instinct of nationality," Brazil's classic novelist Machado de Assis wrote in 1873. "Poetry, novels, all … dress themselves in the colors of the country." The result was that Brazilian literature was mostly a literature about Brazil, and only to a much lesser degree a literature written by Brazilians. It was local, regional, and patriotic, written by self-conscious Brazilians dedicated to creating, or opposing, a certain image of Brazil. They celebrated the country's particularities—its natural beauty, its history, its popular culture, the heritage of the Indian and the African—and they denounced its social problems, its poverty, its injustice, its failure to live up to its apparently limitless potential. Most often they did both.

This literature, above all, was materialistic, rather than spiritual, which is why Mário de Andrade, despite his reservations about the book's artistic and social qualities, welcomed Lúcio Cardoso's *The Light in the Basement*. God had, indeed, returned to stir the waters. Lúcio was not the first godly writer to appear in those years: there was the "introspective school," whose concerns were less social and national than internal and spiritual. Many of these writers were Catholic, and many, like Mário de Andrade himself, were gay. In that time and place, the alliance with religion made more sense than it would later seem. The Church was a logical home, and not only because it had always been full of gay men, offering redemption to those weighed down by the awareness of sin. Such people did not see art as a way of addressing social issues, or of refining the national language, or of asserting the preeminence of one political party over another. Their mission was much more urgent: they sought to be saved through art. Writing was for them a spiritual exercise, not an intellectual one.

•

Fellow writer Clarice Lispector was not the only one to fall in love with Lúcio. He was strikingly handsome, brilliantly witty, and endlessly creative. "It just poured out of him!" said a friend. He would sit in cafés, writing one page after another, tearing one sheet out of the typewriter and immediately beginning another. He completed his novel *Inácio* in a mere four days. "What a verbal talent he had, my God, Lúcio Cardoso," another friend recalled. "And what an ability to work, even though he stayed out all night drinking. He got up early and wrote, wrote, wrote. What he published isn't half of what he wrote."

Lúcio was a natural writer, a natural talker, and a natural seducer. On his first meeting with Luiz Carlos Lacerda, a teenager who later became a well-known film director, he scribbled off a poem for him and then took him back to his apartment. Lacerda, young and naïve, assumed they would live happily ever after. A few days later he was devastated when he went to Lúcio's apartment in Ipanema, saw the light on, rang the doorbell, and got no answer. After waiting a while he saw another boy emerge and understood that he had been just another notch on the bedpost.

But Lúcio never had a lasting relationship. As anguished and tormented as the characters in his books, he apparently never wanted one either, though he was constantly falling in love with different men. When he died, Clarice wrote, "In so many things, we were so fantastic that, if it hadn't been for the impossibility, we might have gotten married." Clarice's friend Rosa Cass disagrees, seeing a different impossibility. "It wasn't just that he was gay," she emphasizes. "They were too much alike. He needed his solitude, he was a 'star,' unearthly. The two of them would have been an impossible couple." This was probably just as well, because anecdotes suggest that Lúcio would have made a difficult spouse.

"Lúcio went crazy, Helena," a coworker told his sister when she arrived at his office in downtown Rio. "He sold me a suit because he needed money and now he's amusing himself by throwing bills and coins out of the window, half of what I just paid him." "I went to the window," Maria Helena writes, "laughing myself. Below, the Rua Álvaro Alvim was full of people, and more were streaming in every minute, attracted by the noise of the crowd chasing after the money that was ceaselessly falling from that miraculous window."

The prankishness also had a dark side. Once he told people that he had hired someone to kill him, the better to comprehend the feeling of being persecuted. He did not need to resort to such theatrics. The tenants' union in his building tried to kick him out in a letter that made reference to Oscar Wilde. He himself repeatedly tried to correct his homosexuality, sometimes even punishing himself like a medieval penitent. "This perpetual tendency to self-destruction," he wrote. "Yes, it has long been inside me, and I know it as a sick man comes to understand his own illness." He began to drink.

•

Lúcio features in Clarice Lispector's longest and most ambitious piece of early writing, an enigmatic novella from October 1941 called "Obsession." It introduces a dark character, Daniel, who will reappear at length in her second novel, *The Chandelier*, published in 1946: Lúcio Cardoso, the seductive guide through occult realms. He had a direct hand in her first novel. "Groping in the darkness," she pieced the book together by jotting down ideas in a notebook whenever they occurred to her. At length the book took shape, but she feared it was more a pile of notes than a full-fledged novel. Lúcio assured her that the fragments were a book in themselves, and suggested a title, borrowed from James Joyce's *Portrait of the Artist as a Young Man*: "He was alone. He was unheeded, happy, and near to the wild heart of life." This became the book's epigraph. The title, *Near to the Wild Heart*, became famous, it stands out in Clarice's work, perhaps because it sounds so mannered, so much like the title of a teen romance, so much like—one might say—the title of a book by Lúcio Cardoso. Clarice left Rio soon after its publication, living abroad for the best part of the next two decades.

Lúcio, however, remained in Rio, writing one book after another, trying, almost singlehandedly, to remake Brazilian culture. The boy who had dreamed of film stars in his small backwater in Minas Gerais set up his own Chamber Theater. "Lúcio Cardoso—I remember well—attributed great importance to his work in the theater," said his friend the novelist Otávio de Faria. "It was inevitable, since he himself was essentially more a 'tragedian' than a novelist." His theatrical work was artistically avant-garde and politically far ahead of his time, nowhere more than in racial questions. Though slavery had not been outlawed until 1888, within the living memory of many Brazilians, the country's elite held as a doctrine of faith that the country did not suffer racial divisions. He participated in the Black Experimental Theater of Abdias do Nascimento, an early Afro-Brazilian activist, writing a biblical drama called *The Prodigal Son*, performed with an all-black cast. If such productions were radical in the United States, they were unheard-of in Brazil.

Despite all the group's efforts, the play flopped. His sister recalled her "anguish seeing Pascola, the most renowned theater critic of the day, snoozing in the front row." Undaunted, convinced that theater was a weak area in Brazilian culture, Lúcio produced his own *The Silver String* in 1947. "I cannot recall a more carefully prepared, better worked-out, more impressive spectacle for our little group around Lúcio," Otávio de Faria recalled. "Ester Leão was the director and Lúcio Cardoso submitted (though, it is true, sometimes almost screaming) to all her demands. Sometimes I saw him on the verge of tears. It doesn't matter. The play opened, and the actress Alma Flora got almost all the applause."

Enthusiasm ran high, as always with Lúcio's undertakings. "I remember it like it was today," de Faria continued, adding:

> Lúcio Cardoso, wild about the new "diva" (he never got over his "passion" for Italian film divas), ordered up a huge "banquet," at Lapa 49, to commemorate Alma Flora's breakthrough. No end to the beer and the fresh crabs—except that there wasn't any money to pay for it . . . and there, in the middle of the table, a magnificent centerpiece of red roses (red, of course! . . .) dedicated to the diva being honored. It was a great party, one of the few happy, successful ones I can remember. It really was a breakthrough—not for Alma Flora, nor for Maria Sampaio (another actress, splendid, by the way), nor for Ester Leão, a notable director—but for Lúcio Cardoso, one of our greatest playwrights.

The inevitable hangover soon arrived. "Despite this great success, even '*d'estime*' (in relation to the earlier plays), it was still a complete professional failure. It vanished without a trace."

But it was typical of Lúcio to infect a group of Brazil's most talented artists, an astonishing number of whom participated in this production alone, with his extravagant dreams. "Ipanema ought to be called 'Lúcio Cardoso,'" one friend said. "I am not a writer," he himself said, "I am an atmosphere." His sister Maria Helena captured the power of his irrepressible enthusiasm:

> I remember Nonô [her pet name for him] so joyful, his head full of fantasies, especially when thinking of traveling, and still young, with several books published and many still to be written, deciding to be a rancher

> someday. Infected by his enthusiasm, by the power of his faith and of his imagination, I seriously believed in all his whims, even the most impossible things. For me, it was all feasible, nothing was impossible for him, whom I admired above all else: novels, poems, beautiful plantations conjured out of nothing. His slightest dreams were realities for me, such was the force of his imagination.

Yet his failures, too, were typical. Despite his volcanic creativity and the admiration he inspired from the leading artists of his generation, Lúcio would never enjoy the fame to which his talent seemed to entitle him. His theatrical ventures had come to nothing, and his writing was met with incomprehension. In 1959 he published his masterpiece, *Chronicle of the Murdered House*, a long novel set in his native Minas Gerais, an attack on "Minas, in its flesh and spirit," a meditation on good and evil and God.

Its setting, the decaying mansion of the once-grand Meneses family, and its themes, including the ways that one generation's sins are visited upon its descendants, are redolent of Faulkner; but its charm resides in the ways Lúcio marries those themes to what can only be called camp: as if Bette Davis had wandered, bewigged and in full makeup, into Yoknapatawpha. The figure of Timóteo, the semi-deranged cross-dressing scion of the decadent dynasty, has no precedents in Brazilian literature, and, almost certainly, no descendants: a not-quite-caricature of a man trapped between his own nature and the expectations of family and society, and who, unable to escape, wavers between alcoholism and hysteria. The character of Timóteo may be seen as representing all those gay people, in Brazil or anywhere else, for whom an adequate language had not been found, and who desperately sought some means of expression.

There had always been certain limited places for gay people in Brazil: they had taken a leading role in making Rio's Carnival the most opulent in the world; and a leading role, too, in religion: in

Catholicism and, even more notably, as priests, soothsayers, and palm readers in the African-descended religions. Shut out of so many areas, they became gatekeepers of their own domains: organizers and collectors, tastemakers and decorators. One area they were shut out of was literature: they had turned up occasionally in Brazilian books, notably in Adolfo Caminha's short *Bom-Crioulo* of 1895. But even gay writers (Caminha seems not to have been gay) wrapped a *cordon sanitaire* around gay lives: Mário de Andrade's story "Frederico Paciência," for example, was only published posthumously, and though it was ahead of its time—it was begun in the twenties and appeared in 1947—its hesitations and implied condemnation of homosexual love leave it far behind ours.

Appearing in this context of no context, Lúcio Cardoso's *Chronicle* predictably scandalized the more predictably scandalizable critics. In words that hint at Lúcio's affinity with Clarice Lispector, his champion Otávio de Faria answered those critics: "Are we going to leave off on our attempts to reconstruct the world, this tremendous responsibility, on which our salvation may depend, in order to obey a half-dozen prejudices?"

•

On December 7, 1962, a lifetime of heavy drinking and drug abuse finally caught up with Lúcio Cardoso. To what extent did these addictions have to do with his sexuality? Even in our far freer times, and as evidenced in numerous studies and articles, substance abuse is notoriously higher among gay people, a toll largely attributable to homophobic discrimination and bullying.

Earlier that year, in May, he had had a warning. Arriving at his home in Ipanema, his sister Maria Helena "saw the muscles in his face ceaselessly trembling, while he, in the greatest affliction, tried to calm them with his hand." The crisis passed, but the doctor was clear. "Look, Lúcio, what you had was just a spasm, leaving your mouth a bit crooked and that drawling way of speaking. Thank God, because it could have been much worse. With time, if you keep doing your exercises in front of the mirror, everything will return to normal. But from now on don't overdo it, don't drink, don't wear yourself out partying, try to lead a calmer life, since if you go on like before something worse can happen." Despite his sister's desperate attempts to help him, he refused to heed the doctor's warning. "I'm not a child for you to be taking care of me," he told Maria Helena. "Don't touch those bottles! If I want to drink, neither you nor anybody else is going to stop me." Later, Maria Helena would write:

> I'll never forget that date: December 7, 1962. It was a calm day, completely normal, until the afternoon. Between six-thirty and seven the phone rang.
>
> "Lelena, I'm at Lazzarini's house, helping out with a dinner for his friends."
>
> I recognized the voice of Nonô, whom I hadn't seen in more than two days. He sometimes vanished like that for a week, which worried me after his spasm.
>
> "Be careful, don't drink, don't take any pills."
>
> "Relax, I'm being a saint."

Later that night, not having heard from him, she went to his apartment, directly behind hers. She found the door unlocked, which she thought was strange. She went in and discovered her brother gravely ill. Terrified, she called an ambulance; that night he fell into a coma. He emerged from the coma, but a massive stroke had left him permanently paralyzed. He would never again be able to speak normally. His writing career was over.

Maria Helena cared for him for years, always hoping that their attempts at rehabilitation would allow him to resume his career. It was a painful struggle, days of hope punctuated by weeks and months of despair. In a moment of frustration, trying to get him to do his exercises, Maria Helena told him:

> "You're very stubborn, that's why so much has happened to you. Remember when you had your first sickness, just a spasm? I begged you, but you kept on drinking and popping pills. Did it work, your stubbornness?"
>
> He got even more irritated and to my surprise said:
>
> "It did. I died."

Nursed by Maria Helena, Lúcio eventually become a talented painter, using only his left hand. The little watercolor on my shelf eventually grew into full-fledged scenes, and before his death he would show these paintings in four different exhibitions. In the eloquent memoir Maria Helena published at Clarice's suggestion, she records his painful, fitful, exhausting progress—until, miraculously, he finally managed to start writing again.

"Can be 100 years—I have in the spirit young—life, happiness, everything!" he scrawled. "I, writer by fate." "I looked at him with great affection and admiration. God had tried him in the cruelest way yet he had more happiness and love in his heart than sadness and bitterness. The dark days passed quickly, followed by light, much light." After saying it for years in order to keep up his spirits, Maria Helena could finally exclaim, this time with conviction, "Darling, the day is not far off when you will be able to write novels again."

The end soon followed, on September 22, 1968. When he was already in a coma, Clarice visited him. "I didn't go to the wake, nor to the funeral, nor to the mass because there was too much silence within me. In those days I was alone, I couldn't see people: I had seen death."

Chronicle of the Murdered House

Contents

"Take away the stone," he said. "But, Lord," said Martha, the sister of the dead man, "by this time there is a bad odor, for he has been there four days. Then Jesus said, "Did I not tell you that if you believe, you will see the glory of God?"

—John 11, 39-40

I.

André's Diary [conclusion]

18th . . . 19 . . . – (. . . what exactly does death mean? Once she's far from me—her mortal remains buried beneath the earth—how long will I have to go on retracing the path she taught me, her admirable lesson of love, how long will I keep trying to find in other women, in all the many women one meets throughout one's life, the velvet of her kisses—"this was how *she* used to kiss"—her way of smiling, the same rebellious lock of hair –and who will help me rebuild, out of grief and longing, that unique image gone forever? And what does "forever" mean—the harsh, pompous echo of those words rings down the deserted hallways of the soul—the "forever" that is, in fact, meaningless, not even a visible moment in the very instant in which we think it, and yet that is all we have, because it is the one definitive word available to us in our scant earthly vocabulary . . .

Yes, what does "forever" mean, save the continuous, fluid existence of everything cut free from contingency, of everything that changes and evolves and breaks ceaselessly on the shores of equally mutable feelings? There was no point in trying to hide: the "forever" was there before my eyes. A minute, a single minute—and that, too, would escape any attempt to grasp it, while I myself will escape and slip away—also forever—and like a pile of cold, futile flotsam, all my love and pain and even my faithfulness will drift away—forever. Yes, what else is "forever" but the final image of this world, and not just this world, but any world that we bind together with the illusory architecture of dreams and permanence—all our games and pleasures, all our ills and fears, loves and betrayals—it is, in short, the impulse that shapes not our everyday self, but the possible, never-achieved self that we pursue as one might pursue the trail of a never-to-be-requited love, and that becomes, in the end, only the memory of a lost love—but lost where and when?—in a place we do not know, but whose loss pierces us and, whether justifiably or not, hurls every one of us into that nothing or that all-consuming everything where we vanish into the general, the absolute, the perfection we so utterly lack.)

. . . All day I wandered about the empty house, unable to dredge up even enough courage to enter the drawing room. Ah, how painfully intense was the knowledge that she no longer belonged to me, that she was merely a piece of plunder to be manhandled by strangers without tenderness or understanding. Somewhere far from me, very far, they would be uncovering her now defenseless body, and with the sad diligence of the indifferent, would dress her for the last time, never even imagining that her flesh had once been alive and had often trembled with love—that she had once been younger, more splendid than all the world's most blossoming youth. No, this was not the right death for her, at least, I had never imagined it would be like this, in the few difficult moments when I could imagine it—so brutal, so final, so unfair, like a young plant being torn from the earth.

But there was no point in remembering what she had been—or, rather, what *we* had been. Therein lay the explanation: two beings hurled into the maelstrom of one exceptional circumstance and suddenly stopped, brought up short—she, her face frozen in its final, dying expression, and me, still standing, although God knows for how long, my body still shaken by the last echo of that experience. I wanted only to wander through the rooms, as bare now as the stage when the principal actor has made his final exit—and all the weariness of the last few days washed over me, and I was filled by a sense of emptiness, not an ordinary emptiness, but the total emptiness that suddenly and forcefully replaces everything that was once impulse and vibrancy. Blindly, as if in obedience to a will not my own, I opened doors, leaned out of windows, walked through rooms: the house no longer existed.

Knowing this put me beyond consolation; no affectionate, no despairing words could touch me. Like a stock pot removed from the flame, but in whose depths the remnants still boil and bubble, what gave me courage were my memories of the days I had just lived through. Meanwhile, as if prompted by a newfound strength, I managed, once or twice, to go over to the room where she lay and half-open the door to watch what was happening from a distance. Everything was now so repellently banal: it could have been the same scene I had known as a child, had it not been transfigured, as if by a potent, irresistible exhalation, by the supernatural breath that fills any room touched by the presence of a corpse. The dining table, which, during its long life, had witnessed so many meals, so many family meetings and councils—and how often, around those same boards, had Nina herself been judged and dissected?—had been turned into a temporary bier. On each corner, placed there with inevitable haste, stood four solitary candles. Cheap, ordinary candles, doubtless found at the bottom of some forgotten drawer. And to think that this was the backdrop to her final farewell, the stage on which she would say her last goodbye.

I would again close the door, feeling how impossible it was for me to imagine her dead. No other being had seemed safer from, more immune to extinction. Even in her final days, when there was clearly no other possible denouement, even when, terrified, I understood from the silence and the stillness that she was condemned to die, even then I could not imagine her in the situation I saw her in now, lying on the table, wrapped in a sheet, her hands bound together in prayer, her eyes closed, her nose unexpectedly aquiline (I remembered her voice: "My father always said I had some Jewish blood in me . . ."). No other being had ever been more intensely caught up in the dynamic mechanism of life, and her laughter, her voice, her whole presence, was a miracle we believed would survive all disasters.

However hard I try to conjure her back, she is no longer here. So why speak of or even think these things? Sometimes, awareness of my loss strikes through me like lightning: I see her dead then, and such is the pain of losing her that I almost stop breathing. Why, why, I mutter to myself. I lean against the wall, the blood rushes to my head, my heart pounds furiously. What pain is this that afflicts me, what emotion, what new depths of insecurity, what is this complete and utter lack of faith or interest in my fellow human beings? But these feelings last only a fraction of a second. The sheer energy of our shared existence, the fact that she was still alive yesterday, that she touched my arm with her still warm hands and made a simple request, like asking me to close a window, all this restores to me an apparent calm, and slowly I repeat to myself: it's true, but I no longer feel the same utter despair, my blood does not rise up before the undeniable truth that she is dead—and I feel as if I no longer believed it, that a last glimmer of hope still burned inside me. Deep in some passive corner of my mind, I imagine that, tomorrow, she will demand that I bring her some flowers, the same flowers that surrounded her in the last days, not as an adornment or a consolation, but as a frantic, desperate attempt to conceal the indiscreet presence of unavoidable tragedy. Everything grows quiet inside me, and that lie brings me back to life. I continue to imagine that soon I will go down the steps into the garden and pick violets from the bed nearest the Pavilion, where there are still clumps of violets to be found in the undergrowth; I imagine that if I walk around the garden, as I have done every day, I will be able to make up a small bouquet of violets and wrap them in a scented mallow leaf, while I repeat over and over, as if those words were capable of devouring the last shreds of reality: "It's for her, these flowers are for her." A kind of hallucination overwhelms me; I can hear her slow, soft voice, saying: "Put the flowers on the window sill, my love." And at last I see her, intact, perfect and eternal in her triumph, sitting next to me, pressing the violets to her face.

Slowly I return to the world. Not far off, probably out on the verandah, a woman remarks how hot it is and mops her brow. I try to recast the spell—in vain, the voice has gone. Through the window, I see the sun beating down on the parched flower beds. Feeling my way cautiously through a now unrecognizable world, I walk down the hallway to the room where the body has been laid out. I know there must be a look of almost criminal hunger on my face, but what does it matter? I hurl myself on the coffin, indifferent to everything and everyone around me. I see Donana de Lara draw back in horror, and Aunt Ana regards me with evident disgust. Two pale hands, sculpted out of silence and greed, smooth the wrinkled sheet—I imagine they belong to Uncle Demétrio. But what do I care about any of them? Nothing more exists of the one thing that united us: Nina. Now, as far as I'm concerned, they have all been relegated to the past along with other nameless, useless things. I see her adored face, and am amazed to find it so serene, so distant from me, her adored son, who so often covered with kisses and tears that brow growing pale beneath the departing warmth, the son who kissed her now tightly closed lips, who touched the weary curve of her breast, kissed her belly, legs and feet, who lived only for her love—and I, too, died a little in every vein in my body, every hair on my head, every drop of blood, in my mouth, my voice—in every pulsing source of energy in my body—when she agreed to die, and to die without me . . .

. . . on the penultimate night, as we were waiting for the end, she seemed suddenly to get better and allowed me to come to her. I hadn't seen her for days because, out of sheer caprice and because she was generally in such a foul mood even the doctor was frightened, she had forbidden all visits and ordered that no one should enter her room: she wanted to die alone. From a distance, and despite the darkness in the room—for she only rarely allowed the shutters to be opened—I could make out her weary head resting on a pile of pillows, her hair all disheveled, as if she had long since ceased to care. At that moment, I confess, my courage almost failed me and I could take not a single step forward: a cold sweat broke out on my brow. However, it did not take me long to recognize her old self, since she immediately addressed me in her usual reproving tones:

"Ah, it's you, André. How could you be so inconsiderate when the doctor has plainly said that I must have complete and utter rest?"

Then in a slightly gentler tone:

"Besides, what are you doing in my room?"

Despite these words, she knew perfectly well, especially at that precise moment, that there was no need for either of us to pretend. I hadn't asked to come in, she had been the one to order that her bedroom door be opened—giving in to who knows what impulse, what inner need to know what was happening outside her room? Perhaps she knew that for hours and hours, and days and days, I had not left her door, alert to any sign of life within—a thread of light, a whiff of medicine, an echo—for the slightest sound or sight or smell was enough to make my heart beat faster with anxiety. And so I bowed my head and said nothing. I would do anything, absolutely anything, to be allowed to stay a little longer by her side. Even if she were dying, even if the breath were slowly fading from her lips, I wanted to be there, I wanted to feel that human mechanism continuing to vibrate until the final spring broke. Seeing me so silent, Nina raised herself up a little on the pillows, gave a sigh, and asked me to bring her a mirror. "I just want to fix my face," she said. And as I was about to leave, she called me back. This time her voice sounded quite different, almost affectionate, very like the way in which she used to speak to me. I turned, and she asked me to bring not only a mirror, but also a comb, a bottle of lotion and some face powder.

She said this in an almost playful tone, but I wasn't fooled and could sense the silent, bitter agitation beating inside her. I hurried off to find these various things and returned to her side, eager to detect in this gay façade some flicker of genuine joy. She took the mirror first and, as if to avoid a nasty shock, very gingerly turned to regard her reflection—she looked at herself for some time, then again sighed and shrugged, as if to say: "What do I care? The day is sure to come when I'll have to resign myself to not being pretty anymore." It was true that she was very far from what she had been, but the same mysterious attraction that had once so captivated me was still there. That simple shrug of the shoulders was proof to me that the idea of dying was further from her mind than it seemed. This impression was confirmed when, leaning slightly on my arm, she asked in a voice that struggled to be confidential, but succeeded only in expressing a certain repressed anxiety:

"Tell me, André, does he know the state I'm in, does he know I'm at death's door? Does he know this is the end?"

She was looking at me challengingly, and her whole being, concentrated and intent, was asking: "Can't you see that I'm suffering in vain. You can tell me the truth, I know I'm not dying, that my hour has not yet come." I don't know now what I said—what did "he," my father, matter?—and I turned away, precisely because I knew her hour *had* come, and that she would never leave what was now her deathbed. Nina saw what I was thinking and, placing one hand on my arm, said, trying to laugh as she did so:

"Listen to me, André: I'm better, I'm well, yes, almost better, I've none of the symptoms I had before . . . So don't go thinking you're going to rid yourselves of me just yet."

And wrapping me in her warm, sickly breath, she added:

"I can't wait to hear what he'll say when he sees me back on my feet . . ."

I almost believed that her astonishing energy had finally triumphed over the germs of death deposited in her flesh. Reclining against the pillows—she was always demanding fresh ones, stuffed with light, cool cotton—she was busy smoothing her tangled hair, while I held the mirror for her. A divine fire, a marvelous presence seemed once again to be stirring inside her.

"The good times will return, won't they, André?" she said as she struggled with her hair grown dry and stiff with fever. "And everything will be just as good as it was in the beginning, you'll see. I'll never forget . . ."

(How I longed to be free of those "good times"! She, alas, would not continue in time at all, but I would, and who would keep me company on the long journey ahead?) When I said nothing, she turned and winked at me, as if to prove that the memory of those days was still alive, days I was trying in vain to bury. And oddly enough, despite that attempt to put on a bright, vivacious, youthful air, there was a stoniness about her face, which lent that wink a grotesque, melancholy quality.

"Yes, of course, Mother," I stammered, again bowing my head.

She shot me a glance in which there was still a remnant of her old anger:

"*Mother*! You've never called me 'Mother' before, so why start now?"

And I was so stunned that the mirror trembled in my hands:

"Of course, Nina, of course the old times will return."

She continued struggling to untangle the knots in her hair, which formed a kind of halo around her head and seemed to be the one thing still alive: through its resurrected waves, a new spring, mysterious and transfigured, was beginning to flow through her veins.

"You need never be angry with me again, André, and you need never again spend hours sitting on the bench in the garden waiting for me." And suddenly, as if giving in to the memory of that scene, her voice took on a velvety tone, tinged with a childish, feminine melancholy, in which I, deeply touched, felt all the pulsating force of her loving soul. "I'll never again hide as I did that time, do you remember? And I'll never pack my bags to go traveling alone."

Tears, landscapes, lost emotions—what did any of that matter now? In my eyes, she seemed to be dissolving like a being made of foam. It wasn't treachery or lies or even forgetting that was causing her to drown (and with me unable to save her), it was, instead, the impetus of what had once been and that she had so cruelly summoned up.

"Oh, dear God, please don't!" I cried.

Then, still vibrant with emotion, still with the comb in her hand, she looked at me as if she had just woken up. And a great darkness filled her eyes.

"You don't understand, do you, you're too stupid!" she said.

And her hands—what proof did she need, what forgotten testimony, what lost memory?—reached greedily across the bedspread in search of mine. She leaned forward and I glimpsed her thin breasts beneath her nightdress. Intercepting that glance, she quickly adjusted her clothes, not that she was ashamed to reveal herself naked to me, but ashamed, rather, of her present ugliness. I turned away to hide the tears filling my eyes. And she, poor thing, had been so beautiful, her breasts so full and firm. Driven by some diabolical impulse, she suddenly, brutally, undid her nightdress and shook me hard, saying:

"Fool, why shouldn't the good times come back? Do you really think it's going to end like this? That's just not possible. I'm not as ugly as all that, they haven't taken everything from me, look . . ." and she tugged at my arm, while I kept my gaze firmly averted. "You see, it's not all over yet. Perhaps we can move to some big city where no one will know about us." (Did she really believe what she was saying? Her grip on my arm relaxed, her voice quavered.) "Ah, André, how quickly everything passes."

She fell silent, and I could see that she was breathing hard. The entirely fictitious color in her cheeks fled, and her head lolled back. It wasn't those wasted words that seemed to dispirit her most, but the vision of that false paradise she had been evoking. I tried to cheer her, saying:

"No, Nina, you're right. We could move to Rio perhaps, where no one will know us."

And I thought to myself: I could never hate her, it's beyond my capabilities. Irrespective of what god or devil had conceived me, my passion was above all earthly contingencies. I knew only the feeling of that body breathing hard in my arms, and in the hour of her death, for she breathed exactly as she had in those moments of passion. In my innermost thoughts, I was sure nothing could save her, and that the pieces we held in our hands were of no use to us now. Love, travel, what did those words mean? On the empty board, fate had finally made its move. The solution no longer depended on our will alone, nor on what we did, regardless of whether our actions were good or bad—the peace for which we had so longed, would, from now on, be a time of resignation and mourning.

And yet even I wasn't sure what provoked those thoughts—perhaps I was exaggerating, perhaps it was the influence of my naturally melancholic temperament. She was, after all, feeling better, she was talking and making plans, just as she used to. But something stronger than me, stronger than my own sad certainty and my clumsy interpretation of the facts, was telling me that it was precisely those words that spoke of the inevitable end, and that death had nailed to her bedhead the decree announcing eternal rest. She could make one final effort, she could laugh and insult me, or say she was leaving and abandoning Vila Velha forever, or simply devour me with hungry kisses—but I knew she was looking about her now with eyes that were no longer of this world, and I was capable of anything except lying to those eyes. What I saw rising up in them was like the sap rising up the trunk of a tree—except the branches were all dead, and no flower was about to bloom in that dying landscape. Yes, she could still kiss or caress me, but both kisses and caresses were directed at me as if I were no longer there. It wasn't her soul, but her lips—impregnated with a thick saliva that was like the last residue of earthly passion and fleshly effort—that were trying to revive the delirium of the past. In the depths of that search, faces, situations, and landscapes bubbled away. And I said nothing, too moved to speak. In her struggle, she must have felt my silence. In her febrile state, she must have thought it was simply a remnant of ill feeling from one of our old arguments—and she perhaps blindly imagined that I could still be seduced by the future she laid out before me, a future in which I no longer believed. For I knew this was the final act, and an unstoppable sob rose in my throat and remained stuck there, preventing me from saying a word. Then, slowly, she ran her hand down my cheek to my lips.

"Ah, so that's how it is!" she exclaimed in a voice of inexpressible sadness. "That's how you show your gratitude to me for allowing you to come to my bedside? You've clearly already forgotten everything, André."

Her fingers continued for some time to stroke my cheek and play upon my lips as if trying to cajole some laggardly word from them, and then, sitting up in bed, she again began mechanically combing her hair. Her eyes occasionally flashed like a gradually dying light, but it was the sign of a storm that was already moving off, leaving the ravaged countryside to sleep. And I could not have said what darkness it was that I sensed covering the landscape of her body, what moldering, grave-like smells already emanated from her words.

"You're right, André," she said at last. "You're right. I understand now: you've finally found your path. All it took for you to realize you were on the wrong path was for me to step out of the way." Her grave voice became enticing, wheedling. "But I know you, André, I know you can't live without women. I bet you've already seduced one of the housemaids . . . an easy enough conquest, eh?"

Overwhelmed by grief, I cried:

"Nina!"

And when I leaned toward her, she pushed me away, almost violently.

"Don't call me that. I forbid you to call me by my name."

I withdrew, cowed by that voice so reminiscent of the old, authoritarian Nina. She regarded me in silence for a while, doubtless pleased with the effect of her treacherous words. Quietly, like someone gauging the impact of what she was about to say, she went on:

"I bet you're already anticipating the hour of my death. You want to be free of me . . ."

"No!" I cried out desperately, flinging myself forward onto the bed. "How can you be so cruel, how do you even dare to say such things? You like to see me suffer, Nina, you always have . . ."

Yes, I knew this, but what did it matter now? All that mattered was being able to embrace her, cover her in kisses, and tell her one last time, before she departed, that we alone existed, and that heaven and hell and everything else were futile, childish notions. Scrabbling at the blankets, my head buried in them, I finally allowed my tears to flow freely—and I felt her body tremble beneath my touch, first withdrawing, then allowing itself to be caressed, as sensitive as a plant battered by a furious wind. Only then, when I had revealed my utter devastation, did peace seem to reign in her heart. She slowly stroked my hair.

"I'm so unhappy, André, so jealous. And yet you must stay and I must go . . ." and she sobbed quietly, as if not daring to make too much noise or to wipe away the tears streaming down her face. I looked up and dried her eyes with one corner of the sheet.

"Nina, I swear there's no one else in my life. How could there be when I've known you?" Tentatively, and when she made no objection, I lay my head on her breast. What did I care if she was ill, or if the cracked, thirsty mouth of decomposition were about to burst from the very flesh my greedy lips had so often kissed?

Then she grasped my head firmly between her hands, and her hollow eyes fixed on mine:

"Swear again so that I can believe what you're saying! You wouldn't dare lie to a woman about to depart this world, would you?"

"Never," I lied, and my voice sounded calm and decisive.

"Then swear, swear now!" she begged.

But swear what, dear God, swear that there was no other woman in my life, swear that she wasn't at death's door? And yet, with my face pressed to her bosom, I did swear and, if her peace of mind had depended on it, I would have sworn whatever she wanted me to and committed all kinds of perjury. When I looked up, she was gazing into my eyes, and in her eyes I saw the frightened, disoriented expression you see in the eyes of certain animals. It was as if she were staring beyond me and beyond my words into a world she could no longer understand. She let out a sigh, pushed me away, and went back to combing her hair. She must have exhausted all her strength, though, because the comb fell from her hands and she turned deathly pale, crying:

"André!"

I took her in my arms and gently repositioned her so that she was once more leaning against the pillows. She was breathing hard. Silence fell, and in that silence, all the objects one usually associates with illness—medicine bottles, rolls of cotton wool, pills, the whole accumulation of things that, for a moment, I had managed to ignore—suddenly reasserted themselves, as if tearing their way through a mist that had, until then, been omnipresent. I stood looking at her, and an unfamiliar machine, weaving who knew what dark, mortal web, began to function again inside her. I couldn't say how long we stayed like that, until finally she came to and said:

"What happened? What's wrong?"

I tried to calm her, saying that she was still weak and had probably talked more than she should have. She shook her head and answered in a strangely serene voice:

"No. That moment was a warning. There's no doubt about it, André, the end is coming."

She again took my hand in hers and lay very still. Someone, not that far away, gestured to me in the darkness. I had to leave. But I could feel time flowing through my whole being and fixing me to that spot as if I had put down roots. The doctor came over to me, touched my shoulder—he was a shy young man, who had only arrived from Rio a few days earlier—and indicated the door as if to say there was no point in my insisting. The world regained possession of my dream. Before leaving, however, I looked back one last time: Nina was sleeping, but nothing in her face bore any resemblance to that of a living person.

(That night, I walked endlessly about the garden, prowling up and down beneath the lit window of the room in which she lay. The doctor's shadow came and went against the white backdrop of the wall. At one point, I saw my father bending over her; he looked even wearier than usual. What would he be feeling, what emotions would he be hiding in his heart, what sense of sad and entirely inappropriate pride? I even considered speaking to him, and in my mind there stirred something like an impulse to console, but my lips refused to utter a word and, when I met him on the steps, as he, like me, came down into the garden in search of solitude, I let him pass, my face a blank.)

. . . When I placed the flowers on her lap, she opened her eyes, and I saw then that she appeared already to have left this world. She could still repeat the same gestures as the living and even say similar words—but the vital force was leaving her body and she was standing on that impenetrable frontier from which the dead gaze back indifferently at the land inhabited by the living. And yet, out of some kind of survival instinct, or maybe it was mere habit, she took the violets in her hand and raised them slowly to her nose, just as she used to do in times past, except that she no longer breathed in the perfume with the same eagerness, and her face was now soft and expressionless. Her arm fell, and the violets scattered over the bed.

"I can't," she said.

Her voice was no longer recognizable either, it was a cold, mechanical thing, a sound uttered with great difficulty, still audible, but soft and insubstantial as cotton wool. I didn't have the courage to say anything and simply stood by her side, asking God, with lips that lacked the flame of faith, to give me a little of her suffering. Roused perhaps by the flicker of consciousness that allows the dying briefly to distinguish some tiny detail in the surrounding heap of agglutinative shapes, she suddenly looked at me. Then, in a flash of recognition, she tried to conceal what was happening to her and turned away. And there we were, so near, so far, separated by that powerful presence. I had promised myself I would be sensible and would force the grief in my heart to keep silent, not because I cared what others might think, but purely in order to avoid creating the tense atmosphere of farewell that surrounds the dying. However, seeing her already half-immersed in night, and as far from me as if her presence were a mere memory, I felt beating in my breast a pulse of despair, of irrepressible anger. And by some bizarre coincidence—or perhaps it was simply the ineluctable nature of the hour—I sensed that both our memories were filled with images of times long gone. (Her, sitting by the pond on the day when I was so filled with desire for her and she touched my lips with her fingertips, saying: "Have you ever kissed a woman on the mouth?"—or on that other day when, sitting on a fallen tree trunk, she suddenly slapped my legs, crying: "Why, you're almost a grown man!" And many other memories came flooding in, multiplying as if under the influence of some narcotic, forming a gigantic, colored spiral, in which her resplendent figure could be seen, like a sun visible from all angles.)

She turned to me as if she had read my mind:

"Ah, André, if only we could live again as we once lived!"

Not daring to take that thought any further, a thought too full of sinful ideas, ideas that should be repelled at that supreme moment, her hand brushed against one of the fallen violets and she picked it up as if trying to pluck a humble witness from the past, then let it fall again—and the flower dropped to the floor.

"But perhaps . . . perhaps . . ." I murmured, not even knowing what exactly I was trying to say.

At that word, a desperate flame, possibly her final plea to the fast-retreating material world, flared into life.

"Perhaps!" and her voice echoed around the room. "Ah, yes, perhaps, who knows, André?"

And she tried to sit up. Her cold, bony hand drew me toward her and, once again, with the same thirst the traveler feels as he pours out the last few drops of water from his canteen, her eyes sought mine—devouring my outer and my inner fabric, my final shape and form, my very being, in order to go beyond that sad, enclosed thing that is the very heart, the umbilical cord, of the material self, and to wander, lucid and uncertain, through my essential self, looking to see if the love that had bound us together was true—seeking, too, the final word, the farewell, the power, the suggestion and the love that had made of me the unique creature chosen by her passion. A cloud obscured my vision and I had to lean on the bed to steady myself.

"Who knows?" she said again. "Maybe this is not the end of everything. So many things happen, so many people recover."

And drowning me in her burning breath, she added:

"Do you believe in miracles, André? Do you believe in the resurrection?"

When I did not immediately reply—feeling as if I had been hurled violently against some hard, dark wall—she shook me, dredging up strength from her impatience:

"You promised you would tell no lies. Come on, speak—do miracles exist?"

"No," I answered, and was myself startled by the calm voice in which I said this. "Miracles don't exist. And there is no resurrection either, Nina, for anyone."

The silence that followed was so vast that I felt as if an unexpected twilight had descended upon us. The objects sitting coolly in their places were growing dull and turning into still, metallic shapes.

When she spoke again, her voice sounded as if it were rising up from the depths of a well:

"We'll go somewhere far away, André. I hate this town, this house. And there are other places, there are, I swear, where we can live and be happy."

I could stand it no longer and tried to free myself from her grasp. This went beyond anything I could bear. I would have preferred distance and solitude and never to see her again, rather than this face-to-face interrogation, in which not the smallest subterfuge was allowed. She sensed my reluctance, and her eyes filled with tears.

"You want to run away from me, don't you? You want to run away, André. It's not the same as it once was."

I don't know what superhuman energy was driving her just then, but thanks to those feelings, she had managed to sit up in bed, despite the beads of sweat running down her thin face and despite her broken breathing, as if she were about to faint. Now, instead of holding me only by my hand, she was tugging at my arm, my whole body, in a last effort to force me to submit. I struggled, because I was afraid she might die in my arms. I bent lower, although still without entirely giving in to her will, and since, in this ongoing battle, she continued to tug at me, her face sometimes touched mine and I felt rising up into my nostrils the stale smell of an ailing body that has spent too long in bed. This awoke in me only a feeling of intense, desolating pity for her. Our struggle lasted perhaps a minute, and when she finally realized she was going to lose, some instinct, some wounded, outraged female essence gripped her—and she raised her hand and slapped my face. It was a rather feeble slap, but I stared at her in astonishment, with eyes that held not even the faintest glimmer of resentment.

We gazed at each other and she managed to gasp out:

"You're running away, André, running away from me. And that slap is so that you will never forget, so that you can say one day: she slapped my face to punish me for my indifference."

And in a quieter tone, with a smile so sad I felt my heart contract:

"And so that you will never unthinkingly betray me, André. So that you will never lie and say: yes, I sinned, but it's not something I'm proud of."

Only then did the tears come into my eyes, not out of grief, because, by then, I was incapable of any emotion, but because I knew then that I could not help that poor, unfortunate creature still clinging to the last glimmerings of life. And what a life that had been, what a past, what a future she was evoking, making one final effort to imprison me, when nothing could now save us on that well-trodden path. Nothing. And how wretched we were, and how I felt in my own flesh the despair of that condemned creature. When I turned back to her, she saw the tears on my face.

"I'm a fool, André, I have no right to talk to you like that. I know that you and I, that our love can never die. How could you possibly forget me when I taught you everything you know?"

She fell silent, but kept her eyes fixed on mine, as if she wanted to drag from them the truth about the situation in which we found ourselves. It was easy enough to say that we, that our love would never die—but how to believe it, if all around us everything was slowly fading? Gravely, almost solemnly, she spoke again:

"I want you to remember, André . . . in case . . . in case anything should happen. I want you to remember and for your heart never to lose sight of me. I want you, on certain nights, to remember how I touched you—never to forget the first kiss we exchanged, next to that big tree by the Pavilion. I want you never to enter a garden without remembering the garden that was once ours. I want you never to wait for anyone else without remembering how you would wait for me on that bench where we used to meet. I want you always to remember the warmth of my body and the things I said when you took me in your arms. I want . . ."

I slowly knelt down. With almost frightening strength, fueled by a kind of yearning, she forced me to lay my head on her breast, to brush her cheek and her lips with my lips. But little by little, the pressure waned and, exhausted, she let her head droop to one side, her eyes closed.

....

The last night I saw her . . .

....

When I learned that Timóteo, my uncle, had been asked to leave the room and that it was now empty, I went straight there in order to say my final farewell. On the threshold I saw a figure with his back turned to me and realized at once that it was my father. He turned around as soon I approached and he seemed to me to have aged considerably, although he was still very erect and had the same irritatingly smug air of the country gentleman. I don't understand why I felt so drawn to him just then—given that we didn't even speak when we passed in the hallway. I think I'm right in saying, though, that only then did I fully grasp that the Meneses as a family no longer existed. I had come to say goodbye to a corpse—and, for a few seconds, it was that man who held my gaze, as if I had suddenly stumbled upon a dead body. A dead stranger, whom I had never seen before and did not know, who, as far as I was concerned, had no name and no identity. I stood rooted to the spot, anxiously asking myself if that feeling of estrangement was not the result of a long, patient process of separation. But, as I say, the odd thing was that I regarded him with an indifference that was there in my flesh, my blood, my nerves—I regarded him as if he were a being from another world whom we struggle to clothe in some kind of humanity. Perhaps drawn by my gaze, he walked toward me, but the coffin lay between us—then, automatically, and almost without being able to take his eyes off me, he approached the dead woman, removed the sheet covering her face and stared down at her. With that gesture, his humanity returned to him—and I felt sure that I was face to face with a complete stranger.

As soon as he moved away, I went straight over to the coffin and stopped short: it had been made by Senhor Juca and was a very simple affair, with metal handles and a plain fabric lining. Wrapped in a sheet, the body lay there without so much as a flower to adorn it. Perhaps she herself had requested that bare, Spartan simplicity.

Unhurriedly, and as timidly as if I were disobeying some secret law, I bent over and lifted one corner of the sheet. That was the first time I had ever seen the face of a corpse, and I had the strangest feeling, as if a distant, delicate music were playing inside my mind. How could a human face change so quickly! Her gentle, perfect features had suffered a violent transformation, from her almost excessively long eyelashes, to her pale, almost too broad forehead and the exaggerated curve of her nostrils, which lent her an unexpectedly semitic appearance. Rigor mortis had placed around that face an impenetrable aura. Death was clearly no joking matter; in death, the original being, roughly shaped out of clay by God's hands, cast off all disguises to triumphantly reveal its true essence. It was clear, too, that there was nothing more to be said between us. Any unspoken words were useless now, as were any caresses not bestowed and the flowers with which we could still adorn her. Free now, she rested there in a state of ultimate purity. Everything, apart from fury and acceptance, was pointless. No answers, as if we creatures deserved nothing but mourning and injustice; it all ended there. And everything that had existed had been only a dream, a magnificent, fleeting sensory illusion. Nothing could ever remove the heavy weight pressing on my heart, and in that ruin already touched by corruption I found it hard to recognize the person who had once been the object of my love, and no tears came into my eyes, not even tears of pity.

In the same unhurried way in which I had lifted the corner of the sheet, I bent over and kissed the woman's cheek—as I had done so many, many times before—but this time I felt the kiss was meaningless and that I no longer knew her.

2.
First Letter from Nina to Valdo Meneses

. . . Don't be alarmed, Valdo, to find this letter among your papers. I know you haven't expected any news from me in a long time, and that you essentially consider me to be dead. Ah, how things change in this world. With an effort of will that paralyzes the hand I'm writing with, I can even see you sitting with your brother and your sister-in-law on the verandah, as you used to do, and in between two long silences, I can hear you saying: "Poor Nina ended up taking the only path that lay open to her . . ." And Demétrio, who has never taken any interest in other people's problems, folds up his newspaper and looks out at the garden with a sigh: "I warned you, Valdo, but you wouldn't listen to the voice of reason." (Yes, "the voice of reason," those would be his exact words, with his usual lack of modesty when it comes to talking about himself.) Ana perhaps says nothing, her abstracted gaze fixed on the sky growing gradually dark as night falls. And so it has been for years and years, because the Meneses family is very sparing with its gestures and has rarely ever instigated anything. And suddenly, on the usual dust covering your bedside reading, you will find this letter. It might take you a while to recognize the writing and it might also take you a while to think: "It's that poor woman Nina again," while your heart beats a little faster.

For once in your life, Valdo, you will be right. That "poor woman Nina," even poorer now, is once again standing humbly at your door, having sniffed her way home like a dog abandoned on the road. I should perhaps warn you that women like me are very hard to kill off, and you'll have to make a few attempts before I actually disappear. But don't worry, my dear, my objective this time is very simple, and once I've gotten what I want, I will return once more to the silence and distance to which the Meneses family relegated me. I don't intend to return to the Chácara (although I do, sometimes, on a wave of nostalgia, remember the quiet drawing room, the imposing sideboard laden with dusty silverware, and above it, the painting of *The Last Supper*, which does not quite cover the obvious mark left by the portrait of Maria Sinhá that used to hang there long ago), nor, indeed, do I intend ever again to use the name of which you are so proud, and which for me merely marked the beginning of a series of errors and mistakes. No, I want only to reclaim what I judge to be rightfully mine. You once said to me that people who are always demanding their rights show a lack of love, which might be true in part, because despite all the love that may perhaps still exist between us, time has not changed me, Valdo, and although you may often have misinterpreted both me and my actions, I believe there is still a remnant in your heart of the sentiment that first brought us together—and, given my current situation, I feel it only right that I should demand the things I believe to be my due. You are doubtless looking a little alarmed now, asking yourself what those things could be—and I should, at this point, remind you that we are only separated, that there has been no legal separation, something so repugnant to your brother Demétrio, always so wary of anything that might tarnish the honorable family name. It is, therefore, only logical that I should enjoy the same help I would expect were I still by your side. Now do you see what I'm getting at? In the eyes of the law, I am still your wife, and while, during all this time, I haven't received a single penny from you and you have proved tight-fisted almost to the point of propelling me into poverty, it is still your duty to watch over me and help me in difficult times.

I can see your furrowed brow, the suspicious expression you always adopt on these occasions, and the false accusations you're storing up in your mind. I can foresee the suppositions and suspicions you have about the life I lead and my current situation. Don't worry, Valdo, I'm not coming to you in order to satisfy mere whims or so that I can afford things that you deem to be luxuries and therefore unnecessary. I can guarantee that in this respect I am more than fortunate, because I do not lack for male friends who help me and give me what I need, and who are, to be frank, sometimes surplus to requirements. Yes, I do have male friends, I won't hide the fact, and some of them occasionally say of me: "Nina has never looked lovelier"—men whom, I'm pleased to say, and you will be pleased to hear, I keep at a distance and even treat with a certain disdain. No, my problem is of quite a different nature. Imagine, for example, always assuming you're capable of imagining such things, and that those things are capable of touching your heart, that a woman of my status, married into such a family—and what higher status could I have in the eyes of a Meneses?—finds herself obliged to live in a cramped apartment that reeks of poverty and of that unmentionable thing: the life of a woman abandoned by her husband. By now, you, who were always trying to second-guess my motives, will have said to yourself: "It's as clear as day what she's trying to get out of me!" I can't deny it . . . ah, Valdo, how we honest souls do suffer, how we cover ourselves in unnecessary shame when it comes to dealing with certain of the world's material values. On the other hand, consider that in the Chácara, where you enjoy a life of relative plenty ....

....

.... and of all my friends, the person who takes the fairest view of the matter is the Colonel. He says that, even when legally separated, a wife deserves the full consideration of the man who was her husband—even more so when there is no legal separation. I can see Demétrio leaning over your shoulder like a shadow and roaring: "The lengths that woman will go to . . ." May God forgive me, but I very much doubt that any sensible person would take your brother's opinions seriously, for they are fueled by prejudice rather than by any kind of fair, reasoned judgment. So think carefully, Valdo, especially since I am really not asking for very much at all. And even if I were, right would be on my side, I would have my reasons and my justifications. For example, the allowance you promised—do you remember?—and that never materialized, and for which I waited in the hope that the family situation would ease, even though, deep down, I was sure you would never get out of the cul-de-sac you have chosen to go down. I say this because I know now that building the Chácara, not to mention maintaining it, has been a complete waste of money, and could have been avoided if you weren't all convinced that abandoning Vila Velha and this mansion of ours would be an act discrediting the family. The fact is that rather than dismembering the old Fazenda do Baú and dividing up the lands among creditors who could perfectly well have waited a little longer, you would have done far better to accept the situation and simply refurbish the old house that is now moldering away in the hills. I have to say that on the occasions when I rode up there, I felt it had a poetry and a dignity I did not always find in the pretentious mansion where you live today . . . If you had done what I always advised and sold the house, auctioned the furniture, dismissed some of the servants, divided the land up into lots and come to an agreement with the rest of the creditors, we wouldn't be in this state of ....

.... which are the same as before. This increases the not inconsiderable amount I'm having to pay out. I actually think that, at times, I might have gone hungry had it not been for the zealous male friends I mentioned earlier. Among them, Colonel Amadeu Gonçalves, who never lets a day go by without visiting me, encouraging me to despise men's evil nature and, at the same time, bringing me a word of comfort. It's hard to believe such men still exist: the devotion of the man, the constancy of his friendship, his selflessness; I sometimes find such qualities frightening. What would become of me were it not for his paternal zeal? Sometimes he arrives and finds me in tears, and then he says: "Nina, I don't want to weigh you down with any more suffering, you have quite enough to cope with as it is, I just want you to know that I come here as a father and that you can depend upon me as if you were my daughter." He was, of course, the only real friend my late father had, and I cannot but feel grateful, especially when he goes still further and often leaves lying about, as if absentmindedly, varying sums of money that have been my sole source of income. I sometimes say to him: "Please, Colonel, don't do that, because I really don't know that I'll ever be able to repay you . . ." He smiles and shakes his head: "Don't be silly, one day you'll pay me back in full." I feel ashamed, Valdo, because I know that day will probably never come. And I feel sorry for that quiet, humble, helpless man at my side. He, for his part, rails against the way you have treated me, saying: "Really, a woman of your quality, who deserved only the very best, who merited every respect!" In writing this letter, I only wish I could tell you all the sympathetic things he has to say about my situation. Perhaps only then would you understand that this world, whose opinion you seem to value so highly, is not on your side, but on mine. Yes, I am the person being wronged and persecuted, despite all Demétrio's efforts to portray me as a flibbertigibbet, a femme fatale who would lead any man to his ruin. And strangely enough, the rumors you so fear are not about me, as you might expect, but about the Meneses family. The Meneses of Vila Velha, that ancient trunk whose roots reach down into the very origins of Minas Gerais. I can't help but feel a certain pleasure when I say this and imagine Demétrio, tremulous with resentment, and Ana, disdainfully sticking her nose in the air whenever she passes me, meanwhile peering at me through every window and shutter she comes across. As I say, this world does not accuse me, it judges you as severely as the Colonel does.

I stopped writing for a moment to wipe away the tears filling my eyes. It's hard to write and harder still to write when what rises to one's lips are words of love that the heart silences beneath the weight of bitter grievances. No, Valdo, my situation could not be more wretched, and you could not possibly blame me were some misfortune to occur. I don't sleep, I'm feverish; I pace back and forth, remembering how things once were, wondering what force it was that drove me to turn my back on everything that made up my life. It wasn't me, you can be quite sure of that, I didn't want it to end like this, it was someone else, prompted by secret powers bent on destroying me. I'm not accusing anyone, because I can't say for certain that it was this person or that, and I can't even pinpoint the motive, because I can't say it was for this reason or that, but the truth is that I always felt a distinct lack of love and watched as the atmosphere I had always imagined to be warm and affectionate slowly turned to ice. When I wake in the night and sit up in bed, listening to the dogs barking in the darkness, behind the railings and gardens that surround more fortunate people—and when I imagine, although I don't know why, that some horrible fate awaits me, and that death is tearing off the pages from the calendar of my allotted time . . . ah, Valdo, is there no pity in your heart? Are you Meneses not made of flesh and blood? Can you never forgive me, never forget an outrage I never actually committed? And can you not sympathize with my situation now, can you not see how you tore my heart in two? The worst thing is the active part played in all this by your brother. The day will come when you will understand what he did to me, the influence he had on my behavior. Until then, until that day, banished and forgotten, I must endure the painful insults heaped on me. (And yet I will say this: you should have seen the way he used to follow me with his eyes down the hallway, pretending, of course, that he wasn't, but devouring my every gesture and opening any doors behind which I tried to take refuge—you should have felt the greedy touch of his hands, on the few occasions when he dared to touch me, revealing the sick desires that lay behind the Meneses mask—you should have heard the cry he let out—the only time—one afternoon when I was crossing the verandah aglow with sunlight. I was just about to open the door when I heard that strange yelp—Nina!—and it was as if the black, stagnant water of his lust had spouted forth from the very depths of his being . . . I hadn't even seen him, but I could sense his presence behind me, the galloping beat of his heart. I swear I didn't even turn around, but all that night, I could feel his eyes fixed on me, as if they could penetrate walls—the eyes of a lunatic, a starving man not brave enough to touch the food set before him. My hand fails, the pen falls from my grasp: how can I possibly describe the devil you have living in your house? But nothing I can say will convince you, Valdo, because you'll think it's just another of my extravagant claims.) And yet someone, even if that someone is me, needs to warn you against your own credulity. What kills us is nearly always the unrecognized cruelty of those around us. If only I could make you recall certain facts . . . certain long-past situations . . . the early days . . . life in the Pavilion. That day, Valdo, when you stood on the steps strewn with dead leaves and embraced me, saying: "Nothing will ever part us, Nina!" But we did part, and with each day that passes, we find ourselves further away from each other. At that moment, though, it appeared to be true, the air was filled with the scent of jasmine, and the whole burgeoning world around us seemed to approve and to promise that our love would remain alive. But what evil spell was cast on us, how was it that everything changed so quickly? What happened to me, what happened to our love? Are there no certainties in life, do we engender only forgetting and distance? Do words mean nothing at all, can they not be used to seal an oath? What are we, we who pass through life like so much foam, who leave no trace once we are gone, only a handful of ashes and shadows? I ask myself these questions, my heart in my mouth: does anything endure, does anything remain untouched by the rage of time, are there feelings that never die and are never betrayed?

But we have been here before. I can feel you retreating into sullen silence and staring off into the distance. Distance is the image of our weariness. There, where not a hint of me, not a shadow of my gestures, not an echo of my words will ever enter, there will you take refuge in your certainty and dig my grave with gnarled, heartless fingers. I am definitively dead for you, a vast, formless tombstone stands permanently between us. And that is what most wounds and consumes me. Imagining you far off, giving not so much as a pitying backward glance at what we were. Imagining your silence, the way you have completely forgotten what you swore and promised, and feeling that I was nothing but a name spoken long ago in a vast and now vanished garden. A name like a petal that falls. Ah, Valdo, Valdo!

On one such day, grown tired of thinking and suffering, I went to a pharmacist's to buy a sleeping draught. I came back and sorted out all my things—boxes, ribbons, hats, the silly little bits and bobs I always have with me and that I find so helpful—putting everything in order so that, after my death, it could all be given to a friend of mine, a nurse. Then I scribbled a note to the Colonel, asking him to forgive me for not being the daughter he wanted me to be—and asking him to forget me, because things weren't well with me. Lastly . . .

Anyway, you can imagine the letter. Then I filled a glass of water, emptied the whole contents of the tube into it and waited until I had courage enough to drink it. No, I'm lying, Valdo, that wasn't the letter I wrote with the glass there before me. I wanted to write something that would be a summation of my life, my testament. I wanted the cries in that letter to echo through the vast spaces of your house and make the guilty parties tremble in their hiding places. I listed Demétrio's crimes, stating that I would never forgive him, in this world or the next. I laid out all the reasons he would come up with once he learned I was no longer in this world. The adulteries and the sins he imagined I would be committing on the other side. It gave me such pleasure writing that letter, imagining my body lying there with a candle at each corner, to be gawked at by the curious. The dead have a language of their own and send a message that is, at once, a warning and a condemnation of our lives. I don't know how much I wrote, but there were pages and pages of the stuff—and I don't know what I wrote after that, what tears and pleas and curses I flung down on the paper. I know only that it was all very confused, that you would never have had the patience or the desire to decipher it. I can't remember either how long I spent writing the letter, I do remember that it was already dark by the time I finished, and the pen had fallen from my hand when the door opened and I heard Colonel Gonçalves saying almost in my ear: "What were you thinking? Are you mad? Have you lost your reason?" I turned around; the floor was covered in sheets of paper. Gripped by a single thought, I made a grab for the glass, but the Colonel snatched it up and poured the contents down the sink. "Have you forgotten that you have a duty to your friends?" he went on. He helped me to my feet: "We must be patient with life." He tilted my chin and shook his head reprovingly at the sight of my tear-filled eyes: "You need to get out more and have a little fun." He gathered up the sheets of paper from the floor and tore them into pieces, then took me to a casino. I followed him like an automaton, blinded by the lights, feeling ill and weak. And yet I won thirty thousand *cruzeiros*. I have never known such luck. "You see!" exclaimed the Colonel "Fate is on our side." I ended up almost forgetting my woes. We dined at a restaurant by the sea, the moonlight glinting on the water, we drank champagne, we danced. It was almost dawn by the time we came home: the sun was rising and lighting up the harbor. It was then that I decided to do as the Colonel advised, to forget and let my heart rest easy.

Don't go thinking, though, that money was the cause of this transformation. You know very well that money has never been of great importance to me. What saved me was the Colonel's disinterested friendship and concern. I know he's not handsome or cultivated, and certainly not young, but there is genuine warmth in his gestures and sincerity in his words. We went everywhere together and, because he considered it to my advantage, he always introduced me as his niece. He would say: "She's been living in Europe. She's an artist." For my part, I didn't much care what anyone said. I knew I was being looked at and whispered about, but felt I had gone beyond worrying about what other people might think of me. Time seemed to pass infinitely slowly, and I would sigh, looking at people and things with equal indifference. But I made new acquaintances, even a few lasting friendships. I can see you smiling scornfully and murmuring: "Riffraff." But what do I care about riffraff or dubious friendships: friendship can be a flower blooming on a dung heap, from which it draws its color and its sap. My whole life gradually changed. During that time, I must confess, not a day passed without the Colonel visiting me bearing gifts: "a souvenir, a memento of our friendship." Now, Valdo, we come to the crux of the matter. If I were a free woman, I would have no hesitation in accepting gifts from this stranger. His courtship, because the truth demands that I call it that, would be justified, and I would not have the nagging sense that I'm leading someone on whose feelings I cannot reciprocate . . . I keep remembering that I have a legitimate husband—and I find the Colonel's constant attentions troubling and vaguely humiliating. Despite this ....

....

.... unable to continue in the same tone. I find myself in a ridiculous position and, thanks to your lack of foresight in not paying me my agreed allowance, I have to resort to various stratagems and hope that other kind folk will take pity on me. No, a thousand times no, I cannot go on like this. When you swore those oaths of eternal love, little did I think this was the path that awaited me. Now it's too late to shed any tears. What I want is for you to come to my aid and send me the promised money, to do something so that I can at last disabuse the poor Colonel and live in peace with my conscience. You have the right to expel me—when I think about it, my departure was precisely that, an expulsion—to deprive me of my son's affection and deny me your name, and, as you have been doing, even expose me to public execration. But you cannot deny me the help you owe me, indeed, to do so now would be an act I could only describe as the lowest of the low. If, as I expect, you claim to have no money, then sell one of those useless bits of furniture cluttering up the Chácara, yes, sell one of those dead artifacts and come up with the necessary money to feed someone who is still living. Some things are worth more than mere furniture, and they could even be the bringers of justice. Remember that when I left your house, having been accused of the most horrible of crimes, I took nothing with me but a few handkerchiefs with which to dry my tears as I wept over my misfortune. It is time, then, for you all to think of me other than as someone to be accused and insulted. I am not alone in the world, thank God, and I know how to stand up for myself, even if that takes my last ounce of strength and my last drop of blood. Take heed, Valdo, and don't force me to take extreme measures. (Again I tremble and my eyes fill with tears: no, Valdo, I feel that I can still trust in the memory of the love that once united us. I know that everything will be resolved quietly, that you will send me the money I need in order to live—and thus an act of justice and understanding will give succor to a woman who was once so ignominiously forced to abandon her own home.)

3.
The Pharmacist's First Report

My name is Aurélio dos Santos, and for many years I have been established in our small town with a business selling medicines and pharmaceutical products. Indeed my shop could be considered the only such establishment in the town, for there is little competition from the stall selling homeopathic remedies on the Praça da Matriz. Thus, almost everyone comes to me to make their purchases, and I have even written prescriptions for the Meneses family.

I well remember the night he came looking for me. I was sitting with a lamp immediately beside me so as to make the most of its poor light (our town's electricity supply leaves much to be desired), consulting a dictionary of medicinal powders printed in excessively small type. Night had just begun to fall and the shop was filled with moths circling ever closer around the lamp. This bothered me and, since both my hands were occupied in holding the thick volume, I had to keep shaking my head to chase them away. I had left the door ajar, just in case a customer should appear even at that late hour. Hearing a gentle creaking, I raised my head and caught sight of a hand pushing the door open; then a face slowly emerged, not with the intention of producing any dramatic effect, but merely to avoid startling me. The person stepped forward and I then recognized who it was. He looked paler than usual, his movements hesitant, his eyes distrustful.

"Good evening, Senhor Demétrio," I said, naturally somewhat surprised by such a visit.

I should perhaps explain why his arrival did not strike me as an everyday occurrence. The reason is simply that they, the Meneses, whether out of pride or conceit, were the only customers who never set foot in my establishment. Any errands or prescriptions or bills to be paid were dealt with by their servants. I would see the men of the Meneses household passing by reasonably frequently, distant and disdainful, and almost always dressed in black. I would say to myself: "It's the Chácara brigade," and content myself with tipping my hat in the time-honored manner. Furthermore, I should add that Senhor Valdo and Senhor Demétrio were almost always together. At home they may well not, as rumor had it, be very close, but in the streets they were always to be seen side by side, as if there were in this world no better brothers. On one solitary occasion I saw Senhor Demétrio in the company of his wife, Dona Ana, who, again according to rumor, remained obstinately confined to the house, weeping over the mistake she had made in marrying Senhor Demétrio. She wasn't a Meneses—she came from a family that had once lived on the outskirts of Vila Velha, and little by little she had been worn down by the dull, dreary life led by the inhabitants of the Chácara. Her fate was widely lamented and some even said that, although somewhat lifeless, she was not entirely devoid of beauty.

"Good evening," replied Senhor Demétrio and stood there, quite still, no doubt waiting for me to initiate the conversation. I don't know what strange malice took hold of my heart at that moment—oh, those Meneses!—and out of sheer capriciousness I remained silent, with the dictionary open in my hands, staring at the face before me. I should first of all explain that it belonged to a man who was short rather than tall, and extraordinarily pale. Nothing about his physical appearance stood out, for nature had charged itself with molding a series of flat, featureless contours, all somewhat randomly thrown together around a central point, for the only object discernible from a distance and the only one to attract immediate attention was his nose—large and almost aggressive, an authentic Meneses nose. The most noticeable thing about him was, I repeat, his sickly appearance, appropriate to those who live in the shadows, cut off from the world. Perhaps this was due merely to his wan complexion, but the truth is that he immediately gave the impression of being a creature of unusual habits, a night bird dazzled and laid bare by the sun.

"I would like your advice," he said at last with a sigh.

I nodded and set the book down on the table, indicating that I was at his disposal. He did not attempt to elaborate on what had brought him there, preferring perhaps to be asked, and he continued staring at me, his beady eyes darting from side to side.

"Of course, if I can be of any assistance . . ." I ventured.

These simple words seemed to lift a great weight off his mind. Something in his face flickered dimly, and he leaned over the counter in a gesture of greater intimacy. I would not say his voice was entirely steady, but it gradually overcame its difficulties to the point where he was able to speak with relative calm. He confessed to me that his wife had lately been much concerned by a strange occurrence at the Chácara. Then, after a brief digression about the perils of life in the country, he stopped and scrutinized my face to see if I believed what he was saying, and I don't know why, but in the unexpected silence that arose between us, I had the instinctive feeling that he was lying, and that he earnestly wanted me to believe his lie. Now, for a Meneses to come to my house, something of real significance must have occurred, given that it was being presented to me swathed in such an elaborate lie. I stood up, my attention now entirely awakened, and leaned over the counter beside him. Thus, with his face almost touching my own, not even the most fleeting of emotions flitting across it would escape me. Such close attention seemed to displease him and, watching me out of the corner of his eye, he returned once again to the strange occurrences that were worrying Dona Ana. Now, everyone in our quiet little town knew very well that anything to do with the Chácara was of almost no interest to Dona Ana and that her days were filled with weeping and bemoaning the misfortunes of her life. So it was inconceivable that she should interest herself in any "strange occurrence" that might have occurred in the Meneses household. I remained silent, however, and he would have been far better off contenting himself with that silence. My head bent low, leafing randomly through the yellowing pages of my dictionary, I heard him give me the curious information that a strange animal was prowling around, causing concern to the inhabitants of the Chácara. There was nothing apparently outlandish about such a piece of news, but his emphasis on the word "strange" and the particular manner in which he described the noises made by the creature and the footprints it left behind, brought an unwitting smile to my lips. He noticed the smile and repeated the phrase with a certain vehemence.

"A strange animal?" I asked, trying to catch his eye.

"Yes, a wild dog or a wolf."

Once again there was a short silence. I shut the book firmly and enquired:

"In that case, how can *I* be of assistance?"

He reached out and placed his hand on my arm, and by the way that hand trembled I understood that we had reached the crux of the matter.

"What do you advise?" he asked. "It is for this, and only this, that I have come."

It must of course be true, for nothing would induce me to suspect a lie lurking behind such a bold affirmation, but even so I could not help but laugh:

"But, Senhor Demétrio, I know nothing about hunting! You would perhaps be better off asking . . ."

He shook his head violently:

"No! No! There are reasons why I have come to you. You could, for example, suggest to me a poison, or some deadly substance that could be placed in a trap."

"One does not kill wolves with poison," I said, and ostentatiously put the dictionary back in its usual place on top of the cash register.

The precise meaning of my gesture, its willful indifference, was not lost on him. He stared at me, and with such hard eyes, filled with such sudden, aggressive resentment, that I felt a shudder run through me. There was no doubt he had come here for some other reason, of that I was certain, and, since he feared broaching the subject directly, he was equivocating, circling around the problem, waiting for me to come to his rescue. He could see that I had not the slightest intention of helping him out (why should I? For a very long time, indeed since time immemorial, there had never been the slightest hint of affection between the Meneses family and me), and it was this that had drawn from him such a piercing look of rage. Instead of encouraging him in his confession (or whatever it might be), I changed the subject completely, as if that story about a wolf had never been mentioned. As it happened, one wall of the pharmacy was in a very bad state due to a small explosion caused by an inexperienced assistant. I pointed to the exposed bricks and ruined plasterwork, adding with a smile:

"These are hard times we live in, Senhor Demétrio! Just look at that wall in dire need of repair. For two months now I've been trying to raise the necessary funds, but I still haven't enough to purchase even one brick!"

Standing before me, motionless, he followed this apparent digression with the utmost attention. He was probably trying to find in my words a hidden meaning, an insinuation of some sort. All I meant was that the wall needed repairing and I did not have the necessary funds. Nevertheless, he had a sudden flash of inspiration, and his eyes lit up as he once again reached out his hand and touched my arm:

"Perhaps I can help you. Who knows? A brick or two here or there; we're always glad to help our friends."

I was standing with my back to him as he said these words. I turned around slowly and looked deep into his eyes. I thought I could see stirring in those depths a glimmer of something like hope—what kind of hope I could not possibly say, so shrouded and secretly did it flicker before me, so seared into the sad depths of that soul. He did not look away; on the contrary, he offered himself to me like an open book, and we stood for several seconds as there passed between us, rapidly and invisibly from one to the other, incoherent thoughts, fragments of ideas and feelings, things that the subconscious barely brought to the surface, but through which we were able to reach an important level of mutual understanding.

"A few bricks . . ." I murmured, "are exactly what I need."

"Shall we say . . . a cartload?" he suggested, leaning familiarly over the counter.

He was certainly breathing faster, and his now bright eyes avidly scanned my face, searching for a word of ready acquiescence with an almost shocking degree of haste and lack of decorum. Even so, I shook my head sadly:

"A cartload? Let's say three, Senhor Demétrio. I could scarcely fill that gaping hole with fewer than three cartloads of bricks!"

Something akin to a smile—a minuscule, meager smile of victory—appeared on his pallid face. As I was expecting, he nodded his agreement. We had reached a place from which it would be impossible for me to retreat, and so it was in the serenest of voices that I returned to the initial subject:

"A wolf on a country estate is always a dangerous thing. Nevertheless . . ."

He repeated that word back to me, as if pronouncing it took enormous effort.

"Nevertheless . . ."

I took a few paces around the shop, trying to behave as naturally as possible.

"Nevertheless, there do exist practical means of eliminating them, without having to resort to poison."

"Such as . . . ?" he prompted.

I left him without an answer for a moment and stepped through into the rear of the house. I should explain that my private quarters consisted of a small, dimly-lit backroom with treacherous floorboards, whose only advantage was that it offered me a place to lay my head at night right next to the shop, and thus enabled me to attend to any customer who might appear at a late hour. However, news had spread that some thieves were operating in the town and this was probably why I had taken to keeping a small revolver among the linen in the top of the chest of drawers. "They won't catch *me* unawares," I said to myself. So I opened the drawer, rummaged through the sheets and soon found what I was looking for. I returned to the pharmacy as silently as I had left, and placed the gun on the shop counter.

"What's this?" asked Senhor Demétrio, not daring to touch the object.

"Oh," I exclaimed, "just a little plaything. It's very easy to handle, but will put paid to any wolf."

He seemed to hesitate, staring all the while at the gun, still not touching it. I don't know what conflicting thoughts were doing battle deep within him, only that in due course he slowly reached out his hand, took the revolver, and, raising it almost to eye level, examined it closely.

"It's a woman's gun," he said, polishing the mother-of-pearl inlay on its grip.

"It belonged to my mother," I explained.

He turned the revolver this way and that, and I could clearly see the satisfaction in his eyes.

"Does it work all right?" he asked, pointing the barrel toward the back of the shop.

"Perfectly."

And, trying to dispel his last remaining scruples, I added:

"They don't make guns like that any more."

From that moment on, he was, you might say, fully convinced. Watching him, I wondered whether he had come to my house specifically to obtain the gun. Would the Meneses, so richly endowed in resources and stratagems, really not already have such a weapon? In what circumstances would they use it? What reason would they have to compromise some other person by a course of action that they were, in all likelihood, about to embark upon? And if the matter did indeed concern a wolf—the idea seemed almost ridiculously naïve—then why did they not find a simpler way to kill it, with a trap, for example? I shrugged my shoulders: it was a transaction that suited me well.

Senhor Demétrio squeezed the trigger, swung out the cylinder, even rubbed the barrel on the sleeve of his jacket. It was evident that all this filled him with an intense, secret pleasure, as if, in the dim light of the pharmacy, he could already sense his enemies being felled. He eventually finished his examination and stared at me, and I swear that behind the smile that spread across his face lay a very deep, possibly ancient sentiment, shamefully immoral and cruel—ah, yes, the shrewd smile of someone who feels perfectly confident in the value of the transaction he has just entered into. At the same time he placed his hand on my arm:

"Thank you, my friend. I do believe there could be no better method for killing wolves."

I returned his smile and we bade each other goodnight. Senhor Demétrio made his way out into the street, clutching the revolver in his pocket, while I, shaking my head over the mysteries of human nature, returned to my dictionary.

4.
Betty's Diary (i)

19th – The mistress (I think that's what I'm expected to call her . . .) was supposed to get here today, but, at the last moment, we received a telegram saying she would only arrive tomorrow. It didn't really matter to me, after all, a few hours here or there makes no difference, but I could see how badly the news affected Senhor Valdo. I saw the sad look on his face as he stared out of the window, the telegram still in his hands. Despite the persistent fine rain, he had gone out into the garden himself to pick some of the loveliest dahlias. While we were tidying the house—moving furniture, plumping cushions, discovering old objects dismissed as redundant, but which somehow gave the house an air of discreet luxury—he seemed extraordinarily lively and happy. He told me not to worry if Dona Nina did not at first understand my position in the family, because it wasn't necessarily easy for someone new to realize that I wasn't just one of the servants, but had occupied the rather different position of housekeeper since before his mother's death. When I remarked that, with the arrival of Dona Nina, there would perhaps be less need for a housekeeper, he mentioned Dona Ana and asked if her arrival had lightened my load at all. I laughed and said, no, it hadn't, and he assured me that it would be just the same if not worse with his wife: she hadn't the slightest notion of how to run a house, especially one as large and complicated as this. And then he was so jolly, so full of joshing and jokes, that old Anastácia, who never normally leaves the kitchen, said, her eyes full of tears: "It's a real treat to see the master so cheerful . . ." When the telegram arrived, the atmosphere changed, just like that; Senhor Valdo didn't say another word, but simply folded up the telegram, put it in his pocket, and went to his room. I felt so sorry for him, because Senhor Demétrio had been making fun of him, saying that he had already been to fetch his bride once and come back alone, and that now he might have to resort to violence to drag that "beauty" away from Rio de Janeiro. But then that's what this family is like, always going into a sulk and hiding away in their rooms when things don't go to plan. A great silence descended on the house and, finding myself alone again, I was just getting started on another task when I heard a very insistent "psst" and a voice calling me: "Betty! Betty!" At first, I thought it was Senhor Valdo with some further piece of advice, but soon realized that it was only Senhor Timóteo. I still did not move, for I had been given strict instructions to ignore him, but then from the hallway came another cry of "Betty," this time sounding so urgent and anxious that I could not simply turn my back on him. Ever since the rift between Senhor Timóteo and the rest of the family, one famous evening when he smashed half the family's glass and china, I had only rarely entered his room, firstly, because I had been made to promise not to help him in any way as long as he persisted in his eccentric ways, secondly, because I found his sad obsession so upsetting. Personally, I think people should be allowed to do what they like, as long as they don't offend others. Senhor Timóteo's behavior seemed to me more of an oddity than a perversion—or whatever other term the others chose to use.

That occasion was further proof of the bizarre habits that had essentially become the norm in his world: when I turned, I saw that Senhor Timóteo, fat and sweating, was wearing a fringed and sequined dress that had belonged to his mother. The bodice was far too tight around the waist and here and there a little imprisoned flesh was bursting out of the seams, tearing the fabric and making any pleasure he might take in dressing up seem like a real torment. He moved very slowly, setting the fringes swaying and, all the time, fanning himself vigorously with a sandalwood fan, which wrapped him in a cloud of sickly perfume. I couldn't quite say what he had on his head, it looked like a turban or a brimless hat, from beneath which emerged lush blond curls. He was, as usual, wearing make-up—taken, like his clothes, from his mother's room after she died, for she, in her day, had also been famous for her extravagant way of dressing—and make-up only highlighted his enormous nose, so characteristic of the Meneses family. His nose, however, was his only markedly masculine feature, because although he wasn't yet as plump as he later became, the excess fat smoothed and softened his features, reducing any lumps or bumps and creating new dimples and indentations in his rose-pink flesh, so that he rather resembled a vast, splendid china doll, shaped by the hands of a rather incompetent potter.

"Sit down, Betty, sit down," he said, pointing at a chair with his fan. "Do sit down—if, that is, you still care about me."

"Why wouldn't I care about you, Senhor Timóteo? As far as I know, you have never done me any harm."

He shrugged and his whole heavy body shuddered:

"No, I haven't, but oh, I don't know . . ." he said with a touch of nostalgia.

And coming over to where I was sitting, this time pointing his fan at me, he said:

"When I decided to be independent . . . Betty, do you believe that one should listen to the voices in one's blood?"

"What do you mean, Senhor Timóteo?" and there was not a hint of pretense or false surprise in my voice.

His eyes grew suddenly very serious.

"I am ruled by the spirit of Maria Sinhá. Have you never heard anyone speak of Maria Sinhá, Betty?"

"Never, Senhor Timóteo. Don't forget, I've only been employed here for a few years. Besides, talking isn't exactly one of the family's strong points."

"Yes, Betty, you're right, you're always right. That's the good thing about you simple folk."

"Who was Maria Sinhá?"

"Oh," he began, and his voice was filled with genuine emotion, "she was the purest, most noble, most misunderstood of our forebears. She was my mother's aunt and the marvel of her age."

He fell silent for a moment, as if trying to damp down the enthusiasm provoked by the thought of Maria Sinhá—and then, in a calmer voice, he went on:

"Maria Sinhá used to dress like a man and go for long rides on horseback—why, she could ride from Fundão to Queimados faster than any of the best riders on the estate. They say she used a gold-handled whip to beat any slaves she encountered on the way. No one in the family ever really understood her, and she died alone in a dark room in the old Fazenda Santa Eulália up in the Serra do Baú."

"Well, I've never heard anyone speak of her," I said, convinced that this was all pure invention.

"Well," he said with a laugh, "who but I would dare to speak of her? For many years, when I was a child, there was a portrait of her in the drawing room, immediately above the large sideboard, with a black crepe ribbon tied around the frame. The times I would stop and imagine her swift horse galloping through the streets of Vila Velha and envy her outrageous behavior, her freedom and her whip . . . When I began to reveal what the others so delicately term my 'tendencies,' Demétrio ordered that the painting be hidden away in the basement. I, however, feel that Maria Sinhá would have been the pride of the family, a famous warrior, an Anita Garibaldi, had she not been born in this dusty backwater in Minas Gerais . . ."

His voice shook with anger, as if he were not quite in control of it—and since the whole story seemed very strange to me, I remained silent, thinking of the family's long history of failures. He noticed my silence and went back to fanning himself, saying in a different tone:

"What do they say about me, Betty, what do they accuse me of?"

And with a touch of childish pride, he added:

"I'm in the right, though, as you'll see!"

I looked at him, as if expecting some explanation. He sat down heavily beside me:

"Yes, one day you'll see, Betty. The truth will out."

And he laughed again, for longer this time and with a certain relish, his head back.

"After all, what does it matter how I dress? How can that possibly change the essence of things?"

I couldn't help but admire him in a way: there he was, complete with plump, padded bosom and glittering sequins. The sequins were like a symbol of him: rather splendid and completely useless. What could have brought him to his present state, what contradictory, disparate elements had shaped his personality, only for it to explode, unexpectedly and forcefully, under the pressure of the inherited prejudices of the entire Meneses tribe? Because that strange sexless being was a true Meneses—and who knows, one day, as he was predicting, I might well see the old family spirit resurface, in its profoundest, most rustic form, the same eternal wind that had driven the fate of Maria Sinhá.

Senhor Timóteo got up and, as he did, his dress unfurled about him in majestic folds.

"There was a time," he said, almost with his back to me, "there was a time when I believed I should follow the same path as other people. It seemed criminal, almost foolish to obey my own law. The law was a shared domain from which none of us could escape. I wore throttlingly tight ties, mastered the art of banal conversations, imagined I was the same as everyone else. Until, one day, I felt I couldn't possibly go on like that: why follow ordinary laws when I was far from ordinary, why pretend I was like everyone else when I was totally different? Ah, Betty, don't look at me, dressed as I am, as a mere allegorical figure: I want to present others with an image of the courage I lack. I wear what I like and go where I like, except, alas, I do so in a cage of my own making. That is the only freedom that is entirely ours: to be monsters to ourselves."

He fell silent, overcome by emotion. Then, more quietly, as if talking to himself:

"That is what they have done with my gesture, Betty. They have turned it into a prisoner's maniacal obsession, and these clothes, which should constitute my triumph, merely adorn the dream of a condemned man. But one day, do you hear, one day, I will break free from the fear holding me back, and I will show them and the world who I really am. That will only happen when the last of the Meneses lets fall his arm in cowardly surrender. Only then will I have the strength to cry: 'Do you see? Everything that they despise in me is the blood of the Meneses.'"

He spoke these last words rather more loudly than usual, but he quickly recovered, fixed me with an intense gaze and, doubtless overcome by a sudden wave of embarrassment, hid his face behind the fan.

"But, my dear Betty, what mad things I'm telling you, eh? How could you possibly understand what I mean?"

"I don't understand everything," I said, "but some of those things seem very real."

"Real!" and he went back to pacing the room, and as he fanned himself, the scent of sandalwood grew still stronger. "Betty, don't tell me that the only real things are those that exist in my blood. Shall I tell *you* something? I believe I was born with my soul in a ball gown. When I used to wear those throttling neckties, when I wore the same clothes as other men, my mind was full of sumptuous dresses, jewels, and fans. When my mother died—she, who in her youth, was famous for her extravagant clothes—my first act was to take over her entire wardrobe. And not just her wardrobe, but her jewelry too. Locked away in that chest of drawers I have a box containing the most beautiful jewels in the world: amethysts, diamonds, and topaz. When I'm alone, I take them out of their hiding place and, on sleepless nights, I play with them on the bed, I roll them around in my hands, jewels that would be the salvation of the whole family, but which will never leave this room, not at least as long as I live. That's why I said to you that the spirit of Maria Sinhá is in my blood: she was always dreaming of the different outfits she would wear. They say that on moonless nights, she would go out into the streets dressed as a man, smoking a cigarette and with a dark cape over her shoulders."

I confess that I was finding this whole conversation deeply troubling, especially since I did not believe what he was telling me and could see that it was leading nowhere. I sighed and stood up.

"This is all a bit over my head, Senhor Timóteo. But if it makes you happy . . ."

He turned around almost violently, and his face grew dark:

"No, Betty, it has nothing to do with happiness. I wouldn't bother to defy anyone if it was merely a matter of my personal happiness. This is about the truth—and the truth is what matters."

"I believe so too, Senhor Timóteo."

Then something like a long tremor of pleasure ran through his voice:

"Well then. Truth cannot be invented, it cannot be distorted or replaced—it is simply that, the truth. However grotesque, absurd or fatal, it is the truth. You may not understand what I mean, Betty, but that is what is there at the heart of all things."

He again fell silent and stood next to me, breathing hard. Then, as if he had revived old, possibly painful memories, he went on in a voice full of an insinuating nostalgia:

"As a man—or, rather, as a shadow of a man—nothing aroused any passion in me. It was as if I didn't exist. And what is this world without passion, Betty? We must concentrate, we must squeeze every drop of interest and passion that we can out of things. But if there's nothing inside me, if I am merely a ghost of others . . ."

I wasn't following his reasoning at all now and felt slightly bewildered by these vague ideas. I saw only the sequins that glittered as his chest rose and fell with emotion. And he must have noticed my distraction, because he placed one hand on my shoulder.

"Whereas now," and his voice lit up, "my free spirit embraces everything. I love and suffer just like anyone else, I hate, I laugh, and, for better or worse I stand among the others as a truth, not as a mere fantasy. Now do you understand me, Betty?"

I nodded, fearful that he would get even more carried away. What was the point of all those justifications, where did they get us? If it was the truth he was after, and if he had, as one of God's creatures, managed to find a place within the mechanism of the universe, why then boast about what he considered to be his victory? And how could I, a poor housekeeper, used only to running a household, how could I comprehend such paradoxes? As he stood before me, breathing hard, he must have followed the arc of my thoughts, for, like someone coming down to earth again after some transcendent vision, he shook his head and said:

"No, you don't understand. No one understands. The truth is a solitary science."

He shrugged and laughed:

"And how absurd it would be, Betty, if they did understand, not everything, but at least what I represent. The fact is, my reasons are secret reasons."

His laughter, like a fragment of brief, inconsequential music, hung in the air—I felt that the last word had been spoken. Slowly, still fanning himself, he went over to the window, which was permanently covered by thick curtains. What would he see, what landscape would he unveil behind those eternally closed curtains? He merely held up one finger, as if repeating an automatic gesture made dozens and dozens of times, before, as if mortally tired, he lowered it again. Then he turned and started slightly, as if surprised to see me there:

"But we're friends, aren't we, Betty?"

"Of course, Senhor Timóteo, we'll always be friends."

His whole face lit up with a look of great pleasure—no ordinary pleasure either, but a great, dense exhalation of pleasure, a kind of belated, silent flash of lightning that dissipated the continual gloom of his isolation—and he came closer and leaned over me, saying:

"For those words I will be eternally grateful," and he kissed my forehead, a soft, warm, prolonged kiss. And while his lips were touching my skin, I could hear the beating of his heart, like the murmur of an ocean kept under lock and key.

"Senhor Timóteo . . ." I began to say, unable to hide the tears filling my eyes.

Then he stood up, took two steps back and said almost gruffly:

"But that isn't why I asked you here, Betty."

If I had hurt him, that had certainly not been my intention. I wanted to say something that would show him I had understood, but the words stuck in my throat. I felt like taking him in my arms and murmuring tender words, the words one says to children. But with his back to me, he had become a silent, impenetrable block of ice.

"Senhor Timóteo . . ." I began again.

He turned and said with extraordinary calm:

"Betty, I wanted to know if 'she' had arrived."

He was clearly referring to the new mistress. I told him that a telegram had come and that everything had been postponed until the following day.

"Again!" he murmured in a voice as desolate as if something crucial, vital even, to his life hung on that one fact. "Again!" he repeated.

Then, in one of those impulses so peculiar to him, he rushed over to me, clutched my hands and said:

"Betty, I wanted to ask you a favor."

"Of course, if I can help . . ."

I could see Senhor Demétrio's implacable orders before me, as if engraved in stone.

"Yes, you can, you can help," he said. And before I could respond, he explained: "I want to see her, Betty, I need to see her as soon as she arrives. Will you promise to give her a message from me?"

I hesitated, but his eyes remained fixed on mine, and so I said:

"Yes, I promise."

"Thank you, Betty, thank you," and he gave a sigh of relief. "I just want you to go to her and say: 'A person wishes to see you as soon as possible, about a matter of extreme importance.'"

"Is that all?"

"Yes. You swear you won't forget my words."

I held out my hand:

"I swear."

And with that oath we parted company.

21st – I think I was the first person to see her when she got out of the car and—oh!—I will never forget the impression she made on me. It wasn't just admiration I felt, because I had seen other beautiful women in my time. But never before had my initial feeling of amazement been edged with anxiety, that slight breathlessness, it was not only the certainty that there before me stood an extraordinarily beautiful woman, it was my awareness that she was also a *presence*—a definite, self-assured being who appeared to give off her own light and her own warmth, like a landscape. (*Note written in the margin:* Even today, after all this time, I don't think any one thing has ever impressed me so much as that first encounter with Dona Nina. She was not only graceful, she was subtle, generous, even majestic. She wasn't just beautiful, she was intensely, violently seductive. She emerged from the car as if nothing else existed outside the aura of her fascination—this was not mere charm, it was magic. Later, as she deteriorated, I watched as the fatal illness left its marks upon her face, and I can honestly say that her features never became coarse or anything less than noble. There was a metamorphosis, a shift perhaps, but the essence was there, and even when I saw her dead, wrapped in the sad winding sheet of the despised outsider, I could see the same splendor as on that first day, flickering, sleepless, rootless, like moonlight glinting on the wreckage of a ship.)

She paused for a moment, one hand resting on the car door. We were lined up before her, with Senhor Demétrio, Dona Ana, and Senhor Valdo slightly ahead, followed, as befitted my station, by me, then old Anastácia, who had been Senhor Valdo's nursemaid and was in charge of the black servants in the kitchen, then Pedro and the other servants. Such ceremony, such solemn faces, slightly embarrassed her.

"Valdo! Valdo!" she cried. "Help me unload the luggage."

Senhor Valdo beckoned to me and I stepped forward, closely followed by old Anastácia. I began the task of unloading suitcases of varying sizes, endless hat boxes—why so many?—and an infinite number of smaller items. Even while I was engaged in doing this, I still had time to observe the welcoming party. The mistress went over to Senhor Valdo, and I noticed their slightly awkward embrace, even though they were newlyweds. He was doubtless wounded by her continual postponements and wanted to make his feelings clear. As for Senhor Demétrio, he gave her a far warmer reception than I would have expected—as if he were both surprised and excited by Dona Nina's beauty. As soon as she had extricated herself from her husband's arms, Senhor Demétrio immediately stepped forward and kissed her on the cheek, saying how delighted he was to welcome her to the Chácara. At the same time, he pushed poor Dona Ana forward, but she showed not the slightest glimmer of pleasure at meeting the new arrival. That was the most difficult moment for all those present: the newcomer merely offered Dona Ana the tips of her fingers, as if she had no great interest in meeting this new acquaintance either. Dona Ana turned even paler than usual and murmured a few words that no one understood. Finally, they all went into the house. At the very foot of the steps, I saw the new mistress crouch down and pick a violet that was growing among the clover. "My favorite flower," she said.

Helped by Pedro and Anastácia, I took the luggage to the newlyweds' room, which was right next to Senhor Timóteo's room—so close that, outside, the windows almost touched. This meant that, for some time, I lost track of events. When I returned to the drawing room, Senhor Demétrio and Dona Ana had already withdrawn. Standing at the window, looking out onto the verandah—although what was there to look at in that sea of mango trees?—were Senhor Valdo and the mistress. They must have been quarrelling, because they both seemed very ill at ease. Not noticing my presence, he turned to her and said:

"You are *never* right, Nina, and the worst of it is that you don't seem to realize it."

I saw her spin around, aflame with indignation:

"Is that why you wanted me to come here, Valdo? So that you could pester and threaten me with your jealousy? I've already explained the reason for my delay, that I had to say goodbye to various friends. As for the Colonel, I've haven't seen him since. Now, if you think . . ."

"You don't understand, Nina," he said, interrupting her.

Those words seemed to raise her anger to a new pitch. She began pacing furiously up and down, and I withdrew discreetly into Senhor Demétrio's study, intending to tidy some of the bookshelves. Since his study immediately adjoined the drawing room and I had left the door open, I could still hear fragments of their argument. As far as I could make out, it was about some money that Senhor Valdo had failed to send to her in Rio de Janeiro, with, according to her, the "base" intention of forcing her to start out for Minas earlier than expected. (Ah, Minas Gerais, she roared, the ugly, silent people she had seen from the train, people who had seemed to her both sad and mean, qualities she loathed.) Standing at the window, doubtless pointing at the dense host of mango trees outside, she declared in her most eloquent tones: "You cannot imagine how I hate all this!" She was doubtless sincere in this, for she had never lived in the countryside, and that low, flat landscape, with its bare expanses parched by the summer sun, did not speak to her at all and aroused in her only a genuine feeling of anxiety. I think it may well have been that aversion, expressed on innumerable occasions, in every possible tone of voice, that laid the foundations for the hostility between her and Senhor Demétrio, who was so deeply rooted in Minas Gerais. More than anything, though, he loved the Chácara, which, in his eyes, represented the tradition and dignity of the local customs—which were, according to him, the only authentic customs in all Brazil. "People may speak ill of me," he used to say, "but not of this house. It dates back to the days of the Empire, and represents several generations of the Meneses family, who have lived here proudly and with dignity."

The fact is that, once the argument between Dona Nina and Senhor Valdo was over—it was early days for them to have any truly bitter disputes—they both went out into the garden while they waited for lunch to be served. I have no idea what they did or talked about as they walked up and down the sandy paths—I saw only that when the mistress returned, she was holding a small bunch of violets. "Alberto the gardener gave them to me," she said, as if not wanting us to think they had been a gift from Senhor Valdo. Senhor Demétrio and Dona Ana were already seated at the table, and perhaps because they had been kept waiting, the ensuing conversation was not exactly animated. When Dona Nina praised the flowers in the garden, Senhor Demétrio commented vaguely that Alberto was, indeed, a good gardener, but rather too young for the job. He lacked the necessary experience for dealing with certain more difficult plants. Dona Nina mounted a rather lively defense, saying that precisely because he was so young, he was more likely to be open to adopting new methods. Talk turned to the Pavilion, and for some reason, Senhor Valdo suddenly began to list some of the Chácara's shortcomings.

"The facilities here are far from perfect, Demétrio, and have long been in need of renovation."

I saw Senhor Demétrio first stare at him in some amazement, then slowly put down his knife and fork.

"You astonish me, Valdo. Since when have you taken any interest in 'the facilities'?"

"I was looking around with Nina today and . . ." Senhor Valdo began tentatively.

"Today!" and Senhor Demétrio's voice was ripe with irony. "Only today, and yet the house has been falling to pieces for a very long time! I congratulate you, Nina, on your miraculous powers. Really, only someone totally irresponsible . . ."

Quickly and as if wanting to prevent his brother from going any further down that route, Senhor Valdo broke in with:

"We need to do some work on the house, Demétrio. For example, as I mentioned, the Pavilion . . ."

Senhor Demétrio glanced first at Dona Ana, as if to make sure that she, too, was aware of the absurdity of what they were hearing, then at Senhor Valdo, who was trying to look as unruffled as possible, and lastly at Dona Nina, who was the only one following the conversation with visible interest—then he gave a soft, delicious gurgle of laughter:

"Work! On the Pavilion in the garden . . . That's ridiculous, Valdo!"

It was Senhor Valdo's turn to put down his knife and fork.

"I don't see why."

"Don't you?" and Senhor Demétrio's laugh, which continued to light up his face, suddenly stopped. "You really don't see why? You know perfectly well what we are: a bankrupt family living in the south of Minas Gerais, a family that no longer has any cattle to graze, that lives from renting out the pastures it owns, although only when they're not parched dry, a family that produces nothing, absolutely nothing, to replace sources of income that long ago dried up. Our one hope is that we simply disappear very quietly here under this roof, unless, of course, some generous soul"—and he shot a quick glance at the mistress—"comes to our rescue."

"You're joking, Demétrio," murmured Senhor Valdo, turning pale.

"No, I'm not," retorted his brother. "I assume that in order to carry out such work, repairs on the Pavilion in the garden and who knows what else, you're counting on a loan from your dear wife."

Dona Nina remained utterly impassive—she merely raised her eyebrows and said coolly:

"I married a wealthy man."

"Wealthy? Is that what he told you?" cried Senhor Demétrio.

"Yes."

He had been leaning forward across the table, but he fell back now, so violently that I feared he might take the chair with him.

"He doesn't have a penny to his name! We owe money to the servants, to the pharmacist, to the local bank . . . No, really, this is too much . . ."

Only then did the mistress appear to lose her composure. Throwing down her napkin on the table, her lips trembling, she said:

"Valdo, this is too humiliating!"

I thought for a moment that she was going to get up and leave the room, but after a few seconds, with the atmosphere still just as tense, I heard Senhor Valdo say:

"Don't worry, Nina, my brother always exaggerates."

I had my back to them, pretending to be preparing the plates for dessert—this was a special day and on such occasions, among my other tasks, I would serve at the table. And so while I couldn't see the look on Senhor Demétrio's face, I heard him laugh again, his laughter muffled this time by the napkin pressed to his lips.

"So I exaggerate, do I?" he said. "It should be easy enough then to explain why you didn't send Nina the money she was expecting, and why you didn't order the room she'll be occupying to be painted, a room that is, by the way, merely a cubbyhole at the far end of the hallway." He stopped, almost hesitated. Then he added more quietly, but very firmly: "And where will you find the money to pay for all the dresses and hats she's brought with her?"

"Oh, Valdo!" I heard Dona Nina exclaim.

I turned and began serving dessert, not that anyone noticed me. Something was clearly about to explode—a struggle, a misunderstanding that could last a lifetime—and only Dona Ana was indifferently stirring the cream sauce I had set before her.

"Oh, Valdo," Dona Nina said again, and suddenly hid her face in her napkin.

"Don't you meddle in my affairs," roared Senhor Valdo, almost out of control. "I'm perfectly capable of paying my own bills, and it won't be with my wife's money."

Then, more softly, and emphasizing every syllable, as if to savor the pleasure of what he was about to reveal, Senhor Demétrio murmured:

"That's just as well, Valdo, because then I won't have to dip into *my* wife's savings, as I have on other occasions."

I heard a stifled cry, and Dona Nina sprang to her feet, trembling. A few tears glittered on her eyelashes—the easily provoked tears I would often see later on—and in a gesture of impotent rage, she was still clutching her crumpled napkin. I realized then that we had reached the critical moment and that, whatever followed, nothing would be as potent or as far-reaching as what was happening at that very minute, because it was the kernel from which everything else would subsequently emerge. With a bold movement, which appeared to be a declaration that she would never submit to the economic strictures of the Meneses family, she pushed back her chair and was about to leave the room when Senhor Demétrio stopped her:

"I'm sorry, Nina, but all those hats and dresses of yours will be of no use to you in the country. Because this *is* the countryside, you know. Here," and he pointed casually at his wife, "women dress like Ana."

The mistress had no option but to look at the person indicated, and the enmity that sprang up between them had its beginnings there and then, I think, in the haughty, horribly scornful look that Nina bestowed on Ana. As she stood there, a few steps away from the table, a venomous smile appeared on her lips. Dona Ana, still seated, endured that examination with head bowed: she was wearing a faded black dress, entirely unadorned and entirely out of fashion. This rapid examination must have been enough to satisfy Dona Nina, because, without responding, without even turning to look at Senhor Demétrio, she stalked out of the room, her chin defiantly lifted. Senhor Valdo shot a glance at his brother—a glance of pure hatred—and followed his wife. Alone at the table, Senhor Demétrio and Dona Ana drank their coffee and, in that shared silence, I realized there was a new and tacit understanding between them.

Hours later, when I went out onto the verandah to shake the table cloth, I found the mistress there, lying in a hammock. She looked completely exhausted. She appeared to have been crying too, for her eyes were still red.

"Come here, Betty," she said.

I went over to her, and she took my hands in hers.

"Dear God, what a dreadful start. Did you see how they treated me today?"

"Senhor Demétrio is always like that," I said, trying to offer her a small crumb of comfort.

She let go of my hand and set the hammock swinging slightly.

"And yet Valdo really did tell me that he was a wealthy man and that here, in this house, I would want for nothing. Why did he do that, why did he deceive me like that?"

"Perhaps he didn't want to lose you, Dona Nina. And Senhor Demétrio does tend to exaggerate . . ."

She again took one of my hands and said:

"I'm surrounded by enemies here, Betty, but I don't want you to be one of them."

"Of course not, Dona Nina," I protested warmly, thinking how beautiful she looked, lying there in the hammock. (*Note written in the margin*: Such an odd impression. There was still a remnant of warm, golden evening light on the verandah. Her pale skin and her almost auburn hair emphasized her shining, liquid eyes, and yet everything about her spoke of a certain strength. I would never have said that she was, overall, a real beauty: no, she was beautiful in every detail, every line, almost exasperatingly perfect in every respect.) "I would never be your enemy," I concluded after a brief pause. "But aren't you yourself perhaps exaggerating too?"

She gave me a sharp, enquiring look.

"No, I'm not exaggerating."

Perplexed, I asked:

"But then why, Senhora, why?"

She let go of my hand and once more set the hammock gently swinging. When she leaned her head back, the branch of an acacia tree cast a shadow over her face.

"I don't know, I really don't," she murmured. "These old families always have a kind of canker at their heart. I don't think they can bear what I represent: a new life, a different landscape."

And as if on a sudden inspiration, she added:

"And maybe they're afraid too."

I said nothing, doubtless hoping she would explain what she meant. The shadow came and went on her face, and a mischievous glint appeared in her eyes.

"The family may be bankrupt, but this house must be worth a lot, Betty. I noticed that around back there's open pasture as far as the mountains."

"It's the grazing land that belonged to the old Fazenda Santa Eulália," I said.

And half sitting up in the hammock, Dona Nina asked:

"And what would they say, these ancient Meneses folk, if I were to give birth to an heir to all this?"

I nodded silently, because I felt she was quite right. Senhor Demétrio, who was older than Senhor Valdo, and who, because of the latter's incompetence and indifference, had always been in charge of the business side of things, would lose all rights to the Chácara, since he had no heir. Yes, it was quite possible; and beneath the pressure of that inquisitorial gaze, I forgot about the wear and tear inflicted by time and suddenly saw the garden and the Pavilion, and even the surrounding mountains, as a great hope of wealth and resurrection. Dona Nina read my thoughts and, leaning toward me, she clasped my hands in hers, saying:

"Don't leave me, Betty, be my friend, I need your friendship. At least as long as I'm living here."

Those were almost the very words I had heard in Senhor Timóteo's room. I remembered my visit there on the previous day and the favor he had asked me. Then, seizing the opportunity, I said:

"A person wishes to see you as soon as possible, about a matter of extreme importance."

Those, I believed, had been his exact words.

5.
The Doctor's First Report

I don't remember exactly what day it was, and I couldn't even say what time, but I can say that the call came as no surprise to me, for it had been evident for some time, even to outsiders, that all was not well at the Chácara. Perhaps I should rather say that our little town, and even other towns in the district, were full of gossip, ranging from the naïve to the scurrilous, about what scandals might conceivably be engulfing the house of the Meneses. For example, Donana de Lara, who had come to consult me about her son and, in the last few days, had been even more agitated than usual, had even suggested that Father Justino should be summoned to ask for God's blessing for the Chácara: according to her, the evil was deeply ingrained in the misdeeds of all those past Meneses, who had poisoned the whole atmosphere of the house. But to return to the incident in question, I assumed, and soon found out how wrong I was, that the call was to attend Dona Nina, whose more or less recent arrival had aroused everyone's interest. While I was getting dressed, I kept imagining what might have happened. People said she was dangerous, fascinating, capricious and imperious, and having seen our little circle come to the boil and then cool off over so many other different people, I asked myself what it was about her that made her such a lasting topic of conversation. "Perhaps it's just because she's an outsider, and a beautiful woman at that," I thought. And as I prepared my medical bag, I sensed deep down a certain pleasure, because I was, at the time, extremely curious to find out what went on at the Chácara.

It was not, however, Dona Nina who needed my attention—and this was the first of my disappointments. The second, which followed immediately afterward, was that there was no scandalous scene for me to witness, for what I found was a fait accompli. I shrugged and tried to hide my dismay. As I climbed the steps from the garden, I was immediately informed that Senhor Valdo had injured himself while cleaning an old gun. I was accompanied by an old negro woman by the name of Anastácia, one of the long-time servants at the Chácara, and I had great difficulty in understanding her half-African, half-country dialect. In any event, I soon found myself in a room plunged in darkness, where the wounded man was lying on a couch. The first thing I noticed was the strange atmosphere; the second was that the man seemed more gravely wounded than I had been led to believe. The only person with him was Senhor Demétrio, and, perhaps in order to feign indifference and thus inspire me with a confidence I did not share, he was sitting on a low chair, his legs crossed, pretending to read a newspaper. I saw at once that he was extremely irritated; indeed, that sense of irritation was the most noticeable thing about his attitude, which one would normally have expected to be one of concern and anxiety. He stood up as soon as I entered, greeted me with the customary reserve of the Meneses, and asked if I wanted him to turn on the light. "Naturally," I replied, and he went over to turn the switch. As in almost all country districts, our town lacked a reliable electricity supply, but at the Chácara, which had its own generator, things were even worse: the yellowish, flickering light brightened and dimmed according to the strength of the current. I saw instantly that the room was not exactly a bedroom, but one of those storerooms they have in large houses, and which get used for all sorts of things. So quickly had Senhor

Valdo been carried to this cubbyhole—for that was what it was—that there had been no time to prepare anything: he had been thrown in among the furniture like just another useless object. He was lying on a tattered couch that they had covered with a faded red shawl. One of his shoes was missing and he was wearing a rather worn linen dressing gown. Beneath that loosely fastened gown I could see his white, blood-soaked shirt. The wound itself wasn't immediately visible because they had covered it with ice, from which the water, mingled with blood, was trickling from the couch onto the floor. He showed no signs of life and his eyes were closed. I asked if that was the only place he had been wounded, and Senhor Demétrio said "Yes," although he did not believe that the bullet had affected any vital organ. He spoke quickly, as if to dismiss the matter as one of little importance. I started by removing the ice and cleaning the surrounding area, which was covered in thick, coagulated blood. It did not take me long to find the wound itself: it was just beneath the heart, and the bullet must have grazed his ribs. It had clearly missed its target but, despite this, he must have lost a lot of blood, which is probably why he had fainted. I asked if anyone had heard the shot, and how they had found him. Senhor Demétrio appeared somewhat annoyed by these questions, which seemed perhaps more appropriate to a police investigation than a medical inquiry, but he nevertheless told me that his brother had been cleaning the revolver since early that morning; that he, Demétrio, had several times voiced his fears that something untoward might happen with a rusty old gun like that; that he didn't know who the gun belonged to; that he hadn't heard the shot nor indeed had anyone else; and that, shortly before my arrival, puzzled by Senhor Valdo's prolonged silence, he had found him, in his dressing gown, stretched out on the drawing room floor. He also told me that there had been a pool of blood on the floor, which he had told the housekeeper to clean up, while he carried the wounded man to this, the nearest bedroom. Senhor Valdo had not opened his eyes since then, and he, Demétrio, who found such recklessness inexcusable, was waiting for his brother to regain consciousness so that he could explain himself. I asked whether he really had been cleaning the gun since early that morning and, barely containing his irritation, Senhor Demétrio repeated: "Yes, since early this morning," while I thought how very odd it was for a man to spend an entire day cleaning a rusty gun. But then the Meneses are capable of anything. Seeing me hesitate, Senhor Demétrio declared:

"Everything points to it being an accident plain and simple. Any other explanation would, frankly, be a betrayal of the facts," and he shot me a furtive glance to see if his words had convinced me.

At that precise moment—and it was as if he were doing so deliberately to annoy his brother—Senhor Valdo opened his eyes—and I confess that I have never seen so absolute an expression of revulsion, anger, and discord as in that first exchange of glances between the two brothers. There was no doubt about it: the accident, or whatever it was, had enraged Senhor Demétrio. This troubled me and, while the wounded man groaned softly (for I was probing his wound), I found myself staring at Senhor Demétrio somewhat unguardedly. He must have realized what was going through my mind, for he placed one hand on my shoulder, in a gesture at once amicable and commanding:

"My brother is not yet able to speak about the incident," he said. "He has lost a lot of blood in this silly stunt of his, and is probably still not capable of thinking very clearly. But soon . . ."

I watched the wounded man make a great effort to draw himself up into a sitting position, sweat pouring from his brow:

"Yes I am," he murmured. "And you know very well, Demétrio, what I have to say."

Although spoken with difficulty, his words were entirely audible.

"What? Speaking already? Well, I'm delighted," Senhor Demétrio said with feigned pleasure, as if he had not heard what the wounded man had said. And he added somewhat scornfully: "Do you really mean to say it wasn't just a reckless joke?"

Senhor Valdo gave him another long look as if formulating an accusation, but, overcome by weariness, he groaned and let his head fall back on the couch, at the same time clawing at the blanket in a gesture of rage and impotence. I waited for his temper to cool and his strength to return, but he merely turned his face to the wall in a gesture of utter exhaustion. I then began the medical treatment proper, applying gauze and bandages, even though I was not entirely sure how effective they would be, since, in emotional crises such as these, the mood of the patient often counts for more than any form of palliative care. When I had finished, I saw that there was nothing more for me to do: the patient, his chest now swathed in bandages, appeared to be sleeping. Much as I may have wanted to, I could not justifiably prolong my presence there. So I covered the wounded man with a sheet and was about to leave when I felt him grasp one of my hands. It was an unexpected and extraordinarily significant gesture: I leaned over and saw his pleading eyes, in which I saw an evident cry for help, insisting that I stay. Not knowing what to do, I stared first at the wounded man and then at Senhor Demétrio, until the latter decided for me what path I should take:

"Come," he said, "I think that more than anything else the patient needs rest. There will be plenty of time for talk later."

He slightly tightened his grip on my shoulder as he said this. After making a few further recommendations, I left the room, ignoring the supplicant look in Senhor Valdo's eyes. I confess I found the calm, silent atmosphere in the house very strange. No one would have thought that such a serious incident had occurred only a short time before, one that could so easily have turned into tragedy. I met no one else as I passed through the various rooms, and since I could think of no rational explanation for this—other than its being a very large house with spacious rooms in which each inhabitant could be alone—I imagined that it was probably due to orders issued by Senhor Demétrio himself. He felt under no obligation to show me to the front door and, after asking a few banal questions about the patient's general state of health, he bade me farewell and, unprompted by me, declared that he felt entirely at ease regarding his brother. "It's no more than a minor disaster brought on by his own recklessness," he concluded, and as he spoke, it was clear that he was utterly incensed by this incident, which he insisted on describing as "reckless." What he said next was further proof of this: "He shouldn't have gone poking his nose in where it wasn't wanted." Alone, I passed through the drawing room and walked across the verandah as far as the steps down into the garden. It was only there, when I turned to take a last look back at the house, so crammed with secrets, that I noticed a few lights coming on; then a door slammed, a voice rang out, probably from the kitchen, as if normal life were returning to the house, leaving me, a curious onlooker, standing on its forbidden threshold. Once again I shrugged—what else could I do?—and went down the steps, which seemed about to be overwhelmed on either side by the encroaching greenery.

Just when I thought my visit was at an end, I noticed a figure appear from behind the shrubbery, as if whoever it was had been waiting for me. Straining my eyes—for my sight never was very good—I saw that it was a woman and, I confess, I couldn't help but feel a certain satisfaction at the thought that I might perhaps leave the Chácara knowing a little more about the mystery than I had expected. For, right from the start, I had been in little doubt that there *was* a mystery to be unveiled, and that behind what appeared to be a simple accident lurked the kind of grave and painful feelings that churn away in the hearts of all families. The woman drew closer, and I saw that she was dressed for a journey. (Let me be more precise: she was wearing a black woolen cape, gloves, a green scarf around her neck, and one of those berets women used to wear when traveling.)

"Doctor," she said, stopping a few feet away from me, "I need to speak to you urgently."

Her voice was calm and somewhat imperious.

"Of course, Senhora. How can I help?"

And I bowed, quite certain that before me stood Senhor Valdo's wife, whose beauty was already legendary. Even in the darkness, I knew that I was in the presence of the most beautiful woman I had ever seen in my whole life.

"I was just about to leave," she said, "when all this happened. My suitcases are over there, by the steps."

She stopped for a moment. Then, without betraying any of the emotion she must certainly have been feeling, she asked:

"Is it serious his condition? Is it very serious? How is he now? Is there any hope?"

She asked all these questions one after the other, without giving me time to answer her first question. I was still more struck by the fact that she had no doubt whatsoever as to the gravity of what had taken place, despite her apparent calm and even coolness. There may have been one or two tremors in her voice, but I put this down to a certain degree of suppressed irritation at events that had doubtless disrupted her carefully-laid plans. It was easy enough to tell what those plans were: she was on the point of leaving the Chácara, probably hoping to say goodbye to it forever, and that "reckless" incident had prevented her from doing so at the very moment of her departure.

"Please," she continued, without giving me time to say anything, "I heard that it was nothing, merely carelessness . . . but I have to say that the person who told me that is not to be trusted. When he said it was merely a reckless accident, I immediately thought Valdo might die this very night. Is there such a danger, Doctor?"

This time she sounded almost anxious. When she stopped speaking, I noticed that she was breathing hard as if she had just returned from a long walk. What a strange woman, I thought, and wondered what peculiar feelings stirred in the depths of her soul. I shook my head and, sensing that she was hanging on my every word, said:

"No, there's absolutely no danger of that. It's only a superficial wound."

"Superficial!" she cried. "Do you mean he isn't fatally wounded, Doctor? Betty told me she had to clean up a large pool of blood from the drawing room floor. When I heard that, I imagined he must already be at death's door."

"No, he is very far from that."

"Oh," she exclaimed, "so it's true then. Demétrio was right. It was merely a foolish gesture, an act of . . ."

She stopped and bowed her head. For a few moments, she remained silent, lost in thought. The wind caught a few strands of hair that had escaped from beneath her beret. But when she looked up again, she suddenly gave a laugh that echoed through the shadowy garden. I shuddered, sensing the repressed malice my words had unleashed.

"So," she said, "that's how they want to play it. Well, they don't fool me. They clearly do not know me or what I'm capable of. Tell me, Doctor, now that we're alone, what did he say, what lies did he invent about me? Did he mention anything about a gardener . . ."

She clapped her hand over her mouth as if wanting to catch those words spoken seemingly involuntarily.

"Who do you mean?" I asked.

"Valdo. Who else?"

I explained that Senhor Valdo was not yet able to speak, due to the shock he had suffered and the large quantity of blood he had lost. She murmured: "So he lost a lot of blood, then," and continued rather absently to listen to what I was saying, as if the subject no longer interested her very much. As soon as I finished speaking, and seeing that she had not moved, I wasn't sure whether I should stay or go, and I had just decided it would be best to leave when her apparent indifference abruptly turned into a state of great agitation, stopping me in my tracks. As if suddenly waking up, she hid her face in her hands, crying and laughing at the same time. Then, overcome by emotion, she leaned against a tree letting her arms droop despondently by her sides, and repeated over and over: "Oh, my God! Oh, my God!" I tried to intervene, and went as far as to reach out my arm to comfort her, but nothing seemed capable of drawing her out of that agitated state and so I decided to do nothing, like someone waiting patiently for a tornado to pass. Eventually, she calmed down, resting her head against the trunk. The moonlight fell directly on her face, and I could see the tears streaming down it. I suspected that such distress had no ordinary cause, and realized from her slightly swollen body that she must be pregnant. Ah, how beautiful she was! A hundred thousand times more beautiful than before, more beautiful than all the women I had ever seen.

"I think you would be better . . ." I mumbled.

She gave me a look that seemed to contain all the feelings ravaging her soul:

"Don't give me any advice, Doctor. I don't need advice, and I don't want anyone to concern themselves with my life."

At the same time, she silently contradicted these words by linking arms with me and drawing me along with her toward the end of the avenue, where the fence separated the garden from the road. The sand crunched beneath our feet, and great pools of moonlight alternated with great pools of darkness. I don't know why (perhaps I was already under the influence of the restless atmosphere in the Chácara), but I was afraid someone might see me in such close proximity to that woman; for there was no doubt that she was someone who paid little heed to convention. But there was in her beauty (for, from time to time, I was able to cast a furtive glance at her), a hint of tragedy. As we walked, she told me her story, although her words were so garbled, so jumbled by emotion, that I could scarcely grasp their meaning.

After an argument with Valdo, she had that very day decided to leave the Chácara forever. Or rather, she had already decided this some time before, when she found out she was pregnant. However, she had not taken this decision lightly; on the contrary, she had thought about it long and hard, for it would indeed be the end of a period of relative tranquility in her life, "relative" because she was sure she could never be entirely happy living with the Meneses, although she had done her best to cope, by moving away from the house and into the Pavilion. She sensed, however, that her presence was displeasing to Demétrio, and he had been the cause of her last argument with Valdo. Because Demétrio had invented the most fantastical stories about her. Oh, she knew very well that he only wanted to get rid of her: he was afraid of the soon-to-be-born future heir of the Chácara. At least that's what she thought, since she could find no other reason for her brother-in-law's peculiar attitude toward her. They had, at times, even argued about whether or not the child should be born at the Chácara. Valdo was opposed to her leaving and implored, even threatened her, but Demétrio, claiming that there were no adequate medical facilities in either Vila Velha or the surrounding area, insisted that she should leave and wait in Rio for the child to be born. She had hesitated because of her husband, but had then suddenly felt so very weary of it all that she had decided to leave. When he saw her mind was made up, Valdo had turned very pale: "Is there no other way, Nina? Are you really leaving?" No, there was no other way; she was leaving. Then he had compounded his brother's insults with one great, definitive insult of his own: "I don't know why God punished me by making me fall in love with and choose a prostitute to be the mother of my son. Because that's what you are, Nina. It's written all over your face, branded on your forehead: you're one of those sluts who follow men in the streets . . ." She had sprung angrily to her feet, and it was there and then that she had decided to pack her bags and leave the Pavilion where she had, albeit briefly, been so happy. Now she was determined to put an end to this charade, once and for all. There was no love between them; there was nothing at all. He had met her at a time of great difficulty for her, when her father was ill, and as soon as her father had died, Valdo had showered her with love and attention and convinced her she should accompany him to the Chácara. That was all. Since she'd arrived, however, she had realized that she would not be able to live there for very long. She was from Rio and used to life in a big city. Here, everything displeased her: the silence, the local customs, even the landscape. She missed the restaurants, the hustle and bustle, the cars, the closeness to the sea. Taking advantage of a brief pause—we had almost reached the fence by then—I asked what kind of feeling it was that bound her to Senhor Valdo if it was not love? It was my only question. The reply she gave was characteristically confused, as if she had never before given the matter serious consideration. It was, she said, a difficult feeling to describe: irritation mingled with fear and a touch of fascination. To her, Senhor Valdo represented many things she had not had: a family, a house, the kind of upbringing she had never known. But she was perfectly aware that she needed to leave and return to the little room where she had lived before she was married, to the friends she had left behind, before she and Valdo became mortal enemies—which was sure to happen sometime soon. While she was dressing, her cases already packed and waiting on the bed, Betty, who had been told to order a cart to transport her luggage, heard a shot ring out. And it was Betty who had burst into her room, crying: "Senhora! Senhor Valdo has shot himself!" She couldn't believe it, couldn't imagine him capable of such an act. So much so that she did not even unpack her suitcases. Ah, she was still very far from imagining what mad lengths her husband would go to in order to keep up their little charade. She was still too stunned even to leave her room, imagining Valdo dying or perhaps already dead in a pool of blood. She paced up and down, unable to decide what to do. It was then that Senhor Demétrio had appeared, even stiffer and more formal than usual. "Nina, it is my duty to inform you of what has happened. My brother has committed a reckless act, but from what I can see, it's of no great consequence. A mere graze. If you still wish to leave, please do not feel you have to stay." She could see that he was extremely angry, and that he would never forgive Valdo for something he considered to be utter foolishness. She knew very well what he wanted, and what those words uttered with such calculated slowness meant. Everything about that man was studied and false. And turning to face him, she was about to apologize and say she wasn't going to leave after all, when she caught in his eyes a gleam so fixed, so cold, that the words died on her lips. She was sure, beyond any doubt, that Demétrio was concealing some criminal intent. For some moments they stood in silence, he accusing her with all the force of his hostile presence, she doing her best to defend her helpless self, ready to grasp at any straw. Steeling herself, however, she asked: "Suicide? Did he try to . . ." Senhor Demétrio grew even more distant, even stiffer and colder: "Yes, he did, but, as I say, there were no serious consequences." There was a faint note of irony in his voice. When she did not move, he opened the door and left. From that point on, she had felt unable to stay in that room a moment longer and leaving her bags packed and ready on the bed, she went down into the garden, looking for a servant from whom she could obtain more information. Finding no one, she had summoned up all her courage and gone to the small room where Senhor Valdo was lying. Her hands were trembling, her whole body was trembling. What if Demétrio had lied and Valdo was gravely wounded, how could she possibly face him? She found Senhor Valdo on the couch, his shirt stained with blood. Unable to bear the sight for more than a second, she ran from the room, certain that she had indeed been the cause of that absurd tragedy.

For a while, she remained absorbed in her thoughts, not speaking, her hand resting on my arm. We had reached the fence, beyond which lay the road leading to Vila Velha. Fireflies glowed in the darkness, and not far off, an invisible stream sang and babbled.

"Tell me, Doctor," and she turned to me again, her voice noticeably softer, as if she were about to give voice to the heavy matter weighing on her heart, "is he really not in any danger?"

"None," I confirmed.

“Is it possible,” and by now she was almost whispering in my ear, “is it possible that it was . . . an attempted murder?”

I have to say that her question, far from surprising me, found an echo in my own thoughts. I remembered the look the brothers had exchanged when Senhor Valdo came around, his threat to reveal all that he knew and, as there seemed to be no proof that it really was an “accident,” I had no qualms in affirming that the possibility of a crime could not be entirely dismissed.

“In that case, everything changes,” she said. “If this isn’t some new charade of Valdo’s, then I won’t leave. I shall stay, and I shan’t rest until . . .”

A bright, decisive light appeared in her eyes—I saw that she had finally reached a decision. The mimosa-covered fence blocked our path and we could go no farther. What’s more, we were bathed in moonlight and thus easily visible from the windows of the Chácara. It was then that Dona Nina seemed to remember that this was the first time we had met and that, with her customary impetuosity, she had just entrusted her secret to a man whom her family did not even consider to be a friend of the household.

“Thank you, Doctor,” she said, taking my hands for the last time. “Forgive me for everything I’ve said.”

I declared with a certain warmth that there was absolutely no need to apologize, and said goodbye. The moon was shining brightly, the stream was singing close by. I took a detour to reach the gate. I was feeling somewhat uneasy, sensing a new element in my life. Well, perhaps only for an instant, but it had been like a poetic ray of light. A remarkable woman and a remarkable story. From a distance, I turned again and saw her walking resolutely through the darkness toward the Chácara.

6.
Second Letter from Nina to Valdo Meneses

. . . An era, all that I suffered while living in utter penury. Ah, Valdo, I became so disillusioned that I almost came to believe that the love between us had been but a dream. I spent days and days in a state of utter despair, slumped on a sofa, unable to move my legs. The doctor, who diagnosed a form of nervous paralysis, said I might never return to full health, that the illness was very difficult to treat, and then he rattled off a string of complicated names I can no longer remember. I wept copiously, indeed, my eyes are still swollen from crying. These were not the easy tears you always found so irritating, these were the genuinely desperate tears of a poor paralytic. If only I had simply died and put an end to my suffering once and for all, then I would not have to rely on other people's charity in order to live. Sitting in my room, looking around at the few pathetic objects that are a testament to my penury, I realize that I am surrounded by strangers, that I am no longer any use to anyone, that no one even bothers to ask after me. Yes, Valdo, I must finally give in and acknowledge the truth I have tried so hard to avoid: in the face of your silence, I have no alternative but to consider you a stranger. However much thought I have given to our situation—and I have thought about it endlessly, tossing and turning in my bed—however hard I have tried

to find a solution to the painful times we are going through now, and for which neither of us is actually to blame (and I say again, and will continue to say until the end: there are malevolent influences at work, on the part of our enemies, people who have nothing to do with our problem, which should be left to us alone to resolve. On the night of the "accident," and in view of the happy days we had spent in the Pavilion, I had decided to stay—and I would have stayed, if, in addition to his crude accusations, Demétrio had not then produced his so-called proof . . . He was the one who forced me to leave the Chácara. And you and I were too innocent, too trusting of loyalties that did not exist.) I have studied and examined our situation from every angle, but have found nothing that could help us in our affliction. We are condemned to a hatred we did not want. As far as I am concerned, Valdo, I have never harbored any cruel feelings for you in my heart. And there was a time when we loved each other ....
.... the ingratitude of others, the evil of the world. They are the real culprits, and were we to appear in court, what judges would we see before us, what hypocritical faces, what false friends revealed at last as the liars and slanderers they really are? As I write, my eyes again fill with tears. Everything around me is so ugly, this apartment with its tiny windows, the concrete courtyard where children play, this mean little room—I have never been any good at being poor. Meanwhile, Valdo, in order to retrace the path of that old story, we need to probe certain secrets and rummage around in the ashes of that sad night. Up until now, out of a kind of foolish scrupulousness, I have always refused to comment on what happened. Largely because that would mean naming someone who no longer exists, and who, through his suicide, freed himself from a slander he could not bear. And besides, what's past is past. I take up my pen now to write about those tragic events because I have a plan of action—and I warn you, Valdo, that nothing, not even my son's life, will stop me from following my chosen path. Besides, it is time I got my own life back and restored the purity of my name for

the sake of that poor angel. He and he alone is the motivating force behind what I now intend to do. Forgive me if I occasionally cut a slightly pathetic figure, it is simply that this whole business causes me more than mere disgust—it drives me to extremes of humiliation and despair. My very blood cries out to be avenged for the injustice of which I was the victim. From now on, Valdo, no one will have the right to throw my sins in my face. There are no sins, they never existed. You'll say I'm mad, that I'm playing a role no one takes seriously. But you must believe me, Valdo, you must take me seriously, because I need you to and would not, otherwise, know how to go on living in the way I have been living until now. Or is it my fate to go from door to door protesting my innocence? What is this guilt with which nature has tainted me from birth? Yes, Valdo, from now on, you have but one duty: to understand me and to judge me in the true light, and not allow others, purely in order to salve your conscience, to interfere in our lives and trample on the little that is left to us.

.... in the Pavilion in the garden, where we had decided to spend part of the summer, firstly, because we would feel more at ease there, secondly, because we would thus spend most of the time far from your brother. (I repeat, and this is important, Valdo, there was always an element in Demétrio that I never quite understood: he hated me in a way that verged on the abnormal, as if he were constantly accusing me of a crime, but what that crime was I never knew. He hated me with a hatred that veered between exalted enthusiasm and utter repugnance.) When I realized this, I became convinced that you and I could only stay together if we lived apart from the rest of the family. Time proved me right, but in those early days, I still had no way of knowing just how right I was. You were not opposed to my idea, on the contrary, you supported me, certain that we would be happy, despite the Pavilion's isolated location, away from the main house. And it was there, if you remember, that we spent the happiest days of our married life. There, in that abandoned, ivy-clad Pavilion, with its tall windows—their glass panes mostly intact—which glowed in the afternoon sun and lived in intimate contact with the surrounding greenery; it was there that I learned about love and waited for our son to be born. Ah, Valdo, you only have to close your eyes to recall those summer nights, with the cicadas whirring away among the ancient tree trunks and the scent of jasmine filling the air—the peace of a tranquil, old estate, belonging to an old and very wealthy family, and which was exactly as I had dreamed it would be when I still lived in the city. Long, slow, sleepy nights and days . . . and it was only later in my pregnancy that I began to think it impossible to continue living in that place where I felt so happy, because it was so far from any medical help I might need and because of the lack of comfort, well, the Pavilion was not exactly luxurious. But only then did I fully understand the peace that surrounded me and the sober beauty of those walls. I can honestly say that only then did the Chácara, at whose heart lay that haven, the Pavilion, only then did it take on a different meaning.

But all was not silence and happiness, one might say that adverse forces, jealous of our quiet lives, were watching and waiting for an opportunity to burst aggressively in upon us. And so it was that Demétrio—who never visited us—one day abandoned his various tasks to come down to the Pavilion and to find kneeling at my feet, as if in a carefully staged act of adultery, the poor lad who looked after the garden. I had often seen the boy before, had even noticed his submissive manner, the strange way he looked at me—but to think that I, especially in my heavily pregnant state, would allow him to be so bold—no, that really is too much. (I can go further in my recollections, because they are still so vivid it seems like only yesterday. The most he had dared to do, and I swear this is true, had been to plant a bed of violets for me—a modest little bed, surrounded by white stones, and which, being not far from the Pavilion, was watered by the nearby stream.) He was indeed kneeling before me, Valdo, but I swear and swear again and will always swear that this was the first time it had happened.

It was Timóteo who told me everything that night. (I was in my room, lying on the bed, with a damp cloth on my forehead—the only thing that helped relieve the constant waves of nausea. I heard someone scratching at the window pane and sat up, startled, afraid it might be the gardener again. After the scandal of that afternoon, when Demétrio had openly accused me of choosing to live in the Pavilion as a cover for my criminal love affair, I did not want to see the boy ever again, feeling that I lacked the necessary courage, even though he was not in the least to blame and even though I had already decided to leave. When I opened the window, I heard an insistent "psst" and leaned out, trying to see who it could be. If it was the gardener, I would tell him: go away, never cross my path again, you have already disgraced me forever in the eyes of the Meneses. And at the mere thought I began to tremble and burn up with fever. But it wasn't the gardener, nor would I ever have an opportunity to say those urgent words to him—to my surprise, it was Timóteo. He was still wearing women's clothes, but had a man's jacket draped hastily over his shoulders. He whispered: "Open the door, Nina, I have something very important to tell you." I never did find out how he had managed to cross the whole garden dressed like that—just as I never found out what mysterious reason had made him leave his room that night. True, there was the reason he gave during our conversation, but I sensed, like a tune playing secretly and incessantly in his soul, another reason that he was not telling me, but which was equally important. For some reason, when I saw him, I instantly distrusted him, fearing that he might deceive me—after all, he was a Meneses too—and while he was speaking to me, I tried in vain to guess the real motive for his visit. But that was probably one of those secrets I would die without knowing. When I opened the door, having turned on the light, I saw the sweat running down his face, and he looked utterly exhausted. "You shouldn't have come here," I said. He embraced me, then fell into a chair: "Ah, Nina," he said with a laugh, "imagine my brother's expression if he were to find me here . . ." He was still breathing hard and it was clear that he was unaccustomed to exercise of any sort. Before he began to speak, and as if he were recovering from his exertions, he looked around him with great interest. "What a good idea coming to live in the Pavilion, far from everyone . . ." And then he sighed and added: "But I miss you. Ever since you moved, everything seems so much darker somehow . . ." I sat down near him: "I couldn't go on living up at the house, Timóteo." And, at the same time, very discreetly so as not to frighten him, I observed the change that had come over him since last we met. He was not the same person at all. I had first known him when he was still young, before he had become so fat, before his face had taken on that ravaged look. I wasn't in the presence of a human being, but a swollen, amorphous mass. I knew he had taken to drink, as if to blot out some terrible memory, and that he gave all his money to the servants (I don't know if I ever talked to you about that, Valdo, but I always thought it was a mistake to allow him to keep his part of the inheritance in his room) so that they could buy him the drink he needed, but I had no idea his decline had been so rapid nor that the alcohol had had such a devastating effect on him in such a short time. And then, and I say this with no desire to shock, there was the way he used make-up, not as a woman would, but in an excessive, intemperate way, furious and uncontrollable, like someone who has lost all sense of taste or moderation—or worse still, someone bent on debasing himself still further. The sight of that poor, strange, crazed creature moved me to tears. There was always plenty to cry about at the Chácara, Valdo, where happiness was a rare commodity. Timóteo placed his hand on mine: "I think they'll kill me if they find out I've left my room." And suddenly changing the subject, he added almost brusquely: "Nina, why did you leave me? If you knew how it upset me . . ." I looked at him, bemused: "As I said, Timóteo, it was better for me." He groaned: "The things that are better for others are always worse for us . . ." I took pity on him and said: "But Timóteo, you could still come and visit me now and then . . ." He stared at me, almost panic-stricken: "No, no, what would be the point? Besides, Nina, I came tonight to talk to you about an extremely serious matter." I again tried to distract him: "I'm really worried about you, Timóteo." He gave me a long, tender look, and again I was aware of his breathing, but this time his breathlessness was caused by something other than weariness. "Thank you, Nina, but I didn't come here to talk about my life . . ." "About what, then?" Again he sighed deeply: "I don't know if you realize, Nina, but they want to send you away." His voice sounded calm and not in the least angry. We sat in silence for a while, until I asked: "But why?" He thought for a moment, then said: "Because of a young man, a gardener, whom they found kneeling at your feet." I turned to face him: "And you . . . do you think that's true?" His whole being seemed to tremble: "Oh, Nina, why ask me that question? You have no right, you can't, that is the one thing I refuse to answer." I asked coldly: "Why?" And falling to his knees, he said: "Nina, I don't judge you, I accept you exactly as you are, good or bad. Besides, in my opinion, all the kings of the world should fall at your feet." I helped him up and made him sit down on a chair again. He was confused and upset. "What else did you find out?" I asked. And he said: "Betty told me everything. I asked her to come and tell you herself, but she said she didn't have the right, that it was her masters' secret, but that I . . ." "But what did she tell you?" I demanded impatiently. "That Valdo and Demétrio were talking in the study—that's where they get together whenever there's something important to discuss—and that Demétrio was the one who spoke most loudly. He said 'I always warned you to be careful with that woman. She should have left already, she has no place in this house. Besides, we don't have the right facilities here for her to give birth. Whether you like it or not, Valdo, she has to leave. I would never tolerate . . ." "Ah!" I exclaimed, "so that's what he wants. Well, I'll leave all right. And I won't come back, not even if the whole Meneses family were to come to me on bended knee!" I was saying these things because I was aflame with anger. I knew he had accused me of choosing to live in the Pavilion to conceal my illicit love affair. Isn't that what he said, Valdo, isn't that exactly what he said? Timóteo again took my hands in his: "Don't leave, Nina. That's why I came here. Do you remember our pact? We need you with us." "No, no," I cried, "if I stayed, I would be constantly humiliated and constantly under suspicion." We talked for a while longer, but nothing he could say would change my mind: I was convinced I should and would leave, regardless of that business with the gardener. I well remember the rage that overwhelmed me when I thought of all the promises you made me, Valdo . . . I leapt to my feet and, with Timóteo still there, started picking up any object I could find and smashing it to the floor. I had been wrong to give in that first time, and how stupid of me not to have left on the night of the gunshot . . . There I was, utterly humiliated, and I could do nothing about it because no one ever told me anything, all of them too busy plotting against me in the shadows. The sound of things breaking brought Betty running to the Pavilion: "What is it, Senhora, what's happened?" My eyes must have been blazing, my body shaking, and the sight of me surrounded by broken shards must have been far from reassuring. "Ah, Betty, you know perfectly well what's happened." She turned pale and begged me to calm down: no one was going to harm me. When I continued pacing furiously back and forth, not even listening to what she was saying, she turned to Timóteo, who had remained silent all this time, watching me. "Ah, Senhor Timóteo, it's you . . ." And from his corner, Timóteo said: "Isn't she superb, Betty? What a woman!" They exchanged a few more words and concluded that I had, indeed, been deeply wronged. (And you know, Valdo, while this was going on, none of us gave a moment's thought to the gardener as a real being with a real existence: for us, he was merely the catalyst that had set the whole thing in motion, an instrument used by Demétrio. And what did I care if the gardener existed and had, in a moment of madness, thrown himself at my feet? I remember that for one minute, one single, fleeting minute, I had abandoned my hand to the fury of his hungry kisses—what was it, what could it mean the wild, animal sob that rose to his lips in the form of a caress? He wasn't strong enough to sweep me up in the whirlwind that possessed him. But it must have been then that Demétrio opened the door—and even all this time later, I ask myself how long he had been outside watching and waiting. Did he merely see the gardener kneeling at my feet or did he linger a little longer, in which case he would have seen the energetic way in which I ordered the gardener to get up? In either case, how can he judge me on what he saw during that one moment, how can he base all his anger and feelings of revenge on that one brief lightning flash? He would only just have shut the door when Alberto was on his feet again: I can remember clearly how Alberto ran his hand over his head, as if trying to drive away a bad dream, then said: "I don't deserve to be forgiven for what I did, but I will be eternally grateful." I didn't understand and asked: "Grateful?" And moving away from me, he said: "Yes, for your mere existence, for having been allowed to know you." Ah, Valdo, it was only later, much later, after many, many sleepless nights, that I really began to think about that boy. In fact, I couldn't get him out of my mind. It's terrible the suffering we inflict on others, and in the whole ensuing drama—by which I mean that stupid gesture of mine, throwing the gun into the garden—his was the most tragic of all our fates. I can see him so clearly, still almost a child, standing before me, trembling. Only on the long nights I experienced later did I begin to wish I could meet him again: what would he say, what could he say when he was still so young, what words would he use, would his love be made of some incandescent matter? I began to imagine him not as a lover, but as a son, to whom I could teach things and warn of life's dangers, saving him from himself and from others. Son, lover, what does it matter—loneliness is full of such traps. My solitude led me to fantasize, to imagine someone who would remain faithful until death, who would have eyes only for me. I'm sorry, I'm quite mad at times, sadness has that effect.)

Timóteo was still sitting down, with Betty by his side, both of them doubtless waiting for me to do something. Hatred was churning around and around inside me like a perpetually turning wheel. And I was constantly asking myself: "What will they be saying now? What will they be plotting?" And I kept repeating softly what Demétrio had said: "That's why she chose to live in the Pavilion . . ."

You know how happy we were in the Pavilion, Valdo, you know what good times we had there, and the strange, sudden way in which everything seemed to be reborn between us. Time slipped by like silk. Amazed at this transformation, I would hold you in my arms and say: "Valdo, we love each other, everything is possible." It was a simple, inarticulate thought, one that millions of women have expressed before—and yet I felt that, for us, the world really had entered a different orbit. Do you understand, Valdo? I had exactly what I wanted, the absolute, the infinite. It was unimaginable to me then that you would listen to such a lie, that, at the very moment when I considered we were safe, you would be infected by the accumulated venom of your brother's hatred for me. The proof was there before me in the form of the only two friends I could count on at the Chácara, both sitting there in silence waiting for me to act. And it was then, and only then, that my decision rapidly became an unshakable intention—and throwing my suitcases onto the bed and hauling my clothes out of the wardrobe, I cried: "Betty, let's get these bags packed so that I can leave—forever. I wouldn't stay now even if, this time, he really did kill himself . . ." Betty got up, and I saw that Timóteo was doing the same, all the while staring at me wordlessly, probably not daring to stop me, so deeply did he respect my decision, and yet the look in his eyes was so unutterably sad, full of deep, lacerating pain ....

.... I can do nothing. This is my destiny, and we cannot escape our destiny. Believe me when I say that I have only a few more days to live. And remember: this is all I am asking of you. Besides, Valdo, this is not a request, but a command: the dead have their rights, and I feel I am in a position to make one last demand. You never answered me, never replied to my letters. Perhaps you never even opened them, and all those complaints and recollections, all that invective, remained dumb and covered in dust on some desk, waiting, who knows, for some generous soul to unseal the envelopes. On other occasions, I made different appeals, I wept, I cried out for help that never came. No matter, although that silence could well be what has gradually destroyed me. I never imagined I would die like this, spurned, and without a friendly eye to accompany me on this difficult journey. But I can still imagine what is mine by rights, and it is now, when I have so little strength left, and when I can already begin to sense the definitive peace awaiting me in the tomb, that I am prepared to reclaim, for good or ill, what is mine and what was so unjustly taken from me. (Even now, it's up to me to refresh your memory. When I left the Chácara, I never expected to see the person who came knocking at my door months later. I can see her now, all in black, her face utterly devoid of emotion. Yes, she was the one you sent to fetch our son. And it was to her, all in black, that I gave the only possible answer: "I would never keep a child belonging to the Meneses family. He's there somewhere, in the hospital where he was born." But I wasn't being honest when I said that, and Ana, who had come to Rio for that express purpose, had no right to take my son from me. But that, alas, is what happened . . .) Believe what you like, but I can guarantee that I will never again seek to justify myself or beg you on bended knee to listen to me. No, Valdo, my strength is at an end. Listen carefully, so that you are not taken by surprise later on and cannot tell me off or accuse me of having acted frivolously and hastily: I am ready to return to the Chácara to take up my rightful place, until I die and for as long as I have the strength to do battle with Demétrio and possibly with all the other Meneses too.

There is no point in refusing me, because by the time you receive this, I will already be on my way. I have the right to live out peacefully the little time I have left. I know I did nothing to offend you, and I will not allow you to keep me away from my son because of a mere calumny. Are you listening, Valdo, do you understand what I'm saying? ....

....

7.
The Pharmacist's Second Report

It was around this time that the most disparate and divergent rumors concerning the Chácara began to circulate. Nobody knew for certain what was going on, but all manner of things were suspected, even an actual crime. (Dr. Vilaça, the doctor who attended the Chácara, had even let slip something to that effect . . .) It has to be said that the general atmosphere was highly conducive to such gossip, and the more intrepid of the local busybodies even took to strolling along by the fence surrounding the grounds, in the hope of seeing something. In vain: the trees filling the garden prevented any clear view of the Chácara, and the most they could report was that they had seen Dona Ana, or even Senhor Demétrio, strolling along the avenues. Any mention of the Meneses was accompanied by a wry smile, a shrug of the shoulders, a knowing shake of the head; and the old house that had for so long been the pride of the whole municipality soon began to be tainted by that aura of suspicion and drama. Despite this, less and less was seen of its inhabitants. At one point, it was said that Dona Nina had been spotted with a stranger, close to the old slave cemetery on the road to the Chácara; then it was reported that Senhor Demétrio had his bags packed ready to go traveling, that he was going abroad and that no one knew when he would be back. However, none of these reports was confirmed, for the Meneses kept themselves to themselves and rarely called on any of their neighbors. Even so, it is fair to say that they remained immensely important in the locality, and there were no festivities, charitable occasions, or public ceremonies to which they were not invited. In short, while they were neither friendly nor kind, they were, nonetheless, indispensable to the life of the town.

Now, it was in this climate of high drama that Senhor Valdo one day appeared at my pharmacy, even though the shop was having work done to it and was partly closed to customers. He came not once, but two or three times, always trying to look as nonchalant as possible and pretending there was nothing he was looking for, but all the while paying close attention to everything around him. I was not surprised by this, not least because I was accustomed to that family's curious manners. His pretext for coming was in order to have a wound dressed, for he had sustained a gunshot wound to his chest, which was not healing well. (I believe, moreover, that this was the origin of the rumors filling the town.) As discretion required, I asked no questions, but he told me he had wounded himself "accidentally." I said nothing, even pretending that the story did not interest me in the slightest. It was, I believed, the only way of putting him at his ease, and thus more inclined to talk. On the other hand, it occurred to me that he may simply have been sounding me out, as a way of gauging the extent of the townspeople's curiosity. In any event, I kept my silence, which is another way of saying that I asked nothing and presumed everything. Since they were in the habit of summoning me whenever they needed anything, I assumed that, this time, they wanted to keep me away from the house precisely so that I would not see whatever it was they wanted to hide from me. I have no idea what it was, but it clearly existed, and those visits to the shop by Senhor Valdo were the proof, breaking as they did with such a well-established modus operandi. There was also, I must say, a certain nervousness about his movements, and he, unaccustomed to my cool demeanor, occasionally shot me a worried, searching glance.

On his last visit, he unceremoniously sat down on a pile of bricks next to the counter, resting his hands on the crook of his umbrella. (He had come on foot from the Chácara, even though a storm was brewing; to the south where the railroad tracks stretch off into the distance, thick black clouds were gathering.) As I've already mentioned, his wound was a minor one, and the dressings could well have been changed at the Chácara itself. Perhaps, since the departure of Dona Nina, he was unable to find anyone there to help him, and it was this, among other things, that had brought him to the shop. He was, like all the Meneses men, a man of few words, but on this occasion, so as to break the silence into which we were gradually sinking, he let out a sigh and said:

"Ah, yes, the good old days."

Which probably meant nothing at all, or at least, no matter how hard I tried, I couldn't see what he was referring to. He said it several times, though, and hearing the words repeated so often, I ended up thinking that they must contain some deep meaning, which I, in my ignorance, could not apprehend. He spoke with his chin resting on his hands, which were, in turn, resting on the handle of his umbrella in a pose that struck me as particularly characteristic. He was gazing into space, as if he really was traveling incalculable distances. Such theatricality, whether feigned or not, must have concealed some purpose, and I waited patiently for that purpose to become apparent. But looking at him, I felt troubled—his suffering seemed so disturbingly real. I had often seen the suffering on men's faces, but nothing like that, hemmed in by so much reticence and scruple. It must be said, however, that there was a certain dignity in everything to do with Senhor Valdo, and at the same time, a feeling of such sadness, such constant loneliness, that those attributes, by their very force, became factors of indisputable prestige. Women, who are particularly sensitive to such refinement, can sense it from a distance, and never fail to be captivated: "How manly, how romantic, such refined manners!" And it was undoubtedly the case that almost all of them considered him their very own small, personal god.

I always hoped he would tell me some clear, concrete fact about the Chácara and its goings-on, because it was precisely those facts, and the enigma surrounding them, that most interested me and the rest of the town. Even the most restrained of men have their moments of weakness, but during all those visits (for I deliberately lengthened the period of his treatment, and the visits lasted for over three weeks), he was always very discreet, and I never heard him utter a single word to deny or confirm the myths swirling around the Meneses.

He did speak to me once, on one single occasion, and with the exuberance and emotion of the very timid, who, in the depths of their heart, feel the wall of ice imprisoning their most cherished feelings suddenly break. He spoke to me not because it was me, but merely because he had a need to speak to someone, indeed anyone. Listening to him, the story seemed so much his own and so disconnected from any Meneses family business, that I wondered whether that wasn't his real reason for coming to my pharmacy: an excuse to relive those events, to ponder them in the presence of someone else, and thus escape from the siege and isolation imposed on him by the other inhabitants of the Chácara. I must stress that this was the only time I saw a Meneses in a confiding mood, and what he did confide to me was only remotely connected to the Meneses. (Indeed, perhaps before telling you what he said, I ought to revive an old recollection of my own, for it fits with everything I heard later on, and agrees with what is known of the person in question. I cannot emphasize enough the impression that Senhor Valdo's unexpected marriage caused in Vila Velha, and the excitement with which the first news of his wife-to-be was received. It isn't easy, however, to gauge the impact of this without bearing in mind the almost universal esteem in which Senhor Valdo was held and the deep interest felt by everyone regarding the

Meneses. By the time he married, he was no longer what could be termed a boy; saucy tales and anecdotes abounded concerning him and his adventures, whether true or not, with all sorts of women. There was even one, a certain Raquel, who worked at a place called "Half Past Midnight" and who was said to have received a large sum in payment for several hours of her favors. Indeed, to put it plainly, he was assumed to be an accomplished womanizer: silent and arrogant, of a kind very common among wealthy provincial folk. His manners, his noble bearing, his immaculate elegance, albeit somewhat old-fashioned, contributed greatly to this reputation. Half of these affairs were quite possibly invented and he may never even have set foot in that place called "Half Past Midnight," such were the tales and imaginings the Meneses men aroused. But then, as they say, there's no smoke without fire. To the outside world, Senhor Valdo, with his faintly supercilious air, cut a figure that perfectly fitted the legends that circulated about him. On many occasions I saw young girls of marriageable age leaning out of their window whenever he passed by, flashing him sly looks or giggling, and this trail of excitement would last at least as long as his stroll around the town.

When it was finally announced that he was to marry, there was general excitement, and the only topic of conversation was who the lucky woman might be. It was said—by those recently returned from Rio de Janeiro—that she was the most beautiful of women, rich and endowed with all the attributes one might expect in a wife chosen by a Meneses. Someone who swore he had seen them together in a smart coffee-house in Rio, said: "They make the perfect couple."

So there was great expectation when Senhor Valdo left to bring her back to the Chácara: for days and days, when the train from the capital was due to arrive, our little railroad station was packed with people. And this expectation turned into a great torrent of whisperings and mutterings when he returned alone after several days in the city. It was reported that she did not want to come to such a backwater and that she hated the thought of leaving Rio de Janeiro.

And so, before they even knew a single positive fact about her, the majority already felt hostile to the new bride, declaring her to be a conceited woman who would neither look at nor speak to anyone. However, this was all mere supposition, and it all changed on a certain afternoon when Dona Nina stepped off the train at our little station, which by that time was completely deserted. She may well have merely been waiting for interest in her to wane so that she could arrive peacefully and quietly. She arrived laden down with luggage and, I swear, I have never seen a more beautiful woman in my entire life. She wasn't particularly tall and was perhaps slightly too thin, and she was clearly of a highly-strung disposition and accustomed to being treated well. The purity of her features—only her nose was perhaps a little too aquiline—combined to create a strange, tempestuous atmosphere that, even at first sight, made her an irresistible creature to behold. The whole town—for as news of her arrival spread from house to house like a lit fuse, every window filled up with onlookers—wondered what it was that simmered inside her to make her gaze so melancholy and her attitude so warm and irresolute. And everyone agreed that the delay, and her subsequent arrival when everyone had forgotten about her and the station was deserted, all worked in her favor. Many rashly proclaimed that she deserved an apology from Vila Velha, and since there was no means of delivering such an apology, they instead heaped her with exaggerated praise, declaring her "a queen who did not deserve to be exiled to this dull, dusty place." So from the moment she set foot in the town, she became the focus of attention, driving the Meneses themselves discreetly into the background. Little by little, however, this interest, for lack of nourishment, became gradually corrupted—and what had previously been unalloyed praise turned into a game of doubts and probabilities. From calling her a queen, they judged her to be, rather, a failed cabaret singer, and there were even those who recalled seeing her face in certain "specialist" magazines. Others, more romantically, persisted in considering her to be a mysterious blue-blooded heiress.

But the majority obstinately countered with: "No, she's a singer, and in a revealing pose that leaves little to the imagination . . ." The truth is that nobody really knew anything about her, and so it remained for a long time.)

"I can remember perfectly the moment I first saw her," he told me, his chin still resting on the handle of his umbrella, eyes still gazing into the distance, as if pursuing a vision he feared might break up on the rocks of time. "It was a hot summer's afternoon, and I was walking along the shore at Flamengo. I was looking for the address of a friend, who I was told was living in a luxurious guesthouse somewhere near Glória. But we country folk always seem to go astray when we get to the city. And so that's how I came to be knocking at the door not of a luxurious guest house, but of a very modest hotel. It was situated in a vast old two- or three-story building with a wide, steep, dark staircase with wooden banisters. The doorman was half-deaf and pointed me in the direction of a room on the second floor, and as I went up, I was assailed by the characteristically tepid smell of food and ill-disguised poverty. I couldn't find the room number I was looking for and was about to turn back, when I overheard the sounds of an argument coming from one of the rooms off the hallway. I stopped, out of curiosity and a desire to see for myself how people lived in such confined surroundings. They were discussing a marriage. One of the speakers had the hesitant, fitful voice of an elderly, ailing man, possibly an asthmatic. Each sentence was interspersed with gasps and coughs and choking. The other speaker was female, and she had the warm voice of a young girl. Listening to her replies I instantly wanted to know who she was, and as I stood there, I imagined her to be small, blonde, and blue-eyed. When the door was flung open following a particularly angry riposte, I saw just how wrong I was: she was dark-haired, almost a redhead, of medium height and with bright, shining eyes. I was immediately struck by her appearance, or rather, by her pallor and her nervous, pitiful tone. She wasn't wearing any make-up and was dressed very modestly. My first thought was: 'So beautiful, and yet she will never be happy.' Why? What led me to prophesy such a dark future? Then I asked myself who she could be, and before I could answer, I heard the argument coming to an end. 'I can wait until tomorrow,' said the old man. I was hiding behind one of the newel posts on the staircase, and I peered around it to see who the speaker was. He was indeed an old man, his hair and moustache entirely white, and he had a very kind face, but he was, alas, sitting in a wheelchair. 'Paralyzed,' I thought to myself. There was still a glint of anger in his eyes." (Ah, I thought, while Senhor Valdo continued talking: what a strong impression this incident must have made for it to remain so clear after all this time!) "I saw the woman turn around and say with extraordinary passion: 'Never. I would rather die.' The old man started to move his wheelchair, trying to catch up with her: 'You've always done exactly what you wanted, you've never once considered your father. Perhaps now . . .' She slammed the door shut without answering, rushed past me and went down the stairs. Suddenly everything in the old building went quiet. Cautiously, I followed, breathing in the trail of perfume she left behind. It was growing dark and the sky, still blue over toward the sea, was beginning to glow a fiery red. I walked along distractedly, thinking about what I had just heard, when I saw her standing beneath a lamppost. She must have been waiting for a bus or some other means of transport. I stopped and saw her take a handkerchief out of her handbag to wipe her eyes. I felt a searing pang of pity. I kept my distance, though, not knowing whether or not to approach her in her present distraught state. At that moment, a car stopped by the curb and I saw a man's hand push open the door. She got in and the car drove off. I caught a sudden gleam of stripes on a uniform, shining in the darkness. I assumed therefore, with some disappointment, that she was the lover of some soldier.

"On an impulse, I returned there at the same time the next day. Throughout the night, during which I endured the exhausting, sleepless rigors of a Rio summer, I could not drive from my mind the image of that beautiful stranger. I hoped to find her under the same lamppost, and sure enough there she was, clutching her handbag and waiting for the car. It did not take long to appear and everything happened exactly as before. It was clearly a regular occurrence, and, as if they were of crucial importance, the same questions kept going around and around in my head: Fiancée? Lover? Wife? I observed this same scene on the following three nights, prompted by an interest it seemed pointless to conceal. Then, on the fourth night, I finally resolved to approach her. I needed to act at once, before the car arrived. When I went over to her, she gave me a look more of sadness than surprise, and that impenetrable sadness, which seemed to have its origins in some unending inner agony, never failed to touch me. 'I don't know who you are,' she said simply and in a formal tone that somehow in no way suggested rejection. I shrugged as if to say 'what does it matter?' while the girl glanced down the street, no doubt imagining that her soldier would appear at any moment. But that day, to my good fortune, he must have been delayed. 'I need to talk to you,' I insisted. She looked at me again, slowly this time, from head to toe, as if trying to determine exactly who I was. I surmised from her look that she had judged me rightly. Oh that wicked thing, female intuition! I must also confess that I had no intention of hiding anything from her. Standing there, already somewhat distracted, she was trying to contain the only emotion holding her back: a mixture of anxiety and irritation at the imminent arrival of the man whom I presumed to be her lover. At last, she reached a decision and, taking me by the arm, said: 'Let's go, before he arrives.' She said this quickly and with evident relief, and we walked down to the beach so briskly that in no time at all we found ourselves some distance from the lamppost where they had arranged to meet. As we walked we exchanged not a single word, for we felt that no explanation was necessary; the impulse that had begun our friendship was explanation enough.

"That same night, tucked away in the corner of a bar in Copacabana, she told me everything: the soldier, an army colonel, was a friend of her father's. Or rather, his only friend. Her father had also been a soldier, and had served in a garrison in Deodoro until a terrible disaster had befallen him—a grenade going off unexpectedly. He had then retired from the army and, being of an irascible, even violent temper, he had lost all his friends and acquaintances, driven away by his angry outbursts. His injuries made matters even worse, for he was still a young man, imprisoned in his wheelchair and seething with anger. His one remaining friend was Colonel Gonçalves, Amadeu Gonçalves, who endured his old comrade's virulent mood swings not out of friendship exactly, but . . .

"Every night they played interminable games of cards. They had started with simple games like *escopa*, *rouba-monte*, and *ronda*. But gradually they moved on to playing more seriously, for money, which, as the night wore on, left them flushed and excited. When the money ran out—for now they always played for money—they played for whatever was at hand: books, tables, chairs. They did this without a flicker of shame, and she allowed it to happen, because it was the only way for her father to forget his sorrows. 'I'll bet you this watch,' her father would say, apoplectic with rage after a long-drawn-out defeat. The Colonel, who had more valuable items at his disposal, always kept his cool, hid his cards from prying eyes, and always won. The daughter, who was a witness to these daily spectacles, thought it would be better for her father to refrain from such unprofitable games, but she held her tongue, aware that he saw no one during the day, and that it was the Colonel who formed the only bridge between him and the outside world and kept him up-to-date on military matters with a meticulous detail that would be the envy of the very best gazettes. A judicious observer could not fail to notice a certain touch of sadism on the part of the Colonel. For example, when the subject matter was particularly thrilling, as was often the case, for the Colonel showed a truly histrionic talent—he was a man who reveled in farcical incidents, piquant details, unexpected discoveries—he would often stop suddenly and fall into a deathly silence. 'What is it?' her father would cry out anxiously. And slowly, rubbing his chin with his hand, the Colonel would say: 'You know, I can't quite remember what happened next.' Her father would reach his hand across the table and touch his companion's arm: 'For the love of God, man, don't stop now, not before you've told me the rest. Don't just leave me in suspense!' The Colonel would shake his head: 'No, I don't remember. It was a lance corporal who gave me that particular piece of information. I need to go and find him again.' The father, distraught, tried to jog his memory: 'Which lance corporal? Was it Mamede from Pernambuco?' The Colonel smugly shook his head again. The old man spluttered: 'In my day . . .' And the Colonel interrupted: 'In your day, Colonel, but these days it's all very different. It wasn't Mamede from Pernambuco, indeed, I'm almost certain it was Libânio from Paraná.' 'Ah!' exclaimed the invalid, greatly relieved. And he would repeat, as if it were the most delightful thing in the world: 'Libânio from Paraná!' But the other man wouldn't give in so easily and would once again shake his head: 'No, no, I'm wrong, it wasn't Libânio. Libânio was in the Third Division, and if I'm not mistaken, this story took place in São Paulo. Oh dear, this memory of mine.' Then the father, bereft, his forehead dripping with sweat—the world, movement, the sensation of life itself were all disappearing before his eyes—would scan the almost bare room: 'I'll bet you that photo album over there—do you see it? It's a family heirloom. Look carefully. It has silver clasps!'"—(At this point in his story, Senhor Valdo paused briefly. The silence was so great that we could hear the leaves rustling outside. Then he started speaking again, in a different, more emotional tone: "I well remember the last time I saw that room. It was after her father had died of a heart attack, shortly before the wedding. There was nothing left at all, and his corpse, far too thin for the uniform they'd forced his body into, lay stretched out on a mattress on the floorboards. You might say that after living so long in that cramped room, he had drained it of everything; he had gone and left nothing behind. And here's a curious fact: it never occurred to Nina, who wept bitter tears, that she could not carry on living there after his death. She still hadn't given me a definite 'yes,' and her life, seen from outside, resembled a strange, disturbing adventure. I should have mentioned that the window looked onto a stretch of the Glória seafront: through it wafted a gentle sea breeze and you caught glimpses of the unexpectedly blue water, the one luxury left to adorn that humble death.")—Senhor Valdo went on: "On hearing the old man's proposal, the Colonel deliberately played for time: 'What would I do with an album with silver clasps? It's the sort of thing that could only be of interest to your family.' The father began to grovel and beg: 'I'll bet you that chair over there, then. It's the last one, you know. Or that Panama hat you like. Or I'll bet . . .' (and his gaze ran desperately around the room, then returned to the table, stopping at his own hands). 'I'll bet my wedding ring!' Sometimes, in the silence broken only by the ticking of the clock, the Colonel would give in and tell him the rest of the story. Then it was as if a river of light flowed invisibly through the room. At other times, though, hard, immovable and as silent as the grave, he would simply leave. On those occasions the father would sleep badly, tossing and turning, waking up shouting in the middle of the night: 'What is it? Where's the Minister? Who took the message?' When he returned to his senses, he would apologize to his daughter, sip a glass of water and wash his face. 'Colonel Amadeu didn't tell me everything. Lord, what suffering. It's like being condemned to death,' he would say.

"Now, it was in the midst of one of these stories that the most incredible bet of all took place. Colonel Amadeu had stopped telling one of his tales at a key moment, just as he was about to reveal some great political intrigue in which government ministers and generals were implicated. An ex-Minister of War, plotting against the new government, had been secretly transporting arms to a far-flung region of Mato Grosso, where he was training a bunch of badly-paid half-castes and Indians to form a small rebel army who would trigger the revolt, in conjunction with key underground cells established at various locations across the country. It had all been carefully planned by many fine army men, Colonel Amadeu assured him, nodding his head mysteriously. In this intrigue, somewhat improbably, the father himself had figured, for according to the Colonel, 'they needed him to provide certain reports, and to carry out certain checks that should properly be exercised outside the purview of the Ministry.' The father was thrilled by this sudden possibility that he might be needed—him, a cripple!—and that he might, even at a distance, play a small part in events which proved, even after his long years as a retiree and an invalid, that he still existed and that in the world of his former comrades, where all that was meaningful in his life had occurred, they still remembered him and valued his contribution. Daydreaming and with his eyes half-shut, he could almost hear them: 'General, it's that colonel who had the accident—don't you remember? The one who served for many years at the district headquarters. A splendid fellow; you couldn't find a better man for the job.' This, then, was the final, most diabolical and perfect part of the Colonel's invention: suddenly bestowing on the poor old man a reason to live, implicating him in the most sensational intrigues of the day. 'Don't you remember?' he would say. 'It was back when they were repairing the tank at the regimental depot . . .' Beside him, the old man was anxiously racking his brain, scarcely daring to draw breath: 'Yes, I remember it well . . .' 'Moreover, the matter concerns a major, who was just a lieutenant back in your day.' 'Yes, yes,' the father replied. 'I remember that lieutenant very well. To judge from the sloppy way he saluted me, he seemed very full of himself.' Sensing that the old man was hooked, the Colonel stroked his chin: 'Indeed . . . But the damned thing is I can't quite remember . . .' The father cried out: 'For the love of God, man!' And the Colonel: 'Quite. It's a funny old business. It's always at exactly this point that my memory seems to fail me.' The old man shook him: 'Please, please, carry on . . .' But the Colonel had cruelly decided to stop. Suspended at its very climax, the story hovered in the air like a slowly evaporating cloud. Already on his feet and standing motionless before him, the Colonel said: 'It's late, my friend, and it's quite a walk home.' He was blinking as if struggling to pick up the threads of a memory. 'For pity's sake,' groaned the cripple. But the other man, unmoved, was shaking his head: 'It's a terrible thing, unbelievable really, but I can't remember a thing about what happened next.' The father wrung his hands: 'Not one more detail? Nothing?' 'Nothing.' 'A snippet? Anything at all?' The Colonel was implacable: 'Alas, I've completely forgotten—don't know what's come over me.' And all just as the Colonel was beginning a tale about the regimental depot, at the time when the old man was still a serving officer. A deep sigh filled his chest, as if his own life were escaping him. And that night the Colonel rose and bade him a chilly goodbye, as if the father had mortally offended him. A great silence fell upon the room. Then the father began to shout and foam at the mouth. He was having an attack, just as he used to in his younger days. He spent the rest of the night in a bad way, his body rigid, his eyes bulging. The next day, his face pale and drawn, his very first question was: 'No message from the Colonel?' 'No,' replied his daughter, standing by his bed. 'Oh God, I'm suffocating! I need some air!' he exclaimed, and pressed his hands to his chest. The strange thing was that, for three nights, three interminable nights of permanent agony, the Colonel failed to show up. The father sniffled and sobbed over his misfortune. His daughter tried in vain to distract him, but he became even more irritated, calling her 'lazy' and 'slovenly' and any other insults that came into his head. 'Calm down, father,' she replied. He twisted and turned in his wheelchair, saying he was done for, abandoned by God and by man, one foot already in the grave. He stretched out his hands, examining them: 'Do you see, Nina? This is what used to happen to me as a young man. I nearly died.' 'Hush,' she consoled him, 'I'm here beside you. Nothing's going to happen to you.' Then he told her she was just like her mother—a mediocre Italian actress who had run off back to Europe saying she was homesick—and that one of these days she, too, would abandon him. His was a terrible fate, and why? What had he done? Nothing, nothing at all. There he was, rotting away in that room, with no friendly voices and not knowing what was happening in the world, or even how his former comrades-in-arms were faring. Oh, it was all too much—what a miserable fate, what indignity! Finally, on the fourth day, the Colonel reappeared, and found a broken man, crushed by adversity. 'I'm a dead man, my friend,' the father declared as soon as he saw the Colonel, who went over to him, feigning complete ignorance. 'But what happened? What can have brought you to this state, and so quickly?' The old man smiled, the sad smile of a defeated man: 'I'm a dead man, Colonel.' The Colonel sat down then and whispered: 'I'm sorry I haven't been able to come for the last few days.' Then added mysteriously: 'Things have been happening at the barracks . . .' This insinuating statement made the father's eyes gleam. And reaching out one trembling hand, he touched his companion's arm. 'Shall we play today?' There was a long, painful pause. Slowly, however, the Colonel's features revealed his true feelings: 'I'm sorry, my friend, but today is quite impossible.' A kind of strangled cry rose to the father's lips: 'You mean you're not going to tell me the rest of the story?' 'Please believe me, I'm very sorry, but it's quite impossible.' 'Why?'—and the father, who for years had not risen from his chair, found himself almost standing, ready to prevent his friend's sudden departure. 'Because . . .' He stopped, and for the length of that pause it really did seem that the very existence of a human being hung in the balance. 'Because I don't remember the rest of the story.' He said this coolly, and it was clear from his wan smile that he had just told an enormous lie. At that instant, there must have passed before the father's eyes, like a flash of lightning, the empty nights, the silence, the absence of any human companionship, nothing but those four walls, and, ashen-faced, he fell back in his chair. 'What do you want?

What do you want of me?' he groaned. The Colonel shook his head without saying a word. 'Just say it. Take whatever you want, but don't treat me like this: have some pity on a poor old man.' His voice trembled, his eyes filled with tears. The Colonel, a few feet away, looked impassively down at the broken man before him. 'To tell the truth . . .' A faint warmth seemed to revive the old man's exhausted body. 'Yes . . .' The Colonel leaned over the table, ready to play his winning card. 'I've been thinking . . .' The father waited silently, his eyes fixed on the eyes of his friend. The other man, sighing, as if removing a great weight from his soul: 'We get on so well with each other—I tell you my stories and you listen.' 'Yes, yes,' the father stammered, like someone who can hear joyful ringing deep inside him. Then the soldier, his mind made up and with an impudent gleam in his eye: 'Well, then, we could be friends, we could even be relations!' The astonished father merely repeated: 'Relations!' as if he suddenly saw the possibility of supreme happiness in this world. 'Relations . . .' he said again. Then rapidly recovering himself: 'But how?' 'Well, for example . . .' the Colonel hesitated, looked at his friend as if not yet entirely sure of victory, then a confident smile reappeared on his lips: 'For example, here we have a pretty young woman of marriageable age.' 'She's my daughter!' exclaimed the father outraged. 'Yes, she's your daughter,' repeated the Colonel coldly, realizing that he had gone too far now to turn back, 'so what if she's your daughter? Your daughter also needs to marry, and if we agree . . . In any case, I think I have all the necessary qualities. Or do you have some objection? I may not be exactly young . . .' The father interrupted him impatiently: 'But . . .' The Colonel continued unabashed: 'There are no ifs or buts about it. Unless, of course, you can think of a better suitor than me? I'm not some down-and-out, I know a thing or two, and, what's more, there's my position in the army.' 'And you want me to gamble away my own daughter?' The Colonel stood abruptly to attention: 'It is not your daughter you are gambling away, it's her happiness. And I think we can agree it is a bet you are sure to win.' This argument seemed decisive. The old man tried to resist, wrung his hands and muttered something inaudible, but, seeing the Colonel about to leave, he bowed his head. 'It's true,' he said, 'but I don't know . . .' 'Don't know?' The Colonel loomed forbiddingly over him. 'You don't know what? Because I do know: girls of that age have no right to want anything; they must do what their father decides.' The old man tried one last time: 'That's exactly what I was going to say. She . . .' The Colonel gave a contemptuous snort: 'She? I'll take care of that. Once I have your consent . . .' The father thought it over for a minute and came to the conclusion that the request was not so unreasonable after all, and that they could very well come to an agreement, given that the Colonel himself was offering to speak to his daughter. When he heard the old man's answer, the Colonel sat down again, pulled his chair closer and picked up where he had left off: 'So then, my friend, as I was telling you the other day, you were unwittingly at the very fulcrum of the story. At the time, the district headquarters . . .' The details poured forth and multiplied, but for the entire duration of the Colonel's report, the father's eyes remained inexplicably wet with tears."

"I don't know," said Senhor Valdo, finishing his story, "if that was the end of the matter. Colonel Gonçalves wasn't at heart a bad sort. He helped Nina many times, but the truth is he never managed to master her. Nina wasn't as needy as her father, although they both had the same lust for life. And as was to be expected, the Colonel ended by losing the bet—the only time he did."

That was the report given to me by Senhor Valdo. Once or twice, he broke off in order to rein in some particularly strong emotion. Leaning on the counter and feigning an indifference I certainly didn't feel, I repeatedly asked myself what it was that had made him go so far, what was the secret and pressing motive that had caused him to unburden himself to me in such a manner. Ah, how little we know of the human heart. Deep down, in that unfathomable place where the final scene of a comedy without spectators is played out, perhaps he was merely reacting against the wrath of the Meneses, their constant and oppressive tyranny.

He stood before me for some time, his head bowed, as if he had summoned up those memories purely for his own pleasure. However as soon as he raised his head, I saw his now shadowless face and realized that, during all that time, he had been speaking about someone who had already died, a being who had undoubtedly once been very dear to him, but whose irremediable absence had only be softened by the passing of time. I felt a shiver run through me, imagining the courtship that had preceded their nuptials: the Colonel, with no reason to come up to their rooms after the father's death, pacing around downstairs waiting for Senhor Valdo to leave so that he could speak to Dona Nina—his pleas, his possible threats, his astonishing proposals—and then the final capitulation, the sublime flowering of that late passion, the wedding, and, at last, Dona Nina's arrival . . .

And for all my digging into that past that did not belong to me, I learned nothing more than that Senhor Valdo spoke of his wife with all the indifference, gravity, and distance with which we sometimes interrupt our work to recount an anecdote about someone long since dead.

8.
Ana's First Confession

Father Justino, you may never receive this letter.

I may never have the courage to send it, and may simply keep it, crumpled up, in my bosom. When my heart beats, it will feel against it that piece of paper wet with tears—and one day, when I'm dead, maybe they will find only an envelope from which the address was long ago erased by the cold sweat of death. And yet, who else, apart from you, would be interested in these pathetic words stopping my mouth? When I used to visit the sacristy of our old church, such thoughts as these often led me to think of some way of delivering this letter into your hands. True, I would never have the courage to give it to you personally, indeed, the mere possibility makes me catch my breath—but alone in the shadow of the images that fill the sacristy, I imagined leaving it somewhere, between the pages of your prayer book or perhaps among the vestments you put on to say mass. I was convinced, though, that you would recognize my writing and would perhaps steal five minutes from your sacred duties to read, possibly with interest, everything that my fever and my impatience now set down.

I don't honestly know where to start; before beginning this confession—because that is how I want you to see it, Father, since only then will my heart find some relief—I thought it would be the easiest way to explain myself, that the words would come naturally. I see now how wrong I was, and I hesitate, stumbling over sentences like a schoolgirl struggling with a class composition. This is because I am not writing about an actual fact, a palpable revelation that I could present as definitive proof—shall we say—of everything I saw. It is not even my intention to affirm anything, and what follows is merely the outpouring of my soul and its horribly confused contents. That is the truth, Father, the only one I can set down in this letter—and yet, in order to begin this confession, I needed a certainty that even today causes me to quake, for a keen, tormented conscience is worth more than any testimonial. And besides what *is* the truth?

It is, I think, something more often intuited than put into words. Father, I believe I have seen the tangible presence of the devil, more than that, I have, with my own silence and, therefore, my acquiescence, contributed to the silent destruction of the house and family which have, for many years, been mine. (Forgive my vehemence, Father, but ever since I entered this house, I have learned to refer to it as if it were a living entity. My husband always said that the blood of the Meneses had imbued these walls with a soul—and I have always walked between them rather apprehensively, feeling fearful and puny, imagining that huge ears were listening to and judging my every action. I don't know whether I was right or wrong, but the house of the Meneses bled me white, like a plant made of stone and whitewash that needed my blood in order to live. My whole childhood was a preparation for crossing that sacred threshold, from the moment, that is, when Senhor Demétrio deigned to choose me as his partner in life. I was still only a girl, but from then on, my parents tried to bring me up as the Meneses would wish me to be brought up. I never went out alone and wore only dark, unflattering clothes. I myself (ah, Father, now that I know better, now that I can imagine having been another person—there are days, moments, when I think of the forests I could have explored, the seas I could have sailed!—I feel a great bitterness, a heavy weight on my heart), yes, I myself struggled to become that pale, artificial creature, convinced of my high destiny and of the important position that awaited me in the house of the Meneses. Before we married, Demétrio used to visit me at least once a week, to make sure I was being properly brought up. My mother, conscious that I had been specially chosen, would exhibit to him the colorless being she was creating for the satisfaction and pride of those who lived in the Chácara: she would make me parade before him, and I would nervously carry out her orders, eyes downcast, wearing clothes that any reasonable person would have found ridiculous. At the time, I had no idea what a genuine emotion was . . . a passion, for example. I was a faded figure, stitched together out of childish, watery threads, and I imagined life to be like a story glimpsed through a window. My bloodless, mechanical gestures resembled those made in some tedious and now empty ritual. Allow me, Father, to speak to you like this, now that my dead and poisoned heart expects nothing more from the world. I repeat, I knew nothing of love or passion or any other earthly graces, the only flowers that grew in my soul were the sad creations of a timid, imprisoned imagination, and now I see everything filtered through the incoherence of others, their injustice, their baseless fears, their anxieties, their greed—and yes, why not, through my own anxieties too, my own vain, belated revolt . . .)

Demétrio would declare himself satisfied with the examination—turn to the right, smile, show how you must curtsy when in society—and say to my mother: "Excellent. You must always remember that she is being brought up to be a Meneses." He would dismiss me then, but first, bending down a little—only just enough to breathe in the perfume of my hair—he would add: "As you know, one day we will be visited by the Baron himself. I want to be able to present to him a wife worthy of me, someone who, with her graces, can dazzle the Baroness he brought with him from Portugal." At the time, I did not know that, for Demétrio, the Baron's visit was like a disease, his dearest obsession. Or rather, to be fair and to make plain everything

I saw and heard in this respect, it was, I would say, the obsession of the entire Meneses family. Because, in our district, the Baron's family was the only one that considered itself superior to the Meneses, not only in terms of wealth, which was said to be immense, but in terms of tradition, for they were the direct descendants of the Portuguese Braganças. The families appeared to be on good terms, and always greeted each other and exchanged a few words when they came out of mass, but, either because the Baron was all too aware of his own importance or merely in order to punish the pride of the Meneses, he had never once visited the Chácara, although, with the easy magnanimity of kings and princes, he was always promising to do so. Thus, year after year, that ever-postponed visit became a wound, a tumor in the soul of the man who would be my husband. Everything he did or thought turned in some way on that possibility—it was as if he expected the Baron's visit to give him the final seal of approval, the definitive proof of his own glory and of his family's reputation.

Shortly after we were married, I was witness to an argument between Demétrio and Timóteo. I'm not sure if you know, Father, or may perhaps suspect from the malicious rumors that are rife in our town, but Timóteo has always been a very strange man, with extremely eccentric habits, which have obliged the family to shroud him in silence, as one would a shameful illness. Initially, when I first came to live in the Chácara—which, at the time, retained a little of its former glory—I would catch an occasional glimpse of Timóteo when he returned from town with some of his friends. In my room at the end of the hallway I could hear the sound of their laughter and talk wafting up from the garden. (I should say, out of respect for the truth, that Timóteo almost always arrived home completely drunk—he was an utter wastrel, who squandered the money left him by his father, mocked his brothers' meanness and generally heaped scorn on them.) This behavior infuriated my husband and, once, when he burst in on one of Timóteo's private parties, he told him a few harsh truths, the kind, I imagine, that should and can be said only once.

Timóteo laughed and said that his brother was nothing but a puffed-up fool; and as for the Meneses, who were, Demétrio felt, sullied by Timóteo's behavior, they were merely the rotting shoots of a family doubtless of bastard origins. My husband started shouting then, and for some reason, he mentioned the Baron, perhaps because, in our household, regardless of the circumstances, his name is unavoidable. "He'll never come here," sneered Timóteo. "Do you really think a nobleman would cross our grubby threshold?" I must confess that I had never before seen Demétrio in such a rage; all the insults Timóteo had come out with up until then were as nothing compared to that. From then on, their shouted exchanges became so wild, so frenetic, that I couldn't understand what they were saying; feeling frightened, I left my room and heard my husband threatening to take away Timóteo's inheritance and, if he continued to live as he did then, to have him locked up in a lunatic asylum. In some families, "inheritance" is a sacred word never to be taken in vain. There was a pause, and the tension eased. But I think Timóteo's strange decision never to leave his room dates from then, fearful lest his brother should carry out his threat. Perhaps, deep down, the Chácara does mean something to him as well—perhaps inheritance is a disease of the blood. Those stones form the inner fabric of the family; the Meneses are made of concrete and whitewash, just as other families pride themselves on the nobility of their blood.

And of course I met Timóteo on other occasions too; I particularly remember walking down the hallway one afternoon and seeing him peer around his bedroom door. He stared at me for some time with a look of complete and utter disdain, then he laughed: "*You're* a Meneses too." And as if suddenly recollecting that I had been a witness to that earlier angry scene, he added: "You can tell my brother that his dream will never come true: the Baron will never set foot in this house." I didn't pass on these words, but one day (recently in fact), Demétrio again mentioned the Baron, and I commented, without really thinking about it, that he would never come to the

Chácara. He turned on me, eyes blazing: "The only person you can have heard that from is my fool of a brother! He's doubtless planning to besmirch our name forever, but I won't let him leave this house as long I'm alive. He's basically an atheist, a revolutionary, a man who believes in nothing—he would be better off dead than trying to destroy the Meneses name with his dissolute lifestyle . . ." I bowed my head, sorry I had ever spoken.

So you see, Father, that is the lens through which I have always viewed the family of which I am a member. I began this long parenthesis as a way of explaining my own role in everything that happened subsequently and in order to beat my breast, convinced of my own guilt . . .)

It is hard to continue my confession, especially, as I said, because what I am setting down is not so much an indisputable truth as a presentiment. I cannot pinpoint at what precise moment the transformation occurred—but she was here among us, having arrived only shortly before, and was already making her influence felt in the febrile times we lived in then. I had always gotten on well with my husband, even though I did not love him. That, Father, is the first time I have ever said those words, which seem to come stumbling to meet me, strange and rebellious—but if I cannot tell *you* the secret that has lived inside me all this time, who can I tell? As I say, I did not love him and never have, indeed, sometimes, I almost hated him—that is the sad truth. But ever since I came to this house like a fruit picked when still green, I had remained green and slightly hard, with a few bruises and lacerations here and there, but intact, preserved—and for me, the world was stuck fast in that permanent state of coldness and deceit. Until the moment when, standing in front of my mirror, I suddenly understood my husband's look and saw in it all the disdain he felt for me. I didn't feel humiliated exactly, or unhappy, because I didn't care what he thought about me. But that look, born of such anger, somehow revealed to me the palpable reality surrounding me: I woke up and, for the first time, looked around in astonishment, not quite understanding what was happening. What surprised me most was the silence; I had never known such stillness, a complete absence of rhythms and dissonances; it was icy and fluid, as slippery as the sleep of death—and that was what alerted me to my own mediocrity. There must be a place in hell for the mediocre, and Satan himself, trident aloft and looking down on his inert prey, must ask himself, slightly perplexed: "What am I supposed to do with this thing, when its mere presence makes even suffering dwindle in intensity?"

I looked in the mirror then and was startled by my pale skin, my dark clothes, my inelegance. I repeat, and will do ad infinitum: this was the first time such a thing had happened to me, and I was gazing at my own image as if at a complete stranger. This could have lasted no more than a minute—that was me, that being looking at herself in the mirror, my eyes, my hands, my silently moving lips . . .—and I must confess, Father, it wasn't fear, anger, or resentment that so abruptly turned me against my husband. After that look, which had woken me up to the real world, he did not leave the room, doubtless waiting to see the effect of his words. He had gone over to the window, and I went after him, grabbed his arm and shook him furiously: "You despise me, don't you? You despise me!" He pushed me away nervously, impatiently, and as if sensing the approaching storm, asked uneasily: "What's gotten into you today? I've never seen you like this before . . ." Never. I stood there like a pathetic creature abandoned by its creator. I could easily have retorted that I had never *felt* like that before, either. My whole being was filled by the most disparate, intoxicating feelings. I said: "It's Nina you adore, isn't it? I've seen the way you look at her . . ." I said this slowly, as if someone were whispering the words to me. He turned pale, looked deep into my eyes, then shouted: "You must be mad! Wherever did you get that idea?" I don't know what I said in reply, but the effort was too much for me and I collapsed onto a chair, sobbing and laughing at the same time, covering my face with my hands. By the time I had calmed down, he was no longer in the room.

Ever since that moment I have felt like a different woman. Oh, I continued to live like everyone else, as I always had up until then, but a fire burned ceaselessly inside me. Whatever I did, whatever distractions I came up with, I couldn't take my eyes off my sister-in-law. She was so beautiful, so different from me. Everything about her was bright and animated. She was surrounded by an aura of interest and sympathy, whereas I was an opaque, clumsy being, plumped down in the world, with no gifts of warmth or communication. One day, I found her sitting in the sun, combing her hair, and I went over to her and, on an irresistible impulse, ran my hand over her hair. She started at my touch and spun around; when she saw it was me, she hesitated, then smiled: "Do you think I have pretty hair?" she asked. I rather shamefacedly said that I did, but dared not go any closer. And yet what a whirlwind was in my heart! "I always take very good care of my hair," she said with an almost voluptuous nonchalance. "Men love pretty hair." She shook her head, making her beautifully combed, coppery locks ripple and shine in the sunlight. "See?" she said. And she went on mischievously: "They like to stroke hair like mine, to rub their face and lips on it . . ." She looked at me and, seeing my embarrassment, concluded: "But men are terrible creatures, aren't they!" "Shut up!" I cried, tormented by an unbearable feeling of unease. She got up then and came over to me: "You wish you were like me, don't you? Come, admit it, what wouldn't you give to have hair like mine?" I felt my eyes filling with tears. Nina must have realized she had gone too far, because she moved a few steps away in silence, then said: "Forgive me, I sometimes forget who I'm talking to . . ." Her kindness wounded me more than her previous words. For a few days, we avoided speaking to each other or even meeting, but the truth is that I never lost sight of her, I followed her like a shadow, peered through shutters, through half-open doors, through windows, wherever I could catch a glimpse of her strange, magnetic figure.

It was around this time that she moved to the Pavilion. I'm not sure if you remember it, a wooden structure at the far end of the garden, it used to be painted green, but for a long time now, it's been no particular color at all, scarred by time, battered by the rains, with patches of mold and cracks opened up in the walls by the damp, all of which made it look rather grubby and unpleasant. Yet at the time, I envied her because she was free of us, of the Chácara—oh, she knew exactly what she wanted!—and free, too, if she wished, to lead a completely separate life, with not a thought for the Meneses. Oddly enough, though, alone now in the big house, I could find not a moment's rest, always imagining what my sister-in-law might be doing, her plans and thoughts. I would look at my ancient shoes, my frumpy clothes, my prim manners, my prematurely old smile, and feel an unhealthy curiosity to know what Nina might be wearing, how she had learned to choose her clothes, what she did and what it was about her that attracted men. It was this same curiosity that revealed to me the silent presence of the devil. Don't judge me, Father, don't go thinking that I'm rushing to judgement, trying to squeeze the facts into a narrow rationale. By dint of sniffing and watching and following like a cautious, hungry animal, I finally came upon the infernal trail that would lead me to the fire in which I am burning today.

My husband always used to take a nap after lunch, whether in a hammock on the verandah or in our large bed in the warm shadows of our shuttered room. I took advantage of those moments to go out into the garden and slip quietly down to the Pavilion, spying and suffering and imagining the life that must be going on inside—and, yes, why not say it, Father—eaten up with melancholy and envy. There were flowers everywhere, and I would sit down among the flower beds, crushing some small petal against my cheek and trying in vain to calm my fever. Again and again I would catch a glimpse of Nina through the curtains or hear her voice far off, as if we were separated by an impenetrable wall. One day, though, when the sun seemed even hotter than usual and the poppies were wilting in the heat, I suddenly saw her coming down the Pavilion steps at a speed which, at first, I thought languid and, later, judged to be cautious. She was wearing a flimsy pink negligée tied at the waist with a velvet ribbon. I give these details so that you can picture the woman and understand what a very disruptive presence she was. For a moment, dazzled by the sun, I saw her whirling around among the flowers, her clothes fluttering about her. She seemed entirely untroubled by the brilliant light and set off purposefully. I don't know what dark force impelled me to follow her. You may no longer remember the exact layout of that part of our garden, Father, but you often went there to hear my late mother-in-law's confession; you walked together there on innumerable occasions, or so the story goes—and no one would, I think, be better equipped to identify the place where we were heading. It was to the right of the Pavilion, where there used to be a clearing with a statue at each corner, each representing one of the four seasons. The only survivors were Summer and the lower half of Spring, inside which, as if it were a vase, a vigorous fern grew, overflowing the broken edges. The plants and trees had grown taller, and yet the clearing remained untouched, as if it were a redundant space, floating in the midst of that dense vegetation. That—a place no one ever went to—was where Nina was heading, and this only intensified my curiosity. I continued to follow her, hiding behind trees as I went. My fear of being seen meant that I missed part of what happened next. When I got closer to the clearing, I hid behind the trunk of an acacia tree, and I saw Nina, trembling with rage, talking to Alberto, our gardener. I moved closer still and hid behind a tall clump of ferns, not wanting to miss a single word of what they said. However, everything must have happened very quickly, because I saw Nina raise her hand and slap the boy. He dropped the spade he was carrying and stepped back, putting his hand to his cheek. The strangeness of the scene left me momentarily stunned—and I had barely recovered from my shock, when I saw Nina give the boy a shove, then stride off in the opposite direction from which she had come. Alberto was left alone, rubbing the cheek she had struck. He clearly lacked the courage to do anything else and merely followed her with his eyes until she had disappeared from sight. I don't know what I did then, I must have slipped or lost my balance, because he immediately turned toward me. "Ah, it's you, Senhora," he said, and there was no surprise in his voice. Only then did I notice how he had changed. When people are of no interest to us, they fade into the background like insignificant objects. For me, Alberto had always been the gardener, and I had never thought of him in any other way. Now, simply by virtue of Nina's presence, I discovered him just as I had discovered myself. This, Father, must be the devil's main talent: stripping reality of any fiction and placing it naked, in all its impotence and anxiety, in the very center of a person's being. Yes, for the first time I really saw Alberto and I saw him in various ways simultaneously: first, that he was young, second, that he was handsome. Not handsome as he was in that precise moment, but handsome as he must have been before meeting Nina, pure and serene in the simplicity of his small, provincial soul. Now, split in two, the old him and the new came together in that same dark beauty, and there he was, as if by chance, looking slightly disheveled, like those gods whom the myths conjured out of foam or wind. I sensed the person he would have been, retrospectively, if you like, not as Nina loved him, but as I might perhaps have loved him. He was different now, but I knew he was different. There was a weariness about his face, the sadness of knowledge in his eyes. I spoke to him as if for the first time, and my voice shook because I was speaking to a human being and not to an abstraction. "What's wrong, Alberto?" And the odd thing is that he addressed me then as if *I* were an abstraction, as if I did not exist or were merely the colorless being he was accustomed to greeting. "Did you see how she treated me?" he said, by way of a response. At the same time, this was spoken in such a clearly confessional tone that I could not possibly misunderstand, and a wave of bitterness rose up in my heart. I turned away to hide my tears. And yet there was nothing special about what he had said to me, except that, for him, the veil had not been torn asunder and he saw me as he did every day: the same poor, sad, empty being I had always been. Forgetting I was there, he exclaimed again: "Did you see the way she treated me! But she'll pay for it one day, and pay dearly, the slut!" That last word shocked me, and I spun around. He seemed then to wake from his dream and muttered an awkward: "Sorry . . ." I confess I was still trying to control my own feelings, and so, pretending not to have heard the insulting term, I went over to him and asked again: "What's wrong, Alberto, what happened?" But he did not answer and had grown distant again. At this point, I began talking, and it was as if another being had entered me and was using my lips to utter those strange words: "I know exactly what's going on. You're probably in love with her and dream night and day about her beautiful hair, isn't that right? Of her white skin, Alberto, her body, which you cannot have . . . Be a man and have the courage to confess, you're madly, hopelessly in love with her, aren't you?" I was holding him and shaking him, completely out of control. He came to his senses then, stared at me for a moment in amazement, and then began to laugh. I did not at first understand that laugh, which had the affect of a cold, concentrated beam of light that quickly dissipated the shadows on his face. And then I understood: how ridiculous I must look in my dark dress, my hair caught neatly back in a bun, my thin lips pressed together, braced for the first insult, the first lie, the first offer . . .

I could not bear what, for me, was not so much a laugh as an offence of the gravest order; I recoiled, turned, and fled, feeling that, without even having met him, I had already lost him forever.

9.
Betty's Diary (ii)

5th – We haven't had a moment's peace since she arrived. She's constantly asking for things and is never happy, complaining about the servants, the house, the weather, everything, as if we were to blame for what is happening to her. I haven't yet seen her at rest, and I don't honestly think she knows how to rest. She is always pacing back and forth, doing something or thinking of something to do—this gives her a feverish, almost hostile appearance, which creates an uneasy, expectant atmosphere. In the servants' quarters, the maids complain, and in the house itself the masters and mistress sit around, grim-faced.

It's odd, but despite all this activity, and right from the very first moment, she struck me as not being in the best of health. She complained of headaches and looked very pale; dark shadows appeared under her eyes. Once installed in her room, she began unpacking the many suitcases she had brought with her. I asked why she needed so many dresses, and if she planned to wear them all, adding: "Because the family hardly ever goes out." She responded tartly: "What do I care what the family does or doesn't do? I will do exactly as I please." Then she asked what amusements were to be had in town—dances, theaters, meetings of some kind. I couldn't help but laugh as I continued to unpack quantities of capes and dresses. Seeing the angry glance she shot me, I told her straight out that there were no dances and no theaters, that the Baron very occasionally invited a few families to his house, but that we never went. "Why?" she asked, still helping me unpack. "That's how Senhor Demétrio lives," I said. She dropped everything and gave me a hard look: "I don't want to live the way Senhor Demétrio lives," she said. I merely shrugged, imagining the battles that lay in store for us if she really intended to live a different kind of life. I said nothing, but was filled with dread for the future. When she had finished unpacking, she dropped into a chair, exhausted. "I can't do any more." Her forehead was beaded with sweat, which seemed excessive after carrying out such a minor task.

"Are you feeling ill?" I asked.

She slowly shook her head:

"No, not ill. But I haven't felt well since I arrived. Perhaps it's the atmosphere in this house. I'm afraid I won't be able to bear it. Oh Betty, if you knew how unhappy I am!"

I don't know why, but I felt she was telling the truth. The way in which she spoke those words left no room for doubt, and my heart ached for her. If you asked me to explain, I couldn't, but it was clear to me that she was suffering from some unnamable malaise.

"I think you should rest a little, Senhora. Then you can think about the future more calmly."

She fixed her eyes on me again, and this time they were filled with scorn:

"I never rest, Betty. What kind of a woman do you think I am, to waste my time lying in bed?"

My suggestion filled her with a disgust verging on terror. I finished putting away all her clothes, then dusted the furniture and was about to leave, when she called me back:

"Betty, who sent me that message when I arrived?"

"Senhor Timóteo."

I imagined she would want to know more, but instead she remained silent for a moment, before exclaiming "Ah, yes!" as if she knew all she needed to know. Then she thoughtfully bowed her head.

I assumed I would be able to leave then with no further delays, but I again heard her voice behind me:

"And where is his room?"

"Right next door."

She thanked me and I left, leaving her sitting in the chair.

7th – I was talking to the maids in the kitchen—all of whom were surprised to see the mistress—when I was told that Senhor Timóteo wanted to speak to me. Before going to him, I wondered what excuses I would give to Senhor Demétrio if he should find out, because he had already forbidden me several times from answering his brother's calls. I had never obeyed those orders and now, drawing myself up, I went straight to Senhor Timóteo's door—what did I care about family squabbles? Senhor Timóteo himself came to greet me.

"Good morning, Betty," he said cheerfully, quite unlike his usual self. I could see that he was happy and wanted to show how happy he was.

"Good morning. You were asking for me."

"Indeed I was, Betty," and before I could do or say anything, he dragged me inside.

He was dressed in his usual eccentric fashion and, as always, the curtains were carefully closed. Nevertheless, it was easy to see from the dust on the furniture and the dirt on the floor that the room had not been cleaned for a long time: the air was warm and fetid, as if it were Senhor Timóteo's own personal climate, as though it were the only element in which he was allowed to exist. While I was looking around me, I suddenly spotted someone moving in the gloom and it did not take me long to identify who that person was.

"It's me, Betty," came my mistress's calm voice. "If Senhor Valdo asks for me, you can tell him I'm here, visiting my brother-in-law."

At these words, a strange, guttural sound emerged from the spot where Senhor Timóteo was standing. It was impossible to describe it as a laugh or any other normal manifestation of joy.

"Did you hear that, Betty?" and he came over to me, his voice brimming with excitement. "Did you hear what she said? She came especially to see me. I think the Meneses will have many reasons to be glad today . . ."

This was clearly an exceptional event for him, first, because he was getting to know his sister-in-law (who could become an ally, although who knows by what means or by what secret affinities?), second, because he was doubtless secretly plotting against his brothers. Oh, I knew the Meneses tribe well. Meanwhile, as I stood there, I was trying in vain to understand why that visit should give him such extraordinary pleasure. What game was he playing? What future possibilities was he conjuring up out of a gesture that was probably nothing more than an act of courtesy? I went a little closer, trying to see my mistress's face—and her eyes, which glinted for a moment in the warm shadows, revealed a confidence, and yes, why not, almost a sense that she was quite at ease in that exotic atmosphere. How mysterious those two hidden natures were: that room, where none of us breathed easily, was the one place where she seemed comfortable. Slow and majestic (I don't know if I mentioned that Senhor Timóteo—who was beginning to drink too much, perhaps in order to escape from the oppressive monotony of life between those four walls, perhaps for some sadder, more hidden reason, a kind of slow suicide—was growing visibly fatter, and his mother's lavish, extravagant clothes, which had once added such luster to the social world of the Chácara, were now literally bursting at the seams, torn and ripped asunder by the first, irremediable signs of his excesses) Senhor Timóteo came toward me as if defying my gaze. Then, standing before me, he said:

"Betty, I want you to go at once and fetch a bottle of ice-cold champagne. I want to celebrate this memorable day."

From her armchair, the mistress appeared to give her silent consent, and so, having no alternative but to obey, I left the room, closing the door behind me. As soon as I reached the end of the hallway, however, Senhor Valdo suddenly leapt out at me. I tried to avoid him, but he grabbed me by the arm:

"Where are you going? Where have you been?" he demanded.

"I was in Senhor Timóteo's room," I answered, trying to pull away. However, he simply tightened his grip on my arm and pushed me against the wall.

"From Senhor Timóteo's room?" he repeated, aghast. "And who else is in there?"

"The mistress," I answered.

"The mistress!" he repeated, as if I had said something utterly outrageous.

I merely nodded and he stared at me in silence, perhaps waiting for me to provide him with more details. When I remained defiantly dumb, he let go of me, and his voice regained its usual polite, almost gentle tone.

"And where are you going now?" he asked, before immediately adding, as if he no longer cared about that question and wanted to get straight to the point: "What were they doing? What were they plotting against me?"

"Senhor Valdo," I exclaimed, "how can you imagine such a thing? No one was plotting against you. They didn't even mention you!"

"Ah," and he gave a rather strained laugh. "So what were they doing then, shut up in his room?"

"Senhor Timóteo asked me to bring him a bottle of champagne."

"A bottle of champagne!" he cried in horror. "But my wife never drinks. Why today?"

I shrugged:

"I know nothing about that, Senhor Valdo. I merely carry out orders."

He looked at me again, repeating the word "champagne," and his thoughts were obviously far away. Then a mischievous glint appeared in his eyes.

"You can get back to your normal duties, Betty, there will be no champagne."

"Why not?" I asked hesitantly.

He laughed:

"Because I have the key to the cellar."

I felt I should take a sterner stance:

"But what will they think, Senhor Valdo? I really don't believe it's right for a Meneses . . ."

He was already moving away, but at the name "Meneses," he turned:

"What will *they* think, what will *they* say?"

I corrected myself:

"She might think we're mean. And she would be right, Senhor Valdo. After all . . ."

"After all what, Betty? Why do they need champagne? They want to get drunk, do they?"

"No, not drunk. How can you think such a thing of her . . . of your wife? Senhor Timóteo is simply pleased to have met Dona Nina."

He shook his head, as if unsure what to do. For a moment, seeing him standing obstinately before me, I thought it was merely a matter of jealousy, one of those spats that seem to be commonplace between newlyweds. But then, when he spoke again, I realized there was something more serious troubling him.

"It isn't as innocent as it seems, Betty. Timóteo will not rest until he has destroyed us all."

There was such certainty in his voice that, for a moment, I thought perhaps he was right, that the normally reserved Timóteo really might be plotting some treachery. What was he planning? Why had he told me to fetch champagne? What kind of alliance was he trying to forge with the newcomer? And I thought about that room, its suffocating atmosphere and the way in which Senhor Timóteo had spoken to me.

"Here it is," said Senhor Valdo, handing me the key to the wine cellar. "Fetch the champagne."

And then, as if he could no longer contain his innermost feelings, he blurted out:

"Take it to them and tell him he can besmirch the family name for all I care, but if he so much as touches Nina . . ."

He left the sentence hanging and made a threatening gesture. I had never seen him so angry; he, who never lost his composure and never got carried away, was suddenly overwhelmed by rage. And yet, strangely, his fury was merely a display of his own powerlessness. True, the mistress was in his brother's bedroom, the brother whom everyone considered a reprobate, but if Senhor Valdo had been brave enough, it would not have been so very hard for him to open the door and tell his wife to leave that place of dissolution. Why did he not do that, instead of prowling furiously around outside the room and talking to me, when I had nothing to do with the matter and was in no way responsible for what was happening? He stared at me dumbly, and I could see that there was no peace in his heart: his troubled eyes betrayed the contradictory emotions battling away inside him. When he saw I was about to leave, he went on:

"Yes, tell him . . . You can even say . . ."

He stopped in mid-sentence, as if he had run out of breath, then leaned against the wall, bowing his head.

"Enough is enough," he said. "It doesn't matter. She hates us all far too much to accept him as a friend."

He said this as if it were the last of his confessions, and left as abruptly as he had appeared. I stood watching him, and it seemed to me that he stumbled slightly as he walked. Somewhat apprehensively, I went and fetched the champagne. And despite everything, my hands were trembling, my whole being was trembling, and I didn't know who I should believe: that strange creature who kissed me and called me "her friend," or that man who had suddenly revealed to me his intense suffering.

8th – Today, for the second time in two days, the mistress returned to Senhor Timóteo's room. There was no champagne, but a modest pot of tea, which I prepared. Unable to forget Senhor Valdo's words, I confess that I was surprised by this second visit so soon after the first. While I was serving tea, I tried to linger longer than usual, in order to gauge the degree of intimacy that had grown up between these two new friends. What could two such different people find to talk about? At first, they chatted about our town, Vila Velha—and she complained about its bad roads, saying that while there had been improvements made in Mercês, Queimados, and Rio Espera, there was no sign of anything similar happening in Vila Velha. Senhor Timóteo agreed, laying the blame on the mayor, who, in his opinion, was a fool and a thief. Gradually, though, I saw that, beneath the apparent superficiality of that conversation, there existed between them a mutual understanding—it was as if they had talked long and hard and reached an agreement on some matter of great importance. Without knowing quite why, my heart contracted. What would he be capable of, that man whom others said was not quite right in the head, and who did indeed behave like someone mentally ill? He might not be dangerously mad, but who knew what he might do? Immersed in these sad thoughts, I pulled a small table into the middle of the room. I also noticed that, at one point, they stopped talking, as if waiting for me to leave—and on purpose and in order to affirm my independence, I began painstakingly polishing the cups, occasionally glancing across at the mistress and at Senhor Timóteo. Then Dona Nina said something I didn't quite catch, but which must have been very funny, because Senhor Timóteo erupted in a series of muffled laughs, exclamations and yelps. Then, as if they had noticed my determination not to leave, they began another boring, banal conversation about fashion or some other such nonsense. The conversation changed then and became faster, more energetic. They were talking about the Chácara, and Senhor Timóteo launched into a passionate description of what the garden used to look like. Dona Nina grew equally passionate and said that flowers were the thing she loved best in the world. No jewel, no diamond, no turquoise was worth as much to her as a few rosebuds about to open. Senhor Timóteo suggested that this was perhaps because she had been brought up in a city. Dona Nina was not sure what the reason was, but spoke nostalgically about the flowers that a friend, a colonel, used to bring her. She concluded, saying:

"They were so lovely, the roses. But they are not my favorite flower."

"What's your favorite, then?" asked Senhor Timóteo, sipping the tea I had poured him.

"Violets," she said. (And I remember that, suddenly, as if her thoughts had entered some shadowy zone, her eyes grew dark. And her voice, abandoning its earlier frivolous tone, became suddenly more serious.). "Timóteo, will you promise me one thing?"

"Anything, my angel."

"I'm sure that I will never go back to Rio . . ."

"Why?"

She shrugged:

"I don't know, but something tells me I'm going to die here."

"What a sad thought!" protested Senhor Timóteo.

"Sad or not, it's the truth. And I want you to promise me one thing."

"Of course, anything," he said. "But tell me, why would you die now?"

"I'm not talking about now, but we all have to die one day, don't we?"

He tried to lighten the tone:

"Yes, but I'm likely to go before you do."

"No, no," she said firmly. "I'll go first. And I want you to promise that you won't forget me and will place some violets on my coffin."

At this unusual request, Senhor Timóteo was touched and took her hands in his:

"I will do anything you wish, my angel. But you mustn't think like that. I bet it was my brother who . . ."

She covered his mouth with her hand and the conversation moved on. It was hot, and the sun was visible through the closed shutters. In some dark corner of the room a bee was buzzing. Dona Nina got up, kissed her brother-in-law and left, saying that she needed to write a letter to Rio. Senhor Timóteo and I were left alone, and I was just about to leave too, when he called me back.

"Betty, do you remember Father Justino? When my mother was alive, he often used to come to the Chácara."

"Of course I remember, sir," and I was surprised at the abrupt shift from unaccustomed frivolity to his more usual grave, reserved manner.

"Father Justino," he went on, "sometimes said some very true things. Nothing very profound, you understand, because a provincial priest can't be expected to know very much, but one day . . ."

He paused as if trying to recall the priest's exact words, then went on:

"One day, in the garden, he told me that a sin is almost always something very tiny, a grain of sand, a nothing—but that it can destroy an entire soul. Ah, Betty, the soul is a strong thing, an invisible, indestructible force. If a tiny pinch of sin—a nothing, a dream, a nasty thought—can destroy it, what will a large dose of poison do, a sin instilled drop by drop into the heart you want to destroy?"

I didn't really understand what he meant, but I stared at him in alarm.

10.
Valdo Meneses' Letter

Post-script written in margin:

Make no mistake, Nina, you will find things here very different now. I don't love you in the way I once did, and all you can expect from me is an honest, compassionate coolness. I will meet you at the station, and together we will rebuild the relationship between us that should not have been severed in the first place, but which, alas for us, now lies in ruins. But just remember that I am only doing this for the sake of the dignity of the Meneses ....

....

Yes, you can come—of course, no one can stop you returning to the house on which you so high-handedly turned your back all those years ago (fifteen years, Nina—fifteen years!). I was not at first going to reply to your letter or give in to your entreaties . . .

However, on reading your most recent letter, I see there is no putting you off and that I will have to drain this poisoned chalice to the dregs, and silence will help neither of us: we will have to look each other in the eye, and I know that, just as I will not have the heart to refuse you my protection, so you will not have the courage to live without it. Perhaps everything will be different now: my brother, about whom you complained so much in the past, is older and more irascible than ever, and my sister-in-law has grown even quieter and sadder. The house is just the same, but time is visibly taking its toll: yet more windows that won't open, the green paintwork growing ever darker, the walls cracked by the beating rain, and the wilder parts of the garden invading the flower beds. There's no denying it, Nina, things have changed since you left—as if an engine, dependent entirely on its own momentum, had suddenly stopped working—and the calm that descended on the house after your departure brought with it, too, the first signs of death that so often reveal themselves in our moments of repose; we have stopped in time, and our slow progress toward extinction has created a climate to which you will probably never be able to adapt. Despite all this, the eternal spirit of the Meneses family remains and for that we are thankful, for it is the only thing that cheers and sustains us, like a steel joist holding up crumbling masonry. You will find us, immutable, at our posts, and the house exactly where it has always been. As time goes by, many things may get lost along the way without us even noticing, but others will grow and gather strength within us, and so, in some ways, due to circumstance or fate, we are more Meneses than ever—as you will see the moment you set foot once again in the Chácara.

For us there remains, like weeds clinging desperately to a ruined wall, the nostalgia for what might have been, had we not destroyed it through our own weakness or negligence. No, Nina, don't think I am accusing you of some crime or blaming you for everything that happened. I long ago lost my old rigor. I now believe we were both to blame for all the things that went wrong between us; and if we were to blame, then we were also the victims.

What surfaces in my mind now, in particular, is the night you came to my bedside to say goodbye. How I loved you at that moment, Nina, and what unspeakable pain and turmoil your presence aroused in me! The doctor had just left, and I was still convalescing from that senseless act of folly; and I committed that act not because I was finding it harder than usual to bear the Chácara, Demétrio, and all the other things you found so hateful. No, my reason was more straightforward: I simply couldn't face life without you by my side. Demétrio had placed the lamp behind my head, which meant that I could see the whole room without others immediately being able to see me. I remember you were dressed very simply in a dark woolen cape. We were alone, and you stood in the doorway, no doubt waiting for your eyes to grow accustomed to the glare. Ah, how well I recall that silence; you cannot imagine how ignominious and wretched I felt while it lasted. All the things we could not say to each other, all the things left unspoken and that formed part of our unremitting sadness and isolation, all those things we knew so well without ever having been able to give voice to them, all the torment that always constitutes the most painful portion of any kind of love, all hung there between us, vast and tangible. For that whole minute, I could measure exactly how low I had fallen in your estimation; and at the same time, Nina, I was aware of the utter absurdity of my despairing gesture all those weeks earlier; I know you were never convinced by that gesture, but it was that feeling more than any other, intermingled with so much shame and humiliation, that led me to abandon everything and let you go, let you leave—at that moment, in the silent way you looked at me, I understood that it was all over.

"I came to say goodbye," you said coldly, taking a step forward.

My days spent recuperating in the Pavilion had proved very beneficial, and although I wasn't in any pain, I was still very weak. I tried to sit up, failed, and let out a groan. You looked at me from afar—from miles away it seemed—and a chilly smile crept across your lips.

"Well, you're certainly not going to die of your wounds, Valdo, and not even this silly pantomime of yours is going to keep me in this house a moment longer."

"Nina!" I cried, trying to grab hold of one of your hands in an attempt to revive old times, when, despite everything, and however great my humiliation, I could still count on having you by my side.

It was not to be, though, and I could tell you were trying to contain your own tumultuous feelings; and as you turned away you seemed to me taller than usual and somehow more of a stranger. When you turned around again, your voice was even calmer and more composed.

"I was hoping to leave on good terms, Valdo, with no ill feelings and no resentment. But this ridiculous accusation . . ."

"Please, Nina," I said. "No one in this house hates you; here you are among friends."

(It was true: one or two longer than usual silences from my brother, a few rebuttals on his part, a misunderstanding here and there—how could such simple things, so common in the day-to-day rhythm of family life, be interpreted as signs of irreparable enmity?)

"Friends!" and once again a smile spread across your lips. "Listen, Valdo. I met Demétrio in the hallway just now, and he walked straight past me without saying a word."

From your lofty position standing there beside me, not even deigning to look at me on the sick-bed where I lay, what were you afraid of, what benevolent feelings did you fear might be triggered in your heart of hearts were you to look me straight in the eye, as I had always done with you? But no, your cruelty knew no limits. You chose blindness and, by rejecting me outright, you consigned all my suffering and despair to oblivion. I said:

"It was doubtless all that silly nonsense at the Pavilion . . ."

Then, for the first time, I saw you tremble, and you bent down as if to crush me with your words:

"It's a lie, Valdo! All lies! As you know very well, that man barely brushed my fingertips with his lips."

I said nothing. What was to be gained by revisiting such painful events when we were about to say goodbye? That was when you began to pace the room. With your every movement I could smell the perfume given off by your body—that particular sweet, feminine scent—and I remembered—oh, how I remembered!—what we had lived through in those final days together in the Pavilion, all the minute details of that life, still so potent and yet already dead, quite dead. You suddenly stopped pacing and knelt down beside me—the only time you did that, Nina, the only time!—and whispered almost in my ear:

"You know very well why he wants to drive me away."

Yes, Nina, I knew, as I still do today. These things are never forgotten, but they are things that go beyond our understanding, and all we can do is keep a dignified silence. You stood up again.

"Even if he really did hate you," I said, grabbing hold of your skirt, "even if he really wanted to see you driven from this house forever, thrown out into the street like a dog, you could still count on me, Nina. You could always count on me. I swear that no one would ever dare touch so much as a hair on your head . . ."

"Ah!" you cried, startling me. "Is that what you think? Oh, but you're so naïve, Valdo!"

I sensed your gaze wandering about the room, evidently looking for something. How well I knew you, Nina, especially at times like that when you were in the grip of anger and your gleaming eyes darted about enigmatically, like an animal sensing danger. How well I knew you, and how much I loved you, trembling and ready to pounce on the first object that might serve you as a weapon. The object you were looking for—and I knew this just as well as you—was the revolver I had used for my ill-fated suicide attempt. You probably realized what was going through my mind too, and as my gaze instinctively fell on the chest of drawers, you rushed over, opened the top drawer and triumphantly pulled out the gun. Demétrio had wrapped it in a handkerchief so as to hide it from my view.

"Here it is!" you cried. "The murder weapon. Only you, Valdo, only you could try to deceive me about such stupid things."

At that moment, I confess, I feared for your sanity. We were in one of the rooms farthest from the drawing room, a narrow storeroom containing the old couch on which they had laid me all those years ago. If you really had gone mad—which, after so many days of inner struggle, could not be entirely ruled out—how would I summon help? With some astonishment, I observed your growing agitation, your abrupt manner, the wild, harsh way you spoke.

"It wasn't a suicide attempt," you went on. "It was murder. Who does this revolver belong to, Valdo? How long has it been paraded about in front of everyone, displayed in the most visible place in the whole house, tempting you, leading you on to that moment of folly?"

I felt a tremor inside me, for your words contained a glimmer of truth. The revolver belonged to Demétrio, who had come to me that night saying: "It's an old model, unusual too. Senhor Aurélio promised me I wouldn't find a better one anywhere in town." I took it in my hands and examined the trigger. "It's certainly old," I agreed, "but it works perfectly well." For some time he continued twirling the gun around in front of me, then he placed it in a prominent position on the sideboard. And it's true that every time I passed by I saw it there. Even Ana, when she was tidying the drawing room one day, asked: "Why don't you put that gun away, Demétrio?" He replied somewhat drily: "No. Guns must be kept on display so that they're immediately at hand whenever they're needed." I don't know what need he was referring to, probably nothing in particular, for I could never imagine that I would use that gun. But viewed from a certain angle, maybe you were right? My brother has always had a very labyrinthine way of thinking, and neither I nor anyone else ever managed to penetrate its paths. It's possible that he was trying to tempt someone, but I don't believe that person was me. You yourself, Nina—what might you have done in a moment of madness? Despite everything, I tried to dissuade you:

"Mere appearances, Nina. I'm sure you're mistaken."

"No, no," you shouted. "I'm sure he planned to kill you, but probably didn't have the courage to do it himself."

"But I tried to take my own life," I retorted.

I remember you studying the gun carefully and then, all of a sudden, as if something outside had caught your attention, you rushed over to the window and leaned out into the darkness. There was nothing to be seen, apart from the treetops swaying in the wind. I asked what had happened and you, without turning around, answered:

"I don't know. I thought I saw someone."

I tried to convince you that it had only been a shadow, the branch of a tree perhaps, but you continued to insist that it wasn't a shadow, but a real person lurking among the bushes. As you turned away from the window there was a new expression on your face. You calmly tossed the gun from hand to hand, turning it over, and then, suddenly, as if gripped by some new idea (what could you possibly have been thinking, Nina, for your eyes to shine like that?), you threw it out of the window, saying:

"I just want that wretched gun out of here—it can damn well rot in the garden!" you said, as the revolver flew from your hand in a single, smooth arc. We didn't even hear it land among the leaves.

Those angry words and that gesture seemed to close an entire chapter of our story. The air suddenly felt lighter, and I gazed at you with a smile of contentment. You were standing right next to me by then, almost within reach. There was a pause, however, and when I looked at you, I realized that you were there merely in order to say your final farewell.

"Is this forever, Nina?" I whispered.

"Yes, Valdo, forever."

A few minutes later—or seconds, rather, for so brief was the illusion of your presence—all that was left in my hands was the faint trace of your perfume. A mere trace, nothing more. I tried to get up, and considered looking for the revolver again and repeating my desperate act. But I had lost a lot of blood and, as the room began to swim around me, I let myself fall back onto the couch. After that, I don't know what happened; the wound wasn't that serious, but I believe I would have died if it hadn't been for Betty's unstinting care and attention. I would have died of sorrow, neglect, and nervous exhaustion. It's true, however, that there is no ill to which the human

soul cannot accustom itself, and by the time I was able to leave my bed, your absence was already less painful. I learned to be even more taciturn than before and to hide my thoughts from others, to distance myself from everything that causes me pain. This was the reason for my silence during all these years, and so it would have gone on were your return not imminent. I don't know what else to say, Nina: at this moment, the thing that hurts inside me is like an old stitch, muted like a distant tune, a memory, perhaps remorse. I can't imagine what will happen when you return. In any event, you can be quite sure that I never ....
....

11.
The Pharmacist's Third Report

After the work on the pharmacy had finished, carried out with Senhor Demétrio's assistance, I must confess that my greatest wish in life was to own a dog. I wasn't thinking of a pedigree dog with silky, well-groomed fur, nor one of those fierce hounds they keep on the big country estates up near Rio Espera and Queimados, but a medium-sized animal, perhaps some kind of mongrel, but with a strong, gentle appearance, always ready to come when called. You could well say, and I would not necessarily disagree with you, that such are the dreams of an old bachelor. For those, like me, who are accustomed to solitary conversations, it is always good to find a listener, even one who cannot reply. I would call this dog Pastor, which seems to me an appropriate and even poetic name. I've often imagined him lying beside me, and me saying to him: "Such is life, Pastor. Each to his own." It wouldn't matter that he couldn't reply and merely wagged his tail, looking at me with the tender eyes of a true canine friend. I would thus be sure of having a faithful listener, one who would never contradict my opinions, as could all too easily be the case with one of my own species.

This is not the only reason that makes me wish for Pastor to arrive. With the increase in stock and a subsequent increase in value,

I find that I no longer sleep easily in the back room, mainly because of all the reports of thefts and burglaries in and around our town (Vila Velha is coming on in the world, of that there is no doubt . . .), sometimes almost in broad daylight. Just now, for example, to everyone's alarm, people are saying that the notorious Chico Herrera has returned and is already up to his old tricks over in Serra do Baú. So in addition to being a faithful companion, the dog could also stand guard over the shop. I heard that outside the town, over by Fundão, there was a man who wanted to sell a dog, a fine rat-catcher, but which had recently taken to chasing his hens. I pounced: it was exactly the animal I needed, since I kept no poultry in my back yard. This rat catcher, I confess, was nothing to write home about: thin and bony, with a snout gouged with scars left from previous encounters with hedgehogs and wild pigs; he barked little and spent most of his time crouching in the corner. But although not exactly what I had imagined, he served my purpose. I trained him carefully and he grew accustomed to sleeping at my feet while I did the accounts and made up the cashbook. I like seeing him prick up his ears at the slightest sound, and listening to him snarl at the most imperceptible of noises. It's the old rat-catcher in him, as if he could sense his prey out there in some dark, invisible wood.

It was precisely such a warning signal that caught my attention one night just recently, during a heavy, relentless downpour. I didn't hear the knocking at my door because of the streams of water running off the roof, and it was only when Pastor suddenly jumped up, ears pricked, that I realized there was someone outside. It was late and the pharmacy was already closed—who on earth could be looking for me at such an hour, and in such foul weather too? Of one thing there could be no doubt: it was clearly an emergency. So I got up, closing my book and muttering under my breath, not wanting to get out of the habit of grumbling, went to the window and pulled up the sash:

"Who's there?"

I saw a shape moving in the darkness.

"You're needed, doctor."

Hearing that muffled voice and seeing a figure that seemed more anxious to hide than to reveal itself, I hesitated.

"Sorry, you've made a mistake. The doctor lives farther along, next block down."

Then the man moved closer and I was able to see him properly: he was dark-skinned, middle-aged, and over his shoulders, like a cape, he wore a sack made of coarse cloth. I remembered having seen him a couple of times near the Meneses' house. He told me that he'd already gone to the doctor's house, but that the doctor was on a call in Fundão.

"But what do you want?" I asked, not without a certain impatience, looking out at the pouring rain.

"Senhor Valdo sent me to get you. He said that if I couldn't find the doctor, you would do."

"Oh, he said that, did he?"

"Yes, he did, he said that you could stand in for the doctor."

"Is it Senhor Valdo who's sick?"

"No, it's the mistress."

It's true, some patients did from time to time seek me out when they couldn't get hold of the doctor, so this certainly wasn't the first time. But even so I shook my head and wondered. Going to the Chácara in that weather was no laughing matter. I imagined the muddy track, rutted by carts and stray cattle from the surrounding countryside. I asked once again if Senhor Valdo had expressly told him to knock at my door, and when he said yes, I realized that I had no choice and that I would have to go with him. I asked him to wait and went to get dressed. While I was doing so, Pastor kept growling by my side, as if he wasn't at all pleased. "You see?" I said to him, "I have to go out in weather like this, and I'll be paid a pittance." He agreed, and I promised him I'd be back shortly. Putting on my thick drover's cape, it occurred to me that there might in the end be some recompense, at least in terms of finding out some gossip about the Meneses family. "And what's more," I continued out loud, "it's all part of the job. Whose idea was it set myself up as a pharmacist in a poor town in Minas Gerais? I should have been a civil servant in Rio, that's what I should've done." Once again Pastor agreed with me and accompanied me, tail wagging, as I gathered together the things I needed. I closed my case, bade Pastor farewell and within a few minutes I was at the dark-skinned man's side, heading toward the Chácara. We took a shortcut along a narrow path that left the main road and ran alongside an old slave cemetery, weaving between the clumps of crocuses that carpeted the marshes on either side of us. A muddled orchestra of frogs were croaking so close by that they seemed at any moment to be about to join us. Puddles of water glistened in the darkness, and the rain continued to fall, dripping softly on the leaves. Hoping to break the monotony of the walk, I asked:

"What happened?"

And he replied:

"The mistress suddenly felt unwell. She was sitting at the piano, and had an argument with her husband . . . I don't know. I think she fainted."

I couldn't resist exclaiming disapprovingly:

"Honestly, that family!"

And we continued in silence, me snug in my thick cape, he sheltering as best he could under his sack. Through the rain, I could make out a few rough crosses and the remnants of whitewashed tombstones that glowed in the darkness: it was the old slave cemetery. The Chácara, therefore, wasn't very far away. Now and then, I stepped into a deep puddle as I tried to keep to one side of the path, since I didn't like having that man walking behind me—he was, after all, a stranger. It wasn't long before we rejoined the road leading to the main gate of the Chácara. I must confess that as we drew near, its avenues seemed even gloomier than usual. In the distance, I could make out the dark shape of the house, with a couple of windows lit.

It was filled by a dense air of secrecy, of a life lived apart. "Strange creatures, those Meneses," I thought again. And the whole landscape gave off a coldness that came not so much from the rain as from the hostility emanating from its silent, austere occupants.

Senhor Valdo was waiting for us at the top of the steps, a lamp already lit. As soon as he saw me, he exclaimed:

"You certainly took your time! I thought you weren't coming."

"You forget, sir, that I am a mere maker of medicines," I replied, with a certain irony.

"At times like this," he replied, "your assistance will be invaluable."

As I set down my case and removed my dripping cape, I tried to find out what had happened. Senhor Valdo told me that just after dinner, Dona Nina had sat down at the piano, feeling overcome by a sudden illness. She was feeling better now, thanks to some lemon balm tea she had drunk, although she was still very weak. Since she did not generally enjoy good health, he had thought it best to call someone, for he himself had little understanding of medical matters. In the absence of the doctor, the task had fallen to me: there was no one in the town better qualified. He added that he hoped I would forgive the inconvenience, but that he would reward me generously. Clearly he knew who he was dealing with, and this promise did indeed encourage me somewhat. As he was explaining all this, he led me to the drawing room, and, with my customary pleasure and curiosity, as if I were attending a magic show, I revisited those surroundings so typical of such families: heavy, antique furniture of mahogany and jacaranda that spoke of an illustrious past, of generations of Meneses who led perhaps simpler and more tranquil lives, whereas now a vein of disorder and dissolution adulterated those finer qualities. Even so, it was easy to see what they had once been, this country nobility, with their crystal gleaming gently in the darkness, their dusty silverware attesting to a faded splendor, their ivories and their opals—yes, one certainly had a sense of comfort there, and yet it was merely a survival of things long gone. In this slowly disintegrating world, there seemed to be an evil gnawing away inside it, a latent tumor deep in its guts.

Dona Nina lay stretched out on a couch (a tattered chaise longue over which they had spread a red shawl) and she was visibly pale, her forehead glistening with sweat. But even in that state I had to admit that she was a very beautiful creature, endowed with a delicate, decadent beauty very much in keeping with the spirit of the house. Her breathing was irregular, and she followed my movements with eyes that seemed both fearful and suspicious. She said nothing to me, but I was aware she was studying me intently. I sat down beside her and took her pulse, which was very fast. I asked how she felt, and she said it wasn't the first time she'd felt nauseous and feverish, with blurred vision and other peculiar symptoms. I called Senhor Valdo to one side:

"She's pregnant!" I exclaimed.

His eyes widened:

"Pregnant?" and he stared at me as if I had just said something utterly outrageous.

I nodded my head gravely and returned to finish my examination. Without me needing to say a word, Dona Nina had understood everything. With her head resting against the wall, she appeared apprehensive and even paler.

"Oh, good Lord," she said, "I'm not ready for this."

I told her that all she needed was rest. Finally coming to his senses after the shock of the news, Senhor Valdo went to the door and called for his sister-in-law:

"Ana! Do you know what Senhor Aurélio has just told me? We're going to have a child in the house."

Dona Ana gave me an indefinable look—I believe I even saw in it a faint touch of irony—and said simply:

"Well, it's high time there was a Meneses heir."

Her husband also appeared at the doorway, but did not enter. He was swathed in shadows and seemed to be held back by an inexplicable timidity. On hearing Senhor Valdo repeating the news, he shook his head:

"In that case, she must be taken to Rio de Janeiro. We don't have the facilities here to deal with that kind of situation."

Senhor Valdo erupted:

"We don't? Nonsense, Demétrio. Nina will stay right here. The Pavilion suits her very well and there she will find all the rest she needs."

Senhor Demétrio cut in coldly:

"The Pavilion is not to be recommended. It's downright unhealthy and, besides, it's too far from the house."

He had a point, for the Pavilion, where the couple was now living, was little more than a long-abandoned, glorified gazebo with no home comforts. But Senhor Valdo, thrilled with the idea of becoming a father, ignored all such remarks and immediately began to plan out loud a series of renovations that he maintained would completely transform the Pavilion and make of it a magnificent residence, better even than the house itself. The boy—he was quite sure it would be a boy, indeed it could only be a boy—would receive every possible care and attention. Perhaps even Betty herself might want to look after him—why not? And so he paced from one side of the room to the other, rubbing his hands, and it was a pleasure to see him so full of manly enthusiasm. His enthusiasm, however, was not shared by the others. A strange silence had descended on the room as if everyone else had lost interest in the subject, making Senhor Valdo's delight seem disproportionate and futile. Still lying on the couch, Dona Nina had picked up a magazine and was pretending to leaf through it. I noticed, though, that she seemed agitated and her hands were trembling. Dona Ana had turned away and appeared to be absorbed in some detail of the room that no one else could quite determine; and as for Senhor Demétrio, he was waiting, head bowed and hands folded, for his brother's high spirits to cool. Senhor Valdo, as if none of this were of any importance to him, or indeed as if he hadn't even noticed what was going on, came over and stood beside his wife:

"You'll see, Nina. Everything will turn out just fine," he murmured, taking one of her hands, which she allowed to lie limply in his.

Only after he had repeated these words a couple of times did she put down the magazine and look calmly up at him:

"Perhaps Demétrio is right, Valdo. There are no facilities of any kind in Vila Velha."

He, however, was not about to give in:

"We can go to Queimados—there's a hospital there. It isn't very far, and that way we would avoid a long journey."

Dona Nina merely said: "Queimados!" But it was clear she wasn't thrilled by the suggestion, perhaps because the little hospital in that town was not exactly famous for the care it lavished on its patients, indeed she had heard that it was more of a poorhouse than anything else. Senhor Valdo was clearly not listening and he continued elaborating his many plans. Finally, turning again to me, he asked what type of treatment should be provided, what would be needed, what should be done and what should be avoided. I set out the usual facts I would have assumed were common knowledge, and was rather surprised that the Meneses did not apparently know them. He interrupted me once or twice, in order to clarify some detail he hadn't understood. Then, at last, when he had tired of this, and judged he had exhausted all the advice I could possibly provide, he sat down beside Dona Nina, and the two of them carried on a whispered conversation whose meaning I could not make out. At that moment, seeing them sitting so close to each other, I had no doubt that the greatest possible harmony existed between them. The rumors that had at one time been circulating in town must, I thought to myself, be completely unfounded—and I couldn't help but regret that such a fine, decent couple, who, in their own home, conducted themselves in such a sincere and amicable manner, should be exposed to the frivolous, indiscreet comments of half a dozen idlers with nothing better to do. It was at this point that Senhor Demétrio came slowly over to me.

Taking me by the arm with a familiarity I found somewhat disconcerting, he led me to the window, saying that he, too, required my services. Before I could even answer or remind him that I was not a doctor, he said that he wished me to treat the subject of our conversation with the utmost secrecy. This preamble aroused enormous curiosity on my part and banished all the negative thoughts that had been forming in my mind. Immediately grasping the meaning of my silence, he then asked if I had noticed his wife, Dona Ana. I said that I had, and he asked whether I thought her somewhat pale. I replied that I hadn't noticed anything in particular, but that I had always found Dona Ana to be somewhat pale. "No, no," he said to me, "she's much paler than usual." He paused, as if searching for the precise words to tell me what the problem was. "Well," he eventually said, "I've noticed that she's not herself lately, that she seems agitated, even feverish." Perhaps he was expecting me to say that these were the symptoms of some serious ailment, but I merely shrugged, in the hope that he would provide more information. In the face of my continued silence, he decided it was best to carry on, and told me that he was very worried, indeed, he could see no practical solution. "Why?" I asked. He replied despondently: "She's such a very reserved person, she could easily fall gravely ill before she said anything to anyone." I remained silent, but this time I was seriously considering how I could help him. It was difficult, though, since no precise illness had yet been identified. I asked whether this was all he knew or whether there might, by any chance, be other symptoms, some overlooked detail that could help me form a rational opinion. He said no, and that it was all a matter of probabilities. At that point, and so as to bring the matter to a close, I suggested that perhaps she needed a change of air. Women, after all, are such strange creatures. My words clearly made a strong impression on him, and he nodded repeatedly: yes, women certainly were very strange creatures. Perhaps a change of air was exactly what she needed, and he should, therefore, send her away on a trip somewhere. I thought it strange that he should so immediately take up my suggestion; one might almost say that this was not the first time he had thought of the idea, and that I was merely corroborating something that had already crossed his mind innumerable times. In any event, not wishing to appear indiscreet, I did not press the matter further. He thanked me for my concern, and bade me goodnight with an effusiveness I found somewhat suspect.

What was happening in that house, I thought, was certainly extraordinary. I went over to Senhor Valdo to say goodbye and, taking me amicably by the arm, he said he would accompany me to the front steps. "You have brought me some very good news, Senhor Aurélio," he said. And as we walked, he added, sighing:

"Oh, yes, it will be a boy. I haven't the slightest doubt that it will be a boy. And I can guarantee that this time my brother won't get his own way: the boy will be born right here, just like all the Meneses, and he'll be called Antônio, just like my father."

We came to the top of the steps, and he said goodbye in the same contented mood. Some time later, I heard that Dona Nina had left for Rio de Janeiro, which meant that the child would not be born at the Chácara. Later still, I heard that it had indeed been a boy, and christened not with the name of Antônio, but André.

12.
Betty's Diary (iii)

13th – Today, there was a slight panic in the house because Dona Nina woke up feeling ill, complaining of a headache and nausea. Senhor Valdo wanted to stay by her side, but was unable to, because he had to go to Vila Velha to sort things out with the bank. (I also heard him say he had a meeting with a farmer from Mato Geral, who was prepared to buy the land in Benfica that they haven't yet been able to sell, because the soil is so poor and dry.) So he asked me to stay and keep his wife company. "She's not yet used to the Chácara," he said, as if this were the only possible explanation for Dona Nina's ailments, which, I thought to myself, might be truer than he imagined, because this dull, country life, with no diversions, could hardly be to the taste of someone accustomed to the hustle and bustle of the city. When I first arrived here, I too found it a real struggle—indeed, it was hard to believe normal human beings could live so completely cut off from the world.

Dona Nina was lying on the bed, a towel placed over her eyes.

"Ah, Betty," she exclaimed when she heard me come in, "could you please bring me a little salt water?"

I did as she asked and, having soaked the towel in the salt water, began to massage her forehead, without really believing this would bring her any relief. She explained that she often had such crises, and a cloth soaked in salt water was the only thing that helped reduce the pain.

"Could it be the weather?" I asked.

She shrugged:

"Possibly."

"You should go out more," I said, "there are some lovely walks around here."

She smiled:

"I'll tell you a secret, Betty: I loathe landscapes. I feel much better in an enclosed room like this."

"Why?"

She sighed:

"I don't know." Then, after a pause: "It's so lonely here."

I tried to win her over, listing the most picturesque places to visit: the slave cemetery (and for a moment, I could see those mounds of earth, the dilapidated, roughly carved crosses, many of which bore ancient dates and strange names—Joana, Balbina, Casimiro—which seemed more like the names of people you had known and loved and long ago forgotten than those of poor slaves who had grown old on the estate . . .), or the waterfall at Fundão and, if she wanted to travel a little further, there was the ruined house in Serra do Baú.

She listened to all this in bored silence. Then she said:

"There's too much space, too much land. No, I can't, Betty, I can't."

She asked me to open the window, because she did sometimes like to look out at the garden. The old flower-beds, which lined the path leading to the front door (many of them edged with upturned empty bottles) were, in her opinion, the best thing on the estate. "Besides, I enjoy watching the gardener at work," she added. When the sun was not too hot, she would walk alone in the garden, where she would pick a leaf from a mint bush or from a geranium and breathe in the scent. And she would ask the gardener to teach her the names of the plants, wanting to know which could be used as remedies and which were merely weeds. On one side of the Chácara, behind the Pavilion, there was a stream, where she would go and sit with her bare feet in the water.

"Now that really is nice, Betty," she said, "feeling the water tickling the soles of your feet."

Thinking that something had finally aroused her interest, I told her that the same stream had once worked the flour mill at the old house in Baú, and then she removed the towel from her eyes and asked:

"What house is that, Betty? Why don't you tell me about it?"

"It used to belong to the Meneses," I explained.

She half-sat up, saying:

"Show me where it is."

"From here you can only see the tops of the mountains—it's that bluish streak in the distance. Behind it—can you see that dark line even further off?—is the Serra dos Macacos. They say the gypsies lives there, but I've never seen them."

"And does no one ever go there?"

I shook my head:

"Almost never. When we used to make a nativity scene in the house at Christmas—when Senhor Valdo's mother was still alive—we would ride out there looking for moss and the like. But now . . ."

I gradually began to tell her what I knew, about how important the old house had been in the area, how its owners used to welcome visitors from the towns of Leopoldina and Ubá and other nearer towns—and how, later on, the land was divided up and sold off, and about the death of Maria Sinhá. When she heard that name, she asked me almost urgently:

"Who was Maria Sinhá?"

This was a subject about which I knew very little! I had heard only the occasional comment, because Senhor Demétrio did not like to talk about her. There used to be a portrait of her stored in the basement, next to Anastácia's room. Dona Nina immediately became interested:

"I want to see that portrait!"

Giving in to her enthusiasm, and seeing that her melancholy was fast fading, I promised that we would make an expedition to see it as soon as she was well.

"I *am* well," she said. "I want to go now, today."

"But Dona Nina . . ."

"Betty," she said, almost begging me. "Can't you do me that one favor?"

"I can, I could, but . . ."

She made an imperious gesture—she was born to command!—waving away any further objections on my part, as if there were nothing in the world she wanted more than to see that portrait. When she realized that she had got what she wanted, she asked if there was anyone else in the house who knew about Maria Sinhá. I said that when Anastácia was a girl, she had seen Maria Sinhá, already very old by then, accompanied by a faithful slave.

"How very fascinating," she said.

And she declared her intention of going to speak with Anastácia. I laughed: Anastácia was so ancient she barely made any sense any more. Dona Nina would not be denied, though, saying that she would know how to separate reality from fantasy and adding:

"Besides, this house suffers from too much reality. It could do with a little fantasy."

We agreed that, when it got dark, I would come and fetch her and we would visit the basement.

Undated – After supper, when the house was plunged in the most absolute silence, I went to fetch Dona Nina. She was waiting for me, looking out of the open window. (She has lived in that room, next to Senhor Timóteo's, ever since she married Senhor Valdo. It has quite a large window, covered by an iron grille, and a person standing outside could easily reach up to it with their hand. I'll explain why: the Chácara is built on a slope, and while it is very high on the side where the verandah is, it reaches its lowest point at Senhor Timóteo's room, which is the last room and shares part of a wall with the kitchen, which is, of course, also at the lower end of the building. I explain all this now so that, later on, if necessary, I'll be able to remember everything. Dona Nina was leaning at the window, a dreamy look on her face, and, almost without turning around, she said: "Do you know, Betty, a few days ago, I found a bunch of violets on the windowsill here. Who could have put them there, do you think?" "An admirer," I answered jokingly. She looked at me very seriously: "Well, his admiration only lasted a day, because there's been nothing else since.")

We left the room as quietly as we could and went out through the door that opens onto the area near the fountain and the garden. It was cloudy, but not raining as yet. Beneath the arch leading into the basement, we found Anastácia, sitting on the ground, plaiting some wool. We asked her to open the door, and with much groaning and grumbling, she got to her feet. While Anastácia was turning the large key in the lock, Dona Nina tried in vain to get some information out of her. Anastácia must have been drinking because her words were slurred and she kept spitting. She finally managed to open the door, though, and we entered a dark, damp, musty space with huge beams on the ceiling.

"You shouldn't have come, Dona Nina," I said, "the air in here is almost unbreathable."

"And what's wrong with that, Betty?"

We advanced slowly, and Anastácia lit a small lamp hanging from the ceiling. In the half-light, in the corners, we could see various objects piled up, some of which I recognized, for example, the furniture that had belonged to Senhor Valdo's mother when she was alive—large wardrobes, the doors hanging off the hinges, sideboards and low stools. There was also a prayer desk, on which the velvet upholstery on the kneeling pad was torn, revealing the cotton stuffing. Against the wall stood a huge mirror, cracked from side to side, and our figures moved silently about in its still untarnished surface. And finally, slightly to one side and turned to face the wall, was a painting—it must have been about a yard tall—the frame still perfect. We turned it around and saw that it was covered by a thick layer of dust. From one side hung a frayed black crepe ribbon, and for some unfathomable, unfounded reason, we both felt suddenly sad and troubled. Anastácia dragged the painting into the light and wiped the surface with a cloth, and slowly, as if emerging from the still depths of a lake, a face began to appear, and the clearer the features became, the faster our hearts beat, as if we were violating a secret that should have been left sleeping in the dark past. It was the face of a woman, there was no doubt about that, but so stern, so unemotional, so detached from any mean, everyday thoughts, that it was more like the face of a man—a man, moreover, utterly disillusioned with the vanities of this world. There was no promise of serenity, none of the greens and pinks that conceal barely suppressed laughter or the twinkle of a sudden burst of youthful spirit—no. Everything about that face was dense and mature. The colors were the grays of tamed passions and the ochers of contained violence. It wasn't the face of an old woman, but of a woman at the outer limits of herself, with nothing to cover herself but the truth itself, whose caustic effects might or might not be dangerous. We could only really see her head, and it was difficult to make out much else, apart from the velvet choker around her neck, and her hair, unadorned, caught up neatly on the top of her head. Hers was not an unfamiliar face, on the contrary, it immediately reminded us of someone we knew very well—the strong, aquiline nose, the shape of the eyes and the line of the jaw were to be found to a greater or lesser extent in the faces of all the Meneses, more obviously so in one person than another, but nonetheless identifiable, like threads of water flowing from the same well-spring that contained the germ of all the family's energies and characteristics. We stood there for a while, trying in vain to comprehend what lay hidden behind those eyes—and the odd thing was that the portrait, with its enormous sense of authority, its sober masculine atmosphere, had doubtless been painted by one of those traveling artists who used to visit farms and estates. It was clear that Maria Sinhá was accustomed to obeying only her own will—the determined shape of her mouth, with not a hint of docility, was that of someone used to giving orders, and her haughty gaze to seeing only obedient gestures. I once heard someone say, I can't remember when, that she would ride the fields even in the rain, helping the cattle hands with their work—and that no one was better than her when it came to lassoing a calf and bringing it down, or breaking a wild horse. The people, heads bowed, said she was a woman without religion, as she proved when a priest disobeyed her orders by entering the estate uninvited in order to administer the last rites to a dying slave. Grabbing the priest by the cassock, she dragged him out onto the road and, with astonishing strength, threw him off her property, leaving him cut and bruised. I told these things to Dona Nina and saw that she grew thoughtful—and as the face of that woman before us was taking shape again in time, it was as if a very faint, distant music were gradually becoming clearer, louder, purer. Old Anastácia must also have been able to hear this through her fogged mind, because, when I turned to her, I saw her make the sign of the cross before that portrait exposed now to the light. As we put the painting back in its place, it occurred to me that it was a memory, a memory of times that will never return.

Undated – Dona Nina was exhausted by the time we got back to her room, and she asked me to bring her a cup of coffee. While she was drinking this, we talked further and she asked more questions. She clearly wanted to broaden her knowledge of the family, perhaps as a sign of good will and an attempt to become acclimatized. At one point, however, she sighed and said that her life at the Chácara was far from easy, and added in a murmur: "It's so quiet here, so monotonous."

"You should do some physical work," I suggested. "For example, you could work in the garden. Or plant a flower bed."

The idea seemed to interest her:

"Yes, it would be good to plant some flowers," she said.

But then, putting down her cup, she added firmly:

"No, Betty, there's nothing here to interest me."

"Nothing?" and I paused, as if testing her out. "I thought you already had some friends here."

I don't know what she understood me to mean, but she spun around, as startled as if I had said something truly outrageous.

"Friends? What do you mean?"

And at the same time, before I could explain, a look of terrible weariness came over her face, and I felt not only pity, but rather that I was able to gauge precisely and perfectly just how much that exile must weigh on her. This, I confess, worried me: what might happen here to a beautiful young woman, alone with her thoughts and guided only by the impulses of her own imagination? I remembered how I, too, had initially felt suffocated by all that greenery and how long it had taken me to adapt to that way of life, so different to the life I was used to. And I wasn't unstable in the way Dona Nina was, with her febrile nature and her very different reasons for being here. Because it was clear that she loved Senhor Valdo—but not enough to bear the solitude in which he lived. I might delude myself for a minute or two and imagine that her enthusiasm would overcome all the obstacles imposed on her by that life, but I knew she would always reach the painful conclusion that she was not made for such a quiet existence, nor was it what she had imagined as her definitive ideal.

"I presume you don't mean yourself," she said, "because I know that you are my friend."

"No," I said, "I don't mean me."

Again I saw in her eyes that same look of either alarm or surprise, I'm not sure which.

"Who then?" And after a second: "You're not suggesting . . ."

"I mean Senhor Timóteo, Dona Nina."

The name evoked no immediate response, and she remained silent, as if carefully weighing my words. Suddenly, as though giving in to some inner pressure, she began to laugh—a brief, nervous laugh.

"Oh, Timóteo," she said.

Still smiling, she poured herself more coffee, but I noticed that her hands were shaking; she was not exactly surprised to hear his name.

"Timóteo doesn't count," she said after a while.

"Why not? If it's because you think him a little eccentric . . ."

She put down her cup, shaking her head.

"No, it's not that. I've known plenty of eccentric people in my time."

I shrugged to indicate that I didn't understand what she meant. Dona Nina tried then to explain:

"No, Betty, that isn't it, it's not because of what other people think either. What do I care what the world thinks about things I myself have no right to judge? No, that's not the reason. But I think Timóteo has an excess, a superabundance of personality. He shut himself away in his room because he believes that nothing else exists outside. And all that exists *inside* is Timóteo and his problems."

I remembered everything he had told me in the past—"the truth, Betty, only the truth matters"—and I felt even more intrigued by what she was saying.

"So you believe that . . ."

"There's too much originality in him." (Dona Nina was trying to speak emphatically, quietly laying the stress on certain words.) "Originality in the sense of purity: he's too original."

"I don't understand, Dona Nina."

She laughed again at my frankness.

"Ah, Betty, I could easily put it in simpler terms."

"What then?"

She looked at me mischievously, doubtless trying to gauge whether or not her words would frighten me.

"I mean that he's not normal, in the ordinary sense of the word."

"You mean he's . . ."

"Mad."

I had finally understood. Darkness was gently falling about us. Outside, in the encroaching dusk, the birds were settling like leaves. A startled swallow, its white breast heaving, alighted for a moment on the iron grille. And the sweet smell of pomegranate blossom wafted in on the air. Dona Nina was still talking, and her warm voice divested itself of those thoughts like someone revealing herself naked to another person for the first time. It was very simple, but—after all, how else describe such a fleeting impression?—there lay the nub of what she had said about Senhor Timóteo. And it was this: whenever she went into his room, she felt as if he were leaning over her to peer into her soul. Literally leaning, like someone looking down into a well for some lost object. And she was sure it was not just curiosity, but a conscious effort, a slow, cool examination. He was obviously sounding out whether or not he could count on her for something—but unable to understand what that something was, she had begun to feel afraid, because a man like him was capable of anything.

"Oh, Betty," and she blurted these words out with a strange urgency, "oh, Betty, he is certain I will die!"

It was my turn then to stare at her in astonishment.

"He doesn't want me to die," she explained, "but he's sure my death is on its way."

We did not continue the conversation, but for the rest of the day, Dona Nina was extremely agitated. She asked me to bring her paper and ink, because she wanted to write a letter. However, she then abandoned the idea and threw herself down on the bed, weeping. Then, with her face wet with tears, she embraced me and begged me "in the name of all that is most sacred" to go to Rio on her behalf. When I asked why, she shook me by the shoulders, saying that she needed me to deliver a very important letter. Without my asking, she added: "But don't go thinking it's a letter to a man, no, it's to a woman, a nurse. Her name is Castorina." To calm her, I promised that I would, and thinking that her agitation was the result of drinking too much coffee, I surreptitiously carried the coffee pot off with me to the kitchen.

13.
The Doctor's Second Report

I don't particularly like revisiting things I consider dead and buried, even if not all of them have been properly explained, and not everything should be taken as an accusation of the people involved. I believe, furthermore, that a family like the Meneses, who have added such luster to our local history, are entitled to the silence they have sought over the years but have so signally failed to find, on account of the violent events that have overtaken it—events that nonetheless deserve only to be understood and then forgotten. It weighs on my conscience, however, to conceal facts that could shed light on some of the mysteries that so shook our town at the time. Indeed, that is why I am here, once again peering into the past through these thick lenses of mine, with one tremulous desire: to serve the truth. Not that it is easy for me to exhume those people and events, for they are intimately attached to the person I myself was and to my emotions at the time. And yet what happened is still so vivid that it seems like only yesterday: I can summon up the scenes so easily and the house rises up, bright and perfect, from the sleep in which they have since been shrouded.

I can no longer recall whether it was on the second or third occasion that some unusual circumstance took me to the Chácara. I say "unusual" because I had, of course, already been there on numerous occasions, but it was only the first or second time that I had been summoned there for what could properly be described as an extraordinary occurrence. As before, I was not surprised when they asked for me, since the goings-on at the Chácara had become the subject of ever more persistent rumors throughout the town. No detail was spared in the telling, as if it were a spectacle offered up for the amusement of all. Some of the more outspoken townspeople, wishing to show themselves better informed than the rest—Senhor Aurélio at the pharmacy, for example—raised the possibility that a crime had been committed, and this was insisted on so vehemently that we would long ago have sought the assistance of the police had we not been perfectly aware that everyone was safe and well behind the fortress walls of the Chácara.

I remember that it happened soon after Senhor Valdo's supposed accident. In Vila Velha and other towns further away such as Mercês and Rio Espera, that so-called accident was already being openly talked about as a case of attempted suicide, on account of his wife wanting to leave him. This country tittle-tattle, stirred up outside the pharmacy door or in the course of a monotonous journey on horseback, was eagerly received, as indeed was any other snippet of information that reflected badly on the inhabitants of the Chácara. The news quickly gathered momentum, fueled by "facts" that were as likely to be false as true—for example, that Dona Nina was demanding an enormous pay-off from the family, that Senhor Demétrio had threatened her with legal proceedings, that a summons had already been filed with the judge in Rio Espera, that someone madly in love with Dona Nina had sworn to kill Senhor Valdo, etc.—all of which, of course, was accompanied by dire predictions and the most disapproving of comments. Others, including those claiming to be better informed than everyone else, maintained that Dona Nina had been caught *in flagrante* with a lover, that she was already on the verge of leaving, and that she had flung the very worst of insults at the Meneses. Some were even bolder and swore blind that all these things had not only taken place, but had done so in the presence of the Baron himself, on the occasion of his official visit to the family. This had caused an enormous scandal, and the Baron had declared to his circle of confidantes that he had never seen anything more shameful in his entire life. This version, however, was hotly disputed, since it was widely known that, despite frequent and repeated invitations from the Meneses, the Baron had never, and would never, set foot in the Chácara. And so the gossip simmered away, and, whether true or false, all it achieved was to create some idea of the atmosphere surrounding events at the Chácara. It goes without saying that I never said a word about what I myself had witnessed, still less about my meeting with Dona Nina in the garden, for I knew that anyone I spoke to would, in the first place, distort my words, and, secondly, would retain only what was deemed most likely to contribute to the continued slandering of the Meneses. In any event, and thanks to the sixth sense I consider part of my professional calling, I was ready for the summons I received some days after my visit to Senhor Valdo. I could not say exactly how many days later, but it cannot have been many, because the facts of that visit were still the main topic of conversation among the idle classes. I was at home, and my wife, with unusual vivacity, ran in to tell me that someone was at the door asking for me. She had no doubt recognized the messenger, and I saw that it was the same black servant who had come for me on the previous occasion and who was standing waiting on the pavement.

"What is it?" I asked. "Has Senhor Valdo got worse?"

Turning his straw hat around and around in his hands, he said that no, Senhor Valdo was getting better, but that someone else at the Chácara was ill. He was staring at me wide-eyed and was so reticent that I realized at once that something of exceptional importance had occurred. It seemed inappropriate to try and obtain further details from a servant, especially from one who, to judge by his appearance, was among the lowliest at the Chácara, and so I went back indoors, gathered the things I needed and said goodbye to my wife, who insisted on accompanying me to the door, no doubt hoping that the neighbors would be watching. However, the street was completely deserted, and she was obliged to go back inside, although not before trying to detain me with goodness knows how many useless pieces of advice.

It did not take us long to reach the Chácara. Again I was surprised by the family's peculiar manners, for no one came to greet me, as one might expect upon the arrival of a doctor. As always, the house appeared deserted, and there was not the slightest sound to be heard. The silence was thrown into even sharper contrast by the racket made by a flock of parakeets which, arriving suddenly from somewhere near the mountains, had perched on a coconut palm close to the verandah. As we paused, however, I caught a glimpse at one of the windows of what I thought was a pale, anxious face. I didn't have time to see who it was, but something about the clenched, fugitive features made me think it belonged to Senhor Demétrio's wife. Of this I became almost certain when I noticed on the verandah a swaying hammock, which still bore the impression of a body. Our arrival must have frightened her and, on reaching the drawing room, she'd had just enough time to glance quickly at us through the window. I asked my guide where the patient was, and he replied: "In the Pavilion." "The Pavilion!" I exclaimed, even more surprised than before, for I could not think what any member of the family, still less an invalid, would be doing in the Pavilion, which I knew to be far from the house and in a state of some abandon. He asked me to wait a moment in the drawing room while he informed Senhor Demétrio of my arrival. Left alone, I seized the opportunity to have a good look around me. At the far end was a sideboard full of glass, opal and silver, gleaming softly in the darkness. Above it, clearly visible on the wall, was the mark where a painting had once hung. I was about to take a closer look when the black servant returned: Senhor Demétrio had asked that I go on ahead, saying that he would come and meet me later. With a shrug, I prepared to follow my guide, wondering why anyone would choose to leave those sequestered rooms. We walked back through the garden, and I was again impressed by its dignified air of repose and the sheer poetry of its tall trees, hung with lianas. But as I walked, I became more and more convinced that the Pavilion was hardly the ideal retreat for an invalid: the paths grew narrower and narrower, and instead of flowers, the teeming undergrowth began to close in. "It must be someone from the lower orders," I said to myself, "to be left in such a place." For there was no doubt that it had seen better days and been better cared for—thick clumps of gourds and bitter melons overflowed what had once been flower beds, their borders still picked out by a few lines of white stones and upturned bottles. Finally, we reached the Pavilion, and one glance was enough to take in the gaping cracks in the foundations, splitting apart the thick wooden piles and cracking the stone base, displaying a neglect that had begun many years before and which would no doubt bring the whole thing crashing down—perhaps not immediately, but the first accusatory signs were plain to see. My guide stopped in front of the closed door:

"In here."

He was clearly expecting me to enter first and he gave me another of those hesitant, distrustful looks. Since I had, after all, been called to see a patient, I waited no longer and pushed open the door, which was half-concealed beneath the foliage, and found myself in a space I could scarcely call a room—it was more a kind of annex, square and low, the ceiling crisscrossed with thick wooden beams, which showed the same signs of decay I had seen outside. (It was evident that the Pavilion was not as solidly built as the Chácara itself, but had been hurriedly thrown together with ill-fitting, roughly-finished timber—like so many other houses in the countryside—making use of local materials and the most rudimentary of construction methods.) There was so little light that, although it was still daytime, an oil lamp had been lit. The melancholy flame cast a long black stain across the whitewashed wall.

I carried on until I came to a low door, which the servant opened, ushering me into a narrow space full of gardening implements and illuminated by a single round, barred window, through which could be glimpsed some of the greenery outside. On a narrow pallet bed covered only with a thin mat, beside a bench strewn with medicine bottles and rolls of gauze and cotton wool, lay a man. There was nothing to indicate that he was still alive; indeed, it was hard to believe that anyone could possibly live in such a place, devoid of all comfort. However, the tools of his trade (a few rakes and spades, two or three watering cans, and a container of plants that had not yet been put to use) confirmed to me that I was in the gardener's sleeping quarters, or at least the place he used as a storeroom. I moved closer and saw that the man had one hand under his head, resting on it like a pillow, while the other trailed on the floor. I should add that what first caught my eye was his extreme youth. I imagined he must be asleep or something similar, and when my guide pointed to him—as distastefully as if he were pointing at some disgusting or shameful object—I took the oil lamp from beside the bed and leaned over him. An initial inspection confirmed that the case was even worse than it had at first seemed: the patient's breathing was labored, his lips were purplish and his face ashen. As I leaned closer in order to take his pulse, the bedclothes covering him slipped off and I was shocked to see that the whole of one side of his body was covered in blood, his chest visible through his torn shirt. In fact it did not take me long to ascertain that he was literally soaked in blood—the dark, sticky substance surrounded him on all sides, spreading out across the mat on which he lay and dripping slowly onto the dusty floor.

"What happened?" I asked my guide as I felt for the wounded man's pulse.

"I think he shot himself," he answered, his voice as uncertain as his gaze.

"Accidentally?" I asked.

This time he merely shrugged. I observed that the wounded man's pulse was extremely slow; the incident must have occurred some time ago and he had lost a lot of blood. On closer inspection, I noted that the bed itself was damp, and that the stains, recent and red, were spread over the wall, as if he had struggled, or as if someone, for whatever reason, had tried to lift or drag him over there by force. I was about to stand up and fetch a syringe from my bag when he shifted in the bed, opened his eyes and moved his lips, as if wanting to say something. More out of curiosity than anything else, I leaned closer, trying to make out what his bloodless lips were saying. One single, effortful word came out: "Forgive." Forgive what? Why? At that age, still barely molded into the flesh of manhood, what sin could he possibly have committed, what irremediable fault could have driven him to such an extreme? I stared in bewilderment at the lad, who was already slipping toward his final, dying breath. His hand kept obsessively, mechanically stroking his blood-soaked chest. Then he would raise that same blood-red hand, only for it to fall limply back down again. From beneath his feet, the dark stain spread, sinuous and unstoppable, like the hidden roots of a tree; it would not be long before his blood-drained body found its final rest. "Forgive? Forgive what?" I repeated to myself, feeling powerless to solve this drama in which I sensed the hand of God; and the word grew and grew, echoing in my ears, like a long, inexplicable groan. Forgive what? Then, in answer, I saw his hand, palm open, rise up one last time in an effort to express what his lips could not, only to fall back lifelessly, pulling his shirt open and exposing the wound, almost exactly over his heart. An overwhelming stillness overtook his body; he was breathing, but already his limbs had softened, like bundles of dead grass lying splayed on the bed. Some urgent first aid was clearly needed, for he had received none up until now. I turned to the servant, who was standing a few feet away, leaning against the door, and told him to bring me a basin of boiling water. He hesitated, and I was about to shout the order again when, looking back at the young man, I realized that these were indeed his final moments and that in just a few minutes more he would be dead.

"There's no need, not now," I said, while the servant continued to stare at me impassively. I leaned over the boy, examining his lips—I saw them quiver with the faintest of breaths, then everything went still—and he lay there, inert, benighted, as if sleep had suddenly snatched him from the midst of all that blood. Almost as if by some sort of miracle, a sweet smell hung about him, some secret perfume from his lost childhood. I paused for a moment, entranced by the peace that had descended over his features—the power, the silence, and the magic of those landscapes that the dead suddenly lay before us—and I could not fail to notice that I was trembling, in sympathy for the death of one so young, so eloquent in his simplicity, now so far beyond us and all our miserable earthly concerns.

"There's no point," I said to the servant, who had not moved. "The boy's dead."

He received this news with the same indifference he had displayed all along. Was he merely insensitive or was he under orders to show no emotion? I don't know, but it was as if I had just announced the most banal of facts about the most ordinary of mortals.

"It's the gardener," he said, as if apologizing for the dead man's lowly social status.

"The gardener!" I exclaimed, taking a step back. And at the same time, I took one last look at the boy lying on the bed. "Who should I tell?"

"Senhor Demétrio," said the servant. "He's waiting for you up at the house."

Lacking the courage to look again at the corpse, I left that suffocating cellar. At the door, I took a long deep breath of the cool breeze blowing through the garden and, for the second time, I thought I could make out a pair of restless eyes watching me. As I turned into the avenue, I saw who it was: standing motionless behind a tree was Dona Ana, waiting for me to pass.

"There's someone hiding back there," I whispered to the servant, as soon as we had gone a few steps farther. He glanced back in that direction and, if he did see who it was, he gave no indication. When I reached the top of the steps, I again scanned the garden and this time clearly saw Dona Ana scurrying toward the Pavilion. (I may have been mistaken, but I thought I saw a dark shape accompanying her—a woman in black, or a priest perhaps?) If it was a priest, he would, I presumed, be on his way to perform the last rites—so I merely shrugged, inclined to forget what I had just seen. Senhor Demétrio was waiting for me in the drawing room, hands resting on the back of a chair. His studied, solemn pose made it clear that he did not want to know any more than was strictly necessary. He seemed to me to have aged somehow—he was one of those men who can age from one minute to the next, like rotting fruit—and despite his energetic appearance, I noticed a look of weary submission. He had dark circles under his eyes; his lips drooped in two lifeless folds.

"So how is the lad?" he asked abruptly, dispensing with any greeting.

I looked him straight in the eye, trying to discern the secret that he would no doubt never tell:

"He's dead," I said. "He died just now."

He lowered his eyes and, just for a moment, which could as easily have indicated annoyance as pity, his lips trembled, and he said not a word. During that single, solitary moment, what image must have passed through his mind? I had no doubt there was a secret locked deep in his heart. Everything about him said so, from his expressionless face, his pale hands, his old-fashioned clothes, even his tight, willful self, which, in the shadows of that dimly lit room, seemed to be armoring itself against any threat to his dignity, as he stood, a timeless figure, reflected in mirrors that endlessly repeated his image, and only his image. But then, as if from far away, I heard him say:

"How very odd. So young too—I don't know why he would do something like that."

He seemed sincere in this assertion—or, rather, his voice had taken on a slightly different timbre, and there was in it a degree of astonishment, as if something deep inside some secret, private zone was being forced to acknowledge this proof of the mysteries of this world.

"Did he kill himself?" I asked.

"Yes, he did," he answered. "We were on the verandah when we heard the shot. My wife went to see what had happened . . ."

(Curiously, it wasn't hard for me to imagine the entire scene: the various Meneses on the verandah, Senhor Demétrio in the hammock pretending to read a book, Senhor Valdo nearby drumming his fingers on the balustrade, Dona Ana hunched over her embroidery. I could even describe the precise moment that followed the shot—a long, anguished minute-long pause, during which, suddenly torn from their innermost thoughts, they all looked at one another foreseeing some unimaginable nuisance.)

"Poor boy," I exclaimed rather unconvincingly. "He must have suffered terribly to do something so desperate."

Senhor Demétrio looked at me with evident disapproval, as if I had said something utterly foolish, or something that in some way or other impinged on the honor of the Meneses.

"Will you fill out the death certificate?" he asked.

I shook my head:

"Not until you have informed the appropriate authorities."

He looked at me, and there was such surprise in his eyes that it took me all my strength not to waver.

"What did you say?"

I repeated what I had said and his expression froze and became even more inscrutable than before.

"It would be the first time the police have ever entered this house," he said.

Despite his attitude, though, and for reasons I could not fathom, the usual pride and resentment in his voice had gone, to be replaced by an enormous sadness, such as only accompanies an awareness of impending disaster. For a moment, sitting quite still in front of me, his hands impassively resting on the back of his chair, I had the impression that his attention was fixed on something far beyond us, a scene revealed by that sudden presentiment and by shame—perhaps, who knows, the ruin of his own house. But, I repeat, I saw in him no sense of outrage, only resignation, together with that selfless indifference adopted by martyrs in the face of their imminent sacrifice. In one of those flashes of insight that often come to me, I saw what that man must already have suffered and the high price he had paid for his pride, for him to have reached the end of all his dreams like this, naked and resigned. Because there was a serenity in his manner, a final, dramatic gesture of acceptance and abdication: the house of Meneses was crumbling around him, burying him in its rubble and enveloping him in darkness. It wasn't only the house he was renouncing, but his own self, for he could not hold on to the house if his pride was not intact.

People might say that all this was nothing more than my own wild imaginings, but the truth is that, for a long time, I had sensed some sort of evil gnawing at the foundations of the Chácara. It had once been a stronghold, a monument to tenacity (and one which I had learned to respect and admire since my childhood, back when the road still twisted and turned between tall, majestic mahogany and aroeira trees and was rich, in equal parts, in treacherous marshes and bandits), but now it lay before me, fragile and defenseless in the face of its imminent destruction, like a gangrenous body invaded by the poisons coursing through its own blood. (Ah, how often I would return to that image of gangrene—not now, but later—in order to explain what I felt and the drama unfolding around me. Gangrenous, rotting flesh, purple and numb, through which blood no longer flows, its strength vanished, to reveal the poverty and eloquent misery of human flesh. Veins furiously throbbing, enslaved to the delusion of another hidden, monstrous being, famished and dissolute, who has taken charge of this final stretch of our existence, raising throughout the conquered land the scarlet standards of its deadly, purulent victory.)

"Is there anything else I can do for you?" I asked, aware of the growing silence between us.

He started, as if waking up.

"No, no. Thank you."

I said goodbye and left, expecting at any moment to see the pale face I had spotted twice before. I don't know if it was my imagination or if it had any basis in reality, but I certainly thought I saw that same face for a third time, hiding near a tree. Ah, yes, this time there was no doubt about it: an inner voice was telling me that the Chácara was now in its final days. As I walked, I was seized by a strange feeling: that everything around me was pure, senseless illusion. Where was Dona Nina? Why didn't she come to meet me and lean on my arm, as she had done once before? I walked on, my footsteps slower than I wished. When I reached the gate, I turned around, hoping that a miracle might yet happen, but everything was still and the somnolent air that hung over the house was as thick and dense with meaning as the air surrounding the poor suicide in the cellar.

14.
Ana's Second Confession

My intention in writing this memoir is not, as many might think, an exercise in self-justification—or written in the hope of being seen in a better light after my death. Because should some human eye alight upon these pages when I am gone, it will matter very little what that person thinks of me, because I will be nothing but a pile of ashes, and it may be that no one will even remember the woman bent now over this sheet of paper. Before beginning this confession, I thought I would deliver it to Father Justino, who has long been part of my life—I made my confession to him on the occasion of my first communion—and his advice has often proved useful. What I want is to get at the truth, a complete truth that does not frighten or make me blush, but which is the exact expression of the silent being full of compromises that I represent. The first truth, if I am to be honest with myself, is that lately I have been something of a stranger to the Church and to the sacraments, so much so that I am not even sure I would know now how to kneel before a priest. And yet here I am, and I ask myself what is the point of this vague litany of woes, this continual lament that I cannot keep locked in my heart? May Father Justino forgive me for what are possibly the worst, the harshest, and most contemptible of feelings, but even I do not understand what is wrong with me, because I feel so utterly changed. Everything to do with the Church seems to me pointless and absurd, as does everything else in this world. I was quite content until the moment I realized that I was drowning in darkness, in this darkness, which never weighed on me before, but now leaves me with the unbearable feeling that I am being poisoned. It's as if I were struggling for air in some soft, viscous element; in the depths of my being, some force is trying in vain to break through the crust of habit, to reveal itself and impose its power on me, a power whose origins are unknown to me. I repeat, I do not know what is wrong—silent and troubled, I drift past people and lack the courage to tell them what is wrong with me, although I am lucid enough to be certain that a monster exists inside me, a booming, urgent being who will, one day, swallow me up. Ah, what is this voice that demands to speak, what is it that makes me walk along with head erect, what is it that propels me forward, like a creature wounded by the dart of suffering? I cannot go on, Father, you are the one person I should speak to, it is your pity, your understanding as a man, as a saint, oh, what am I saying . . .

You must understand now why I am avoiding going to church and avoiding your eyes too, eyes that must know all possible human weaknesses. On several occasions, I saw you looking at me anxiously and perhaps I should have stopped and tried to explain to you the crisis engulfing me. But Father, damnation is a fire that burns in solitude; sometimes one person burns, sometimes two, sometimes a whole community, but we are each alone in our own particular flame, sole owners of what we might call our evil or our crime. That is why I could not kneel at your feet or share with you the fierce fire consuming me—that would be a sacrifice beyond my capabilities. I know that I began this confession as a letter intended to survive my death; I think now, though, that this is my last and most desperate attempt to find myself again, and to feel, in my dull, cold state, not happy as I would like to be, but indifferent as I always was. I know you have been worried about me lately, have noticed my absence at morning mass. I know you have spoken about it with this person and that, asking if I was ill; that you have approached various acquaintances asking if it is work that occupies my mornings—oh, I know all this, and can probably imagine the rest, you shut up in your little sacristy, your face buried in your hands, thinking how very hard it is to drive God's sheep through this world. It would be pointless trying to hide, you know what is wrong with me, even though I myself cannot put a name to the mysterious malaise afflicting me. You may remember the last time you saw me: it was in the afternoon as I was leaving the church, after making fruitless efforts to recover enough inner peace to pray as I so often had in the past. My heart refused to hear my plea, and I merely sat, motionless, muttering words that no longer had any meaning for me and feeling the beating of a heart that seemed dead to any kind of hope. Does that frighten you, Father? Hope is the most important of all the theological virtues: without it everything shrivels up, without it nothing can exist, and without hope's constant presence, not even charity can warm our heart. Behind me, high up, the bell was tolling and the sound of its ringing spread out across the town and was lost somewhere along the dusty roads. I got up and hastily made the sign of the cross—and it was then that I saw you, immediately in front of me, leaning against one of the pillars, talking to another parishioner, who was presumably arranging the date of a baptism or a wedding. Ah, the shudder that ran through me at that moment, as I wondered if I would have the strength to confront your searching gaze. I quickly realized there was no escape, because you were looking at me as if waiting for me to pass. This so bothered me that I considered hiding or escaping through one of the side doors—and it was then, as I moved off to the left, that the string on the scapular I wore around my neck suddenly broke. I had worn it for many years, that small Agnus-Dei made of white felt, so begrimed that its original color had long since been lost, and which had been given to me by my mother. Now, there it lay between us, in the great pool of red light flooding in through the stained-glass window. If I bent down to pick it up, you would see me do so and rush to help me, and then there would be no avoiding the conversation that would inevitably ensue. I felt I could not bear that. I don't know what came over me, but I pretended not to have noticed the fallen scapular and walked away, head high, as if nothing had happened. I was deluding myself, though, because you saw my maneuver for what it was. Taking two or three steps in my direction, you bent down, picked up the scapular and held it out to me. At that moment, we were both standing right in the middle of the scarlet light coming in through the window. Half-blinded, I pretended not to have seen your gesture and, greeting you coldly, continued on my way without even a glance at the hand returning the scapular to me.

Please forgive me, Father Justino, now that misfortune has returned me to myself.

....

It was precisely four o'clock in the afternoon when I saw him, and I was in a state of great agitation. I don't know if you remember him, Father, the gardener my mother-in-law brought to the Chácara as a child. (She and my husband would often talk about how he arrived wearing a black beret and turned-up trousers and still speaking with a Portuguese accent.) As soon as I saw him looking around as if he were searching for something—as I found out later, this was merely the nervousness and confusion of someone so young—I imagined that perhaps this would be the day, and that we would not reach nightfall without something strange occurring. And what happened was perfectly in keeping with the heavy atmosphere, full of foreboding, in which we were living at the time, frequently shaken by those electrical currents that zigzag through the apparently still air like lightning flashes illuminating the horizon, and which were brief interludes in that apparent state of bucolic peace. I put down the embroidery I was working on—if I am being strictly truthful, I should say that I wasn't really doing anything at all, absorbed in watching the boy from the verandah and only pretending I was busy with my sewing. I didn't want him or anyone else to guess what I was thinking or feeling. Slowly, as if I were merely going for a walk, I went down the steps and followed him into the garden. Not far away was an oitizeiro tree from behind which I could easily see the Pavilion, because I was still spying on Nina at the time, still obsessed with knowing what she might be doing. In these closed-off places, in this tight-knit world of country houses, we are so few and so few things happen that we miss not the slightest flicker of life that appears before us. I had gathered from Alberto's agitated state—the gardener's name was Alberto—that something important must be going on, that some drama was about to unfold. The whole place was steeped in that troubling atmosphere; in the distance, dogs were barking as if they could sense something strange in the air, while the trees, with unusual restraint, stood utterly still, as though waiting. Hiding behind the oitizeiro tree, I admit that I felt slightly ashamed: seeing the sky still blue above me and the centuries-old serenity of the things around me, it seemed to me then that I was distorting or exaggerating the facts. Perhaps the tumult I was feeling existed only in me—perhaps I was being misled by the blood flowing so ardently through my veins. But no, I would soon be given ample confirmation of everything I was imagining. From where I was standing, I distinctly heard a shot—a single sharp shot cutting through the silence like a sword—and Alberto came running down the path. Shortly afterward, I heard another shot. What filled my consciousness was neither fear nor terror, but a quite different feeling, cold and inhuman—a feeling of joy or, rather, peace, knowing that my predictions were coming true. It was not hard to imagine what had happened: indeed, I was almost certain what it was, the facts fitted so logically together. Father, when you judge these words of mine, please remember, with all the indulgence you can muster, that I was suffering greatly at the time; more than that, I had grown weary of suffering. I could not bear the presence of that woman any more, watching as, day after day, she sucked up all the life around us, brazenly and disrespectfully garnering all the good things always denied to me. Yes, I was thinking smugly that, in his despair, Alberto had shot her dead. I admit I was trembling, and Nina's hair, caked in blood, seemed to wave endlessly before my eyes. I waited a while, until I saw him run past me, dripping with sweat—and then, dizzy and indifferent to the blinding sun, I did not hesitate to leave my hiding place and grab him.

"Alberto," I cried. "Where are you going?"

He tried to push me away.

"I'm going to fetch a doctor," he said.

I was so certain of what had happened that I clung to him, determined to keep him there.

"No, no, please, don't pity her, don't go back. She needs to die!"

He stared at me in astonishment:

"She?"

In my madness, I thought I had perhaps not been firm enough and had failed to dissuade him from fetching a doctor and that he had not yet recovered from his state of shock.

"Yes," I said, "Nina."

"But she didn't do anything. Don't you understand, it's him."

I finally released my hold on him and took two steps back—what a strange figure I must have cut, my hair all disheveled, the red glow of the setting sun lighting up my face, my lips half-open in a scream that never emerged.

"Him?" and as if roused by the clamor of a distant alarm bell, the mean soul that normally inhabited my body hurriedly regained its composure.

"It's the master," he said. "He's hurt."

"Valdo?"

He repeated the name back to me in a neutral voice:

"Valdo."

I let him go and remained fixed to the spot. Night was falling with astonishing speed, the flowers hung limply on their stems; far off, an unexpected wind was blowing. Above me, the leaves of the oitizeiro tree were already stirring. Then, slowly, I went back to the house.

So it was Valdo. Perhaps he had tried to take his own life. Perhaps he was the victim, the unexpected victim of the crime for which I had waited so long. And if he died, perhaps Nina would succumb to Alberto's passion, perhaps she would surrender to him, despite all the problems this would cause. I trembled. I trembled even more than I had at the thought that such things could happen. Father, I cannot describe the feeble, tormented creature who climbed back up the steps, clinging to the rail. The wind was blowing hard now, and I could feel it beating on my face, but what did it matter, what did anything matter? By the time I reached the verandah, I was like a mortally wounded animal. There were people there, moving about. I again pretended that I knew nothing, that I hadn't even heard the shot. I didn't care what had happened to Valdo. Soon, all movement stopped, and it really was almost as if nothing had happened. I did notice my husband, as if through a veil, and he seemed to be waiting for someone or something. He spoke to me, but I didn't understand what he was saying. He got angry and shouted at me, but still I did not understand. Then he walked over to the verandah and back, and I myself doubted that anything of any importance had occurred—for example, that Valdo might be dying from a gunshot wound. I waited. I waited for hours in the darkness, slumped in an armchair in the drawing room, listening to the strangely clear ticking of the clock and staring at the old family silver gleaming on the sideboard. It could not be true, it was all some monstrous mistake, someone would come and bring me news; I would be rewarded. It was night now, and the wind continued to blow—a strange, slow wind, circling and buffeting the house again and again with mortal gusts. Then I heard the sound of footsteps not far off, perhaps near the steps, perhaps even closer. I listened carefully and was aware that the person outside was walking very slowly as if wanting to go unnoticed: I got up then and went over to the verandah, where I leaned against the wall. From there I could see what was happening both inside and outside the house and in the garden too, as far as the Pavilion. I did not need to look that far, though, for only a few feet away was Alberto. He had his face pressed to the wall, and appeared to be crying. I went over to him and he looked up. When he saw me, he set off into the garden almost at a run. In that brief second, I realized that something very strange was going on.

"Alberto," I called, "where are you going?"

He stopped by the fountain, his back to me, as if he had recognized my voice. I called again, he turned and came toward me dejectedly. It was as if he were asleep or in some kind of hypnotic trance. I emphasize that word "hypnotic," just so that you can understand the power that woman had over him. However hard he might try to clutch his secret to him, he could not fool me.

"What's wrong?" I asked again, shaking his arm, unable to control my impatience.

Then, uttering a single, violent, tearless sob, he covered his face with his hands. Seeing him in that state—and I swear, Father, this was the first time—I was filled by something far stronger than pity, and the rigor of all those years spent keeping a distance, maintaining that mechanical mistress-servant relationship, fell to the ground like a useless, rusty piece of armor.

"Speak," I cried, shaking him even harder, "for God's sake, speak! If it wasn't her, if she's alive, why are you so upset? Can't you see that I'm your friend, Alberto?"

He was so distraught that not even these extraordinary words caught his attention.

"Speak," I went on, still shaking him, and it was like trying to shake a body made of marble, whose soul has been snatched away by some occult power. "What was it, what happened, what's wrong with you?"

Finally, he could hold back no longer and he spoke—not because he was moved by my questions, not because he was giving in to the silent fury of my feelings—for I, too, could keep silent!—but simply because he was too young, and everything locked inside his heart needed to break through the narrow walls of the prison in which it found itself enclosed. Slowly he began to unfold his secret—or *en*fold himself in another far denser secret from which there could be no escape. His story was a simple one; or at least what he told me of it was simple. Because someone like Alberto would never reveal himself entirely—that would be tantamount to destroying himself. Such people *are* their silence, their refusal to speak, and forcing them to confess would be like climbing over forbidden walls and entering territory that a permanent, congenital modesty defends from prying eyes. He said nothing really about his love, or only what I already knew, but again and again, like a fateful, agonizing leitmotif, the name of that woman appeared on his lips and never have I heard a name pronounced with such pain and such delight.

He said that Nina had walked past him without so much as looking at him—at him, the man who had planted a whole bed of violets behind the Pavilion, a bed he watered morning and evening, hoping it would produce some truly beautiful flowers . . .—and all because, every day, standing at her window, she would ask him for a bunch of violets. "Now don't forget, Alberto . . . You can't imagine how I adore violets." And then she had just walked past him as if he didn't exist. When he met Betty by the fountain, he asked her what had happened, and Betty, who was dusting off some suitcases, told him that the mistress would be leaving first thing in the morning. That was all. Stunned, he had waited there on the verandah, hoping to see Nina again, to find out if she was still speaking to him. The flower bed was doing well, the sweet smell of violets surrounded the Pavilion; he had kept his promise—so why was she leaving and behaving so coldly toward him? While he was waiting, he saw not Nina, but Demétrio come out. He was deathly pale and had about him the threatening air of contained fury. "You should leave this house, Alberto, and as soon as possible." "Why?" Alberto had asked.

Demétrio seemed momentarily lost for words because, according to Alberto, he did not respond at once. But when Alberto stayed where he was, with that indecipherable look in his eyes, an explanation was finally given in a low, penetrating voice: "Because of what happened at the Pavilion." He fell silent then, as if remembering the scene, not the scene with Demétrio, which mattered very little to him, but the other scene, the one in the Pavilion, where, he told me, Senhor Demétrio had caught him kissing Nina's hands. Only her hands, nothing more. There was something in his voice I could not quite pin down, as if he found telling this story very hard; and seeing the suffering provoked by that small, almost fictitious betrayal, I imagined what he must be concealing—the great, tumultuous passion Nina had awoken in him, the meetings they would have had, the words exchanged, none of which I would ever know about, in this life or the next—and he selected from his small vocabulary the exact words that would leave no room for error. "Just because of that?" he asked Demétrio, still unable to believe what he was hearing. "Yes, just because of that," my husband answered in a firm voice. And then everything became perfectly clear in his mind: she had ignored him because she was about to leave. Simply because he had dared to kiss one of her hands, and Senhor Demétrio had caught him in the act. He may have been sincere in what he said, Father Justino, and his surprise may have been genuine, but the truth is I was eaten up with jealousy, it was as if a deadly acid were flowing through my veins, and I was cruel, cruel in the way one can only be to the dying, to whom one refuses a final word of comfort.

"Ah," I said, "you didn't fool my husband, just as you didn't fool me that day when I saw you in the garden, do you remember? You only kissed her hand, you say! So what were you doing together in the clearing, then, and why did she slap you?"

He looked at me in horror, as if he had only just realized that I had seen them together in the garden. We were facing each other, both of us breathing hard, staring into each other's eyes. And suddenly he began to talk, very loud and fast. I knew we could be heard, that Demétrio might come out at any moment, which would only cause more scandal—but I had neither the courage nor the desire to stop him. She had slapped him for no reason, because of the violets. Every day, he carefully placed a bunch of violets on her windowsill—but she called him a liar and said that he never left anything. He couldn't understand and insisted that, every morning, religiously, he left her some flowers—and he had even started to keep watch in case someone was stealing them or to see if they were blown away by the wind. He couldn't solve the mystery, and Nina had grown angry then, saying he was taking her for a fool, but that she would teach him a lesson. How could she possibly think that of him, when he had planted a whole bed of violets solely to please her? And yet, despite this, what pleasure, what joy he had felt, knowing that she appreciated his gift, that she was demanding it of him, because, in her eyes, it was valuable. It was then, realizing her mistake and realizing that she had gone too far in revealing her feelings to that man, who, however simple and rustic, understood what she was saying, it was then that she had slapped his face as a punishment. But there was nothing to be done, because those violets, whether real or not, were a tie that bound them together—perhaps the first and only tie.

(Moments later, Father, I caught a glimpse of that joy in the warm, true light that flowed from his eyes, and it stripped me bare as though it were tearing away the veils in which I had long been buried. As if lit by a flash of lightning, I saw myself for what I was. Losing him, knowing that I had lost him forever, transformed me instantly into the stiff, colorless being I am today. Now do you understand why nothing matters to me, neither God, nor my husband, nor even that scapular? Now do you understand, Father?)

My rage on hearing his story knew no limits. I began to pound on his chest (you cannot know and never will know the wild delirium that filled me, Father, me, a mature woman, whose flesh had never once trembled with love . . .) and my eyes filled with tears:

"You're lying, Alberto, you're still lying! When has anyone ever slapped someone's face because of a bunch of violets? That wasn't the reason, and besides, you never did leave flowers on her windowsill . . ."

He stood transfixed and uncomprehending. Overwhelmed by sobs, I finally slumped against the pillar, defeated. He came toward me, he tried to explain that he wasn't lying—although what did I care about his wretched violets?—and that he had only kissed her hand because he had gone there to ask her forgiveness. He wanted to know why that was so very bad, how could they condemn him when that was all he had done, when he was even prepared to admit he had been lax and, yes, he had sometimes forgotten to leave violets on her windowsill? And he said other things too, excuses, threats, who knows what else, but I did not respond and continued to weep, my face pressed against the cold stone. He must have felt very awkward, not knowing what to do, and although I knew I was making a complete fool of myself, I couldn't help it. When he timidly touched my hand, I begged him:

"Go away, for God's sake, go away!"

And as he moved off, I continued to weep, my gaze turned now on the vast darkness of the garden.

15.
Continuation of Ana's Second Confession

Father Justino, I cannot describe to you what those first few days after Nina's departure were like. Apparently, the gossip in the town was that she had been driven out, and I really do believe that my husband played a major part in her leaving the Chácara. It was odd, though, because once we were free of her presence, none of us felt any real sense of relief. It was as if we were forever prisoners of that woman's magic spell. My husband hardly spoke, and I think he felt responsible for everything that had happened. I can recall almost word for word a conversation I heard one night, when he and Valdo lingered after supper, when he certainly had no qualms about accusing Nina of adultery. On that point, he was immovable and brought his fist down hard on the table to confirm this. I remember Valdo's voice: "You're mad, I don't understand . . ." And Demétrio: "You're the one who's mad, and if it wasn't for the current precarious state of your health . . ." I have no idea what veiled threat lay behind those words, but I imagined he was in possession of some hidden proof, of facts that the whole family would prefer to keep secret. Valdo had left his bed sooner than expected, but, were it not for Betty's ministrations, he would doubtless have succumbed to the seriousness of his wounds—it had not been a mere act, as Demétrio sometimes implied: Valdo genuinely had attempted suicide. Betty took charge of everything, as if she were the mistress of the house. And she was really, because I took no interest in what was going on around me, only occasionally receiving news of my brother-in-law's condition from other people, for I never asked anything myself.

On the other hand, while we were living this tense, silent life, I kept my eyes fixed on Alberto. I must tell you now, Father—so that one day you can reconstruct the truth—about something that happened on the night of Valdo's failed suicide attempt. I have already described how I was left sobbing and gazing out at the dark garden. Well, moments later, I saw Alberto once again go creeping past. He had only just left my side, I myself had begged him to leave me, I could even hear the echo of his footsteps—but I couldn't bring myself to lose sight of him, and so, drying my tears, I waited until he was lost among the trees before I myself went down the steps. The impulse that drove me on was that of a broken, troubled being, an irresistible need to rebel, which had the effect on me of a toxic drug. Stepping lightly, I too plunged in among the shadows. I think it had rained, because everywhere there was the smell of damp flowers and leaves. It did not take me long to find him—there he was, crouched behind a clump of ferns, watching someone moving about inside the house. Since the light was on in the window, it was not difficult to see who it was: Nina. She was clearly silhouetted and was talking to someone we could not see. Perhaps Alberto could hear what was going on and may even have heard part of the argument—judging by Nina's gestures, she seemed extremely angry, so it was clear that this was indeed an argument—but I could not hear a single word, however hard I tried and however close I got to Alberto. I was constrained by the fear that a dry twig might crack or the sand crunch beneath my feet, and that Alberto would then realize I was spying on him. Nevertheless, it was clear that the person Nina was talking to was lying down, and since this was the couple's bedroom, I assumed she was speaking to Valdo. At one point, when I raised my head a little, I saw something metallic glitter in her hands. She strode over to the window and threw the object out into the garden—it arced through the air and fell into one of the flower beds. Alberto gave a cat-like leap and began rummaging among the plants. He did this urgently, as if time were of the essence. Suddenly, he appeared to find what he was looking for: the object Nina had thrown out of the window. I soon learned what it was, because he came trampling through the bushes onto the path. When he emerged into the light, almost opposite me, I saw that he was holding a revolver—a small nickel-plated weapon, which I had noticed before, some time ago, on the large sideboard in the drawing room. Alberto was turning it over in his hands as if examining some strange, unidentifiable object. The dreadful idea had probably not yet entered his mind, he was doubtless still far from imagining what extremes he would go to, but I already knew what would happen later on—more than that, I realized that Nina had seen Alberto outside and had thrown the weapon out of the window precisely so that he would pick it up. This realization so shocked me that I almost gave myself away, revealing my hiding place. Alberto must have heard a noise, because he quickly stuffed the gun inside his shirt and whirled around, expecting to see someone. I stole away into the thick undergrowth and, had he been less agitated, I am sure he would have spotted me. I saw him almost break into a run as he approached the Pavilion. I confess I was afraid he might kill himself in the cellar, that he might do the deed there and then, without further delay. Slowly, afraid now that I might be seen by the people inside the house, I followed him, taking occasional refuge behind a tree whenever I thought he might look back. He never did, though, too consumed by the idea leading him on. I reached the place where he had entered through a low door, half-hidden among the foliage, and which was the sole entrance to the cellar. It occurred to me for the first time that this was where he must live, and I was touched. I had never been there before, because it seemed to me so uninhabitable, so neglected—and now, standing before the door, I was surprised that such a young man could live in such a gloomy place. There were a few barred windows in the ivy-clad wall, but the bars were all broken, so it was easy to see how dark it was inside and that the walls were black with damp. I went over to the door and, looking inside, saw a small lamp flickering in one of the rooms. I went in, trying to avoid bumping into the furniture and the piles of old crates, and managed to reach a spot where the light was brightest. There, too, the door was open and I was able to hide behind it, peering in through the crack. Alberto was in the middle of the room, shirtless now, but still holding the revolver. I don't know—how could I?—if, at that point, he had already considered killing himself, if the insidious idea had already taken hold of his mind and begun to flow through the wild, healthy, youthful blood in his veins. I think it had, because, with one tremulous hand, he slowly raised the gun to his heart, first higher, then lower, like someone rehearsing a scene. He did this very carefully, as if he were weighing up the possibilities of a task in which there was no room for error.

I knew he would not kill himself then, Father, that he would have many inner struggles first, that his youth would do battle with the mad urges of an innocent heart. But I decided, at that precise moment, not to intervene, but to allow the boy's fate to run its course. Ah, Father, all I ask is that you understand what was going on in my soul. I know that my decision implied a tacit complicity, that I could have been compromising my soul by maintaining a stupid silence in that game of chance. I could have intervened, it's true, I could, at that early stage, have prevented him from destroying himself in an act of extreme desperation. But for me to have done that, I would need to have been in an entirely untroubled state myself, my heart at rest and feeling at one with the people and things of this world. That was the first reason justifying my silence. The second, and possibly the most important reason, was that I wanted to preserve for myself that proof of Nina's treachery. I did not know how or when I would use it, only that one day I would be able to throw that horrible truth in her face and call her a murderer, proving that it was all her fault, and that I had seen her toss the gun into the garden. (As time has passed, I have gradually lost my way, and I am no longer sure I have the right: Could she really have known what she was doing when she threw the gun out of the window? If it had been an unthinking gesture—and how could one ever know the truth?—then almost all the blame would fall on my shoulders, and I would be the criminal, not her. But at that moment, how could I not give in to the voluptuous pleasure of gambling and risking everything? This was almost my only opportunity to destroy her.) The pleasure I felt when I imagined this was almost a guarantee of impunity. Later, long after I had abandoned him to his fate, my heart grew troubled, and I no longer knew what to think. It was horrible to have before me that blood-stained body, as I did later on. No, he no longer exists, there was nothing in the world to stop him killing himself—neither beauty nor youth nor the strong beat of a warm, generous heart. Now silence has fallen forever in his small room, in which his twenty years of life were consumed with no possible escape or remission, I am guilty of having preferred to lose him because I knew he could never be mine. I cannot conceal that fact, Father, if I intend to be honest and open in my confession. I say again—and the tears flow from my eyes as I do so—it was my love and my despair that abandoned him to his death.

I was still watching him from a distance, through the crack in the door, still admiring his splendid body, his bare torso, which took on a coppery glow in the lamplight. I had never seen a male body naked like that, because I imagined that my husband's unclothed body—the body he occasionally pressed against mine to offer me a bitter, fleeting caress—would be lifeless and ungainly. Alberto's was an adolescent body, the matte pink of human flesh when it is still pure, ready for the great leap into sin; he had only just become a man, and I could sense the energy in him, as clear as music in the air. Now I understood why Nina could not possibly have failed to notice him, and I imagined her running expert fingers over that tender flesh, provoking in him his first tremors of pleasure and getting the same pleasure herself from that discovery. I confess, Father, that I was half-blind with jealousy. No, I could not help myself—since he would never be mine, I would rather lose him forever than know he was in the hands of another woman.

Alberto did not kill himself that night, and many more nights passed before he committed that final act. I barely let him out of my sight, following him everywhere with my eyes—and he must have been aware of being watched, if, that is, he was still aware of the things of this world. But following Nina's departure, which happened immediately after the argument in the bedroom, his heart was no longer here; he would go back and forth, pretend to be packing his bags as Demétrio had demanded, or perhaps weed a flower bed—but we both knew he lacked the strength to do much more than that, and time passed, and inexplicably, my husband no longer insisted on his leaving. (Did he also think the gardener would kill himself? His impassive features gave nothing away.) A strange torpor fell upon us, as if we were helpless to do anything until overtaken by some sudden, dramatic event. I don't know if all of us were aware of the turbulent emotions filling the gardener's heart, but I knew its every beat, and, ah, what rage I felt, what despair, to be unable to anaesthetize that mind poisoned by the image of the woman with whom he was obsessed! He came and went, fussing about in the garden over violets that no one wanted any more. I would follow his movements from the verandah, where I sat with my embroidery on my lap, watching out of the corner of my eye. If he disappeared behind a bush, I would immediately stand up and stretch, as if I had suddenly grown bored with sewing. Demétrio, who was always by my side, immersed in a book—and how often I caught him, too, staring off into space—would sometimes jump when I started to my feet.

"What's wrong?" he would ask.

And I would lie shamelessly:

"I thought I heard someone . . ."

And he would say: "It's only the gardener," and go back to his reading, as if he could not tear himself away from it.

Yes, how often I would sit absolutely still, head bowed, heart pounding, trying to listen—and I would imagine footsteps, people running, the hasty gestures of people shaken by some grave incident, and which existed only in my mind. "When will it happen?" I kept tirelessly asking myself. And equally tirelessly, I kept staring at the paths beneath the hot light of the unforgiving sun, where things seemed so fixed as to appear eternal. And so the days crawled by and nothing happened. I felt almost impatient sometimes: "How can he, how does he have the courage to drag things out like this?" And out of that long soliloquy was born a kind of secret, insalubrious joy that appeared on my lips in the form of a sad smile: "Perhaps he didn't really love her so very much . . ." And again I would start listening, but nothing disturbed the peace of the day. Far off, a bird would unleash its harsh, repetitive, monotonous cry, and I would go back to my embroidery, my hands trembling with impatience. When I had not seen him for a while, though, and spotted his hoe abandoned in the sun, I would stand up. I had grown so inured to the idea of his suicide that not even the sound of a shot would have startled me. And yet he had only to disappear from view for me immediately to spring to my feet.

"Whatever's wrong with you?" Demétrio would ask, putting down his book.

"I'm tired, my legs have gone to sleep," I would say. "I'm going for a walk . . ."

"In this heat?"

I would try to look as nonchalant as possible.

"Yes, why not? There's plenty of shade beneath the trees."

I don't know, perhaps it was simply my imagination, but I felt that he looked at me for longer than usual, although without betraying any nameable emotion. I came to loathe him then, but was still able to conceal from him what was happening in my heart. I would walk down into the garden and, pausing before a flower here, a bush there—he was, of course, still following me from the verandah with his eyes—I would finally reach the protective shade. A silent rage made my heart beat faster: the calm he affected, that horrible indifference! And head down, I would follow every crushed leaf, every bit of scuffed earth that indicated Alberto had come that way. And I would say to myself: when, oh when will it be? The blue sky did not answer, and the birds flapped serenely past on the horizon. I imagined then that he was perhaps already in his room, that he would kill himself in the next few minutes or seconds. I would listen intently for the shot. Then I would walk on, unconsciously quickening my step. I was dripping with sweat, but that did not stop me: even if my husband did see me, even if I permanently compromised myself, what did it matter? I wanted to be present at his death. I ran—and when I stopped, exhausted, my eyes clouded by a slight dizziness, I felt the strangeness of my situation. No shot rang out, and my eyes filled with tears. I would walk back to the house then, aware of another hopelessly peaceful evening coming on.

He did kill himself, but on a day so calm that any violent act seemed utterly impossible. We were sitting at the table, and I was just thinking about him when Betty came to say that something had happened, that the gardener was lying, wounded, in the Pavilion. Despite my long training in repression, I leapt to my feet. Demétrio gave me an indefinable look and, as he had before, kept his eyes fixed on me for a long time.

"Are you going?" he asked.

"Why shouldn't I?" I answered, and I myself didn't know why I said that.

I knew I must have turned pale, and I could not for another second control my emotions. What was the point of lies and pretense at that supreme moment? Demétrio continued to look at me, as if challenging me—and I turned to face him as if for the last time, as if I were saying goodbye, bidding him a final farewell—without rancor, without scorn, but strangely detached. I left the room without a backward glance, certain that, as always, his eyes would accompany me as far as they could. I went down the steps, my heart beating only a little faster than usual, my vision slightly blurred. I did at least have solid reasons for doing what I was doing. But even if no one else agreed, even if they were all suspicious of me and pointed to me as the worst of sinners, even then, I would still have gone, despite Demétrio's unspoken anger, because the woman I had been up until then had ceased to exist, and in accepting that death, I was accepting my drama, my passion, and everything that existed outside the ordinary orbit of that house. And there I was going down the steps from which I had so often gazed with yearning eyes—there I was walking along the sandy paths of the garden I had so often probed and studied from a distance, imagining it to be the garden of all possible delights. Except that now it was very late, and the sun was cold and the color of lead.

Alberto was not yet dead, and I asked Betty to send at once for a doctor. In my impatience, I even gave her a shove, but there was peace in my heart, and in my mind the certainty that he was already doomed, and that no one, not even the doctor, could do anything to save him. No, Alberto had not yet died, but what good were those faint, lingering glimmers of life? Standing there, frozen to the spot, I looked at him as if for the first time, so accustomed had I become to the image I myself had created, so very different from the reality confronting me now, however hard I tried to mound real-life flesh to dream. He was lying on the bed, one hand beneath his head, the other trailing on the floor, revealing his blood-soaked chest. He could no longer recognize me, he was breathing hard, his eyes closed—and yet still I was afraid to go any closer, dumb and dry-eyed with respect. A pinkish foam was forming in the corners of his mouth, and his face was taking on a greenish hue: death was not far off. It was this thought, I believe, that gave me the strength to approach him—because I could hold back no longer—and, kneeling by his side, I pressed my lips violently to his foam-tinged lips. What I said then, Father, even I could not repeat—incoherent words, insane ramblings, that seemed to be spoken by someone else, and which, when I recalled them later, filled me with panic and shame. A hoarse voice was speaking those words, while I embraced that wounded body, my cheek resting on his chest, where my tears, free at last, mingled with his still-warm blood. At last, I could touch him, and touch him while he was still alive, feeling that every tremor shaking my body was draining the strength from his, and that each of my all-too-passionate kisses brought his death a little nearer. There was a moment when I saw him open his eyes and look at me as if he understood what was happening. A wave of hope ran through my being, and I believed for a moment that I could yet be redeemed, even if only through a word or a smile, and that the hatred in my heart could be purged forever. A single word, a smile, not of love or complicity, but merely of understanding—that was all I was hoping for. His lips moved, he was about to say something, perhaps a word of farewell. I leaned closer, not wanting to miss that supreme message—and then I distinctly heard him say a name—NINA. Oh, Father, I do not know what madness gripped me then, but seeing him close his eyes again, I kissed his lips one more time, and said: "It's Nina, my love, it's me, Nina, here by your side." I don't know how often I said those words, rubbing my face over those foam-smeared lips—however, nothing now seemed capable of drawing him out of the torpor into which he was sinking. I made one last effort and tried to lift his head, repeating: "Can't you hear me? It's me, Nina, here by your side." But his head fell back so limply then that I knew he was dead, and I again clung to him, saying: "Goodbye, Alberto, goodbye."

His body stiffened beneath my hands, his head drooped to one side, and that was how the doctor found us moments later.

16.
Father Justino's First Account

I saw her even before I had finished giving the benediction; she was half-hidden behind one of pillars in the nave. Since my eyesight is poor, and her dark silhouette was easily confused with that of many other women in the congregation, I looked again, and that is when I realized she was hiding from me. This confirmed me in my belief that it was indeed her, for what other woman in the parish would be capable of such conflicting impulses, simultaneously seeking me out and fleeing from me? It could only be her—she had come specifically to see me and yet she was avoiding me, lacking the courage to show her intentions openly. That lack of spontaneity was one of her fundamental traits, and seemed to me representative of what I called the "Meneses spirit": a desire to stay safe within the bounds of solid realism and never go beyond a certain sphere of common sense so essential when dealing with worldly practicalities. As soon as I had finished saying the rosary, and the murmur of accompanying voices behind me had stopped, I made my way to the sacristy, certain that she would follow me there. And indeed before I had even removed all my vestments, I became aware of someone softly opening the door and standing there, presumably waiting for me to turn around. I could easily imagine how difficult it must have been for her to do such a thing and so, to allow her time to compose herself and prepare an explanation for her visit, I kept my back to her while I carefully folded up the chasuble and stowed it away in the large chest. Only when I heard a dry, somewhat impatient cough did I turn around.

"Oh it's you, Dona Ana," I said, trying to sound as natural as possible.

She was leaning against the doorframe, a black shawl over her head, and she seemed even paler than usual, if such a thing were possible. Or perhaps not pale exactly, but wan, with the dull, greenish complexion of someone suffering from a liver condition. Contrary to my expectations, she did not appear agitated; indeed with her frank gaze and head held high, I would go so far as to say that I had never seen her so calm. She exuded an air of forthright determination, which, for some reason I found most troubling. I had the distinct impression that the struggle within her was over and that what was driving her now, far from being the clash of opposing forces, was the sense of certainty that she had reached her final destination, like a swimmer at last touching dry land. What that destination was scarcely mattered—her face, like a land laid waste, showed very clearly the price she had paid and the kind of serenity she had found through that process of pacification. She did not respond to my words, which I had tried to make cordial and friendly, nor did she make the slightest attempt to enter the room, merely leaning more heavily still against the doorframe, waiting for whatever kind of invitation I might make. "Ah," I thought to myself: "She's come only to tell me that it's too late." And as I searched in vain for something to say, realizing that whatever I did say would inevitably bump up against the wall of her hostility, I heard her say, precisely and firmly:

"Yes, it's me, Father Justino."

I stepped toward her:

"Won't you come in?" I asked, and then, pointing toward the vestments: "I haven't quite finished putting these things away."

She shook her head:

"No, thank you. I won't stay long."

I did not press her, fearing that she would prove still more elusive or, in her embarrassment, lie about the real reason for her visit. Noting my silence, and possibly realizing that there was not much I could do without her help, she took two steps toward me, but still she said nothing and merely stood there, breathing faster than normal. In the sunlight streaming in from one of the side windows, I once again noticed that green, bilious tinge to her skin—everything about her, as if she had been very hastily thrown together, was excessively gloomy, to the extent that, seeing in her face all that suppressed rage and disappointment, I could not help but shudder.

"Have you come to confess?" I asked.

Once again she shook her head, and so, setting aside all caution, I asked what had brought her there. She answered in a low but perfectly natural voice that she had come to ask me to accompany her to the Chácara. I was surprised and told her that I couldn't just go like that; I had, at the very least, to wait for the sacristan to return—he had gone home for dinner and would not be long. This seemed to upset her and she muttered several times: "Oh, really!" as if I could have no other choice but to go with her immediately. She added that it was a very grave matter, indeed *extremely* grave (which I took to imply that I was needed *in extremis*), but she did not provide any further details. To see if any more information might be forthcoming, I asked if it was someone else who had sent for me, and she simply answered: "No, no one else." However, I could tell from her manner that she was not going to leave without a formal promise from me and, with a deep sigh, I promised that as soon as I had finished changing my clothes and locking up the church, I would go and meet her. She agreed to this, saying that she would wait for me at the Chácara's main gate.

And only a short time later, that is where I met her. She was waiting impatiently, leaning on the fence, her eyes fixed on the road. As soon as she saw me, she hurried toward me.

"I thought you weren't coming," she said. There was a note of irritation in her voice.

"Why?" I asked good-humoredly as I dismounted.

"Because it's getting late."

I looked at her and there was something about her that only increased the sense of disquiet that she always provoked in me. I did not reply and we walked together up the avenue, with me leading my horse by the reins. Neither of us said a word, but I knew perfectly well that something was troubling her. Night was coming on, and the clumps of trees cast patches of deep shade over our path, even though, up in the sky, there were still great swathes of blue. To my surprise, instead of continuing up the main avenue, we turned down a side path bordered by a hedge and followed the course of a stream burbling over its stony bed. Along with the clip-clop of the horse's hooves, the sound of frogs and crickets began to fill the gathering gloom. We carried on walking for some distance until we reached a kind of gazebo plunged entirely in darkness, with low branches covering the entire façade; there was absolutely no sign of life. I assumed we would go up the steps, but once again I was mistaken: Dona Ana skirted around the front of the building and made her way toward a low, barely-lit side door. (The weak wavering glow coming from within suggested that the only light was an oil lamp.) Dona Ana finally turned toward me and pointed to the door:

"In here."

I must admit that, at that moment, I was unsure whether to enter or not, for that whole adventure struck me as extremely odd. However, having come that far, how could I waver now, especially since my assistance had been sought as a minister of God? I entered and, from the very first second, I was taken aback by the suffocating air of that dank cellar. Turning to the left, Dona Ana led me to an open door, from where the light was evidently coming. Without a word, she stood to one side and motioned for me to enter. I obeyed the commanding look in her eye and found myself in a smaller, even narrower room with an even lower ceiling (I could almost touch the beams), and which was ventilated by a single, circular window that gave onto the garden. (Later, much later, other circumstances would take me back to that same unbreathable atmosphere—and the most extraordinary thing is that, all those years on, the new episode would attach itself to the first to make a single whole, like two parts of the same tree. And on both occasions it was the absence of God, rather than His work, that I was to witness.) Looking down, I saw a body stretched out on a miserable pallet bed. It was a young man, covered in blood. Moving closer, I saw that he was dead. I was gripped by confusion and doubt: it had clearly been a violent death. But how? How had it been spilt, all that still-fresh blood staining the walls and darkening the floor where I stood? I turned to Dona Ana, unable to contain my feelings.

"It's him," she said simply.

Him! And for a moment I tried desperately to work out who she meant by that, going through all my memories, the names of people I had met, the stories, and even the confessions I had heard. She sensed my consternation and sighed:

"Ah, you didn't read my letters! You don't know who it is!"

It was only at this outburst that I remembered who it must be, and, with unexpected violence, that dark, tortuous tale thrust itself once more into my thoughts, bringing with it the same deep unease as before. So it was him, the gardener. He was what this was all about. Turning to look at her, I felt genuinely afraid for the first time: an undefined but very real fear, like that of someone slowly realizing the danger he is in. What did it really mean, this woman's coldness, her apparent self-control, her resignation in the face of a drama that must have deeply affected her?

"How did it happen?" I asked.

"He killed himself," she replied.

So it was all over—despair had consumed the one person who was perhaps the most innocent of all, the one whom destiny had most cruelly entangled in its web. But for us wretched mortals there is no destiny, only the will of God. In their silent, eloquent simplicity, those blood-soaked remains were an exact representation of man's rebellion against God and his refusal to believe in Divine Providence.

"He killed himself, Father," repeated Dona Ana, in a tone that made me turn immediately toward her. Then, more quietly, as if saying something she could not believe: "He killed himself."

Suddenly, unable to hide her true feelings, she exclaimed:

"He killed himself, or at least that's what they say. But as far as I'm concerned, he was murdered."

I waited for her to offer some explanation for this outlandish statement. Coming a little closer, but without taking her eyes off the body of that poor soul lying on the bed, she told me that Dona Nina was the cause of all this. It was she who had thrown the revolver out of the window and thus created, you might say, the opportunity for a suicide. Ah, yes, and she knew why too: Dona Nina was about to leave, indeed was obliged to leave, and she knew the gardener would kill himself the moment he knew all hope was gone. And here, lying before us, was the proof. He had picked up the revolver that had landed in the garden and taken it as if it were an order. The loyalty of such simple souls was unimaginable. (As she spoke, into my mind came the nagging question that has never left me since: was Dona Nina really conscious of her actions? Would she have been quite so cruelly aware that she was ordering the gardener's death? How much of it was her fault, and how much that of the others? I have no idea, or rather, I have never found out. Over time, I have made many inquiries, but have never been able to pin down that woman's role in such a tragic event. I was never able to tell whether she had acted out of wickedness, which is something I don't believe in, or whether she had been driven by jealousy and the fear of leaving him behind, which seems scarcely more likely. There then remained the most plausible explanation: that it was one of those reckless, impetuous gestures, which, from what I have heard, was typical of her. I don't know why, but this seemed to me the most convincing hypothesis. In any event, one can only agree that this was a still graver shadow to be added to the many dark shadows left trailing in her wake and adding to the portrait of that strange, remarkable person—an enigma of God.)

The force with which Dona Ana said those words had now faded, and she sank groaning to the floor beside the body. She stayed there for some time, her head resting on the edge of the pallet, not so much crying as wailing; a long, harsh, rasping sound like the cry of a dying animal, and which was merely the sign of a broken soul, unprepared for such strong emotions.

"He's dead," she wailed, and I wondered to myself how many times she had repeated this to herself when alone. "He's dead. Gone. What will become of me now?"

"My dear child," I said, going over to her and trying to help her to her feet, "everything that happens is by the will of God."

"Of God!" she exclaimed. And she raised her head so I could see the scorn glinting in her eyes. "Of *God*! Oh, Father, how can it be that of all the creatures in the world God should choose *this* one?"

"We can never know what He desires of us," I replied.

Once again she slumped to the floor. For some time the whole of that small space echoed with the sound of her tears, like the mournful cry of farmers calling their cattle. Then, feeling calmer, she turned to me:

"He's gone, gone forever. He's not here any more." And as she said this there was such sadness in her voice, such poignant melancholy, that it was impossible not to see that there lay the crux of all her ills: a deep, constant, desolate absence of Hope. The young man's death did not signify for her an act of God's will, nor the beginning of another existence, nor the possibility of a future life—it was simply death, like a blank wall against which there was no point in throwing oneself. (Wasn't it precisely this absence of Hope and this sense of the precariousness of worldly things that had for so long weighed on her poor benighted spirit? I saw her again some time later in equally dramatic circumstances, and then, as now, she exemplified for me what it is to despair of divine assistance and to think of this world as a place with no possibility of rescue or redemption. The world, with all its limitations, filled her entirely, and there was not the tiniest crevice in which so much as one leaf from the tree of fraternal joy could grow and flourish.)

I don't know if it was pity or simply a need to say something, but I placed one hand on her head and said, in a tone which I intended to be joyful:

"Not forever. For it is written that we shall all be restored to life, and the fewer our sins the younger and more beautiful we shall be."

"Young! Beautiful!" she cried, astonished.

"Don't you believe in immortality? It does exist."

"Oh, Father!" And she began to weep again, not with the same harsh gasps as before, but frankly and openly, as if something had given way inside her, and the tears flowed freely down her cheeks. "Oh Father, don't you understand?" she stammered, her voice choked by tears. "It's now that I want him, right now, here, living and breathing in front of me. And yet there he lies, stiff and cold."

How could I respond to such a cry, filled as it was with her utter incomprehension of God's divine mercy? I bowed my head and begged God to shine a light into that poor, sad, imprisoned soul. As I prayed, my thoughts were filled with a vision: a vision of what she and all of us were lacking, a lack that was probably the cause, for many, of a hard, daily battle: Christ's presence. Or rather, a vision of his absence. An absence so absolute and so tangible that, around us, it created a kind of vacuum, an intense, accusing reminder of that absence. The truth came spontaneously to my lips:

"You must understand, my daughter, that God wanted you to lose him."

She stopped crying and laughed, a soft, sinister laugh that made me shudder. Then she began to clamber to her feet by a series of oddly contorted movements, first heaving herself up onto the edge of the bed then sliding up the blood-streaked wall until, finally, she was standing. And there she stood, facing me, eyes shining, leaning against the wall as if she might fall at any moment.

"No, it wasn't God. It was me who wanted to lose him. And the worst of it, Father, is that even if he had been mine, all mine, I might still have wanted to lose him. It was too much for me, too much for my meager strength."

She took two steps toward me.

"After he killed himself, I finally understood everything: living without him was worse than living with him. A thousand times worse. Day after day of emptiness, coming and going, not caring about anything. Now that he can no longer hear or reply to anything I say, I'm horrified at what happened. I can't bring myself to do anything, to walk or eat or talk to anyone. That's why I came to find you, Father."

"That's why?"

She drew even closer:

"That's why." (She paused briefly and looked at me. Her deep, inquiring gaze made me feel suddenly uneasy.) "Do you know what people say about you, Father? They say you're a saint."

She didn't laugh, but stared at me again as if testing me. "Ah," I thought to myself, "what does she want? What lengths will she not go to?" I shrugged, as if to say that people said all sorts of silly things. Then I detected a tremor in her fervent voice:

"Don't you believe me? That's what everyone says, Father. Not just here in Vila Velha, but farther away in places like Rio Espera, Mercês, and even Ubá! Everyone says you're a saint. And I believe them, Father. I believe that you are a saint."

I don't know where I found the strength to reply:

"There is something more important than believing in this or that. Do you believe in God?"

She again fixed me with her gaze, and this time her eyes were vacant, with no fear in them now, only exhaustion, complete and utter exhaustion.

"I don't know," she said. "I don't know what I believe in. Is it important? Look," she added brusquely, "I believe in what I can see."

"That isn't believing in God," I replied.

"Does it matter?" She spun toward me, finally laying bare her intentions: "If you perform a miracle here in front of me, then I'll believe in God."

"You must be mad!" I exclaimed.

She laughed again, that same strange, soft snicker.

"No, I'm not mad. I know you could very easily perform a miracle. It's just a matter of stretching out your hand . . ."

I took a step back and, for the first time, it occurred to me that what was happening to that woman was more serious than I had thought. In the cellar's dim, flickering light, I stared at her, and she stared back at me. I could see that something in her had changed and she no longer looked like the person I knew; she had grown taller, thinner, and strangely self-assured. I don't know how long we stood staring at each other, but it seemed to me an eternity, and while it lasted, as if by some ingenious conjuring trick, an extraordinary rearrangement of her personality occurred. (That's when I truly discovered that human beings change, that we are not fixed structures but moving forces, always advancing toward our definitive form.) From where I stood, I watched her slowly circle the bed—even her way of walking was different—and take up a position at the other end, almost at the dead man's head. From there, erect and resolute, she dominated the space now separating us. There was something in her that struck me as profoundly masculine: even her face, usually softened by despair, had taken on a hard, greenish, sculptural quality, and in her pale eyes I saw a being I had never known before.

"It isn't me you should turn to," I said, holding her gaze, "but to God's mercy."

The voice that echoed around the room sounded breathless, as if pressed for time, and, although it was still human, it was no longer a woman's voice, still less that of the woman who stood before me. It was a man's voice, and a man who had run a long way before he arrived at that spot. "I don't believe in God. Who is God? What can He do for me? But you, on the other hand . . ."

I felt dizzy and feared I might collapse. The rasping voice from the other side of the room continued:

"Only you, only you can do anything for me. He was young, Father. He was handsome, he was charming. Just look at him resting there like a sleeping child. Look, Father, how can you not feel pity when you see that face?

"Yes, I can see that," I replied. "But didn't Christ tell us to let the dead bury the dead? There's nothing more I can do, neither I nor anyone."

"A miracle, Father," she begged. "You must make a miracle happen."

Suddenly she moved, stepping forward and almost shouting:

"Bring him back to life, Father. Bring him back to life and I will believe in God and everything else."

"How can I . . ." I cried, recoiling.

Her trembling hand pointed to the corpse:

"If you give the word, he will rise. All you have to say is: 'Arise, wipe away your blood and walk.'"

I raised my hand, not to do as she asked, but to make the sign of the cross over her. She ignored my gesture and, coming closer, continued gabbling furiously:

"A man from Mercês said that you performed a miracle. I believe him, Father. I believe him. He was short and fat, he wore boots, he was riding a horse and was covered in dust."

"What did he tell you?"

"I was sitting on the verandah. He didn't even dismount, he just looked at me and said: 'I have just seen great things, Senhora.' I asked him: 'Where?' and he pointed to the road: 'Over toward Fundão.' I asked what he had seen, and the traveler told me: 'A priest has performed a miracle.'"

"And you believed that?"

"I did. I asked him 'What miracle?' And he replied: 'He brought a man back to life, a man who already stank of death.'"

"It's a lie. There was no miracle."

"None?"

"None."

"Not even that man . . . ?"

"I don't know that man."

Then she threw herself at me, shaking me so violently that I almost fell to the floor.

"What does it matter who it was? What does it matter whether or not you know him? Perhaps there never was such a man and I've merely invented this story to get through to you."

Silently, I again made the sign of the cross. She shrank back, but she had not given up. She was still breathing hard, but her voice was fading as if she were ready to depart this life

"Bring him back to life, Father. They'll say you're a saint. Your name will be known throughout the state, even the entire country. A saint! Our very own Brazilian saint! And here in our little provincial backwater we'll proudly say: 'Yes, it's a priest from Vila Velha who's performing those miracles.'"

No longer able to contain my emotion, and confronted by that pathetic voice flowing around me like a river of darkness, I hid my face in my hands and began to pray. I don't know what I said—snatches of prayers that came to my lips and which I recited willy-nilly, while in the depths of my heart I implored God to have mercy on her poor tormented soul. Seeing me praying, she shook her head:

"No, it isn't saintliness that interests you."

"Not that kind of saintliness," I whispered.

She turned to me one last time, her eyes blurred with tears:

"Who knows? Perhaps you don't believe in God either. These things happen: false priests who prey on people's good faith."

"May God protect you . . ." I began.

She looked at me scornfully:

"From what?"

I imperceptibly lowered my voice:

"May God have mercy on you."

She shrugged and seemed suddenly to grow distant, forgetting my presence altogether. She fell into her usual apathetic state. She sat down beside the bed and stared sadly at the corpse, at the single black bloodstain spreading across his chest. She pulled her shawl around her, as if she were cold. The lamp was burning out. I realized it was time for me to go, that there was nothing more for me to do there. But I left with the certainty that I would never forget the image of that small, frail woman sitting beside a corpse—for no other image would ever give me such a profound, tormenting sense of human solitude.

17.
André's Diary (ii)

15th – I was no longer expecting her to come and had assumed she had forgotten her promise. Yes, I repeated to myself once, twice, innumerable times, that she must have forgotten, there was no doubt about it, and that thought, by dint of being repeated and chewed over like a humiliation I chose not to forget, made me turn pale with rage. She had deceived me, had made mock of my hopes, my feelings, my friendship, in short, everything—and the most painful part of all was that it was entirely unnecessary. Why promise to visit me when, before she spoke, I had not for a moment expected she would even deign to knock at my bedroom door? Now there was no avoiding the sad truth: she was treating me like a child. Her very gesture, which I had seen as a sure sign of her unequivocal liking for me, was revealed for what it was: banal and empty. (And yet she could transfigure everything, from the simplest of laughs to the most distant, fleeting glance . . .) How often I had relived that gesture in my mind, my heart beating like a schoolboy's! The hours were slipping by, and there I was still sitting on my bed, staring into the darkness. I could remember it perfectly, and would probably do so for the rest of my life: she was leaning on the piano—the piano in the Chácara, which was almost never used—leafing through some music, while my father played. I can't recall exactly what he was playing, or the names or titles on the score, because I was interested only in her. There was something so abandoned, so intensely lonely about the way in which she leaned on the piano, that I could never drive it from my memory. After all, what are our memories but an awareness of an elusive, fugitive light hovering over the truth of things? Oh, she was certainly beautiful, singularly beautiful, as she bent nonchalantly over the music, her elbows on the piano lid, possibly reading, possibly oblivious to everything, or, as I would often see her later on, immersed in endless, feverish thought. I was thinking how everyone was saying that she was not as beautiful as she used to be, that she had aged and was very different from the person she once had been. With great difficulty, like someone traversing dark, difficult terrain, I was trying to imagine what she would have been like then, when everyone bowed before her, acknowledging her as one of the most beautiful women of her day. Younger perhaps, more carefree, unmarked as yet by such things as a knowledge of certain fixed and irremediable truths or of secrets finally penetrated, things that lent her face a stern maturity.

My eyes filled with tears and I turned away so as not to betray my emotion. Maybe that sudden movement made her gaze fall on me. Now, alone in my room, I think that perhaps she did not see me, but merely looked at me with the empty eyes of the indifferent—at the time, though, carried away by my own enthusiasm, I thought she really could see me and, worse still, had discovered my secret. I turned even paler, I trembled and, unable to contain my unease a moment longer, sprang to my feet, my brow beaded with sweat. This time, there could be no doubt: she had seen me fully and completely, right down to the very core I was trying so hard to hide. (Why? What was this guilt I carried within me and that already singled me out as quite different from the others?) I saw a smile appear on her lips—and it was a smile that was, at once, gentle, meaningful, and dominating. My father continued to play—this time a selection from *The Gypsy Princess*. She came over to me and murmured my name:

"André!"

Moments before, I had turned away in order to avoid her eyes, but now I slowly turned back to face her, as if her voice had torn me from some deep distraction.

"André," she said again, sensing that I was pretending, "what's wrong? Are you feeling all right?"

I was clearly not all right, for I was extremely pale and dripping with sweat.

"It's nothing!" I cried in a tone that attempted to sound surprised. "Nothing." But my face must have given the lie to those words.

"Nothing?"

And her eyes gazed into mine with the glare of a sudden, golden light.

"Nothing," I said again, but my face said otherwise. The effort was too much for me, and my eyes filled with tears. There could be no deceiving her now. Her face darkened suddenly and, taking my hands in hers in a tender, intimate gesture, she blurted out, like someone in a hurry to confide a secret:

"Tonight, before I leave the house, I will come to your room. We have much to talk about . . ."

At those words, a tremor of love ran through me. I squeezed her hand harder still, as if afraid she might break the promise she had just made. She smiled, at the same time looking across at the piano.

"Be sure to come," I said, adding more softly and with my eyes fixed on hers: "I will wait up all night for you."

She let go of my hand and patted me on the cheek, and that intimate gesture, a clear indication that she still thought of me as a child, plunged me once more into the somber mood I had been in ever since her arrival. But now was not the time to respond, because my father had just finished playing and had turned to look at us.

"How well you still play, Valdo!" she said. "And how that music takes me back to a time I will never forget."

Her tone of voice was so calculated, so intentional, that I could not help but tremble—whether what she said was true or not, what strange resources of mischief and pretense that woman had, how easily she could create the perfect atmosphere for a lie with a mere gesture, a look, an insignificant word! My father was clearly happy, for he stood up, took her in his arms and kissed her:

"What an excellent memory you have, Nina."

She was looking at me over his shoulder, as if seeking my approval for her words. And again, for some reason, I felt suddenly, unexpectedly ashamed.

15th – Unable to sleep, I got up, feeling in the dark for this notebook. The room was not entirely in darkness, however, because a shaft of moonlight was shining in through the window onto the foot of the bed. I found the chest of drawers and was just about to open one of the drawers, when I heard raised voices. I froze, trying to work out what was happening. The voices were not far off, but with the door closed, it was impossible to know precisely where they were coming from. If I opened the door, I might be seen, and then my efforts to find out more would be in vain. I remained standing for a few moments longer, then, realizing that the voices were not so very close and that those engaged in the argument would not, therefore, notice me, I finally opened the door and went out into the hallway, which, fortunately, was pitch-black. I could tell at once that the voices were coming from my father's room, although the other person involved was not Nina, but my uncle Demétrio. Disappointed, I was about to go back to my room, when I distinctly heard Nina's name. So, although she was not there herself, they were talking about her. This immediately revived my interest and, tiptoeing along like a stealthy criminal, taking advantage of the still darker shadows in the corners,

I crept toward the one visible line of light. Once there, I had no compunction in pressing my ear to the door. I heard my uncle's cold, measured tones:

"You are completely and utterly insane."

And my father's higher-pitched, less assured voice:

"Why? What do you imagine . . ."

My Uncle Demétrio must have been pacing up and down, because his voice came and went in volume:

"You're forgetting what happened before, Valdo, but fortunately I have a very good memory."

"What is the point in dredging up such things?" my father said. "Nina is here again, and where I go, she goes. I have no reason to doubt . . ."

My uncle's voice exploded, as if he had just heard the most heinous of insults:

"What about the Baron?"

My father mumbled some confused response, doubtless something about not caring a fig for the Baron—and the voices moved over to the window. I did not need to hear any more, that was quite enough. They had been having the same discussion over supper and felt I knew quite enough about the matter. It was the Baron's birthday; and, as they did every year, my father and my uncle would have to attend a reception at the Baron's house. This time, however, they were arguing over whether or not Nina should go too; my father wanted to take her with him, and my uncle, doubtless fearing gossip about past events, was opposed to this. I don't know who won the argument, because I returned to my room. How little I cared about that family bickering! For a moment, standing in the dark, it occurred to me how very removed I felt from everything and how the people I lived with were like strangers to me. The only thing that united us was the roof over our heads. At the far end of the hallway, my other uncle, Timóteo, was sleeping, the uncle I never saw and about whom no one spoke. What did I care about him, either? I had other, quite different reasons for staying awake so late. I was vainly trying to piece together the sequence of events that continued to obsess me—events that had happened long ago and which surrounded my birth like an impenetrable fog. Despite all my efforts, the only figure I could glimpse in the midst of all that mist, was the person I now know as my mother.

16th – She came, although I was no longer expecting her and was lying on the bed, staring into the dark, my mind crisscrossed by all kinds of crazy, confused ideas. (For example, what if she wasn't my mother, and we had met somewhere else and in different circumstances? Or what if there were no one else in the house, just her and me?) It was then—I don't know the time exactly—that I heard the door open and, looking around, saw a figure framed in the doorway. I couldn't see who it was, but my heart began beating wildly—it could only be her. Before she even spoke a word, the smell of her favorite perfume wafted over to me as if through a window flung open onto a courtyard full of flowers. She still did not move, doubtless wondering whether she should come in or not, whether I would already be asleep, and she would be disturbing me—meanwhile, I, in my impatience, could feel her calm, pulsating presence in the tiniest details, from the silk of her dress, so different from Aunt Ana's dresses, to the curve of her breasts. Everything I had imagined earlier, the retreats, the obstacles, all seemed to fall away, and there we were hovering above the world, as if in a chosen land, far from all human interference.

"Mama!" I cried, and that word seemed to me insubstantial and meaningless.

"Ah, you're still awake," she said, while I heard the rustle of silk and felt her moving toward me, her perfume pushing through the air ahead of her, growing stronger.

"You said you'd come and see me, so I've been waiting."

She sat down beside me and took my hands in hers—I felt the weight of that body touching mine, the caress of silk on my skin, the warmth of her breasts. How long did I remain like that, my feverish hands in hers, while our shining eyes sought each other in the darkness?

"You mean you've been waiting for me all this time?" she said, her lips almost touching my cheek. "You poor thing! If I'd known . . ."

"It doesn't matter," I said. "I knew you had to go to the Baron's house first."

Her voice quavered:

"The Baron's house? Who told you I was going to his house?"

The answer took a while to emerge from my lips:

"I was in the hallway, listening, outside my father's bedroom."

She let go of my hands:

"Oh, so you listen in on other people's conversations, do you?" she said sternly.

I wanted to explain that it had happened accidentally, because I had heard them mention her name. But what was the point? How could she possibly know what was going on in my head? I said nothing and, for a second, an awkward silence reigned. And yet she was so close I could almost hear her heart beating. I have to confess that, even though I was sixteen then, this was the first time I had been so close to a woman. Everything I knew about women I had gleaned either from books or from what I sensed in the silences of my elders. And often—when I went into town with Betty or with my Uncle Demétrio in his buggy—I would follow with wandering, dreaming eyes the young women I saw in the street. But that was as far as it went, and I could not but think with a certain dread of the time when my uncle, seeing me glancing furtively at some female passersby, had rather gravely announced: "So you've already got an eye for the ladies, have you? One of these days, you'll have to get to know them at rather closer quarters . . ." Beside me now was the woman I had been physically closest to so far, since I could not consider Aunt Ana or Betty as proper women, but merely dull, familiar, domestic beings with whom I lived. Yes, there she was, intoxicatingly close, the mother who was a stranger to me, and who, in my eyes, was so thrillingly real and possessed of all the heady fascination of the female sex. That is what I was thinking while she remained silent. Then suddenly, with a sigh, she returned to the subject of the Baron:

"No, I didn't go to the Baron's house," she said.

"Why not?" I asked for no other reason than to fend off another weighty silence. A single, long sob shook her body, and she buried her face in her hands. I felt alarmed that a simple question could arouse such feeling and I sat on the edge of the bed, my legs dangling, trying to think of some way to console her. She removed her hands from her face—in the gloom, I could make out her pale features and burning eyes—and she again clasped my hands, only this time her fingers were wet with tears.

"My poor child . . . If you knew how I have been treated . . . the injustices I have endured!"

I knew what she was referring to, and on hearing those simple words, the fog of facts again began to circle about me. And yet, however hard I tried, I could not find the right words or provide her with the consolation she needed. How I hated all those things from long ago! To me they represented my absence, a time before I existed—and ironically enough, it was precisely those past events that dominated everything that happened in the house! What troubled me even more at that moment, more than that intense feeling of revulsion, was the darkness, her presence, her hands in mine. In other circumstances, I might have been able to find my way to some appropriately consoling gesture, but I was too paralyzed to do anything but bear anxious witness to her sobbing. Eventually, she calmed down, and only a few sobs still shook her body. Finally, she stopped crying altogether and, in the dark, I could feel only her hands letting go of mine and beginning a terrible, unexpected caress. At that very moment, her soft, tender hands were touching my shoulders, the back of my neck, my hair, my earlobes, almost my lips. It may be that she meant nothing by this caress, that these were simply mechanical gestures, perhaps those of an affectionate mother—after all, what did I know about what mothers did and did not do!—but the fact is I could not contain my feelings, and a shudder ran down into the very depths of my being, and I was filled by a spasmodic, agonizing feeling of pleasure and annihilation. However often I kept repeating "she's my mother and I should not be having these feelings," however hard I tried to convince myself that this was how all mothers behaved toward their sons, I could escape neither her intoxicating perfume nor the sheer force of her female presence; and my tumultuous sixteen-year-old self could not help but be aroused by those simple feminine gestures. Everything I imagined to be female attributes—the physical warmth, the soft, alluring touch, the smell of flesh and accumulated secrets—was there beside me, and in vain I invoked the mother who had been a stranger to me for sixteen years, in vain I repeated her name respectfully and responsibly, tenderly and reverently—I was lost and blind, and in the depths of my shaken, confused self all those feelings were being slowly annihilated. Her fingers came and went and just as I was struggling hard not to be entirely submerged, she drew me to her and pressed my head to her breast.

"Here, close to my heart," she said, "I want you to promise me something."

I knew what that promise would involve, but what did I care? What possible act of betrayal could compare with the mere fact of her presence?

"Yes, anything, I'll promise anything," I cried.

She pressed my head still closer to her bosom, and I felt her breath on my cheek:

"Promise that you will never take sides against your mother. Promise me that—whatever the situation, whatever the circumstances."

In a low, breathless voice, I promised, but all that existed in me at that moment was an intense awareness of the body on which my head was resting, and more than her body, her breasts rising and falling with each calm, clear breath, and whose curve lay almost within reach of my dry lips.

"Then nothing will ever separate us!" she said.

And, eyes closed, I repeated:

"Nothing!

With that word, she squeezed me so tightly, so passionately, that I was afraid I might fall and take her with me. It was as if she wanted to pluck something out from deep inside me, something as fundamental as my breath. (*A note in the margin in a different handwriting*: Only long afterward did I understand the passion in that gesture: it was like an act of witchcraft aimed not at my body, but at my soul. Poor Nina. Even then, she was pure instinct: in her efforts to make others submit—an impulse that was, to her, life itself—she crossed frontiers and headed straight for forbidden territory.) I don't know what happened next, but utter darkness filled my mind, and, swept along by an irresistible force, I raised my head and kissed her between her breasts—no, I didn't kiss her, I almost bit her, a furious, wild, mortal bite, such as can only be given by an adolescent suddenly wounded by the discovery of love. She accepted my kiss and did not draw back, as if it were merely a more than usually ardent homage from a son. However, when that kiss appeared to last longer than most simple manifestations of filial affection—ah, she would be thinking, the gaucherie, the extravagance and excess of a closed, timid heart!—she raised my head, saying:

"We're agreed then, André. That is the promise I wanted you to make. After all this time, it's as if they had finally given me back my son."

Those were certainly not the words I was expecting to hear, and my disappointment was reflected in my silence. There was something

I could not fathom: Had she understood the meaning of my kiss? Or had it all been in my imagination? Was she just playing a role, or would she actually accept the passion springing into life inside me? Now there was a distance between us, and we seemed to have said everything we needed to say, as happens with lovers when they have taken stock of the situation. Perhaps I would never solve that mystery; perhaps she would never know my secret. I saw her get to her feet and stand motionless before me. At least that was clear: it was the moment to say goodbye, for the chaste farewell kiss, while my whole helpless, tormented being shuffled off into a zone of utter desolation. She still did not leave, though: she was waiting, as if the last word had not yet been spoken.

"I still haven't had a proper look at you," she said in a voice that was surprisingly uncertain in one accustomed to certainty. "Turn on the lamp, I want to see you in the light."

I rather reluctantly did as she asked. I did not need light in order to feel her presence, so what did it matter if she couldn't see my face? Brightness flooded the room, and rather than her being able to see me, because I was almost covered by the bedclothes, I saw her, whole and smiling and magnificent. More than that, I understood then why she had wanted to see me. Despite the slightly troubled look in her eyes, she seemed to be offering herself to me, and I understood then that she knew everything, and that we were both setting off along a path that was no longer the path of innocence.

17th – I cannot close this diary without finishing my account of what happened last night. She was standing there, motionless, and I was gazing at her admiringly, almost enraptured. I had never seen such a beautiful woman, she was not just the sum total of every perfect feature—her beauty was a combination of everything about her, her hair, her eyes, her skin, down to the smallest vibration of her being. Even though she had not gone to the Baron's house, she had nevertheless dressed for the party, an artifice that only added to her fabulous beauty. (*Written in the margin in a different handwriting*: I have no hesitation in describing that dress, it's engraved on my memory and I know I will remember it always. I would go further: whenever I try to relive those early years of my adolescence, I find something chaotic and troubling, but what stands out, clear and elegant, is that strange ball gown—a masterpiece of frivolousness and style, of the fascinating, intimate nothingness that makes up the external appearance of a woman.

It was made of a heavy, dark-red fabric, as soft to the touch as satin. It was very simply cut, almost like a tunic, that fell loosely over her breasts to form a wide, sweeping wave. Covering the tunic was a veil of black gauze sewn with beads that glittered with every move she made—and she was so keenly aware of her own charm, now stopping, now moving with studied ease, an infallible quality in women who understand their clothes. I could see her from the bed, and, following with my gaze the contrast of the black gauze against her white arms, I felt she was becoming a painting in oils, and that those basic colors were making of her a timeless, definitive portrait.) She went over to the door, and I assumed she was about to leave without saying another word, when she stopped and turned, her eyes almost closed:

"When I left the Chácara that first time, André, you did not yet exist. I don't know what memories or feelings you may still have of the time when I lived with you . . ."

She let go of the latch and came back to the bed, where she leaned over me:

"Tell me, do you really remember nothing at all?"

And although her eyes were fixed on mine, and she asked that question as gravely as she could, it still did not ring quite true; it was as if she were playing a part she had rehearsed earlier. It was clear that any secret depended on my response, but that the actual words I used would not, in themselves, be of any importance or significance. I wondered what it was she needed—what word or tender gesture or acknowledgement of what had clearly been a very painful time in her life? Then, as if speaking out of the silence inside me, I lied:

"No, I do remember."

And I saw her shiver, and a new music began to play between us.

"Where? How?" And she touched my shoulder.

"I'm not sure where . . ." and I tried to imagine where it could have been, more accurately than I suspected. "In a garden. There was a tree, a big tree and I used to sit in its shade. But it's all very vague, and it was such a long time ago!"

"Ah, a garden!" she exclaimed, and there was disappointment in her voice.

Then, after a silence, she spoke again, and her words were so cold they appeared to roll lifelessly around in the vacuum surrounding us:

"You must mean the Pavilion where we used to live."

That was all, and I realized then that she did not believe me. A kind of sob rose to my lips:

"Aren't I allowed to forget?"

She looked at me as if she could no longer see me:

"Goodnight, André. Go to sleep, and we'll talk again tomorrow."

Those were the last words she spoke, and we had obviously reached the end of that particular path. My importunate question still hung in the air. I heard the door close; I turned off the light and found myself once again in the darkness. However, I was less alone now, because from the four corners of the room, not in the form of a lie now, but as a real, tangible building, there arose the image of that Pavilion where, who knows, I had possibly been conceived.

18.
Letter from Nina to the Colonel

. . . Everything that happened after I left. Given your naturally fatherly heart, I can imagine you must have been very shocked. I can even see you taking a handkerchief out of your pocket and furtively dabbing at your eyes, but without saying a word against me. Ah, Colonel, my own eyes fill with tears at the thought. And yet, it isn't hard to guess why I left, I couldn't go on living like that, I was haunted by the image of my son. I felt guilty and had a horror of dying without seeing him and being able to kneel at his feet and beg his forgiveness. You do not perhaps understand a mother's heart, but there is nothing in the world more potent than the idea of the being who was born of your own flesh. You also may or may not remember that I had written to my husband demanding some money that he had promised, but never sent. (The evenings I spent alone in that narrow apartment with no one to help me. The perversity of the world and of the indifferent creatures filling the streets and whom I could see from my window. I think I would have succumbed to despair were it not for your generosity. I especially remember that night when we went to the Casino together and I won a not inconsiderable sum, a decisive event in my life, because I was definitely prepared to die at that point. I had even bought some poison and kept it always within reach, ready for the moment when I finally summoned up the courage. When I returned home in the early hours that night, I opened the drawer in my bedside table, removed the envelope containing the poison, threw it away, and replaced it with my winnings, saying to myself: "God made the decision for you, Nina, and the hour of your death has not yet come." It was then, whirling blithely about the room—I hadn't felt such a sense of freedom in a long time!—that I thought about refurbishing the apartment and replacing the old furniture. You encouraged me in this and, breaking the silence of years, I wrote to my husband, asking him to send me some money. When I met Valdo, I was, I admit, an innocent who knew nothing of the world. I lived closeted in that boarding house where you used to come and visit my father, do you remember? It was Valdo who taught me about good taste, about what one should and shouldn't wear. And so, Colonel, my idea of what an elegant apartment should look like came from Valdo and his advice, and I imagined it furnished with pieces identical to those I had known during the only really happy time of my life. For days and days, I waited for his answer, and never had the place where I was living seemed sadder or more cramped. Leaning at my window, I would stare out at the horizon, and my entire life would parade past me in my thoughts, and unconsciously, things I had believed to be long dead would rise to the surface, and I suffered all over again, but with a new intensity, a new sense of injustice at the way I had been treated. I could not for a moment forget that my husband was living in the quiet abundance of the Chácara, while I pined away in that bare, uncomfortable apartment. It was then that I showed the first signs of a strange illness, a kind of paralysis, which the doctor diagnosed as being psychological in origin. You were tireless in your help then, Colonel. No one could possibly have had a better guardian angel. Not a day went by without you visiting me, bearing sweets and flowers, and you went even further, always leaving some small, secret gift, sums of money hidden under the towels, loose change that you deliberately forgot and left behind, checks that you silently slipped into my handbag. We never spoke about this, I felt too embarrassed, but the moment has come to confess that my soul felt grateful unto death. Whenever you left me, I would burst into tears. Ah, Colonel, what a strange, ungrateful thing the human heart is. While you were heaping me with presents, my thoughts returned again and again to the home I had lost. I could not sleep, I could find no peace, I could not drive from my mind the idea of the Chácara as a place of refuge. Because for years and years, that thought had been working away inside me, slowly and surely, until it manifested itself in that physical paralysis, which kept me confined to my room. I was sure that what afflicted me was nostalgia and that I would not survive unless I satisfied that deep-seated yearning. (I talked to my husband today about that time and about the illness that confined me to a wheelchair. I saw him almost smile, doubtless thinking it was pure invention. And the truth is that, seen from a distance and in the silence that surrounds us here, it does seem more like a fantasy, an unconscious lie, a private trap, rather than a genuine illness. His eyes seemed to be saying: "Really, Nina, the things you invent!" And I could only agree and bow my head.) At the time, weary of suffering, I wrote a second letter to my husband and gave him a frank description of what my life was like. I wanted to set off to the Chácara whether he agreed or not. When you read these words, you may well accuse me of duplicity and consider me a sly, treacherous creature. There I was planning to leave and abandon you forever, while still gladly accepting the presents and flowers you brought to me each day. You would be wrong, Colonel, even though, at the same time as I was accepting your gifts, I was equally sure that I could not possibly go on living in that apartment. To do so would have been to accept my own death, a form of suicide more certain than poison. That is why, sitting trapped and still in my wheelchair, I began to feel a kind of nausea, an exquisite, deep-seated loathing for that furniture, those paintings, for all the things that made up the sad atmosphere in which I dragged out my existence. The Chácara and its comforts had seeped into my very bones. I wasn't angry with you, Colonel, but with my surroundings, the way some people with a high fever become consumed with anger for everything around them. I would fall asleep, but, despite my dreams, would wake up surrounded by those loathsome objects. Alone, I would weep and hurl insults at those cold walls, at what seemed to me a lifeless world.

I vividly remember the moment when I decided, once and for all, to leave. You had just closed the door and left a large amount of money on the bed. The day was fading fast, all was silence and nothingness. I knew it was now or never, and, throwing aside the blankets covering me—I could still hear your parting words: "Wrap up warm, my dear, the nights are getting cold"—I tried to get up. You will be surprised that I still had the strength to stand after such a long illness. I can assure you, Colonel, that the only thing driving me at that moment was the desire to see my son again, to see my home and the trees of the Chácara. That alone was enough to bring me back to life. I cannot describe what happened next, the feverish way I packed away my things, the journey to the station, and then the train. I was trembling, and had to force my poor body to do the bidding of my will.

Even though I had written on ahead, there was no familiar face at the station. The Meneses are very slow to forgive, and I feared they would not give me the warmest of welcomes. Added to this was a certain embarrassment, because I knew I was badly dressed and that my illness had left me pale and debilitated. I had always been a woman noted for her elegance; now, in a situation requiring me to look my attractive best, I arrived looking like someone who had suffered terrible privation. I know this will surprise you, bearing in mind that you had done your utmost to ensure that I lacked for nothing. I will go further, though, and confess that I fabricated and skillfully created that modest exterior in order to touch my husband's heart. I wanted him to be troubled by what he saw and to say to himself: "Is this the same poor Nina whom I so mistreated?" I would say nothing, but my silence, my black clothes, my cheap necklace, would speak volumes. No, don't protest, Colonel, I know I have lovely clothes and lovely jewels, but when I packed the little luggage I had brought with me, I deliberately chose the oldest, cheapest items. (Perhaps because I no longer felt I had the right to wear all your gifts.) Anyway, when I got off the train, I immediately realized that I was not exactly the most welcome of guests. No one was waiting for me, and I had to make my own way to the Chácara. A few people in Vila Velha had spotted me, and a group was already gathering in the pharmacy, opposite the station. Soon the gossip would reach fever pitch. But what did it matter? I called a cab and asked to be taken to the Chácara. Throughout the ride, I felt I was being stared at, and even though I knew it was just a ridiculous provincial town, I suffered, nonetheless, because I saw in those eyes a curiosity verging on malice. More than my own pale skin, what marked me out was the name of the Meneses.

Only Valdo was waiting for me in the garden and he held out his hands to me far more cordially than I was expecting. Before I could say a word, my eyes were already saying beseechingly: "Where is André?" He said softly: "Don't worry, you'll see your son soon enough." And I may have been imagining it, but I thought I heard in his voice a faint tremor of jealousy. He stood back from me a little:

"But you haven't changed a bit!"

He sounded so genuine that I felt all the care I had taken had been in vain. I attempted a smile:

"Oh, Valdo, I've changed a lot, I'm a different woman. After my illness . . ."

He replied rather too briskly and with a look in which I sensed a certain irony:

"On the contrary, you have never looked better."

Those were the only words we exchanged. I went up the steps—those worn stone steps, in whose cracks grew the occasional stubborn weed, steps I used to know by heart—wondering how the others would receive me. That was the most serious obstacle, and I was determined to face it with my head high. I said to myself: "Those Meneses will see that I have as much character as they do." When we reached the drawing room, though, my strength failed me. At the far end, next to the sideboard, were Demétrio and Ana; sitting slightly apart from each other, they formed a solemn, hostile pair. How stupid I had been to think I would have the strength to confront them: I would never be able to cope with their terrifying dignity. Especially Ana, who to me seemed as much a part of that atmosphere as if she were one of the rooms or a detail on a piece of furniture, as immovable as if she were a judge handing down the most unappealable of sentences. I pretended to feel dizzy, cried out: "Valdo!" and fell limply into his arms. I heard him say to the others:

"The poor thing. She must be exhausted . . ."

Then I heard Demétrio speak for the first time, and his voice sounded quite close:

"It's nothing. She's just a little pale."

"No, it's more than that," said Valdo, and I was pleased to hear him speak so warmly in my defense. "She's still recovering from a serious illness. I think the doctor may even . . ."

I didn't hear what else they said because they moved off into another room. I opened my eyes and saw the figure of Ana not that far away; she wore her usual hard expression. (That expression had the power to drag me back to a previous climate I could not quite identify, and in which we suffered as if we were chained one to the other.) I looked at her too: something had clearly happened to her. When I left, she had been simply a sad, graceless woman; now I saw before me someone wrinkled, worn down, prematurely old, as if shaped by some furious inner fire. For a while, I stared at her in astonishment, and then, slowly, a sort of smile appeared on her lips, an indefinable smile, because I don't know whether it was scornful or accusing, but which illumined that physiognomy with a dull, tentative light.

Just then, Valdo returned bearing a bowl of soup, which he forced me to eat, saying that I must be weak with hunger. Even Demétrio came over and took my pulse. I may be wrong, but I thought his hand trembled. Cold, inaccessible Demétrio! I tried to catch his eye, but he fled, turning away. Did he regret what he had done to me? I went straight to my room, saying that I felt unwell: in fact, I merely wanted to gain time, analyze the situation, and perhaps savor my triumph. Because I was sure I had won, and that victory was to me the sweetest of pleasures. It was there, in the quiet of my room—the same window, the same bars, the same view . . . and from outside, like a continual exhalation, the scent of violets and mallows filling the whole garden—that Betty suddenly appeared, despite my asking not to be disturbed. She was the same old Betty, with her spotless apron and her maid's bonnet covering her hair, which had not yet turned entirely gray, and her own quiet presence, which made her not a superior housekeeper, but a distinguished, shy, polite being, untouched now by the miseries of this world.

"I'm so glad to see you again, Betty," I said.

She sighed and shook her head:

"And I am even gladder to have you back, Senhora. You cannot imagine how much you have been missed . . ."

These were precisely the words I needed to hear. I knelt on the bed:

"Oh, Betty, what good is an old woman like me?"

She laughed and said I was exaggerating—I was still the same lovely creature whom everyone admired. In a confidential tone, she told me that, since my departure, the sound of laughter had been completely absent from the house. And even André, who barely knew me . . . When I heard that name, I shuddered, lacking the courage to ask about my son. She noticed my reluctance to speak and said his name again: "André." I put my arms around her waist and drenched her with my tears. Where was he? I hadn't seen him in the garden or the drawing room or anywhere. Why had he not come to greet me?

Had someone forbidden him to do so? Betty fell silent before that rush of questions. Then, when I insisted, she said:

"Don't worry, he's gone hunting in the Serra do Baú."

"But didn't he know I was coming?"

She lied, saying:

"No, he's been gone since yesterday."

And she indicated some vague point on the horizon. My curiosity knew no bounds, and I made her sit down beside me, while I asked her what he was like, who he resembled, if he enjoyed those brutish sports. She answered only that last question:

"Senhor Valdo makes him go hunting, but I don't think André much enjoys such violent sports."

"I see," I said, but that barely quenched my thirst for information.

She tried to get up, but I made her stay, asking her what he did, what he thought, what his interests were—and she told me that he was, by nature, reserved and taciturn. Not very tall and not very strong either. He enjoyed reading and would steal books from her room. A silence fell between us, and, fearfully, lowering my eyes, I asked if he ever spoke about me, if he knew I existed, if he had been told of my arrival. I saw Betty hesitate, and a shadow crept across her face.

"Yes, he knows. Senhor Valdo told him you would be arriving today. But I've never heard him mention it. I think it's a forbidden subject."

"But has he never said anything to you?" I asked urgently.

She looked at me, almost shocked:

"I'm just a servant to him . . . an old woman!"

I could not conceal my disappointment:

"So he's a true Meneses, then."

She thought for a moment, then said:

"No, on the contrary. He's not like a Meneses at all."

I placed my hand on hers:

"Thank you, Betty, you can't imagine what a relief it is to me to know that."

Despite those words, she could see how sad I was.

"On the other hand," she went on, as if trying to console me, "there's another person who never stops talking about you."

"Who?" I asked, and the dying flame flared up in my heart.

"Senhor Timóteo. He's the one who sent me to see you."

I nodded somewhat indifferently. Betty pretended not to notice, but I knew she was watching my every look and gesture. Senhor Timóteo wanted me to go to his room, she said, he had much to tell me. You probably don't remember who Timóteo is, Colonel, despite the interest and curiosity you have always shown regarding family matters—doubtless out of consideration for your ungrateful friend—nor will you understand why he, more than anyone else, should want to see me. It's hard to explain, especially since, in the Meneses family, Timóteo was far from being its dullest or its least unusual member, on the contrary, but to describe his personality, I would have to speak not so much about what he did or felt and more about the dense, unstable, electrically charged atmosphere that surrounded him—like the atmosphere you might find in certain smoky bars. Were I to describe his actions and feelings, they would be like mere supports propping up the foggy world he inhabited. He navigated his room like some splendid, deep-sea fish in the small maritime stronghold of his aquarium. What he said could seem abrupt and disconnected to those who merely heard him speak, but for anyone who understood him, there was a complete coherence between the things he said and the turmoil of his thoughts.

But it's late, Colonel, and I must leave this letter and my visit to Timóteo until tomorrow. I do not complain about my life, because I am responsible for what happens to me, but you are still very far from being able to judge what my life has been . . .

19.

Continuation of Nina's Letter to the Colonel

. . . A melancholy I cannot disguise. I will continue writing this letter, but I know you will never receive it. It will never leave this house, because nothing that belongs to me ever manages to cross its frontiers. That has always been the problem here: my sense of being a prisoner, alone and hopeless. I knew this from the very first moment, ever since I set foot on that first stone step, when the familiar scent of violets wrapped about me like a fatal sigh uttered by the earth itself. And yet still I came—I myself opened the door of my prison, because some more potent force was driving me on, and I came to meet my fate. No, you will never receive this letter, but I will continue to write it, because that is the only way I feel I can still talk to you, my one friend, my other life. I will continue to tell you interminable tales about Valdo, Timóteo, and the Meneses family generally, and I hope you will listen to me as willingly as ever, and I may even hear, above the clamor of some clumsy phrase of mine, some words of advice whispered in my ear. Ah, Colonel, were I brave enough, I would admit that I am already beginning to regret this latest adventure of mine, but I am sure some of us are fated always to make mistakes, until the day, who knows when or where, we are given a final explanation for mistakes that have left us feeling so uncertain and so wretched.

Going back to what I was saying before, I decided that I must visit Timóteo, since, in the past, he was the only one who had ever shown me any friendship. Although I had better not go now, I thought a moment later, because they might doubt that I really had been ill. No, later, a little later, when I could say that I was feeling better, and then no one would have any reason to suspect me. How cunning I had become, and quite shamelessly so! However, seeing Betty there, still apparently waiting for my answer, I decided instead to go and see him at once. Smoothing my hair with my hands, I went to that room I knew so well. The door stood open, as if Timóteo were expecting me. As usual, darkness reigned. My eyes were still adjusting to the gloom, when, from behind the piles of furniture—what a mess it was, this room that always used to be so scrupulously tidy!—I saw a huge, misshapen figure emerge, and I did not at first recognize my old friend. When I stopped, he rushed toward me, and only then did I recognize his warm, husky voice:

"Oh, Nina, I knew, I knew you would come back!"

He dragged me over to the window and only then could I see him clearly: he looked so very strange that initially I felt unable to react. He was not the person I had known before, but an exaggerated, over-exaggerated caricature. Yes, monstrous even, but extraordinarily touching. His still bright eyes had disappeared beneath a flaccid, sallow mass of flesh, which formed two large folds on his cheeks. His small, thin lips could barely articulate the words, which emerged like a sigh or, rather, like the hiss of air from a bellows. He was still in his feminine guise, but he had long since ceased to be a proud, magnificent *grande dame*. He was the mere wreckage of a human being, so decrepit and obese that he could scarcely move and had already reached the point where humans begin to resemble animals. The impression of utter decay was confirmed by the clothes he was wearing; what had once been splendid garments were now tattered rags that struggled to cover not the body of a middle-aged lady still capable of dazzling certain young men, but of an old lady defeated by neglect and dropsy.

"My poor Timóteo," I stammered, unable to find the right words.

"I am so happy to see you, Nina, your very presence here restores me to life!" he hissed in that strange voice, while he took my hand in his, the damp, limp, weightless hand of certain creatures that live in the dark.

I don't know why, but I found those words unimaginably touching; he had the ability to draw me instantly into that climate of overwrought sentimentality. I slumped down in an armchair, while the tears came into my eyes, tears so genuine that I could not even bring myself to stop them. Timóteo, possibly slightly shocked, came closer and placing one hand on my head, said:

"I understand you so well, I know exactly how you feel!" and his voice almost broke with emotion. "You know, I've often sat in that very chair and imagined seeing you again and unburdening myself to you. I wondered if you would have changed or if you would be the same Nina I've always known, the same eyes, the same hair. Ah, Nina, once we begin something, we must finish it. And we did begin something, do you remember? We began, Nina, and you were my only hope. Ever since you left, the Meneses have grown in strength, become the sole formidable power here. Nina, we must destroy this house. I mean it, Nina, we must kill the Meneses family. We must leave not a stone standing. When you left, I wept out of pure rage: I would never see my work finished, never. They were stronger than me, too loyal and determined for me to out-think them. They will end up burying me in this room. Ah, Nina, how often I have loathed myself, loathed my ugliness, my lack of dignity. Sometimes I would curse myself and my feeble blood! How often have I sat in that same chair and wept loudly, vainly, calculating what time and what resources were left to me! Sitting by this window, in the dim light, I would touch my swollen arms and legs, my distorted face. I knew I was ill, and that I was nothing but a heap of sweetly rotting manure. The very humus I am made of was a mixture of bad perfume and salt. Yes, my days were numbered, and my defeat, the defeat of my own will, would see the rise to omnipotence of the Meneses. The truth, Nina, it's the simple truth."

He fell silent, breathing hard. Then, drawing up a stool and sitting down beside me, he went on:

"I knew what was devouring me. I knew that the smell of decomposing jasmine in this room was the smell of my own cowardice. It was the absence of fever, my unimpugnable heart. It was my whole white, futile self. I would look at my white hands, my white feet, my white flesh—and a cold, pitiless wave of nausea would rise up within me. Ah, chastity is a terrible thing. Chastity, that is what was devouring me. Chaste hands, chaste feet, meek, chaste flesh. And I would weep, Nina, because nothing would ever set my blood on fire, and it was on this limp ruin that the Meneses were building the indestructible empire of their lie. Do you understand now why I wanted you, why I fantasized about your return, and why, sitting there, I so often talked with your absent self."

No, I could not honestly say that I did understand, because everything he said seemed to me the fruit of a delirium. I sensed an echo, a tremor that spoke to me of some old and, who knows, possibly genuine cause, but how to connect that wild monologue with our past conversations, a monologue, which, not being based on any logical fact, took for granted a unanimity that bound me to him, not intellectually, but through a shared feeling of revulsion that existed in some opaque area of my consciousness? Through my tears—because I was still crying—I told him that I felt the same, and he, in a sudden burst of enthusiasm, kissed my forehead and my hands. Perhaps I should not have lied to him, because he was counting on me for what he called "our pact"; perhaps I should have told him that I found his words obscure and meaningless. But even though I did not understand, in my mind I did agree, I somehow understood him without understanding, I felt I was on his side, even though I did not know what side that was.

Timóteo talked for a while longer, demanding that I tell him everything. And for some reason, Colonel, he was the first and only person I told about our friendship. I must have spoken with some affection, because he was touched. "You're so good, Nina, and how good that we have a friend!" he said more than once. When I had finished, he led me over to the window and drew back one corner of the curtain, so that the daylight fell full on my face.

"Ah," he cried, "so this is the rare being with whom ministers and colonels fall in love! I want to see her, I want to see her from close up, to touch her with my own hands, to be quite sure that she really is here by my side."

Holding back the curtain with one hand, he stroked my face with the other. There was nothing sensual about that gesture, it was more the meticulous pleasure that an artist takes in his work. He ran his fingers over my eyebrows, jaw, neck—and slowly slid his hand down to my throat.

"You are beautiful, still beautiful, very beautiful," he said with the grave satisfaction of a blind man who no longer fears being betrayed by reality.

Before me, I saw only that swollen face, which should have been expressionless, and yet which, at that moment, despite everything, was lit with the light of a concentrated fire. He released me with a sigh, at the same time allowing the curtain to fall:

"You must remain exactly as you are, Nina, to the despair of all men. Ah, how your beauty must make them suffer!"

In the darkness, he again gently ran his fingers over my closed lids, one last time:

"But come now, dry those tears; what is the use of them? Tears are very little valued in the world. Besides, a strong woman like you should never cry."

And saying this, he moved away. I saw him disappear into the shadows, leaving in his wake a vague scent of jasmine. I remained seated and, inexplicably, had the impression that he was sinking into an even greater darkness than before.

20.
André's Diary (iii)

4th – I knew I could not ask about her, that no one would tell me anything, and yet she was the one thing that interested me. I could easily pretend not to care or, for the nth time, recount one of those hunting stories my father seemed to enjoy so much. (He would listen to me with more interest than usual, but his thoughts were clearly far away.) I could not, I felt, lie to myself though, and I knew that nothing, not the hunting trips, not my father, not my studies, were as important to me as my mother. On many nights, I lay awake, propped on one elbow, imagining what she would have been like—tall, fat, blonde, or dark. I had never seen a picture of her, no one had ever spoken to me about her looks. And what did it matter what she had looked like? All that mattered was the mystery shrouding her life. They all pretended and lied and changed the subject whenever I went into the drawing room—in vain. I knew there was a secret, and that only intensified my curiosity because, despite their silence and despite her name being like a dead object in our house, everything I touched, everywhere I went, the garden, the verandah, it all spoke of her. She had existed, she had lived in that same atmosphere, and everything had witnessed her passing. Again and again, leaning on the railings around the verandah, I would gaze up at the sky and think to myself that, in another time—precisely when I did not know—she must have done exactly the same and, staring up at the blue as I was now, felt the same pleasure.

I remember, when I was still only small, opening a cupboard that was, at least tacitly, forbidden territory, and finding myself wrapped in a strange, sweet perfume, which soon impregnated the whole room. I bent down and started rummaging around among the things filling the wardrobe: I pulled out various unfamiliar items of clothing, doubtless thrown in there as being of no further use. Remembering the whispers I had heard about Uncle Timóteo, my first thought was that these things must belong to him. I was quietly continuing my investigations, when my father came in, alerted, above all, by the perfume filling the room. He leaned on a chest of drawers and I, hearing a noise, turned and saw him there, saw how terribly pale he was, as if he were about to faint. Thinking that he must be feeling dizzy, I went to help him, but he held up one hand to stop me. I stood, frozen, in the middle of the room, still clutching bits of clothing and studying him with a joy in which there was a considerable dose of mischief. I was thinking of all the things that had been kept hidden from me, and looking at that shadow of a man, I realized that I had finally stumbled upon the very heart of the secret. I slowly raised my hands to show him my plunder: everyone was constantly running away from those memories, but there they were for all to see, and rather than merely resurrecting the perfume of a dead woman, what I was showing him was the ineluctable evidence of a life. He could not bear to see this and covered his face with his hands. For some time, he appeared to surrender himself to the great tide of memories washing over him—deep inside him, they must have been still throbbing and vivid and dripping blood. He lowered his hand, and while his distraught face clearly revealed how much he was suffering, he was completely oblivious to everything around him, as if, at that moment, nothing else existed. Like someone carefully observing a strange phenomenon, I took two steps forward, and only then did he look up, and a faint moan emerged from his lips.

"Oh, it's you! How long have you been there?"

I was about to respond, but instead I raised my arm higher and showed him the clothes I was holding. He stared at them again, without, at first, understanding, then a kind of horrified shudder ran through him and, as if I were offering him some truly repellent object, he asked:

"Where did you find *that*?"

"In the bottom of the wardrobe," I said.

"Put it back," he ordered. "And don't go looking in there again." He hesitated, then in a steadier voice, added: "Unless you want to be punished."

He rarely spoke to me in that stern manner. I went back to the wardrobe, threw the clothes inside and closed the door—but I did not leave the room. I stood there, my whole rebellious being burning with a single question: Why? Why? We remained like that for a while, until I sensed that he had calmed down. Standing there, he looked smaller, more vulnerable. His silent rage had vanished, and what lay between us now was a sense of terrible desolation. There was no point in saying anything, because all words were meaningless, apart from the one word that interested me—and he knew that. For the first time, we were being open with each other, and in his eyes, I had ceased to be a small ignorant child and had become, instead, a possible judge. I looked at him again, so that he would not forget that moment. Keeping my eyes firmly trained on him, I raised my fingers to my nose and breathed in the perfume still clinging to them. That way he would know that my mother did still exist, and that her presence was still there between us. He must have understood this, because he allowed me to walk past him in silence and, in silence, to go out into the hallway and from there into the drawing room.

I don't know how long I wandered about the house, bound to a presence I did not even know. The places, the objects, even the people seemed closer somehow. When the first lights came on, I was still struggling to retain that perfume, which was already fast disappearing, like a color absorbed into the night. I was once again on my own.

7th – Today, Betty and I were together in my room, looking out of the window, and the sky was more beautiful than ever. The garden was bright with moonlight, and the shadow cast by the house reached as far as the tree-lined path. Amid the surrounding peace and the serene light, I fixed my thoughts on her, only her, like someone drowning in an absent love. Oblivious to everything else, I tried to recreate the time when she had walked those sandy paths, immersed in unknown dreams and hopes. So intense were these imaginings that I thought I could see a figure moving about near the flower beds. My heart beat faster, and hot tears filled my eyes. I spun around to face Betty and asked in an urgent voice:

"Why does no one ever talk to me or say anything about her? What happened, what did she do, why do they keep everything hidden from me?"

Betty looked embarrassed and avoided my gaze. Seeing her so distressed and noticing that her eyes, too, were fixed on the garden, I imagined for a moment that perhaps her thoughts were not so very different from mine.

"Speak to me, Betty," I went on, shaking her. "You must tell me what happened. You have no right to keep it from me!"

This was the first time I had questioned her so directly; up until now, however frustrated I felt, I had made do with her silences and the occasional escapes from the house that she afforded me. There must have been something in my attitude that told her this situation was at an end. Or perhaps in the grip of one of those impulses peculiar to people of a generous nature, and which occur almost against their will, she had reached the conclusion that it was only right and just that I should be told the truth. I know only that, in the face of my earnest pleading, her usual stiffness melted, and poor Betty stood before me, trembling, as if she had been caught committing some grave misdemeanor. When I saw this, I softened my voice, but still spoke firmly:

"Tell me, Betty. One day, I will have to be told everything."

Again, she averted her gaze, saying:

"I can't, André, I can't."

"Why not?"

Her voice became faint as a sigh:

"I promised . . . I swore . . . a long time ago."

"Who did you swear to, Betty?"

"To your father."

There was a pause, during which I tried in vain to catch her eye. Betty was driven more by duty and by the fact that she had sworn an oath than by a genuine feeling that she should not talk about the tumultuous memories filling her mind. I did not need to ask again, for she began then to speak, and her soft voice gradually unfolded before me the panorama I had so often dreamed about.

She could no longer remember when it was exactly that my mother had left. One evening, she was sitting beside my cradle when my father came in, shutting the door behind him.

"Ah, it's you, Senhor Valdo!" she had said.

He had grown very thin and he stood beside her in silence, staring down into the cradle. After a while, he had sighed and gestured to Betty to follow him:

"I need to talk to you, Betty."

They had both left the room and, once in the hallway, he had pressed her against the wall. What he had to say was very serious and required all her attention. Betty nodded. Then, slightly awkwardly, he asked if she had heard about or even witnessed certain strange incidents that had taken place at the Chácara. Yes, she had, she said, and had been most surprised by some of what she had heard. Senhor Valdo placed one hand on her shoulder: that was precisely it. He needed her to swear, and to swear on whatever was most sacred to her, that she would never, ever, under any circumstances, mention to the child now sleeping in that room the name of the woman who had been his wife. He wanted the boy to know nothing about her, not even that she had existed. Betty had duly sworn by the thing most sacred to her—the memory of her mother. And she had never broken her oath: if she was doing so now—may her late mother forgive her—it was because André was no longer a child.

When she finished this account, she turned to me, her eyes brimming with tears:

"Do you understand now why I cannot possibly . . ."

Yes, I understood, but the pain overwhelming me was no less intense for that. I moved away from the window and fell onto the bed. There was no point in trying to hide, in burying my face in the pillow: there they were, the same obsessive questions: Who was she, where was she, and what great sin had she committed? No one would answer me: outside, the sandy paths glittered in the moonlight. My one consolation was to think that, once, she might well have walked that path, not distracted or absent, but with a heart as heavy as mine.

9th – Today I had one of the biggest surprises of my life. I was on the verandah, cleaning the barrel of a rifle, when my father came over to me.

For reasons I had never attempted to understand, there had always been a certain awkwardness, a certain unease between us. He was not the most expansive of people and usually kept his distance, and for my part, I never liked him enough to make him my friend. I did as I was told and even satisfied some of his whims. In the matter of sports, for example, I took up whatever interests he advised, even though they went contrary to my true nature. I collected all the rifles and shotguns he gave me, but never fell in love with hunting. I accepted his gifts in order to please him, because as he always said, firstly, any boy born into the Meneses family had to practice a sport and, secondly, any normal adolescent should take part in some violent game if he wasn't to turn into a spineless creature like Uncle Timóteo. However, the truth is that, although I became a reasonably good shot, I never really enjoyed hunting, much to my father's disappointment.

"It's good to see you engaged on such manly tasks," he said.

"I like to keep it well oiled," I answered, thinking that, as on so many other occasions, the conversation would end after that banal exchange. I was wrong though, because he stayed where he was and continued to watch me work, as if he found the task deeply interesting. Troubled by his continued presence, I removed the ramrod from the barrel and was about to put everything away, when he said:

"Could you spare me a moment?"

Only then did I realize that he had not come simply to watch me maintaining my rifle. I put it down on the edge of the verandah and looked at him: he seemed paler than usual. His usually frowning face betrayed some secret fear.

"I have something very sad to tell you, my son," he said with a sigh.

He pointed to the wicker chairs and invited me to sit by his side. I obeyed and my heart began to pound in much the same way as certain atmospheric changes indicate an approaching storm. We sat down, and he stared into space for a moment, as if trying to dredge up some fact from his memory, or searching for a way to begin the conversation. We were sitting so close that our knees were almost touching, and I was able to examine him in detail, and he really did seem much older, with lines around his eyes. "My father," I was thinking, searching my mind to see if, somewhere deep inside me, there was even a remnant of some tender feeling. I felt nothing, my heart was silent and indifferent. I certainly did not consider him to be a monster, but neither could I forget how I had been brought up, without any show of affection, and handed over entirely to Betty's care. Ana, with whom I spoke one day, told me that I had not been born at the Chácara, and that she, on my father's orders, had gone to Rio de Janeiro to fetch me. I found this odd and wanted to know more details, but, as if regretting that untimely confession, she immediately reverted to her usual mute state. So not even my birth had aroused his interest; he had not even been the one to bring me to the Chácara, and I was horrified now by those events that had shaped me—I don't mean having been born far from here, but being brought back to the Chácara instead of being allowed to remain with my mother. Had he just realized this, was he hoping to make up for that deception, was this an attempt to get closer to me? I felt this would be a vain enterprise, and that even if he did make the effort, we would simply become still more alien to each other.

"I see you're planning another hunting trip," he began, like someone finally determined to take the bull by the horns.

"No, I'm not," I said. "I was just cleaning this particular rifle."

"That's a shame," he said, "because you going off on a little hunting trip now would suit me perfectly."

"Why's that?" I asked, studying his face in the hope of uncovering his real feelings.

"Because . . ."

He stopped, and I could see that he was waging an inner battle. For a while, he sat with eyes downcast, perhaps trying to find the right words to express his reasons—the reasons of a proud man, who never normally had to justify his preferences or desires.

"Because it's necessary, André, that's all," he said abruptly. "Don't ask me why, because I can't tell you right now, but I need you to stay away from the house for one or two days."

This was the first time he had ever spoken to me in that almost pleading tone. It was the first time, too, that I had seen him almost humbly admitting that his motives were not entirely fair. Then a flash of intuition lit up my mind, and it was so quick, so bright, that I sprang to my feet:

"Is it her?" I asked.

And then without waiting for a response:

"It is, I'm sure of it. It's to do with her."

He looked at me in amazement, and I feared for a moment that he might withdraw into his customary reserve. However, this time, he nodded slowly:

"Yes, it is to do with her."

What other words did we need, what other possible explanations or explications could there be? A sudden feeling of serenity took hold of me, and I said:

"Then I won't go, Father, I won't go hunting."

He continued to study me as if he were thinking: "So that's how it is, is it? She means that much to him."—and he showed no surprise at all. He, too, stood up and took a few steps about the verandah, his hands behind his back. The deep frown line between his eyebrows seemed to indicate that he was searching for some way of resolving the matter. Finally, he turned to where I stood waiting.

"If you think I want to stop you from seeing her, you're wrong. All I'm asking for is a little time."

"So she is coming, then?" and my voice died in my throat.

"She is."

He hesitated, then went on.

"I think she may even be coming back for good."

In that case, what did I care about a breathing space of two or three days, or even a month, when I had already waited all those years? And when I made as if to speak, unable to contain the throng of feelings inside me, he told me to say nothing, because he was going to explain everything. In fits and starts, struggling to find the right word and often failing, he said he had forgiven a past full of errors, and that she would soon be back home. He was worried about our first meeting because it would inevitably trigger all kinds of emotions, and she was, as he understood it, still very weak. This was why things needed to be handled very carefully. He said, too, that, according to the letter he had received, she was suffering from a grave illness, which is why he had agreed to forgive her. He wanted at least one day's respite so that Nina—and when he spoke that name, his voice faltered—could readapt to the house and to the situation. If I was in agreement, then I should go off on a hunting trip that would last just long enough for her to settle in. He was counting on my good sense and understanding, to protect an already frail person from a succession of emotional shocks.

That, at least, is what he said, but what did I care what he said? What did anything matter, as long as she was, at last, about to arrive? The time was approaching when all barriers would fall, all oaths be broken, and I could finally satisfy my curiosity—no, what am I saying, my passion. When we were alone, and that ineffable moment would surely come, I would tell her that I had known her for a long time and had always felt her presence around me. I had never been deceived by the silence of the others and knew that their thoughts were equally full of memories of her, and that the house itself, its stones and pillars, had only remained standing because she had once lived there. My father must have sensed the turmoil inside me, because his eyes were following the changing expressions on my face with a mixture of unease and astonishment.

"Do you swear . . . swear that she will never again leave us?"

He replied very simply, in a voice of total surrender:

"I swear."

Then I didn't mind leaving or even forgetting about her for a few hours, knowing that when I returned, she would be eternally there to quench my thirst for her presence.

"Don't worry, I will go hunting," I said.

He held out his hand:

"Thank you."

He stood up, and I felt that he could not forgive the joy in my eyes, which despite myself, revealed an intensity of feeling that had sprung up in secret and spread its roots throughout my whole being.

10th – I left at dawn, having said that I preferred to go alone and without a servant. When she heard this, Betty came out into the garden to tell me to be very careful with the gun and not to venture too far into the wilds. I promised her that I would not be going for a long ride, and then, without a backward glance, I spurred on my horse and rode off like a man in flight. I wanted to be alone with my own thoughts. Giving my horse free rein, I took the path that led to Fundão. At that early hour, the thicker vegetation still lay in shade, although here and there, the pools I passed were already glittering in the pale pink morning light. Above me, the sky was still dark, and Venus was guiding me with her silken blue glow. "This is the last time that planet will shine on me in her absence," I thought. And this prompted me to take up the reins again and ride more quickly, as if that would make the time pass faster.

Two or three huts emerged out of the mist and familiar voices greeted me. I had ridden by there so often and yet never before had I felt my heart beating as it did then, as if this were the first time I had noticed the harsh reality of country life, and it touched my heart. (*Written in the margin of the diary*: This all happened years ago, those huts no longer exist, and the valley is dry and barren. From this hill I can see the whole of Campo da Cruz Vazia; I peer through the mist—the mist at least hasn't changed—looking for traces of the adolescent I was then and I feel nothing, hear nothing, see nothing, because my heart is no longer light, and not even the purity that once was mine can bring back the sweet music of that moment.)

Riding on, I saw before me the trees laden with blossom and mistletoe, the white ginger lilies—and I imagined making a bouquet of all these things and placing it at her feet, as a homage from the countryside. She probably liked flowers, and so on some mornings, I would ride out, exploring the caves and the hillsides in search of rare specimens. Or else we would go together and she would ride ahead of me, while I, filled with pride, would glance at any passersby as if to say: "She's my mother."

The parakeets and the saracuras would fly happily about and dazzle the woods with the flapping of their wings. The nightlife in the heart of the marshland would be abuzz with joy. And I would not raise my rifle against that life, not because I respected it, but because, since the arrival of my mother, nothing else mattered to me. I don't know if this is how other people experience love, if they all feel like this about their mothers, but for me it was something unique and all-consuming, something that absorbed every ounce of warmth and will. And besides, what did I care about what others felt? As far as she was concerned, it was that thirst that had always driven me on, even if it was only now that I knew for sure it had not been in vain, that I had not squandered my love on a ghost. What did the others and their reasons matter?

I felt full of energy, I knew that the world was waiting for me, my whole being was as alive and vibrant as if a clarion call were echoing through it. Nothing else existed, nothing else counted but my fever, and so I set my horse galloping ever faster along paths and tracks, over plains white with dew; in the distance, the tops of mountains were waking to the dawn, while everything inside me was dawning too, and the day was becoming ever brighter, slipping into my inner self—and I rode faster still, my horse drenched in sweat, its mane flying, and I felt sure there was little difference between my sun and the one lighting up the landscape.

....

At last I saw her. It was already dark by the time I arrived home the following day. When I reached the garden, I could see through the tangle of foliage that the verandah light was on. A very dim light which was never usually lit, even on really important occasions. "It's her," I thought, advancing through the leaves as cautiously as a hunter following a trail. Farther on, I noticed that the main drawing room door stood open, although there seemed to be no one on the verandah. I crept up the steps and suddenly I saw her, she was lying, very still, in the hammock. She had her faced turned so that it rested on one of her arms and her eyes were closed, although it was clear that she was not asleep. I leaned against one of the pillars and stopped to look at her. She was not the creature I had imagined, she was paler, more languid, and much older than I had expected. At one point, she set the hammock swinging, moving her arm and letting her head loll back. Then, when the light fell on her throat and the curve of her breasts, emotion overwhelmed me. What strange sorrow pierced me? I tried to get a clearer look—and realized that the sudden feeling of pity rising up in me was provoked not by what was there before my eyes, but by the atmosphere surrounding her. She was a beautiful woman, of that there was no doubt, a woman who, above all, *had* been beautiful, and yet she appeared to be carrying a secret guilt, some stigma that seemed to forbid her human company. (*Written in the margin of the diary*: Only much later did I understand this; at that moment, she seemed like an island, complete and inaccessible, swept by winds that were not of our world. She could get up, talk, and even laugh as others laughed, but some force separated her from other people and created around her a troubling field of light from which she was constantly reaching out to those who passed.) I drew back, my heart pounding. I had never seen such a solitary, needy creature, desperate for affection or for male attention. So powerful was this impression that, for a while, I could not move—meanwhile, the night, with its myriad stars, boomed around me.

When I finally summoned up the courage to move, she started and opened her eyes and sat on the edge of the hammock. The atmosphere slowly dissipated, like a threat retreating into the shadows.

"Who's there?" she asked.

I moved closer, not daring to respond. She came to meet me:

"You're André, aren't you?"

"Yes, I'm André."

"I knew it," she said, and there was such certainty in her voice that I stared at her in astonishment.

She gazed at me from out of her world, as if wanting to lessen the distance between us. And without another word, she took my hand and made me sit down beside her.

21.
André's Diary (iv)

10th – I spent the whole night awake, still under the influence of that first meeting. Leaning at the window, eyes wide open to the darkness, I was turning over, one by one, the words I had heard, remembering the sound of her voice, the light in her eyes, her gestures, all the elements, in short, that formed her presence. They were certainly not the words I had hoped to hear, nor those I had dreamed of hearing during the long years of waiting, but they were as full of warmth and tenderness and sympathy as I had imagined they would be. There was also a touch of inexplicable anxiety, and sometimes I even felt that she was having to make a real effort to surface and to utter the banal words essential to human relationships, as if some dense, magnetic force in the very depths of her nature were holding her back. I was the only person awake in the house, and I went over and over what she had said, which was really very little, a few simple words of affection, the occasional more personal question or fond observation. It was not what I had so anxiously been waiting for, and which seemed to fit the image forged by my imagination and gleaned from what other people had told me. No, but what did this matter given that she actually existed and had sat by my side, and I could touch her, as one can touch those things that are closest and most sensitive? The day might come when she would say the words I was hoping for; the moment might come when I could fully understand the mystery that was there in her consciousness. Until then, it was enough to know that she was only a few steps away from me. If I got up and went to her bedroom door and pressed my ear to it, I might even hear her breathing, and if I called, she would rush to my side, alarmed, smoothing back her disheveled hair with one hand. What more could an impassioned heart like mine desire?

I was listening in the dark to the ticking of the clock, and it sounded different to me, as if it were marking off the minutes of a new life. I remembered how, in the garden, abandoning her apparent aloofness, she had suddenly taken my head in her hands, fixed her eyes on mine, and with a strange tremor in her voice, said: "My son, my son!" And strange though it may seem, it was as if those were words of love; not the words mothers usually say to their sons, but the words women reserve for the object of their passion. My hand does not tremble when I write this, no remorse clouds my conscience; indeed, I cannot imagine how else to describe the feelings that bound us together in that embrace. There was such torment in her face, and her words were like the cry of a helpless, wounded animal. I don't know why, but almost without my realizing it, my eyes filled with tears.

11th – I saw her again, quite suddenly, and almost without my expecting it. I say "almost" because ever since she entered this house, I have lived in a state of permanent expectation. So it would not be true to say that I was not expecting to meet her, on the contrary, I went looking for her all over the house, following the sound of voices I could not identify, peering through windows and around doors and even following the trail of the perfume she left behind her. It was a strange perfume, I'm not sure if I have mentioned it before—a bit like the scent of violets, but mingled with some kind of human essence that somehow diluted it and made it less banal. I knew very little of such things, but I imagined that it was a truly feminine perfume, the kind I had read about in novels as being characteristic of romantic heroines. Perhaps the image I created for myself of the woman wearing that perfume was slightly bookish, but I liked that, because the warm scent marked her off as quite different from the other women I knew. That is what I was thinking when I saw her before me, standing motionless in the drawing room, as if she were waiting for someone. She was leaning against the sideboard where Demétrio displayed what remained of the family heirlooms, and she was somewhat distractedly and indifferently examining the various objects, as if they had no meaning for her apart from their existence as mere domestic items. As soon as she saw me, she cried:

"André!" and there was no mistaking the joy in her voice.

I was troubled by that encounter, as unexpected as it was desired; the words got stuck in my throat. She guessed what was happening and drew me over to the sofa:

"André," she said tenderly, "where have you been hiding all this time?"

"I've been looking for you," I answered, and an image flashed into my mind: her looking for me, while I was wretchedly pursuing her. It's extraordinary, there was nothing wrong with a mother looking for her son like that or a son looking for his mother, and despite that, we seemed to be under some kind of spell, as if there were something reprehensible about our behavior.

"You were looking for me!" and as if she were grateful to me for that, she took my hand in hers and squeezed it. "How kind you are, André. Ah, if you knew how much I love you . . ."

(*Written in the margin, in a different colored ink*: How much truth was there in what she said, what was it about her earnestness that failed to communicate any real enthusiasm, and what exactly did she intend by those words? I don't know now and I didn't know then. Only one thing seems certain: at the time, she was struggling to readapt to the rhythm of life at the Chácara, and anything, any show of friendship, was like a piece of wreckage to cling to. It did not much matter if it was me, but it was almost better that it was. She needed an anchor, a safe mooring post, given the hostility surrounding her, from the monotony which, despite her best efforts, she found utterly unbearable, to the memory of past events, which she had hoped to drown in the depths of her consciousness, but which, with every minute, kept muscling their way up into her thoughts and even—why deny it?—into her flesh.)

"Don't leave me," she said in a soft, pleading voice, and she looked at me for the first time and for the first time made me feel that she was actually looking at me sitting there beside her, and not at a ghost. "Don't leave me. If you knew everything that was going on here . . ."

I think the kind of relationship we formed was influenced by the feeling of intense insecurity she gave off; indeed, from that very moment, a sense of pity, like a permanent mist, began to grow inside me, a pity I could no longer disguise. Ah, poor, strange woman, what was the sin she dared not reveal and that made her tremble before her enemies, and which I did not even need her to reveal to me in order to guarantee her all my support and all my love?

Still with my hand in hers, she went on:

"Now, no one can steal you away from me. We know each other, we know who we are. And you must tell me what you've been up to, where you've been. I want to know everything. A son should have no secrets from his mother."

I found the straightforward tone in which she said these words quite extraordinary—it was as if she were both doing herself a violence and expressing a tenderness, a concern that she either did not really feel or kept carefully preserved beneath a layer of excessive shame. Then, abruptly, she fell silent. (Did I already mention that we were sitting on the sofa in the drawing room? The light was fairly dim, kept out by the curtains. I could still see her eyes, though, and they continued to scrutinize me, and I was so shocked by the genuine anxiety and affliction I saw in them that the blood rushed to my face.

There was something about the whole situation that defied common sense—this could not possibly be the usual way in which mothers spoke to their sons.)

"Please don't look at me like that," I said.

"Why not?" and letting go of my hand, she tried to create a more normal atmosphere.

I shrugged, and for a while we sat in silence, unable to shake off the feeling of constraint that wrapped about us. Gradually, the room grew darker. On the sideboard, the silverware gleamed dully. Suddenly, as if she had made a decision, she put one hand about my neck and drew me toward her, meanwhile saying very tenderly:

"Little fool. I bet you've always been a little fool . . ."

I tried to pull away, unable to interpret that gesture; and when she did not release her grip, but began stroking my hair with her free hand, I felt afraid, and for the first time wondered if perhaps she was not quite right in the head. She felt me trying to draw back, but, instead of letting go, she tightened her grip, saying:

"Don't move away, don't be afraid."

"I'm not afraid," I said, despite my deep unease.

Then she leaned forward and kissed my forehead and my cheeks:

"I want you to promise me something. I want you to swear . . ."

I could still feel those warm moist lips on my skin:

"I swear," I stammered, astonished at her intensity of feeling.

"No, don't swear anything, at least not now."

She did let go then, and when I looked at her again, I saw that her eyes were full of tears. It was my turn to take her hands in mine—and I was amazed at my own audacity.

"If there's something wrong . . . if you need me . . ."

"One of these nights," she said, "I'll come to your room and then, if you like, we can talk."

She was already standing up when she said these words. I thought perhaps I should say something, just to keep her there, but I saw that it would be pointless: she had not really seen me, had not really recognized me, except for a fraction of a second, and had now moved off again into that distant place of which I knew nothing, and which was reflected in her eyes like the memory of some underwater world. Any attempt on my part to get closer would be utterly futile. Without a word or gesture of farewell, she left as suddenly as she had arrived.

I stayed where I was, feeling as if I had been abandoned forever or as if some element that was very dear to me, essential even, had dissolved inside my heart. I sat on in the dark for some time, then slumping forward onto the sofa, I burst into tears. I had never felt as unhappy as I did at that moment.

12th – Every detail of last night's scene keeps running through my mind. I don't know why I reacted like that, whether it was anger or merely my response to the terrible strangeness of everything. I only know that, unable to control the emotional confusion within, I lay there sobbing for some time, leaving the sofa wet with tears. I say "confusion" because there is no other word for what was going on inside me; I had no idea what I wanted or what anyone else wanted. As I lay there, I felt as though something were flowing out of me, carrying me along like a hidden, boundless river, making of me a different person, full of nameless contradictions. Perhaps I was growing up or had simply outgrown the childish being I had been up until then. Life seemed touched by a new meaning, dense and obscure: the boy taking on that new shape was doing so with an awareness entirely novel to me. There was no vanity in this, only a certainty that I would now have to face up to the obstacles awaiting me like a man, and experience the hard task of living and continuing to live despite all the little deaths that would inevitably occur as I came into collision with life's events. It was only when I became aware of someone else's presence that I emerged from these thoughts. In the secret hope that they had not seen me, I stayed where I was, my head buried in my arms. However, that person came and placed a hand on my shoulder. I turned: it was Betty. I tried to push her angrily away and again hid my face, but she forced me to look up and anxiously examined my face:

"What's a boy like you doing crying like this!"

All I could say was:

"Oh, Betty!"

And pressing my face to her bosom, I began to cry again, as if, far from comforting me, those words had only increased my despair. She silently stroked my hair and that tender gesture somehow made matters worse, because I hated being or having been a child; and while my tears diminished, long shudders still ran through my body. I felt too exhausted even to raise my head. We stayed like that for some time, and when, with a sigh, I finally looked up, night had fallen and the shadows in the room had grown still more impenetrable.

"A boy like you!" Betty said again and she appeared to have no other words with which to express her displeasure, shaking her head and looking at me reprovingly.

Now that we were in almost total darkness, she could not see the traces of tears on my face nor understand how very weak I was. And I confess, my pain was so great, I felt so alone and helpless before the problem looming before me, that I really did not care about anything else—whether good or bad, whether she could see me or not, and I quailed before facts whose real dimension was quite beyond me. Only one thing was sure, I had just made a discovery, one that I judged to be so very grave, so full of consequences for my future, that I could not hold back my tears—and it was that discovery that had surfaced inside me and revealed a terrain I had never known to exist, but which could well be the stepping-off point into the most dangerous of feelings. It was that vision perhaps that made me again press my head to Betty's bosom, and she again began silently stroking my hair. Then in a very low voice, she said:

"It was her, wasn't it?"

I nodded. She must have understood, because I heard her sigh and say:

"Never mind. Everything passes."

She was about to say something else, some further words of consolation, when I, giving in to the heavy weight on my heart, exclaimed:

"It was so strange, Betty. She was talking to me and looking at me as if I wasn't there. I didn't even understand what she was saying. It was as though there was someone else in my place or as if she was talking to someone other than me."

"And is that what upset you so much?"

I shrugged, unable to find any other way of giving expression to my feelings.

"Yes, Betty, it was."

How could I explain how distressing I had found her sudden departure, her plunging off into some distant, all-absorbing place, a memory, a lost past, a painful image that never left her heart? Betty respected my silence and seemed to be thinking, gazing off into space, as if searching for the motives I could not find and never would, and with which I would always struggle vainly and desperately, like someone hurling himself against the shifting, insubstantial walls of mist. After a while, she stopped stroking my hair, sighed again, and said:

"There's no point thinking about these things, André. Maybe it was all in your imagination. Besides, your mother was always like that: if you had known her earlier, you wouldn't find it so very strange. Best forget all about it."

Then she stood up, bringing our conversation to a close with those sensible words. I remained where I was, unable to quiet my thoughts, my mind occupied by a single idea: *she* had promised to come to my bedroom one night.

22.
Letter from Valdo to Father Justino

. . . forgive me for writing to you like this, but I find myself in a state of the utmost perplexity. While I have never been much of a churchgoer, in the present circumstances, I know that neither a doctor nor even a friend could help me. And you, although not exactly a doctor, are accustomed to dealing with all manner of human ills—besides, you are an old friend of the family, a man whom my dear departed mother trusted implicitly. Even if that were not the case, there remains the incalculable gift of Christian charity, which must surely incline you to look with compassion on my wretched state ......

....

I don't know whether you have ever had the chance to meet my wife; she, too, has strayed from the Sacraments and from the Church. After being absent from our home for many years due to regrettable incidents entirely beyond my wishes or control, she has now returned on the pretext that she is gravely ill. After fifteen years, that was the only reason that could possibly move me. Since her arrival, however, I have discovered that she is not so very ill after all, and apart from looking slightly worn by time or, more likely, by her lifestyle (she was never a person of what one might call temperate habits), I have seen nothing that could have justified her returning in this manner. My brother, who played a decisive role in her departure, blames her return on my weak character. At first, I disagreed, but I am now beginning to wonder if he might not be right, as he usually is. And yet if you were to ask me precisely why I say this, I would be unable to give you an answer. Up until now, my wife has given me no reason to reproach her for her conduct. She behaves like any other normal person, walking, talking, going about her business—and yet, Father, there is about her something distinctly ambiguous, not to say dangerous. I cannot put my finger on what exactly it is, because it isn't anything specific. It is as if she were preparing some kind of revolution or attack, which one senses to be imminent, but without knowing exactly when it will be. She gives off an air of subversion, but I have no concrete evidence with which to confront her. There have been certain silences, certain omissions, one or two absences at key moments, yes, but that is hardly enough for me to make the kind of grave accusation I am making. How can I expose her without running the risk of accusing her of things that exist only in my imagination? And the truth is that it became apparent to me long ago that she was the carrier of a certain disease or, rather, that she behaved toward others in an arbitrary, cynical, or even, to put it bluntly, criminal manner. I can now easily believe that the passion we shared fifteen years ago was a mere product of the feelings she gives off. I don't know if these things can be said, if it is possible to accuse someone of such imponderables, but if I do so now, even against my will (for it reopens old wounds that have long since healed), it is because I foresee even graver situations, with possibly even more dramatic consequences than in the past. That woman will never stop, for the simple reason that she doesn't know how to; she is a loose cannon, a force of nature, and if we still lived in the dark days of the Inquisition, she would doubtless die at the stake. Yes, Father Justino, once again there is a storm brewing over the Chácara, and it is an agglomeration of all those wicked, aimless feelings that I see once again building up over the heads of innocent people ....

.... one of my concerns, before I gave my full consent to her return, was my son. Now him I'm sure you do know, and so it's easier for me to talk to you about him. He may, alas, have inherited a lot of his mother's character, because he shares those same wild, extravagant tendencies. He's a sensitive soul, for whom the world of fantasy counts more than reality. Many, many times I have warned him that this will be the cause of much suffering should the gifts of intelligence not come to his aid. I have of course limited myself to warning him, since true to his nature, he is strong-willed and extremely thin-skinned. Knowing his origins, and knowing, too, that some ills are incurable, I have tried to set him on the right path without wounding his sensibilities or inhibiting his natural spontaneity. My brother often said: "You're raising a savage." And to my shame, I have to admit that he has once again proved to be right.

The truth is that ever since I told the boy of his mother's return, I've noticed a marked change in his behavior. When I told him, he seemed to receive the news in an agitated, almost febrile way. There was a peculiar gleam in his eye, and I was aware that while I was speaking, there were questions he was burning to ask, but did not dare. What questions? Why? When he had never before heard a word about her. What sorcery was it that could cast its spell from so far away? My surprise was all the greater given that, since Nina's departure (I hope you don't mind if I call her by her name) I had forbidden anyone to speak to him about her. I kept my feelings of astonishment to myself, all the time pondering the possible consequences of her return.

I did not witness the climactic moment of their meeting, but I could imagine what must have occurred, knowing that my wife, despite a penchant for melodrama, was never much given to displays of emotion. Despite this, I saw the full impact of that encounter the next time I saw my son. The change, Father, was extraordinary. That spirited determination of his, which I had so admired as evidence of his self-control, was gone. Hesitant and pale, with dark circles under his eyes, he was the image of someone who had assumed the burden of some great sin. We were in the hallway, and when he saw me coming toward him, he pressed himself against the wall as if afraid. I had never before seen him do something like that. I quickened my pace and stopped in front of him. For a moment, we looked each other in the eye, and my gaze expressed not condemnation, but a desire to understand and forgive; his, however, was evasive and terrified, apparently struggling not to give away a possibly criminal secret. You may well think, Father, and with good reason, that I am exaggerating, and that I was being too hasty in drawing such conclusions when it could all have been mere happenstance. I too wondered about that, but subsequent facts, together with some more general observations, justify my saying all these things.

Nina had already been back with us for some time, and I had noticed that not only had *her* behavior changed, for she had become more silent and more restless, as certain animals do when danger approaches, but that my son's behavior was also becoming ever stranger and more rebellious. I considered it my duty to intervene, and spoke to him about it. He refused to be drawn and fled the room. On another occasion, I tried to grab him by the arm and he, who had never before dared to talk back to me, looked at me, eyes blazing, and said: "What gives you the right?" And I let him go, feeling slightly ashamed, as if the fact of being his father really did not entitle me to take such stern action. Indeed, I felt myself to be a stranger. (I know what she would think if she read these lines: "Jealousy, Valdo, your eternal jealousy." Perhaps that was the accusation I saw in my son's eyes. But then, Father, what is jealousy if not our desperate concern for those we hold dearest? How could I possibly abandon André to the rage and fury I felt was imminent?) If I had never really been what might be called a loving father, at least I had managed to establish with my son a relationship of mutual manly respect and honesty. Now, unexpectedly, I found myself cast in the role of enemy, excluded from all his interests and anxieties, little better than a stranger. I searched in vain for a solution to the mystery. Or rather, although my intuition already knew, deep down, what was going on, I tried to run away from it, like a man fleeing from certain secret evils. But I could not equivocate for long, and I soon discovered what really lay behind all this. It was Nina, of course; and the corrupting influence of her personality—the same influence I had seen her deploy so cunningly and seductively in the past—was beginning to take hold around me. At that moment, Father, I trembled from head to foot, for I understood full well the peril my son was in. And it was then that I glimpsed the full extent of my mistake. For there could be no doubt about it, I had made a mistake, and a terrible one at that. Nina should never have returned. You may suspect, Father, another reason for my pounding heart; that I was troubled by something I did not even dare confess to myself; that not all my feelings had died and that I did still love her, perhaps as much as I had loved her in the early days. And I would deny this, and say that I feared only for the safety of the young adolescent living under my roof. Nina is not to blame, I know; she may not even be aware of what she does, but evil is part of her nature, and everything about her gives off the unbearable stench of decay. How I must have loved that creature, in the days when I did love her, to be aware of these intimations of my own death and the possibility of my own destruction, and yet still embrace them! Or—and here I scarcely even have the courage to suggest it—might it not be precisely the vision of my own death that had held me in thrall to her? And yet, despite all this, I found myself unable to make the slightest gesture; frozen, vanquished. Once again, I would have to witness all the conflicts provoked by her presence, and once again I would have to watch the drama swirling around my door, unable to do anything to prevent it, like some helpless victim who has brought about his own downfall.

I think it was my keen sense of what was going on that led me to speak to Nina. It was nighttime, and she was getting ready for bed, wearing a dark dressing-gown, tied around her waist, that only emphasized the paleness of her skin. (Ah, Father, I must finally confess, since this letter is rather like a confession, that despite everything, and to my eternal misfortune, that woman has always exercised a pernicious influence over my senses. I was never able to look at her without a tremor of desire. Even now, after fifteen years of absence during which I imagined her defiled and sullied by the hands of others, the fire within her gone, burnt out, I still cannot look at her without a thrill of excitement, such is the power of her beauty and the feminine grace of her movements, even when disguised beneath a man's bulky dressing gown.) After watching her in silence, I went over to her:

"Nina," I said, "I want to talk to you."

She looked up at me, her face still utterly impassive. Would she, just from those few words, remember other similar situations and understand what was going through my mind? In any event, the mere thought of it made me freeze. She waited, her eyes fixed on mine. In response I sat down beside her and, trying to sound as sincere and sympathetic as I could, said:

"Nina, what I have to say is very difficult. Not least because there's no pleasant way of putting it."

I must have hesitated, and, seeing my discomfort, she smiled—not as a normal person might smile in such circumstances, but cynically, almost defiantly. Her attitude immediately made my blood boil (ah, we are so weak, Father!) and the words came out before I could stop them:

"Don't play games, Nina. This is serious. This time around I won't allow a repetition of what happened before."

Her expression changed, grew serious, and she gave me a hard look.

"What are you accusing me of?" she asked. "What have I done now?"

I hesitated again, not knowing how to express my thoughts. It was almost impossible to tell her, just like that, what I was accusing her of.

"It isn't exactly an accusation."

She eyed me warily.

"Coming from you it can only be an accusation. Well, come on, Valdo, I'm ready for anything."

I looked down and, beneath her half-open dressing gown, I could see her breasts trembling with emotion. This troubled me even more, and not only did the words escape me, but reason itself seemed to desert me, and I could no longer remember why it was I had come to see her. She was waiting calmly, alert to every flicker of emotion in my face. Then, painfully, realizing the ridicule I was exposing myself to, I stammered:

"My son . . ."

At these words she stood up, as if touched by an electric current. I raised my head and saw the fire in her eyes, her body tense as if ready to lash out in defense.

"Is there nothing you would not stoop to, Valdo?"

All I could say, almost in a whisper, was:

"And you, Nina . . . is there nothing you would not stoop to?"

She tugged at her robe and drew herself up in a gesture of anger or pride—and that simple movement offended me more than any words. It was almost a modest gesture, and I had assumed her to be beyond all modesty.

"Are fifteen years not enough to drown your jealousy?" she said with bitter irony. "And after all the wrong you did me, it's not *your* son, but *our* son who . . ."

What she was suggesting did not bear repeating and, succumbing to the outrage she felt, whether justifiably or not, she turned her back on me, and leaning on the tall chest of drawers, she began to cry. From the bed, where I remained seated, I watched her body shaken by sobs, and to my surprise I found that it did not move me as much as I might have expected; watching her, I asked myself whether this might not just be another of her performances.

"I am not exactly accusing you, Nina," I replied after a pause. "I just want you to tread carefully. André is still a child."

She turned to face me, her eyes full of tears:

"But what exactly are you suggesting? No, Valdo, I can't imagine you capable of such monstrous thoughts."

When she turned, her robe had come loose again, and it fell open slightly to reveal the curve of her breast. You may well wonder if this was her final, desperate bid to seduce me.

"And yet . . ." I added coldly.

"No," she cried, hurling herself at me, "this is all your jealousy, your horrible jealousy. That's what's driving you, making you suspect even your own son. Ah, if only I'd known!"

And she fell onto the bed, sobbing. She clawed at the crumpled bedspread and, strangely, she seemed to be not so much in the throes of grief as of unbridled pleasure. Then, gradually, she calmed down and fell asleep. I took one last look at her body stretched out on the bed, my mind troubled by ideas of various sorts; seeing her lying there, so defenseless, I couldn't bring myself to hate her. I tiptoed out of the room and went to lie down in the hammock on the verandah.

So that's how our conversation ended that night, Father. It is also everything I know. However, once I had recovered from my momentary agitation, neither her tears nor her behavior convinced me of anything. I see my son becoming ever more restless and withdrawn, and yet have not one piece of evidence to incriminate her. Perhaps it really is just a figment of my imagination; perhaps I still suffer from that lingering, poisoned residue of jealousy. In both these matters, only you can advise me, no one else. I have reached the point where I can no longer solve anything myself: I lack both the necessary clarity of mind and the impartiality. I shall anxiously await your letter or your visit here to the Chácara. It is the uncertainty that torments me most, for that woman can make one doubt everything, even reality.

23.
Betty's Diary (iv)

26th – A pig was slaughtered yesterday, and the black servants were busy in the kitchen preparing sausages. I went to chivvy them along because Senhor Demétrio always complains that the smell of fried pork-fat gives him a headache. The maids were standing around three large wooden troughs, their hands deep in the soft meat—and the usually quiet kitchen seethed with laughter and chatter, while Anastácia, whose sight was already failing, was seated on a stool before a basin of warm water, cleaning the intestines. I sat down with her, and it was then that I received a message saying that Senhor Valdo was asking for me. Since he never normally asked for me, and since I was not normally to be found engaged in such domestic tasks, I thought it odd, and, for some reason, felt a touch annoyed. However, I was just about to go looking for him, when he appeared at the kitchen door. At the sight of the servants working away, he hesitated, looking somewhat sheepish, as if he had committed some fault deserving of reproof. But seeing that I was occupied, he came over to me, all the time glancing furtively around him.

"Betty, has my brother been in here?"

"Senhor Demétrio never comes into the kitchen," I said quietly, while the black servants, noticing him for the first time, very slightly lowered their voices.

"Did you want to talk to me about something?" I asked.

"I did," and there was an almost pleading look in his eyes.

"If you'll just wait a moment . . ." and I had already begun taking off my apron, when he said:

"No, no, Betty, there's no need for that. We can talk right here."

He glanced around him and noticed, at one end of the room, the large pine table where the servants usually took their meals.

"Let's go over there," he said, pointing at the table.

I imagined the comments this would provoke.

"But Senhor Valdo!" I cried.

"What's wrong? At least no one can accuse us of hiding."

He was right, and so we went over to the table, which, as well as being away from the other servants, was closer to the smoking, crackling fire.

"Are you sure the smoke doesn't bother you, sir?" I asked, perching on the end of one of the benches.

"No, not at all," he said, "Besides, what I have to say won't take long."

He sat down on the same narrow bench worn smooth by all the many servants who had sat there in the past, and which gave the rough-hewn seat a human dignity it had lacked before. Seeing him sitting there, saying nothing and drumming his fingers on the cracked wood of the tabletop, I started talking, in an attempt to break the awkward silence. I said that, lately, Senhor Demétrio had been conspicuous by his absence, not just from the kitchen, but from the hallway, the drawing room and any of the other rooms too. (I kept to myself most of the other things I had noticed, namely, Senhor Demétrio's increased irritability and nervousness. He wore a permanent frown and was displeased with everything, as if nothing in the house was right. I had even caught him sniffing the air, as though sensing the imminent arrival of some misfortune—and symptomatic of these changes was that he and his wife—who usually kept well away from each other, so much so that they were rarely seen together—now appeared to have found a common enemy and thus a reason to join forces and support each other. It did not take much imagination to guess who that enemy might be, and so it was hardly a surprise when, one day, out in the hallway, I heard Demétrio saying: "Ana, from now on, I want my meals sent to my room." She merely nodded and said nothing. But he added, with a sigh: "We are living through dark days, Ana, and who knows how it will all end." Dona Ana did not answer, but her attitude could not have been more eloquent. It was impossible not to see her reserved manner as a distillation of the Chácara's long tradition of disapproval. I could have told Senhor Valdo this too, but felt this would be anticipating matters and so I kept quiet, waiting for a better opportunity.)

When I finished speaking, he nodded thoughtfully:

"So you haven't seen him, Betty?" Then stroking his chin, he said in a quieter tone. "It's never a good sign when my brother disappears."

"Why don't you go and knock on his door?"

He did not answer, but from the look he gave me, I could tell that he was trying to win my trust. I was touched by this, since, he was generally very aloof and barely acknowledged my presence, despite all the years I had worked there.

"You can say whatever you want to here, Senhor Valdo," and, as a guarantee, I glanced across at the servants hard at work at the far end of the kitchen.

"The fact is, Betty," he began, "it isn't Demétrio I want to talk to you about."

"Who then?"

He looked at me again, and this time I felt he was struggling for air. Ah, if I could only meet him halfway and, by touching on the matter that so paralyzed him, help him lay down that heavy burden and thus bring a little relief to his poor troubled soul. He must have sensed this impulse in me, because, leaning closer, he suddenly put one hand familiarly on my knee:

"Betty, I desperately need your help. If you knew how much a word from you would mean to me at this moment . . ."

"Oh, Senhor Valdo!" I cried, and my eyes filled with tears.

He bowed his head, as if searching for the best place to begin, and he was so overwhelmed by emotion that he was almost panting. (My thoughts inevitably went back to another time, many years earlier, when, again, he had summoned me in order to ask me to keep a family secret—and when I compared those two occasions, it seemed to me he had been less upset and had got to the point far more quickly on that earlier occasion. Perhaps the difference was simply that he had aged, and, sitting there before me, he seemed to be blindly grappling with some deeply shameful matter. But then, as now, I could not help him, and whatever it was he wanted to tell me, he would have to do so of his own volition, not prompted by my pity.)

"Ah, Betty, Betty!" and with that cry, he turned to me like a vast open sky torn in two by a flash of lightning. "Betty! What can I say? I need your help, *she* is here, and it's just terrible!"

So that was it. That was the cause of his suffering, and I wasn't in the least surprised, because, the moment he came into the kitchen, I knew what it was about. However, I had never imagined things had gone so far, nor that he would feel so defenseless in the face of danger, so hopelessly indecisive. If there really was a danger, as Senhor Demétrio had so often pointed out to him, should he not have taken steps in order to safeguard not just his own happiness, which would require no effort at all, but also the untouchable purity of those around him? What I was hearing was the despairing cry of a man surrendering to fate. And if so, if he lacked the strength to condemn her outright, this was because his suspicions had not yet put on flesh, and the evil seeds sown by his brother had not borne the fruit of justice that should have destroyed her forever. But how could they think such dreadful things about a person? He had already tested me out on another occasion, and in different circumstances, and then he had received from me only what the truth told me I should say. And now, again, I had to be bold and say what I thought.

"Senhor Valdo, I think what people say about her is a gross exaggeration. How could the poor . . ."

He brusquely stopped me in my tracks, and only then did I realize how ill-disposed he was toward Dona Nina:

"Don't tell me, Betty, that you've already taken her side."

I slowly shook my head:

"No, I'm not taking her side or anyone else's."

I watched his eyes slide away from me and, for a moment, there was a glint of madness in them, as though he were losing his grip on reality and no longer recognized his surroundings, as if his head were spinning. However, the silence calmed him, his will resurfaced, and he added:

"Don't be angry with me, Betty, but I need to know . . . Forgive me, it's just that I find myself in such a very painful situation."

"I understand, Senhor Valdo."

And he shot me a grateful glance.

"I have my suspicions about several things. Nothing positive, but if they proved to be true, it would be truly horrible."

"May I know what those things are?"

He turned to me so abruptly that the heavy table shook:

"Betty, what is going on with my son?"

We had reached the nub of the matter, and the as yet unnamed thing floating thinly about inside me like a tattered cloud suddenly came into sharp focus, took on form and name, and I shuddered, not daring to face that now confirmed suspicion. For a moment, I considered running away, escaping the unbearable pressure of feelings that did not belong to me; after all, I was of no importance in that house, so why should I get mixed up in things that would weigh so decisively on the fate of people who were my betters? Guessing my thoughts, Senhor Valdo touched my arm and shook me:

"Betty! Betty!"

Then I covered my face with my hands and remained like that for some time, turned in upon myself, on my shame, on the wild beating of my heart. Suspicions, yes, but what are suspicions worth, what do mere doubts mean when it comes to making a judgement against which there can be no appeal? Senhor Valdo, meanwhile, must have understood what my response, or lack of it, meant, because he kept repeating in a low voice, like a moan:

"Oh, Betty . . ."

I let my arms drop and, slowly, despite the shame burning my cheeks, I told my very first lie:

"There's nothing going on with your son, Senhor Valdo, nothing at all."

27th – I spent a horribly agitated night. Yesterday, when I told Senhor Valdo that there was nothing going on—and this was the second time in recent days that he had asked me such a question—my mind had been flooded with memories. It was almost as if they had been waiting for me to say those words in order to rise up and reveal their true meaning. I went back to work, helping the servants wash and fill the sausages, but I was so troubled, my hands so shaky, that I was hardly aware of what I was doing at all. I was remembering not just gestures or snippets of conversations, but actual scenes, real events that had occurred in my presence, and that were now causing me such concern. A day before—exactly one day before—I had found André lying face down on the sofa in the drawing room, sobbing his heart out. He had always been a nervous, sensitive boy, but I had never seen him cry before. I was even more surprised to find him there alone on the sofa. I sat beside him, stroking his hair, and he did not react at all. Such was his pain that I felt a pang of animosity toward "her": there had never been any tears in the house before "she" came. Still stroking his hair, and in as neutral a voice as possible, I asked if "she" was to blame. He shuddered and, when he turned to look at me, I saw that his eyes were still wet with tears. I don't know what turmoil he was going through at that moment, but, instead of the flat denial I was expecting, he began to talk, and I saw that nothing had actually happened and that what was hurting him was merely an impression, but one strong enough to make him open his heart to me, so great was his need for help and understanding. Whatever others may say, I understood him and believed everything he was telling me, which was nothing coherent or palpable, but rather a feeling of emptiness and futility, a lack that he did not know how to dismiss or to fill. It had begun the very first time he saw her. Whenever Nina spoke to him, she seemed absent, as if she were merely going through the motions, without really being aware of the person she was speaking to. "I feel," he said, "that I could talk about anything at all, and she would respond in the same way, not even conscious of what she was saying, because she's never really present when she speaks." I myself had noticed such absences, like spaces through which her words slipped, not strong enough to fix on the matter in hand. Is that what she was really like, was she putting on an act, or did she inhabit a world to which we had no access? That was what he found so troubling, and as he described his distress, I felt, too, that he was moved by a need, a desire, to exist, to be real and to be part of the emotions she embodied. He felt canceled out and, worse still, he was sure that no power in the world could make her see him as a real physical being. Torn apart by his own feeling of powerlessness, he, at one point, grabbed me by the shoulders and shook me, saying: "Betty, is that woman really my mother? Is there no chance there could have been a mistake, some monstrous mistake?" "No, there's no mistake." And I was truly sorry that there was no mistake and I could not offer him even the tiniest crumb of comfort. Whichever way he turned, he would always bump up against the same four walls of that reality, the limits of his prison. And now, as I felt the foundations of that drama growing around us like a dark jungle, I was trying to imagine what it must be like in that world only she could penetrate, and I could not help but recall what people said about her, about her past, and her turbulent life in Rio de Janeiro. When she spoke, what images lay behind her words, what men, what places, what guilty secrets lay behind the façade she went to such pains to present to us? As I stroked André's hair—he was still such a child, still so inexperienced—I myself drifted into thoughts of those far-off days—about which I had promised Senhor Valdo I would never speak—summoning up some forgotten face or an expression, the key to which I had already lost, and which, in the light of new events, might take on a new aspect, perhaps a clearer meaning. Was it those bloody scenes, Dona Ana's reaction, and the rumors I had heard on my occasional visits to Vila Velha or Queimados—rumors that I tried to drive from my mind like someone pushing her way through a bramble patch—was that what bubbled up to the surface, insidious and indestructible? No, I refused to believe that the beautiful creature who so fondly called me her friend could possibly be a woman of such base appetites, such unbridled, shameless feelings. No. If it were true, the world would take on a new and terrible meaning. Would it not be better to withhold judgement and allow time to clarify what seemed so obscure? And that is what I did, telling André that perhaps he was mistaken; that Dona Nina had always been a little vague, and that, had he known her for as long as I had, he would not find this in the least strange. André shook his head and did not answer, but I could see that my words had failed to convince him. At least I had succeeded in making him stop crying, which was a more than satisfactory outcome. Everything else would, possibly, calm down of its own accord.

When I left him, though, something odd happened: I began to feel a weight on my conscience, not because of my silence when Senhor Valdo had spoken to me, nor because I had not told him all that I knew. No, for the first time, and in an insistent, insinuating way, I understood what that woman's presence really was—a seething, rotting ferment. She herself may not have been aware of this, she simply existed, with the blithe exuberance of certain poisonous plants; but the mere fact that she did exist as an intrusive, disruptive element filtered into the atmosphere and gradually destroyed all vital signs of life. And just as those ardent, beautiful plants spring up from arid soil, later on, she would flower alone in a parched, sparse terrain ravaged by death. And there was no point in hiding: everything in that house was impregnated by her presence—the furniture, day-to-day life, the passing hours and minutes, even the air itself. The normally calm, untroubled rhythm of life in the Chácara had altered completely: there was no shared timetable, no general law to which everyone submitted. It was as if we were living under constant threat of some extraordinary event, which could happen at any moment. In the peace of my room, where I had taken refuge in order to think freely about these things, I realized that the whole spirit of the house had changed. And all my efforts to justify Dona Nina and find reasons for what she represented seemed futile, for she was, like a scandal, beyond justification. And up until then, I had always felt there was nothing worse than scandal—it was like the summation of all evil. That at least is what my mother had taught me, and she, too, had been brought up according to strict puritan teachings. At the same time, though, the graceful image of Dona Nina would rise up before me, and I would shake my head incredulously and wonder fearfully if I, too, had fallen under her spell.

28th – I have been thinking and thinking about these things for two days now, and there is one idea I cannot shake off: André will be the one to suffer most. If only I could find some way of making him speak and thus influence his behavior . . . I can't forget that I was the one who brought him up and so am directly responsible for him. Everything that happens to him is the result of my teachings. In my defense, I would think, well, that's easy enough to say, but who can stop a plant from growing and spreading freely? How could I possibly imagine the germs at work deep in his nature, the poisons that might predispose him to do who knows what? I had no doubt what my duty was, but what about everything else, himself, the consequences of his total lack of experience? Dear God, how difficult and complicated everything was. Not really knowing what I would say, I went looking for him and found him in his room, lying on the bed, a pillow covering his face. I sat down beside him:

"André," I said, "what's wrong?"

He removed the pillow and stared at me, his hair all disheveled:

"Nothing's wrong. Why do you ask?"

"What you told me . . ." I began. Then I stopped, imagining how difficult it would be to resume that conversation.

He reacted immediately and with unexpected brutality:

"What's it to do with you anyway? Why are you meddling in my life?"

That was the first time he had ever spoken to me in that tone of voice, and I instinctively thought of Senhor Valdo and the question he had asked me that day in the kitchen. The person who had alerted him to this change in the boy was probably Senhor Demétrio, who was always quicker to notice such things. In this case, he had been right, because clearly something very serious was troubling André.

"It's not me," I said after a while, "it's the others who find your attitude strange."

"Who, for example?" and he looked at me defiantly.

"Your uncle, your father."

For a second, the light in his eyes grew dim, and his voice sounded sadder and less certain:

"Oh, Betty, don't tell me you're on their side too."

So it was true. There *were* different sides. Those words more than confirmed all my suspicions. Some corrosive action was at work, the family was being torn asunder. Suddenly, in the midst of my shock at this realization, I thought of Senhor Timóteo—what part would he be playing in all this? Because I had no doubts now: if there were different sides, if the dividing lines had been drawn, Senhor Timóteo would never ally himself with his brothers, whom he had always hated, but with the others, and he would be one of their biggest supporters. I stood up, horrified:

"No, André, you're wrong. I'm not on anyone's side, a mere servant can't take sides. Because you're right, I am just a servant."

He merely shrugged:

"So what the devil did you come here for?"

"I came to help you." I saw him shudder. "But not like that . . . not like that."

I left the room, feeling that I could say nothing more. However, I could not drive from my mind the image of that house being torn to shreds, as if it were a living body. And I, alas, knew where the attack was coming from.

24.
The Doctor's Third Report

. . . I am now happy to recount the things I witnessed back then, even though those events are now so old that it's unlikely any of the people involved are still alive. That, perhaps, is why I have agreed to take up my pen again, and if my writing is sometimes a little shaky, that is because age no longer allows me to write with the ease I once did, nor is my memory as quick to come when I call. However, I believe I do recollect the day you mention. In fact, your enquiries have proved very useful to me, since they oblige me to pin down facts from the past that would otherwise be left to drift on the tides of memory.

It was shortly after the return of the woman we all knew as Dona Nina, and although I can still recall every detail, the truth is that, despite my being the Meneses' family doctor and having often been called out to attend the Chácara's inhabitants, I had not been there for a long time because no one had required my services, as if life and its ills had called a truce up in those parts. So the sudden summons from Senhor Valdo took me by surprise and, for the reasons I have just given, that visit stands out among all the many others I made to the Meneses family during my time as a doctor.

It was, I recall, a rainy morning, and I was looking through the open window at the trees being buffeted by the wind. Senhor

Valdo drove up to my house in a buggy, and I noticed at once that he was extremely agitated. He was always so calm and so impeccably dressed—his outward appearance a perfect match for his inner feelings. On that occasion, however, he seemed extremely flustered, his hair unkempt, and—a detail which, on its own, would have been enough to reveal his state of mind—he wasn't even wearing a tie. Now I could accept many things, but not, I confess, the notion of a Meneses without a tie. Despite the rain, I rushed out to meet him, since I was already imagining some grave event at the Chácara. I opened the door even while he was still reaching for the bell.

"Ah," he exclaimed with relief, "I thought you might not be at home."

"But you hadn't even rung," I replied.

"Well, I don't know," he answered. "I always assume that you'll be out attending to some other patient."

These opening words reassured me, and I assumed that the reason for his visit was not so urgent after all, and so I said jokingly:

"Patients are getting few and far between—nobody falls ill in this town any more."

He sighed and, since the rain was getting heavier, I invited him to come in. He accepted and while we stood rather close together in the cramped hallway, I could see he was wondering how best to explain his reasons for coming. He turned suddenly, and I saw his lips trembling, evidently from the nervous effort of having to explain his mission.

"You have often come to our aid at various difficult times in the past," he said.

And he paused again and stood staring into space. Perhaps he was remembering all the many times I had gone to the Chácara ever since my very first visit there to attend his poor departed mother. For a moment, I, too, allowed myself to drift back into the past, and we both stood there silently facing each other, as if we could see those potent shadows circling around us. It was he who broke the spell, moving closer and placing one hand on my arm:

"Come with me," he said. "We have need of a doctor at the Chácara."

By the way he spoke, he did not appear to be referring to an illness as such, but to some sort of incident that required a doctor's help and advice, and which was grave enough in itself to take on the characteristics of an illness. It would be pointless to set down here all the words we exchanged—and I certainly don't think it would help you in your objective. Besides, I don't remember all of them, which have become so mixed up in my memory with the echoes of other words, and because so much time has passed since they were spoken. I remember only that I tried to get him to explain why exactly they needed my help, and that he gave me a somewhat garbled explanation about someone in the family suddenly falling ill and that my help was urgently required. I hesitated no further, and took my place beside him in the buggy. And so we set off toward the Chácara, the old Chácara that had always been a source of legend and of pride for the little town where we lived. I recalled fights, quarrels, and rivalries—the Baron, for example, richer, nobler, and more illustrious than the Meneses, who lived on a large estate far from the town, but whose house and name, despite everything, did not have the same romantic prestige as the house of the Meneses. Where did it come from, the prestige that lent their decadent mansion its enduring fascination, like a poetic inheritance undimmed by time? From its past, purely from its past, all those masters and mistresses who had been the aunts, uncles, cousins, and grandparents of the Senhor Valdo sitting beside me in the buggy—every one of them a Meneses, who through their affairs and escapades, their myths and marriages, had created the "soul" of the house which would always survive intact, as if hanging in the air, even if its representatives were to sink forever into obscurity. Those were my thoughts as the buggy entered the main gate and slithered down the soggy, sandy paths. And yet I still felt a pang of nostalgia as, even in the rain, I could make out the distinctive scent of the Chácara's garden; little did those Meneses know what they meant in the imagination of others, the value of the legend surrounding their name, its mysterious, dramatic force, the poetry that illuminated them with a dim, bluish light. Yes, those old houses kept alive an identifiable spirit, capable of pride, of suffering, and (why not?) of death too, when dragged down into mediocrity, down to the level of mere mortals. And was that not exactly what was happening with the last dregs of the Meneses, who could no longer live up to the prestige of their ancestors? Peering ahead through the heavy rain, I could almost sense the gaze of the old building seeking me out, streaks of blood running down its martyred stones.

Senhor Valdo brought the buggy to a halt, not at the steps leading up to the main house, but alongside a separate building known as the Pavilion, with its large frosted-glass windows. I had never been inside and must confess that I entered it then with considerable curiosity since, for good or ill, anything connected with the Meneses was to me a subject of the utmost interest. The Pavilion must have been abandoned long ago, because the steps were almost overwhelmed by greenery and puddled with rainwater. The walls, too, were showing the effects of time, and beams poked randomly out from under the roof of broken tiles. Before stepping inside, Senhor Valdo turned and rather roughly grabbed my arm:

"I don't quite know how to begin . . . but it concerns my son."

He seemed to hesitate again, and his eyes—which were not vacant exactly, but uncertain—looked away from me in search of some other external support, and in them I saw all the wild feelings filling his soul. And then, like someone embarking on a dangerous journey, he added:

"I myself don't really understand. I need you as a doctor and, perhaps, as a friend. Ah, if I were to tell you everything . . ."

He steered me toward one corner of the verandah, where there was a pile of wicker chairs. He extricated two, made me sit on one, then himself slumped down in the other. The rain was hammering tirelessly down on the roof. With a sigh, his eyes half-closed, one eyelid twitching slightly, he began his story, and it was curiosity rather than any clinical interest that held me in thrall to every tremor in his voice.

He began by saying that he had noticed recently that his son, André, was behaving very oddly. Nothing very alarming at first, he merely seemed somewhat overwrought, and there was about him . . .—he stopped for a moment, searching for the right expression—. . . a sly, angry air, like someone trying to conceal some profound inner turmoil, all of which could, of course, be put down to adolescence. However, the first symptoms had coincided with the return of André's mother—and at this point, he stopped again and stared at me, then lowered his eyes as if embarrassed—after an absence of fifteen years. For family reasons—and he eyed me uneasily, almost pleadingly—her name was never mentioned in the house, and the shock of meeting her at last could well be the reason for the boy's troubled state. Senhor Valdo fell silent, no doubt so as to compose his thoughts, and I took the opportunity to ask if the boy had always exhibited such tendencies, that is to say, was he naturally of a nervous disposition. He said that he was, adding that his son had always been an enigma to him, full of abrupt mood swings that he had never understood. I then asked him for details of André's more recent moods and odd behavior. Once again he fell silent, looking at me uneasily as if afraid that I would never be able to fully grasp what was going on. He then asked, rather oddly I thought, if I knew his brother Senhor Demétrio. "Of course," I replied, "I've known Senhor Demétrio for many years. I believe, at one time or another, I've even treated some illness of his." He then told me that Senhor Demétrio had been the first to notice that there might be a problem and had long ago warned him about the boy. "It's quite extraordinary," he had said. "He's simply not like other boys." Senhor Valdo had never quite understood what his brother meant by this, but, deep down, he felt afraid, because his brother's predictions and misgivings had so often proved true. He could remember one or two occasions . . .—and for a moment, the words almost came to his lips, but he drew back and, instead, merely sighed. It was best to say nothing, he said, because those past events had absolutely no influence on what was happening now. Nevertheless, he had begun to observe André more closely (when he said his son's name, I noticed a faint tremor in his voice, a slight dissonance, as when people are fearful perhaps of betraying a non-existent intimacy or of revealing some overpowering emotion—and remembering that he had always referred to the lad as "my son," I couldn't help but think, with some concern, that the evident effort required in saying the boy's name might, first and foremost, be an attempt to overcome some kind of secret repugnance), and that closer scrutiny had confirmed that the boy did, indeed, seem deeply disturbed. He had decided to intervene and on more than one occasion had tried unsuccessfully to talk to the boy, who, having been raised in total freedom, refused now to submit to any degree of control. That upbringing had been a terrible mistake! Urged on by his brother, who was clearly worried about the situation, he had attempted to act more decisively. Two days ago, when the boy was refusing to eat, he had summoned up the courage to go and see him in his room. He had immediately noticed the unhealthy atmosphere—the lights off, pillows scattered on the floor, everything in complete disorder. André (I noted that his tone was now more robust, the name pronounced more firmly, as if he were finally acknowledging his paternal responsibilities) was crouching in one corner beside the chest of drawers and, even in the dark, his eyes had a strange glint in them. "This won't do," he had said, "either you're very ill, or else . . ." The boy had slowly gotten to his feet, leaning on the chest of drawers. Lacking the courage to complete his sentence, Senhor Valdo had instead changed tack and spoken more gently and affectionately, in a desperate bid to win over that rebellious heart. "If you're not ill, you need to go outside and get some fresh air. You can't live in here on your own like a convict." André had laughed: "Are you saying I can't live the way I want?" And Valdo had seen then that any attempt to draw him out was doomed to failure, and that if he wanted to achieve anything he would need to have more influence over the boy than that of a mere father. (This time his voice had grown noticeably quieter, and at the sight of that bowed head, that unexpected show of humility in one who had always been so proud, I could not help but feel sorry for him.) In the end, all he could say, with a sad shake of his head, was: "You're still little more than a child. No one at your age lives the way they want to live." But then something inside the boy seemed to snap, and Valdo watched in astonishment as André flew into a furious rage: What did he care about his advice? What did he care what he thought? What did he care if he considered him still a child? What did he care about anything? And he had propelled him toward the door, beating on his father's chest with his fists like a creature possessed. Something very grave must be happening for him to get so worked up at the mere mention of his age. André again took refuge in one corner of the room, angrily repeating: "A child! A child!" Senhor Valdo had not wanted to offend him, and his failure in that regard left him paralyzed. Now he understood what his brother had always told him: "You don't know how to raise that son of yours, and you're laying the foundations for a bleak future for you both." He had approached the boy again to attempt a reconciliation—possibly for the last time. "You don't understand. I'm only saying these things for your own good." The boy was still trembling with rage. "What do you know what's good for me? What do you know about me at all?" And then he had once more exploded with rage: "For God's sake get out! Just get out of my room. I don't want to see you. I don't want to see anyone." And he had pushed him so hard that Senhor Valdo, fearing he might trip and fall, had left the room. From that moment on, he had been pondering what course of action to take. (There was a new note of despondency in his voice: But what course of action? Spiritual assistance? He had written a letter to Father Justino, but had received no reply. In any case, there didn't seem to be much that God could do in a case like that. A doctor, that's what he needed.) He had felt his sense of responsibility growing within him: measures must be taken and the more draconian the better. Meeting his brother in the hallway, he decided to tell him what had happened. Demétrio's response was decidedly cool: "So what are you going to do?" Senhor Valdo had confessed his doubts, and his brother, shaking his head, had commented. "It may already be too late." Senhor Valdo felt a shiver run down his spine when he heard those words, which rang out like a death knell. "It can't be too late, it just can't—we have to do something." Then in an almost off-hand manner, Demétrio said: "Let me think about it. I'll give you my opinion later." (Another tremor in Senhor Valdo's voice: "And yet," he said, as if he were talking to himself now, "I had the impression that Demétrio had already formed an opinion, that he had known about all these things before I did and had thought long and hard about them, although I may, of course, be mistaken. Standing there before me, Demétrio seemed ready to fend off any further questions from me on the subject.") "However, before he gave his promised verdict, we received unexpected and decisive confirmation of the boy's madness." (Once again, in that broken narrative, he appeared to hesitate—not as he had done previously, but more profoundly, more frankly, if I can put it like that. It was a hesitation of despondency, and his silence seemed to carry within it the bitter gall of all human despair.)

Then he said very bluntly: "I don't know if you've ever met my other brother, Timóteo. He's an eccentric fellow, a complete madman really. In fact, he's even worse than that . . ." (Perhaps it's my age, or my habit of listening with eyes cast down, not looking at the speaker, but, curiously, the years seem to have increased my ability to notice the subtlest nuances in a person's voice. Perhaps it's a talent honed by experience, I don't know. What I do know is that not the slightest shift in his tone of voice escaped me, and I saw with utter clarity that there was not a hint of sorrow or discomfort or regret, as one might expect when one brother speaks of another, and which was so evident when he spoke about his son, but, rather, a deep-seated loathing that went far beyond contempt, a loathing that informed everything he felt about his brother. This was apparent in the confidence with which he expressed himself, almost as if he were handing down a judicial sentence, an unappealable verdict, consigning Timóteo to utter ignominy, and I, who had often heard tales of this elusive Meneses brother, sensed that he was exaggerating, even though I knew beyond a doubt that the family considered Timóteo to be the blackest of black sheep.) "And even worse," continued Senhor Valdo, "he is a sick, evil creature, unfit for human company. I don't know why I'm telling you all this now. It's as if I were finally giving vent to my deepest feelings." He then told me that this infamous brother of his was at the heart of all that was wrong in the family. Timóteo had not left his room for many years, and never saw either of his brothers. Only the maid visited him, reporting back afterward to Senhor Demétrio on what she found. André had been brought up completely ignorant of the situation, and had never been told the truth about his uncle. Once or twice he had tried to breach the walls of the mystery and actually meet his uncle in his self-imposed prison. Senhor Valdo had intercepted him at the last moment and, when the boy insisted, he felt no compunction about lying. "You can't," he had said. "The doctor won't allow anyone to enter that room." Astonished, André had asked: "Why?" And Senhor Valdo had replied: "He has a highly contagious disease." André had gazed at the door to the room almost in horror—and since then had never again broached the subject. Recently, however, the maid had told them that Timóteo was not at all well. And this was no doubt why Nina (another brief pause) had decided to visit her brother-in-law. Senhor Valdo explained that his wife was now a frequent visitor to Timóteo's room; indeed, she seemed to take a secret delight in his company, and, ever since the very first occasion fifteen years ago, this had always been a source of discord between them. Deep down, he was convinced it was not that she was seduced by his brother's saccharine compliments, but by a real desire to annoy Senhor Valdo and to wound his pride, for there was nothing in that house more likely to cause him pain than her friendship with a person of such abnormal habits.

On that occasion, however, he had not seen her go to Timóteo's room. A few minutes later, the whole house had been shaken by André's shouts as he pounded with his fists on the door, screaming "Let me in!" And then even more loudly, redoubling his efforts: "What's she doing in there?" Obviously, Valdo was to blame for planting such fears in the boy's mind with the idea of a contagious disease. For years and years he had made the boy avoid that room as if a leper lived there. And then when the boy saw his mother entering that accursed place, all his instincts, curiosities, and misgivings had awoken, and, blind with rage and anxiety, sensing perhaps that the person he adored was slipping away from him, crossing the forbidden threshold (goodness knows what dangers he imagined hovering over Nina's head), he had hurled himself at the door like a lunatic, determined to penetrate its secret. That, at least, is what Senhor Valdo had thought initially, but this was not the conclusion reached by Senhor Demétrio and his wife, Dona Ana, who both rushed to the scene, drawn by André's shouts. André was in a terrible state: disheveled and sobbing, still pounding at the door, resisting all efforts to pull him away. He repeated again and again: "Let me in! Let me in! What's she doing in there?" Helped by his wife, Senhor Demétrio had finally managed to subdue him. "The boy has gone completely mad," he said. "This calls for the severest of measures." Senhor Valdo did not dare to intervene, convinced that disaster beckoned. André seemed to be having some kind of seizure and, when they finally and with great difficulty managed to restrain him, he had been brought to the Pavilion—Senhor Valdo indicated the faded tiles of the verandah—and locked in one of its rooms. This is what his brother had decided, and he had gone along with it on condition that he was allowed to consult a doctor about the matter, so that André could undergo a suitable course of treatment. Demétrio had chosen the Pavilion because it was far from the house, and so that the boy would be safe from what he considered to be pernicious influences. (It was hard to say what these influences were—whenever any mention was made of them, Demétrio always retreated into impenetrable silence.) At first, the patient had reacted violently, but, little by little, his strength gave way and he fell into a state of extreme prostration. For several hours he would neither speak nor eat, and this was why Senhor Valdo had been in such a hurry to seek medical advice. He wanted a detailed examination, for upon my diagnosis hung the decision of whether to send the boy away from the Chácara or not. No sacrifice would be too great and he was even ready to send him to Rio de Janeiro, perhaps to a spa on the coast. This was what he told me, and he concluded by declaring that he hardly needed to say how much he was relying on my clear judgment and knowledge of the facts—it was almost his only hope of seeing his son return to normality.

Thus ended Senhor Valdo's explanation. I remained seated after he had finished speaking, my head bowed. Although many things remained unclear to me, I now knew why I had been summoned and what was expected of me. I needed to tread with caution, though, for I sensed I was walking through a minefield. Senhor Valdo must have grown impatient with my silence, for he cleared his throat, sprang to his feet and began pacing up and down the verandah. I could hear the monotonous sound of the rain dripping from the gutters. When my silence continued, he stopped pacing and stood in front of me: "So what do you think of all of this?" Only then did I raise my head and look at him—the expression on his face was one of anxiety. "There are certain other things I would like to know," I replied. "What other things?" he asked, glaring at me and making no attempt to conceal the note of defiance in his voice. "For example, during all that commotion, did no one open the door, even out of simple curiosity? Did no one respond to the boy's pleas?" His answer came quickly: "No, my brother considers himself to be some kind of enemy of the world." I nodded to indicate that I had understood, then said: "When you talked with André in his bedroom, was that all he said?" This time he did not reply quite so promptly. I looked at him again and, although this may only have been an impression, he seemed to turn pale and to have difficulty formulating the right words. I stood up too and looked him straight in the eye. He flinched and turned away, but did not have the courage to lie: "No, that wasn't all—he told me something else as well." "And could you tell me what that was?" I asked. His voice grew very quiet and he suddenly looked old and weary. "I don't know what strange idea, what obsession, has taken hold of him. He told me I had only come there out of jealousy, that I couldn't bear seeing him so close to his mother, and that my intention—and here I really couldn't grasp what he meant at all—that my intention was to destroy them both."

Standing motionless on that verandah, I felt myself slowly slipping further down the dark, narrow path that was the life of the Meneses.

25.
André's Diary (u)

Undated – Although I could not be sure that she had received my note—I hadn't left it anywhere very visible for fear it might fall into the wrong hands—as soon as supper was over, I ran to the proposed meeting place. (It would perhaps have been easier to speak to her directly, during a pause in one of the unbearable conversations at the supper table, but, afraid that someone might notice, I chose instead that difficult and ingenuous stratagem.)

I have no doubts now—I know exactly what I want. I am not blindly engaged in a struggle that might have possibly surprising results; I have weighed up all the possibilities and I know exactly the result I want. What do I care about what the others think and have always thought? I feel extraordinarily free: the walls imprisoning the old me have crumbled. Like a man who has been sleeping for a long time at the bottom of a well, I have woken up now and can face the light of the sun full on. This feeling is not maturity, as I once thought, it is plenitude. Aren't my flushed cheeks, my restlessness, my arrhythmic heart—are not all those things proof that I have really started to live, that I exist, and that life has ceased to be a fiction gleaned from books?

What frightens me most about what I see around me is the poverty of other people's lives. I am astonished that, up until now,

I have been able to live with only my father, Betty, and Aunt Ana for company. They lack all understanding, are so narrow-minded, so immune to grand emotions, that they have come to symbolize for me everything I have spontaneously left behind. Only with her arrival could I perceive my mistake. I compare her to those other people and I cannot but feel the vast difference, the thrilling, expansive air she seems to breathe as opposed to the stuffy atmosphere that has always surrounded me. Following that period of depression in which I began to explore my new discoveries, a wave of enthusiasm suddenly swept through my being like a fresh spring breeze: I even performed a solitary waltz around my room. I leaned out of the window, breathed in the dry air from the fields, and gazed over at the distant blue silhouette of Serra do Baú, and life seemed to me suddenly very grave and beautiful, filled with a meaning I had never known until that moment, but which existed and gave color to the trees and the leaves, to the clouds and the sky, to everything that glowed and pulsated with infinite love. I felt glad to be alive, and even considered kneeling down and giving thanks to God, whichever God that might be, for having made me aware of all those marvels. I know, too, that certain forms of madness are also composed of such moments.

After this, I decided to change all my habits. I began by collecting together the books Betty had lent me—naïve tales by English authors—and gave them back to her. She was in her room and, as it happened, was dusting her bookshelves, carefully piling up the books covered in brown paper. "Why are you giving them back?" she asked when I placed the small pile of books beside her. And doubtless assuming that these were authors who no longer interested me, she said: "I have a very good novel here, by José de Alencar." "No, Betty," I said gently, "I don't want to read books like that any more." "But this one's really good!" she insisted. And holding it out to me: "It's *The Silver Mines*. Have you read it?" I shook my head. And sensing her disquiet and knowing that she was trying to read my thoughts, I said: "I'm not a child any more." I left her alone with her books, and she silently watched me leave, her eyes full of the pain I was inflicting on her.

That night, though, I found it hard to sleep, my mind troubled, as if a vague notion of having betrayed someone were weighing on my conscience. A friend perhaps, the thought of whom painfully, ceaselessly circled around and around inside me, and in those dark places, where the light of understanding had not yet penetrated, I tried in vain to revive the echo of promises I had trampled underfoot. I got up several times, went to the window, breathed in the night air; I came back, opened the drawer and took out this notebook, trying to soothe myself by writing. I gave up in the end and went back to bed. And yet, whenever I had felt restless before, those things had always worked: the night air used to bring me the consolation for which I searched in vain now, and this notebook, my faithful companion for so many years, had always gladly welcomed my confessions.

I was thinking about her. Not as she was now, but as she had been when she had lived here before. The garden and the pale moonlight on the trees were just as I had always known them, ever since I was born. What had happened before, who would have gone to meet her along those same paths, and what event or human image from that time illumined the depths of her mind? Slowly, and as if I were about to set off in search of those same paths, I returned to the window and peered at the shadowy shapes of the trees, the moonlit patches of sand, the dark swathes of undergrowth, from which there came a faint breathing, as if the spirit of the darkness itself were present. I could not explain my suffering, nor the many strange reasons jostling inside my head, but of one thing I was sure: I was alive in a way to which I was utterly unaccustomed, but I was alive—painfully, wretchedly, suffocatingly, voluptuously alive.

Undated – She came, she finally came to meet me, just when I was beginning to lose all hope. It was quite a cold night, and I had over my shoulders an old cape I normally never wore because it was now too small for me. Whenever I thought I could hear footsteps—it was windy and the sudden gusts made the branches creak—I would immediately take the cape off and throw it down on the bench, preferring to shiver rather than have her see anything that might remind her of the child whom I considered to be dead. I even rehearsed what I would say, words in which she could not fail to sense my new maturity. I adopted a deliberate, slightly cool tone of voice, a tone I remembered hearing my father use, and which seemed to me appropriate for the current situation. Despite all these precautions, I think it was precisely that remnant of childishness that she noticed when she confronted me in that secluded place. Despite keeping a close watch on the path and continually peering into the darkness, I did not hear her arrive, because a particularly strong gust of wind was rustling the leaves in that hidden part of the garden. I suddenly turned and saw her standing there, tall and still, and doubtless expecting me to notice her, in the belief that her mere presence would be enough, and I felt then how foolish all my preparations had been and was tormented by the thought of my pointless attempts to stage-manage our encounter. What I would have given to overcome my shyness, and to appear bold and frank during what was our first real meeting. Because, for good or ill, that *was* our first meeting, the initial moment of everything that would happen afterward, almost a commitment—and, yes, a hidden bond between us, given that she had agreed to come and thus consented to being an accomplice in an affair that was just beginning to unfold. Contrary to my expectations, she was the first to speak:

"Here I am," she said, taking a step forward. And then in a clearly reproving voice, she added: "Are you quite mad, sending me that note?"

Even while she was saying this, there was such an intense sadness about her that I felt my heart might break. She was, I felt, so very lonely, imprisoned in a world of dead emotions, empty of all hope, and those feelings chimed perfectly with my own, like an echo of my own emotions. Such passionate fellow feeling gave me the courage to answer:

"I needed to see you, somehow or other . . ." and the hesitancy I had so wanted to avoid was evident in the breathless, uncertain tone in which I spoke those words.

She shook her head:

"It's ridiculous to take such risks. Have you thought what your father . . ."

"My father!" I said scornfully.

She appeared not to notice this interruption and continued to scold me:

"If you wanted to see me, if it was as important as you say, then why didn't you just seek me out in the drawing room or somewhere else in the house?"

"No, no," I blurted out.

And more softly, as if I was ashamed of my words:

"It would be impossible inside the house."

She gave me an indefinable look:

"Why?"

I shrugged, unable to find words to justify what I had said. Then she came a little closer and looked deep into my eyes:

"I hate such subterfuges. No one in the house is plotting against you. Besides, such behavior is only justifiable between . . . lovers."

She said this almost dismissively, and yet I felt my face flush scarlet with shame as if my secret had been uncovered. No, I should not say that she had *perhaps* uncovered my secret, because she had seen it for precisely what it was, had stripped it bare before my eyes. I could see it now, I understood everything: I was the one who had gone too far and dared to imagine what should never have existed even in my thoughts. What folly, and how typical of the still childish me, full of absurd presumptions. She would have been perfectly within her rights to slap me or punish me in some other way, to relegate me to the humble position I should never have abandoned. Feebly, like someone repeating a particularly meaningless lesson, I kept saying to myself that the woman before me was my mother, and however crushing I found that horrible truth, I could not escape it if I did not want to return again and again to the dubious, compromising situation in which I found myself. She doubtless noticed my confusion and examined me in silence, including the cape I had not had time to take off, and which lent me the cowed air of a schoolboy caught committing some grave fault. I could almost see myself in her silence: thin, tremulous, trying in vain to conceal my own fragility. I was just considering fleeing that place, when she came closer still and placed one hand on my shoulder:

"Listen André, you're still just a child, but I know, I understand these things," and again a kind of mist wrapped about what she was saying, and I noticed in her voice the complicit tone that had so struck me before, "but this has to end. What do you take me for? Despite your youth, you must behave like a man."

More than her words, which, in that brief time, had run the gamut of many different emotions, I think it was her hand on my shoulder that decided me. It was still there, and what she was saying was exactly what she should say in that situation, but rather than dismissing me or imposing her authority, she then raised her hand to my face in a slow caress, running her fingers over my chin, my lips, where they lingered for so long that they set my whole being aflame.

"Yes, like a man," I said blindly, feeling those fiery fingers touching my cheek. And gripped by a sudden, diabolical fury, I desperately grabbed the hand stroking my face and cried: "But it will never end, and you know why! You're the one who wants it, the one who calls to me. Ah, if you knew . . ."

I had finally dared to break my silence and confront her gaze. I saw then that her pale face, her fragile, poisonously malevolent beauty, had changed completely at my words, as if a veil had been torn away: her eyes closed and a tremor ran through her body as she said:

"Me? Oh, André . . ." and it was impossible to know if she was genuinely shocked or merely pretending.

I let go of her hand, and she took a step back, but that movement, far from repelling me, drew me in, as if it were not a rejection, but an incentive to my boldness.

"Yes, you," I said. "You. Why do you toy with me like this if you consider me a mere child? Why do you clutch me to you and agree to meet me at the far end of the garden?"

These words were dictated by my own febrile state, and I wasn't even aware how unjust I was being, since any mother would have responded to such an appeal from her son. I, however, was at one of those decisive moments when the subterranean truth, still too formless to withstand the light of day, bursts to the surface like a wave of dammed-up water. She must have felt the same, realizing that we would not emerge the same from that moment, that my words had shattered the fantasy world she was trying to impose on us and that we stood now, alone and naked, at the very center of an irrefutable truth. She must have felt she needed to make a supreme effort, some quick, brutal gesture, in order to confirm or deny her response or her revolt. Accordingly, she raised her hand and slapped me hard on the cheek. Everything whirled around me, the garden, the house, the sky—and I was so utterly calm, so absolute was my determination and my certainty, that I could count every beat of my heart, and smell on the wind the errant perfume of this or that flower, and even count the stars turning in the firmament. No words were necessary, the mystery had been forever resolved—my heart overflowed with wild joy, the joy of victory and maturity, the joy condemned men feel when they discover that death is not a harsh act of sacrifice and consummation, but one of self-realization and freedom. Because in that simple slap I saw not an insult, but an affirmation, and sensing that I at last had her cornered, I dragged myself to the very brink of salvation, even if it meant my eternal ruin.

Undated – She said not a word more, but looked at me, and what an intense, devouring gaze that was! Seeing her in that fearful state, I understood various things, feeling that everything else was mere cloud and fantasy in the face of my strength and my will. She was unveiling me only to reveal new depths, a dynamic, irreducible vision of my very being! She looked at me as if her whole frightened self were begging for clemency. I feel no shame when I say—because I am sure that never, in my entire life, will I see such a pure vision—it was as if her clothes had fallen away and she had emerged, female and naked, into the darkness of the garden. At one mad stroke, I had revealed what constitutes the difference between a man's body and a woman's, and there it was, fragile and delicate, like an open vase waiting for me to fill it with my blood and my impatience. She was still staring at me, and as she did so, by a strange process I could not understand, I felt myself growing in her eyes, maturing and taking on definite form: I was someone. For the first time, she was actually seeing me, not some other person who lay behind my personality, an echo, a shadow from the past. Just then, I was the one who existed, and she was listening intently, observing on my face the signs of that metamorphosis, that new self being carved out. While this impression did not last long, it lasted long enough to fill the whole world with a powerful magic, overflowing all the usual boundaries, taking on physical form and washing about us like some absurd, luminous matter—then everything returned to its former narrowness, as if the only reality, the fundamental truth of that transfiguration, were a lightning flash too bright for our human nature, one that instantly abandoned us once more to darkness and lies.

The lie was there, and it was me and my pathetic cape and the female shape beginning to grow before me. She was slowly gathering strength again, like a vast, secret, poisonous sunflower burgeoning in the shadows. I felt she was about to leave me, that her decision to flee was already there in the air, a decision with its roots in skepticism and incomprehension. I cannot begin to describe my anguish, seeing the dream that had glowed for a moment in my hands suddenly dissolve. She turned her back on me and began to walk briskly away toward the main path. It felt as if some external force was wrenching vital fibers from my being, leaving me helpless and drained of life in the now pitch-black garden. So powerful was that feeling that I took a few steps after her and called softly, but still loud enough for her to hear:

"Mama!"

The surprise of that word, and the pain, which, despite my best efforts, must have been apparent in my voice, made her stop—and then, the miracle occurred again, and I managed to cancel out the existing atmosphere and superimpose on the ordinary world the real world dwelling within. Softly, so that she, too, would feel the wild excess of the word, I said again:

"Mama . . ."

And I saw then that, although still with her back to me, she appeared to be waiting. I paused, imagining the inner struggle she must be engaged in, the concessions she might make if she did turn back, if she accepted the implication behind that word. But there she was, frozen, and the fact that she had stopped was clearly not a rejection. Through the trees came a powerful smell of lemon blossom—she raised her head, as if breathing in the perfume wafting to her on the breeze. Then slowly, so slowly that I barely noticed, she turned and came back toward me. Now there she was before me again. My impulse was to hurl myself into her arms, to cover her with kisses, to bind her forever to my passion. I held back, though, and waited, knowing that she would be the first to speak.

"Child!" she exclaimed in a dull voice. "Child, what do you want of me, tell me, what do you expect?"

Only a fool would have heard in the way she spoke the faintest glimmer of rancor or revolt. No, those words contained only infinite tenderness, almost surrender, unable now to fend off the fury of desire she sensed growing inside me. But seeing her so helpless, another feeling was fermenting inside me, and I was wondering how often she would have said the same thing, in identical situations, and to how many different men . . . How could I know her entirely and possess her without the moment being contaminated by memories of other men she had loved and who had doubtless left deep scars on her soul? And that very male jealousy made me realize that all childish feelings had died in me. Another self was beginning to rise up, aggressive, imperious, full of an absolute hunger and thirst, like an animal waking in some primitive forest.

"What do I expect, what do I want?" I said, feeling my whole self vibrating from head to toe. "I love you, I adore you, I want you for myself alone!"

And I rushed toward her and took her in my arms. Despite my own feverish state, I noticed that she was not trembling, that she did not refuse my embrace, as would have seemed plausible. (No, I do not want to accuse her: what would be the point? After all, what excuse could I find for my own fault, if it can be considered a fault?)

We sat down on a stone bench, while she kept murmuring, as if invoking some invisible witness: "Dear God, dear God, what should I do, what should I do?" My one impulse, like a fire devouring me, was to crush that doubt, that last defense, to disable that final remnant of fear that seemed to make her hold back. I knew now that she would not have the strength to withdraw or to refuse me anything, but I delayed my victory, because I wanted her entirely, with not a trace of remorse or doubt. But words were of no use, and we could only know each other now through the attraction driving us into each other's arms and that finally brought our lips together in the first and most desperate of loving kisses.

26.
André's Diary (v – continued)

Undated – There is not much more to say. After that kiss, everything changed. I thought I had won a final victory, but soon realized that, for her, this was merely a passing fancy, one of those moments of weakness so common in a certain type of woman. (*Written in the margin in a different hand:* I did not know about women then, or only in my fantasies. However, with astonishing speed, Nina taught me all I needed to know.) Not because things did not go as I had foreseen or as I had assumed they would with any woman once certain barriers had been overcome, but because a change took place in her, and what changed her and distanced her from me was the very thing I thought would bring us closer. That kiss, like the touch of a magic wand, ran through her from head to toe, and she closed her eyes, as if unable to fend off that wave of emotion. The shock must have been so great that she tried to struggle and, taking my hand, clung to it as if she were afraid of drowning.

"Oh, André!" she cried in a strange voice.

And spoken like that, my name sounded like the name of an absent being, a stranger, and yet it seemed to me that nothing had changed. The bench, the night, the garden were all the same, but that feeling of strangeness, which had sprung so quickly into life, was nothing to do with us, or not at least with me, and I was overwhelmed by a presence that divested me of all personality. I was tempted to shake her and say: "Yes, I am André, but I am not the person your voice calls out to, nor am I the person your gaze is fixed on. But why?" At the same time, though, I realized how futile those words would be and how far that kiss had driven us apart. Because, for her, any kiss was but a memory of another kiss exchanged, possibly on that very bench, on an identically windy night, a kiss that, by dissolving the present reality, cast a spell capable of replacing it with a vanished time, which, though utterly destroyed, was, nevertheless, still strong enough to return from exile. She must have sensed what was happening from my silence, from my impassive face, both of which betrayed the depth of the feelings gripping me, and then, raising my hand to her lips, she covered it with moist, lingering kisses, saying:

"Ah, what will become of us? What utter madness is this? Who knows where it will lead?" and in those words, in the tragic way in which she pressed my hand to her face, there was a certain coldness, which, far from deceiving me, repelled me. What shocked me most was that her words had no roots in any genuine feeling of perplexity; they were merely an attempt to adapt to the situation, there was no sense of any inner struggle, but, rather, a desire to restore the balance and lead me quietly back to some kind of natural status quo. This was a mistake on her part, which I found outrageous and repellent, because I was very far from considering this to be the kind of adventure one might have with some free-and-easy maid, and when I held her in my arms and kissed her lips, I was knowingly stepping into a part of the world that would never be seen as acceptable, and in which I would have to travel alone, a journey that would make me not the happy, much-loved son, but the guiltiest and most knowing of lovers.

I tried to oppose that coldness, that attempted deception, with my glad acceptance of the situation, embracing her and crying:

"Who cares what happens? What can anyone do in the face of what is happening to us now? We exist."

She let out a moan and stared at me in astonishment:

"Ah, my poor André . . . what do you know . . ."

I covered her mouth with my hand, afraid she might say something irrevocable.

"Let me speak, André!" she begged, drawing back.

"No, no! Don't say anything . . ."

And in my struggle to overcome the phantasmagorical atmosphere she had created—when had that other man existed, whoever he was?—I felt crumbling about me not just the fragments of that vivid memory, but also the whole image of what we represented—and which did not yet exist. Perhaps I pressed too hard with my hand and—as I hoped—she felt slightly threatened by me, because she stood up, and a sob shook her whole body, an explosion of emotion the truth of which could not be doubted. She turned away as if not wanting me to see what was happening, and, for some time, not daring to interrupt her, I watched her back shaken by her sobbing. And I could not have said who she was crying for, whether for me, who did not yet exist, or for that other man, who no longer existed. At that precise moment, I understood how terribly alone she was, and it was like glimpsing a landscape peopled with random shadows and lit by a dying light. I too stood up and slowly put my arms about her waist, resting my cheek on her shoulder:

"Nina," I said. And added more softly still: "My love."

Just when I was hoping to triumph and see the ghost of that absent being banished forever by my tenderness and my understanding, he threw off his disguise and fearlessly presented himself to me in the look on her face. She said:

"Yes, call me Nina, just like that . . . very softly."

Ah, how her face was transformed, even frighteningly rejuvenated, as if, after enduring years and years of pain and struggle, her torment had finally returned to its starting point, and was there, resplendent, magnificent, triumphant in its refusal to submit. The woman standing before me was not the one I knew, even though there was still the trace of a tear in her eyes; she was the same, but different, and what overlaid her present anguished appearance was the warmth of a passion I could only glimpse, not share, an imitation of the pleasurable, peaceful look on the faces of lovers at a moment of supreme revelation. Like a rose touched by the dew and about to open and burst into life, her whole being appeared to tremble with a still fresh emotion, to be made new, revealing a hidden energy revitalizing her whole being, her enthusiasm for all love's febrile lunacies. I did not dare to move or to say anything, aware only that she was giving off an energy that both burned me and drew me to her. Realizing what was happening, she took my hand and began to lead me away: I allowed myself to be led, not knowing where we were going.

We came to the end of that path and headed down another still darker one. This was one of the least frequented parts of the garden, and the path itself emerged near the Pavilion, in a clearing whose four corners had once been adorned with statues, each one representing a season, of which only Summer had survived. She stopped in that clearing and, still holding my hand, glanced around as if looking for someone. My sense of that other presence was so strong that I shuddered, and in her troubled, shining eyes I saw something like a reflection of that lost time, a reflection so insistent that I could almost make out a man's face, and through that face, a name, which should, I felt, never be spoken. She was so clearly looking for someone that, at one point, I found myself looking too, expecting to see him step out from the undergrowth. But I saw no one, and when I turned to her again, I realized that what she was doing was pure, obsessive habit. Again, I had the feeling that I did not exist, and even though she still held my hand in hers, I knew she was in another time altogether, doubtless in that same place, but in the midst of events that had vanished and dissolved many years before. I don't know how long she stood there, gazing at that moonlit scene. The statue of Summer rose serenely from behind a dark bush, a clump of ferns sprouting out of it as if from a vase. She again tugged at my hand and leaned against the statue, and it was as if she were listening to words spoken in the distant past, because her eyes shone with visionary energy, and her whole being gave off an intense feeling of happiness, like a blue wave. That was what obliged me to keep silent, even though I was suffering inside and understood little of what was going on.

"Call me Nina again," she said softly.

And I obeyed:

"Nina."

I don't know why, but this felt to me like the repetition of a scene from years ago, as if through my mouth another mouth were breathing the sound of that other voice. The wind was growing colder, the stars were fading—what time would it be?—and the trees were beginning to stir quietly and rhythmically. Then a shudder ran through me and, releasing myself from her grasp, I began to shake her:

"No, Nina, no! We need to live, but we need to live *now*, don't you see?" And I did not know who was telling me to say those words or what power was wrenching them up from my very soul.

Somehow she awoke from that dangerous state of distraction and again took my hand. Then, walking at an unexpectedly fast pace, she headed off toward the Pavilion. I confess I was intrigued, because the Pavilion, an old wooden building, had long since been abandoned, and as far as I knew, no one ever dared enter what was now the domain of mice and cockroaches. I myself rarely ventured into that part of the garden, which, in its neglected, overgrown state, was hardly the most alluring or most picturesque part of the Chácara. Nina, however, strode confidently ahead, as if the path held no surprises for her and she had often trodden it before in a different time and, doubtless, in a very different situation. (When, though? When she had lived there with my father? But the undergrowth was far denser now, and the place almost unrecognizable. Later? But in what circumstances? Why would she go to the Pavilion, what business or what idea would take her to that almost forbidden place? I did not know the answers to any of those questions, and so I accepted what was happening, convinced that, sooner or later, either by my own efforts or with the mere passage of time, I would eventually learn the truth.)

We reached a low, narrow door, which was clearly a servants' entrance, presumably with access to the rooms above via some stairs. She tried the door, but it was locked. (It may have been my imagination, but, at that precise moment, when the moon suddenly appeared from behind a frayed cloud, I turned my head and, not far off, thought I saw the leaves stirring. My first thought was that someone was watching us, but I immediately rejected the idea because the leaves stopped moving and I thought then that it was probably only the strange atmosphere and the bright moonlight helping to create those illusory, shifting shadows.) After a moment's hesitation—only a moment, like someone finally reaching a decision—Nina went over to one of the window ledges and felt nervously with her hands for some object that should have been there, but clearly wasn't. After feeling about for some time, she gave an irritated sigh. I did not at first understand what she was looking for, but when she again ran her hand along the ledge, I realized that she must be looking for a key. After this fruitless search, she lost patience, went back to the door and pushed hard, first with her hands and then with her shoulder, trying to force it open. The stubborn lock soon gave and, slowly, with a dull creak that echoed through the garden, it turned on its hinges, revealing the dark cellar within. I thought I saw signs of some previous experience in the skillful way she had opened that door. I went closer and felt a damp musty breath on my cheek. She grabbed my arm and said:

"Come here."

I obediently followed the sound of her voice, because I could see nothing and my heart was pounding ever faster. There seems little point in telling lies in a notebook intended exclusively as a place in which to describe my emotions, and the truth is that I felt not so much afraid as convinced that something grave and decisive was about to happen, something in which I would, perhaps, be an unwitting participant. For a few seconds, we stumbled over various objects and piles of tools, which toppled and fell as we collided with them, until we reached a point I could still not identify, but which she clearly thought was the place she was seeking. She stopped, ran her hand along the wall in a circular gesture and must have found a latch, because before our eyes a door opened with a creak just like the outer door—those hinges had clearly not been oiled for a long time. I could not help but admire her knowledge of the darkness, and a far from scornful smile appeared on my lips. Holding out her hand to me, she continued to lead me on, skillfully avoiding any further obstacles, as if she knew precisely where they were, and as if guided by an instinct or a sixth sense, which aroused not so much my surprise as a sharp, unexpected pang of jealousy. So it was until, a little further on, she sat down on something, giving an enormous sigh of relief as she did. I sat down too and found myself sitting on a tattered old couch covered with a musty shawl, and which had presumably been relegated there as a useless piece of junk. Mice and cockroaches scurried about in the darkness, and sitting there, motionless, for a moment, I could hear that whole prodigious concerto of sounds and sense the powerful breath of death filling the place. It must have been a servant's room, cramped and dirty—on one of the walls was a single barred window, through which I could see a sliver of sky, as if we were in a prison cell.

"What are you thinking about?" she asked, and I could feel her breath on my neck. "We need to live now," and I realized she was repeating my words back to me, but without a hint of scorn or any wish to offend.

Bending over, I sensed that she was so close I had only to turn my head in order to touch her face, which I did, and our lips met again. True, one part of my conscience remained in the shadows, although

I still felt it as a very present, albeit intangible weight; besides, what did I care about those remnants of conscience, when, for the first time, the body I had so desired in secret was there before me, alive and willing? She lay back and I followed suit and we rolled about on that old couch—and for as long as I live, I will never forget the feel of her breasts beneath my hands, her soft throat beneath my lips, the warm, sweet perfume she gave off, like a whole bed of crushed violets. And I cannot even say I was unaware of the extent of my sin because, however often I repeated to myself that I was caressing and biting the very body that had borne me, at the same time, I took a strange, mortal pleasure in that, and it was as if I were leaning over myself, and, having always been the most solitary of creatures, I was now plunging into a perfumed tangle of nerves that was me, my most faithful image, my conscience and my hell.

I gently ran my hand over her body, my whole being prickling at the touch of her skin, and as if this were a long-familiar path along which flowed all the world's dissonances, I placed my hand on her soft, moist cunt, which, like a sucker, trembled beneath my touch. Her whole body shuddered and heaved, and as my fingers probed more deeply, I felt that hidden flower opening and frankly laying bare its mysteries, like a mouth uttering not its own name but that of its invited guest. I again ran my hand over her body, overwhelming her with the sheer force of my affections, and finally, like a shout, the spell broke, and that body's dark, red cleft half-opened with a laugh so youthful and so vibrant that it seemed to ring with all the music that had ever existed.

To say that we made love would be to say but little; allowing myself to be absorbed, I, in turn, tried to absorb her, and out of that fusion I gained my first sense of love and its abyss. How often we made love would be hard to say, for the act of love and my own emotional ecstasy were too intertwined. The sheer sacrilege of it drove me on; imagining it to be an affront to both human and divine laws, I delighted in clutching her to me, in squeezing and biting her breasts, reinventing the pleasure of being a child and imagining the deep, narrow path that was now mine and which, independently of myself, had once brought me into this world. I, we, what greater madness was there than this desperate coming together of flesh, annihilating time with our deviant love?

Finally, overwhelmed by exhaustion, I fell back beside her, drenched in sweat. (The same sweat, I sensed, the same sticky sweat, cold as ice, that I would, alas, meet again later, on the walls of the room in which she lay dying, the same sweat that would absorb her last trace of perfume, her final tremor—her final living breath. The same oily sweat—the common denominator of those two moments of rupture, creating that barrier of separation against which I began to struggle as soon as I rolled over and she began to breathe alone and far from me, solely herself, cut off from our joint escapade, a mere woman, and she fell asleep, exhausted, like an anemone closing, like a rejection or a condemnation.)

I do not know how long we lay there, but it must have been very late when we heard a noise, probably a spade or a hoe falling over in the darkness. It could easily have been caused by a scampering mouse, but, for some reason, I remembered the leaves stirring outside and imagined that someone really was following us. I betrayed my cowardice then:

"I think someone is spying on us," I said, sitting up.

She laughed softly:

"Are you afraid?"

I hesitated:

"What if it's my father?"

She did not reply at once; she must have been weighing up just how cowardly I was. Then, with extraordinary calm, she said:

"Well, whoever it is, you had better leave. They mustn't find you with me."

I confess, and I blush as I write these words, that I was only waiting for that excuse to run away. I wanted to be alone in order to evaluate the extent and depth of those experiences. I fled, stumbling over the tools in my path. My forehead was bathed in sweat, my shirt stuck to my body, and I gave a sigh of relief when I saw the sky again and felt the night breeze on my face.

27.
Ana's Third Confession

I, Ana Meneses, am writing this even though I have no idea who I am writing it for. It's pointless, more habit than necessity, but such is my despair that I resort to writing so as not to give in entirely to my distress. I used to write to Father Justino, and even if such confessions did not always reach him, they often served to calm me. Writing created a kind of artificial serenity in my inner self. And perhaps that is what I am still hoping for: to forget, to sink into a lethargy that would change nothing, but would at least allow me to forget myself, as if I were under the influence of a narcotic. Now, though, I don't know who I am writing for, nor who could possibly be interested in these neat, symmetrical lines with which I am laboriously filling this sheet of paper. The only thing I do know is that everything around me feels terribly hostile and I myself have become a sad, cold creature. How hard it is to put those two words together—sad and cold—knowing that they correspond precisely to what exists inside us, to that heavy, insensitive thing that is our heart. I often stand in front of the mirror and take a long, cool look at my reflection. It's me, there's no doubt about that, because it moves when I move, and wears the same familiar shabby clothes, as inalterably mine as my hands, my eyes, my mouth. Despite this, I cannot help asking myself: who does that face belong to? And slowly, cruelly, I gradually reconstruct that familiar physiognomy, which, needless to say, causes me such revulsion. How I hate and despise myself, how I dislike my external self. The snuff-brown skirt, the plain, faded blouse, the unkempt hair, are all proof of how mean and vile I consider myself to be. There is, alas, no Christian sentiment in that statement. I loathe myself in vain, just as one might loathe a snake or a toad, but this does not imply any leniency toward the rest of the world, because I loathe the others just as much, not because I feel they are better than me, but because, in my opinion, they are equally ridiculous and despicable. I loathe everything and everyone, and it is at such moments, standing before the mirror, that I realize the extent of the coldness inhabiting me—a bottomless, inconsolable thing, oppressive and stagnant, as if everything inside me had been scorched by a fire that had destroyed any possibility of tenderness and forgiveness in my soul. I cannot say why I am like this, perhaps someone else could, maybe Father Justino, were he ever to read what I am writing here. But I no longer believe in Father Justino—I never did; besides, I am not interested in what he might have to say. All that remains is that creature in the mirror: she moves from side to side, winks, smiles, but has long been dead, and what is dead cannot be resurrected out of mud or sterility.

That is why I clung to the remnants of the one thing that, for me, represented existence. That is why I defended those remnants, like someone defending the image of their only chance of happiness in this world. I cannot remember when Father Justino said this, but I can hear his voice telling me: "You cannot imagine the blood, the turmoil, the negativity of those souls made for love, and who are betrayed by their own destiny." It was not hope that made me kneel so earnestly before that grave, because I have no hope. (I am perhaps the only creature totally without hope. Time does not exist for me, nor does the past or the future, everything is irremediably permanent. That is what hell is like—an empty space with no frontiers in time.)

I repeat, it was not hope that made me tend those poor remains so zealously: it was a need to justify myself, to have in my hands unmistakable proof that there was once a moment when I truly existed.

That is the only reason I was waiting for her, ready to bar the way along that path forever. She did not see me at first, and she must have had a shock, because I was so still and so calm. I can see myself there, all in black (and so very still it was almost as if my heart had stopped beating), and leaning against the pockmarked cellar wall. I watched her draw closer and then I moved, just once, barely visible in the darkness, but enough to show her that the way was blocked. She stopped and I could see her breathing quicken. We did not have much to say to each other, silence was enough. We stood there, and I could feel her struggling to contain her emotion. That was when she said in a voice rich in sarcasm:

"I know who you are," she said. Then in a different tone: "And I know that you've been following me for a long time."

It was ridiculous of her to say such a thing, especially when these were the first words we had exchanged in fifteen years. I say again, the silence was enough, because everything that contains a death, even a death cast and recast over fifteen years, needs only a moment or a glance to makes its presence felt. That is why I simply laughed, and maybe my laughter was too brief or too fierce, but those fifteen years of effort were finally finding their release through that small crack.

"What are you laughing at?" she cried. "What?"

I did not respond immediately—I wanted to have her there for a while at my mercy, to see her squirm before my eyes like a wounded reptile. And, of course, that unfamiliar darkness in which she was thrashing about—she must have forgotten it, just as she had forgotten the garden, the trees and the whole backdrop to her sin—was for me the element in which I lived and breathed each and every day.

"What? Tell me." And she launched herself at me, coming so close that I could feel on my cheek the furious blast of her breath.

"No reason," I said, "or only one. Yes, I've been following you, but not because of you."

"Why then?"

"Because of him."

"Oh!" And then her voice, too, sounded more like a laugh. "So you want to defend him as well . . . you want . . ."

I was so taken aback, all I could say was:

"Who?"

She said nothing and took a step back. She was probably calculating how best to wound me, now that we were face to face; more than that, she was probably working out just how long we had waited for that moment and even perhaps how often we had both imagined that scene—that particular scene, unique among all others. Then, as if she had finally reached a conclusion, she shrugged and clothed herself in coldness. In that look, the look of someone judging another person touched by madness, I saw how much she must despise me, how much she thought she knew about me.

"I know who it is," she said. "It's the boy, my son."

I looked up, surprised at this unexpected statement, and laughter rose once more to my lips.

"Nonsense," I said. "How could you possibly think such a thing. I have absolutely no interest in your son."

She seemed troubled and again recoiled slightly, examining me from head to foot. Ah, what pleasure I took in feeling superior to her, safe with my sly secret. It was as though she no longer understood the person before her and were cautiously trying to sniff out some hidden threat. She had understood nothing, not then and not before. All my imaginings were just that, the whims of a feeble imagination immersed in its own deliriums. There was no rival, no enemy, nothing existed, except a life I had thought was real and in which no one else had a part—a mockery, in short, of my own pathetic vanity. Blindly, I took a step forward, while these words came quickly to my lips:

"You're mistaken. I have no interest in André whatsoever. I know what's going on, because that is my punishment in this house: to know everything. But what do I care if you consort with him in dark corners, like a bitch in heat? That is your personal hell, your personal misery."

There, I had said it, and she was waiting, standing slightly apart from me. I expected her to be angry, to attack me, to commit some desperate act. Instead, in a soft, singularly calm voice, she asked:

"So why are you following me, then? What do you want from me?"

My sense of victory vanished like smoke: I felt lost. Everything inside me was so fragile that all it would take to shake me to my roots and expose my weakness was a word, a withdrawal, a show of serenity.

"Because you . . ." I stammered, but lacked the courage to go any further.

It was hard to say—it was almost like betraying myself and handing myself over to my enemy bound hand and foot. Was this why I had lied all those years, endured life within those cold, uncharitable walls, spoken only to my own sad, numb, hopeless heart? To speak would be to offer her the comfort of an explanation, and she must have understood this, because her voice rang out with a note of triumph:

"Answer me. Why are you following me? What do you want? Are you in love with my son too? Is that what you want? If you were brave enough . . ."

And then she revealed the depths to which she had sunk:

"Ah, if you knew what soft skin he has . . . how he kisses and caresses . . . A grown man couldn't do it better."

Then she stopped. In the darkness, I could feel her waiting for some response. Those provocative words hung in the air. However, my silence must have frightened her. She withdrew still further and leaned against the wall, hiding her face in her hands. I thought she must be crying, but could hear no sobbing. Finally, she fixed her dry eyes on me:

"What am I saying?" she cried. "How dreadful! I must be mad."

And more quietly, as if trying out the effect of the words on herself:

"My son."

I coolly corrected her:

"Your lover."

She said nothing, but I could see her eyes shining in the darkness. After a while, as if she had recovered her strength, she said:

"If it's not him, then why are you following me?"

This time, I smiled to myself—she clearly didn't understand at all! I didn't know what to think, was this one of those acts she was so good at putting on, or was she really so utterly removed from everything that had happened? No, I could not forgive her, still less understand her. For me, she would always be the woman I had imagined her to be. I did not want her carefree and flighty, blissfully ignorant and light of heart; I needed her to be hard and fierce, defending her territory inch by inch, as ferociously as someone chained forever to a guilty passion. With infinite calm, I began to speak:

"Because I made a promise to myself . . . ever since that time, don't you remember?" (And I had never before spoken like this; it felt so very strange that I could hardly believe that the words "that time" had suddenly appeared there between us, clear and palpable, like a piece of terrain suddenly revealed before our cowardly steps.) "You could come back whenever you wanted, you could wreak havoc again just as you are doing now, but you cannot harm me any more than you already have. Does that frighten you? No. You are doubtless playing a part for me, just as you do for everyone else. But I know your secret. I swore to myself, you see," and I advanced on her almost threateningly, "I swore that I would seal up this room—the very room from which you have just emerged—and that no one else would ever set foot in it. Only me, when, on certain days, my sense of loss grew too much and the pain of the world unbearable." (She, of course, would never understand that "pain of the world." So intense were my feelings when I spoke those words, that an involuntary sob escaped me.) "When I saw you come back, I was afraid you might remember this small room, which is the only thing that belongs to me, the only possession I have."

I could no longer hold back my tears and my voice was drowned by my sobbing. I noticed, though, that she did not draw back, on the contrary, she was watching me intently. Ah, I could bear anything but that woman's pity. I managed to get a grip on myself, dried my eyes and went on:

"And you headed straight here . . . to this room, to my hiding place. Do you understand now that I really don't care if you're bedding your own son, perverting him, teaching him to enjoy base pleasures? No, I swear, I really don't care. I know that both of you are made of base matter, and so I'm sure you'll get on like a house on fire. But I don't want you using this room, you hear me? I don't want your laughter and your moans to waken the dead. Use any bed but this one." My voice had grown softer: "The bed that still bears the bloodstains of the man you killed."

She said nothing, but I could tell from her ever faster breathing that she was moved, and perhaps, who knows, those words had led her back to her permanent reality, to the feelings and memories now filling her mind. Perhaps there was no need to imagine her utterly devoid of a soul; she must have a soul, a cold, egotistical one, but a soul nonetheless, capable of experiencing ecstasy and grief, even if that grief were unjustified, even criminal.

"How cruel you are," she said. "Believe me, I could demolish with a single word everything you have just said. And you're so confident too . . ."

And suddenly she began to laugh, and I saw her eyes shining brightly in the darkness. I was troubled by her nonchalance, by her reaction to my offensive remarks. I know only that she spoke and for a long time, not as if she were remembering things that happened years before, but with the vivacity and warmth with which one speaks of present-day events. I used to imagine the remorse, the sad thoughts that must now and then surface in her mind. (Ah, I had seen him when he first arrived to tend the garden, still just a boy, almost André's age. He had about him the inscrutable aura of the eternally innocent. And I had been the one to press his dying head to my bosom, the one to feel his heart—pierced by a bullet—stop beating in his youthful chest) and, in moments of greater calm, I even succeeded in imagining her feeling a tiny spark of tenderness and giving a smile intended perhaps for the poor dead lad. That, I felt, was what she must imagine love to be, like alms given out willy-nilly, a chance gesture devoid of any personal intent, a random gift. It had never occurred to me to idealize that repressed rage, the hot, long-buried rush of words to her lips. She spoke—and although she said nothing I did not know already, it was as if this were the first time she was revealing what had happened back then. I felt a new me being born, despite my certainty that, over the years, my jealousy would remain unchanged.

"If you must know . . . if you still don't know everything that happened . . . then be assured that I loved him, loved him madly, and in this very bed that you tell me is still stained with blood. He was a boy, but I made him a man. I left my mark on him so that he would never ever forget me. Those who imagine love from afar, like a fruit they have never tasted, have no idea how delicious suffering can be—simultaneously terrible and sweet—because to love is to suffer. How can you speak of love, you, who have only ever known one repellent man? How dare you confront me and demand payment for a sin whose price you do not even know? He would lie in my lap weeping and begging me for a kiss, a caress, and at first, I would refuse him everything, only to give myself to him entirely later on. It's strange to say his name now, especially because I have never once said his name out loud since then: Alberto. I'll say it again—Alberto,

Alberto—and you cannot take that name from my lips, because it's as much a part of me as my own blood. Do you think he ever actually saw you, that he even noticed your presence? Never. But I knew, I was sure of it, I was watching you and knew you were following me. What delight I took in making you suffer, in seeing on your face, day by day, hour by hour, minute by minute, the signs of your sad passion. Do you know, I even hoped you *would* touch him. I wanted to see him besmirched by another woman. For a long time, I went around with a knife, imagining how I would kill you. Because if you had so much as touched him, I would not have hesitated, I would have murdered you at once. But the only image in his eyes was mine. He was glad to be blind. I would follow him too, when he wasn't by my side; I would threaten him, promise to reveal everything so that he would be expelled from the Chácara. How he trembled then, saying that he would die outside, like an abandoned dog. All those things, though, only fueled our love. The afternoons we spent, our faces pressed together, hatching plans that never came to anything, but which were intoxicating just to imagine. It was good like that, I would breathe in his breath and we would touch each other as if we were one and the same body. When I came to my senses, I remembered that I was married to the Meneses, that I belonged to this house, that there *was* a reality. That was what finished me off, finished us off. Today . . ."

She stopped talking for a moment, apparently focused on her own thoughts, no longer talking for my benefit, but merely responding to an interior dialogue that must have been going on inside her for years. She continued in a very different tone, as if the heat of passion were cooling in her voice:

"I didn't know how to accept my sin, if it was a sin. That is why now, when André holds me in his arms, I say to him: 'André don't deny it, accept your sin, embrace it. Don't allow others to make a torment of it, don't let them destroy you with their assumption that you're a coward, a man who doesn't know how to live his own life.

The most authentic thing about you is your sin—without it, you would be a dead man. Promise me, André, promise that you will take full responsibility for the evil you are committing.' And he swears, and with each day that passes, I see that he is more and more convinced of his victory."

There was a diabolical fervor in those last words. She was moving away from my problems, from everything I knew and had assumed to be inherent in human nature. That woman clearly carried something within her that went beyond anything I was capable of. As I stood there, I hardly recognized her, it was as if I were seeing her for the first time—and I could not deny that she was beautiful, very beautiful, with those extraordinary words burning her lips, so potent that they seemed to bathe her in an infernal light.

"Anyway," I said, wanting to have the last word, "you will never come back to this room." (I tapped my chest, as if there lay source of all my strength.) "I have the key here: this door will never again open to you."

She laughed as she was moving away:

"I don't need a key," she said. "It's easy enough to open these old doors just by giving them a good shove. Besides, the room doesn't mean anything to me any more."

Those last words were spoken from a distance. And I soon found myself alone, with darkness closing in on me.

28.
Father Justino's Second Account

I wasn't intending to go in, since I had only come to ask for a donation. Holding my mule by the reins, I leaned against the post at the bottom of the steps and waited for the maid to announce me. It was almost midday and the sun was glittering on the wet sand of the garden paths. Senhor Valdo soon came out onto the verandah. I saw from the way he leaned on the balustrade that my visit was more than just a surprise, it was almost an auspicious event. "Ah, Father Justino," he said to me, "what a pleasure! It's been quite some time since we've seen you around these parts." He seemed to be expecting me to come up the steps. I explained that I had come to ask for a donation for the forthcoming church festival. "But of course, Father!" he exclaimed and insisted that I come up. We could have a chat; he wanted to hear all about the construction of the new parish church. I noticed that he seemed nervous and somewhat preoccupied. It had indeed been a long time since I had been to the Chácara, although I used to go there frequently to visit my good friend Dona Malvina, Senhor Valdo's mother, paralyzed in her wheelchair. I had not been back since her death—one somber evening that seemed to presage the Chácara's present decline—first, because she was the only member of the family who showed any real interest in me, and, secondly, because with her death my work here was, alas, done, and other tasks called me to other parts of the parish. And so up until that day my contact with Senhor Valdo had been somewhat limited; you might even say that I did not really know him at all. He looked so exhausted and so much older that I wondered whether he had always been like that, if the anguish in his eyes was a permanent feature. Something was clearly gnawing away at him inside. I tied my mule to the post and went up to the verandah, trying to suppress the memories that swept over me with each step I took (Dona Malvina in her wheelchair, a blanket over her knees, her face twitching from the effects of her stroke: "Ah, Father Justino, I fear for what will happen when I'm gone. This house . . ."). Although I could not say that there had been a major transformation in the physical appearance of its inhabitants (it's strange how suffering imposes its own particular mask on people's faces; at that moment I could not quite recall what Senhor Valdo had looked like before, but it seemed to me now as if another face had been imprinted on his, and, strangely enough, that new face was Dona Malvina's. The man standing before me was filled with the same eagerness, the same inquisitive gleam and even the same tics that had characterized my dear friend during the last few years of her life. The only difference was that, in her, all those things had been genuine, while, in him, they seemed borrowed or stolen, the result of some strange subterfuge. And yet there he was, installed in that place so laden with memories for me, with all the deft ease of a successful impostor), I could, however, at least state with certainty that the house itself had undergone a radical transformation. The verandah, for example, with its row of colored glass panes around the top, seemed larger because much of the furniture had been removed since my previous visits. The pillars were chipped around the edges, and the trees from the garden clung with intimate abandon to the slope outside and threatened to invade the house itself. An insolent branch of flowering jasmine had almost reached the middle of the verandah. Ah, it was clear that the voice of Dona Malvina was no longer to be heard in that world, which was undergoing a slow process of disintegration that was gradually eating away at the solid, austere name she had left behind.

Senhor Valdo was still standing in front of me, and the two of us stood there awkwardly until he decided to break the silence. "Do sit down, Father Justino. You know you are always welcome in this house. In fact, I would very much like to talk to you . . ." I sat down. (And everything seemed to return to a certain order: the branch of jasmine stopped in its tracks; the chipped pillars took on a familiar air; the atmosphere itself grew calmer, as if, beneath the midday sun, everything around us were being numbed by dull, tepid everyday life.) "I don't quite know how to talk about such things . . ." he began, and his voice, interrupting my thoughts, almost startled me, ". . . the truth is that I have never been much of a churchgoer and have always managed without the assistance of the sacraments." "What things?" I asked. He shook his head, perplexed: "I don't know how you would describe them . . ." I tried to be as undogmatic as possible: "For me, some things are a matter for confession and some are not." He shook his head again: "No, it isn't a matter for confession." "Well, then, is there something you'd like to ask me?" I could tell from his silence that he was trying to gather his thoughts, searching for the best way to say what he wanted to say. "For example . . ." he continued. Then, breaking free of all constraints, he suddenly burst out: "Father, what is hell?" This was not the question I was expecting and I stayed silent for a few moments, looking at the sun beating down on the tiles of the verandah. As if in the grip of some superior force, I was filled with an overwhelming desire to reply: "Hell is this: this house, this verandah, this homogenizing sun." However, I did not and turned to look at him: "Ah, my son. Hell by its very nature is the most changeable of things. When all's said and done, it is the manifestation of all of man's passions." He seemed at first not to understand and repeated softly: "Passions?" I nodded: "Passions. The very deepest of inclinations. A desire for peace, for example." As I said this, I sensed that I had perhaps been somewhat arbitrary in invoking the house, the verandah, and even the sunshine itself. Senhor Valdo bowed his head, deep in thought. Everything around us was silent, a pause within the already long noonday pause. A sweet smell of roses filled the air; far away, a bird taking flight let out a shrill cry. It would be hard to overcome that bright atmosphere, and yet, like an impulse rising up from the static surroundings, I felt a beating presence, a sinuous, unstoppable movement, a liberated spirit wheeling around above us. It made me shudder, and I turned to face Senhor Valdo just as he looked up and began to speak again: "Are you referring to this house, Father?" A mocking smile appeared on his lips: "There's no peace in this house; quite the contrary." He stopped, eyed me intensely, then concluded abruptly: "If the devil exists, then it is he who has destroyed the peace of this house." Perhaps he was waiting for a gesture of protest or surprise from me, but I merely shrugged: "The indifference, you mean . . ." He stared at me again with undisguised astonishment: "What are you accusing us of, Father?" Once more, I gazed with infinite weariness at everything around me. He must have understood, for he, too, looked about him and gave a sigh. "Must we . . ." he replied in the voice of someone whose strength was gradually ebbing away, "must we believe in God in order to know that the devil exists?" Once again he had wrong-footed me, and I chose my words tentatively. I could, of course, answer immediately and settle the matter once and for all, but would I not then be ruling out the chance of hearing what he had to tell me? It would not be difficult for me to say, for example, that signs of the devil's presence—after all, is he not the prince of this world?—were usually far more obvious than those of God's presence. Or at least bolder and cruder. However, I limited myself to asking him a question to which I already knew his answer: "You don't believe in God, is that it?" How, in the torpid heat of that verandah, was it possible to believe? He laughed again, and there was a roguish edge to his laughter that displeased me. "No, I don't," he said. Once again I felt that strange blind presence whirling about me. I thought of saying: "So there you are: that's what peace is," but I merely stared down at the floor and listened to the birds singing. (Into my mind came the memory of Dona Malvina, propelling her wheelchair along the garden paths and waving her stick: "Leave the birds in peace, boys. I don't want any traps in my garden!"). When I came to, Senhor Valdo was staring at me with open curiosity. I needed to say something and so, leaving the spell of the past to the warm embrace of the light around us, I asked: "And the devil? Do you believe in him?" I saw him tremble and glance over at the other end of the verandah as if he sensed someone's presence there. "Yes, I do," he replied in a voice so faint I could scarcely hear him. It was my turn to look up then, as if obeying an order—and it was then that I saw her, modestly dressed and leaning in the doorway to the drawing room, providing a strange contrast to the radiant midday air.

29.
Continuation of Ana's Third Confession

I had no intention of following them, nor did I care what they got up to, until pure chance revealed their secret to me. I had been wandering about the house, eavesdropping on the servants' silly conversations, and vainly watching the slow hands of the clock, when I found myself in the drawing room. At that hour, the windows were closed and the curtains drawn. It was then that I saw André—I hadn't seen him for three days, because Valdo, alarmed by one of his son's hysterical outbursts, had shut him up in one of the rooms in the Pavilion—anyway, I saw André creeping very cautiously toward the verandah, like someone about to commit a crime. What prompted me to follow him was, as I say, merely the terrible idleness that hangs over a household like ours. Everything is so firmly fixed in its place that the most insignificant of incidents attracts attention. I had never really thought much about André. Not even to consider his defects or to try and understand his foolish passions, as I had done with his father, but I had, of course, noticed him coming and going, I was aware of him as a living, breathing being who lived alongside me, and I even went so far as to try and imagine what kind of person he really was—a solitary creature like all the others, trapped inside his own deficiencies and errors—but I had never felt interested enough to ponder his real nature. That evening, though, I got a slight surprise: when I went over to the window, in the furtive, silent manner I had adopted ever since Nina's return—you will perhaps say that I was spying, that I was following a trail like an animal in search of disaster—I noticed André placing something, a note perhaps, under one of the loose bricks along the edge of the verandah. It was growing dark, and the garden was plunged in a diffuse, purplish glow that reached as far as the colored glass frieze under the verandah roof. Possibly because of the cold, André was wearing an old cape he had worn as a child. Silhouetted against the light from the garden, he lingered for a moment, glanced around him, then disappeared. I thought I saw him gesture to someone I could not see, but I was too far away to be sure. I was about to abandon my hiding place and go out onto the verandah when I saw Nina approaching; she was walking slowly, tentatively, as if afraid she might be seen. She stopped at the same spot and deftly lifted the brick, removed the note, and unfolded it. I noticed that she was looking for somewhere bright enough to read it. This took only a moment, then she screwed up the note and threw it down; I made a point of noticing the exact point where the ball of paper fell. She did all these things very impatiently. She did not immediately move away, she paused to think, and I saw the dreamy expression on her face. Maybe it was just the light, but I realized again how very beautiful she was. Leaning on the balustrade, head back, her lips parted as if to drink in the cold air of the coming night. What would she be thinking, what inner battles was she waging? I don't know and I never will. But, still keeping well out of the fading light, I continued to observe her, recalling, one by one, with utter clarity, the details of everything that had happened between us. Seeing her still so young and so alluring, I understood, but how could I forgive her, when to do so would be to accept God's manifest injustice? I saw her utter a deep sigh, then, with the same cat-like steps, she left the verandah. I waited a little longer, afraid she might come back, but when the night had completed its invasion of the verandah—apart from one piece of the glass frieze, which glinted stubbornly red like a phosphorescent eye—I left my hiding place and went outside. There was the screwed-up ball of paper, and, I confess, my hands shook when I picked it up. It was pointless trying to read it in the dark and, besides, someone might find me. I ran to my room, bolted the door, and turned on the light. My heart was beating fast—I was finally about to be given the key to the secret. I smoothed out the paper and saw that it was written in a pale, tremulous hand, as though by someone in the grip of a powerful emotion. The light was rather dim—this had always been one of the Chácara's fundamental failings—and so I went over to the prayer desk at the far side of the room and took out the little lamp that was always lit to illumine the image of Our Lady of Grace. By that light I read these words: ". . . they let me out today, and I need to see you immediately—alone. How can you be so cruel to me? I will be waiting for you in half an hour, in the clearing next to the Pavilion." Those words, read by the unsteady flame of an oil-lamp, did not surprise me in the least. Nothing that Nina did would surprise me. I thought only: Ah, so it's incest! And I was filled by a kind of dense peace. She was clearly capable of anything, I had said as much time and again, and what could a woman driven by such desperate energies do except hurl herself against the walls of the atmosphere surrounding her, before that same atmosphere smothered her? I almost envied her, envied that brutal impulse, that blind search to satisfy her appetites! What astonished me was the speed with which everything had happened, and now, sitting on the bed, clutching the sheet of paper once more rolled into a ball, I was thinking that things must already have happened, and that I was merely seeing the emergence of events that had long been fermenting in the hearts of those more than willing participants. I don't really believe in fate, that would be foolish—what is fatal is our human tendency to slide toward the abyss and chaos. That potently fertile soil, loneliness, had enriched those vulnerable fields. Nina would love anything, anyone; it would be impossible for her to live like a plant alone in its flower bed. She would send out roots, spread her seeds on the wind, until she overflowed the boundaries of the bed and found some defenseless, will-less bush. (*Written in the margin*: Only later, much later, did I realize that this was not quite true: Nina was simply reacting. To what? To whom? I hardly dared think. But the helpless, solitary plant I imagined was, in my opinion, a hard, spiny cactus. She was reacting against that savage love—in order not to die, in order not to be torn to pieces.) I stood up, muttering: "Just like before, just as she always does," and I could not conceal my bitterness. Still standing, I repeated: "Just like before." Then the thought of the Pavilion rushed in on me, and I heard in my ears the words I had read in the note: "I will be waiting for you in half an hour, in the clearing next to the Pavilion." This was almost exactly what had happened before. The Pavilion was still there, and Nina would be waiting next to it, possibly in the dark and with the same perfume floating on the air. Except that now, everything had changed, and I had promised myself that no one—no one—would ever again enter the room where he had breathed his last. I had often seen her sloping off down to the Pavilion, and I knew where she was going: to that room, that poor, dark, cramped room that had served as the stage for their secret love. (I remember his chest covered in blood, the pink foam bubbling out from the corners of his mouth, the gardening tools piled in the corners, the precise hour and, in particular, my own pain. I remember as if it were yesterday. I remember, to my own great torment, that his lips had uttered a single name, and what I said, what I did, is lost forever in the great flood of facts exemplifying the futility of all human effort.) But everything was different now, and I kept the key close to my heart. It wasn't a medal or a scapular pressed to my beating breast, it was merely the key to the room where God had so cruelly wounded me. That is probably the supreme problem, God and man, but however hard I try, I cannot imagine God without love, regardless of what kind of love that might be, even the most sinful kind, because I cannot imagine man without love or man without God. Perhaps that is why, ultimately, Nina does not frighten me; what I hate about her is that she got in my way. She can sully whatever she likes, she can destroy whatever she can lay her hands on, but, even if it costs me my life, she cannot enter that room, where I built my altar. (I know that voices will be raised against me—to serve God one must renounce human love. In that case, I prefer not to serve God, because he made me human, and I cannot and do not wish to spontaneously renounce what constitutes my own self and forms part of my very essence. What kind of God would require us to renounce our own personality, in exchange for a marvelous kingdom we cannot even glimpse through the mist? I know, it's a question of Grace, but for a poor, limited, earthbound creature like me, how can I see renunciation and saintliness, goodness and peace, other than as an act of criminal violence perpetrated on the spirit that inhabits me?)

I hesitated not a moment longer: I covered my head against the cold night and set off into the garden. Absorbed in my own thoughts, I hurried down the avenue that led to the clearing. The air was utterly still and, despite the chill, the roses were lifting their heads attentively in the darkness. When I arrived, there was no one there, and I had plenty of opportunity to find a place to hide. This was not the first time I had done this when following in Nina's footsteps, and doing so all those years later made my heart beat as hard as it had then. I did wonder if I was acting out of pure habit, but when I noticed my frozen hands, tight, dry lips, and heavy heart, I realized that rather than these being the signs of dull habit, they were evidence of another, far stronger feeling driving me on. (I can even hear voices saying: What about the love of God? But what do people who can no longer express ordinary human love know of God's love?) If it weren't for the fact that all the trees and shrubs had grown enormously since then, it was almost as if my observation post had remained unchanged. I was just settling down behind a clump of ferns, when I heard footsteps. I kept very still and saw someone walking toward the clearing, although I could not yet see who it was. The otherwise calm air was occasionally shaken by a sudden gust of wind, and then, high up, the clouds would thicken and cover the moon, plunging everything into deep gloom. It was at one such moment that I spotted my nephew, André. I confess that when I realized it was him, I felt a twinge of curiosity. It was almost as if I were seeing him for the first time. Oddly enough, he seemed older and less familiar than I imagined. Thin, and with his straight hair falling forward over his face, the cape slung over his shoulders, he could have cut an almost childish figure, were there not something very grown-up about his gestures—a certainty, a determination of which I had no idea he was capable. I should make it clear that I felt no pity for him, but was thinking coldly: so he was the sinner, the most recent prey to fall into Nina's talons. How would he cope? Would he be up to the role reserved for him?

I don't know how long we waited, with him shifting restlessly about on the bench, alert to the slightest sound, and me in my hiding place behind the clump of ferns. Finally, she appeared; I saw her dark figure emerge from the avenue and walk slowly toward the bench. I could gauge his excitement from the way he sprang to his feet. However hard I strained my ears, I could not hear what they were saying. There was a moment when she seemed about to leave, but then she turned back and continued talking to him. What would they be saying, what could they be talking about that could be of any interest to me? It would just be a string of vacuous inanities, the kind of things lovers say to each other. In the circumstances, it was hard to imagine anything more ridiculous. Having never heard or spoken such things before, he might have the right to say those things, but what right did that woman have to deceive him, having sullied her lips with every possible false promise? Time seemed to stand still, and I looked up at the moon drifting across the sky. Finally, I saw that they were heading for the Pavilion—ah, so she had given in—and I thought to myself: "It's time." I had brought a small flashlight with me, but felt it best not to turn it on. If she went into the room, I would not hesitate to do so, though. I was hoping that when Nina found the door locked, she would give up, but I hadn't realized how fragile the door had become. All it needed was a hard shove from either her or André. (No, I should be more precise: I was convinced, as I still am, that she was the one who did this.) From where I was, I heard the door creak wearily open. Anger flooded my heart and seemed to blind me, and I walked toward the Pavilion, my flashlight in my hand. It wasn't hard to locate the exact point where they had entered. Standing before the open door, I trembled, breathing in the musty smell emerging from the darkness, as if they had just desecrated a grave.

30.
Continuation of Father Justino's Second Account

It did not take me long to realize my mistake: Senhor Valdo was unaware that a third person had joined us on the verandah. He may still have had something left to say, but, noticing my eyes fixed on the door, he turned and saw his sister-in-law, still uncertain as to whether to come forward or to retreat into the drawing room. It was already too late to withdraw, though, and she moved, glacially, toward me. (As I stood up, I understood why I had come to that house: the reason that had brought me was something more decisive, more imperious, and I no longer had the slightest doubt that the reason was standing there before me. How she had changed! And even though she kept her eyes prudently lowered, how fiercely they burned compared to that day long ago when she had summoned me to the bedside of the young man in the Pavilion. My first act—and I had known this for a long time—would be to tell her: "Don't worry, it's of no importance," but from the very first glance I sensed that she was quite literally on her guard, and that any soothing words of mine would be a mistake.)

"Father Justino," she said to me, "how are you?"

Nothing in her voice indicated any kind of emotion. On the contrary, it was the most banal of greetings, so banal indeed that it could have been addressed to anyone. I held out my hand and, to my surprise, found that it was trembling. Senhor Valdo must have noticed my discomfort, for I saw him bow his head slightly as if deep in thought.

"You . . ." he began, staring first at me and then at his sister-in-law.

Dona Ana realized what he was about to say:

"No! No!" she exclaimed vehemently and made as if to leave.

I do not know what inner force impelled me to intervene:

"Senhor Valdo, I have a couple of things to say to Dona Ana."

I saw his arms drop disconsolately by his side and noticed that he was biting his lip. He nodded and said:

"In that case, I'll go in and fetch that donation I promised you."

We were left alone, and the light on the verandah seemed to grow still brighter. She was standing quite close to me, but in her hostility, she had all but turned her back. I might have thought she was studying something happening out in the garden, but when I looked more closely I could see that her eyes were half-closed, doubtless dazzled by the intensely blue sky.

"My child . . ." I began.

(Ah, how ridiculous we priests feel at times! I was sure she knew what I had to say to her, and I was assailed by a keen awareness of the impossibility of my position—but how to express myself? How could I penetrate the depths of her soul? My words seemed old and tired, and if the means I had to move her seemed inadequate, it was because I needed gestures, and gestures of love are both difficult and dangerous. I ought to speak to her as a priest, mouthing the same old truths and much-repeated revelations, whereas what was really needed was something stronger and more spontaneous, a single, definitive gesture of tenderness and compassion issuing forth from my whole self to her broken soul. And yet, poor wretch, there I was—and even before I began, I knew that everything I said would be in vain, like the seed that fell on stony ground. But a priest has his vocation, I said to myself by way of consolation, and I must be a priest, even if I had no faith in my actions.)

"My child," I repeated, and she must have noticed the uncertainty in my voice.

She turned so quickly then that I felt almost afraid.

"Father Justino," she exclaimed, "I heard every word you said to my brother-in-law. For quite some time now, my sole occupation has been listening at doors."

She stopped, and I was about to speak again—oh! the futile pride of these rebellions, the poor heart that castigates itself with a supposedly humiliating confession—when once again she interrupted me:

"If hell exists, Father Justino, then it exists right here in this house. You cannot imagine what disorder reigns . . ."

Suddenly, as if by divine grace, I found the means to reach her heart. Nothing but the truth—and only the truth—because in goodness as in evil, truth is the only thing that can satisfy those souls who thirst for absolutes.

"I know," I said in a voice that had regained its self-control, "I know, and more than you think. When I arrived here, I brought with me a great secret. And here it is: the devil took hold of this house long ago."

She covered her mouth with her hand, as if to hold in an exclamation. When I remained silent, she lowered it again and I realized that she had simply been hiding a scornful smile.

"That's no great secret, Father Justino," she said.

I looked up then, although I still felt small and insignificant, as indeed I had since setting foot on that verandah; perhaps it was the effect of the sun.

"The devil is not as you imagine," I continued. "He does not signify disorder, but rather certainty and calm."

Now that I had begun it was easy to carry on. She was still standing almost with her back to me—no doubt on account of the feelings of disgust and nausea I aroused in her—but that no longer mattered to me. She was listening and that was enough. What I had concealed from Senhor Valdo, or, rather, what I had not dared to tell him, now came rushing to my lips:

"What do you think a house ruled by the power of evil is like?" (I skated clumsily over those words—*the power of evil*—ignoring their poverty and vulgarity.) "It is constructed very much like this one, firm in its foundations, secure in its traditions, conscious of the heavy responsibility of its name. It isn't tradition that takes root in it, it is tradition as the sole defense of truth."

I paused—just for a moment—while a lingering ray of sun once again dazzled my eyes.

"It is what we could call a solidly built home." (I could not help noticing that my voice had become singularly calm.) "There is not a single crack through which heaven can enter."

She had slowly turned toward me, and I saw that the look of revulsion had vanished from her face, like an unravelling cloud. She was breathing faster, but this revealed both her excitement and her total surrender to the words I was saying.

"Often, in times gone by,"—it was my turn now to confess—"I wondered what made this house so cold, so soulless. And it was then that I discovered the formidable immutability of its walls, the frozen tranquility of its inhabitants. Ah, my friend, trust me when I tell you that there is nothing more diabolical than certainty. In certainty there is no place for love. Everything that is solid and firm is a denial of love."

She reached for something to hold on to and let herself fall into the chair that Senhor Valdo had occupied moments earlier. It was as if nothing separated us now and that we were both in the same abyss, discussing identical passions.

"I don't understand, Father," she stammered.

I sat down too, and tried to explain myself more clearly.

"It is perhaps difficult for you to accept your own reality. Deep down, we are horrified by what we really are. Imagine, for the sake of argument, that heaven was not at all a place of peace and tranquility, but a land of torment and anguish. Let us imagine, if we can, a heaven far beyond our own limited possibilities. Because if it were like that, what would they go there to do those who, all their lives, have enjoyed only rest and repose?"

She had turned very pale and merely shook her head:

"I still don't understand, Father."

Then I leaned closer and placed one hand on her arm:

"I am talking about sin, my child." (I knew how difficult it was to say that—but how else was I to touch that heart of stone, how else lead her where I wanted to go? As I said, the only key to some people's souls is the brutal truth, the uncompromising revelation.) "I want to make you conscious once again of sin, because you long ago banished it from your thoughts and replaced it with certainty, which, in your eyes, is the only manifestation of good. There is no chaos or struggle or fear in the depths of your soul. I repeat, I want to reinstall in you an awareness of sin—not for fear of sin itself, but for fear of heaven. Let us imagine a heaven so heavenly that the thought alone of the Son of God's death robs us forevermore of our peace of mind. My child, the abyss inhabited by the saints is not a harmonious place, but a cavern of warring passions."

I stopped speaking, almost breathless. I don't know if I had been entirely clear in my explanation, but the spirit that moved me was genuine. I had not perhaps wished to do so initially, but I had, in the end, succumbed to the violence of my own ideas. I bowed my head and waited for my feelings to subside. She must have understood what was happening, for she asked me almost humbly:

"Do you mean . . ."

The ray of sun had broadened into a great shaft of light filled with dancing motes of dust. Staring into it, I continued:

"I mean that our essence is of this world, and for us to imagine salvation as seen through our unworthy eyes is to diminish the greatness of God. Let us first assess the extent of our defeat, for such is man's lot, and only then the triumph, which is God's alone. For there can be no triumph over something that does not exist—what is virtue without struggle, or conquest without turmoil?—and without the existence of sin there can be no triumph. Now do you understand?"

She did not reply at once. She bowed her head as I had done moments before and then, looking up again, said simply:

"Father . . ."

The moment had arrived. As if a wall inside her had come crashing down, the words began to pour forth from I know not where, loud with the somber eloquence of long-suppressed thoughts. I no longer remember exactly what she said and I could not repeat what I heard, but I know that it concerned everything that was most intense and enduring in her being, possibly in her soul itself, torn between her inhibitions and her desires. It would have been pointless to talk again about God as I had once before—what she was giving expression to was the world, indeed the most violent thing that exists in this world: passion. Perhaps the passion of the flesh, which is the most ferocious of all, for it labors within like a cancer. I don't remember the name nor what it was all about, even though there is nothing to stop me revealing everything here since what I heard was not subject to the secrecy of the confessional. But such facts are unimportant; what counts are the consequences. Furthermore, she was probably not even interested in who was listening, for she talked almost mechanically, as if her only wish was to free herself from that silence. Listening to her, I thought to myself that this was exactly as it should be, for who could listen to her better than that other side of her own self, that constant warrior who had perhaps been her greatest adversary? The details were banal enough, even if they seemed exceptional to the person telling them, but I was more than used to witnessing such unchained emotions and was not shocked by what I heard. Now, as I write these lines, I remember a young man like any other (a gardener, if I'm not mistaken), lying dead in some cramped cellar, while she, in a fit of despair, implored me to bring him back to life. Is that right? Does it matter? There is nothing more touching than that youthful lust for life, for it is often in its bright, lithe allure that death sets its most perfect trap. I remember that her voice became quieter and quieter, until it faded and then ceased completely—the way water from a spring gushes forth then slows. I stared at her. She had raised her hand to her breast, feeling for some hidden object, which I somehow realized was a gun. As she stood up, her eyes wet with tears, she said:

"And *her*, Father. What punishment does she deserve now?"

31.
Continuation of Ana's Third Confession

. . . And so I walked back to the house, following more or less the same route she had taken. I had no doubts now about what was happening, and I was being guided by a certainty, a cold, calculated certainty. Had I not heard it from her own lips, had I not been given a description of their love in all its detail? Her words were still ringing in my ears, or, rather, not the words exactly, which mattered little to me, but the sound of her voice, the ecstatic way in which she had spoken about Alberto. What I had sensed in the heat of her words, behind the mere sordid details, was the passion and the crime. Maybe that wasn't true love, but what did it matter if the flame burned anyway? There was only one punishment for that woman's crime: death. Death pure and simple. Inside me, my old anger was ebbing away; I had finally reached the end of a long, long wait. It was so easy to comprehend, but I had needed that extended period of time in order finally to realize the truth. Nina had to disappear, and I must be the one to make that happen—with my own hands too. And just as she had derived pleasure from my torment, so I would achieve peace with her death. I was not in the least bit feverish when I thought these things, no, I was filled, rather, with an immense calm, and the only noticeable difference was that the world seemed clearer, and I looked around me with more than usual clarity. My sensibility had grown more refined, I felt a kind of inner music flowing through my veins, and I was astonished to find that everything still existed, even though I had never realized it before. For example, walking down the avenue, I noticed how very long it was, that the flower beds had become neglected, that the Chácara, framed by the trees, looked grubby and sad. Precisely when had the house become frozen in time like that, what had silenced it, a house that had always prided itself on being so full of life, so full of flowers? I could still remember Dona Malvina early in the morning, secateurs in hand, as a black servant pushed her wheelchair down the sandy paths glittering in the morning sun. Then, life and health still filled those now rotten foundations. Dona Malvina's presence had vitalized a whole generation of Meneses condemned to die. At that moment, I felt I had the right to do anything: any attack would merely drag down into the dust the architecture of a family that had already half-disappeared.

While these ideas were gathering strength in my mind, I was remembering, too, that I still had the revolver that had been used on that tragic night. It was an old thing, with a bluish barrel and a mother-of-pearl grip. I had checked that it still worked, and its first owner, who had been fond perhaps of that small instrument of death, had clearly taken special care of it. Another question occurred to me, directly linked with that weapon: why had it been left lying around for someone to pick it up and use it? (Everything became suddenly very clear at that moment, when I recalled the abandoned revolver, perhaps waiting for some convenient fit of rage. Someone had put it there, with his eye on a particular pair of hands, but whose hands? What other object in that house deserved to be destroyed? The sentence passed at the time was still valid. Nina had to disappear, and had stood condemned ever since that first episode. Trembling, not daring to probe too deeply into my suspicions, I asked myself: Who hated her enough to desire her death? Who in that house would prefer to see her dead to seeing her going about her daily life? The name came to my lips, but I refused to speak it. Poor Alberto had been the victim of a mistake.)

Still immersed in these thoughts. I was greatly relieved to find that everyone had retired to bed, which meant that I could walk, untroubled, through the house. However, the moment I entered the hallway, Betty opened the door of her room:

"Do you need anything, Senhora?" she asked.

"No, thank you, Betty," I replied. Then, stopping, I asked as casually as I could:

"Is everyone home?"

"Yes, Senhora, apart from Senhor Valdo. He's gone into town."

This was precisely the information I needed. I thanked her and continued on my way. When I reached my room, I noticed a light under the door opposite mine—Nina and Valdo's room. "Nina must be awake." And a tremor of joy ran through me: she would lose nothing by waiting. I opened the door to my own room, turned on the light and saw that my husband was asleep. It was odd, lately he had been taken by an irresistible need to sleep, whereas in the past, he had always been such an active man, something that had led to him being considered the head of the household. Normally he was always going on about ledgers and accounts, and complaining about the servants. Now, however, he was clearly not at all well—it was as if he were being eaten away by something inside. I leaned over the bed, curious to take a good look at that pale face, its lines deeply etched by age. He gave off such an air of weariness, as if he were being rapidly worn down by the rigors of time. So rapid was the change, he looked like someone who would not live for very much longer. I leaned closer, but could not explain why I felt so very curious. His forehead was bathed in sweat and I could hear his shallow, labored breathing. I don't know if this was true or if it was just my imagination, but I felt I was in the presence of a dying man.

I tiptoed over to the chest of drawers and, from one of the drawers, removed the small revolver hidden under the sheets. I checked that it was loaded—of the five bullets it had contained, three had been used, two on the occasion of Valdo's accident and the other . . . The remaining two would complete the sequence of deaths. I slowly closed the drawer and crept out into the hallway again. There was still a light under Nina's door, and I wondered what a woman like her would be doing all alone. Would she be praying, thinking about God or merely telling the beads on the rosary of her crimes? I really didn't care. I pushed the door, which was not quite closed, and saw Nina sitting on the bed, her back to me, and still wearing the clothes she'd had on in the garden. At first, that was all I could see because of the extremely bright light next to her. However, when I advanced further into the room, I saw that her back was shaking and realized with some astonishment that she was weeping. My surprise lasted no more than a minute. She must, I thought, be feeling remorse for all her horrible sins. As I stood there, I could have given in to a feeling of pity—touched by the sight of such grief in a frivolous creature like Nina—had it not been for the memory of Alberto and the room in which he had died, that and the revolver I was clutching in my pocket; both those things anaesthetized any capacity I had for emotion. I walked coolly over to her; and she, sensing another presence in the room, looked up.

"Oh, it's you!" she said in a loud voice and with little show of surprise. I said nothing. "It's you," she said again, and, oddly, there was a note of recrimination in her voice.

"Yes, it's me," I said at last. "I came because we didn't quite finish our conversation."

She gave a scornful smile:

"What more have you got to say to me?"

"Nina," I said, and this was the first time I had ever called her by her name. A kind of complicity bound us together, perhaps a sense of imminent violence. "Nina," I said again, "I made a promise to myself."

After the words we had exchanged in the garden—and especially after everything she had revealed to me—those words did seem to surprise her. She stood up and looked at me—ah, those eyes! Almost forgetting why I had come, I searched them for the aggressive, mutable light that had seduced so many men. I had never seen them from so close up, eyes that, in my silent, jealous thoughts, I had imagined to be all-devouring and full of treachery. I saw now that they were perfectly ordinary eyes, almost childish, possibly even slightly alarmed at the mysteries of this world.

"What has that got to do with me? Why have you come to my room?" and she, too, looked deep into my eyes.

I waited a moment for us both to calm down. What I had to do allowed for no sudden shocks, no hesitations. I wanted the serenity of accomplished fact to hover over those final words.

"I promised myself," I went on, "that I would kill anyone who went into that room. I can't forget and I can't forgive, and that is why I am here."

I spoke as slowly as possible. Meanwhile, those childish eyes remained fixed on mine. And suddenly she spoke almost gently:

"Did you love him so very much?"

It was my turn to smile:

"What do you care how much I loved him?"

She continued to look at me, and I confess that her insistent gaze began to trouble me. I had never before revealed so much of myself to anyone, and I was doing so to her of all people.

"I'd like to hear you say it in your own words."

"Why?"

"So that just once I can imagine you as being slightly more human."

"So you know," and I turned away, fleeing those implacable eyes.

She came up behind me:

"It's a shame we both loved the same man."

I spun around, my heart again filled with rage:

"*You?*" I spat out the word in a tone of utter contempt.

She smiled sadly:

"Yes, me, what's so strange about that?" And with a look on her face in which I recognized the old Nina: "Do you think I wouldn't be just as capable as you of loving a gardener?"

Ah, how the truth, even one you have lived with all your life, even one mulled over minute by minute in the depths of your mind, even one drenched in secret tears and watered with futile, sacrificial blood, how very different it seems to us, how brutal and cynical it sounds on someone else's lips! In the garden, she had spoken and even moaned at the recollection of their moments of pleasure, but only now did I *see* that they really had loved each other. Why? What had rendered me indifferent to the revelation made only seconds before? I don't know, it's something I will never be able to explain. But just then, through the magic of a few banal words, I understood not only the love that had bound them together, but love itself, the love I had never known. Dear God, it had only lasted a moment, but what did it matter if that moment still illuminated her life? No, I could not bear the brutal truth of what had been spoken between us, as if, up until now, I had been lying to myself, imagining a feeling I would be the first to dismiss. She must have sensed my confusion, because she leaned closer:

"I loved him," she said in a soft, calm voice. "I loved him and he loved me, what more do you want? Haven't we said all we need to say on the subject? What more do you want me to tell you? Do you want to be humiliated, do you want me to say that his full lips crushed my lips when we kissed, that he used to put his tongue in my mouth, that he nibbled my breasts? Is that it?"

And in that hushed, whispered voice I felt the tremor, not just of those words, but of the secret caresses, the shared madness, the ecstasies that had never been mine—everything I had so long imagined, about which I had felt such a piercing jealousy, and that had become a mere accumulation of suspicions, but never certainties—and which now revived a truth I had never fully acknowledged, peopled as it was by the specter of gardens and darkness and kisses, the sheer compelling impetus of a mutual love, one that would never ever be mine!

This caused me such intense pain that I covered my face with my hands and collapsed onto the bed, on the very spot where Nina had been sitting. The warmth of the bedspread only filled my mind with still more terrible and obscene images: from every side, like mushrooms springing up in the shadows, I felt hands sprouting, fingers interlacing, touches, sighs, wild nights of love. Still covering my face, I sat very still, waiting for my blood to quiet. Nina was doubtless savoring her victory. And yet, when she spoke again, there seemed to be a note of pity in her voice.

"When you spoke at the Pavilion about him . . . about . . ."

Staying exactly where I was, I waited for her to say the name again, like a final slap in the face. She understood and said instead:

". . . about André."

"As I said, I don't care about André."

There was another pause, as if she lacked the courage to go on, either because the words were too painful or because she feared touching on a subject she preferred to leave alone.

"Despite everything," she went on, "despite everything . . . if you think about it . . ."

No, that wasn't the tone of voice I was expecting: Nina was talking as if she were dreaming, as if she were speaking to herself about things she was unsure of and had never dared say to anyone. I stood up and went over to her, as if drawn to her, and she seemed so absorbed in her own thoughts that she didn't even notice, didn't even turn around, but continued to talk in that rather slow way:

". . . if you think about it . . . there is a certain resemblance. The full lips, the fine, strong fingers, the smell of his hair." (Gradually, the image of the man rose up before me: through her, through a miracle of transposition, I began to see Alberto again, a new Alberto, one I had never known, but who pulsated as though he were still alive, almost within reach, a loving, complicit Alberto. Nina took two steps toward me, I took two steps toward her, and by taking those few steps, we were united, we became one, and I was drinking her in, making her mine, because I wanted to drag from her lips the presence of that lover, made eternal and formidable by her eloquence.)

"André . . ."

That name brought me abruptly back to reality. I retreated slightly, trying to recover my lost calm.

"What do you mean?"

She, too, seemed to wake up; she smiled and shook her head:

"Nothing. But there are certain similarities. Eyes and lips. Have you never noticed?"

She was standing directly in front of me now and, again, her eyes were probing mine suspiciously. This was not because of what we were, two unfortunate women in a room together, but because of the memories traced on our faces by the past, by what had been and was now transforming us into ghosts. So it was true then, she had loved him and she did have a heart, just like everyone else. All her betrayals, all her shameful deeds could be redeemed by that one genuine feeling—and it was that love, or its shadow, that was binding us together now, one in front of the other, like sisters.

"Are you suggesting . . ." I began, then foreseeing what was about to happen, I stopped, too weak to go on.

"That André is Alberto's son, that he was never a Meneses."

Slowly, while those words were still vibrating in the air, I took out the revolver and pointed it at her.

"This is why I came," I said. "To kill you."

Nina's face betrayed not a flicker of emotion; her eyes merely went back and forth between the weapon and my face, as though she were troubled by other emotions, not fear, but feelings or memories or, who knows, the past events in which that small revolver had also played a part, but which had long since disappeared, only to be revived now, hard and bright and eloquent in the light of the lamp.

"That gun . . ." she said very simply.

". . . is the same one," I answered, completing her sentence. "There are two bullets left. I think that now . . ."

An icy smile spread across her features:

"You want to kill me?"

"I made a promise," I exclaimed.

There was another brief pause, and while I still awaited some violent reaction on her part, her face remained unchanged, and she stood there, utterly calm, as if I hadn't said a word.

"What do I care?" she cried suddenly, turning her back on me. "André will still have the same father. No amount of spilled blood—not even his father's do you hear?—can ever erase the memory of the pleasure with which he was conceived. Or that night of passion . . ."

"Shut up!" I yelled, in a tone that was more pleading than commanding.

Again she turned to face me, eyes shining:

"What do you think I'm looking for in him? When we fall into bed together, what kind of satisfaction do you think I find?"

"He's your son," I murmured, feeling that, despite everything, she would never grasp the enormity of her crime, that it was not in her power or her nature to comprehend the gravity of that incestuous passion, which was merely one of a thousand possible kinds of madness, with no hope of a cure or restored lucidity.

"He is my son," she went on, "but he is the son of a father who no longer exists. How I would love that man, how I would throw myself at his feet and kiss the ground he walked on if he did still exist. I go to bed with André as an attempt to find in his face, his body, in being possessed by him, the man who disappeared."

Now I understood—and my amazement, which rose in me like a great flame whipped up by the wind, made me lower the revolver. I understood, and took a cruel pleasure in imagining the sinful effort involved in that attempt at resurrection. I had dared to ask a priest to bring him back to life, I had been brave enough to go to the outer limits of heresy and blasphemy, shaking a lifeless body that no human force could ever breathe life back into—but that woman had gone further still and invented a substitute, raising up her own son as a monument to the sin she could not forget. Seeing my astonishment and seeing the hand holding the gun hanging loose by my side, she laughed:

"You came here to kill me, didn't you? So why don't you?"

"I can't."

Doubtless realizing that I had fully understood both her crime and her pain, she turned and threateningly shook her fist at me:

"No, you can't, and I'm going to tell you why. Because you're a Meneses, because the blood of the Meneses, which is not your blood, has infected you with the same disease. Because you would never shatter the peace of this house with a gunshot—the sacrosanct peace of the family—nor would you commit incest or murder, nothing that might besmirch the honor they claim as theirs."

"That's not true," I murmured.

And despite everything, possibly prompted by what I had just heard, the memory of my sleeping husband suddenly appeared in my mind with a strange clarity. For me, he *was* the Meneses family, and, suddenly, I could not rid myself of the image of his pale face, his sweat-beaded brow, his lifeless, moribund features. To condemn him, though, would be to condemn myself, for he had carefully been molding me into a Meneses almost since I was a child. She was absolutely right—and how humiliating that was! Standing there, with the revolver still in my hand, I had to admit that she had beaten me, me and all the other slaves to habit, to a single truth, to a teaching they dare not destroy or repudiate.

I don't know how I made it to the door—all I can remember is Nina's extraordinarily calm voice saying:

"And don't go deceiving yourself. You never loved Alberto. It isn't love that binds you now to the image of the person he was, it's remorse."

I stopped, still with my back to her. I did not dare to look at her, I wasn't strong enough, nor would I ever be, not at least until, like her, I felt capable of committing any crime and any sin. She came a little closer and said with a passion that almost undid the cruelty behind her words:

"Not remorse for having given yourself to him—just once—not that it matters. But because you have always been a complete nonentity, utterly incapable of being anything more than that. You weren't interested in him—how could a Meneses possibly be interested in a gardener?—but in your own freedom. Or what you imagined to be freedom."

Unable to bear it any more, I opened the door and ran out into the hallway.

32.
End of Father Justino's Account

I looked at her hard, but did not answer her question. She returned my gaze and then, as if reaffirming her challenge, she turned the revolver over and over in her hands.

"I wanted to kill her," she said, "but I didn't have the courage."

She then told me, in detail, what had happened between her and her sister-in-law. She spoke haltingly, revealing the battling emotions within, and I could not say there was anger. No, not anger. With anger there is a certain warmth, a vigor that reveals the true nature of the soul. What I perceived in the woman standing before me, slightly hunched, her head tilted to one side, was something stagnant and inhuman that gave her, alas, an unmistakable air of eccentricity. What distances she must have traveled to arrive at that point, and how she must have turned and turned within her own solitude until, suddenly, unable to contain herself any longer, she had given vent to her spite before my astonished eyes. It was not difficult to surmise what she was thinking: she considered that the only thing the other woman merited was destruction, pure and simple, with no regard for sin or justice. She was absolutely convinced that hers would be an act of self-defense rather than violence. "What do we do with poisonous snakes?" was what she seemed to be asking. And so on and on she talked; I don't know how long for—I only remember that the sun was setting and that through the trees I could see a faint, reddish glow. Bathed in this light, the pillars of the verandah were growing less substantial and the invading branch of jasmine was shrouding itself in shadow. Finally, she stopped speaking, and I touched her arm:

"Have you ever thought," I asked, "that this woman might not be the capricious, wicked creature you suppose, but a human being just as capable of suffering as any of us?"

"Oh, Father!" she exclaimed. "How could that be? How could she suffer, being the way she is? Beauty is a cruel thing."

This time I could hear the fear in her voice, and she seemed less sure of herself, but it wasn't her rival who frightened her: it was beauty, the secret power of beauty.

"My child," I replied, making a final effort to break down the barriers that separated us, "everyone's suffering is different. What do you know, for example, about what God holds in store for her?"

Staring at some point in the distance, she said softly:

"God is unjust; he denies one person everything in order to shower all the others with graces."

I must admit I shuddered when I heard that word. She was talking about human grace, the thing she was confusing with beauty and which was mortal and transient. For me, what was important was divine Grace. But either way, I can swear to you that I had never in my life seen a creature so devoid of grace, whether God's or any other sort. The person I saw before me was entombed, deaf to any appeal for kindness as if somehow set apart by a perverse and stupid law. From whatever angle I looked at her, everything about her was dull and leaden.

"You always talk about God as if He did not exist."

She spun around:

"If God exists, then why . . ."

Her voice faltered.

"God exists," I replied firmly. "You just lack . . ."

I was about to say the word, but stopped myself, sensing how fatally I would wound her. She seemed, however, to understand and completed my sentence for me:

"I lack His grace? Is that it? And by any chance . . ." she sighed deeply, ". . . by any chance does God's Grace also exist?"

(There was no irony in her voice, but for some reason, I shuddered again. Rebellion is such a strange thing! Feeling a little lost, I asked myself what Grace really was. A prize? If so, who were its recipients? Who did God turn to first? Yes, God exists. But if we waited eternally on our knees for Him to distribute His gifts . . . ah, and I a priest was saying this! And was that not the crux of all my past struggles, of my battles with theories and theological scholars? Then all that is left for us is to contemplate the long line of our fellow creatures who have failed to hear His voice.)

"Yes, Grace exists," I replied. "But it is not so much a gift from God as an effort made by man. God waits in hopeful anticipation, but we do not have the right to think of Him as a judge distributing gifts. He has a greater role, as the last supreme resort for man to unburden his despair. Because lack of hope is man's greatest sin. May God preserve me from believing in nothing—because that *nothing* is merely the reverse side of the absolute certainty of those who are capable of believing in God."

Was I right or wrong in what I was saying? It scarcely mattered as long as I managed to reach the reclusive center of her soul. It scarcely mattered even if God was not what I said, but an omnipotent creator from whom injustice flowed like a never-ending river of blood. She turned to me almost tenderly:

"Father, let's just say that I do believe in God. Who am I to boast shamelessly of my doubts? Yes, I have often thought that she is human, that she also suffers, spinning blindly in her own orbit like all the rest of us. I could even forget all about her if she were far away. But how am I to forgive her, how am I to trust in God's justice when I see her living and breathing among us, wreaking havoc and fomenting all kinds of evil? And then my thoughts get confused, my words get muddled and I pray in a way I don't want to pray. 'Lord, have mercy on that woman,' I say. But immediately my suffering begins again and I rebel, beating my chest with my fists: 'Lord, punish that woman; prove that you exist and strike her down.' Didn't they teach me from an early age that He does exist and mercifully answers all our prayers? So I wait until evening falls, thinking to myself: 'She hasn't returned yet; she must be lying dead somewhere in the middle of the road.' And as soon as it's dark I run out, I open the gate, I walk and walk, I search everywhere—but her corpse is nowhere to be seen."

"What do you expect?" I barked. "Do you really expect God to be the servant, the mere instrument, of your passions?"

She drew herself up, looking very pale. I could see she was straining to control her anger:

"And if she were human, as you would have me believe, if she suffered just like any of us, if she were good, would that change anything?"

I shrugged:

"In that case, I don't know what to say. I cannot understand what evil afflicts you."

I sensed that I had deepened still further the rift between us, and the ill feeling provoked by what I had just said was now almost palpable. There was no doubt that I had failed in my attempt to find the right words to touch that stony heart. For I was absolutely convinced that there was no wrong that could not be righted—it was I who, in my weakness, had fallen short of my priestly mission. I stared down dejectedly at my worn cassock. How useless it all was, how overpowering the ways of the world and how bitter its impulses. I stood up, convinced that I could go no further. Then she turned again and took a step toward me, as if to hold me back.

"It's me, Father, that's all. It's simply the way I am."

And there it was: she would never give way, forever anchored to her resentment as if to one of those immovable iron bollards on a quayside. The other woman wasn't merely a rival, an enemy; she was the very image of the world, that same world which only a few minutes earlier I had been deploring, together with its vanity and all those things of which she felt unjustly deprived. Human logic, even that which seems to us most absurd, often contains its own secret coherence. I shook my head, and she, too, with a rapid blinking of the eyes that did not escape me, understood that we had reached the end. Then, slowly, unable to stop that nervous tic, she slipped the revolver back inside her blouse and looked at me one last time:

"It may well be, Father. But nothing will deter me. I am incapable of fear. And believe me, there's nothing I can do but accept myself as I am."

"Rest assured that I will pray for you."

She shrugged, and a sort of smile spread across her face. Then she bade me a silent farewell and walked away. I watched her reach the door of the drawing room and disappear into the house. I did not dare to leave and stood there, immobile, my eyes fixed on the door through which she had vanished. Her voice still rang in my ears: "It may well be, but nothing will deter me." I looked at the pillars, formidable and perfect in the dark. And I thought about how all houses, in their fixity, sooner or later become bastions of evil. Who knows, perhaps the love of God lives only in the open countryside and in places of restless instability.

33.
End of Ana's Third Confession

As soon as I left Nina, I understood that, far from hurting her, I had merely succeeded in wounding myself. Her words, which were, I felt, filled with poisonous intent, began to seep slowly into me, penetrating my blood, and thus rekindling the anxiety that had once been my normal state of mind. (I remembered, in particular, the time I summoned Father Justino—Alberto was still lying dead in the cellar—and asked that he resuscitate him, work a miracle and make him live again. Never had I sunk so low in my despair—and later, as I calmed down and found myself in the sea of detritus that was me, I was horrified by the sterility of that empty, unsettling time, when I barely recognized myself. The return of that old affliction filled me with a kind of terror and, feeling my heart again weighed down by those memories, I ran to the bathroom, splashed my face with cold water, dabbed alcohol on my temples, imagining that it was the effect of a fever, and that it was all just a passing delirium. Alberto was well and truly dead. I had found it very hard to accept that horrible idea, but had been obliged to submit, because there was no chance that he would return to the world, nor that I would ever see his face again. At first, I told myself over and over that he was dead, knowing that I was merely repeating an empty, meaningless word—yes, he was dead, but that was like naming a tree I had never set eyes on or a place in the world where I had never set foot. I never really penetrated the reality of that death or assimilated the stark fact of his disappearance. I wandered aimlessly about the house, paced up and down the avenues in the garden, visited the places where I used to see him. I imagined that I would meet him unexpectedly and wave to him, thinking: There, didn't I say as much? He's still alive. Alberto is immortal. I don't know whether it was pride or rebellion that drove me on, but thinking of him dead and gone forever was an absurdity I simply could not grasp.

Very gradually Alberto did die for me, minute by minute, hour by hour, day by day, and I, silent and lucid, watched that agony, which lasted years. Yes, he died countless deaths in me; now in a tree he had leaned against, and which lost its magic to become a mere tree; now in one of the avenues in the garden that lost all its charm—the times I had walked down it!—to become an insignificant path I never bothered to walk again. Thus, everything that had surrounded him, that had lived with him and of him, or had served as a witness to his passage through this world, slowly lost its power, grew old and stiff and joined the ranks of all the other anonymous, boring things. That is how Alberto died, a long death, longer than his actual existence. What remained of him was what remains of any death—a grave. If the body wasn't there, it didn't matter: for me, his human form had long since become a myth. His grave, in my view, was the Pavilion, where he had breathed his last. Those bloodstained walls, which, afterward, I often caressed with trembling hands, provided the only space where I could watch over his memory. There I wept and remembered him; there I accepted that he had died, and often, lost in my grief, wondered if it had been a dream, if Alberto had ever been a real flesh-and-blood human being, if, like everyone else, he had actually existed. I did not know his soul or his passions, I had no idea if he was generous or selfish or pure—I did not know the sound of his laughter or, indeed, if he did laugh or what made him laugh—if he cried or if he had plans for the future. Dying so young, he had, in that brief time, become the very image of youth and was as fixed and remote as any other emblematic image, and was now like an errant breeze rippling the surface of beautiful, tender things, rather than a being who had been positively alive and loved, idealized and dreamed of like any other. Obviously, this was all in my imagination, and I had created an Alberto more fictional than real. But is not love a series of probabilities that we bestow on others? Alberto's vitality came precisely from those gifts I endowed him with, and if I imagined him as happy, healthy, and full of noble intentions, it was because this suited my fantasy, and my passion needed only that Alberto and no other. Those feelings faded, of course, and the day came when I grew tired of imagining him as kind or loving; then I replaced those old feelings with others I invented, with interests and situations that had never existed, but which, momentarily, filled his empty flesh and gave me the certainty, the flavor, the verisimilitude that the truth denied me. For example, I would imagine him engaged in humble, day-to-day tasks—gardening or kneeling by the stream and washing his thick plaid shirts. Or by the fence surrounding the estate, tending the roses that had been planted by my husband's mother. That was enough to take me down to the stream, where I would gaze into the waters, which no longer served any purpose, or walk over to the fence and pick one last bloom that the winds had not undone, all the while thinking: This is what he used to do, he used to care for these plants. When my imagination no longer came to my aid, I would dig furiously into my memory, so desperate to find some sign of his life that I would see him again, blurred as if in a dream, but still present—walking along such and such an avenue or bending over that bed planted with mallows. Ah, I would say to myself, this was his favorite avenue, his favorite corner. I would then visit those places often, struggling to find the exact emotion he would have felt, and thus drinking in, yet again, like a toxin, his presence and his memory. It was, I know, a feeble consolation, and a day did come when I could imagine him as neither passionate nor bold, neither this nor that, because it all blurred into one, until it reached the stage when I lost sight of his identity and even his name. Alberto, became a name identical to all other men's names. I was gripped by panic then: who was Alberto, what real human being did he represent? And I discovered sadly that the Alberto I had so loved, for whom I had made so many sacrifices, to the point of forgetting myself and my duties, had no eyes, no hands, no face, no other characteristic physical feature—he was merely a vague recollection. I was sorry then that I had no photo of him, no drawing, nothing that would have firmly fixed his face in my mind—and sitting for long hours, staring into space, I would vainly, patiently try to recompose him as he had once been and restore to the poor ghost who now inhabited my dreams his exact nose, the color of his skin, the shape of his eyes. How many deaths did he die, the one I loved, how many deaths before he reached this definitive, inconsolable death that left only a name floating on the surface of my memory? No, not just a name, because Alberto left something else. The cellar room, the wall still stained with his blood, and that bed covered with an old mat, where he had lain dying, and which represented him, splendid and real, in his final moments, and that would, for me, fix him forever in eternity. (Sometimes, succumbing to damp or simply time, a bit of plaster would begin to come loose, and I would carefully stick it back in its original place, as if I were restoring an image about to fade, a body lacking vital parts, and which would only survive over time thanks to my efforts and my patience.) That is what led me back to the cellar and made me protect it from any stranger's gaze, like an altar that should be kept safe from profane eyes. I alone could penetrate that space and trace the outline of that stain, a dark continent extending over the whitewash, opening up like a web at either end, then rising up in one sharp line and, finally, exploding like a noiseless, lightless firework. (I remember—and the memory always rekindles my passion—I remember, when I was alone with him and realized he was dead, how I hurled myself desperately upon him, hoping to wrench from his body the final breath I imagined must still exist in his shattered heart. How I clung to what remained of him and tried to lift him up, begging, weeping, swearing, struggling with the weight of his body, which I propped against the wall, marking the whitewash with those signs whose meaning, later, I would so often try to decipher . . .)

Well, it was that same fleshless being into which Nina's words breathed a little life. "André. Certain similarities. Eyes and lips. Have you never noticed?" That is why she loved André, why she gave herself to her own son. Then, in wonderment, it was my turn to ask: did she love Alberto so very much that she was prepared to trample on all conventions, break all moral laws, to defy God himself, by sleeping with her son? That woman must know what she was doing, must know what kind of love she was dealing in. Cheap slut, I said to myself, the worst kind of prostitute, amoral, monstrous creature—and yet what did any of that matter? She was a woman, very much a woman in her madness. How often she must have trodden the paths of that guilty love, followed the meanders of that rich, young flesh, of a love exacerbated by age and desire. The vision of that itinerary rose implacably before my eyes, making my head reel: Alberto's skin, his manly smell, his vigor. How they must have loved each other, in the four corners of the Chácara, as if in the wild tangle of a new Paradise. And she was repeating that adventure with André, with her own son, because she found in him such strong echoes, such similarities, enough to provide a substitute for those earlier, unforgettable pleasures. No, it was not some mythical Alberto who now appeared before me, it was a ghost finally made flesh. And, it must be said, Nina's words had given him that dangerous identity. I needed only to add a slightly scornful air, a mere sketch with no human substance, and there was André, and I had never noticed, never even looked at him, or seen the miracle happening right before my eyes. The reason was clear: it had never occurred to me that André was not Valdo's son. I was brutally sure now that he was the gardener's child. Ah, if Valdo ever found out, if the Meneses ever knew the truth . . . I smiled to myself at this possibility, imagining the family gathered together to resolve the matter, with me feigning surprise—the Meneses, ever the victims. The money Demétrio would spend, the emissaries they would employ to clear the matter up, to investigate. And the key to that secret lay with me. Only I could say, and with absolute certainty, that the person André most resembled was the gardener. The idea set my blood boiling—and I imagined going off at once in search of André. But how to broach the subject? What words to use? I had never been close to him, so how could I now justify my sudden interest? Petty concerns, it's true, given that what mattered above all else was the truth. (No, I was lying: I wasn't interested in the truth, but in André. No, not André, Alberto. What did I care if André was or wasn't Valdo's son? It was those echoes and reminiscences of which Nina had spoken that I wanted to see in his face.)

I confess, I did not hesitate for a moment. I opened my bedroom door and went out into the hallway. Everyone was asleep, and the house was plunged in the most absolute of silences. I went to André's room and knocked—to my surprise, I saw the door open very slowly, and, from inside, my nephew's voice asked softly:

"Is it you?"

Who did he think it would be? Who would he be waiting for at that hour of the night? Any doubts I might have had about their illicit romance were instantly dispelled. I pushed the door open and, in the darkness, because he had not turned on the light, I felt his ardent breath on my cheek.

"You came!" he cried in a voice quivering with emotion.

I moved closer, not saying a word, and our faces almost touched. He stammered something else, probably another "you came" made incomprehensible by sheer emotion, and then, suddenly, with a muffled cry, he drew back. From my troubled breathing, the smell of my hair, or simply the secret fluid given off by lovers and which only they can recognize, he must have realized that I was not Nina.

"Ah, I thought you were . . ." he said, alarmed.

"You thought I was Nina," I responded. "Well, I'm not."

He murmured:

"Aunt Ana!"

He could not have sounded more astonished, and perhaps imagined I was spying on him and had come there merely to tell him off. How wrong he was. This was the ideal moment—while he was still too embarrassed and startled to react—to find out what I had hoped to discover and to gauge the truth of what Nina had said.

"What if I am Aunt Ana?" I said, and I took a certain pleasure in my own shamelessness. "You were, after all, expecting a woman, weren't you?"

He said again in the same astonished tones:

"Aunt Ana!"

I stepped forward, orienting myself in the darkness by the sound of his voice:

"I'm not Aunt Ana. I'm not anything. I am simply a woman like any other."

I touched him and felt his trembling, transfixed body. With a violence that took even me by surprise, I flung my arms around him:

"I am Ana, just Ana. You go to bed with your own mother, so why not with your aunt?"

"You're mad!" he cried. "You're my aunt . . ."

I tightened my embrace:

"Not your real aunt."

This time, he said nothing, but I could hear his breathing growing increasingly agitated. He was probably recovering from the initial shock and thinking how to respond, whether to retreat or allow me to continue with what he must be thinking was sheer insanity. That pause gave me the strength to go further—and I wrapped my arms still more tightly around him, like a serpent its prey, and I felt for his lips with my own parched lips, fondling him, squeezing him, feeling beneath his clothes his warm blood and his vibrant masculinity.

"Please don't do that!" he begged.

But I was already pressing him against the wall and running my hand over face, lips, jaw, ears. Impervious to anything but that wild impulse, I murmured:

"I want to know what you're like. Ah, if you only knew how much I need this . . . I want to touch your nose, to feel your lips against mine. Kiss me, André, kiss me the way you kiss your mother or as you would any other woman, even a woman of the streets."

While I was speaking, I continued to caress that fugitive face, feeling it hot beneath my fingers, forcing him to accept my caresses, controlling him with the twin yoke of surprise and shock, for he was still afraid and did not yet dare push me away.

"You're not a child any more, André, you won't tell anyone, you won't betray my secret. Just one kiss, just so I can feel the shape of your lips . . ."

And when I ran my hand over his lips again, he suddenly bit me, and the pain made me release my grip.

"You little fool!" I cried.

He was still breathing hard, but he had managed to put some distance between us, and I sensed in the darkness that he was ready now to defend himself. Clutching my wounded hand to my chest, I tried again to reach him—what did I care what he thought or said!—but André, as if he had again gathered sufficient strength, ran over to the door, opened it and left me standing alone in the middle of the room.

34.
Betty's Diary (v)

3rd – I had been busy restoring some kind of order to the damp, mouse-ridden pantry, and hadn't seen the mistress for some days. Yesterday, though, when I was walking down the hallway, I heard her calling me from her room. I put down the mousetraps and the other things I was carrying and went in. She was sitting on the bed, with a few clothes scattered around her. Since, as I've said, I was the one responsible for ensuring that the house was kept clean and tidy, when I saw the wardrobe doors wide open, I thought she was going to tell me off about something that had been left undone. Instead, she pointed to the clothes on the bed. These were her famous dresses, all of them made in Rio de Janeiro and of little use to her in the Chácara. I recognized a few of them because she occasionally wore them at supper when she felt like getting dressed up like "people in Rio" or on mornings when she was feeling particularly cheerful and would parade up and down the avenues in the garden, but I was seeing most of the dresses for the first time. I had never really had much time for fashion myself, being too busy with household matters, but even I could see how pretty and expensive those glittering outfits were. She was silently lifting them up and shaking the dust off them, then despondently putting them down again.

"They're no use at all, Betty, so old-fashioned. This one, for example," and she held up a blue dress decorated with sparkling beadwork. "It cost me a small fortune, and I can guarantee you that the first dance I wore it to . . ."

"But you don't need such clothes here," I broke in.

She looked at me, almost scandalized:

"It isn't just the clothes, Betty. One should always dress well. And if the day ever comes when I don't, I won't feel I'm me any more."

"But I hardly ever see you wearing them . . ."

"Oh well, what does it matter anyway," she said, and her voice was filled with sadness.

"You mustn't talk like that," I said. "You're still young and pretty. There's not another woman around to compare with you."

She smiled and clutched the dress to her with unexpected ardor:

"Ah, if only that were true, Betty, if only that were true!"

I had never heard her talk like this before. She had often made such grave statements, and I even recorded some of them in this diary, but they had always been rather mocking, off-the-cuff remarks. Now, though, there was an unusually mournful tone to her voice. She wasn't joking, she was genuinely bemoaning her fate, which both surprised and troubled me.

"If you like dressing up, then why . . ."

I was leaning toward her over the bed, trying to establish a kind of intimacy to support my would-be words of advice. Seeing me so close, she threw the dress across the room, stood up with a sigh and said:

"There's a time for everything, Betty, and I think my time for wearing pretty dresses has passed."

Hearing her putting on that cold tone, I assumed she did not mean what she said. Perhaps she simply wanted to know what I thought; perhaps, as was often the case with her, she had an ulterior motive that I had not yet picked up on. I stayed where I was and watched her walk over to the window, draw back the curtain, then return, and it was as if she were preparing to tell me something very important, but could not quite bring herself to do so, waiting, instead, for the atmosphere between us to grow warmer. She must have decided it was not the right moment, because she again picked up one of the dresses and held it to her, saying:

"Isn't this red dress just lovely? I can remember the first time I wore it. The seamstress had sent it to me several days before, but I hadn't been able to wear it because I was ill. That was when the Colonel turned up—I've told you about him before, haven't I? He was an extraordinary man, a great friend of mine—and he took me out to the Casino. When I went in, the men almost knelt down before me. He got rather jealous and said: 'You see how you are adored, Nina.' And I was, Betty, I was adored by all the men."

I liked to hear her talking like that, because when she did, she gave off such warmth and enthusiasm. Her eyes briefly took on a new light, and she looked almost happy. This was the first time I had heard her mention a colonel, but that didn't matter, because it fitted perfectly with the scene she was recalling.

As if those good memories had been vanquished by an awareness of her present situation, she slowly lowered her arms and let the hem of the red dress drag on the floor.

"How time passes, how everything changes! I was almost happy then. There was the Colonel, there were other friends. Everything would have been so different if I . . ."

A sob rose up in her throat, she pressed the dress to her face, then ran and flung herself on the bed. I was so astonished I didn't know what to do—should I console her, should I wait so as not to interrupt the wave of memories that had provoked that sob? Selfishness won out. Firstly, because I didn't know what to say or what kind of consolation to offer without knowing the cause of her distress, and, secondly, because, like most people, I longed to find out more about her obscure past. Often, when absorbed in some mechanical task, I would ponder the mystery of that existence, an absurd enterprise really, pure conjecture. People said so many things, there was more and more gossip doing the rounds, and yet so little was known about that strange creature! Thanks to my privileged position in the household, I was able to find out a lot of things and adapt them to my imaginings, and thus create a fairly convincing figure. However, when I compared this to the real-life model, it fell far short of the reality. Dona Nina eluded any amount of conjecture, just as it was impossible to find out anything definite and clear-cut about her, whether good or ill. One thing was certain, she never failed to arouse people's interest and even, sometimes, their passion. Now, seeing her weeping so disconsolately, I realized that I had never been able to imagine her life as anything but brilliant and magnificent, the sort of life led by an artist or a famous singer. And yet there she was, not brilliant or magnificent at all. When I still said nothing, she looked up. A few tears still shone in her eyes.

"How strange life is," she said. "We never really know when we are happy. We look back at a particular time as being most unfortunate, and only later do we understand that we allowed an opportunity for a little peace to pass us by. Anyway . . ."

She got up, threw the dress down on the bed and began pacing again:

". . . I have never been as unhappy as I am now." (Given her agitated state, it was clear that, for her, happiness meant peace.) "I know, I know," she exclaimed when she saw the look on my face, "I have everything I could possibly want, a house, a family, a husband. But happiness, Betty, is a very personal thing. I wasn't born to be happy in the same way as other people."

What did she mean? Probably that material things were not enough, which was true. But what about her husband, and the comfort of his constant presence? I had heard countless times that she was the one who had brought about the reconciliation. If she had been so happy during her time with that colonel, why then had she given him up in favor of exile at the Chácara? No, what she should have said was that she simply wasn't made to be happy, that, unlike other people, everything about her aspired to a continual, insatiable state of unhappiness. I had never known such people personally, but I knew they existed: for them, unhappiness was as necessary as the air they breathed. Watching her pacing up and down, imprisoned by the mechanisms of her life as if by the bars of a cage, I realized that she had never loved her husband and had probably never loved anyone! For what characterizes people greedy for misfortune is a deadness of soul, a disquieting lack of love. When I grasped this, I understood her misery and could not help but feel sorry for her, because it seemed to depend less on her than on the baleful influence of some planet full of negative energy.

She paced a little more, then came back and stood before me:

"You probably think I'm a bad person. Most people do. It's always so easy to judge others. But I can assure you, Betty, that appearances have always been against me. I have only ever been bad unintentionally or because I could not be anything else." She fell silent for a moment, as if weighing her own words. "Although it's true to say that I have never tried very hard to be good either . . ."

I had never thought about such things or paused to consider such deep problems, but a thought suddenly occurred to me, one that almost rose to my lips in the form of a shout: What is goodness? How could one judge or evaluate it when in the presence of a blind, impulsive being like her? I may well have been deceiving myself, I may merely have been giving in to her charm, but wasn't that what redeemed her and made her different from anyone else I had ever met?

And suddenly, she said in an extraordinarily calm voice:

"We are always cruel whenever we try to be ourselves." (I looked at her: she had her back to me now and was silhouetted against the window.) "But what about the others, those who impede us and block our path . . . what about them?"

She turned and fixed me with an intense look:

"No, I was never bad. When I look back, it seems to me that I have merely been weak." (I was thinking: Weak? When everything about her bespoke determination and boldness? Yes, perhaps she was weak in that she had lacked the courage to embrace her natural impulse, that of death and destruction.) "I could have done some things differently . . . or avoided them . . . But who can say that they have never sinned?"

She slowly went and picked up the clothes she had thrown down on the bed:

"When I used to wear these dresses, I believed in them, I thought I was beautiful."

"But you still are beautiful," I protested.

She shrugged impatiently:

"No, now I am wounded, and these clothes are of no use any more."

"Wounded?" I could not help but exclaim at the strangeness of that word.

She said sadly:

"The woman who wore those clothes, Betty, no longer exists."

"Dona Nina!"

And everything in me cried out at that attack upon herself. No, in my eyes, she was not a simple human being, but a construct, a work of art. She did not have the right to wound herself, to rot and die like other people—she was untouchable in her majesty. I pressed my hands to my breast, as if to hold in the feelings flooding my heart. She noticed this and must have understood what was happening: a new energy ran through her, she straightened up, raised her head, and the wind blowing in through the window ruffled her hair. Then she came over to me, her eyes bright with determination:

"Betty, I can't resign myself to being just like anyone else. I have to follow my own path until the end, I have to be myself, pitted against everything and everyone. Timóteo said to me once: 'Nina, you are the one who will avenge us all.' How can I possibly betray him now by giving in?"

I did not entirely understand what she was talking about—I certainly had no idea what she meant by "giving in." However, I knew that I was ready for anything, that I would defend her come what may, and that she could count on my help. In silence, as if she had sensed exactly what was going on inside me, she pointed to the clothes on the bed, then, while I gathered them up, she went over to the wardrobe, took out all the other dresses and, still in silence, went over to the door. I didn't know where we were going, but I followed, carrying my bundle of dresses. Fortunately, we met no one else on the way. In the kitchen, she picked up a box of matches. The servants eyed us with evident curiosity. We went down the stairs to the basement and into the backyard, where she put the clothes down next to the outdoor sink. There were a lot of them, and she had to organize them into a neat pile with her foot. I stood beside her, watching and fascinated. With no further hesitation, she struck a match and set fire to the dresses, and I could not help give a gasp. She looked at me as if trying to instill me with some of her courage, and I bowed my head, ashamed. The flames grew quickly. For some time, the dresses burned brightly in the midst of great billows of smoke, and I occasionally saw a buckle gleam as it shrank in upon itself like an animal, or caught the greenish-yellow glint of glass beads, like cat's eyes. Frills and flounces and ruffles in lace or satin were quickly consumed and the pile gradually dwindled down to nothing. Soon there was only a handful of ashes—all that was left of the beautiful dresses that had so excited the Chácara and the town and had shone at so many famous suppers and family reunions. Rooted to the spot, I was remembering the boxes and the trunks arriving from the station, the lines of servants picking them up, Dona Nina herself, so young at the time, glancing hesitantly around her, a veil covering her face. Without knowing why, as if I were witnessing the end of an era, I could not bring myself to look away from that little heap of ashes, and my heart felt horribly heavy. It was then that I felt the mistress's hand on my shoulder.

"Let's go."

I looked up and saw that she was smiling. I went with her, unable to speak. She, on the other hand, strode ahead, as if she had made a decision to start life anew.

Undated – I've felt really worried since the mistress burned those dresses, trying to work out exactly what that gesture meant. She had never before spoken to me so spontaneously, and as time passes—seven days have gone by—I still feel shaken by what I saw. And despite everything, I can't forget the sense of sadness she provoked in me; on the contrary, with time, the atmosphere I had always felt surrounding her has grown denser, as if it were driving her toward some ineluctable fate.

35.
Second Letter from Nina to the Colonel

I realize, Colonel, that this is not a letter you were expecting to receive. When you happen upon the envelope in your mail box, you won't even know or be able to imagine what it might contain. However, these very first lines will make your hands tremble, the sentences will blur before your eyes and, still incredulous, heart pounding, you will hurriedly turn to the end of the letter to see who wrote it.

Yes, it's me. I have to say that I myself am not in the least surprised to be writing to you again; I always thought I would one day, not in order to recall the appalling way in which I treated you or how I ran away from Rio or the many other things that belong firmly in the past, but in order for us to speak seriously like two old friends, who, having survived stormy seas, finally come in sight of terra firma, the one place where they can finally reach some understanding. I hear you sigh: "Ah, that Nina always finds a way to disinter the old Colonel!" But it is only with age, my friend, that we do, at last, understand certain truths. Or, rather, those truths finally take on some kind of reality inside us, because reality takes time, and we can only believe in what our age allows us to believe in. And I am being absolutely honest, hand on heart, when I say that I, who never once considered the possible consequences of any of my actions, I, who was so often cruel and unjust with you, do truly repent, now that I find myself in dire need of a good friend . . . (As I write these words, incidents from the distant past surface in my mind—the afternoon, for example, at a bar on the beach, when you gave me a wristwatch . . . There was another friend sitting nearby, and for some mad reason I was expecting *him* to give me a watch, not you. I think a few days earlier, I had mentioned, in your presence, that I needed a watch, and you immediately rushed off and bought me one. And that was what irritated me. I only had to express a wish for you to grant it. And you were not the one from whom I wanted such haste or such resolve. I scornfully closed the box containing the watch and flung it into the middle of the road. The box flew open and the watch lay glittering on the tarmac. You went to get up, and I stopped you, saying: "If you touch that thing, I'll leave." You did not move, but your eyes filled with tears. The other man sitting next to me observed the scene in silence. The watch stayed where it was until a tramp picked it up, examined it carefully, then disappeared around a corner with it. I don't know what happened afterward, Colonel, but whatever it was, I can guarantee that was the last I saw of the man sitting next to me. I don't know if he was frightened or what, but he never came back.

As I say, I always thought I would write to you again one day, and if I do so now, with tear-filled eyes, it is because I am so horrified at what is happening to me; and during what is, for me, a crucial time, the image of all those who loved me—who truly loved me—is horribly vivid. Whichever way I turn, and however many more things happen to me, I will never forget the times we spent together, and I recall everything, absolutely everything: your kindness, the interest you took in my late father, your advice when he died, and even—yes, why not?—your voice, which so irritated me then and which, now, alas, I miss so very much. No, I have not forgotten those things, nor can I remain silent about how much I miss those precious days. I always knew, and this is a confession I make as a homage to your friendship, I always knew how you felt about me. (Yes, this is the moment to be totally honest.) It was clear to me that I was the reason you came to visit us. You may call me fickle and say that I was always more than happy to take, but never had any intention of giving anything back. That is because you do not understand women's hearts, and do not know to what extent we are prepared to sacrifice others in order to satisfy our own vanity. (Ah, the things I remember as I write this! The modest room in which we lived, the window that looked out onto the slums behind. The noise of the children in the afternoon, playing in the street. My father's coughing. His invariable question: "Nina, has the Colonel arrived yet?" And later, when the card games stopped, the sad tone in which he said: "Nina, the Colonel won't be coming to play cards any more." He went rapidly downhill after that, until he died. I remember the funeral, his body laid out in the middle of the room, covered with a sheet. That was when you suddenly reappeared and took my hands in yours: "It's such a shame, Nina, that you find yourself in this situation." And when you left, after one last long look at your dead friend, you left some money on my pillow. At that moment, I did, I admit, consider seeking you out and marrying you. We even met a few times, do you remember? But it was then I met the man who would become my husband and abandoned everything to come and live at the Chácara. I can still remember our last conversation, when I told you of my decision. You made no attempt to hide your horror: "Vila Velha? But that's the provinces, the back of beyond!" It took me a few years to see that, once again, you were right, but that's the way we are, we never know for certain who we will be happy with or where. A rather banal thought, perhaps, but how different it is when we experience the truth of that banal thought in our very flesh.) I feel I should be more explicit: on the few occasions when you squeezed my hand—always very delicately—or looked at me when my father fell asleep, or when you followed me down to the street on the pretext of giving me a present, I was always perfectly aware of the nature of your feelings for me. But I was so confused at the time, how could I possibly have shown you the gratitude you deserved or returned the deep feelings of a heart that was ripe for love? I let everything slip away, and the current that carried me off cast me up here in this sad place.

You know what happened after that. I don't want to describe here all the difficulties I experienced at the time, a time when I often felt completely lost. (And I would have been, had someone not said to me: "Nina, let us make a pact. The power of the Meneses is a terrible thing.") And when, exhausted, I finally decided to leave the Chácara, you were the only one I could turn to. It was raining, and, standing there on the deserted platform, I thought for a moment that you had perhaps not received my letter. How I suffered during those long seconds—an accumulation of years of hopeless suffering—thinking I was all alone, until I saw you peering anxiously into all the carriages, looking for me. My sister-in-law Ana had come with me, and I introduced you to her as my best friend. I can still remember the look on her face. When I announced to her that I would not be going back to the Chácara and intended to make a go of life on my own in Rio, she said simply: "I know, with that friend of yours." And the worst of it was, she said this without a hint of irony in her voice.

We have reached the point I wanted to reach, Colonel. Having fulfilled her mission, which was to take my son away with her, Ana left for the Chácara. Alone and utterly lost, there was nothing then that I would not have promised you—or not in so many words, because nothing was ever said, only silences, unspoken agreements. I know that, later on, you said that by refusing nothing, I had tacitly accepted everything. And it's true, I did accept your proffered hand, but how could I have done otherwise? I knew what your feelings were and, knowing that, I could not have failed to be aware that I was committing myself to repaying your kindness in some other way. Yes, maybe I was fickle and frivolous, but I was never cruel on purpose. I think I'm right in saying that it was around this time that I fell ill and seriously considered taking my own life. The image is still clear in my mind: me sitting in an armchair, you standing by the window. We said nothing and just let time pass. You would occasionally offer me a glass of water or some other drink. You would suggest cooking something, or else warming up some tea long forgotten in the pot, or bring me some biscuits. And one afternoon, unable to bear it any longer, I ran away. I returned in the early hours, extremely drunk, my hair all over the place, and collapsed onto the bed, retching. And without a word, you took care of me as if I were a child. And I liked that. Other similar nights followed, and I never heard an angry word from you. On the contrary, it was as though caring for me brought you a certain peace of mind, as if playing the part of angel of mercy suited certain aspects of your nature. It was probably my fault that we never went any further than that, but then again, you never made any attempt to get closer. Once you had administered your help, you would simply observe me from afar, and that made my blood boil. I have always found indecisive men infuriating, indeed, I think that was the main reason for the failure of my marriage. (Because there's no point in hiding the fact that our marriage did fail, and not just once, but twice. And the reason it failed was because I felt he succumbed too easily to his family's narrow-minded spirit, which appeared to be far more important than me, and to exert a far stronger influence. When Valdo had a chance to leave the Chácara and make a new life at my side, he chose to go in the opposite direction and made a ridiculous suicide attempt.) Your relationship with me, as I'm sure you would agree, was limited to you giving me gifts and flowers, which, while it was clear proof of great constancy, went no further than that. You occasionally lent me large sums of money, and I know that, in exchange for such fundamental favors, I could have broken the ice myself and embraced you or kissed you, thus occasionally showing myself capable of an enthusiastic display of gratitude. For some reason, though, your presence always made me feel strangely cold. Often when I was with other people, having fun, laughing, telling stories—in short, giving every appearance of being happy—you only had to enter the room for the smile to vanish from my face, my enthusiasm to die, and I would start to complain of headaches, a lack of air, and a thousand and one other imaginary ailments. One night, I even said to you: "I can't stand the sight of your face. I don't even like you." We were in a bar, surrounded by other people, celebrating some anniversary or other. You said nothing, but looked desperately around you, finally fixing your gaze on the stained tablecloth. Then, unable to contain my irritation any longer, I said: "What are you looking at? What are you waiting for?" And when you continued to sit there, head bowed, I added: "Get out of my sight—now." But you didn't dare to move, as if you were nailed to the floor. I waited one, even two minutes, and all around us absolute silence reigned. Finally, I found the courage to get up and throw the contents of my glass in your face. The wine dripped slowly down over your white shirt, like a huge bloodstain. Only then did you turn and almost run out of the bar. (Forgive me: we never hurt those about whom we care nothing, only those who, for one reason or another, touch our hearts most deeply.)

For a few days, I was free of your presence, but eventually you came back, your coat over your arm, two pools of water in the spot where you were standing. "What are you doing here?" I screamed. You merely smiled, having completely forgiven me.

As I say, it was sheer cussedness on my part. If I was happy, I would try to conceal the fact. If I was sad, I would pretend to be even sadder than I was. I disliked the aftershave you used, which had a musty smell about it, your brusque, cutting manner, acquired in the barracks, your anecdotes, which I considered absurd, your tastes, which I thought vulgar. If you suggested going for a walk or to some bar or restaurant, I would immediately suggest the exact opposite, just to underline how wrong your suggestion had been. In the end, you didn't dare suggest anything, you merely followed me meekly around, gazing at me with sad, faithful eyes. I don't know what egotistical demon made me behave like that.

We are nearing the end, and, besides, these recollections are pointless now. However, through them, and after so much time has passed, you will doubtless have learned who I really am: a foolish, volatile creature, whose cries of feigned pleasure sometimes became mixed up with the genuine sort. Be assured, Colonel, despite everything you saw and everything that happened, the only feelings in my heart for you were ones of affection and gratitude; I would embrace you now, fall at your feet, kill myself, if you asked me to. Do you doubt me? Then all I can say is that much of what happened already carried within it the seeds of this letter. Sooner or later, you would have understood the true nature of my feelings.

The day has come, Colonel. Here I am, stripped of all artifice. I know full well that without your help I would have perished. And perhaps what irritated me so much was knowing how important you were, how irreplaceable, but I promised myself long ago that I would, at some point, tell you everything. It would coincide with the moment when, once again, I said: I've had enough. I have no one to turn to. The walls of this house are pressing in on me. Your help is even more precious now, and this might well be the last time I come knocking at your door. Does it surprise you to hear me talking like this? Don't worry, I'm not considering suicide again. No. You cannot imagine how ardently I cling to life, yes, me, the one who once tried to flee from it for the stupidest of reasons, and yet now I feel its worth, minute by minute, and I grow pale and tremble just to imagine that one day I will be cut off from its light. Yet despite this sudden rapture of mine, I sense that my days are numbered and that the time is fast approaching when I will have to pay my debts. (I see you smiling and murmuring: "She never changes" and recalling other conversations in which I also talked of death and repentance.) But, Colonel, we never really invent anything, we merely anticipate a scene that we will later be obliged to play for real. And I feel that my role would lack veracity if I did not settle accounts with certain people—you being the first among those.

This letter, then, is a declaration. I find myself suddenly free to speak. For once in my life, Colonel, I want to show you that I do know what love is. At the time, I was a child and could not return the fire of your passion. Let my hand not tremble when I dare to write that word and let it not awaken in your heart some very cruel memories. Let us be simple and human within our own very human limitations, and let us try to do right after so many years of doing wrong, convinced that we can enjoy another kind of happiness in completing, in our maturer years, something we tried in vain to throw away during our less enlightened youth. I swear that you will find in me the seed that, while it did not germinate at the time, has since borne fruit a thousandfold. And in quite a different way from anything you might have imagined, I will be yours, entirely yours, and so definitively that, for as long as you live, the memory of me will be the one thing to illumine your thoughts.

36.
André's Diary (vi)

Undated – Something incomprehensible is happening between us, because I feel we are different somehow. I've been aware of this for some days now: firstly, there is a certain lassitude and a vagueness when she speaks, as if she wasn't very interested in what she has to say, and was only speaking because she felt obliged to; secondly, there's a genuine absence of anything to say, a silence interspersed with sighs, a lack of energy which is not like her at all. Others might not notice these changes, or might attribute them to a momentary indisposition, but I am so used to observing her every mood that I can spot the slightest alteration. And I confess that I tremble, not knowing what to do—could she have grown tired of me? The usual confidences and promises and smiles have all vanished, as have the secret, knowing signals made behind other people's backs, a way of facing down the danger and, at the same time, providing proof of our closeness. Her usual mocking self has disappeared or is disappearing; even when she's with me, she seems preoccupied, almost sad, her thoughts always elsewhere. One evening, I came across her in the hallway, reading a letter. "What's that?" I asked, but she said only: "Oh, it's nothing." I stood in front of her to stop her going into the drawing room. "You've changed," I said. She pulled an angry face:

"Oh, for heaven's sake!" Not far off, a door slammed, and, afraid that someone might be coming, I blurted out: "I want to see that letter." She said bluntly: "Never." I moved toward her, intending to snatch the letter from her, but she pushed me out of way: "You're such a child." And she walked past me into the drawing room. Left alone, I was filled with spiteful rage and, in revenge, I decided not to appear at supper that evening and locked myself in my room. Betty came and knocked on my door. "I don't want any supper," I told her. "Is something wrong?" she asked. "No!" I roared. But I spent the whole of suppertime in my room, with the lights out, my ear pressed to the wall, trying to hear what was going on in there. How it pained me not to be at the table. She had said the same thing to me on other occasions—"you're such a child"—but always in an affectionate way, so affectionately that, up until that evening, when she had spoken those same words with such evident anger, I had felt that the fact of my being a child was what most interested her about me—not that I had ever paid much heed to this possibility. Coming away from the wall, through which I could hear only a confused murmur of conversation and the clink of cutlery, I reminded myself that I had often been told how capricious and unpredictable women can be. Perhaps she was going through one of those phases. And I thought sadly that I should give her a rest, avoid her, make myself conspicuous not by my constant, solicitous presence, but by my absence. I swore that I would adopt this plan of action—because humans are limited beings and tire of everything, even love—and I even came to idealize the days that I would spend away from her side and what I would do in the meantime. My rifles had grown rusty and urgently needed cleaning. I could even go into town and see what was in the shops and buy a book or two. These thoughts, however, lasted only a moment, and reality immediately regained its hold on me; and yet, anxiously going over in my mind everything that had happened recently, I could still find no explanation for the present situation. A thousand possibilities occurred to me, including that of a definitive rupture between us, a return to square one, motivated by fatigue or by late-flowering feelings of remorse. Then I recovered and invented all kinds of reasons that would redeem her for her behavior. After all, she was under no obligation to show me any letters she received. Could I not control my jealousy and realize that my loving her did not mean that she belonged to me body and soul? I went further, imagining that the crisis was already over and that she was waiting for me, possibly ready to explain herself. Borne along on that thought, I left my room and began wandering about the house, in the hope of finding her. That, at least, had the merit of partially salvaging my dignity: if I saw her, it would seem like an accidental encounter and not a deliberate ploy on my part. Immersed in its customary stillness, the house revealed nothing to me, afforded me no explanation. How vast and useless those rooms seemed! Heavens, the things men invented! The very walls seemed impregnated with a habitual, everyday life that felt quite alien. I went over to the verandah and lay down in the hammock and swung gently back and forth, gazing up at the star-filled sky. A single milky stripe traversed the heavens from side to side. A smudge of red on the horizon suggested that summer was on its way. I imagined that, in years to come, that same sky would shine just as brilliantly, and she would perhaps no longer be at my side; a sharp pain pierced my heart then, and I told myself that she had no idea how much I truly loved her. I forgot everything else, who she was, what she had been, what she represented for me and for others, in order to concentrate solely on the extraordinary times we were living through. Losing her would be like losing the light of the world. And however hard I tried to remember the person I had been before she appeared in my life, I could come up with nothing real or substantial, only an obscure, will-less individual. She had created me, given me the power to analyze things, to say what I liked and didn't like; she had given me my identity, making me a man capable of despising anything that did not contribute directly to increasing or clarifying the feelings that inhabited me. The hammock creaked on its hinges as I tried to recall certain particularly charming details—her satin skin, her way of laughing, the inimitable curve of her breasts—and I did so slowly and with infinite care, so that those details did not become distorted or contaminated by images created by my own imagination, and I asked myself, although without receiving a satisfactory answer, if all women were as strange and perfect as her. There was about her something so special, so mysterious, something that made her utterly different from any other woman I could possibly imagine. No other woman had that firm, velvety skin, the subcutaneous light that seemed to illumine her from within, and which had so often made me think of her as a star glowing softly and serenely in the dark. I was always astonished by her lack of modesty—she would happily stand naked before me, with the ease and aplomb of an animal accustomed to a life free of malice or sin. Then there was the way she walked, swaying her hips, confident of her own grace and femininity. I remembered other details too: on one of our encounters in the cellar, I had found her already undressed, lying face down on the straw mattress. She did not just lie down, as others might do, she literally embraced the mattress, surrendering to it, as if wanting to become one with its old and rather musty stuffing. There was nothing superficial about any of her actions, she did everything wholeheartedly, with a passion that was a guarantee of the depth of her impulses, a passion that lent dignity to the way she chose to live her life. For a moment, holding my breath as if afraid I might wake her, I contemplated those magnificently free curves. In the end, though, I went over to her, and she, pretending to be asleep, closed her eyes, which was another way of offering herself up to my gaze.

So powerful and incisive is the effect of her presence that I feel close to her even when she isn't with me; I walk, and my steps seem to correspond to a hidden music that binds us together, and then I know that she belongs to me, as I do to her, and that this is a law no power on earth could ever take away from us. Ah, how strong and powerful we were in our love! And yet, oddly, I cannot describe her as "that woman," still less as "my mother." She is neither one thing nor the other. She is neither a woman who exists outside of me, who can be designated as "this one" or "that," nor the woman who gave birth to me, nourishing me with her blood and her sap. Perhaps I could never feel so closely identified with any other woman. We are not different people, that is the reason, we are one and the same. (Because the god of love is a hermaphrodite god—by bringing together two different sexes in one creation, he created the image of a wise and knowledgeable being, which, in its duality, is the paradigm of perfection.) Woman and mother, what other hybrid being could better contain the force of our feelings? Loving her means becoming easily, seamlessly reunited with the person I was. It's a return to my country of origin. Loving her as a man, I feel that I cease to be myself in order to complete the whole being we must have been before I was born. There can be no shame in this urge to be conjoined, because there's nothing immoral about it. When she isn't there or seems bored with me, I feel as if a part of me had been stolen from me, I feel lacking, incomplete. A whole part of myself is left blind. The stars could plummet from the sky, and the colors of nature promise entirely new seasons, and my eyes would be oblivious to such phenomena. That is why I feel my way about the house, touching the objects around me and failing to recognize them, like a man who has lost his own shadow.

The last time we saw each other (and "see" for me means being alone with her in the cellar), I was keenly aware that she was under the sway of alternating currents of enthusiasm and despair. It was as if she were trying to be the person she had always been, but that, independently of this, some powerful, inner preoccupation was dominating her thoughts. For example, when I asked about her lack of interest in me, she laughed until she cried, then subsided into a deep silence. I tried in vain to bring her back to the surface, but she hung her head and remained very still, eyes fixed on the floor. "What on earth is the matter?" I asked. She did not answer, but got up and went over to stand by the narrow window that looks out onto the garden. What ideas, what memories were adrift in her mind? She seemed so agitated, her expression shifting and changing under the influx of images long since vanished, but whose return evidently provoked a lacerating pain. I could not bear it, and standing behind her, I kissed the back of her neck, trying to restore her to life. She let me kiss her, as if she were dead. On one such occasion, I went further, giving lingering kiss after lingering kiss, determined not to leave her until a little warmth had returned to her icy skin. In an ecstasy, my lips moved from her shoulder down to her breasts. She finally clasped my head in her hands—we were sitting together on the mattress—and looked at me as if she did not even recognize me. I asked again: "What is it, what's wrong?" Then she spoke, and there was such a poignant note of longing in her voice: "Here, many years ago . . ." And I saw then, as clearly as if it were there before my eyes, an identical scene, a love scene, with another man in my place. He must have kissed her as I had done, and that is what had provoked the abstracted look on her face. (*Written in the margin*: So many years have passed since then and yet, even now, I'm assailed by doubt: did she really love me or was she merely looking for someone else whom I closely resembled? The way she would sometimes touch my cheek, as if searching for some trace of a beloved face, the words she would say in moments of ecstasy—fragments of words and phrases that did not belong to any conversation we had ever had, but to her interrupted conversation with that other man; her insistence on certain caresses, certain expressions of love, revealed an intimacy learned from someone other than me—but who and when? Who was he and, given her perennial discretion, how could I ever find out? Even now, I still do not know whether it was me she loved or a ghost, but of one thing I am sure, she was the only woman I had ever loved.) Unable to contain my jealousy, I drew back and, seeing her still immersed in her thoughts, I raised one hand and slapped her face. She gave only a faint moan and turned to look at me, but there was no surprise in her eyes. "You have no respect for me at all," I cried. "You don't even see me, aren't even aware that I'm here by your side." Then, seeing her eyes fill with tears, I took her in my arms. She made me rest my head on her shoulder and stroked me as if I were a child. "Don't be angry, André, all is not yet lost." "Not yet lost?" And again I felt that incomprehensible threat hanging over us, like a shadow. "No, not yet," and she squeezed me so hard, I almost gasped for breath, "not yet. But everything has its end, André." I confess that, for the first time, I felt that she really did not love me. No, she didn't and never would; there was a kind of poison in her veins that made it impossible for her to love me. Perhaps, up until now, she had merely been pretending. And I was so terrified, I felt so lost in that silence, that I covered her in kisses, saying: "No, never, what exists between us will never cease to exist, because that would be the end of me, my death." She realized that I meant what I said and, tenderly stroking my hair, answered: "Don't be afraid." And in another tone of voice entirely, in which I recognized her old self: "From now on, I will be yours in a way I never was before." I closed my eyes, feeling that those hovering threats had been banished and that this time she was not pretending.

Undated – I haven't seen her since that day, which only increases my unease. I dare not question anyone, neither have I been able to glean anything from any overheard snippets of conversation. I even went into the kitchen, hoping to pick up something from what the servants were saying, but they were all unexpectedly silent and ignored me completely. I got angry then and told myself it would be best not to think about it any more and, in order to pass the time, I took my horse and rode along the roads around the Chácara. Everywhere, the ripe maize heads were tinged with red; birds, attracted by the maize, were already flying in over the fields, tracing silent trails across the blue sky. I passed a few mud-built huts, a well, a bridge over a stream. From a distance, the daughter of one of the farmhands eyed me curiously; I noticed in passing that she was pretty and blonde, but that was all. Then I rode along one of the dirt tracks that lead out into the countryside. The farther I went from the house, the farther from any familiar sights, the more alone and desperate I felt. No, there was nothing about that landscape to attract me, I found its very vastness oppressive; it seemed to take from me the pleasure of living and breathing. I reached a bend in the road where a pink ipê tree was in full bloom, then galloped back the way I had come. There stood the farmhand's daughter, carrying a basket full of laundry. The stream foamed about my horse's light hooves. And soon, with some relief, above the old trees I have known since childhood, I could make out the Chácara's rather battered roof. It might be hell itself, but what did that matter if it was where I lived and was the only life that interested me. I dismounted, tethered the reins to a pillar, ready to call one of the servants to take the horse to the stables. And I was just about to go up, when I saw her standing motionless above me. I stopped, my heart beating furiously. She had obviously been watching me ever since I rode through the gates of the Chácara. Now I was the one to congratulate myself. Had I succeeded in worrying her? Had she suffered to think that I had managed to forget her for a few moments and was enjoying myself far from her presence? How good it felt to be cruel, how that feeling helped dissipate some of my anxiety. Having recovered from the shock of seeing her there, I continued on up the steps, saying in a voice in which surprise was mingled with disapproval:

"At last!"

She said nothing, but came down to meet me. I waited, leaning on the handrail. Below me, its reins hanging loose, my horse stood snorting. When she reached me, I grabbed her wrist:

"Where have you been?"

She tried to pull away.

"Be careful, André, your father is on the verandah."

"So what?" I said through gritted teeth. "All these days without seeing you . . . couldn't you at least have said something?"

"André . . ."

And there was such a pleading look in her eyes that I let go of her. The wind was tousling her hair. Rubbing her bruised wrist, she was gazing up at me with a wounded expression on her face:

"You didn't used to be this way . . . you would never have treated me like this before."

I turned away so that she would not see how upset I was.

"I'm going crazy," I said.

She shook her head:

"You must stay calm. If you carry on as you are, you'll spoil everything."

That was tantamount to asking me to leave her alone. Suddenly, as we stood on those steps in the morning sun, a chasm opened up between us. I hadn't been expecting that, and only really noticed when I felt how great the distance had become. And whatever I did, whatever I said—regardless of whether I heaped complaints on her or insults—would only drive us further apart. I just stood there, feeling utterly discouraged. She said nothing more, but in silence, as if accepting that there really was nothing to be done, she went down a few more steps. Enraged, as if this constituted a major affront, I shouted after her:

"Where are you going?"

She turned and fixed me with a serene gaze:

"For a walk."

"Alone?"

She hesitated before answering:

"Yes, alone," she said at last, and her lips trembled.

I caught her up again and this time grabbed her arm:

"Why alone?"

She looked up, and I saw in her eyes that spark of anger, defiance, or sheer determination that I had seen on so many other similar occasions. She said:

"Because that's what I want, André."

Unable to contain myself any more, I seized her by the shoulders and began to shake her:

"Is this how you promised to love me . . . in a way you never had before?"

And I was so violent, so out of control, that she gave a cry and leaned back against the wall.

"Stop it, for God's sake, you're hurting me."

Seeing how pale she was, I immediately released her. She was breathing hard and, with her head still resting against the wall, was rubbing her arm. I saw then how fragile she was, how profoundly, inexplicably helpless, and I did not know what to think:

"Oh," I murmured, "if you only knew . . ."

And even as I was still feeling like an utter brute, my anger was fast dissolving to give way, finally, to the tenderness that had never entirely left me. Words deserted me, and for a few seconds, standing before her, I could find no way of expressing what I was feeling. She was equally silent and continued mechanically to rub her arm. I could bear anything but that passivity, that lack of will in a person normally so impulsive. I couldn't understand why she was behaving like that, nor why she was being so evasive. Was she simply tired—she, who had urged on me the need to embrace my sin, or what she called sin—or was she merely giving in to the corrosive effects of remorse? The expression on her face was not her usual one, but that of someone struggling against intense, physical pain. It was as if she were oblivious to the noises of the outside world and aware only of the secret battle being waged by some emerging, evolving force in the very center of her being. Suddenly, everything I had been unable to see—too blinded by jealousy and distrust—was revealed to me, and I saw how much thinner she had become, how her features had changed, become sharper, her face gaunter, how she trembled before me, pathetic and defenseless. The change was so extraordinary that I even wondered to myself if she had ever been beautiful, if the fascination she held for me was not some diabolical mistake on my part.

Was she just an ordinary woman, the same as all the others? There, in the full glare of the sun, I could easily find the answers to all those questions. And I took pleasure in examining her, in being cruel, and showing how cruel I was, and I enjoyed imagining her to be mean and cruel as well. I even adopted a superior air, that of someone who has suddenly noticed the trap set for him. However, this lasted no more than a minute, the time it took for me to recognize her again, to imagine, with keen, decisive eyes, the illness eating away at her, and which perhaps, out of pity, she was concealing from me. I folded her in my arms, and she offered no resistance.

"What's wrong? Are you ill?"

She rested quietly in my embrace, as if she lacked the strength to do anything else. Then, glancing furtively up at the verandah, she said:

"Be careful. We'll talk tonight."

And pulling away from me, she went down the steps into the garden.

Undated – I waited hours for her in the darkness. My eyes had grown accustomed to the gloom, and I was amusing myself trying to make out the shapes of the old tools piled in the corners, the various crates and other less easily identifiable objects. All those things had once been useful, had had their moment, had been used by skillful hands to create the garden that was now succumbing to neglect. When had that been, who had lived here on the Chácara then, what had their lives been like? No answer came; those abandoned witnesses maintained a hostile silence. An idea occurred to me, a strange thought, doubtless born of those particular circumstances and my particular situation. That part of the Chácara—the Pavilion—had always seemed to me a fateful place, of which no one spoke, and if someone did have to mention it, they would do so only in the most roundabout way and never use its actual name; they would say "there" or "down there," as I had heard Aunt Ana refer to it on more than one occasion. And I myself had never asked why it had suffered that fate. As a child, I had always known that the old garden tools were stored there, and if I ever went "down there," it was only in order to listen to the lizards scampering about or to pick fruit from the overgrown trees. Despite that, and without anyone ever telling me as much, I knew that the Pavilion was linked to the drama that had happened years ago—the same drama everyone took such pains to keep from me. I had grown used now to that heavy, damp, musty atmosphere, the smell had impregnated me, become part of me, it was, you might say, the smell of what was happening to me, yes, why not, the smell of my love. Whenever I encountered that smell later on, the feelings I had then would always come rushing back. And it wasn't only the smell, it was the touch, the feel of certain objects—for example, the cold, damp straw mattress on which I was lying and which gave off the scent of some special herb, was becoming part of what, in my mind, was already a memory, offering me a strange perspective on time, with things emerging from the past, which, even while they were still in the present, were already forming the basis of my future. They pulsated in the darkness with a secret inner life. And while I felt entangled in that silent web, I was still too young to recognize it as the source of that feeling. I say "feeling" even though I cannot pinpoint it exactly: rather, in the surrounding darkness, it was more a vague sense of being caught up in something hidden and violent (some bloody incident—but when and with whom?) and which I could only describe as the smell of evil. An evil atmosphere. And it was clear that the person I loved belonged to that atmosphere. Not because of the thing she called sin, but because of the mere fact that she existed and breathed and was herself, and shared the same tepid, spongy essence as sea anemones. For the truth is that it was the only place where Nina was fully herself, a brilliant, perfumed, ever-fresh flower among all those objects eroded by time. She embodied that musty, subterranean odor. Yes, that fragile creature was the simple, frank embodiment of evil, human evil. This idea filled me with terror, not the kind of terror that suddenly closed around me and rendered me instantly helpless, but a slow-growing terror, which began as a tingle in the soles of my feet, then advanced like a blockade on my heart. However, my poor heart now reacted to so few things in this world. To evil, yes, but so what? Were anyone to accuse me, I would say that evil was all I wanted, all that interested me on this earth.

She found me there, trembling, besieged by darkness. I did not get up, I did not go to meet her, as I would have done on other occasions. She would, of course, notice this change and doubtless think my love for her had lessened, when, in fact, I felt that my love had reached new heights and that everything else was a mere detail with no real existence. Lying there, legs outstretched and numb, I could no longer feel the blood circulating in my veins and was enjoying imagining myself the victim of a poisoning. Nina duly noticed this change and bent down to touch my face.

"What's wrong?" she asked.

"Nothing," I said. And I trembled, not because of all those other things I might have feared, but because I had suddenly realized how very alone we were. The touch of her hand on my skin gave me a clear sense that I was sliding, disappearing into another man's body, another man's will.

"But you're trembling," she said, and her hand continued to explore my face, as if engaged in some intimate guessing game.

"I'm just cold. I've been lying here for ages."

"I'm sorry," she said, "I couldn't get away any sooner."

As if she had sensed what I had been thinking earlier, her voice took on a gentler, more insinuating tone. She lay down beside me, snuggled up against me, radiating a new warmth that wrapped about my whole body. We were reaching the point where words became unnecessary, we were merely listening, and the faintest sounds became monstrous, discordant, animal noises, because we were only interested in one movement, and it was that somber, medieval mechanism that bound us together, uniting us not as two distinct beings, but as one being, made of the same flesh and the same blood. With my ear pressed to her breast, I didn't care if that beating heart was mine or hers; it was ours, and I felt myself to be a branch sprouting from her trunk, as if, in the gloom, we had been transformed into a tree and lost all human aspect, become vegetable and pagan, burning in the fire lit by the night and by our desire. Suddenly, in the middle of the silence, she said:

"Have you never thought, André, that you were once my baby? Has it never occurred to you that I carried you inside me before you were born, and that we were once even more united than we are now?"

"Never," I murmured, "I have never thought we could be more united than we are now."

"We could," she said, and her voice was barely a whisper.

"How?"

"Dead."

I sat up then, the spell broken:

"What would be the point if we were dead?"

She drew me close again and placed her lips on mine, and in her urgent desire lay an invitation that was no longer expressed hesitantly, but decisively, brazenly, like a command. It was not just love she wanted, but fusion, annihilation. And I agreed to die, closing my eyes and hurling myself into the unknown, our bodies becoming one. Time ceased to pass, everything vanished into a frontierless world. I did occasionally recover consciousness and with it came doubt and fear. This, however, lasted only a second and, as I plunged back into the dark, I told myself that were it possible to cross the frontier that we each represent for each other, we had made that crossing.

37.
Valdo's Statement

She stood before me, holding the letter, her hands trembling. My difficulty was explaining how I had happened to burst in on her, for she would never believe me, but it really had been pure chance. I was walking down the hallway when I heard a noise, not very loud at first, but rather like someone moving about between bits of furniture in an enclosed space. The door was locked, and I saw no immediate reason to try and force it. It was only when the noise was repeated, this time accompanied by another sound that seemed to me more like a groan—or a lament—that I decided to investigate. The door wasn't locked after all, and the handle turned easily. I should explain that it was the door to a small room adjoining my bedroom, one that was never really used. My sister-in-law Ana used to go in there sometimes to store clothing or objects that were no longer needed, at least not immediately. Long ago, my mother had also set up a little shrine in there to Our Lady of Sorrows, and it had become the room's centerpiece along with a prayer stool upholstered in threadbare velvet for those who wished to kneel. Some of her personal effects had also been stored there. Demétrio hadn't allowed them to be distributed among the servants, and together they formed the accumulated stock of memories left behind after her death.

When I opened the door, I could not at first make out who was there, only the outline of someone leaning on the chest of drawers on which the shrine had been placed. On seeing the light coming in through the door, the figure turned toward me.

"Who is it?" the voice asked, and I realized it was Nina.

Had I known it was her, I swear I would never have gone in. But now, even if I'd wanted to, it would be hard to convince her that I had appeared there merely by chance, rather than with any firm intention. I considered withdrawing, but that would not have been straightforward either, for I was clearly silhouetted in the open doorway. Then, from where she stood at the back of the room, she immediately went on the attack:

"Oh, it's you, is it? Why are you spying on me?"

Our relations had for some time been conducted on a level of scant cordiality. I had given up trying to understand her, convinced that there was no rational explanation for the way she behaved. I no longer cared what she did, and although I often found myself watching her every move, or trying to fathom the reason behind some gesture of hers, I now limited myself to trying to prevent any major dispute arising between us. And here, suddenly and inadvertently, I had walked right into one of those potentially inflammatory situations.

"You're mistaken, Nina. I swear I hadn't the faintest idea who was in here. I wouldn't have come in if . . ."

She cut me short, and said in a voice edged with anger:

"If you hadn't known it was me."

She waited for me to defend myself or offer some sort of justification, but this seemed to me superfluous, convinced as I was that we would never manage to reach any kind of understanding. So I shrugged and concluded:

"Yes, it's me. What of it?"

As always, her attitude was one of defiance. And yet, there was something about the situation that made me want to stay. On any other occasion, if my presence really had been undesirable, she would have left the room, slamming the door or whatever. Now, despite her words and the irritated tone in which she said them, there was a certain humility in her voice, perceptible only to someone who knew her intimately: a slight fissure, the hint of stealth and desperation of someone straining to hide a secret that was no longer within her control. Or to put it another way, the Nina I had burst in upon was not the Nina who had slowly been revealed to us here at the Chácara, but the other one, the younger Nina, the one who had seemed so in need of my protection when I saw her in the street that very first time. I know, I know: for me to remember these things with such clarity must mean that I still loved her—this Nina or the other Nina, it scarcely matters. But, even if I live to be a hundred, and learn to hold my tongue and control my feelings, I cannot imagine ever meeting another woman who could make such an impression on me. For me she was not some passing love affair; she was the real thing.

"You're wrong, Nina. But now that I'm here . . ."

"You won't leave. Is that it?"

"Not at least before finding out what it is that's troubling you."

No sooner had I said these words than I heard the rustle of crumpled paper and saw her quickly concealing the letter beneath her clothes. Then, in the darkness, she moved toward me.

"What do you mean by that?"

I felt her hands touching me. And I took them and held them fast in mine.

"You're crying, Nina. Why?"

I could feel her shaking and trying to pull away: no, she wasn't going to succumb to my pity this time. But I made her stay, trying to give more warmth to my words:

"Why don't you trust me?" I asked. Then, daring for the first time to address the matter directly, advancing into territory where her possible weakness was my only guarantee of safe passage, I added: "Is this why you came back? Ah, Nina, it would have been far better if you hadn't come looking for me again."

I realized, with a renewed sense of surprise, that my words did not anger her; she did not try to escape, or indeed react in any way at all. Her cold hands stayed pressed between mine. I think it was this acceptance, real or not, that encouraged me to go further—I felt the ice melting between us, and the first stirrings of a sense of trust that had long been lost. At the same time, superimposing themselves on the sad reality of our everyday lives came a flood of images, wistful possibilities and past conquests. I liked to consider myself a mature man, immune to such waves of hope and optimism. However, clasping her to me, I exclaimed:

"We could have been so happy, Nina!"

Even now, her silence had an air of complicity about it. As I embraced her, however, I heard the rustle of the crumpled letter and was immediately plucked from my reverie and deposited back in harsh reality. Who was it from? Why had she hidden it? The post was usually left on the dining table, from where everyone collected the letters addressed to them. But I hadn't seen that letter arrive, nor who had left it on the table. For a second, I hesitated to ask, not wanting to ruin that moment of unexpected closeness. But curiosity and my latent jealousy got the better of me:

"What's that letter? Who's it from?"

She slowly detached herself from me and, once again, her reaction was not what I expected.

"Valdo, I need to talk to you. But we should go somewhere else. I don't feel comfortable in this cramped room."

Whatever it was, I realized we had reached a decisive moment. There was about her a calmness, a weariness, a vulnerability, none of which seemed to me to bode well. Various thoughts rushed into my mind—things I had seen, others I had merely suspected, the occasional concrete fact—all overlaid with images of her and her many shifting expressions; her mysterious reaction on being discovered with the letter now took on a new, incriminating vitality in the light of what she had just said. I don't know if it was Demétrio's influence (he had, after all, been full of dire predictions right from the start), but to me the image of Nina was always linked to some disaster waiting to happen—who knows when—but like all disasters, it would no doubt break upon us when we least expected. And so all my old fears flared up again, and I could see that evil—its name and shape as yet unknown—looming on the horizon.

We left the storeroom and went into the drawing room. At first, I said nothing, waiting for her to speak. For some time, we sat in silence, not an uneasy silence exactly, but one filled with that state of indecision peculiar to those afraid of broaching an important matter, and who merely succeed in increasing rather than diminishing the listener's sense of foreboding. But soon enough she did begin to speak, in exactly the same tone I had heard in the storeroom: muted and hesitant, and full of that same uncertainty. Fear? Indecision? The more she talked, the more the problem revealed itself. She told me she was ill, possibly gravely ill. (Before I continue, I must confess that, initially, despite everything, I did not believe what she was saying. I remembered Betty saying a few days earlier that Nina had burned all her dresses. I thought it strange and went to the wardrobe, expecting Betty's story to prove false. But no, it was true—the wardrobe really was empty. Now would a woman who was gravely ill be so concerned about her clothes? What could it mean other than that she wanted some new clothes?) But at the same time, as I listened and doubted, two important factors weighed in favor of what she was saying: first, her tone of voice and, second, the change in her physical appearance. So I tried to find out from her what this illness might be or what form it took. She paused for a moment, as if searching for the right answer. Then she asked if I couldn't simply accept what she was saying, without her going into any detail. I said she was being cruel, and that she would succeed only in worrying me still more. "That's not my intention," she told me. "I just don't know what exactly is wrong with me." I came to the conclusion then that she merely *suspected* she was ill. I said that this was no reason to despair or, indeed, to weep in secret. At other times, in other circumstances, this remark of mine would only have irritated her. Now, in what I took to be a positive sign, she showed no strong feelings; indeed, she didn't react in any way at all. She just shrugged slightly and said: "I'm so tired of everything." But then why not tell me? Once again, mistrust seeped into my mind. She lacked for nothing, she had everything she desired, lived an easy, carefree existence. So why was she tired? Tired of what? The thought of some hidden, secret life ran through me like a shudder. I asked if she could be more specific, give me some facts about this hypothetical disease. She replied calmly that it was not hypothetical. I felt confused, and did not know what to think. It was she herself who came to my aid: if the worst did come to the worst, she asked me, what did it matter? It has a strange destiny, the truth. Listening to her speaking, I had the fleeting sense that she was not deceiving me. Something serious was going on. And yet I was so accustomed to her subterfuges that this feeling lasted no longer than a moment. I looked at her once again, and was sure she was lying. But there must be some purpose to what she was saying, some hidden objective? The best thing would be to control my impatience and wait for her to hit the target in her own good time. She began to speak again—and for the first time since we had sat down, I felt ashamed of the feelings I had entertained in the storeroom. What she told me was neither banal nor extraordinary—it was merely exactly what a liar would say, and one who believed utterly in the naïvety of the person she was speaking to. She lied, and because she couldn't help it, for she believed utterly in my boundless love (she wouldn't have been so bold if she hadn't) and supposed it to be prey to all the usual weaknesses, even that of not believing and yet accepting the lie as a possible truth. She went too far, and painted a picture of her illness that seemed to me entirely unconvincing. She spoke vehemently rather than dramatically. And vehemence in that woman, at least in certain circumstances, was a rare thing. I could imagine her dead (or dying, which amounts to much the same thing), but I could never imagine her subject to the afflictions and sufferings of an illness. What she was saying—and even I don't have the courage to remember all of it—demeaned her. And as she talked and as the words flowed freely, I paid less attention to the meaning of what she said and more to her presence, her proximity, her perfume. She was testing me, and watching her demean herself in her efforts to appear pathetic, I was wondering if I would still find her touch so very troubling. On that occasion, victory was still hers. I closed my eyes, not listening, simply aware of my whole body tensing up. It was at that point, possibly intuiting my feelings, that she said very calmly:

"I must go. I have to go."

"Why?"

"I need to see a doctor in Rio."

So there it was: we had reached the decisive moment. Once again, the same old thing: leave, face the world, forget . . .—and yet it astonished me. Ah, how persistently, how identically, suffering befalls us: as if pain were minutely catalogued and always afflicted us in exactly the same way. And it was so absolutely the same as before that I looked up, surprised to feel surprised.

"I never expected anything else," I said. "I always knew your stay here was only a temporary solution."

"Let's spare each other the insults and recriminations," she said quickly.

I smiled:

"And then? What else? The mistake we made was starting afresh, but you can be sure by now that I am resigned to anything."

She seemed taken aback by what I said, and put her hand on my knee:

"I need you to believe me."

"Why? Either way you'll go, won't you?"

"Yes, I will."

We sat in silence. Then, as my desire for argument or revenge subsided, I asked when she would leave, and whether she wanted me to go with her. If she really was ill, why shouldn't I accompany her? She might need someone by her side. She replied that she preferred to go alone, more than that, she needed me to let her go alone. Her insistence seemed to me to conceal an ulterior motive. I remembered the burned clothes and could not resist asking her why she had done such an odd thing. For the first time since the beginning of our conversation, I realized that I had succeeded in annoying her. "Oh, the clothes!" she exclaimed, and by her tone it was clear she considered the incident completely devoid of any importance. Nevertheless, as an explanation, she declared that the clothes were very old and out of fashion. "But why burn them?" I insisted. "You could have given them to the servants." She stared at me defiantly and replied, somewhat maliciously, that her illness might be contagious. I said I didn't believe her and she simply shrugged. She had her reasons for burning them, she said. Then in a softer voice: "They reminded me of a time I didn't want to remember." This explanation seemed to me more plausible. Finally, I asked if she intended buying more clothes on her trip to Rio. (This last question wasn't entirely ingenuous; I was well aware that we had less and less money at our disposal, and that Demétrio, with his account ledger in hand, was forever noting down superfluous expenses and inventing excesses where economies could be made.) To this she replied abruptly: "No." And there our discussion ended.

We had not in any practical sense come to an agreement, nor had I given my consent. But when I analyzed the situation, I understood that she would in any case act according to her own wishes, and interpret my silence as consent. We did not discuss the matter again, even though I was sure, in the days that followed, that she thought only of her departure. And so it was that one day she came to me and said:

"I'm leaving tomorrow, Valdo."

I nodded, wondering what on earth I would say to my brother this time.

38.
André's Diary (vii)

5th – That's it: she's gone. I didn't see her when she left the house, but I ran to a bend in the road and hid behind a tree to watch. It was windy, a warm, sultry wind that brought with it from afar a vast quantity of dry leaves; the dark sky promised a storm that would probably never come. As soon as I heard the wheels of the buggy approaching, my heart began beating so hard I had to press my hands to my chest. There she sat beside the driver; she was wearing a shawl that, strangely, concealed almost half her face. Dear God, how pale she was, more ghost than human. I couldn't bear to look at her for very long; my eyes filled with tears, everything grew blurred and I covered my face with my hands. I could still hear the sound of the wheels, though, which gradually diminished, and the pain was as intense as if half of my own self were being torn from me, and the other half relegated to uncertainty and darkness where it would do nothing but weep. Because I *was* weeping, terrible sobs that shook my whole body. I understood then that the price of all human affection is cruel, irremediable pain; I told myself I didn't care if my love were sinful or not, and that my sense of utter devastation was proof that my feelings were pure and real—as if I did not already know that all forms of love are a way of supplanting oneself. I wept, and yet those tears brought no relief. I slid to the ground and pressed my face to the trunk of the tree, my eyes closed. (While I tried to silence the tumult unleashed inside me, I searched in vain for silence; I could hear the trees buffeted by the wind, the cries of birds with nowhere to go, the murmur of a stream—and I was amazed that the world should contain so much noise.) I don't know how long I stayed there, but when I opened my eyes, it was night and the stars were shining. Swift, black clouds were racing along, propelled by the wind. Never had stars shone so pointlessly. I got to my feet, my tears having dried, and began to walk—but it wasn't me walking, I had no conscious will, and no inner force was driving me along, it was something outside myself, or a simple, uncontrollable animal impulse—or perhaps the same unknown impulse that makes wounded or dying animals head for water. Yes, the stars were shining, but it was as if the world no longer existed for me, and the things I saw around me were mere cardboard cutouts with no reality of their own. If you have never known sadness, then you cannot know what that emptiness is like, that absence from oneself, that stillness, which is not the same as peace, but, rather, the stillness of doomed places, which, despite everything, have yet to experience death.

(Sadness—and I have had long hours to ponder its meaning—is not a feeling or an impulse or even an emotion, it's a permanent state, a way of being. Yes, the house is the same, with its verandah, its pillars, its rooms and the potent botanical world surrounding it, and while some essential part—its soul, for example—has been taken from it, its cold stone and concrete structure remains the same. I wander the empty rooms alone, feeling that the air has become unbreathable, and telling myself that it really doesn't matter if the others look at me or what they think of me. What matters is to escape, to save myself, because everything around me is like a shipwreck, and what remains of my instinctive self has taken refuge in the one thing that keeps me from going under: remembering.)

It happened soon after we met. You would think the meeting had been purely accidental, had it not occurred in such a strange place:

a small clearing by the wall of the original house, of which only a few stones remained, with the tall grass surrounding the area like an undulating fence. Someone must have had the idea of planting a vegetable patch or something, because a square area had been cleared, a few trees cut down, and the logs piled up on one side. The work had gone no further than that, however, for beyond that cleared area, the displaced dry clods of earth had already been colonized by ants. We sat down on one of the tree trunks, her in the shade and me slightly more in the sun.

"The sun's good for you," she said. "You're too pale. Why don't you undo your shirt?"

I obeyed and, feeling somewhat embarrassed, undid a couple of buttons.

"No, not like that," she said, laughing.

She tugged at my shirt and rapidly undid all the buttons.

"Like that."

I was breathless with emotion, ashamed to show my chest, which I knew to be thin and still almost childish. She studied me:

"You're not a child any more, you're almost a grown man."

She said this in a calm, flat voice. She picked up a twig from the ground and with one end of it touched my chest and flicked my shirt open wider still.

"You need sun, lots of sun. How can you bear to spend all your time in that old house? Does no one take care of your health?" And she exposed my bare torso, as if casting a precise, disapproving eye over the consequences of that neglect.

I was about to explain that I went riding and hunting and that I was naturally skinny, but I stopped myself, because it seemed foolish and inopportune. Besides, she didn't let me speak, but waved the twig at me and continued talking:

"It would be different if you lived in the city. There, boys go to clubs, swim, live more freely."

At the word "city" something lit up inside me, and for a few seconds I hoped she would tell me about Rio or São Paulo, which I knew only from magazines and photographs, and which, frankly, had never much interested me, despite my father always saying: "You need to find out about the world beyond the walls of the Chácara." But despite the unexpected charm of the subject—listening to her, finding out about her life, what more could I want?—she failed to notice my sudden interest and continued talking about me.

"Given how little exercise you take, I'm surprised you have such a good physique." (She was examining me meticulously, coolly, studying my chest—my ribs visible beneath the skin—pausing to look at a scar or at the point beneath which my heart was beating wildly.) And it was through her eyes that I discovered my own body, which, up until then, had had no reality for me—my ribs, my sparse chest hair, my rather under-developed shoulders became shoulders, hair, and ribs with all the responsibility and weight of a living being taking its place in the world we lived in. Oddly, it was as if she were looking not at me, but at a map, and what was even more frightening was the idea that she might be able to see inside me too and notice my wildly beating heart. The examination continued, while I automatically obeyed her orders:

"Come on, stand up. I want to see what you look like."

I stood up, feeling as though I were naked. I wasn't actually trembling, but was filled with an uncontrollable feeling of panic. And yet her slow voice, more even than her veiled eyes, was breathing calm into me. I gradually began to lose that feeling of nakedness, and the sun, which I hadn't even been aware of before, now slipped warmly and fondly over my whole body like a sweet oil being poured over my skin.

"Excellent," she said at last. "I'm glad to say that you're just as good as those city boys." (She again prodded me with the stick.) "There's a kind of repressed energy in that body of yours, which I like."

Whether unintentionally or not, the twig slid down to my knees.

"Strong legs," she said, "young muscles."

And suddenly, she pressed her lips together and hit me hard on the leg with the stick. A shudder ran through me, and I rubbed the place where the mark would have been, but which I could not, of course, see through my trousers. A strange, impetuous emotion began to rise up inside me; my eyes grew dark. I stood up again and buttoned my shirt. The sun was beginning to burn my skin.

"Sit down," she said in a commanding voice.

I slumped back down onto the tree trunk, my legs shaking uncontrollably. An embarrassing silence ensued: words seemed to elude us, as if unable to cope with an emotion that was as intoxicating as a strong drink. Around us the trees glittered in the hot sun, and everything gave off a kind of metallic steam. From beside the stream came the cry of a bellbird, and on a rock not far off, a lizard, asleep until then, suddenly twitched into life. These insignificant details engraved themselves on my mind. My leg was still smarting, and I again rubbed it slowly. I was actually grateful to her, because when she made me reveal my chest and stand before her, she had not done so as one might with a naughty child, and there was on her face a fascinatingly perverse expression, and in her eyes a severe, grave look. Suddenly, with that short, sharp blow, she had made me aware of my own dignity, and out of the boy she had found sitting in the clearing, she had made a man, still slightly surprised to be a man, but ready to carve out his own path. Many years afterward, when I remembered that blow, I would feel a voluptuous shiver of pleasure, and on other occasions too, I felt the same sensual tremor when, like another short, sharp blow, it would surface in my memory, as if a distant childhood echo were repeating the bitter-sweet taste of her discovery. By looking at me as if I were a man, she had perhaps gone beyond her own intentions, and actually made a man of me.

She spoke again then, some comment about how hot it was or

about life at the Chácara, but what she said seemed strangely meaningless and unreal, like events that had happened in another age or in another place.

Some time later—I remember it with delicious, bitter clarity—there was another incident, which could be seen as a complement to that first one. It had been dark for some time, and the bright moon shining down on the garden did nothing to diminish the heat. I was leaning on the verandah, as I often did, and yet, that night, for some reason, my being there seemed different and intentional, a kind of landmark moment. I saw someone sitting by the small pond in the middle of the garden. (It was an ordinary circular fountain, the stone parapet decorated with shells; the fountain itself, which had several spouts, was always out of order and had as its centerpiece a one-legged stork.) It did not take me long to realize that the person sitting by the pond was Nina. The house was its usual silent self; my father lay snoring in the hammock, and that was, perhaps, the one dissonant note in the monotonous concert of the days. For he never usually lay in the hammock after supper, and if he did so then, it was probably because of the heat, and to take advantage of the slight breeze in the garden. The other inhabitants must have been in their rooms and so there was no risk of bumping into any of them. I went slowly down the steps and, when I reached the sandy path, I set off to the pond as if I wanted to enjoy the moonlight, which was at its brightest there. It shone through the partial canopy of the leaves onto the water, forming a single, vast column of milk-white light. I walked toward it, whistling a tune. She may well already have spotted me when I came out and leaned on the verandah, but seeing me suddenly appear before her, she nevertheless pretended to be startled:

"Oh, it's you!"

"What's wrong?" I said, walking straight over to her.

"Nothing," she said. "I was deep in thought."

"Did I frighten you?"

"A little," and she patted the stone parapet. "Why don't you join me?"

I sat down beside her, so close that our knees were touching.

"It's a beautiful moon tonight," I said as an opening gambit. And in the tremulous, wind-blown moonlight, this banal remark seemed to me neither inappropriate nor untimely.

She raised her head, and I saw the soft, unadorned curve of her throat, its pure classical lines.

"Yes, it is. In the city, people don't even notice the moon." And she gave a somewhat constrained laugh.

"Do you like it?"

"I do."

She looked up at the light silvering the tops of the trees, and I was able to study the grave silhouette of her profile, which gave off an air of terrible melancholy. From that angle, her nose seemed very slightly aquiline, but far from giving her an exotic air, it only emphasized the forceful beauty of her features, which was sometimes lost in the diffuse light of the sun. Then she turned away with a sigh, reached out a hand and trailed it languidly in the water.

"And yet the water's still cold," she said. "We're barely out of winter."

(How could such factors as winter and summer exist for her? I thought of her as being as gloriously indifferent to such things as one of those plants that grows in all seasons. Listening to her, I was thinking that, for me, all that existed was before and after her presence at the Chácara.)

She moved her hand back and forth in the water, making tiny waves. In the dark water, beneath the bright moonlight, her wedding ring glinted, as did her pale, slender hand as it came and went. Like a delayed, but still resonant echo, I felt the same deep emotion as on that day she had struck my leg with a stick. Her feminine curves filled my eyes, like a drug beginning to take effect. Slowly, I was traveling through her toward a discovery of myself. She must have noticed my silence, because she looked up.

"What's wrong?" she asked, and perhaps sensing what was happening to me, her eyes glinted as brightly as her ring in the water. I shook my head and sighed. Then she took her hand out of the water, exclaiming:

"See how cold it is!"

And she placed her hand on my lips. I was more aware of the perfume her hand gave off than of the cold, and was overwhelmed by a feeling of faintness, like a wave breaking over my body. This lasted no more than a second—and then she slowly withdrew her hand.

"Your lips are dry," she said. "It's almost as if you had a fever."

She went back to dabbling in the water, but this time, kept her eyes fixed on my face. I did not move, listening to the music of the water lapping against the sides of the pond, and it was as if I had heard that same music long ago, a time forgotten by myself and by my senses, as if the sound were merely a repetition, suddenly retrieved from the past, but also like a real echo about to be undone by the wind.

"Listen, André," and her voice was softer, more caressing, "I wanted to ask you something."

"What?"

And still stirring the water, she said:

"Have you ever kissed a woman . . . on the mouth, I mean?"

I was tempted to lie—why shouldn't I?—to play the strong man, to impress her with my knowledge, inventing women and experiences lost in the darkness of that garden, outrageous acts, surrenders, separations, but the truth came pitilessly to my lips:

"Never."

Then she bent toward me—if I close my eyes, I can still feel her breasts touching my arm, the perfume of her body rising up to my face—I can still feel her, as vividly as if her skin were actually touching mine—and she again placed her hand on my lips, not as she had before, but pressing against them, almost violently pushing them open, then slowly brushing them with the tips of her fingers.

"That's what it's like . . . like that . . . cold . . . like that."

Then, before I dared say or do anything—I was, you might say, paralyzed by emotion—she got to her feet.

"It's late," she said, "I need to go inside."

She stood looking down at me, and I could feel how fast the spell was fading. She waited a moment longer, then slowly walked back toward the house. I saw her silhouetted in the moonlight. She reached the steps, went up, paused—would she look back at me?—then disappeared indoors. The desert closed brutally about me. An insect with iridescent wings was now moving about on the tranquil surface of the water. And yet my heart was pounding and would do so for as long as I stayed there, lacking even the strength to stand up. The insect skittered about the pond, creating a series of concentric circles on the water, then took off and vanished, buzzing, into the mango trees. For a while afterward, something seemed still to tremble in the air—then everything went quiet. Fascinated, I suddenly plunged my hands into the water and splashed my face, once, twice, three times. However often I did this, though, however often I ran my fingers over my lips, I could not find the origin of the emotion that had me in its grip.

Sitting beneath a tree, or some other place I thought would be free of any memories, I tirelessly relived that and other scenes. What is the point of setting them down in this notebook? None of them, however powerful, will bring back the happiness I lost. (*Written in the margin*: On the day when I wrote those lines, I imagined that everything was lost forever. I still didn't really know what was going on. It would not be long, though, before I understood the exact meaning of "forever" when spoken in a way that allows for no hope, however remote, apart from the desperate hope of saints and madmen.)

And despite everything, I only have to close my eyes to relive this or that episode—the day, on the steps, when she gave me her hand to kiss—another, when she went riding with me and got stuck in a marsh (I remember her, in improvised amateur horsewoman guise, shrieking with laughter among the saffron and tabebuia bushes)—and another when she stripped off in a wild gesture of freedom, in order to bathe in the pooled waters of a river—or more recently, when she pretended to be angry with me and spent the whole day—what torment!—refusing even to look at me—and that other time when I found her rummaging around among my papers—"What's this? A novel? A diary?"—and, finally, the time when she was feeling sorry for herself and complained about pains in her side, and so that I could better understand what she meant, pressed my hand hard against her breast, rubbing slightly, until I felt her nipple grow erect beneath my touch . . .

Is there any point in thinking and remembering? By going over and over these events, I have lost any real notion of them, mixed them up, confused everything—and for better or worse, whether under the influence of a truth or a fantasy—the name doesn't matter—I have relived the hours that were given to me, learning that there are many ways of being a man, the least dignified of which was certainly not that which makes us live silent and alone in the midst of the rubble of all the dreams we create.

(Written in the same hand in the margin, in a different colored ink: So many years have passed, and yet I still have not forgotten. I have loved other women, but that love was never more than a faint echo of this first love. We do not love different people during our lifetime, but the same image found in different individuals. I have felt despair too, until I despaired not of love, but of humanity. And now that I have this poor wretched notebook in my hands again, among other remnants of that house which no longer exists, I tell myself there is not much difference between the person I was and the person I am

now—it is just that, with time, I have learned to overcome what, as a boy, was pure despair; now, albeit silently, I still suffer, but without the darkness that so often hurled me furiously up against the four walls of my own self—a madness that was merely the adolescent version of the deep human fear of losing and being betrayed, which, alas, accompanies us throughout our whole existence.)

39.
The Colonel's Statement

When I arrived, she was already there waiting for me—which was the first time this had happened since we met. She was sitting at a small table toward the rear of the bar and was clearly very agitated: fidgeting in her chair, opening her handbag, looking at herself in her mirror, closing her handbag, sighing impatiently—in other words, showing all the signs of a person who has been kept waiting, a person accustomed to making others wait for her. I noticed at once how she had changed; she looked older, visibly thinner and paler. It was rather as if she bore a remarkable resemblance to someone else of the same height and the same features, but who wasn't her. I should also explain that I had not given much credence to the more-than-friendly terms of her letter and its implicit proposal, but I certainly did not expect her to receive me in a manner so entirely at odds with those warm words, which is to say that she greeted me with a veritable explosion of anger, jumping to her feet as soon as she saw me and crushing and twisting her handbag with unbridled fury.

"So this is how you treat me, is it? This is how you intend to humiliate me?"

Without waiting for an answer, she pushed the table away and began pacing up and down.

"I may have written you that letter, but I won't have you thinking I'm some miserable beggar woman lying in a ditch. I'll never be that. I'm still a married woman and I'm not about to let people walk all over me."

This little scene naturally attracted the attention of the waiters, who lined up at the cash register and were following everything with sardonic grins.

"So what happened? What's wrong?" I asked.

She stopped in front of me, her hands on her hips:

"What's wrong? How can you ask me that?"

"But I've only just arrived, my dear!"

(Later on, going over the scene in my mind, I realized that this was just a woman's way, or at least Nina's way, of defending herself—because, feeling humiliated at having written that letter, she now felt compelled to give me a very frosty reception.)

"Exactly," she retorted, her voice still angry. "That's exactly what I mean. Since when did anyone leave a woman like me alone in a bar like this?"

The bar was no better or worse than any other bar in a big city, although it did perhaps have the distinction of being more secluded than most, rather like a hotel bar, with its frosted glass doors and wooden booths. Moreover, I had chosen it precisely because it was in the center of town and would save her having to walk any distance. There were undoubtedly other fancier or more luxurious bars, but none more appropriate for our particular kind of encounter. Her annoyance, to my eyes entirely unwarranted, almost made me smile—ah, how little time changes people! Nina was exactly as she had always been! And so, knowing her as well as I did, I immediately found the best way to calm her down:

"My dear, you have clearly been away from Rio for far too long! This bar, despite its somewhat modest appearance, is absolutely the latest thing in Rio. Anybody who's anybody comes here, even artists and theater folk."

The words she was about to unleash evaporated on her lips, and she ran her eyes curiously around the room—indeed she almost seemed to be noticing it for the first time. She changed her tone and said:

"The latest thing? Well then, you must be right. I'm obviously terribly behind the times."

She sat down in one of the booths, shifting along so that I could sit beside her. I ordered two aperitifs from the waiter, and she continued talking:

"If you only knew what my life has become . . ."

And she detailed all her difficulties and hardships. As she spoke, I observed her closely, and how could I not believe she was telling the truth? She was badly dressed, worse even than before she had been married. It could, of course, be one of those little ruses of hers at which she had always been so adept, but I had to admit that her pallor and her air of exhaustion did not strike me as a ruse. Furthermore, there was a coarseness about her face and a disoriented look in her eyes, as if she had burned all her bridges. Together, these things completed the portrait of a woman who has lost her way and been deeply wounded. I felt sorry for her, and the old tenderness I had always felt for her, even when she lived only in my thoughts, returned to unsettle me. Once again, I could no longer distinguish truth from lies in what she was saying. For she probably was lying, without me knowing why or how, but in times gone by, on account of that same tenderness, had I not accepted from her all manner of scornful insults? Back then, I had desired her and was capable of committing the wildest extravagances for the most fleeting of her smiles. Now that I no longer desired her (or at least had learned to live by sacrificing my desires), why shouldn't I once again endure her lies and insults in silence, not for what she meant to me now, but in memory of what she once had been? Pity is not a sentiment much appreciated by women, especially women like Nina, and I knew she would never forgive me if she realized that I no longer loved her as before. There was, of course, the pleasure of seeing her again, of hearing her voice, and feeling her warm, invigorating presence—so why not just close my eyes and pretend it was love? Not the old love, but something calmer and more all-embracing.

"You know I am always at your disposal, Nina," I told her. "Nothing has changed between us."

She gazed at me tearfully:

"I knew that," she said. "And I couldn't die without writing that letter."

"I carry it next to my heart," I declared, patting my breast pocket.

She sighed and turned away. From that angle she still had something of her former appearance, and seeing her looking so like her old self, I could only conclude with a certain melancholy that I was the one who had aged, for even though I was still capable of admiring her, I had lost the secret of adoring her.

"I've come to stay," she said, shooting me a sideways glance, "for good."

This statement hung heavy in the silence. She paused for a moment to let those last two words take full effect, then added:

"I know you don't believe me, but I swear that this time I mean it."

It was the same artificial tone she had used all those years ago, the same old story. How could I tell her that it wasn't necessary any more, that I would still help her, that she could have from me anything she wanted; how could I tell her all that while keeping from her my own changed feelings? I did, though, notice a new element in her little drama, something I hadn't seen before: a haste, an almost febrile need to play that familiar role while she still could. That is what most struck me in what she said. What was going on? What was the reason for such urgency? I let her speak without interruption, and as she spoke, her impatience showed me just how much, and how profoundly, she had changed. Her haste wasn't a reason, it was a consequence—she was in a hurry because of something, and that something was slowly revealing to me a reality that could certainly not be described as vibrant, but rather as weak and feeble, an indication of a larger truth concealed behind her anxious expression. The faint lines around her eyes, her slightly downturned mouth, her no longer satiny complexion—how could I not see, how could I not sense that her beauty was reaching its end? My heart was filled with a deep, deep pity—she was just a woman losing her charms, and she knew it. She had not yet lost them completely, but she had lost at least a third, and that missing third must surely haunt her when she looked in the mirror, smoothing away her wrinkles, peering deep into her eyes, replacing that third with a fiction, an emblem of what she no longer possessed. Good or bad, it scarcely mattered—it would never be good enough to fool a man who had once been a slave to every one of those charms. How I congratulated myself on not revealing from the outset how much I pitied her! And how I praised myself for being prepared to maintain that sensitive silence come what may! She took a few appreciative sips of her aperitif, then turned to me:

"But we will go again to all those wonderful places, won't we?"

"Wherever you wish."

"To the casino . . . do you remember? And to theaters, and cinemas, and dances!"

I nodded in agreement even though, for some reason, I felt that all the things she listed were now inexplicably, perhaps impossibly remote.

"But," she continued, shyly lowering her eyes, "I don't have any proper clothes. I don't dress as I used to."

She herself had raised the subject that most intrigued me.

"What happened to all your beautiful dresses?"

She put her hand on mine, as if from the very beginning she had been seeking my approval, without daring to say so:

"I got rid of them. I burned them. They were weighing on me," and here her voice trembled. "They brought back all the wrong sort of memories."

She took her glass and squeezed it tight, as if making a wish:

"I wanted to live a new life, to have new clothes. If I carried on buried like that in the Chácara, I knew I would just fade away, rot. That's why I wrote to you."

"And I replied too. Didn't you get my letter?"

She laughed for the first time, and for a moment there was a fleeting, miraculous, glimpse of her younger self.

"Oh. he went to such lengths to try and find out who I was writing to!"

"He?"

"Yes, Valdo."

She evidently took a mischievous pleasure in having fooled her husband. At times like that I couldn't help but admire her.

"And he never found out?" I asked.

"No." And, after a moment's pause: "Never."

She gave me a look then that answered all my questions once and for all. I thought to myself: ah, so even she is losing her old discretion. Suddenly I felt a great nostalgia for the Nina I had once known, and who meant so much more to me than the one now sitting next to me. Even so, I said to her:

"You will have all the dresses you need."

"I knew you'd say that," she said. "Thank you. It's so wonderful to know that life goes on, that the good times will return!"

Perhaps there was genuine enthusiasm, or something akin to enthusiasm, in the way she spoke, and yet there was also an unmistakable sadness, as if she were talking about something lost and gone, rather than the possibility of a new life that might really bring her pleasure. This feeling cast an invincible melancholy over the rest of our lunch, and I gave a sigh of relief when we finished. She had scarcely touched the dishes she had ordered. (Another significant detail: she hesitated over what to eat, asked the waiter about everything on the menu, then ended up ordering several things and barely eating any of them.)

We stood up, ready to spend the rest of the day shopping. I could see that this was what she most wanted and, although I certainly wasn't rich, I was nevertheless quite prepared to sacrifice some of my bachelor savings for her sake. She gave me her arm, and this gesture of familiarity that would once have stirred such powerful emotions in me, now provoked only a certain agreeable nostalgia, and it occurred to me how we always get, admittedly sometimes too late, the very thing for which we have battled all our lives. She had rather lost her city ways, for she walked cautiously, as if the crowds frightened her.

"Are you feeling unwell?" I asked.

"No," she answered, adding with a wave of her arm: "It's all these people . . ."

I don't know how many shops we went to—shoe shops, dress shops, shops for knick-knacks, and even jewelry. At first, she chose fearfully, looking again and again at whatever it was, almost too timid to touch anything. But as time went on, her spirits picked up and, by the end, she was choosing things almost at random, almost frenetically, her forehead beaded with perspiration.

"There's no rush," I said to her gently, noticing how much paler she had become, "we have lots of time. We can come back for more tomorrow."

She looked at me sternly:

"Tomorrow?" She threw her head back, drawing her lips into a forced smile. "Oh, I see—you're afraid I'll run off again, is that it? Didn't I say that I was here to stay? Forever and ever?"

(Strangely, as she said those words, I had a very strong sense of just how false they were. Now that it's all over, and I'm writing this statement, with no other aim than to reestablish the truth and clear her memory of certain slurs and slanders, I ask myself if I was to blame, if perhaps I unconsciously revealed my skepticism about what she was evidently planning. Because my actions or my lack of reaction, my silence, all carried within them an implicit rejection.

Perhaps I was rejecting her on the one occasion when she was actually offering herself to me? And who knows, despite the false tone in which she spoke, perhaps she really had come back for good, as she so robustly asserted?)

In any event, just then, I felt there was no point in trying to make her understand anything at all—her ambition, her willpower, her whole person, was focused on a single objective and any attempt to divert her from her goal would have been completely futile. So I went along with her minor frenzy: she bought flowers, velvets, silks she scarcely touched, nightgowns, belts and buckles, kid gloves, a hat she thought was the height of fashion and a fur coat for the harshest of winters—all of which, I can tell you, cost me a small fortune. And so went almost all of my carefully husbanded savings. She tried things on, posed in front of mirrors, and even as she did so, throwing back her shoulders to test a décolleté neckline or asking for the waist to be taken in, I realized, to my astonishment, that she did all of this more or less automatically, barely looking at her own reflection in the mirror.

By the time we had finished, or at least when she judged that the time had come to stop for the day, it was already late and the sky was dark. The streetlamps had been lit and the cafés and pavements were overflowing. All around us was the warm, soft buzz of Rio at the beginning of summer.

"How about a nice, cold drink?" I suggested.

"Oh!" she exclaimed, putting her hand to her mouth, "I almost forgot!"

"What?"

"Something important," she explained, eyeing me warily. "You don't mind waiting for a moment, do you?"

"No, not at all."

"You can wait in a bar. I won't be long—I just need to visit someone."

"In a bar? Yes of course."

Then she stopped suddenly in the middle of the street, blocking the paths of several passersby, and stared at me. Given the intensity of her gaze one might almost have thought it was the first time she had laid eyes on me. She gave a stifled cry:

"But you don't love me! You don't love me any more!"

As with many of those whose sense of decorum or truthfulness prevents them from using such loaded expressions, we had never used the words "love" or "friendship" in relation to each other, or any other term or symbol that might approximate to such sentiments. So, on hearing her say this so unexpectedly, almost like a cry of surprise or grief, I suddenly felt ashamed, as if I had been caught committing some grave misdemeanor. And yet I had waited and waited all those years for the merest hint of such a cry, a pale reflection of something resembling not even love or friendship, but simply a little of that fleeting tenderness we sometimes bestow on our favorite objects or animals—or perhaps not even that, perhaps just one of those obliging gestures we would not even deny a poor beggar who held out his hand to us. And yet now there was that effortless, naked confession, and I was embarrassed, because I no longer knew what to make of it or what to say. Slowly, almost sadly, I replied:

"No, you're wrong, Nina."

She leaned on me, as if the ground had given way beneath her feet, and closed her eyes. I could see her trying to contain her emotion, gathering all her remaining strength.

"Nina!" I whispered.

She let go of me then and looked up, as if recovering her poise.

"Wait for me there," she said, pointing to a nearby café. "I'll be back soon."

"Is it so very urgent, this thing you have to do?"

"Yes."

I shrugged and let her go. But I followed her with my eyes for as long as I could. She was battling her way through the crowds, listing slightly to one side as if she were injured. I don't know what impulse, what notion or presentiment—or perhaps all three together—filled me at that moment; I only know that I began to run after her, pushing and colliding with various passersby, trying not to lose sight of her. She kept up the same hurried, lopsided gait. At one point, I feared I was getting too close and that she might turn around and see me, but I put the idea to one side, quite sure that the blind force driving her on would never allow her to turn around. I was so close I could almost touch her. At times, when her pace slowed I could see her face, hard and tense, as if under the influence of some implacable will. She walked a little farther, then stopped in front of a doorway bearing a doctor's nameplate. I stopped too, but I was not greatly surprised. Her sudden haste, her anxiety, could only be hiding something of the sort. But what was wrong with her? What sort of illness could have such a profound effect on her? I watched her climb the steps and disappear inside. Taking cover behind a tree, I decided to wait for her.

Less than a quarter of an hour later she reappeared, with the same resolute air as before. Resolute? Well, perhaps—there was certainly something fixed and fateful in her expression. I almost shuddered when I saw her: she was a different woman entirely. If I had passed her in the street, not knowing that she was back in Rio, I might well not have recognized her. And it wasn't merely the effect of treacherous time or age on her physical appearance: it was something deep and obsessive, whose origins I still did not know and which must always have been there, but was only now coming to the surface, like the debris that lurks at the bottom of a well and one day rises to the top when the water is disturbed. "What a strange and terrible woman," I thought. And that was the very first time such a thought had crossed my mind. Feeling troubled, I allowed her to go ahead of me, then returned to the café where we had arranged to meet. It perhaps goes without saying that I waited for more than two hours, but she never appeared. On that occasion, there could be no doubt: she had revealed herself in all her calculating complexity.

Early the next morning I went to the doctor's surgery. It was a small, cramped room, clearly not a well-known practice. If she was spending so much money on clothes and other fripperies, and if she really was ill, why not find a reputable doctor who could be of some use to her? (There, in that small, ill-furnished and tastelessly decorated room, I still could not understand why, for women who have always been sought after and flattered, illness was a source of deep shame, a terrible sin that must be concealed. I couldn't imagine who might have given her such an address—perhaps she had merely seen it in a newspaper advertisement, but clearly she had come there secretly and she felt humiliated at having to make such a visit.)

The person who appeared as soon as I rang the bell did little to reassure me:

"What do you want?" he asked.

He was short and bald, with thick-lensed glasses, from behind which peered two hard, aggressive eyes. He was wearing a white coat with two red letters intertwined on the left pocket: R.M. His small, soft, chubby hands seemed cold and devoid of any pity. I explained as best I could the reason for my visit. The more I spoke the lower I felt myself sinking in his estimation, and he stared at me sternly while I stumbled over my apologies. When I finished by saying that I wanted to know about the state of health of the woman who had been there the previous day, he held up his hand to interrupt me:

"There is such a thing as patient confidentiality."

I tried to convince him:

"Doctor, you must try to understand my situation. After all,"—and I did not hesitate to lie—"I am her husband."

He stared at me, perhaps trying to work out how to expose my flagrant lie.

"Ah, so you're the husband," he said simply, realizing that there was nothing now he could accuse me of. "In that case, what would you like to know?"

"Whether . . ." My voice trembled and I could go no further. I felt as though I was violating a secret, which, when all was said and done, did not belong to me.

It was this hesitation, however, that saved me: he could see from my evident emotion that if I wasn't the husband, I was at least someone very close to her.

"Yes, her condition is untreatable," he said (and he said this almost emphatically, almost proudly, as if he were praising a particularly fine painting). Then, with a despondent shrug, he added:

"It's too late, alas."

I hung my head, and a whirl of thoughts, memories and echoes raged within me: those long-ago evenings, the room where I used to play cards with her father and where I would so often torture him by not telling him what he was so desperate to hear, and all because of the passion which, day by day, was growing inside me. Then her, her face then, and now. But this lasted no more than a moment. The little bald man was still standing there, staring at me:

"Would you like a glass of water?" he asked.

"No, thank you."

And in a final effort, I asked:

"Did you tell her everything?"

"There was no need. She already knew."

"But . . . it's so sudden," I said, lacking the courage to ask the question directly.

He looked at me in surprise:

"Sudden? She's been coming here for nearly two weeks."

Two weeks! She had been in Rio for nearly two weeks and had only gotten in touch with me yesterday. What had she been doing all that time? Who had she been with? Ah, how vain are our efforts to penetrate the mysteries that surround certain people's lives! We descend ever deeper into the bottomless pit of our discoveries. I went slowly down the stairs, leaning on the bannister. The street seemed extra bright, the people strange. What a bizarre and absurd thing life was. With a heavy heart I began walking aimlessly. My steps took me to the hotel where she said she was staying. Why shouldn't I go up? There could be no more insults or reprisals. I asked the doorman. He said:

"*Madame*? She left last night." (So just a few hours after she had been with me.) "And goodness, what a lot of luggage she had, sir!"

I thanked him and left. That's how it was, and that's how it would always be. What was the point of judging her? I accepted her as she was, for that is how I had loved her. And I sensed, painfully, that the previous evening was perhaps the last time I would ever see her. And indeed it was better like that, since I could then return her to the pedestal from which she should never have stepped down.

40.
Ana's Fourth Confession

Here I am again. In this room where no noise enters, I am writing, as usual without knowing to whom, and what initially caused me such pain, now brings me a certain tranquility. I can say things better when I don't know who I am talking to; there are no impediments, no obstacles, and what I remember emerges unadorned and undisguised.

It's windy, and from here I can see the trees in the garden being ceaselessly buffeted about; and yet the weather is still dry and there are constant clouds of dust along the roads in the distance. So, nothing new, as if it were the repetition of a scene watched many times before. Old fragments of myself come together in a brief harmony, one with which I will quickly find fault. I, Ana Meneses, am a mere repetition of myself. There is nothing original about my jealousy—for how else can I describe the feeling that still wounds me—and nothing original about my loathing of all the others. I am monotonously like anyone else who may have suffered the same misfortunes. And so I get angry neither with the wind nor with the clouds of dust, because their indifference completes my landscape, they are part of me and of the despondency that shapes me. I will go on then, and I sense that other future moments, possibly identical, will come and superimpose themselves on this precise moment in which I am alive, holding this pen and putting my ideas in order so as to set them down on paper, and in which the same Ana, only different, will repeat these same words, which though mysterious to others, for me are filled with meaning. Let us be clear, and I will be brief now so as not to annoy any future reader: what I want to express is the terrible indifference of being alive, which, in a flash of lucidity, someone very sensibly described as a task for mediocrities.

I confess that I felt this most keenly on the day "she" left. It was as if I had been suddenly relegated to silence and abandon, to exile from any manifestation of life. They should not have done that to me, because the feeling that nourished me, whether negative or not, was as strong, as dominant, as friendship or any other enthusiasm of the heart. It was the one thing that kept me alive. But have I not already described all this in painful detail, have I not, in different circumstances, woven and rewoven my inner web? What's left are the facts, and that is what I want I set down here, in a mechanical attempt to travel, yet again, the road that has just come to an end.

I was entirely unprepared, no one had said anything about her departure, and it caught me completely unawares. As has become more frequent of late, Demétrio had complained that morning of feeling unwell, saying he had slept badly and kept waking up in the night with a headache or unable to breathe; he then asked me to make him an herbal tea that was supposed to be good for the kidneys.

"How strong do you want it?" I asked.

"Not too strong," he said, "and with as little sugar as possible."

I took the bunch of herbs and was about to leave the room, thinking how everything in that family was a matter of habit—the tisane was the same one his late mother used to drink, and which he would go on drinking, even though it had been shown to be completely ineffectual—when I heard voices in the hallway outside the drawing room. This was so unusual that I turned and looked at my husband.

"What's going on?" I asked.

He was reading a book or pretending to, and, looking distractedly up at me, said:

"Didn't you know? Nina's leaving today."

"Leaving?" And that word emerged from my lips almost like a scream.

Demétrio closed his book and stared at me as if astonished by my reaction. Ah, how well I knew that calm air, that closed, expressionless face, that way of seeming perpetually amazed by other people's excesses or afflictions, and how well I knew, too, that this was merely proof of how detached he was from his own innermost self, and how sick I was of him, knowing, as I did, that his air of scandalized surprise was entirely calculated and hypocritical. Crushing the herbs in my hand, I shot him one last glance and left the room. I was trembling, my heart racing. She was leaving, she was leaving again. But why? To what end? Why was she abandoning the house she had fought so hard to reconquer? However closely I scrutinized recent events, I could see no hint of a drama, no hidden plot (those that existed were there for all to see!) that might provoke such a desperate gesture, because I was in no doubt that this *was* a desperate gesture. And while I was pondering these insoluble problems, I was surprised, too, that she had so easily escaped my vigilance. Was she perhaps simply tired and in need of a holiday, or was she leaving for good? I would have to investigate and piece together the whole plot in order to assess the significance of such an unusual decision.

I went into the kitchen to prepare the tisane. A few of the servants were standing around the big iron stove and talking about something in low voices. As soon as I entered, they fell silent. One of them began scooping up the ashes from the grate. I went over to the sink and untied the bundle of herbs.

"Anything wrong?" I asked as casually as I could.

The cook appeared from the other side of the room:

"Ah, Dona Ana, we were wondering . . . People are saying Dona Nina's so sick that . . . Is it true?"

I continued to wash the herbs in the sink. Sick? So that was it. But what illness was it, how had it appeared? Since the cook was waiting to hear my opinion, I asked her to fetch me a pot and then, like someone simply picking up the thread of a conversation, I said:

"No, it's nothing serious."

"But, Dona Ana!"

I continued putting the washed herbs into the pot.

"Why? What are people saying?" I asked.

"That's not what they say at all, Senhora. They say she's so sick she's going to see a doctor in the city."

Bent over my task, I was trying hard not to appear surprised. I wanted them to think I was absorbed in my work, and the cook, taken in by this charade, went over to help the other maid cleaning the oven. After a pause, she sighed and, clearly unconvinced by what I had told her, said:

"Poor Dona Nina."

"She'll be fine," I said.

She continued to work very slowly, as though thinking how full the world is of deceptions and frailties, traps and lies. Then, after a few moments, still holding the shovel she was using to scoop up the ashes, she said:

"The other day, she burned her dresses. That's not a good sign."

"Burned her dresses?" I put down the pot and turned to her, making no attempt now to conceal my surprise.

"Yes, didn't you see? Out there in the backyard, behind the house. There was so much smoke, we could hardly breathe in here. Burned the whole lot, she did," she concluded with another sigh.

I continued my preparations, but my thoughts were far away. How strange. Why had she burned her dresses, just when she was thinking of leaving? The idea was growing in my mind that certain things had been deliberately kept from me.

"And when is she leaving?" I asked, still feigning indifference.

The cook looked at me in amazement:

"Didn't you know, Dona Ana? She's leaving today. The buggy's waiting for her down below."

I could contain myself no longer then, and handing her the pot and the herbs, I said:

"Put that on to boil, will you? I'm going down there and will be back shortly."

I did not go down to where the buggy was waiting; instead, I hid behind one of the pillars on the verandah; the wind helped me by setting the thin stems of the climbing jasmine flailing about, and thus allowing me to see everything without being seen. There was the buggy; and the driver, José, appeared to be asleep, despite the wind that set the bells around the mules' necks clanking. Carried off on the wind, that melancholy sound was like a long, distant tolling of bells, announcing a funeral. It may just have been my imagination, but I felt my heart contract; I looked up at the sky, and saw not so much as a sliver of blue; the sky was solid gray, growing darker, almost black on the horizon. A few vultures were circling above, gliding on the wind. I told myself this was simply a sign that rain was imminent, but my heart felt like lead. Voices approached, and I hid behind the pillar, so close to the jasmine that a rebellious stem brushed against my face. Nina soon appeared; when she paused to speak to Valdo, I was surprised to see that he was evidently not intending to go with her, given that he was still wearing his pajama top. I was able, though, to get a good look at her. Was she ill? Possibly, but there was no indication that she had anything very serious wrong with her. She did look different, but only superficially: she had no makeup on and her hair was drawn back in a bun. She was certainly not the beautiful, triumphant Nina I had always known, and despite this, I again experienced the feeling of rancor, antipathy, and jealousy that always swept over me in her presence. I could not and would not see her cast down and vanquished, because I needed her strength, her beauty, her omnipotence in order to live. Even her lack of vanity, her modest appearance seemed to me a betrayal. What lengths would she not go to in order to gain the pity of others?

The scene lasted no more than a few seconds: Valdo clasped her to him, and she, cold and indifferent, allowed him to embrace her, then offered him her cheek for a lukewarm, conventional kiss, as I had always imagined she would on such occasions. Then she went down the steps alone. From the top of the steps, he waved a friendly goodbye. She got into the buggy, holding just one piece of luggage. She would not be away long then. I noticed she was wearing an exceedingly modest black dress, far inferior to the many others she had given to Betty as presents. Either because of the wind, or in order to hide from the townspeople, she was wearing a shawl over her head, which made her look even paler. I could not help but smile. It was all so brilliantly thought out! This was yet another of her extraordinary performances, and the worst thing was that the victims were always the same. I assumed she would maintain that same erect posture beside the driver, but before she reached the pond, almost in the middle of the garden, she turned, cast a long look back at the house and gave a final wave to Valdo. He remained standing, a few feet away from my hiding place, and watched the buggy until it had disappeared through the main gates of the Chácara. The bells, though, continued to ring out sadly for some time, carried back on the wind.

Two weeks later, when she returned, the wind was not as strong, but it was still blowing intermittently, as it does in dry regions that begin to grow still drier with the approach of summer. There had not been a drop of rain, but huge, slow, black clouds were moving southward across the sky. The dark strip on the far horizon had turned bronze, which made one think that the hot weather would soon be here. Swallows, late arrivals, were slicing cleanly through the air. As I went down into the garden, to pick up some fallen mangos, I saw the buggy pull up outside the gates—not our buggy, which was driven by José, but the one that was for hire in Vila Velha. It came through the gates, up the main avenue, around the pond, and stopped by the steps to the verandah. From where I was standing, I immediately recognized Nina, even though she was hiding her face not beneath a shawl, as she had when she left, but beneath one of those traveling hoods, which I knew, from the ladies' magazines, were highly fashionable. I was about to go and meet her, but once I was confident of not being seen beneath the canopy formed by the mango trees, I decided to stay where I was. I was surprised to see her back so soon—just over two weeks!—and again I could not suppress a smile, thinking that the trip, which had raised speculation about some really serious health problems, was merely a front for her frivolous desire to buy some new clothes. I noticed, too, as the buggy passed in front of me, that it was full of suitcases and trunks. That was obviously why she had burned her old dresses. Valdo and the Meneses could foot those very large bills—what did she care if they were ruined, if the warning letters from the bank kept piling up on Demétrio's desk, or indeed if all that luxury was inappropriate given the very quiet, dull life we led at the Chácara. What did she want, what was she after? Who was she trying to impress, which ghost or phantom wandering the rooms of that house was she hoping to seduce? One or, at most, two minutes later, Valdo appeared at the top of the steps. I drew farther back, not wanting to miss a single thing. I could not deny that his face brightened, that he looked happy, almost relieved. Even after all those years, he still loved that woman. (He—I realized then—was possibly the best and most likeable of the Meneses, and his silent nature was a sign not of cold egotism, but of a certain distinction of character. His one sin had been the result of his weakness, when he met and fell in love with that woman. Seeing him and the pleasure with which he welcomed her back, it was impossible not to consider him responsible for the decline of the house, which only by a miracle remained standing and, as it cast its shadow over him, accompanying him to where the buggy had stopped, appeared to be condemning him.) The meeting was as brief and informal as the departure: he kissed her forehead uneffusively—the Meneses men were only capable of loving or being affectionate in a paternal way—then they exchanged a few words, doubtless equally banal. I expected him to notice the suitcases and packages, but he only did so in passing, as if it were a pure formality, then, his arm about her waist, they went up into the drawing room. How many defeats and retreats must that painful, humiliating apprenticeship in love have cost him?

André, who had come out shortly after his father, took charge of the luggage. I then abandoned my hiding place and went over to the buggy to talk to the driver, who was an Italian from the town.

"Goodness," I said as innocently as possible, "did she bring all that?"

"There's more at the station," he said. "I've got to make a second trip."

He climbed back into the driver's seat, cracked his whip, and set off for the gates. Alone, André and I looked at each other, or, rather, I noticed him looking at me, as if he were expecting me to say something. Instead, I stared down at the piles of boxes and suitcases, all of which bore the labels of fashionable shops in Rio. I could not help asking myself that same question: where would Valdo find the money to pay for all that? Without turning to look at my nephew, I went up the steps and into the house, but I could feel his eyes on me all the time, examining me and the baggage, and thinking exactly what I was thinking.

Supper that evening was a slightly more solemn affair than usual. Nina lived up to expectations and appeared wearing a dark green, low-necked gown. It was easy to see that she was trying to revive her first years of living at the Chácara, when she would wear outfits that provoked a mixture of shock and admiration. Ah, but she could no longer shamelessly show off her beautiful shoulder blades; her bones were now too prominent, and that alone was enough for me to see how much she had changed. What's more, for someone like myself accustomed to submitting her to long examinations, it was easy enough to see she had been crying, for her eyes were red and puffy. For that reason, her pale complexion seemed even paler, and there were lines at the corners of her once seductive mouth, lines that had not been there before. What a strange thing time is—there was a haste, a hunger to destroy, which seemed to be the secret sign of Providence. I remembered Father Justino's words: "What do you know of the misfortunes God holds in store for her?" I looked at her again, hard, intently, and was filled with an unexpected moment of enlightenment: for the first time, I believed in that illness. God was revealing himself, and I had been given the grace that would once again make me believe in his existence. And yet were those apparent signs enough to guarantee my belief? No, there was something else, and that was possibly what underpinned my certainty. She had entered the room with a carefully rehearsed flourish, she had clearly prepared herself, and was trying, by sheer force of will, to recover her old aplomb. And she had succeeded, the flame was again burning inside her, but it was, alas, only a borrowed flame. She might deceive the others, but not me, because I knew every little thing about her, as if she were my personal territory, because while she might deceive me about other things, I knew all there was to know about her extraordinary capacity for lying and pretense. And that was why I felt so certain about her illness: her need to lie, to dissemble. So, it was true, then, she was gravely ill. I watched her sit down, watched as she achieved an entirely artificial and rather strange phenomenon: purely by dint of wanting to be beautiful, she did almost succeed in glowing just as she used to. But hers was now an unsteady light, and there was no spontaneity or confidence in her movements. Demétrio greeted her unemotionally:

"How is your health?"

It was years since he had asked anyone such a personal question. He had to take into consideration the fact that she was ill, and was making an effort to behave politely. Nina merely shrugged:

"The doctor says there's nothing wrong with me," and after a moment's pause, as if weighing the importance of what she was about to say: "I just need to rest."

His reply came quickly:

"Well, you'll get plenty of that here at the Chácara."

Nina, who was filling her glass with wine, put the jug down on the table, perhaps so that no one would notice that her hands were shaking.

"But I need distractions too. The doctor said . . ."

Demétrio slowly raised his eyes to look at her—ah, how cold those Meneses men could be when they wanted!—or, rather, not at her, but rather at her décolletage and her jewelry. She bravely held his gaze, with its barely concealed censoriousness:

"I need to go out, enjoy myself."

Somewhat embarrassed, Valdo came to her aid:

"Yes, Nina needs to have fun, and why not? She's young, it's only right that we . . ."

". . . who are old," said Demétrio, completing his sentence and smiling.

Valdo bowed his head over his rapidly cooling soup. Demétrio, without a hint of irony in his voice, went on:

"But there are young people here. André, for example."

I pressed my napkin to my mouth, almost choking. This time, he had gone too far. Before me, as if touched with a magic wand, the colors of the crystal wine glasses glittered brightly. Demétrio could not possibly be so ingenuous as to mention such a painful subject unintentionally. I put down my napkin and observed him discreetly. He was happily drinking his soup as if he had said nothing of any significance. He only looked up—eyes glinting—when he heard Nina say:

"Yes, I could go out and about with André." (She said this with extraordinary calm, as if this were a game she knew and liked and accepted so easily that, for a moment, taken aback, I thought perhaps I was the victim of an illusion; I must be wrong, there was no malice behind those words, and everything I thought I knew was a mere trick of my imagination. "He would be good company."

"Do you like hunting?" Demétrio went on. "I understand André is an excellent hunter."

"I've never tried," she said, "but I could always practice. Is it easy, André?" And she turned to her son, who was sitting, his spoon poised in midair.

(I could not recall her having behaved like this before, even though she had spoken these words as though they were utterly banal and unexceptional. Yet for those who knew her, there was in that very indifference a veiled note of defiance.)

André managed a quavering response:

"Yes, it's easy."

He was clearly not up to the game they were playing. A silence fell, during which all you could hear was the clink of crockery. Even supper was different that night. Perhaps on Valdo's orders—wishing to celebrate Nina's return—or perhaps on her orders, who knows, they had disinterred from the old chest the porcelain dinner service sent from Europe and on which the M of Meneses appeared surrounded by gilded garlands of leaves; the linen tablecloth, edged with lace, reached down to the floor; and the dishes kept coming, roasts and salads, almost regardless of order, but with an exuberance reminiscent of brighter, more prosperous days. André was not drinking, and Demétrio barely touched his wine, whereas Valdo and Nina indulged themselves freely. All these things, and the evident disparity between this behavior and our usual everyday habits, created a feeling of constraint that was growing by the minute. It was in this climate, at the very point when the air began to become unbreathable, that Valdo spoke, doubtless hoping to lighten the atmosphere, but never had he appeared to be more on Nina's side, never keener to cover up or at least pass over her faults and weaknesses, and having witnessed his constant coolness toward her, his air of seething, silent disapproval, in which I had learned to see not repugnance, but the strength of feeling that bound him to her, I was left wondering if there had perhaps been a mitigation, a pause, or even a complete stagnation of his love. In his defense, he was not so much interested in her as a person, as in his need to oppose and defeat Demétrio. It was not, on his part, a protective act, but one of resistance. Or perhaps her illness had changed his way of being. As I was thinking all this, I was promising myself not to miss a single detail of what was happening around the table. Valdo was speaking, and it was clear that he was struggling to make his voice sound as natural as possible. The subject was still hunting and, extraordinarily enough, night hunting. The talk turned to fishing, and he said that the local streams and rivers were full of fish, especially wolf fish, which were small, but very tasty. When it grew dark, they would gather near the banks to sleep, and that was the best time to catch them, because, oblivious to any light, they would not move away when the fisherman approached. I pick out this particular topic as an indication of how trivial the conversation was, but it was precisely the triviality that heightened tensions. He developed his theme, and we, who never talked at supper, were barely listening to what he was saying, trying to work out why he was behaving in this extraordinary manner. As expected, he soon tired of talking, and the supper ended in silence, as if pushed to its usual limits by a force far stronger than us. We left the table and went out onto the verandah to wait for coffee to be served. Convinced that it was all over, I went and leaned on the balustrade: a wind was still blowing, but more gently, in sudden gusts that ruffled the trees, then vanished into the distance, like waves breaking on the shore. It was then that Demétrio, provoked by who knows what malevolent thought (I believe he wanted to add to the artificial tone of the evening), went back into the drawing room and opened the lid of the piano that had belonged to his mother, who had been a great pianist in her youth. He ran his fingers idly over the keys. I heard the sound from where I was, leaning on the balustrade, and I turned around, amazed. What a strange effect it had, that music echoing gravely through the stern Meneses household. After years of disuse, the piano was badly out of tune and some of the notes very flat—but what did that matter? The fingers running over them managed to draw from them a song that filled the whole house. Nina, who had lain down in the hammock, as she always did after meals, got up and, drawn by the music, went over to the piano.

"Ah," she said, and I heard her voice distinctly, "I'd completely forgotten that you played the piano. It's been years since I heard you play!"

And this time, there was no pretense or irony in her voice, on the contrary, she spoke warmly and with a visible desire to move closer. Demétrio did not answer, but when I, too, went over to the door, and a few of the servants appeared at the end of the hallway, I caught a malicious glint in his eye.

"Would you like me to play 'Waves of the Danube'?" he asked. "It was my mother's favorite waltz."

"That would be lovely," said Nina.

Seduced by the affectionate tone of the question, she leaned against the piano, almost bending over the keys. She was clearly very moved, her breast rising and falling. From the other side of the room, sitting on the white-upholstered sofa, André, equally surprised, was observing the scene. And Valdo, who seemed aglow with happiness that night, also came in and sat down beside his son. From outside, cut off from that harmonious picture, I thought to myself that they looked for all the world like a happy family. Pure illusion, because all of them were being eaten away inside by a destructive element. Yes, let them enjoy the pleasure of being together, while I stood there, as if watching a performance from which I was excluded. Again, jealousy filled my heart, and, as I had so many times in my life, I gazed enviously at my sister-in-law—there she was, victorious, as she always would be. She had even managed to make the illness gnawing away at her a reason to triumph and dominate. If only God would come to my aid and punish her as she deserved to be punished. If only he would show how unfair and sinful her victory was. If only he would save me and destroy her. Behind the window I was murmuring the Our Father, pouring every ounce of willpower into that desire for justice. It was then that I saw her go over to André and say:

"Have you really never danced in your entire life? That's shameful! Would you like to try?"

He did not, and made some excuse I could not hear. But Nina, in an ebullient mood and encouraged by the music and by her apparent success—she had finally made the Meneses unbend a little—she insisted:

"Come on, it's easy. You just have to count one, two, three . . . do you see?"

And he did then begin to follow her steps, although he obviously felt deeply embarrassed. He stumbled, tried to stop, but his mother hung on to him. "What a clumsy clot!" she would exclaim whenever he showed himself to be more than usually inept. From my position out on the verandah, I could almost have sworn that the old days of the Chácara had returned, and I found it incomprehensible, feeling that, for some reason or other, they were all betraying me. The delighted servants were now crowded in the doorway, smiling at this remarkable sight. Then, unexpectedly, the music stopped—Demétrio slammed down the lid of the piano, and that violent sound echoed around the room. Nina abandoned her partner, and Demétrio strode off, taking long, determined steps. Left alone between André and her husband, she looked first at one, then at the other, and her eyes filled with tears. Demétrio had just been playing a game. He evidently believed neither in Nina's illness, nor in her reasons for coming back to the Chácara, nor in anything else she said. That, at least, is what we all felt. Unable to withstand the pressure of all those eyes on her,

Nina put her hands to her face and burst into tears; almost doubled-over with sobbing, she had to lean on the piano. Valdo rushed to her side, while André slumped down on the sofa. And it was as though the sole purpose of that whole scenario, so cruelly constructed, had been to heighten the contrast with what was happening now. Valdo tried to embrace Nina, but she pushed him away and stalked out of the room. Alone on the verandah, I saw that the wind was relenting, and one hesitant star had appeared. I said to myself, I wonder how much Demétrio knows about the cellar and its secrets? And feeling utterly serene, I leaned out into the vastness of the night and murmured: "Thank you, God."

41.
André's Diary (viii)

2nd – We were finally alone in the drawing room. I had been devouring her with my eyes throughout supper, so much so that, at one point, I could feel the others staring at me. I blushed and looked down at my untouched plate. Gradually, feeling the tension around me easing (although not the general tension in the room), I resumed my staring, unable to believe what my eyes were seeing. It was her, she had come back, and had said nothing to me, either about her departure or her return. I was in my room, trying in vain to read a book, when I heard the sound of a car crunching up the sandy path. I ran to the window, convinced it was her, that she had come back. It *was* her, and out of sheer joy, my hands gripped the wooden window frame and sweat beaded my brow. The summer was just beginning, although there were still occasional high winds, a warm, gusty wind, laden with the acidic smell of ripening fruit. The weight of all those preceding days dissolved in my heart, and in the agitation that followed directly on from my earlier state of utter dejection, I kept pacing up and down and asking myself how I could possibly have imagined she had left for good, had abandoned me, and so I moved seamlessly from believing myself to be the most wretched of creatures to being the most fortunate and happiest of mortals. What did

I care about what had happened, her possible treachery, her reasons for leaving? What did I care about anything except her presence? She was back, I kept repeating, and that, at the time, was enough. I went over to the window again, looked down at the car parked below, then whirled around my room, whistling. In the distance, the horizon was turning an intense, obsessive red, and the first cicadas were singing. From outside, from the plum trees laden with clutches of yellow fruit, came a sour, exciting smell. I opened the door then and ran out onto the verandah, ready to help her with her luggage—an excellent excuse—if help was still needed. It was, because I had never seen anyone arrive at the Chácara with so much baggage. And I confess that, while I worked, my hands trembled and my vision blurred just to feel her standing not far off, possibly casting furtive glances at me. I looked up, studying the world about me, and felt that the simple fact of her being there again restored the Chácara to its old familiar self. My father came to meet her too and planted a kiss on her forehead, but what did I care if they kissed? She had come back, she was here. Then, arm in arm, they went up the steps. As I sorted out the various parcels and packages, I never once lost sight of her: I saw her go rather unsteadily up the steps, noticed her slender ankles, her slim body, more like a girl's than a grown woman's. When she reached a certain point on the steps, she called to me: "André, can you bring me that parcel over there . . ." I ran to take it to her, and she bent down and whispered in my ear: "Later on . . . I really need to talk to you." That was the only indication that she had noticed my existence, but it was all so quick that I didn't have time to respond. Even so, who could doubt that she had deliberately forgotten that parcel, and that her doing so had instantly rekindled our former intimacy? I gave a long sigh of relief.

Some hours later, we were sitting opposite each other at the same table. She was wearing a beautiful dark-green dress, with a neckline that, to many, would have seemed far too low, but which, to me, seemed endowed with a special charm. I admired her elegance and imagined her among the other ladies of the town; they would no doubt all be fatter than her and definitely vulgar. They would never be able to carry off such a décolletage, or feel so at ease when being examined by those impertinent eyes. And yet, when I scrutinized her further, I noticed that something had changed, not her satin skin, which I knew so well, nor its slightly duller tone, as if under the effects of an early dusk, but I examined her in vain, because I could not pinpoint what it was about her that was different. She was simply not the same. I felt a pity whose origins I myself could not explain, a pity mingled with a sense of danger, as if she had changed or suffered, not for any reason peculiar to her, but because of some factor that affected us both equally. It's true that, at least for that moment, she was filled with animation, with a vibrant desire to spread her wings and enjoy life, which could be mistaken for a natural impulse, but, on closer examination, I could not help but see how much effort and artificiality lay behind this. Yes, there was in her a vacuum, an emptiness that she was trying desperately to conceal. And I think that never again will I find myself before a creature who gave off such a powerful sense of having been betrayed or, rather, shaken to the very core by the violence of a blow that had come completely out of the blue. Nina was struggling to regain a lost equilibrium and, if she failed, it would be because such failures are almost always definitive. While I sipped my soup, I imagined that, if I could only devote myself to her, I could take this analysis still further, but the atmosphere at the supper table remained tense, and I noticed, unsurprised, that everything had been prepared with more than usual care. There was a sense of generous abundance, and among the glasses and the cutlery, tureens of dark, rich, steaming gravy, a speciality of old Anastácia's, were passed around; then a lovingly prepared loin of pork served on a bed of lettuce; and blood sausages too, my Uncle Demétrio's personal favorite. I observed all this and was momentarily dazzled by the light glittering on the crystal glasses. It was clear that my father was happy and, contrary to the Meneses' usual commonsensical approach to things, wanted to celebrate the return of someone dear to him. As for me, I confess that I was barely listening to what was being said around the table, and was counting the minutes until I could finally get up and leave. What mattered, I thought, was escaping from there. This meant somehow making time move faster, bringing me closer to the moment when I could, at last, see her alone. The conversation was interspersed with long pauses, and the trivial words spoken barely covered what was hidden beneath the surface. At one point, though, the talk turned to leisure, and she said she intended to devote herself to sports, and hoped to be able to go out with me walking and hunting. Only I could gauge how sad this comment was—after all, she had always gone on walks and gone hunting with me. So why announce this now as something new? But then, she wasn't saying it for my benefit, but for the benefit of the others. That is why I rather unenthusiastically agreed, weighing the effect those words had on the atmosphere. Had they noticed? Had they found something out? (I mean about our relationship, which hovered like a dark, invisible circle over the brightly lit table.) Yes, they probably had, and I recalled catching whispered remarks among the servants, something Ana had said, certain unequivocal silences—but what did that matter? What did I care if the whole world went up in flames, and the scandal smeared the faces of all those around me with soot? When she and I were alone, I would say: "Do you remember what you said to me? That I should embrace my sin and have the courage to take full responsibility for it? Well, that's what I am proposing now: let us escape, let us leave the Chácara, and confront the world with our love. What do the others matter compared with the love that unites us?" And those words came into my mind with such force that they almost burst from my lips. I found it very hard to keep them in, and it was with enormous relief that I saw that supper had reached an end.

I don't know why, but the atmosphere in the room was electric. Outside, the wind was blowing and bringing with it into the house the smell of ripe peaches. My uncle went over to the piano and started playing some old familiar tunes. Still under the influence of this fictitious excitement, Nina told me off because I didn't know how to dance, insisting that I try, and I obeyed, of course, but it gave me no joy at all. There was a whiff of something putrid in the air and, despite the wind gusting in through the window, I felt as if I were suffocating. It was not long before my uncle slammed the piano shut, prompting Nina to burst into tears, as if that had been a blow inflicted on her personally. She finally left the room leaning on the arm of my father, who did not dare say a word about what had happened. I was left alone, listening to the clock ticking in the background. With all the lights blazing, the crystal glasses still glittered on the table, and there was that lingering acidic smell of ripening fruit; the atmosphere now was that of a party abruptly broken off. I went over to the table and poured myself a glass of wine, which I drank down in one: the liquid burned my throat. I was again aware of the sound of the wind blowing, and it seemed to carry on it the very essence of the rotting garden outside. I poured myself another glass of wine and, for the first time in my life, considered getting drunk. I felt too afraid, though, because some stubborn instinct was urging me to stay where I was. Had she herself not said that she needed to talk to me? I believed her, and it was those words that kept me there, intently waiting. I put down the glass and the bottle and went to lie on the sofa. The tick-tock of the clock sounded closer, perforating the dense air in the room. Through my half-closed eyes, the Chácara seemed to glow, and anyone seeing the house from a distance would have thought the fires of some forbidden party were still burning. It was then that Aunt Ana, who had been standing out on the verandah until then, came inside: wearing her usual drab clothes, she stood for a moment before the cluttered table, then fixed her paralyzing gaze on me, and the hideous things those eyes were saying could not have been clearer. This, however, lasted barely any time at all, and then she, too, disappeared. A few more minutes slipped by—the wind, the ticking clock—and suddenly Nina was there before me. She crouched down, and I saw not just the rise and fall of her breasts beneath her décolletage, but also her moist, red eyes, those of someone who has been crying.

"André," she said.

She looked so upset, her breath was so warm, that I feared she might not have the strength to get to her feet again. I sat up on the sofa and made her sit beside me. She did so with a sigh, as if this involved an enormous sacrifice.

"Whatever's wrong?"

Nina began to cry again and rested her head on my shoulder. My shirt became wet with her tears, and I have to say that I had never before seen her in such a state, so immersed in her pain. All the barriers erected over supper fell, and now, defenseless, she was revealing her terrified inner self.

"Nina," I said, and I took a cruel pleasure in calling her by her name, as if this placed us on the same level, from which there was no possible escape. "Nina," I said again.

She did not respond, but looked up at me and wiped away her tears. She was so close that I could see the traces of tears left on her cheeks. Her lips, which were only inches away, were half-open as she struggled to catch her breath. On a wild impulse, I bent nearer and, for some time, we kissed each other with extraordinary violence. Breathless, she tried to break away, but I held her close, my hand around her waist, forcing her to allow our lips to meet again, and in my mouth, open and eager to taste her, I felt the tang of salt and fever. Finally, with a moan, she managed to free herself, but we stayed there, our heads pressed together, our eyes closed, oblivious to everything apart from the powerful force uniting us. I was stroking her as one would a child, and my hand grew wet with the warm sweat drenching her body. Yet that was not my most important discovery: as I ran my hand down her back, I felt how much thinner she had become. What I had failed to see initially or only glimpsed during supper, became horribly, inexorably clear to my touch.

"You're ill, Nina!" and my voice trembled despite myself.

Slowly, as if those words had awoken ghosts that should have remained dormant, she placed one hand on my lips:

"Don't talk."

"But I knew nothing about it. Why didn't you tell me, why did you never say anything?"

"I couldn't. I didn't have the courage."

I interrupted her, holding her still closer so that if she noticed the irritation in my voice, she would not attempt to flee.

"The torment you put me through. I almost died, thinking you had left forever. How could you? How did you have the courage for that?"

Again her hand brushed my lips:

"Don't talk like that. I'm back now." And in a softer voice, in which was concentrated every ounce of solemnity and certainty she possessed, she added: "Forever."

I found her tone odd, though, because it sounded more than anything like an invocation. They were not mere words, but a confluence, a coming together of every fiber of her will, as if in response to some kind of incantation. Where and when and to whom had she spoken those same deep, decisive words, which were not just a promise, but a manifestation of her entire being, a particular way of feeling and understanding the world? "Forever." And those words resonated so deeply inside me that, relieved, I said:

"Why don't we run away together? Why don't we leave this place? You spoke of sin once, well, what kind of sin would be worthy of the name if it was not disapproved of by the whole world?"

She gave a sigh:

"André, don't talk like that. What I said then . . ."

". . . no longer counts?"

"No, it still counts," she said, "but what do I know about love or sin?"

"What does it matter? What does anything matter?"

"Ah," and again her voice sounded strange to me. "Perhaps I didn't love you. Perhaps it isn't love . . ."

I drew her close to me again, before she could complete that blasphemous sentence.

"If it wasn't love, then it was sin or pure mischief. But that is what I want and nothing else. Let the Devil do what he likes with me, as long as I can be with you. Let's run away, Nina, let's flee this place. You'll get better, you'll see . . ."

She protested, and for the first time that night, she spoke almost vehemently:

"But I'm not ill, there's nothing wrong with me. I'm just bored. I have no appetite. We can go wherever you want, somewhere far from here. We'll go to parties, on long trips. God willing, André, we will lead a completely different life from now on. I've brought plenty of clothes with me and everything I might need for a long journey."

As she talked, I was thinking to myself that it was impossible not to believe what she was saying. Once, seeing how changeable her moods were, I would have wondered if what we felt really was love, until I stopped asking that question, because, regardless of whether it was love or not, her presence was quite simply essential to me. Now she was talking about sin, and what did I care if it was or wasn't sin, as long as I was by her side? Hadn't she been the one who taught me the importance, above all else, of submitting to and embracing sin? The days were long gone when remorse or something like it would keep me awake at night, when I would feel fear gripping my throat, and vainly seek solace for my poor, tormented heart in the darkness of the room. No, everything had changed, we had reached a stage of mutual understanding, and she could no longer play a role. Her ardor was very real, and her words represented a genuine lust for life. I could see her eyes shining, her hands pressed earnestly together as if in prayer. All of this was sacred, and I would have sworn that this ritual was being watched over by some unknown god. I obstinately repeated to myself that she could not possibly be lying. Lies have no place in certain passionate human feelings. And so, despite the instinct telling me that something very grave was happening, despite the uncertainty and confusion which I sensed lay beneath that determined façade, I surrendered to her words, convinced that my raison d'être, and possibly that of the world, was to be found only in her acquiescence. She did not need now to swear oaths or protest her love, it was enough that she was by my side and allowing me to cover her with caresses and kisses. We had crossed the frontier and were walking alone in the silence emanating from all things definitively laid to rest. Very carefully, I made her lie down on the sofa, and she obeyed, although she did look terribly pale. When I bent over her, however, she held me back, pleading:

"No, André, not here. Someone might come in. Be careful . . ."

"But it's been so long," I said imploringly.

"I know, but not today."

And struggling to detach herself from the weight of my embrace, she added:

"From now on, we will always be together. Just wait, and you'll see how I will be entirely yours . . ."

....

42.
The Doctor's Last Report

No, no. The courage to tell everything? Where would I find that? Having been a doctor for all those years, and a poor country doctor at that, obliged to add to my Aesculapian duties the roles of counselor, protector and friend—no, I would never be able to tell all with the calm ferocity the subject demands. But I confess that a shudder ran through me, a mist covered my eyes as, thermometer in hand, I kept repeating to myself: say nothing, reveal nothing, even if it costs you your life. You might ask: was it so very grave? And I for my part would say: how should I know? After all, what do we actually die from? From illness, which does exist, from carelessness, which does occur, or simply from that imponderable thing we call the will to die? I believe that we die because our time has come. That woman of legendary beauty was revealing her secret to me as if she were laying herself bare. It was the first time in my whole career that I felt afraid—not of the diagnosis: what did it matter to me if I was wrong?—but of the inscrutable law that rules human destiny, the one we struggle to give a name to, but which always finds a name that answers to it: the will of God.

There lay the cause of my terror: transcending mere illness, it filled the bedroom, and hung in the air like the shadow of a supernatural existence. It was something more remarkable than an illness, it was a dialogue of unforeseeable consequences between two worlds, because it was not a dialogue confined merely to the things of *this* world. I don't know how long I stood looking at her, snug in bed, and, who knows, perhaps willingly giving in to a slow, elaborate desire to die, to surrender to a will far greater than her own, one that was already inscribing on her flesh, in perishable letters, her ineluctable fate. Or perhaps I was mistaken, and what I saw was only the end of a battle, the wreckage of a half-vanquished army? I don't know; it's not my business to know, indeed, I never will because, whether she was surrendering or not, every separation is also a defeat. It was enough to know that I was there with her, consumed by a profound sense of pity. A poor creature of dreams, I thought to myself, she was barely recognizable now, and how often had I seen her pass by, so absolute in her perfection and her harmony? How primitive our power is, and how useless our unknowing hands; and how I wept for her, that woman laid out before me, the mistress of the Chácara whom, it was often said, the Meneses had never understood.

Propped up against pillows, and neither dead nor alive, her breathing was labored, her eyes closed. And as I contemplated her impassive beauty, I kept tirelessly repeating to myself: Why did they ask me to come? What did they expect me to say? I looked at her and felt I did not have the strength to pierce the veil of that mystery. They had closed the door, and we were alone, face to face. The various objects in the room stood around us, bearing silent witness to the scene. I took two steps forward:

"Dona Nina?"

The body did not move. But, as proof that all signs of life had not yet departed, it gave off the warm, sweaty exhalation typical of patients long confined to bed. She was much thinner, and her copper-red hair, which had always been so immaculately combed and styled, hung in a loose tangle. I leaned closer and took her pulse. There was no reaction, but she wasn't dead, that much was clear, merely plunged in a sleep so profound that it often resembles death. No, not dead, but asleep, the deep sleep of someone whose final rest is steadily advancing toward them, like a date marked on the calendar. Could I have been mistaken? In that case, dear God, who am I but a poor man trying to do the right thing, one who has seen death so often, stripped of its disguise, but nevertheless different from the death before me now? And I cannot even say where this impression of mine came from, for I still hadn't examined her, although, by some kind of sixth sense, I already knew what was wrong; yet she seemed surrounded by an atmosphere of attentive, passive waiting, rather than the intense, muted tumult of a place where death has already pitched its camp. I said again: "Dona Nina," and this time she opened her eyes.

"Ah, it's you, Doctor," she said.

"How have you been?" I asked, sitting down beside her.

She smiled and shrugged:

"I think that this time . . ."

"There's always a chance," I said, interrupting her, opening my case and setting out on the bed the various instruments I needed to make my examination, "so why not this time too?"

"I've already consulted other doctors," she said simply.

"But not me, and I've been your doctor for many years now," I said, trying to convey much more than those words actually said—that is, my devotion and feelings of respect and loyalty for the entire Meneses family.

She sighed and tried to sit up a little. I asked her to lean toward me, just enough for me to examine her chest. She did as I asked, but I noticed that she lacked the simplicity of those patients who deliver themselves totally into the hands of their doctor, and that she moved as if she were defending her own body, and as if I were not merely carrying out a simple examination, but was trying to perform some strange ritual, or surreptitiously steal some secret from her. For she was certainly ill, and I needed no laboratory tests to prove that. The moment I touched her shoulder with my finger, she raised her head and her eyes shone so brightly that I stopped. There was no clearly formulated question in those eyes, but her whole being seemed to be waiting intently for me to speak. Curiosity? Hope? Whatever it was, what could I possibly say? Had she not been told the facts in Rio, had she not heard what the doctors there had to say, did she not know their diagnosis? I studiously avoided her gaze, bowed my head, and continued feeling along her bare shoulder, just above her right breast, then a little lower, moving gradually toward the center, until I reached the most sensitive point. And when I touched that point, she let out a scream—not a normal scream of pain, but something stronger and deeper, as if my fingers had brushed not a vital, living place, but a place where death had placed its lips and stamped upon it the fragile seal of pain. I immediately stopped my examination, and she slumped back onto the pillows, as the door opened and Senhor Valdo burst into the room.

"Is something wrong?" he asked, not daring to approach the bed.

I shrugged:

"No, I just touched a particularly painful spot."

He seemed to lack the courage to come any closer. For the first time, the truth, which he had possibly been avoiding for a long time, came to meet him in all its strength. He clearly did not have it in him to flee and so he stood, arms hanging by his side, cowardly and defenseless in the face of the inevitable. He motioned to me and I felt I had to obey. Together, we went over to the window.

"Is it serious?" he asked, a look of childlike anxiety on his face. (Therein lies one of man's great mysteries: even the strongest and most well-balanced of men—even a Meneses—turns into a little boy when ambushed by that powerful enemy lurking in the shadows.)

I nodded, and he bowed his head. Then, recovering himself, he asked again:

"Is there nothing to be done?"

"I don't know," I replied. "My examination was very superficial. We may need to do some more tests."

"If necessary . . ." he began.

"I'll need to see her again," I said, interrupting him. "And possibly consult other colleagues."

His hand rested timidly on my arm:

"Do you think . . ."

His feebleness irritated me and I was unsparing in my frankness:

"From what I could see, it's quite widespread. She should have sought help earlier . . ."

His face flushed scarlet, almost like a landscape suddenly covered by dark storm clouds. Seeing me studying his face, he made an effort to control himself and, with the Meneses' obscure distaste for any kind of illness—which probably explained why Nina had kept silent about her condition and pretended not to notice that the disease was heartlessly spreading throughout her body, creating small rosy islands, twisting through dark canals and swollen veins, tracing long winding, purple paths, a whole geography of slow, pitiless destruction—he asked:

"Is it cancer?"

"Yes, it's cancer," I confirmed.

"And . . ." His lips could not form the word.

"It has already spread," I added.

"Dear God!" His voice sounded choked and muted. "Where on earth did she get that?"

Since there was nothing more I could do, and because it was he who had brought me to the house, I set about providing him with some facts about the disease. Darkness was slowly filling the room. He remained utterly still, but it was evident that his entire being was under tension, even though the only sign of this was the occasional quiver of an eyelid and a nervous twitch at the corner of his mouth. I told him the banal facts that are known to all of us, namely, that cancer is a disease of unknown origin and, despite the certainty with which it can be diagnosed, it is not yet amenable to any truly effective course of treatment. (On rereading these scribbled notes, lost for so many years at the back of a drawer, I repeat: there was no effective treatment then, and there still isn't now. The only difference is that surgeons have grown more skillful and outcomes are more hopeful: nowadays, no one considers a diagnosis of cancer as an incommutable death sentence, as they did in those days. Today, there are straightforward cases where a complete cure is likely, but the truth is that, then, any prognosis was pure speculation. And you almost always ended up watching death drawing inexorably nearer and being unable to stop it; the doctor simply surrendered his patient to God's will.) I went on to explain that it was an insidious disease, which could disappear only to reappear later on, alive and kicking. While I talked, his head sank lower and lower onto his chest—he seemed so utterly cast down that I could not help but feel sorry for him, thinking to myself how even stubborn, persistent human pride could be reduced to this. I patted him on the back.

"Don't lose heart. Beyond our own meagre human resources there is always God's will, and He can do anything."

"Ah!" he replied weakly, "God's will . . ." And, after a pause, "Do you need to examine her again?"

"I do," I said. "I'll need to make a definitive diagnosis."

"In that case, I shall leave you to it."

There was a clear note of relief in his voice. He left the room, and I returned to my patient's side. She no longer had her eyes closed and seemed to have been waiting for me.

"Did you tell him?" she asked, indicating the door through which her husband had just gone.

I sat down beside her again, not knowing what to say. Should I lie? But she had probably been told all there was to know by the doctors in Rio. Lying would only arouse her distrust.

"Yes, I told him," I replied, aware that she would notice even the slightest change of expression.

"Ah!" she exclaimed, as if a weight had suddenly lifted from her shoulders. Then after the briefest of pauses, she placed one hand on my knee: "Now, please tell me: how much longer do I have to live?" Her eyes looked deep into mine. "How long? Don't lie. I want the truth, the whole truth. How long do you think this wretched disease will let me live?"

I wasn't fooled by the frank tone in which she said this, because I knew she was moved solely by despair, or something worse than despair, sharp and unremitting, fermenting in her soul like a concentrated ache, as ferocious as the thing gnawing away at her body. And it was easy to see why she focused on that question—because she had been beautiful, because she still was, because she had loved and been loved. What other factors could bind her to the simple drive to exist? I sensed it less in her words than in the hand that emerged from beneath the sheets and, like the hand of a shipwrecked sailor, take hold of my knee. And so I lied, I dared to lie, convinced that anyone else would do the same, because truth has its limits and slips away at exactly the point where our need for compassion steps in:

"I don't know," I said. "The disease might go into remission, and you could live for many more years. Or at least, as many years as you wish. There are various examples of cases like that."

My words must have sounded strange in the stillness of the room. She drank them in, but obviously wasn't fooled. She let her head fall:

"No," she exclaimed wearily. "I know there's no hope. But even so . . ." and, lifting her head, she said quietly, almost vehemently: "I just want one or two months."

"Oh, you'll have much longer than that," I protested. "But if one or two months is what you really want, I can guarantee that you will have them. I give you my word."

"Thank you," she said, and sighed. She seemed calmer.

I resumed my examination, and as I became more familiar with the terrain, I began to ask myself whether I might not have been a little hasty in giving her my word. It could also have been the effect of the darkness, and so I asked her to turn on the light. She pointed to a small red lamp attached to the headboard. That should be enough. I turned on the lamp and continued my work. My first reaction had been absolutely right: in the light, what I saw was even more dispiriting. Dona Nina was in a very bad state: various dark blotches radiated out from one side of her breast—which was almost entirely dark purple in color—and extended from front to back, indicating a series of tumors that would be very difficult to remove. The affected area was too extensive, and there would be no point in operating. Besides, she was not in good overall health, for her general resistance and energy levels seemed very low—the skin on her back was broken here and there, like the skin of an overripe fruit, revealing the flesh within. I could not judge the full extent of her illness, but, to put it bluntly, she seemed to be rotting away inside.

I felt too perplexed to continue my examination.

"You should have gone to a doctor long ago," I told her. "What you have done is absurd, almost a crime."

With her head drooping and her hair falling forward over her face, as if she no longer had the courage to sit up straight or to look me in the eye, she said:

"I didn't feel a thing. There was no pain. Even now I can't feel anything, only a kind of tightness, as if someone were pulling at my skin."

There was something childlike—no, something more like anguish—in her voice, into which fear was now creeping. I asked her in a tone of voice, which, quite unintentionally, had something of the confessional about it:

"Since when?"

"Oh!" She raised her head, eyes shining. "A long time. More than a year, I think."

Haltingly, like a wounded man hauling himself forward by stages and stopping to lean against a wall to recover his strength, she told me she'd had a lump in her breast, colorless and no bigger than a cherry stone. One day, quite how she wasn't sure, she had crushed that stone and it had swelled up. She had treated it with poultices and homemade remedies, but to no avail. Then she'd discovered a dark stain under her breast, like a large bruise. When she looked at herself in the mirror, she saw other such stains spreading onto her back. She had prodded them with her finger, but they didn't hurt. Even so, she had begun to feel afraid, but had still said nothing. The truth is, she had never imagined that it could possibly be . . . (She stopped, lacking the courage to say the word. And yet, from inside the nucleus of her fear, the word resounded throughout the room, as if cruelly unmasked by some spirit in the shadows.) She had carried on with her life, and everything that was rational in her strove to forget about the illness. But then she got up one morning and found the sheet stained with blood. Trembling, she had gone to the mirror and run her fingers down her back. When she looked at her fingers, they were covered with blood and pus. That was when she announced that she needed to go to Rio, where, without a word to a soul, she had found a doctor. She had said nothing about being ill, just that she needed to go alone. She hoped I would understand these precautions (there was an unexpected edge of humility in her voice as she said this), and would understand that, for her, illness had always been something shameful. She had watched her own father dying, sitting in a chair, stubbornly refusing to go to bed, never complaining about all his ailments. Finally, she was grateful, infinitely grateful to me, for sparing her the task of telling her husband. She was sure that, until then, he had interpreted her silence quite differently.

I nodded. She stopped speaking, and between us fell the sudden silence that always descends when everything has been said, and we look at the other person and realize that the subject has run its course. I stood up.

"Will you write a prescription?" she asked almost pleadingly.

"Of course."

I went over to a small table, took my notepad and pen from my pocket, certain that all efforts would be entirely futile. Even so, I scribbled a few lines—mere palliatives. I turned and placed the piece of paper beside her.

“I’ll come back later,” I said.

She smiled sadly at me. And as I left, I felt sure that I would never see that woman again.

43.
Continuation of André's Diary (ix)

....

I waited—the next day and the next and several more. I waited a week, two weeks—I waited a whole month. After that meeting in the drawing room, I was unable to see her alone again. My despair, however intense, was mitigated by two overwhelming factors: firstly, the knowledge that she was not far away; secondly, that her absence was not of her own choosing. I knew she was ill, but what that illness was, I could not imagine. And besides, what was the point of knowing, when any illness would inevitably interrupt the course of our relationship. It was enough to know she was gravely ill—I had only to observe the atmosphere in the house, the look on people's faces, the doctor coming and going. It was easy enough, too, to pick up comments made in the hallway, because, with the freedom that such extraordinary events always provide, the servants had crossed the clearly demarcated frontier of the kitchen and begun to invade the house. And if that were not enough, I had only to listen to my own instinct; and my own dread of learning the truth told me everything I needed to know. All day, trying to fill the hours with mechanical, meaningless tasks, I sensed that, at any moment, I was about to bump up against an insurmountable wall, and this, far from slaking my burning thirst, only increased it. Nothing could quench my desire, and, incapable of freeing myself from the image filling my whole being, I realized that what had begun as a fantasy and then become love, had, inevitably—exacerbated by recent events—become an obsession. Those hours dense with waiting had at least one advantage, namely, that I was free to come and go without anyone noticing or bothering me. I did not exist for the others—a curious state—even though the evolving drama kept me implacably imprisoned in its vortex. But what did I know? Nothing, only that permanently closed door. I walked past it several times a day, and when I was sure there was no one else in the hallway, I would touch it and even stroke it with fingers heavy with fever and desire. At other times, I would try to escape and would lie, swaying, in the hammock, my eyes closed to the bright light of day, or I would take up a book, paper, pen, ink, and try to immerse myself in studies I should long ago have finished and which I continually postponed. My father occasionally remarked, although without any great conviction: "You need to do something." But in that house, where nothing was normal, who really cared about that hypothetical thing, my future, who thought about what I should or should not become, or considered what might be good or bad for me, either now or later. During that time, I could already feel, quite intensely, the presence of a phenomenon which I would one day describe as the Meneses' backwardness and basic lack of foresight. We were waiting for something that would not be long in coming; the atmosphere was charged with an intense electricity that seemed about to explode, and that was all we needed, as if any future action depended solely on that.

This inactivity only inflamed my imagination. Unable to see Nina, I felt her ever more present. What she had done in the past, far from moving further off, came closer. And as time passed, those images only multiplied. The book would fall from my hands. I would stop the task I had only just begun and close my eyes: I could see her with such indescribable clarity! Now she was leaning over me, and I could feel her breath on my cheek, now her body was emerging out of the gloom, and I could see every detail of her hips, the curve of her breasts, her elegant legs. The blood would grow hot in my veins, and, blind and choking, I would rush off to splash my face with cold water, hoping to break the spell.

It was high summer, no breeze stirred the lifeless, sun-scorched leaves. And it was as if that same sun had seeped into my very being and, dizzy with light, I would suddenly be overcome by a fever no remedy could dispel. I would wander aimlessly about the garden then, my forehead dripping with sweat, my pulse racing. An infinite rain of white blossom fell from the low canopies of orange trees, and bees, attracted by the acidic scent, filled the shadows with a monotonous, persistent buzzing. This only further exasperated me, and I would flee, and, in my madness, break off a flower, crush it roughly to my nose, and watch as the petals wilted in my fingers. From a distance, I would gaze at the window of the room where she lay and, thinking I saw some unusual movement, would race back to the hallway only to learn that nothing had happened and everything was stuck in the same stagnant state. And the door before me stayed obstinately shut. I would grow desperate, curse myself and others and God; and time, so indifferent to my clamorings, continued to stretch out the long, empty hours. I would take refuge in my room and, there, lying on the bed, would hug my pillows; the obsessive images returned, a bare leg, her throat, her parted lips, and, yes, why not say it, her cunt open and waiting, simultaneously alluring and horrific, like lymph oozing a strange mixture of honey and blood. There were moments then when I would have been capable of anything; the familiar female smell—in which, like orange blossom, sweet mingled with sour—clung to me, dissolved into the shadows cast by my gestures and resurfaced wherever I was, asleep or not, to reimpose its irresistible dominion. Exhausted, I would hear invisible bees buzzing around my head.

Today, at last, the opportunity presented itself. We were in the drawing room—where, lately, my Uncle Demétrio had taken to spending more time than usual—when my father came in, announcing he was going to Rio. He seemed very upset and explained that he intended to consult a specialist, because he could not bear to watch his wife slowly dying. (It's odd, but the death he was speaking of had no reality for me at all. It was as if he were talking about something that was happening to someone else entirely. That death, which I feared and suspected, belonged to me, and could only be revealed by my lips.) He added that he would be back in two or three days. This news appeared to displease Uncle Demétrio, and I watched them talking and gesticulating on the far side of the room. What did I care what they said! My father—never one to change his plans—declared that he would leave anyway. Sitting quite still in my chair, I was struggling to contain the tumult in my heart, because I sensed this would be the chance I had so longed for. Given all the comings and goings in Nina's room, I realized that things were not looking good; and soon, thanks to Betty's efforts, my father was ready to leave. From where I was sitting (in the warm complicity of that corner of the room, with its rocking chair, its shade, its glimpse of garden through the open window . . .) I could hear him issuing his final orders. Confused as to what was going on, the servants clustered in the doorway, looking first down the hallway, then out at the garden where the buggy was due to arrive. When it did, my father said goodbye and went to meet it, carrying just one suitcase. And when the sound of the wheels had vanished completely, and the house, as if nothing in the least unusual were going on, had slipped into its usual state of repose, I got to my feet. No voices, no slamming doors, no clatter of something being dropped—the Chácara, by force of habit, was sinking back into its customary slumber. I set off, determined to cross the frontier that I had, until then, respected. What did I care about obstacles and possible prohibitions? I went over to the window and looked out, then, ears and eyes alert, I peered up and down the hallway; finally, controlling my excitement as best I could, I set off for that closed door.

As soon as I opened the door, I was taken aback by the smell that met me, a faintly nauseating blend of flowers and rotten apples. (A repugnant smell, but nothing like what came later, when she was dying, and in which one could sense, indeed, almost feel, the breaking down of human flesh: a huge and precocious task, as if jealous hands could not wait to undo in the darkness the complicated amalgam that made up that woman's body. No, when I went into the room, I could still feel the presence of an intact being; in the bed lay the one creature I cared about—perfect and alive and whole—and for whom I had been longing all those days. Put like that, it may not seem very much, because words betray us and create a mere appearance of truth, but how else express the feeling that was drawing me to the edge of that bed? Let me explain, if I can: *I* did not exist, I was merely part of a ruined, meaningless alliance. And the person lying beneath those covers, was not *her*, it was *me*, a separate, diffuse "me" doing battle with the darkness and the terror, but which nonetheless represented the most vital and most important part of myself. Is that blasphemy? Will that scandalize the ears of those who hear me or the eyes that see me? I felt that nothing separated us, no air, no wind, and that whether bound together or not in that sacramental act of love, we constituted two pieces of the same landscape seeking each other out in order to live the one existence for which we had been destined.)

I stood, not daring to move, because my whole being was in the grip of a kind of paralysis. I know how difficult it is to talk about love, but however clumsily I do it, will there be no one out there who will understand me? I mean only that I did not exist, did not feel alive when I was far from her. When we were apart, whatever flame burned inside me dwindled down to a mere handful of cold ashes. And yet what I wanted was to burn again, to burn tirelessly, so that the same fire would burn the woman who had inspired me, and if she was destroyed, condemned by whatever cruel law rules our wills, then let me be destroyed too, because what use would we be in the world if one of us did not exist?

Eventually, I began to feel my way forward in the darkness. There she was, her head resting on a pile of pillows, her hair a tangled mass, her eyes open. (That was the first thing I noticed, that she had her eyes wide open.) She was wrapped in a white sheet, perhaps because of the heat, and, when I stood looking down at her, her body seemed longer than it actually was. Did I feel tenderness, excitement? I would be lying if I said yes. I had suffered so much during those last few weeks that I had no time to feel either emotion. What I felt was a dull sense of revulsion and impotence, a rage at my own inability to do anything to stop what I considered to be an abandonment, a desertion. (*Written in the margin:* I did love again, or saw others love in that same violent way. And there was always someone saying goodbye, out of fear or boredom, or for one of those many other reasons that can bring a relationship to an abrupt halt. I also often saw those who, faced by a love that had not yet died, became consumed by some illness or agony of unknown origin, but the roots of which lay in their fear of giving themselves entirely. Abandonment and desertion do exist. They are inherent in human fear.) At the sight of that prostrate body and those eyes now seeking me out—for the silence, a subtle change in the air, a passing shadow or a thickening of the atmosphere, must have betrayed to her the presence of another being, or more than that, the presence of the beloved—I could hold back no longer and collapsed with a moan at the foot of the bed. A moan I said, and I lied only out of shame. For some seconds, transfixed by the terrible pain of being brutally robbed of the one atmosphere in which I could breathe freely, I blindly rolled my head back and forth, weeping and biting the bedspread in an attempt to smother my own frenetic grief, clutching at the sheet in a desperate attempt at a caress. Everything I had kept silent about during those long days, everything I had kept locked up inside me, my respect for the situation, my tolerance of other people, my self-pity, my hope, my exhaustion, my memories, and even my ignorance, all this overflowed, and I did not have the strength to contain the force of that explosion, even though I knew I should, and even though I tried to do so, pressing the crumpled bedspread to my face. I had become extraordinarily sensitive, and every corner of my body, every fold of my skin was trembling as I remembered innumerable kisses, vanished caresses, sudden acts of tenderness, as if the whole of me, in allowing that apparent façade to crack, were suddenly reemerging into the self so laboriously shaped by her voluptuous, willing consent. That was the only time when, in my wretchedness, I dared to curse the love consuming me. The words rose unstoppably to my lips, while I continued to roll my head from side to side and clutch at the sheet.

"You promised me! Why did you break your promise? You said you would come back and be mine again! That you would always be mine! Why then did you leave me? What a fool I was falling in love with a woman without pity, without a heart, without anything! What kind of creature are you, a tart, a whore? Don't imagine I care that you're dying and that yours is the very worst of agonies . . . no! I don't give a damn, I'm leaving, going far away, and I won't come back. I will never again set foot in this house."

I was crying, the tears streaming down my face. And then she rested her hand on my head, so lightly I barely felt it. Poor hand, poor ghost of a hand. It reminded me of the warm, authoritative fingers she had once placed on my lips. I don't know why, but that was the only part of her body that gave me the distinct impression she was already dead.

"What madness, André," and her slow voice was like a breath touching my head. Making a huge effort, she had abandoned her pillows and was leaning over me. "What madness. I can guarantee, I can swear I'm not worthy of your tears. I'm bad, André, worthless."

What did it matter to me if she was good or bad? To me, who had never once asked what she was. Outside of her, what did I care for such concepts? She and she alone was important, and she, for me, was the sole measure of good and evil. I got to my feet and sat on the bed.

"Who cares about what is good or evil," I said. "It's you I love, Nina."

I heard a hoarse moan emerge from her lips:

"André!"

I was cruel then and, standing up, I made as if to leave:

"Do you want me to go and never come back?"

And I took two paces toward the door, but she sat bolt upright then, her tangled hair falling about her shoulders.

"No, André, no, anything but that."

And she fell limply back, at the same time holding out one hand to me. I rushed to her side:

"Ah, you do love me, you do still love me!"

I could not tell if her gesture was intended to repel or to draw me to her; she was shaking uncontrollably, and all her vitality seemed concentrated in her eyes, in the deep, pitiless depths of those eyes watching me from some place far away, where I was not, but where, possibly, there still bloomed the diabolically perfumed memory of who I had been and of the pleasure I had given her.

"André . . ."

And she neither called to me nor sent me away, content with being the beloved, loving and brazen, tremulous and humble, proud and subjugated, in the final moments of her time as a frail human being. I sat down again and took her in my arms, and she let me do so.

"My love."

She moaned:

"Don't do that, it hurts, don't do that."

Emanating from her, from that whole dying, sweating, trembling creature, came the same strong, warm, unbearable smell I had noticed when I entered the room. However, in the brief time I had been by her side, that smell had already become part of her, and in the process of transposition binding us together, it had now become part of me too and was the smell of my own sweat and my own blood.

"My love, my poor love," I said again, kissing her eyes, her cheeks, her mouth; and she turned away, her dry lips parted. For me, though, she seemed far more beautiful in her rejection of me than if she had submissively offered herself up.

I again brushed her forehead with my lips, and beneath my lips I felt her temples beating dully. Locked in that embrace, what words I said, what urgent pleas, begging her to surrender to my hunger! The sheet had fallen to one side, revealing one intact breast, and that was all it took. My hands, as if driven by some external force, pulled down the sheet to expose her whole torso. She fell back, half-fainting, and I felt the weight of her head on my arm, but I could still not make out her features, because the room was plunged in almost absolute darkness. Around us hovered that same burgeoning smell, a viscous, repellent smell that came in gusts, as if someone were stirring warmed-up leftovers in a vat. I let her lie back on the pillows, feeling that the supreme moment had arrived. Her breathing was labored and she was moaning softly, her body twitching now and then as if prompted by the pulsations of an invisible dynamo.

"Nina," I said, and my dull voice echoed strangely in the silence of the room.

In response to that cry—whose meaning she could not fail to understand, and which resounded through every filament of her long-suffering flesh—she called out quite loudly:

"Why? Why did you come?"

"Nina," I said again, "there's no one here, just the two of us."

The echo of those words, "just the two of us," struck a hollow note, like the bass note of an organ vibrating in the darkness embracing us.

"Why . . ." she said again and suddenly sat up, her hair glued to her forehead, neck and shoulders with sweat.

"Just once more, Nina," I said.

She did not respond, but a great shudder ran through her from head to toe, like an electric current. At the same time, her eyes fixed on mine—they were a deep, deep blue, of an indescribable intensity—and after gazing at me just long enough to fully take in my body and to draw from that sight the final revelation of our separate existences, they closed again, and she lay back on the bed. But in that gaze, I saw, like warring elements, not only an awareness of the room (a miserable room, a prison, like all human rooms), but also the memory of our hours of love, our promises, of everything that made up the warm, dark bond of our union. Now her body was lying stretched out on the bed, as if, before death itself came—and it would not be long in coming—another different death might be given to her. I lay down beside her—forgive all these details, but I promised myself to record as much of what happened as possible, so as to preserve a perfect image in my memory—and motionless, I listened for some time to her uncertain breathing. Then her hand, urgent, cold, reached out to find me, touching first my side, then sliding down to my stomach, and coming to rest on the exact place in which all my life force lay concentrated. It was not a touch, but a pressure, and that pressure—there could be no doubt—was an invitation.

I leaned closer and blindly placed my lips on her now entirely unresponsive lips. At first, when mine touched hers, I still felt the warm caress of ripe fruit that comes with any intimate kiss; but as I pushed my tongue into her mouth, I was overwhelmed not by the sense of discovering another person's earthy essence, but by a rancid, indefinable odor, which emerged from within like an excess of the oil that was keeping the dark depths of that human engine working. Those into whose hands this notebook may one day fall will say: madness, youth. Madness or youth, what does it matter, this was my one encounter with death, as it carried out its subterranean work of unpicking and destroying the internal harmony that makes up every living being. The image of the closed door would not leave me. And yet, at that moment, I was intent on savoring not life, but death. I made love to her, I don't know how; it was both a terror and a yearning to find completion in her death. Had she herself not urged me, had she herself not told me it was necessary to go through the wall, to possess and break down and absorb those we love? I made love as I never had before, without really knowing what I was loving or possessing. It was not an interior or a woman or any identifiable thing. I was giving myself to a monstrous absorption, a fall, a gangrenous dissolution. I could feel the darkness itself pressing down on me, and as if caught up in a whirlpool, my very being felt as if it would be shattered by the force that kept me spinning and spinning, and not a single part of me remained immune to the frenzy of that terrifying journey. Until I heard a cry slice through the air, and I woke. She lay limp in my arms, gasping for breath. And down my fists and my fingers ran a liquid which was neither blood nor pus, but a thick, hot substance that dripped down as far as my elbows and gave off a foul, unbearable smell. I released her then, and she sank back against the soft pillows. That slow liquid was still running down my arms. Was she dead? Alive? A pointless question. *I* was alive, amid the debris of that mad experience. *I* was alive, and knowing this made me stand up, overwhelmed by emotion, gazing at the still sensate being lying panting on the bed. From every side, like an invisible, ever-swelling river hurling its furious waves against the banks that we represented, a feeling of failure and impossibility interposed itself between us; I retreated, step by step, to the wall, as if allowing those waters to boil and rise up to our impotent chests and dizzy us with their smell of salt and sacrifice. The world quickly sank into its accustomed silence. For the first time, I shook my fist at the heavens: let God, if he existed, take the better part and pluck from her, at that very moment, her final breath, and impose his law of oppression and tyranny. Let him dissolve us into vile matter and, while we were yet alive, and for his greater amusement, reveal to all the world our pestilential essence of tears and excrement—nothing mattered to me any more. Literally nothing. A vacuum formed inside me, as hard as stone. I was aware that I was breathing, moving, existing, as if the stuff of which I was made had suddenly rusted up. And I had never felt so certain that, for as long as I lived, I would continue to proclaim the news that we human beings are pathetic, wretched creatures, and that, anywhere on earth, all we are ever offered is a closed door. Everything else, alas, is a chimera, madness, illusion. Everything I represented, like an island surrounded by the rough waves of that sea of death, was proof that the human race was doomed forever to a clamorous, oppressive solitude. No bridge exists, it never did: the judge in charge of our case denies us that. And so the power that invented us is equally wretched, for it also invented pointless longing, the rage of the slave, our perpetual wakefulness in this prison from which we will only escape through madness, mystery, and confusion.

44.
Valdo's Second Statement (i)

I really don't know how I managed to make that journey to Rio. I only know that, one day, when I went into our room, I was so shocked by her physical appearance that I decided to set out immediately. I went over to the bed, took her pulse, felt how irregular it was and saw that her face, the familiar face that had once filled me with such tender feelings, was already taking on the sad, disfigured look of someone entering a state of coma. Was I exaggerating? Since my conversation with the doctor, when he had confirmed that the tumors had spread, I had been living in a perpetual state of alarm. But even if what I saw in her was in large part influenced by my own fears, there was no doubt that over the last few days the pace of her illness had accelerated extraordinarily. I went to the drawing room to find Demétrio and discuss with him the details of my departure. I found him sitting in a rocking chair, apparently absorbed in reading a book. André was asleep on the sofa nearby.

"Is it as serious as that?" asked Demétrio without getting up, gently rocking his chair.

"Serious?" My voice trembled. "It's more than serious. I don't believe she has many more days to live."

He stared at me as if I had just said something ridiculous. What did he think? That the Meneses were exempt from mere matters of life and death? And in the brief silence that followed, I was the one to stare at him in disbelief; he looked away and casually leafed through his book. What a strange man, what a strange Meneses. I had known his habits for years and years and what it meant when he broke with them. And, standing there before him, I could not have said that he was exactly ignoring what was going on—no—and as proof of this, I could point to his more or less constant presence in the drawing room during recent days. He knew about Nina's illness and was fully aware of its gravity, but it had probably not occurred to him that death would come so quickly. Looking at him then, and despite all our years of living in the same house, I suddenly realized what was so strange about him: a silence, a reticence in the face of events, and which, despite (for example) his presence in the drawing room, was neither more nor less than a rejection of everything that went on around him. And what had been so imponderable and secret about his nature now became utterly clear: he did not believe in the drama taking place in the house. It was in his nature to repel any abnormal occurrence, and even death itself, which, for others, was a decisive, unalterable fact, was for him an outrage and an affront against which he sternly set his face, and with all the force at his disposal. It might be supposed that these events wounded his sensibility, but I understood instinctively that in him it was not mere fastidiousness, but rather a deep loathing of any kind of disturbance not only to his daily domestic routines, but to the rigid, solitary principles that were his refuge. Death wasn't a blow struck by some superior, ineluctable force, it was a gauntlet thrown down between equals, to which it was necessary to respond by fighting, and he, a proud Meneses, was, like any other human being, uncertain of the strength of his weapons. By sitting there in the drawing room, he was simply demonstrating that he was not running away and, although dazed and bewildered, he was ready to leap into combat—to join battle, as it were. However, and this is what his reaction demonstrated, he did not believe that the citadel was yet in such imminent danger. After a while, discomfited by the way I was looking at him and aware of the continuing silence between us, he said:

"You must take care, Valdo. This is no time to be running up expenses."

His tone revived the atmosphere in which I had struggled all my life: failed investments, shaky banking transactions, loans that were never repaid, a whole series of financial disasters that had brought the family to its present situation.

"I know," I replied as coolly as possible.

Almost ignoring my response, he went on:

"Don't forget that since our mother's death, we have done nothing to add to the money she left us, or, rather, the only business deals we've made were bad ones. The income we have been living off is now practically exhausted."

"I know," I repeated calmly.

He closed his book and looked at me:

"Would it not be possible to avoid such excesses?"

I regarded him coldly—this was no time for arguments.

"I want to make sure she has everything she needs."

"You really believe . . ." And once again he eyed me distrustfully.

"Yes, I do." I replied firmly.

He sighed. "That's different then. You must do as you see fit."

I considered the matter closed and was on my way out of the drawing room, when I heard his voice again:

"Will you bring someone back with you?"

"What do you mean 'someone'?" I repeated, not immediately understanding what he meant.

"A doctor."

"Of course," I said. And then after a slight pause: "That's precisely why I'm going—to fetch a specialist."

I saw a shadow flicker across his face, faintly altering it from within. It was as if some internal mechanism were swinging into action, and, like lubricating oil applied to rusty wheels and cogs, was setting stiff, sclerotic parts moving once again, giving his old face a new expression, even a surprising touch of sympathy.

"Would that make any difference?" Even his voice sounded different.

"What does that matter?" My answer, in this brief exchange so laden with meaning, was also spoken in a tone quite different from my normal one.

With the perspicacity of those who have long been turned in upon themselves, he understood that, with those simple words, he had crossed a line—so iron-clad was his emotional discipline, and so unaccustomed was he to making concessions to mere human frailties. And returning to his more usual manner, he replied with a nod of the head. The meeting was over. Then something happened that I certainly wasn't expecting. I turned to leave for the second time, and I again heard his voice:

"And in the event . . . in the event of . . ."

I turned around. He was standing up, leaning slightly forward, and it struck me that he was markedly paler than before, perhaps on account of the sheer effort he was making. I did not reply at once because a curious change was taking place in my mind. From where I now stood—around ten paces away—I examined my brother and, for the first time in my life, I saw how fragile and alone he was. He wasn't a man who lived by the kindness of others, looking for favors or seeking their indulgence; he had no need of that, and never revealed the slightest flaw in his nature that might incline anyone toward sympathy. On the contrary, he had always hidden himself away, aloof and enclosed as if behind solid walls, incapable of any expression or movement that might arouse the interest or affection of his fellow creatures. For he was completely ignorant of any form of human communication, and since he never conceded anything in such matters, neither did he receive anything in return. His existence, at least as far as I could tell, was identical to that of certain plants, mysteries of Nature, that live a rootless, niggardly existence suspended entirely in the air. But now he was different—and the suddenness of that change made me wonder if everything else was pure artifice. He had stood up intending to utter a cry, but even that, feeble though it was, seemed to diminish him and make him vulnerable to my compassion, shedding a brutal light that cut him in two—one half dense and secret, the other cool and composed, both halves displaying their inner workings like a building that suddenly opens up before our eyes. He looked smaller, a mean, humiliated figure in his dull, dark clothes, his aura of authority dissolving as if by magic. And there, defenseless before me, stood the real Demétrio, in as much need of compassion as any other human being caught in the wheels of the unexpected and the dramatic.

"In the event of . . ." I repeated, not wishing to finish the phrase and hoping he would do so himself.

I saw his lips tremble and he let out a deep sigh:

"In the event of something happening, an accident of some sort."

He was skirting around the danger, not daring to say the word and suffering like all of us. My satisfaction on discovering this was so great that I had to control my feelings before I could reply with the necessary feigned indifference:

"Betty and Ana are in there with her. And André will always be somewhere nearby."

This information did not seem to please him very much; he remained standing, his hand resting on the back of the chair as if he needed support. And so, with a shrug, he finally seemed inclined to let me leave. Before going, however, when I was already at the door, I turned to look at him one last time: he stared back at me, as if waiting for a gesture from me, a word of solidarity, or whatever it was that might save him from himself, from being abandoned there at the mercy of the unknown events bearing down on him. We stood there looking at one another for a moment, and I can guarantee that, just as when a conspiracy is revealed, I suddenly understood his silence, the hostility, the impenetrable Meneses aura with which he surrounded himself, the origins of his supposed superiority to me and everyone else—he, Demétrio, a little man, whose heart certainly no longer functioned normally, and who was now returning to his proper place, gutless and torn apart by timidity and indecision. Ah, yes, I must confess this discovery gave me a frisson of pleasure, and I smiled. It was the first time I had smiled like that, and there was neither triumph nor disdain in my smile, just the certainty that we had reached the frontier he had so feared, and where, finally, it was not just him or me crumbling into dust, but the entire edifice of our despotic family, built upon pride and position and possessions and money. He could see what was going through my mind, for his anger made him turn paler still and I saw him grip the chair-back even more tightly, as if he were crushing it, but the truth was that, just then, he needed me more than I needed him. Why? The question hung, unasked, in the clear, crystalline air. I still did not know the reasons, if any reasons existed, but at that moment, facing each other across the drawing room, which also seemed not to know him—him, the master, the head of the family, the eldest brother—I could swear that there was very little to choose between us, except that he was far, far unhappier than I was.

The door closed behind me and I found myself in the hallway. I had scarcely taken a step when I saw the figure of Ana approaching. I can't explain why, and possibly there was no reason, but every time I saw my sister-in-law I felt a certain unease. However discreet and silent she was, apparently trying as hard as she could to occupy as little space as possible, I could not help feeling that her life was ruled by mysterious thoughts and that her every gesture, even the most banal and meaningless, obeyed some silent motive which she dared not reveal to anyone. In the hallway, unfortunately, it was impossible to avoid her.

"Is she sleeping?" I asked as we passed each other.

She gave me an apparently expressionless look. I repeated the question.

"No, she's awake," she said. "But she seems more comfortable."

She clearly wasn't going to say any more, and was about to move away, when I caught her arm:

"I'm going away, Ana."

She stared at me somewhat taken aback, but waited for me to explain. I told her I was going to find a specialist, and that I probably wouldn't be away for more than two or three days—just enough time for me to find some sensible, responsible doctor who would be willing to come back with me to the Chácara. She was still staring at me dubiously, as if casting doubt not on my words, but on the relevance of my actions. And indeed the more I spoke, the more unjustified my reasons seemed, and the journey suddenly seemed ill-timed and pointless. When I stopped speaking, she merely said:

"Very well."

But seeing that I did not move, she added:

"Betty and I will take care of everything. There's no need to worry."

That was all we had to say to each other. She walked away and, for a moment, I followed her with my eyes and watched as she disappeared into the drawing room. It struck me how completely Ana had assimilated the Meneses way of being; how she had embraced the austere lifestyle of the Chácara and learned to be parsimonious in word and deed. Nina, on the contrary, had never adapted, and had lived there like a perpetual excrescence, always on the point of leaving, always coming back. Even now Ana showed just how much she had entered into the spirit of the family, accepting the current situation without a murmur, lending her silent support without anyone asking her to or even reminding her of her duty. Perhaps there really was some mystery hidden deep inside her, but whatever it might be, I was quite sure it would never surface, for she would rather die than share her true feelings with anyone. As these thoughts were going through my mind, I made my way out into the garden. I wanted to be alone before my departure, so as to gather my thoughts and plan what I was going to do. As I walked through the darkness, I looked back at the house all lit up, its windows open, shadows moving about inside; the Chácara, always apparently so tranquil, looked very different to those of us who knew its habits. It was curious to see and there was even a certain charm about it—a new breeze seemed to blow through the house and it stood there attentively, as if prepared for important events. I couldn't remember ever having seen the house so ready, and I would perhaps have been proud of its new demeanor if it did not bring with it a heavy heart and a sense that, like certain gravely ill patients, it was only opening its eyes now in order to witness its own demise.

45.
Ana's Last Confession (i)

I was the first to discover the bad smell. I was sitting next to Demétrio, the presence of illness in the house having somehow brought us a little closer. He had finally emerged both from his room and, very slightly, from his customary reserve: he walked about the house now, looked at the other people, and seemed even to expect some explanation from them. Once, I even found him going very slowly down the steps into the garden, his hand shading his eyes from the bright sun: with his head of white hair, ruffled by the light breeze, he cut a very odd figure. Indeed, he rather resembled a relic that has stepped out of its casket. Seeing him prepared to sally forth into the daylight made me wonder if he was afraid. Did he feel death haunting the house? Why else would he abandon familiar territory and venture into places where he had never previously set foot?

Spending, as we did, long hours alone in each other's company, we were bound together by expectation. We occasionally exchanged a word or two, although without making any direct reference to the illness, but however carefully we maintained that silence, whichever way we turned, the illness and the room outside of which death was lurking were always there between us. I would often secretly examine my husband, and I became aware, almost moment by moment, of his growing decrepitude. This realization filled me with rebellious thoughts, and I, who had always been his faithful shadow, now took certain liberties, I would occasionally leave his side or deliberately not answer his questions, pretending I was asleep—and he would put up with it. His eyes seemed to be begging me to say something, and without knowing exactly what that something was, I could sense its meaning.

One day, when we were, as usual, sitting side by side, both of us pretending to doze—our mutual defense—I looked up and asked:

"What's that?"

He immediately opened his eyes:

"What?"

"That smell."

He took a deep breath, then, shaking his head, said:

"I can't smell anything."

"It's coming from the hallway . . ."

He took another breath, and this time he agreed:

"Hm, perhaps it's the smell of some medicine or other."

"Yes," I said, "but mixed with something else."

I did not, however, have the courage to name that "something else." We remained sitting in the same position, me patiently knitting, and him staring into space—but the image of the thing we dared not name was there in the air between us, astute and cold. Now and then, he would again raise his head and take another deep breath, doubtless trying to ascertain whether the bad smell was still there or had vanished on the breeze. It had not, of course, and while I continued busily knitting, I could easily feel, with no effort at all, that the smell was growing stronger or, rather, establishing itself and filling all the empty spaces in the house. It wasn't a passing wave, a mere odor wafted in by the wind from some heap of excrement or a dead animal lying somewhere. Demétrio had, by then, realized what it was.

"You had better go and see," he said, fidgeting in his chair.

"Why?"

"To find out what's happening."

I stopped my work, put down my knitting, stood up and, without another word, went to the patient's room. As I approached, the smell grew more persistent, revealing the laboratory where it was being processed. And I should say right away that it was not the continuous, insinuating bad smell that, later, pursued us day after day, impregnating everything—clothes, cups, furniture and utensils—with its saccharin odor of death. Just then, as I approached the room, I still found it bearable, thinking it merely a bad smell, even though it turned my stomach, but it would not be long before I could only walk about the house with a handkerchief pressed to my nose. I had seen other people die, sadly, abruptly and with no smell at all—my own mother, for example, who had died of a stroke—but this was the first time I had seen someone decomposing as if under the influence of some violent internal combustion.

I went into the room and, in the darkness, saw Betty straightening the pillows. She seemed untroubled by that atmosphere saturated with strange odors. As soon as she saw me, she put one finger to her lips.

"She's sleeping," she whispered.

We huddled in a corner and, indicating the handkerchief I had now produced, I asked if she knew where the smell was coming from. She seemed troubled and said:

"I don't know, but something's definitely not right, and she knows it."

"Has she said anything?" I asked, with a hint of prurient curiosity.

She glanced over at the bed, then drew me farther away, as if fearing her patient might overhear her indiscretion.

"Poor lady!" she murmured. "When I was changing the bedding, she said: 'Betty, I think I'm rotting away inside.' I told her the smell was to do with the extremely hot weather. She shook her head and said: 'No, it isn't. If you wouldn't mind, would you do me a favor?'

And when I asked her what that favor was, she said: 'Could you rub my body with eau de cologne?'"

"And did you?"

Betty looked at me, shocked:

"Of course I did. And if you saw the state of her back . . ."

"What do you mean?"

"It's like one big sore."

"But how come," I said, surprised at what she was telling me, "when there's been no sign of anything like that."

Betty pointed to a pile of sheets thrown down in one corner:

"You see those?"

"What are they?"

"Sheets covered in blood."

We stood in silence, listening to the labored breathing coming from the bed. Perhaps hoping to take advantage of my being there, Betty bent down to pick up the sheets. I was filled with a sudden horror of being left alone with that decomposing presence.

"No, let me do that, Betty. It's best if you stay here."

And I took the bundle from her. The smell it gave off was far more intense, and it was easy to see now what it was: bad blood mixed with some other fetid, greenish substance. I again pressed my handkerchief to my nose and left the room, the bundle under my arm. In the hallway I met Demétrio, who, too impatient to wait for me in the drawing room, was pacing up and down in the hallway. As soon as I saw him, I feared I would have to tell him what was happening, but one glance at the sheets was all it took, and I could see that he had understood everything.

I went out into the backyard, in order to put the dirty sheets in the laundry basin. In the dusk now filling the air, I looked back at the Chácara, which, with all the windows open and the lights on, stood out with unusual clarity. We weren't used to seeing it like that. Anyone observing it from a distance would have found its invaded, violated appearance strange. And yet, there was in the metamorphosis it was undergoing, from the roof down to its most secret underpinnings, a silence, a waiting, which gave it a dignified humanity. Looking at it now, it was impossible not to see how important that moment was: as if the house were waiting with rapt attention for the storm to pass. Up above, in the blue air, I could hear the roar of an invisible current, the wind, and the house was also doubtless listening to that gale with its stone ears, stone nerves, stone soul, silent and evocative, like a musical instrument lying dying in the vast countryside. I myself, why deny it, felt I was being transformed too, as if my very essence were dissolving, decomposing, becoming part of the sickly air impregnating everything, and creating for me, in the void, an entirely new situation. Yes, whatever I did, however I struggled and argued with the facts, the truth is, I had not expected her to die, and certainly not like that. To me, this was not a normal end or a solution to many painful, problematic things—this was not a natural fading-away, like a thing disappearing, all sharp edges smoothed away, all dissonances vanished, with everything finally being thrown into the bottomless pit of time—no, this was a sudden, senseless punishment, an act of aggression, a sign of a righteous god's will or wrath. And yet, however strange I found the effect of that death, I had to acknowledge the existence of a divine Providence watching over all of us, and no one could tell me otherwise, not even Father Justino. The proof was that pile of bloodied sheets, and I had no doubt that they bore solemn witness to the fact that my prayers had been answered. As I was thinking this, I clutched the bundle to me, like someone pressing to her heart a token of friendship. What did I care if the sheets stank, what did I care if they were drenched in sweat and in her dying breath: burying my nose in them, it was as if I were smelling a bunch of fresh roses, for what that blood-stained ball exuded was not revenge, but an exciting, carnal odor of blood and spring. I even waltzed around with them; above me, invisible chords were playing a victory song, and I spun around as if I were drunk, and with me spun the landscape in that first and only dance in which I allowed the joy of my entire being to overflow. Anyone seeing me would think I had gone mad, and they would not have been far wrong, because such solitary joy is like a glass of champagne knocked back in one: it immediately turns the head and produces an effervescence very similar to that experienced by those who have lost their wits. I don't know how long I danced around like that in the dark, embracing that ghost composed of crumpled sheets; I know only that I turned and turned, feeling in my nostrils a strong scent of violets and crushed heliotropes, like the scent given off by a drawer in which old ball gowns have been stored away. Finally, panting and sweating, I sat down next to the laundry basin. The bundle fell from my arms. For a while, I sat, motionless, my face resting on the cold concrete base. God does exist, I kept repeating to myself, an unbending God capable of unleashing his thunderbolt even on his favorite creations—even on those favorites, who, like Nina, had infringed the strict laws to which all human beings must submit. Now I could live in peace, because I was sure God had heard me and was not indifferent to my poor prayers. My feeling of amazement had nothing to do with the ferocity of the decree handed down, and knowing that brought me a kind of barren serenity, lacking in subtlety and in joy too. What I was enjoying as I finished my dance was the consolation of a mission completed.

(Yes, what else can I say except that here I end? Now that the cellar door has been opened, the key to which I had so jealously guarded, now that the room has been despoiled, the room where I watched him, Alberto, dying, his chest soaked in blood, I have nothing more to hide or to do. No jealousy drives me on, no other feeling, either positive or negative. I see the house shaking, the foundations trembling, the Meneses themselves collapsing—but, as I said, none of that matters. My life, what I consider to be my portion in life, ends here. At least it would, if that depended solely on my will. I feel I have been assimilated into this landscape like some trivial detail. One day, when the dead mortar allows the first weed to sprout among the ruins, I will set off in search of a pile of earth topped with a few dried flowers. There will be no wall around it, no fence, nothing but a jequitibá tree growing not far off, and covering with its dark leaves one third of that cemetery, where the cattle and the horses graze freely. I will say to myself: "That is where she lies resting, or, who knows, mulling over her past crimes." Above, vast and dull, will hang a heavy autumn sky. I will sit down in the shade of the jequitibá and write her name in the earth with a twig. For a moment, it will be the only part of her to survive oblivion. Then a sudden wind will appear and erase her name, one of those winds that sometimes, out of nowhere, sweeps across the fields, and then all that will be left is the pile of earth, until another wind scatters that, mixing it up with more earth, and then the cemetery itself will disappear, and the crosses too, and the place will return to being open countryside, where other cattle will graze, occasionally finding among the lush grass a fragment of wood that still bears a date or part of a name worn away by the elements. Then, no one will remember that she ever existed. Only I, if I'm still alive, of course, and, in the shade of another jequitibá tree, young and sprouting fresh, new leaves, only I will trample the grass, looking for the place where she was buried, pushing my way through the dense undergrowth, avoiding any pools of water, until I stop at a spot where, unexpectedly, a red flower has just opened—a cactus flower—entirely alone and covered in spines. I will say "it was here" and, for a long time, will gaze up at the sky until evening falls and I hear, like a warning, the sound of cowbells tinkling as the cattle make their way back to the corral.)

Troubled by these contradictory thoughts, I left the laundry basin and walked slowly back to the house.

46.
Valdo's Second Statement (ii)

On my return, I found the atmosphere unchanged. It was clear at once that the patient was still very ill, and every expressive, silent face bore the same look of expectation. This time, however, there was one difference: I was accompanied by a doctor, a young man from the city unaccustomed to our country ways, but whose evident good will had immediately endeared him to me. He examined everything in the house with curious eyes, in which there was, perhaps, just a hint of mischief—how strange we Meneses must have seemed to him, concealing, as we did, beneath a thin veneer of liberality all the difficulties and complexes of a once wealthy family relegated to this provincial backwater. I was even more keenly aware of this when we were met by Ana, who was her usual austere, silent self and wearing her usual drab clothes. She was carrying a folded handkerchief in her hand, which, from time to time, she discreetly pressed to her nose.

"Excuse me," she said wearily. "The smell gives me a headache."

I introduced her to the doctor, and she held out her hand, but in such a stiff, ceremonious manner that it was more as if she were bestowing a distant blessing than greeting a guest.

"What is it, Ana?" I asked.

"Oh," she said, "it's nothing." But then, as if contradicting this statement, she indicated the bedroom door.

I left her to take care of the recent arrival's suitcase and proposed that the doctor should go in and see the patient at once. "As you are no doubt aware, we have already lost a great deal of time." The doctor suggested that it was perhaps inadvisable to enter the room unannounced, and that he would rather hear about the patient's current state from someone who had been with her over the last few days. As it happened, Betty was the one to provide this information, for just as we reached the hallway, she came out of the room carrying a cup.

"Ah, Betty, I'm so glad you're here," I said, drawing her to one side and asking her to tell the doctor what had happened during my absence.

"I'm afraid the news isn't good," she said, shaking her head. "Dona Nina has been very ill indeed."

And while she spoke to the doctor, I took a few steps back so as not to hear all the depressing details. (I can still remember the two of them standing there: she, small and prim in her clean, modest clothes; he, the city doctor, tall, well-dressed, bending down slightly, to hear what she said. A few steps behind them was the closed door of the bedroom where Nina lay. How difficult it was for me not to hope, despite everything: I had chosen a young doctor, very different from the one we were accustomed to, with different methods and experiences—so how could I not feel confident that he might coax from the immutable laws of nature one tiny spark to light our way into the future? I hoped and I believed, and as time went on, instead of despairing, I hoped and believed still more.) I left them to it, convinced that no one could do a better job than Betty. (An image, an old one, surfaced in my mind and, for a few moments it occupied my thoughts entirely, like a clear jet of water: Betty, the young girl whom my mother had employed to teach English to my brother Timóteo, who was then only a small boy. The young foreign woman, scarcely more than a girl, suitcase in hand and umbrella under her arm, replying haltingly to the questions put to her. From then on, she had become an invaluable member of the family. Leaving her with the doctor, I felt almost reassured, for I knew that everything would be that much safer if it lay in her good hands.)

Slowly, for the first time since arriving back, and as my heavy burden of worries started to lift, I began to accustom myself once more to all the familiar objects, feeling my way as cautiously and contentedly as a blind man around a world where I had lived so comfortably and from which dark forces had tried to snatch me. Ah, yes, the provinces—I could never get used to living anywhere else. It was then, in the darkness of the drawing room, that I caught sight of the still, silent figure of Father Justino. I couldn't tell if he was awake or asleep, but he had a book open on his knees and a rosary clasped in his hands. Asleep, probably. Beside him, leaning on a chair, stood the sacristan, a young lad from the town, for whom the gravity of the moment had not yet succeeded in extinguishing the curious, playful gleam in his eye.

"How are you, Father Justino?"

He awoke with a start:

"Ah, it's you, Senhor Valdo! I am as God wills it, my child," he said.

He then explained that he had come on his own initiative, after hearing about the illness and thinking that, if the illness did prove fatal, it would simply not be right to allow someone to leave this life without God's presence. I agreed, thinking to myself that I had never seen Nina take the slightest interest in anything to do with the Church. Did God exist for her? Were there times when she would invoke His name? I was appalled by the idea that we can spend a whole lifetime at someone's side without ever asking the many important, indeed fundamental, things we ought to ask one another. When I remained silent, Father Justino launched into a series of explanations, asserting that the last rites, far from being a sacrament of death as most people supposed, offered hope, an appeal, as it were, to life.

As he spoke—and that word "hope" rang out like the deep, solemn tolling of a bell—I became aware of a smell creeping surreptitiously and stealthily toward me, dense, invisible, a smell I hadn't noticed before and which betrayed the presence in the house not of hope, but of a stark testimony to human frailty and human limitations. The smell was so strong that it made me dizzy and I turned toward the hallway.

"Good God," I said, "what on earth is that awful smell?"

"Ah," said the priest, and his voice was extraordinarily gentle, "can you smell it, too?" Then he added in a tone of excruciatingly Christian resignation: "It's her."

"Nina?" I again glanced toward the hallway in disbelief.

You could almost see the smell wafting in waves out of the bedroom and through the drawing room, onto the verandah and out into the night, where it would be lost in the open air, a smell that seemed to leave the walls around us moist and sticky, the sweet, rancid, sweaty smell of the dying. At that moment, I must confess that the tiny thread of hope I had been clinging to vanished, and I felt afraid; this was not a fear of what might happen, nor of what I might see, but a piercing, urgent fear welling up out of the dark regions wherein lie the primordial fears of all men. Father Justino, who had no doubt watched the change coming over me, placed one hand on my shoulder:

"Isn't it time you went to see how she is?"

"The doctor's in there," I replied somewhat evasively.

"Even so . . ." and I caught a slightly scolding tone in his voice.

I agreed, but if truth be told I had absolutely no desire to cross the threshold into the room that was the source of that stench. Then, as if by some prearranged signal, so timely was her appearance, Ana walked into the drawing room, and above the handkerchief with which she was rather exaggeratedly covering almost half her face, I could see two hard, piercing eyes that, far from expressing concern or dismay, showed only a cold, calculating awareness of what was unfolding around her. She made me feel ashamed of my initial hesitancy and I touched Father Justino's arm as if doing penance for that minor error. He too must have realized what was going on, for on seeing Ana, he bowed his head as if not wishing to bother her with his gaze. We made our way to the bedroom, the priest a few steps behind me, and behind him the sacristan. As I was opening the door, I glanced back and saw Ana in the drawing room, and as she lowered the hand holding the handkerchief to her mouth, she seemed uncertain whether or not she should turn and follow us into the bedroom. In the end, she joined us as we were about to go in. "Probably better that way," I thought.

When the door opened, the warm stench filling the room made us almost stagger back, but this time it was not simply a wave rolling over our heads, but an element in itself, something real and tangible, into which we plunged with no hope of rescue. This first impression paralyzed me, and from where I stood, unable to move, I looked over at the bed—and there she was, Nina, entirely wrapped in a sheet. So close, and yet no movement or sound betrayed her presence: she had lapsed into one of those periods of repose that so often precede a major crisis. Besides Betty and the doctor—the only ones not holding a handkerchief to their faces—two or three other people stood around the bed: a neighbor whom I did not immediately recognize (I later found out it was Donana de Lara), a maid, and a fourth person half hidden behind the curtain and therefore impossible to identify. Their eyes were all fixed on me, waiting for me to step forward. But the smell curled about me in successive waves, encircling me tighter and tighter, breaking again and again against the walls, clouding my vision, turning my stomach, and threatening to suffocate me, while I stood there incapable of movement. And there I would have stayed, inert, arms hanging limply by my side, if Betty had not beckoned me over to help her. When I reached the foot of the bed, I saw the doctor waiting for me, grim-faced.

"There's nothing to be done," he said.

And, responding to the question he saw forming in my eyes:

"This woman is dying."

That last word reverberated through the air and hung there for a moment, frozen and pure, as if it were a concept beyond our understanding, before sweeping brutally into the consciousness of all those present. So it was too late; there was nothing to be done. The thing we had not feared, because we judged it to be impossible, was happening right there in all its violent reality. My vision grew blurred, and I steadied myself on the edge of the bed.

"Is it possible, doctor?" I stammered.

"You must fetch the priest," he said bluntly.

Father Justino, who, up until then, had been standing behind me, stepped resolutely forward. The sacristan followed, clutching the holy vessels. Abandoning her post by the door, Ana immediately went over to the chest of drawers and began lighting a candle. During the long pause that followed, none of the others dared move. Ana handed the sacristan a plate on which there were a few balls of cotton wool and took from him the flask of holy oils, which she placed at the foot of the cross. Then, as if by magic, the bloodless figure of Christ, standing on the chest of drawers with a small vase of aromatic herbs at his feet, suddenly glowed and glittered. In the shadows, the priest put on his purple surplice and stole. At the same time, Ana signaled to the maid to go and fetch a towel and a bowl of water so that the priest could wash his hands afterward. And so, dressed entirely in purple, he held up the silver bowl in which he dipped his fingers, and began to recite the *Asperges me*. Then, turning to face the sacristan, he handed him the first vessel containing the holy water, and took the second, which contained the holy oils. I noticed that the others were now kneeling and I did the same, barely taking in the fact that the last rites were being performed. Donana de Lara leaned over the bed and uncovered the dying woman's feet, so white and slender they could have been the feet of a child. "Ah, Nina," I thought to myself, "we could have been so happy, if only I had been able to understand you better." I heard a muffled sob in the shadows: the priest, touching the eyes of the dying woman, was beginning to say the *Confiteor* in a slow, measured voice. I felt as if something inside me had been torn asunder, and I again whispered: "Nina!", but not even her name, once so familiar, could achieve the miracle of reducing the distance between us and her. Kneeling, a folded newspaper in her hand, Betty was trying to drive away a particularly persistent fly. Then a dull, rhythmic sound began to echo around the room: it was the patient's breathing, clearly audible in her final moments, growing slowly louder and drowning out all other noises until it became a single, harsh vibration, like the voice itself of the departing moment. I could no longer smell the stench; I could no longer feel anything—everything was meaningless. I stood up and went toward the door. From there I turned and glanced back at the group, so that, later on, the scene would not be totally erased from my memory. For the last time, I watched Father Justino leaning over and touching the soles of her poor abandoned feet with his oiled fingers. Then my eyes filled with tears, and I escaped out into the hallway.

47.
Ana's Last Confession (ii)

In the days that followed, I lost all interest in the room and in everything that was happening there, and concentrated instead on something equally unexpected, and which I found deeply fascinating, namely, my husband's response. Valdo had returned from Rio and brought with him a doctor, who, after the briefest of examinations, declared himself unable to do anything: Nina was dying. Despite this, he said that he would stay until the end, because we might still need help—"one can never predict how long a patient will last"—and perhaps also to justify such a long journey. Father Justino, who had other people to attend to, withdrew, having administered the last rites. A slight calm descended on the house.

With Betty's help, I installed the doctor in one of the rooms at the back, between the kitchen and Timóteo's room. Betty seemed to enjoy the novelty—he was probably the first guest she had seen at the Chácara—for she went out into the garden, picked a bunch of pinks and placed them in a jar on the new arrival's bedside table. To continue my story, I should say that the doctor was no trouble at all; he barely ever came into the drawing room, apart from at mealtimes. And with the exception of a couple of brief local walks "to get to know the Minas landscape," he spent all his time with his patient. He was clearly genuinely touched by her plight, and as he himself put it: "Dying is a very painful business and we should do all we can to alleviate her pain." And often, during those long hours of waiting, from the afternoon to the night, and from the night into the small hours, my husband and I spent more time together than we had throughout our entire married life. I don't know who was to blame for our estrangement, nor do I care; we probably both partook of the shared guilt that afflicts all unhappy couples, each of us insisting that the other was to blame. However, at that moment, I was interested only in him and not in what had gone wrong with our ill-fated marriage. (While I was thinking these thoughts, and like an image born out of two dots suddenly connecting—our unfortunate marriage and Nina's death agony—an old memory suddenly surfaced, so old I could not describe it exactly or pinpoint details: it was simply a memory, and as vague as memories often are. Nina was standing by Demétrio's desk, holding a letter opener in her hand. He was on the other side of the desk, sweating profusely. When I opened the door, I felt as if I had burst in on something; there was a violence, a tremor in the air, an uncertainty, as if he had just that moment stood up. What had they been talking about? Why that charged atmosphere? I looked from one to the other, but they said nothing. And I never did know what had happened. As I say, this was in the early days, and while I was completely obsessed with Nina, she did not even deign to glance at me as she left the room. Now, years later, sitting beside my husband, that image kept returning to me, because I could see something of that same confusion on his face, the same anguished, helpless air I had noticed on the day when I found them together. And however hard I tried, the memory kept coming back, it would disappear for a while, then suddenly return, speaking to me of a relationship of which I knew nothing, an enigma I could not solve, but which lingered obstinately in my mind.)

Seeing him so agitated, he who was always so calm, seeing him so different from his usual self, so strange, I could not help but study him and silently come up with the most bizarre conjectures. Perhaps "agitated" is not quite the right word; no, that typical, cold, reserved Meneses male was simply allowing me a glimpse of what was going on in his heart. As with most people, it was no longer hard to read his face, because he had lowered his defenses and did not even attempt to simulate a different emotion. He was struggling against the power of a sudden, brutal experience. When I say he seemed strange, let me give an example. I had never known him take any interest in domestic matters or in what the servants were up to; I had never even seen him go into the kitchen, an area of responsibility he left entirely to Betty. At most, and almost in secret, he would occasionally send for her to ask about or issue orders regarding his brother Timóteo. Otherwise, he remained completely aloof. Now, however, the situation had changed; because of all the comings and goings, the smell of medicines and the many other things that are part and parcel of dealing with a serious illness, the windows in the house were now left wide open, and this enraged Demétrio, who demanded that the windows be closed, saying that there was absolutely no reason to expose the Chácara to prying eyes.

"It's necessary, Demétrio," I said. "Aren't you aware of how hot it is?"

"It's always hot," he said, "but we've never gone to such extremes before."

"But there wasn't anyone ill in the house then," I protested.

"Exactly. You want to turn the place into some kind of hostelry."

You might think he was prompted by an excess of modesty at the prospect of being exposed to the world's inevitable curiosity, but he was equally intransigent about other matters too. For example, once or twice, he himself went to the main gate to see if it had been left open.

"There's no need for that," he said, "we're not holding a party."

I explained that there was no point in locking the gate, because there were always people coming in and out, and that we could not forbid the neighbors from visiting. He shrugged dismissively:

"Busybodies more like"—and standing on the verandah, with an energy he had never shown before, he threatened to sack the first servant who forgot to lock the gate. "I don't want any visitors. Close all the gates and the windows and tell any visitors there's no reason for them to come sniffing around." He came back in, then, an angry gleam in his eye. However, it wasn't only the windows and the gate he was worried about; his vigilance extended to other parts of the house too, even the kitchen, a place where he normally never set foot, alleging now that the service was not what it used to be, that the servants were neglecting their duties and that there was no reason why normal routine should be disrupted. He cross-examined the servants, opened cupboards, even went so far as to rummage about in the trash cans, saying that the staff were being careless and throwing away valuable items. I couldn't understand why he was so upset, and so I kept a careful watch on him, while he, his forehead dripping with sweat, said to me: "Do you see? If I let them, they'd turn this place into a hospital."

When everything had been closed, the gate securely padlocked, and there were no further checks to be made, all his energy drained away, and, mopping his brow, he looked at me so intensely, so pathetically, as if asking me for help. I understood this, and I also understood that he found my silence particularly irritating, but he could do nothing to vent his fury since he had no legitimate complaint to make against me. At such moments, I clearly saw his lack of humanity. He did not, as other people did, have the possibility of confessing or opening up to someone else about all the accumulated feelings inside him; and since he did not know how to free himself from them, he was doomed to wander restlessly about, waiting for someone to bring him a word of peace or to assuage his torment with a kind or forgiving gesture. And I did nothing, absolutely nothing, because I, too, had been lost for a very long time, but no one had come to my aid or shown one iota of interest in or pity for my sufferings. I merely observed him, and there was no compassion in that, no impulse to console—I watched him in an almost jeering fashion, imagining what secret infernos he would be inhabiting, without the courage to reveal himself, unable to confide in anyone, as hard and cold as a stone ghost in whose existence no one believes.

"Bring me some coffee," he said, sitting down on the sofa.

He sat glumly for a few minutes, staring at his feet. I could almost hear his imprisoned blood roaring inside him.

I brought him his coffee, but he pushed me angrily away:

"No, no, I don't want coffee. Coffee makes me ill."

I stood waiting, and he again looked at me in that pleading way, as a child might do at someone about to punish him.

Just once, hearing a noise, he turned to me and I could see that his heart was almost in his mouth.

"Do you think . . . ?"

I turned to face him, utterly calm:

"What?"

"It's her, Ana."

To disguise my smile, I turned toward the hallway:

"No, it's not the end yet. It will take a while, I should think; after all, she's still young and strong."

He stood up and began once more to patrol the house. His shoes creaked, and that grating noise was all that could be heard. Since everything was closed, and the night outside brought with it a still more oppressive heat, he undid his collar, saying he was suffocating, and wiped the sweat from his brow with his hand.

"It smells terrible in here, Ana. We'd better open the windows."

He flung them open so nervously and impatiently that they slammed against the wall; then he leaned out and took desperate gulps of the warm, still air in the garden. Voices could be heard in the distance, the gate squeaked open, and he screwed up his eyes trying to make out who was coming down the main avenue.

"I can see someone carrying something on their head," he said, turning to me, his eyes bright and staring.

"You're imagining things . . ." I began, lacking the courage to complete my thought.

"It's the coffin, Ana, it must be," and he again stared into the shadows so eagerly that I felt almost nauseated and looked away, wanting to avoid his eyes.

"Ah," he said after a moment, "it's not the coffin, it's a washerwoman with a bundle of washing on her head. Is today laundry day?"

And abruptly abandoning his lookout post, he added:

"They've no business coming here, it's pure nosiness."

He resumed his pacing, his shoes creaking, now louder, now more softly, a dull, rhythmic sound. No noises came from within, the hallway lay in darkness, and the whole house remained immersed in its restorative slumbers. Succumbing to weariness, I lay down on the sofa. He came over, grabbed my arm, and shook me:

"How can you sleep at a time like this?"

Then, hearing dogs barking outside, he left me and ran out onto the verandah. I got up and saw lights flickering in the dark. Leaning on the balustrade, he was peering into the garden.

"Anastácia?" he called.

Receiving no reply, he stayed where he was, his breathing irregular, his eyes fixed on those errant shapes. They must have been servants or local people who insisted on coming in, despite the orders given to the man on the gate.

"They never give up, do they?" he said.

He turned and now his expression was one of utter exhaustion. He walked slowly back into the house and slumped down on the sofa. He gave off a sense of mute despair, his arms hanging limply, head bowed, feet together. I looked at him, and I say again, I felt no pity; coming from the far end of the hallway, I thought I could hear the beating of that other heart still stubbornly clinging to life, and so powerful was that impression that its feeble pulse sounded louder than the ticking of the clock, shrill and imperious above our heads, not like a farewell but an order, calling for resistance and peace.

48.
André's Diary [x]

When I heard Ana's words, announcing that Nina had died, I did not believe her, and I ran to the room from which I had been absent for several hours. I could see that Nina had just received the last rites, because Betty was removing the various things that had been used for the ceremony, and every face bore the peaceful expression that comes with a duty fulfilled, consoled by the certainty that the dying woman would not leave for the next world unaided. After all the agitation around her bed—there were so many people there, some sorting out medicines, others trying to maintain order, and others simply minor players in that important chapter now reaching its conclusion—as I say, after all that agitation there was, at last, a truce. Father Justino asked permission to resume his other duties, and the various visitors went back to their houses. Ana returned to her husband's side, and even Betty, who had proved tireless during those last few days, seemed to succumb to a momentary weariness and asked me to keep watch at the bedside. I agreed—for that was precisely what I wanted—and as soon as the door closed and I was alone in the room, and even though I was standing some way from the bed, I had to press my hands to my chest to still my furiously beating heart. So she was going to leave, and I could do nothing about it, this was our farewell, our final farewell. This was the last time we would be together, the last chance for me to say anything to her and for her still to hear me with human ears, still sensitive to the language of the living, and to respond with her equally human lips. This would be the last time, on this side of the grave, when we might yet be able to understand each other, and when the images and values I knew would still be images and values she might recognize. And whatever happened afterward, when her lips and ears could no longer speak or hear, would be the result of what happened in that moment, of what we had said and sworn, like a final act of defiance in the face of silence and the void.

I went over to the bed and knelt down beside it. I saw that she was still breathing, not in the hoarse, distressing way she had been breathing over the last few days, but almost serenely, as if the sacrament really had brought her relief. Then I took her pulse and felt it beating, rather irregularly, but beating nonetheless, and that was enough to assure me that she was still there. Finally, I carefully tried to prize open her eyelids, so that she could, if possible, see me, or so that I could at least see her, even if she could not see me. If my image could no longer penetrate the place where she now found herself, and I was, for her, merely a dull, meaningless thing, I wanted at least to be able to see my own image in those opaque pupils and feel myself floating on the surface of that world that had once been mine and which, now that it was lost, would bear me up as indifferently as a wave washing over a dead body. And I was thinking this even as I was trying to open her eyelids, which insisted on closing, while, meanwhile, everything inside me rebelled against being made an outcast, an exile, and I wanted her to see me, for my presence once more to illumine her inner world, which was, at that moment, heading into endless night, the desert where she would know nothing about me. I confess, that while I was thinking these painful thoughts, I began to cry; the tears ran silently down my cheeks, and I could not even say that they were real tears, because they were neither warm nor salty, but merely the result of the sadness filling me, of the conscious sadness that so pained me, and which, for some time, had been clinging to me like a weed to a ruined wall. I leaned over and placed my lips close to her ear and called softly—"Nina"—and I repeated her name once, twice, five times, now louder, now more softly, now gently, now more urgently, now more like a moan, in the hope that the sound would penetrate her unconscious state, like a signal from the outside world, and plant deep in her spirit a tiny spark, the merest shred of a desire to live. "Nina," I said, and, at the same time, with my face almost pressed to hers, I was struggling to open her eyes and wrench her from that lethargy. Seeing her still deep in torpor, I again took her pulse, which seemed even fainter, as if it were trying to slip away. Desperately, I began to rub her arm to warm her. I didn't want her to leave me just yet, but to stay by my side for a moment longer, just a moment. There was no doubt now that she was dying, for I could feel her pulse beating not at her wrist, but just above her elbow. Yes, she was dying, and, in a sudden panic, I felt I had to wake her somehow, to do whatever it took to snatch her from that force destroying her before my eyes, while I sat helplessly by. I looked around me for some idea, some inspiration. Time was running out. I decided to try one last thing. I pressed my lips wildly to her poor, shrunken arm and sucked at it, hoping to hold on to that faint pulse, and, in the process, leaving a dark bruise. I did the same again, and, for a few seconds, that fugitive pulse seemed to vibrate inside my mouth, to beat like the heart of an imprisoned bird. It vanished then, and I greedily went in search of that still throbbing, still captive pulse, which would then break away and rebelliously appear elsewhere. My lips moved up and down her arm, trying to return that pulse of life to its proper place. I don't know for how long I did this, her arm lying inert in my hands; I know only that at one point, looking up, I saw a strange thing: from her closed eyes, which I had tried in vain to open, flowed a kind of dense, thick broth, which ran down her cheeks in two large, dull drops. Dear God, she was crying too, and that meant she was alive and still present and could feel my warmth and hear my pleas. So great was the joy filling my heart that I feared I might not be able to get to my feet. I had won. I again put my lips to her ear and called—"Nina, Nina"—and this time, so crudely insistent was my passion, that she shuddered, literally shuddered, and it felt as if a miracle had occurred and she was beginning to come back. Her whole lifeless body now gave off a dull, sluggish aura, like a piece of music suddenly striking up again, strident this time and out of tune. "Nina" I called more loudly and, then, slowly, she opened her eyes and gazed at me, not in a way I recognized, but with a profound look of bewilderment, although no less eloquent for that, for I could feel she was still conscious.

"André," was the word that made her stiff lips move, "André," and the hand lying on mine attempted a pressure it could not manage, "André," and I lowered my head until it was almost resting on her shoulder, "André, why did you do that, why did you call me back?"

A single mighty sob rose to my lips:

"No, I can't let you . . ."

"André," she said, as if she would run out of breath with every word she uttered, "you have to let me die."

And as I bent over her, trying to fold her in my arms and wrench her from that state of apathy, she spoke these terrible words:

"I had already gone, why did you bring me back?"

And there was such suffering in her eyes, such detachment from all things human, that I cried out and leapt to my feet, trembling, and I said, as if someone else were speaking the words through my lips:

"Is this how you love me, you who so often said how you adored me? You lied then, and there can be no rest for you, because you were lying all the time, and never really loved me at all. No, you never loved me, Nina. Why did you do that, why did you mock me like that, why do you want to go away and leave me alone in the world? Take care, Nina, for if God exists, He will allow you no rest on the other side. You can't be allowed to get away with toying with other people's lives. And I will pray every night for Him to torment your soul and never allow you a moment's peace."

I was, as I say, standing up now, and my voice sounded so strange, so full of discordant, jarring sharps and flats, that I myself was terrified.

"André . . ." and that was the last thing she said. Very slowly her eyes closed, and seeing that she really was dying now, I knelt down beside her again. And at the precise moment when I was blindly clinging to the last hint of warmth in her body, an extraordinary thing happened: I thought I heard her say a name, just one—*Alberto*—and it was said in a quite different tone, as if spoken not in this world, but on the threshold perhaps of the next. (That tone of voice was completely different from any she had ever used when speaking to me, and I never forgot it, nor will it ever leave my memory or my thoughts: it wasn't she who spoke that man's name, or, rather, she wasn't the woman I had known, or perhaps she was, very much so, a real and secret person whom I had never known, but who had resurfaced in death, having been buried all those years, deep in her mystery, her despair, and her memory of a time when she, too, had trembled with love—a different love. I had finally caught her out, as one might an animal in a trap. Too weak to withstand invading death, which breaks down even the most securely locked of doors, she was surrendering and allowing that name to reemerge in her last moment of consciousness. Ah, I swear I was dying a kind of death too, and a deathly sweat was leaking out of every pore of my horror and indignation, because I was being forced to accept that my suspicions had been true, and I would never find a soothing balm for that wound, which would inevitably and eternally shape the wretched love consuming me.)

I took a step back, and then I clearly saw the dark shadow creeping over her body, beginning at her feet, moving up to her waist, burying her breasts and surrounding her face which, for a moment, stood out, solitary, cold, and pure, like a flower sculpted out of the air, and finally wrapping about her whole body, leaving her abandoned on the bed like a piece of debris washed up by the night. And I was alone.

It was then, after contemplating her body for a time without really comprehending its meaning, that I felt she really was beginning to die, because, like a fluid gradually draining away, her presence was beginning to remove itself from things, from objects, as if sucked up by a vast, invisible mouth. All her human warmth was flowing out of the objects she had touched when alive and which had retained, up until then, the unforgettable mark of her passing. As if under the influence of some drug, everywhere I looked I could see her presence leaving the furniture, the bed, the windows, the curtains, like slender threads, small, mournful streams, then bubbling up like a spring, solemn and mighty, curling about the curtains, joining forces with all the other waters and, finally, forming part of one great river made up of memories and experiences that would now flow out into the immense estuary of nothingness. (There was a moment when, half-mad, I tried to catch hold, first, of a shadow slipping across the wall—it dissolved silently before my eyes—then of a last surviving sign of life on the carpet—it died between my fingers—and lastly, a breeze that lifted the veil of the window—it became nothing but a piece of crumpled cloth—in short, everything that could have stayed as a reminder of her existence was leaving, flowing silently away, disappearing as if in obedience to a law from on High.)

Her spirit was finally abandoning that poor exterior, leaving it intact, albeit coarse and soulless, and meanwhile revealing, with brazen cruelty, that room, in all its icy, definitive horror, as a summation of what had been. I don't know if all deaths are like that, but now that the body on the bed had grown quite still, it felt to me as if a bell had stopped ringing and a final wave of sound was solemnly unfurling; and I sensed that somewhere else, perhaps not that far away, she was beginning to live, while in the air, made cold by her departure, the rest of that note lingered on, dissolving down to its very last vibration, although that, too, would soon disappear and all that would remain would be the air reshaping itself into the future—or into nothing.

49.
Waldo's Second Statement (iii)

Questions were now building up in my mind and, as if they bore the same hallmark, they all had the same focus and the same origin: her, and what she had been, what she had meant to me, who she really was. And, above all, her true personality, her genuine, unadorned self, the Nina who would emerge only at the most difficult of times. For I was now convinced that I had never really known her, or, rather, that those things in her that were most real had always escaped me. And this bothered me. It was like a painful point in my body that I could not get rid of, or even ease the discomfort. Yet another frustration to add to all the others that our life together had brought us. I felt almost angry, and was gripped again by the suppressed rage that had once been my most constant feeling in regard to her: I realized that, in her final moments, she had once again eluded me, leaving me alone with my endless questions. Yes, initially, I had loved her with all the fury and impetuosity of unbridled passion. I said nothing, kept a lid on my feelings, because that was what the situation required, but only I knew what I really felt in my heart of hearts, and what energy it took to contain those futile, seething emotions. Even later on, when the first flush of excitement had passed, I still loved her, but knowing that I had chosen the wrong woman and was wasting my time on someone who could never love me. I did not condemn her coldness, not least because you cannot condemn anyone for not loving you at all—and when I say not at all, I am perhaps exaggerating, tormented by what I could never have—but deep inside me, I could not help but nurse a certain sadness and imagine that, even if I had made a mistake, things could nevertheless have turned out very differently. I *had* made a mistake, and yet it was just one individual case, for I knew many men who were happy with the woman they had chosen as their wife. And yet despite this, despite this awareness of my own failure, something else still tormented me: a kind of longing or regret that I simply could not justify; in vain I groped my way along the meandering paths of my mind, unable to find the reasons for this pain: a remnant of love? the beginnings of pity? Who knows? In all violent tendencies there is always a hidden impulse of pity. I remembered when I first met her, what a difficult situation she was in, what with her ailing father—was that perhaps the source of everything I had felt afterward? Wiser men than me might perhaps smile at my conjectures, bearing in mind that she was an exceptionally beautiful young woman. But isn't beauty the thing that drives our more or less dormant virtues, and whose presence prompts feelings that so often end in wonderment or terror, in attraction or repulsion? I had always loved her; I loved her from the very first moment I saw her, and, right from the start, she had also aroused in me paternal feelings and a desire to protect her, but she was too headstrong, too violent, and my paternalistic feelings were completely out of place—but at least they never ceased to exist, always pointing the way, silent and disregarded, like a compass lost in the depths of my being. What I was mourning, then, was possibly not the love I had never received, but the defenseless person who had never made use of my better instincts. The truth is, she had never made any use of me at all, and had lived far outside my orbit, beyond the reach of any gesture of mine. But now it was clear to me: marooned by my own bitter resentment, I had never made an effort worthy of the name, and, standing there on the verandah, indifferent to everything going on around me, I began to sense that I had only one authentic feeling: guilt. Why? Where had it come from? Hadn't she been the one who had left me, run away, leaving behind her everything that was rightfully hers? Wasn't she the one . . . But then a loud voice cried out in my head: "No, she wasn't!" and for the first time in my life I understood that she had not been the one to blame. It was me, guilty of a crime I could not identify, of a neglect I could not see, of a lack of love perhaps, that was greater by far than what I believed love to be. This discovery was so overwhelming that I had to lean against a pillar, my heart pounding wildly. What had really happened? What was I guilty of? What unworthy act had I committed without realizing? An unexpected darkness surrounded me. I was lost; a bitter taste filled my mouth. Ah, what a mystery life is, and how dark and senseless the motives that shape our actions! It was at that very moment, with these thoughts passing through my mind, that I heard a voice behind me say:

"She's dead, Senhor Valdo."

I turned around: it was Betty. Her calm air contrasted sharply with what she had just said. But as I stepped forward to examine her more closely, since her words seemed to me so utterly extraordinary, I noticed that her eyes were strangely bright and her face, grown gaunt with watching and worrying, showed the strain of maintaining the reserve she must have felt was the only response compatible with her position.

"Betty," I cried, "is it possible? Is it really all over?"

She nodded. I stood there, unable to move, and for a moment, the air seemed to desert me. Even though this was hardly an unexpected ending, its sheer brutality hit me like a stinging blow to the face. Betty stood there waiting, not looking away. I summoned up all my strength, gently pushed her aside, and went into the house. The stillness I had observed earlier was already gone. Some lights had been turned on, and a few people were moving around. I was so dazed that

I couldn't tell who they were, or even what they were doing. I rushed toward the bedroom, opened the door and stopped: there was no one inside. No one at all, just a bedspread thrown on the floor and a few pillows piled up at the end of the bed. I couldn't imagine not seeing her in that place; I had grown so used to her being curled up in the darkness there. "Nina!" I called out softly, as if she could still hear me. But no voice, no answer came. I stepped forward, suddenly afraid I might be confronted by the mortal remains of the woman I had loved so much. No, there really was no one in the bed; the crumpled sheet pulled to one side marked the place where someone had, until recently, been lying. I bent down and saw a dark, damp stain almost in the shape of a human form. I touched it and it seemed to be still warm. How many minutes had it been since they removed the body? Or was it only seconds? Why such a hurry? Who gave the orders?

"Betty!" I called.

She came quickly. This time I saw at once that her eyes were red, and that she had been crying.

"Where is she? Who took her away?"

She pointed down the hallway:

"She's in the drawing room. Didn't you see them moving her?"

"No." And I thought to myself that it must have been at the exact moment when I had heard the news and bowed my head, overcome with emotion. "And who ordered . . .?"

I didn't finish the question.

"It was Senhor Demétrio," she replied.

There was no hint of criticism in her voice. Perhaps this was how it should be, and Demétrio, yet again, was right. I went to the drawing room and saw what I hadn't been able to see before, and which explained why I had noticed people walking up and down the hallway: the body, wrapped in a sheet, was lying on the dining table, which had been placed against the wall. A single candle burned at the head of the table—it was one of those cheap, white candles to be found at the back of a drawer somewhere in almost every household.

Some women from the neighborhood were kneeling near the body, saying the rosary in a low voice. As soon as they saw me, they respectfully withdrew. I rushed over. "Nina!" I cried and, oblivious to the people around me, I collapsed next to the body covered by the sheet, giving vent to my grief for the first time, tears streaming down my cheeks. Someone placed a hand on my shoulder: "Senhor Valdo!" I didn't recognize the voice, my face still buried in the sheet. As the pressure of the hand on my shoulder increased, I pressed my face closer to the body. And to my amazement, the sheet felt warm, as if beneath it there were still a living soul. I stood up and tried to touch the stiffening body beneath the folds of the sheet. Yes, she was still warm; it wasn't the mere reflection of warmth as it leaves the bodies of the recently departed, but the heat of someone still living, radiating softly through her skin. Astonished, I gazed at the face concealed by the sheet. I was sure I could detect a slight movement, like someone breathing almost imperceptibly, but nonetheless breathing. "No! No!" I cried, trying to convince myself that it was merely an illusion. But giving in to an irresistible impulse, I lifted the edge of the linen sheet. Her naked face emerged into the light like a cry suppressed almost before it was uttered, but I could have sworn she was alive, alive and breathing, even if it was only the faintest of stirrings, like the falling of a rose petal. (Today, when all that remains is the image of the person she was, I tend to think it really was an illusion, or perhaps one of those remnants of life between true existence and absolute death that doctors sometimes call "neutral ground," and of which we know nothing except that it is the gateway leading to a new path, whilst behind lies the old path, still visible in the fading light.) Her face was deathly pale and drawn, her nostrils strangely dilated and there was a greenish tinge to her hollow-cheeked, disease-wracked face. But I swear that there was still not the distance, the coolness, the hostility so typical of corpses. Something secret and difficult to grasp still lingered—the last fading shadow perhaps of human consciousness. I eagerly touched her again: she was still warm, still living. Oh, why hadn't they left her to grow cold in her own bed, and escape to her eternal life like someone drifting off into sleep? Why that pointless cruelty, that excess of fastidiousness in disposing of a human being who had not yet entirely succumbed to death? I turned and left her there, her face uncovered. Slowly, I went back out into the hallway. Betty stood staring at me. Her eyes coldly followed my every movement. I could no longer contain the cry that burst from my lips:

"Betty! How did it happen? Who told them to remove her from the bed?"

Her voice seemed to tremble with impatience:

"I've already told you, Senhor Valdo. It was Senhor Demétrio who gave the orders. I didn't want . . ."

She then explained how Demétrio had appeared in the bedroom, although without going over to the bed, but keeping a distance, slightly turned away, a handkerchief pressed to his nose. Even from that safe distance, he had declared: "She's dead." For the very first time since setting foot in that house, Betty had dared to disagree with him. "She might not be dead, Senhor Demétrio. She might not yet have breathed her last." He had become angry then, removing the handkerchief from his face: "Who gives the orders in this house?" Betty had pleaded with him, citing the days she had spent by the dying woman's side, her past experience of the dead and dying—she had already watched so many people depart this world—and even the Christian sentiments that must be upheld at times like these. He had replied abruptly that he was perfectly well aware of all that. "But Dona Nina is dead, completely dead. All the rest is sentimental women's nonsense." Along with Ana, Betty had gone over to the bed and touched the body again: still warm, the eyes barely closed, the lips half open. Might she not say something? Perhaps ask for something? She had turned to Ana, standing close behind her, and Ana had turned to look at her husband. He, by then standing at the door, had bellowed: "Ana!" and she, automatically, had pulled Betty away and leaned over the bed. She touched the body, but her fingers barely brushed the skin of Dona Nina's face. "She's dead, Betty. There's no doubt." And without a tremor, as if it were a task she performed every day, she began to pull back the sheet to reveal the rest of the body. The cloth seemed to stick to the skin on Nina's breast, as if it formed part of the wound. "No!" exclaimed Betty softly, grabbing Ana by the hand. Ana did not turn around and kept a firm grip on the sheet, although not daring to continue pulling. "What is it?" asked Demétrio from the doorway. Ana did not reply. Indeed, no reply was necessary, for his revulsion was more than apparent. But when he moved as if to come closer, she turned toward him and said calmly: "It's not that easy, Demétrio. The sheet is stuck to the body." Rather than moving forward, he took two steps back, and their eyes met in apparent agreement. Both women waited, Ana holding the sheet, Betty holding Ana's hand. At that moment, Betty said, she would have been capable of anything. Then Demétrio said in a more measured tone: "It won't be necessary to dress her. In cases like this, such formalities can be dispensed with. It'll be enough just to wrap the body in another sheet." And as if there were nothing more to be said or done, he left the room. Betty, seething with rage, tightened her grip on Ana's hand: "But the poor woman . . . Are you just going to wrap her in a sheet? And nothing else?" Ana had turned to her with a smug smile. "No, please, Dona Ana, not like that . . ." she had begged again, refusing to give in, but Ana shook her off and pulled the sheet up over the face of the woman they presumed was dead. "It's monstrous," wailed Betty. "What if the poor woman is still alive?" Ana did not even reply; she went over to the window and, lifting the catch, opened it wide. The light streamed violently in from outside: the body, covered by the white cloth, suddenly appeared even stranger, more forsaken. Leaning her forehead against the bedpost, Betty began to cry—she would never have the strength to help Ana with that grim task.

From the garden came the resinous smell of trees in blossom, and the stench of death began to dissipate. Ana had gone to the large drawer of the cupboard in the hallway (Betty could see her every movement from where she was, without even looking up), and took out a sheet. It was linen, one of the family's best, carefully laid between layers of fragrant lemongrass. She unfolded it in front of Betty: "See? It's one of the best we have." When Betty continued to cry, Dona Ana shook the sheet at her imperiously: "Betty!", and so the poor woman, tears streaming down her face, was obliged to help her in that funereal task. But she had refused to carry the body out, and they had had to seek the assistance of the black maids in the kitchen. They and Ana had taken hold of the body, still not yet stiff, and transported it down the hallway to the drawing room. Off the body went, not exactly a heavy load, but lugged unceremoniously along, sagging in the middle. With every jolt Betty thought she could hear the body protesting, imagining the poor woman with her eyes barely closed and two thick, waxen tears rolling down her cheeks. Then she had collapsed weeping onto the bed, and despite the terrible smell emanating from the sheets, she could still make out a trace of Nina's favorite perfume—the faint scent of violets that had always accompanied her and even now lingered on as a final testimony of her presence, like a last glimmer of light and youthfulness shining through her long-drawn-out death and decomposition.

Betty talked, and as she talked I began finally to understand, not all at once like a revelation, but little by little, relying on old events and memories, things that only now have become entirely clear to me. Yes, whether dead or alive, by then it scarcely mattered, since she was, in any event, more on the path of death than of life. Other problems were calling me, and they, too, were life-and-death problems in grave need of being resolved before her remains left that house forever. So, without giving any explanation and ignoring the people who approached me to talk, I made my way toward the door, walked through the drawing room and down the steps into the garden. From there I began to walk more quickly, almost running, until I reached the road that leads to Vila Velha.

50.
The Pharmacist's Fourth Report

I had been told that the leaves of certain medicinal plants (stonebreaker, for example) should only be ground down into a powder after they have been dried in the sun, since they would lose much of their power if exposed to the heat of an oven. Now, at the time, I was experimenting with various combinations of plants and had discovered several infusions that were giving good results for certain ailments. And so, taking advantage of a very hot day, I had laid out in the blazing sun, on a sheet of zinc, some branches of a fibrous herb that seemed to bring some relief to sufferers of rheumatism. However, as night fell, and with rumbles of thunder coming up the valley, I decided to bring in the leaves, fearing that a sudden downpour would ruin all my good work. I was just putting them in a jar when Pastor, my dog, burst into the yard and convinced me with his loud barking that something untoward was afoot. He kept sniffing restlessly at the fence and pawing the ground, as if there was some stranger on the other side. Not that this would have been unusual, since people were always coming to me not only as a pharmacist but also as doctor, and even as a counselor, for advice on illnesses that were more often than not mere figments of their imagination. There was, then, every likelihood that this was one of those occasions and, despite Pastor's barking, there was therefore no need for me to rush what I was doing and run out to see who it might be. I returned to my task, but then my wife appeared at the door:

"Aurélio! Senhor Valdo from the Chácara is here."

"Oh," I said, turning around. "Senhor Valdo?"

"Yes, and from the look of it, he's in a hurry."

"I'm on my way. Tell him I'm on my way." And without further ado I put the lid on the jar and handed the jar to my wife. I then tied Pastor to one of the fence posts and went inside. Senhor Valdo was waiting, pacing impatiently back and forth. I was shocked by his appearance: he was usually so impeccably dressed and never forgot his fine manners, but now he was in a visible state of disarray—no tie, crumpled jacket, his hair uncombed. But since I knew what was happening at the Chácara and that Dona Nina was not long for this world, I assumed that his lack of composure was a result of his distress, and that, quite possibly, he had come to fetch some urgent medication. As soon as he saw me, he stopped pacing and stood in front of me, leaning on the edge of the counter.

"Good evening, Senhor Aurélio."

"Good evening, Senhor Valdo. How are things up at the Chácara? Is Dona Nina feeling better?"

His voice rang out with unusual clarity:

"Dona Nina has just passed away."

"Oh!" And I was so taken aback that, at first, I could say nothing more. Then: "I am so very, very sorry, Senhor Valdo."

He did not answer me at first; his restless eyes, somewhat reddened (had he been crying?), kept glancing from shelf to shelf, even though I was quite certain that they saw nothing. Perhaps he was merely trying to gain time with this subterfuge, or perhaps he really was weighed down by the emotional pressure of what had happened, and was struggling to find the right words. After some time, just as the silence was becoming embarrassing, he let out a deep sigh and said:

"I have come here about an important matter." He drew his hand across his brow, as if trying to recall an elusive thought. "Or at least one that is important to me," he added. Then, as if he were having great difficulty in getting the words out, he abandoned his rigid position and began his pacing again, his forehead even more deeply furrowed. I wouldn't say that he had aged—for men of his kind are ageless—rather that he had fallen apart, literally fallen apart, and that the fine façade he had for so many years presented to the world now revealed the dilapidated structure behind it. He was no longer a Meneses, immune to any form of insult; he was a poor, terrified creature who, in his affliction, was totally unaware of where he was or who he was talking to.

"And what would that be?" I enquired, more out of a desire to help him than out of any real interest in the matter. (It must be some family problem—didn't they all run around and around after each other, like turkeys inside a chalk circle?)

Once again, and as if moved by some inner resolve, he stopped in front of me:

"Senhor Aurélio, will you tell me the truth? The whole truth?"

"Senhor Valdo!" I exclaimed, almost offended.

"Well," he said, "these are difficult times. And everything depends on what you tell me."

The subject was beginning to interest me. I said:

"You can rely on me. Besides, I have no reason to withhold any information."

"Excellent. That's excellent," he murmured.

I don't know from which dark region he was now trying to extract his questions, but still he hesitated. Hunched over the counter, I observed with some curiosity the changing expressions on that troubled face; it was as if clarity were doing battle with something fluid and imponderable, impotent against the shadow slowly overwhelming his features.

"Senhor Aurélio," he finally said, his voice resolute and resonant, "I heard my brother say, many years ago, that there was a transaction between you and him. Is that true?"

A transaction? The word sounded so ingenuous that I couldn't help but smile.

"There have always been transactions between me and the Meneses," I said.

"I'm not referring to any ordinary transaction," he said with an impatient gesture.

"To what then?"

The same shadow passed across his face, the same anxious look, and we stood there for a minute in silence, facing one another. I don't know why, but on seeing a sudden, tiny glint in his eyes, I sensed something in him that almost resembled a threat. What could he mean by that silence intentionally left hanging between my question and his answer? When he spoke his tone was different, quiet, veiled:

"I am referring to a revolver."

"Ah!"

This time, I tried to look him straight in the eye—so that's what it was. Oddly enough, even though the incident had occurred many years ago (when was it exactly? Images raced through my mind, of the Chácara, of Dona Nina, of Senhor Valdo himself), I had always assumed that one day, someone would come and call me to account for what had happened. "Call me to account" is perhaps an exaggeration, for I had played a purely passive role, but someone would inevitably want to investigate, to discover what had happened, how it had all begun. Because in that respect I had not the slightest doubt—something had indeed happened! And at its heart, fatally, lay the revolver. Yes, I remembered the revolver very clearly: wasn't that what had so influenced my subsequent relations with Senhor Demétrio? Since then, as if we had jointly committed an act whose weight and responsibility would unite us forever (the rapid glance whenever we met, the sidelong greeting, his careful avoidance of my pharmacy when once it had been the only place in Vila Velha he would honor with his presence), that gun had remained a secret point of reference between us. When I say he never again came to the pharmacy, that is not quite true. He did come, only once or twice, but he did come. But why should I have to be reminded of all that now? Who was forcing me to remember and why should I bother? Besides, it had all happened so many years ago! The matter was, in my view, entirely devoid of interest, but Senhor Valdo, as if sensing my desire not to answer his question, leaned persuasively over the counter.

"Don't you remember selling him a revolver?" he asked in a most insinuating tone.

I looked at him again and felt that I could lead him wherever I wanted.

"Yes, I remember," I replied. "It was a small revolver, a bluish color, and the grip was inlaid with mother-of-pearl."

This simple description seemed to make the object itself, until then hidden in the folds of our insinuations, become palpably present, gleaming in that indiscreet beam of light from the past.

"Exactly."

"But why . . ."

Senhor Valdo cut me short:

"It is enough, Senhor Aurélio, that you remember selling it."

"Why? Has there been an accident? If so . . ." and I made the gesture of someone denying all responsibility.

He understood that this path would lead us nowhere, and that I would remain, for as long as I wished, immured in silence. He stood up and said:

"No, don't worry. There hasn't been any accident."

Another brief pause. I kept my eyes trained on him and saw him tilt his head as if he were thinking about what he was going to say next. Then, looking up, he said calmly:

"I would like to know the circumstances in which that transaction took place. You must understand, it is very important to me that no detail be omitted."

(The conversation was beginning to interest me now: he was doing the asking and, all of a sudden, I was no longer the prey. What's more, if it was a favor he was seeking from me, then what might I, exercising proper caution of course, obtain in return?)

"I can assure you," I affirmed, "that I will hide nothing."

Senhor Valdo seemed relieved, more relaxed.

"I also want you to tell me what he said, his exact words. You do remember, don't you?" (He smiled as if wishing to instill me with confidence, but his smile was quite clearly false.) "I don't believe," he added, "that such matters are to be treated as secrets of the confessional. Especially given that they are mere insignificant facts."

"No, I certainly don't treat such matters as confidential. Quite the contrary."

And while I was saying this, I was thinking: Why should I say anything? I was under no obligation. What right does he have to demand this of me? I looked straight at him and told him rather abruptly to sit down. He obeyed without hesitation, and I noticed that his hands were trembling, and, as I absorbed this piece of information, I smiled.

"Would you like a glass of water?"

"No, thank you." And the ensuing silence was eloquent confirmation that, notwithstanding our brief exchange, he had come there with the sole purpose of hearing what I had to say.

I began to speak. Moths were fluttering around the low lamp lighting the pharmacy. From time to time, slowly and silently, Senhor Valdo would brush one of the annoying insects away from his face. I told him how Senhor Demétrio had turned up at the shop one day and had, after some toing and froing, told me that there was a marauding wolf he needed to kill. There was nothing out of the ordinary about this; the drought that was spreading throughout the region was opening the way up for the wild dogs that the half-castes call wolves and which, although they don't attack humans, certainly kill livestock. It was entirely possible that some stray animal was roaming around the Chácara. Senhor Valdo nodded. I then explained that, at the time, the shop had been in need of repair, which was the reason I proposed selling Senhor Demétrio the gun. I recounted our entire conversation, carefully recalling details that were already beginning to fade in my memory. When I finished—and my account was not a long one—I asked:

"Is that all you wanted to know, Senhor Valdo?"

I noted that during the time I had been speaking, he had kept his head bowed and that the veins in his temples were swollen and throbbing. On hearing my question, he seemed to come to:

"No, it's not all."

I waited for him to explain, and he simply asked:

"And you never saw him again?"

I hesitated: should I tell him what happened afterward, during the second visit? I sensed instinctively that therein lay the vital heart of the story, the part that might be of real interest to Senhor Valdo in the tale of the revolver. But, by a curious contrast, and one that would not be easy for me to explain, this was precisely the part of the story that I felt to be strictly off-limits, revealing it would, I felt, be an implicit betrayal of Senhor Demétrio. Or to put it even more obscurely, a betrayal of what bound us together, and whose only manifestation was the look he gave me whenever we met in the street. Senhor Valdo must have sensed my doubts, for he stood up and once again came and leaned on the counter. The light from the lamp lit up half his face and, as he leaned there, his eyes close to mine, I could still see in them that hint of a threat.

"And you never saw him again?" he repeated, still with his gaze fixed on mine. "I need to know all the details. And you can be quite sure, Senhor Aurélio, that I will reward you very generously."

These last words cast an entirely new light on the problem.

"Ah!" I murmured. "The Meneses seem to be very good at sensing when people are in need."

"How much?" and his voice brushed my cheek like a gentle breeze.

A moth flew past me, and with a folded piece of paper, I felled it with a single blow.

"Times are hard, Senhor Valdo. As you know, I have three sons . . ."

He grabbed me violently by the lapels:

"How much?"

I did not reply. I maintained a dignified silence, sometimes looking at his face, sometimes at the hand creasing my jacket, as if to say that I would not speak until he changed his attitude. His grip slackened:

"I'm sorry," he said. "My nerves are on edge, what with the situation at home."

And he let me go. It was the first time he had revealed his motives for coming to see me; for a moment, as I examined his face, I wondered whether or not I should take advantage of the opportunity to find out what he was after. I had long been curious about what went on within those four walls and about which so much had been said and for so long! However, his facial expression, which, for a second, had relaxed somewhat, darkened again: it was clear that I would get nothing more out of him on that subject. I sighed and, smoothing my jacket, said:

"You can give me whatever you think appropriate, Senhor Valdo. A poor man never refuses a generous offer."

"As I said," he declared vehemently, "you will have no cause to regret your decision."

With that guarantee, I began to talk:

"Senhor Demétrio did come back. It was more or less a year after I'd sold him the revolver. I noticed he was nervous and seemed to want to talk to me about something. I asked about the gun. 'Ah, the gun!' he grunted. There was clearly a certain disappointment in the way he spoke. 'Haven't you used it yet?' He shook his head: 'No, no.' 'Why?' He shrugged: 'Because the wolf never reappeared.' I said to him that, frankly, I hadn't heard of any wolves in the area. He smiled: 'Well, they're certainly out there.' I suggested ironically that perhaps the wolves could tell which houses had guns. As if he had missed the irony in my voice, he asked if I really believed that. I replied: 'Of course I do.' His eyes widened and he nodded. 'That's a good suggestion of yours—I should make sure the gun is clearly on display.' I wasn't entirely sure where the conversation was leading, but even so I asked if he'd heard the old saying: 'Opportunity makes the thief.' He laughed, calmer now: 'Indeed it does. There's always wisdom in those old sayings.' I did not respond, feeling that we had nothing more to say to each other."

"Is that all?" asked Senhor Valdo.

"Yes."

Placing one hand on my arm, he asked again:

"Try to remember. Perhaps you've forgotten something. So much time has passed since then."

I tried hard, but the truth is I couldn't remember anything else—one or two words, perhaps, a look, an inflexion, but what did that amount to, set against the overall impression he had given me? I said as much to Senhor Valdo, and he seemed particularly interested in that last remark:

"You said 'impression.' That's exactly what I want: what impression did he give you on that second visit?"

I tried to remember:

"He seemed very agitated. Or, rather, frightened. He was afraid of something, and perhaps didn't dare admit to himself that he was afraid."

A smile spread across Senhor Valdo's lips. And encouraged by this, other recollections came to mind:

"Yes, he was pacing from side to side, just like you were when you arrived here today. From time to time he would rub his hands, and there was a strange light in his eyes."

"Didn't he say anything?"

"Yes, he did. Just once, he turned to me and asked: 'Are you sure that revolver works?' 'I am,' I replied. And he said: 'Then the mouse is sure to fall into the trap.'"

"Nothing else?"

"Nothing else. I'm sure of it."

Senhor Valdo let out a deep sigh and again turned to face me, fixing me with a stare. Then he put his hand in his pocket, pulled out his wallet, took out a few notes and handed them to me:

"Believe me—you have been of enormous help."

I modestly bowed my head. Then, turning his back on me, he left without saying goodbye. I ran to the door:

"Senhor Valdo! Senhor Valdo!"

In the darkness, I saw him turn.

"My wife and I," I said, "will be going to the funeral tomorrow."

He mumbled something I could not quite make out, and carried on walking. For some time, his heavy footsteps continued to echo down the deserted street.

51.
Valdo's Statement (iv)

When I was still far off, I could see the lights of the Chácara through the thick foliage. The front of the house, glimpsed intermittently in the flickering light provided by the failing generator, took on a funereal appearance. When I reached the main gate, I saw that it lay wide open, as only used to happen on grand occasions, in the days when our mother was still alive and the neighbors would all come in to greet her as news reached them that she had gone out into the garden in her wheelchair. Small groups of people, probably locals who did not dare to enter the house, stood around here and there in the darkness. They greeted me, but I could not hear what they said, nor did I acknowledge their nods and waves, which, under the circumstances, seemed to me false and inappropriate. Without even looking at them, I reached the main avenue, where I could make out other equally unfamiliar silhouettes. They too spoke to me, but by now I had but one idea—that only *he* mattered—and so I did not reply and continued on my way. As the shadows fell, the garden gave off the sharp, sweet smell of fennel and magnolia that, in spite of myself, reminded me of happier times.

The Chácara was coming to meet me, revealing its new face: the open windows seemed to be keeping watch over the darkness, their motionless eyes gazing out over some other landscape, superimposed upon the landscape that had once been the old pastures surrounding the place where I was born. My heart began to pound—in the old days, when would they ever have permitted such an invasion, such a breach of the Chácara's laws, such a total capitulation to the curiosity of neighbors who had always been kept at bay by its inviolable walls? Ever since learning the truth (and now, finally, I knew the whole truth in all its startling detail), ever since the lie had burst upon me, I had no doubt that this invasion signified the end, the end of the Meneses. The neighbors were gathering, heralding the end, just as circling vultures in the fields reveal the presence of a dying steer.

As if obeying the same rhythm of destruction, something inside me was also crumbling. I listened in vain to voices seeking to restore a way of life that was irredeemably compromised (Demétrio, his way of looking and speaking, and, hovering over everything, the whole pernicious notion of *family* . . .), or whispering diktats issued by an authority that no longer existed. The sense of collapse was so strong, the vacuum within me so intense, that I even began to believe in some sort of imminent physical disaster—that the Chácara really might crumble into nothing and suck us all down into its vortex of dust.

But these were merely the thoughts of an instant. I ran up the steps and found myself outside the drawing room. There, as in the garden, I was greeted by an atmosphere that seemed more fiesta than funeral. Few, it seemed, were taking any notice of the poor dead woman, wrapped in a sheet and laid out on the table. She had become a non-person, the remote reason for the gathering, and the visitors, forgetting why they were there, were standing around in groups chatting, some of them more loudly than was appropriate. I think I even heard, coming from one end of the drawing room, some barely suppressed laughter. Indeed, the party would have been completely free of any reminder of death were it not for the insistent smell of decomposing matter that had been radiating out from the dying woman's bedroom for the last few days. People talked with an urgency artificially created by the forbidden, with the heat and haste you find in theater foyers or during pauses in an important speech, but then the conversation would suddenly be interrupted by a disconcerting silence, words would die unspoken, a fan would flap more vigorously. And people's eyes, drawn by the undeniable truth, would glance furtively over at the body, the source of the offending smell. But with each passing minute you could sense that the solitary white body was growing ever more disconnected from its surroundings. With extraordinary speed, it was ceasing to be a corpse laid out for viewing, and becoming merely an anonymous, indifferent object. As soon as I appeared, a woman detached herself from one of the groups and rushed toward me:

"Oh, Senhor Valdo, how terrible!" she said, her thick, coarse hand grasping my arm.

It was Donana de Lara. She was dressed entirely in purple, the front of her velvet dress embroidered with beads, and she smelled of incense and sacristies. I pushed her away almost roughly. Her eyes glittered with barely suppressed anger. She stared at me for a moment as if waiting for an explanation, then shrugged and moved away. Once again gathering an audience around her, I saw her, in the distance, angrily waving her fan in my direction, doubtless commenting on my rudeness, and letting one of her "those Meneses" fall from her pursed and withered lips. Farther along, beside the door leading to the hallway, I saw another group who were clearly engrossed in watching something happening outside the room. I went over and heard someone mutter:

"It's the infected clothes."

Pushing past the people blocking my way (they moved aside reluctantly, as if I were depriving them of a fascinating spectacle), I soon saw what was going on. In the hallway, amid a pile of clothes, stood Demétrio. Just Demétrio, and he seemed to have grown in the last few hours: his face, normally so tired-looking, exuded an inner energy, an unbending, righteous determination. Just behind him, watching, but clearly not joining in, was Ana. The first thing I noticed about her was that she seemed almost to be sleepwalking, present but not participating, like a piece of flotsam washed up on the beach. I spoke to Demétrio and sensed for the first time just how hard it would be for me to describe him: all his deepest, most secret characteristics had floated to the surface and, to those who knew him, he was exhibiting his true self with almost dazzling wantonness. Hair disheveled, eyes wild, he was dragging clothes and boxes out of the little storeroom and throwing them all into the middle of the hallway. Not just clothes but shoes as well, along with lace and other bits and bobs—a whole world of knick-knacks that brought back painful memories. Hurriedly, as if time were of the essence, he was hurling all these things onto the floor and kicking them carelessly to one side when they got in the way. I stared at him; he was moving with the nervous, abandoned haste of a maniac. Completely oblivious to the people watching from the drawing room—he, who had always been the most private of individuals—he was carrying out his task as if something vital depended upon it, like saving the world, for example. He interrupted his frenzy only once or twice to wipe the sweat off his glistening brow, but without looking up from the piles of clothes on the floor. At one such moment, however, he did look up and saw me watching, but so intent was he on what he was doing that he didn't even recognize me. He was about to stoop down again when I took a few steps toward him.

"Ah," he said and stood there, motionless among the clothes, still clutching some of them in his hands.

"I don't understand, Demétrio. What are you doing?"

Only then, hearing my words, did he come to his senses and survey the tremendous mess now filling the hallway. He slowly turned and stared at me, as if trying to ascertain exactly what I was thinking. But then, no doubt guessing my thoughts, his face seemed first to swell, then contract, then resume its normal, reserved expression.

"The clothes are infected," he said.

"What?"

He probably thought, as was his habit, that there was nothing more to say. His actions were sufficient proof that what he was doing was necessary and could not be challenged by anyone. Even so, seeing that I expected more of an explanation, he gestured impatiently and added:

"You are aware, aren't you,"—and it was impossible not to detect a hint of irony in his voice—"that Nina died of a contagious disease?"

"Perhaps," I replied.

He turned to Ana as if calling upon her testimony, her infallible testimony:

"Perhaps! That's what always happens, and it's always down to shameful negligence. Two or even three more people might fall prey to the same illness and all because of the criminal recklessness of a few."

"It isn't certain that cancer is contagious," I replied.

"But nor is it certain that it isn't."

No doubt considering that he had explained himself enough, he went back to pulling items out of the storeroom and throwing them on the floor. And just to clarify (for it's an important detail), although I did think it was far too early to be clearing out a dead woman's possessions, I would not have been so shocked had his actions merely reflected his customary zeal. But he wasn't merely removing the offending items; he was literally hauling them out with a violence and a revulsion that were a mortal offence to the person who had once owned them. I don't know why, but that zeal struck me as somehow intended as an insult aimed at Nina beyond the grave. His actions seemed to reach out toward that infinite space, where perhaps someone would understand the sheer extent of his malice. They weren't just garments, a dead person's belongings: they were living things still imbued with energy and meaning. This impression was made still stronger when, from one of the boxes, as if from some deep well, there appeared a green dress she had worn shortly after returning from Rio. We all froze at the sight of it: it was as if Nina herself were there, watching us trampling over her mortal remains. But Demétrio only hesitated for a moment before flinging it brutally onto the pile, as if the dress were a particular affront to his zealous state of mind. One of the straps of the dress got caught on his legs, and Demétrio, trying to free himself from it, kicked it away, so that it landed almost at the feet of the curious onlookers by the door. This was too much for me. As if a terrible cry had pierced the air, I leapt blindly onto the pile of scattered garments and seized Demétrio by the arm:

"Stop it," I cried, immediately letting go of him and snatching another dress from his hands.

Demétrio turned toward me, an irrational gleam in his eyes.

"What do you want?" he asked.

"Just stop it," I repeated, holding up the dress I had snatched from him.

"There's nothing left. It's all gone," he said, gasping.

"It's too soon to be doing this, Demétrio."

He stepped forward, trembling and panting, very close to me now, hesitating as to what he should do next. Seeing that I wasn't letting go of the dress, he said to me in a low, clear voice:

"She's dead, Valdo. She's rotting."

And as if intending to end the discussion with these brutal words, he snatched the dress back from me. I felt the blood rush to my head and reached out to grab it again—he eluded my grasp and was about to throw the dress onto the pile, but I hurled myself on him in an attempt to prevent this final insult. He would not give way and, for a moment, we grappled with each other; from behind us I could hear the onlookers' muffled comments. Ana looked as if she were about to intervene, and two or three other people rushed to separate us. But I had no intention of giving in, and we pushed and pulled our way over to the window. At that moment, we weren't brothers, but two strangers locked in mortal combat. It was clear that I would get the better of him and, when I felt his heavy breathing on my neck, I was surprised that I had dared to go so far and that he had agreed to fight. Something was truly wrong for the Meneses to fight like that in front of so many strangers. As I grappled with him I said to myself, with the sudden lucidity that comes to us in such extreme moments, that it was he, not I, who had the most extraordinary role in all of this, unexpectedly allowing his true self to surface after a lifetime spent trying to conceal it. For a second I thought he was going to have an apoplectic fit; he turned red, almost purple, his eyes almost popping out of their sockets. He couldn't hold out much longer, and when he finally released his grip on me, I pushed him away and he fell back onto the pile of clothes. There on the floor, propping himself up on his elbows, he looked at me with seething resentment. I brandished the dress in front of him:

"Is it from this, from her, that you want to be free?"

His eyes flashed:

"I have nothing to say to you. I don't have to explain myself." And then groaning as he tried to get up: "You should show some respect for your elder brother."

His gaze turned slowly toward Ana, who had clearly decided not to get involved, and his eyes conveyed more of a silent reproach than a cry for help, as if, in that decisive moment, he was finally taking stock of all his failed relationships.

Later on, when I was waiting for the cart from the station to take me away from the Chácara forever, Ana came to find me. That evening, on the sun-scorched road, with the sun already sinking behind the Serra do Baú, she seemed smaller, more shrunken and timid. She said nothing at first and was probably waiting to see my reaction, and when I gave a hint of a gentle smile (after all, compared to the new life that lay before me, what did all these things from the past matter?), she leaned on the fence and sighed deeply. She was waiting for me to speak first, to break the silence that had existed between us from the very first moment she had set foot in that house. Her eyes, always so vague and evasive, were now staring at me intensely, almost begging me to listen to her. I put down my suitcase and, brushing the dust from my clothes, I asked her what she wanted. She replied that she had something to tell me, but didn't know if now was the right moment. I couldn't help smiling at such a declaration from someone who, after living in the same house as me for so many years, had never said much more than hello or goodbye. And for a second, scrutinizing her perhaps more closely than I wanted, I saw her whole personality laid bare before me. With a sense of shock, I realized that there stood one of the central figures in the drama we had all just lived through: Ana—so despised by everyone, and yet who had also perhaps tasted the bitter fruits of love—was the only one whom no one had ever asked to give her version of events. I reached across the hedge toward her, grazing my arm on the thorns: "Well, Ana, it's just us left now. There's nothing to stop us being friends." I saw her face grow so dark, it was like the shadow cast by the surrounding mountains as the sun set behind them. She seemed about to say something along the lines of "it's too late for that," but the words did not appear, and she simply stood there staring, quite still, as if she hadn't even noticed my hand reaching out to her. I shrugged (these impossible creatures!) and then, averting her eyes, and as if repeating something she had already said to herself a hundred times before, she began to speak, and as she spoke, I found that I wasn't so much discovering a new view of events, or adding anything to the story I already knew, but rather that the things I already knew slotted perfectly into the overall picture she was drawing for me. My awareness of events, until then somewhat shaky, became clearer until the whole story lay before me, so vivid and complete that it almost burst out of its narrow frame.

She had known everything for a long time. Ever since she first arrived at the Chácara, dazzled and naïve, she realized that she had been deceived and that her husband did not love her. Or at least that he no longer loved her. Even worse, it did not take her long to realize that he loved someone else. Given the Chácara's narrow horizons, what other woman could attract Demétrio's attention than the one whose presence filled the whole house? The fleeting signs of what had passed between them—a touch, a cry left hanging in the air, an angry gesture, sometimes so much more eloquent than an overt display of love, a lingering look, provoked by who knows what petty annoyance or betrayal or by nothing at all, a certain nervousness, a faint vibration in the air that suddenly alerts us to what is going on, as if we were being blindly propelled by some superior force through disintegrating walls—she had seen all these signs, and more besides, even in a man as guarded and cautious as Demétrio. Love can be hidden to a certain extent, but it will always escape somehow, like a noxious gas. She cited examples from the many she remembered. On one occasion, as she was about to enter their bedroom, she had found Nina on the other side of the door, just about to leave. That was at the beginning, before Nina started talking about going back to Rio, although things were already tense. Nevertheless, when she chanced upon Nina like that, Ana had felt certain that something had happened, something she could not yet pinpoint, but that she could already sense. Nina had stormed past her without saying a word, as if some violent argument had just taken place. Ana had found Demétrio sitting in his chair—slumped, she would almost say—still surrounded by an atmosphere full of inflamed emotions. He did not even turn around when she entered. Then almost not knowing what she was saying, or why, she remarked: "Nina's leaving, isn't she?" She would never forget her husband's look of anger, surprise, and revulsion. If he could, he would have struck her dead that instant. "There are certain things," he said, "that it would be better for you not to know." And he stood up and left the room. From that moment on, Ana had known for certain that he was in love with his sister-in-law. At first, she had thought it was a mere flirtation, a strong attraction perhaps, such as loneliness often produces in certain sensitive souls. Then, as she watched the crisis deepen and saw Demétrio lying awake night after night, suffering in silence, she understood that it was more serious and that perhaps this man of iron really was in love for the very first time in his life. (While Ana was speaking, I myself was reliving the atmosphere in the Chácara then: all of us wide awake and ensnared in an unbreakable web of shared feelings, warily watching each other, sensing the storm building, and unable to do anything about it because we couldn't tell where the lightning would strike . . .) But for Demétrio, love did not manifest itself as it did in other people—for him it was an illness, an unbearable physical malaise. His nature could not tolerate such an intrusion; it overwhelmed him and he was struggling like a drowning man. Slowly, he began to see Nina as a threat to his peace of mind, his well-being and even his integrity, and he ended up deciding that she was a danger to everyone—an evil that, for everyone's sake, must be rooted out. It's true that he never actually confronted the matter head-on (or so at least Ana assumed), and he never managed to come to terms with something that he saw as the result not of his own weakness, but of the diabolical actions of *that* woman. He both loved and hated her—that was his dilemma. However, it would not be too much to suppose that he had succumbed once or twice—perhaps even more, who knows . . .—and Ana had even surprised him once kneeling at Nina's feet. Yes, on his knees, like a besotted lover or love-struck adolescent! Goodness knows what he had said on such occasions—what cries and curses, what pleas and promises might not have come from his lips? Often, watching him sleeping peacefully by her side, Ana would sit up and gaze at him with the intense pleasure of someone capable of reading the deepest stirrings of his soul. On his knees, groveling like a servant, his tears washing the feet that trod the dust in which he knelt . . . Ana's hoarse voice had taken on an unexpected edge of triumph. I confess that I trembled as I listened to her, watching her furtively, not daring to advance down the dark passageways her words were opening up before me. She grew calmer and continued her story. She could almost swear that Nina had never responded to his appeals. (There was, though, one odd and painful detail in our conversation: Ana spoke not with resentment but rather with a certain nostalgia, almost wishing that Nina had indeed succumbed to Demétrio's advances—what angered her was that the other woman had remained so aloof.) She finished by adding: "Nina was born to mock, and she mocked Demétrio as you might an impertinent child or a capricious old man." Those were her exact words. Once again I reached across the hedge and touched her shoulder: "Why are you telling me all this?" She replied simply: "I believe this is the last time we will see each other." There wasn't the slightest trace of the theatrical, nor of suffering or awkwardness, in her voice. She simply believed that here, at this bend in the road, was where our journey ended, and there was no reason why it should be otherwise. I understood—God knows I understood her reasons—but her coldness terrified me. "You didn't have to . . ." I said. This time she looked me straight in the eye: "I wanted you to know, even if it's too late now, that I understood . . . the other day . . . when you had that fight." It's odd, but hearing her talking like that, I felt a certain distrust, an idea that perhaps she knew still more, and that she was only revealing part of the truth. But how to distinguish the truth from all the other inventions conjured out of light, obstinacy and error? The truth is what we make of it.

That really was the last time I saw her. I said goodbye, picked up my suitcase and walked away, but then, as if drawn back by an inescapable force, I turned around again. In the distance, the wind had picked up, sending the dust spiraling skyward. She was still standing there, determinedly silent. I could tell she had been watching me, but as soon as she saw me turn, she looked up as if she had received a shock. I waved goodbye, possibly my only gesture of friendship to her in my whole life. She did not respond, but simply turned and began walking back toward the Chácara.

For some time I watched her black figure growing smaller and smaller. Then, as so often before, she vanished, leaving only the blue sky and, silhouetted against it, the roof of the house where I had been born.

Demétrio lay sprawled on the floor until Ana, as if waking from her torpor, reached out her hand to him. He got up and brushed the dirt off his clothes. Slowly, looking first at me and then at his wife, he ran his hand through his white hair and I noticed that his hand was trembling. Not wanting to show his fear—him of all people!—he glanced furtively over at the doorway where there were now even more curious onlookers.

"You seem to have something against me," he said, turning toward me. "Whatever it might be . . ."

Perhaps he was going to say: "today is not the day," or some other such phrase (and if he had, it would have been the first time he had alluded directly to the dead woman), but I broke in:

"Today is the day. I want you to know that I know everything that happened."

Facts? Mere suppositions? The truth—all of it, finally? I watched these questions run through his mind, and the color drained from his face.

"If you're referring to . . ."

The insinuation hung in the air.

"To the revolver," I said calmly.

There it was, a fact. And suddenly, just when I thought I had him beaten, I watched that old man rally, pull himself together, almost light up, like a young horse rearing and whinnying—and then a shout, a single shout, erupted from his lips:

"But it was the house I was defending, the house!"

An extraordinary phenomenon occurred: around him, like a forest of iron, the reasons sprang up, omnipotent. I felt dizzy, fumbled for the windowsill and leaned on it: Had I been entirely blind? Was I mistaken? Had I been swayed by an influence that was neither right nor just? My forehead was dripping with sweat and, for a moment, everything around me went black. But this only lasted a fraction of a second, and I felt, with every fiber of my being, that I had merely been doing battle with an irrational force, immune to reason. Slowly, as if for the first time, I stared at the man standing in front of me, naked in his righteousness and his beliefs. He had spoken those words with absolute sincerity, but also with real passion. It was as if, in this vale of uncertainty, he had named the one truly sacred object.

"The house?" I repeated, unable to contain my surprise.

He gestured grandly, pathetically, to everything around us:

"All of this. Our property. Our inheritance."

Then, and only then, did I understand that there was no point in arguing with him. How can you argue with someone who no longer speaks your language? How accuse him when the reasons he invokes are palpable, material reasons?

"No, that's not it," I replied, my voice trembling. "No, it's not. The house . . . I couldn't care less about the damn house. To keep it . . ."

Seeing that I was refusing to look at him, he suddenly jumped forward and crouched down in front of me, trying to catch my eye:

"The house!" he yelled. "There's nothing I wouldn't do to keep it!"

Even his voice sounded strange, spirited, almost youthful. Thinking back, perhaps it wasn't even the voice of a man—in its desire to entice and seduce there was something strangely feminine or childish. Who knows, it might well have been the voice of the only true Meneses, who I did not know and had never known, but who now rose before me in all his fateful splendor. I smiled:

"I know you would do anything." And then, in a quieter voice, as if making my own mental calculation: "And for this you have lied, cheated, and betrayed. You never could stand her, could you?" My voice grew louder, a broken sob becoming stronger, almost a howl, which was perhaps my cry of love, standing in for all the words I had not spoken and that had foundered between the four walls of that cold house, between the walls of my own being, possessed by the malevolent spirit of the Meneses:

"All you ever wanted was to destroy her. The revolver was just one of your many ploys. and there were those trips away as well . . . But you would have been capable of strangling her, of shooting her or of beating her to death—it didn't matter as long as she was gone."

Overwhelmed, as if everything I had done that day were suddenly pressing down on my shoulders, I slumped onto the windowsill and wept, freely and purely, feeling that I was at last regaining a little of the self-respect that had long been buried, but which was now returning, terrified and strange, but nevertheless capable of bearing the weight of all my mistakes and feelings of shame. I don't know how long I remained like that, but when I looked up, I found Ana and Demétrio standing before me. I pointed to the pile of clothes on the floor:

"And even now, Demétrio . . . Even now, can't you see? All you want is to banish her memory."

He bowed his head.

I left the windowsill and went over to him, so close that my lips almost brushed his ear:

"And I know why. Oh, yes, I know why," I whispered.

He didn't raise his head, but I could see the sweat dripping from his forehead. And so I left him, head bowed, but unyielding, amid the clothes littering the hallway.

52.
From Timóteo's Memoirs (i)

The only reason I am writing this is in order to remember her. When they told me she was dead (it was Betty who told me; I was lying down with a damp towel on my forehead, prostrated by one of those violent headaches I've been getting recently), the words seemed so strange that at first they made no sense at all—after all, what does death mean to someone like me who has spent his whole life at death's door? But for all her self-restraint, there was in what she told me a cry so human and so plangent that I removed the towel and opened my eyes. And that was when I sensed that everything around me had changed. The room was filled with a strange yellowish glow, as if someone had flung wide the shutters. Inside, the furniture stood stiff and precise in the heavy silence. A feeling rose up within me far stronger than certainty, for it was a glimpse of death itself, the very death that had just occurred in the next room, and its aura came floating toward me in a solemn, all-mastering wave. Disjointed and hitherto shapeless elements—fluids, currents, intimations of destiny and destruction—came together within me to create a perfectly formed face, a clearly defined being, not for the eyes of others, but for me alone to see, sad and secret. It was a portrait drawn by a bold hand, a complete presence, belonging to someone I had once known and which only I, by some miracle of fidelity, could recreate exactly. There was no embarrassment, no nostalgia, no grief—merely the recognition of something familiar, like a private landscape slowly revealing itself in the growing light of understanding.

I remembered the first time she sat down beside me—a long time ago—and how she looked at me with the sad expression of someone who knows everything and condemns nothing. What really struck me about her wasn't her beauty, although she was indeed very beautiful. (Here, I will pause for a moment and ask myself: what is beauty? Beauty is the ultimate goal of our inner fluids, a secret ecstasy, a concordance between our internal world and our external existence. A gift of harmony, you might say. Nina never stood out in any given environment—with the simplicity of all innocent creatures, endowed with all the graces, she was that environment.) From the very beginning, I sensed that she was one of those irreplaceable human beings, a vital, transcendental force, like a sudden wind that wakes us in the dead of night. That she was made of flesh and blood and had a name, that she was brought here on the arm of another man and never stayed for long—what did any of that matter? That is the way with free spirits, they never stay. And the truth is that for me she embodied what I had long been waiting for. Now that she is dead I can call her by her name, softly, as if wanting to see her once again, and yet, for me, that is no longer the name of the person she once was, but the partial, human translation of the power with which she thrust herself into our midst. Let me be blunt: from the very outset and with the special intuition that certain victims have, the Meneses knew that they were faced with a kind of angel of death.

Betty was waiting with a cup in her hand, still trembling from the news she had just given me.

"Did you hear what I said?"

With some difficulty I sat up, while the yellow light swirled around me—an effect of my nausea. (I could have said to her: "Betty, I'm not well. I've got a headache and I'm feeling sick. Anything could happen to me, absolutely anything . . ." But I didn't, for she never believed my stories.)

"Yes, Betty, I heard. She's dead."

I sat on the edge of the bed, waiting for the shapes around me to stop moving. In a minute or so everything returned to its rightful place. My feelings of nausea shifted to my heart, which felt heavy and still. In response to my apparently simple answer, I saw that gentle creature erupt in anger for the very first time:

"Oh, Senhor Timóteo! How can you take such news so calmly? And the poor woman lying next door, rolled up in a sheet!"

I motioned for her to sit beside me.

"Betty, it's all very sad, but what can we do? Everyone must die some day."

No, death definitely did not terrify me. Powerless to contradict me, Betty covered her face with one hand and slumped onto the bed beside me:

"She was such a good friend to you, Senhor Timóteo. She was so fond of you!"

Yes, Betty knew that too, although she could not have known the full extent of our pact. Yes, Betty knew, and as we sat there in silence, alone with our thoughts, the structure of time itself seemed to disintegrate and there came to us suddenly a vision of the dead woman so pure and so implacable that I felt my heart ache. I hugged Betty tight, and, for those few seconds, it felt as if the hostile, senseless world had stopped whirling about me. In our small refuge, as if bathed in a little friendly sunlight, Betty began to talk, and her cautious tones gradually began to clothe that specter already stripped of earthly pomp.

"It was horrible to watch," she said. "By the end, she was in such pain she wouldn't let anyone near her. All she said was: 'Betty, rub a little perfume on my body.' I did, but it didn't get rid of that terrible smell. She asked for a mirror so that she could see herself. Then she combed her stiff, dry hair, then threw the comb down, hid her face in her hands, and wept. Oh, Senhor Timóteo, why does dying bring such suffering? At the end, she was in such a state that we couldn't even dress her."

She described how they had lifted the body, still warm (for a second, she thought she had seen one of her pupils quiver) and rolled her in a white sheet, on top of the other sheet that had become stuck to her body. And there she lay in the drawing room, her sunken cheeks glowing green in the flickering candlelight.

"Who stayed with her?"

"No one." The way in which she said this was a reproach to us all, and she had never dared to go that far before. No, no one at all, and yet the room must surely have been full of people. Or at least no one who truly loved and understood her, who felt some tenderness or compassion for her, or even friendship, rather than the kind of love that scorns the lifeless shell. That is what Betty had come to tell me, and what sorrow, what grief, must have filled her mind as she witnessed the formal trappings of that drama, of which she understood so little. Slowly, like a distant bell beginning to toll dully, dimly—a sound, so jumbled up with past ages, with the dust of events, with old, meaningless objects; a sound, sweeping across the fields, still far off, but already raising up to heaven its heavy bronze voice—and I began to understand that the time had come, and with it the crowning moment of the cause I had so long espoused.

Almost effortlessly, as if propelled by a new energy, I stood up.

"And Demétrio, did he not send word to anyone?"

"Yes, he did," she said. "She had scarcely closed her eyes when he sent a message to the Baron."

At that, I began to laugh, and the sound of my laughter filled the room like a foretaste of resurrection.

"The Baron! Ah, Betty, what a strange place the world is . . ."

I saw from her silence that she disapproved. She must certainly have thought me ungrateful, laughing at the woman who had been the only person in the world to show me a little friendship. Ever since

I had shut myself up in my room, how many people had dared to cross its threshold? How many had exchanged even a few words or sipped a glass of champagne with me? And yet—ah, the mysteries of human nature!—I was glad. Even at a time like that I could laugh, and I felt neither shame nor remorse. And perhaps—why not?—Betty's disapproval extended to the entire Meneses tribe, for we were such a cold, heartless lot. Ah, this is what she must be thinking, poor Betty, and I realized how difficult it would be to make her understand what my laughter really meant. It was like the creaking of an iron gate being pushed open. No, for me there was neither pain nor despair, because it was not death, but consummation. There was no anguish because there was no suffering. There was only a task fulfilled. Nina had gone, and I would go and pay her my last respects, as a soldier pays homage to his fallen comrade.

"Betty," I said, "before she died, Nina asked me to do something."

She looked up at me:

"What was that?"

"She asked me—and this was a long time ago—she asked me to lay a bunch of violets on her coffin."

Betty nodded:

"They were her favorite flowers."

"Well, then, Betty, I want you to gather as many as you can. Lots and lots of them."

She shook her head:

"That's impossible, Senhor Timóteo. It isn't the season for violets."

I flew into a rage—I don't know why—and stamped my foot.

"I want violets, Betty. I *need* them."

This time she did not answer, but merely gave a sigh of resignation. Then, softly, she asked:

"How can I bring lots? I might only find half a dozen, at most."

"Bring whatever you can find." (Suddenly, as if the urgency of the problem had jogged my memory, I remembered an old, very old, flower bed over by the Pavilion. It was exactly that, a bed of violets, and had been planted by a gardener called Alberto, who had killed himself right here at the Chácara. It probably hadn't been disturbed since, and perhaps among all the weeds there might still be a few flowers, which would be enough for what I needed.) "Listen, Betty, there's an old flower bed near the Pavilion. I think you'll find all you need there."

She replied pensively:

"That was exactly where I was planning to go."

With that matter settled, my thoughts turned instead to finalizing the details of my plan. So the Baron would at last set foot in this house that had for so long coveted his presence! There was not the slightest doubt that this was, in all respects, one of the most important days in the entire existence of the Meneses. It was thus incumbent upon me to play my part, even though it would be the very last time my plans would fit in with those of my brothers, for after this, eternal oblivion would bury me far from them.

"Betty!" I exclaimed, turning to face her. "I will leave this room today. I want to see Nina. I want to say goodbye to her."

"Oh, Senhor Timóteo!" And her voice trembled with pleasure.

Curiously, she did not for a second consider how unusual a decision this was, or how ridiculous my gift of a little bunch of violets, or how much my mere presence would offend the others. But what was there to be gained by her knowing these things and being able to gauge the full extent of the cruelty I was about to inflict? It was evident that, for her, the only death that counted was Nina's, and she would never be able to grasp that another type of death was imminent—a cold, calculated killing committed by hands well-equipped for such a dexterous, murderous deed.

"Now pay attention, Betty." I tried to control my voice so she would not pick up the slightest hint of excitement, or notice in my behavior anything other than sorrow at the death of my dear friend. "Now pay attention, so that you don't forget. As soon as the Baron arrives—and not a moment before—you must come running to tell me. The door will be unlocked, so you'll just have to push it open."

"Just push," replied Betty mechanically. Then, suddenly suspicious, she turned to me with a doubtful look in her eyes: "Why the Baron, Senhor Timóteo? Why him in particular?"

"Betty," I replied, "these are personal matters that don't concern you. I've been waiting for this visit for years."

"Oh, Senhor Timóteo! Senhor Timóteo!" she murmured, and stayed where she was, as if waiting for me to explain precisely what I intended.

"This is the only way, Betty. If you don't do as I say, Nina will leave this house without her violets and without my farewell, and you will have committed a grave sin."

"No! No!" she cried, clasping her hands.

"Then swear that you will come and tell me when, exactly when, he enters the drawing room."

"I swear."

Reassured, I lay down again on the bed. Betty stayed where she was, occasionally inhaling sharply as if she were about to say something. Then, apparently changing her mind, she turned and left the room. The familiar silence that ensued felt unexpectedly heavy. I looked from one side of the room to the other, and not a thing moved, as if in expectation of some momentous event. It was only then, as if welling up from deep waters, that the full realization of Nina's death penetrated the farthest corners of my consciousness. Before me, under a shifting, bluish light, I saw her face as if for the first time—and that familiar ghost, restoring to me a long-lost image, seemed to have been fashioned solely for me. I whispered "Nina," and everything around me appeared to tremble as if shaken to its foundations. It wasn't the world retreating into impassive hostility, but a new reality asserting itself, in which there would be no room for peace or generosity. More than ever I felt that I must go to her and that she, wherever she might be, was waiting for me. And I would go just as I had said I would, as her comrade-in-arms. What finer eulogy could I give her?

Yes, I would go. The door would open and reveal the landscape that I had forbidden myself to enter. It did not matter to me that the landscape consisted of nothing but death and ruin, and that it might or might not suit my purpose. The time had come for me to arise and walk, though not, as I had said to Betty, to say goodbye, for people like Nina and I never say goodbye, except to proclaim the truth and give sustenance to men starved of hope. I neither trembled nor feared to speak this word, for there are as many words for "hope" as there are desires in every human heart. To satisfy the bitter hunger of those around me, I would leave a handful of scorched bones. Rising above my triumph, above my own self, right at the very point where Nina's death had given me my liberty, I would declare: "Meneses, O Meneses, remember that all is dust and to dust it will return, just as the dust returns to the earth." Screams and howls and pleas and curses—how would any of those things help once this proud house was no more?

Finally, my march would begin, and it was Nina's corpse that had flung open my prison door. I got up again and restlessly paced the room. Never had it seemed to me so small, so suffocating, so narrow. I knew every one of its nooks and crannies like old friends, and yet here, suddenly, at a simple call of destiny, they had all become strangers to me. Like someone evoking the name of the one who always accompanies all secret designs of vengeance and extermination, I repeated again and again: "Meneses, O Meneses," and delayed opening the door and showing myself and delivering the final blow that would leave my enemy forever prostrated at my feet. While these thoughts raced through my mind, my blood too began to flow faster through my veins and my whole body throbbed like a secret dynamo, whirring away on the plan elaborated during my many days of torpor.

Step by step, like a cat, I moved toward the door, I opened it and listened, and I could smell, washing over me, the scent of wilted flowers and burnt candles that spread from the drawing room throughout the house and finally reached me, like a warm nuptial perfume.

53.
Valdo's Statement (v)

It will not, I believe, be that hard for me to describe some of the main episodes that took place during Nina's wake and which gave Vila Velha so much to talk about. I think they were, in fact, the culmination of a series of events that had long been discussed in hushed tones and which so spectacularly contributed to the final demise of the Meneses' prestige locally, already so weakened by successive scandals. At least, that was when I made my decision to leave behind forever not just the family home, but the whole region—for the entire state of Minas Gerais was no longer big enough to hide my shame, and I intended to head south, to São Paulo or Rio Grande, and there begin a new life and forget all my past misfortunes. But I am anticipating events, and must instead try, first, to describe that gathering, which was already decidedly odd and quite unlike most wakes. My fight with Demétrio had certainly stirred things up, and there was talk of all sorts of bizarre tensions that were, supposedly, about to explode at any moment, although I knew nothing about that at the time, and was merely watching from the verandah as people came and went, and felt sad that so many were taking advantage of that melancholy occasion to invade our family enclave.

It was extremely hot and people were using all kinds of makeshift fans to cool themselves, and there was a constant stream of mourners coming out onto the verandah in search of fresh air, the men tugging at their sweat-soaked collars. Glasses of water and orangeade, cooled by the black kitchen-maids in wells dug beneath the lemon trees, were being passed around. Some visitors restricted themselves to patiently mopping their brow with a handkerchief, while others paced nervously up and down complaining about the unbearable heat. They all knew that the burial would only take place in the afternoon, and yet they were constantly checking their watches as if the time were fast approaching, or as if such a gesture would help to speed time up. In low but perfectly audible voices people were discussing who should carry the coffin, and while one group was commenting unfavorably on Father Justino's absence, another, at the far end of the verandah, was gravely debating whether or not the deceased would be laid in the family vault. I imagined the procession carrying the coffin along the dusty road in the broiling sun to the somewhat distant town cemetery with its whitewashed walls and rather dilapidated tombstones. I was still immersed in these sad reflections when I saw a troubling figure approaching me. She was a tall, middle-aged woman; her hair was still very black, and she was sumptuously dressed as if for a party rather than a wake. Her clothes, however, while clearly very expensive, had an old-fashioned, pretentiously provincial air about them. She came over to me, opening and closing a large fan encrusted with mother-of-pearl.

"Forgive me," she said, "but we are old acquaintances . . ."

I found out later that she was Angélica, the daughter of the Baron de Santo Tirso. She owned several properties in the town and, perhaps out of spite or mere wickedness, people said that she was not quite right in the head. I replied, frankly, that I did not remember her, and she tapped my face with the end of her closed fan and laughed:

"Ah, Senhor Valdo, how time passes. I'm Angélica. Once, with my father . . ."

And as she spoke, she was all studied poses and gestures, as if her whole body were trying to contain something that might otherwise overcome her and escape. I looked at her and shuddered: her white skin seemed to have been pieced together like a patchwork and had an oily, corpse-like sheen.

"Would you care to . . ." I began.

She brandished her fan.

"I saw a lot of clothes lying on the floor. You must forgive me, and perhaps now is not the right time . . ."

"Do go on."

Beneath her long eyelashes, far too long to be natural, her eyes flashed greedily.

"I don't know if you're aware, but we have an orphanage in town for young girls. If it wasn't inconvenient . . ."

I was taken aback: was she actually going to ask me for the clothes? The very clothes that Demétrio was throwing out because they were infected?

"If it wouldn't be too much bother," she continued unperturbed, "I would very much like to make use of the dresses for the poor orphans."

I looked at her, not knowing what to say. Once again she smiled, and once again I felt that same unease.

"But you're aware that . . ."

"Yes, yes, I know. But there's no proof, believe me. The doctors say . . ."

"Mightn't it be better not to take any chances?"

She again tapped me with her fan, as if I had said something foolish.

"Oh, Senhor Valdo, what a silly idea! If you only knew how needy those girls are . . ."

She stopped. We evidently had nothing more to say to each other, and yet she did not move, but stood gazing me through half-closed eyes.

"Whatever you wish, Senhora. Take whatever you wish."

She was about to reply when, from the foot of the steps, came a murmur of voices. I leaned over the balustrade to see what was going on, and saw two or three black servants running toward the house. When the fastest runner reached the steps, he cried:

"Senhor Valdo! It's the Baron!"

Upon these words a sort of electric current ran through the people assembled on the verandah and crossed the threshold into the drawing room:

"The Baron!"

And that lit fuse, infecting those still inside, triggered a kind of strange buzz of excitement: yet more people appeared at the door, pushing each other out of the way in their eagerness to see the new arrival.

But the Baron was still some way off. Baking under the merciless sun, an old car was advancing sedately up the main avenue through the garden, noisily belching smoke and bearing within it the noble family. The car stopped almost at the foot of the steps, in front of a group of gaping onlookers already preparing to bow and scrape as the occasion demanded.

When the gloved chauffeur opened the car door, the first to get out was the Baroness, tall and well-dressed, with a stern, placid, strangely melancholy face. Immediately after her came the Baron: short and very red-faced, and holding a leather satchel under his right arm and looking somewhat alarmed at the commotion around him. He climbed the steps accompanied by his wife and, before he had even reached the top, a pale, emotional Demétrio rushed to greet him, bowing reverentially, and with extraordinary abandon for a man normally so reserved, he threw himself into his guest's arms before the latter had even so much as acknowledged him.

"Such a tragedy, Baron!" he cried.

(Such a tragedy? And he had ordered her to be rolled up in a sheet when her body was still warm, just so as to hasten the Baron's arrival!

I trembled with indignation, thinking of the sheer hypocrisy of it all.) The Baron said a few words to him that I could not hear, and then majestically ascended the remaining steps. Or as majestically as he could, for he was (as I've said) short and fat, and his movements were restricted by the bag he was clutching to him as tightly as if it contained something very precious. Nodding desultorily to the people on either side of him, he made his way over to the far end of the drawing room, away from the exposed corpse, and sat on a velvet banquette placed there especially for the occasion. His feet, shod in ankle-length boots, did not quite touch the ground. He looked around inquisitorially—the look of a rough and ready Portuguese peasant—and so everyone sensed that they should find something else to do and dispersed around the room, some of them contemplatively gathering around the corpse. Then the Baron, who had quite possibly been waiting for just such an opportunity, took the satchel from under his arm, opened it and, reaching into it, pulled out something to eat—perhaps a sweet of some sort. (By that time, he was already possessed by the demon of gluttony that would eventually bring him to a cruel and long-drawn-out death; he was never to be seen without that bag of food and, wherever he was, whether visiting or at home, he was always chewing. His sly, shifty eyes glinted in his flabby face, the eyes of someone sensing that he has been caught red-handed and who, for that very reason, is always ready with an excuse. As he chewed and sucked, a sickly sweet substance dribbled down his chin, giving his face the repugnant appearance of a piece of greasy ham, as if the essence of the foods he was so constantly and laboriously ingesting were oozing out of every pore in his body.)

Scarcely daring to glance at him (it was said he was one of the wealthiest landowners in Portugal), people at the other end of the room began commenting, without a hint of outrage: "The Baron is eating," as if it were entirely appropriate for a member of the race of barons to bring a bag full of sweets to a wake. Not even five minutes had passed after the Baron's entrance when the most remarkable event of the day occurred, an event so outrageous and scandalous in its repercussions that it completely overshadowed the intended purpose of the gathering, that of marking the death that had occurred in the house. I am referring to the appearance of my brother, Timóteo.

The excitement caused by the Baron's arrival had abated somewhat, and everyone had settled down to watch him devouring a pastry when a swishing sound, like a pent-up stream of floodwater, came surging down the hallway and into the drawing room, where it frothed against the four walls. Suddenly, without warning and with the shock of the entirely unexpected, there appeared before our eyes the spectacle of Timóteo reclining in a hammock carried by three black servants, probably the same three who had come to announce the arrival of the Baron. Such a short space of time had elapsed between the two events that I even thought it must be some sort of set-up—but who in that house would have dared follow the orders of a creature who was generally considered to be completely mad? In any event there he was: the hammock, carried by two men at the rear and one at the front, swayed in the doorway, and, at first, no one had the slightest clue who or what it was.

Let me explain: it was one of those perfectly ordinary, loosely-woven hammocks so commonly found in the countryside. Its one distinguishing feature was that it was clearly rather old and worn, as if it had been hurriedly salvaged from a storeroom. However, what was so extraordinary was the person in the hammock, whom I recognized at once. Ah, but how he had changed, what a toll time had taken on him! He was not just fat, he was enormous, already exhibiting all the morbid signs of the slow, suppurating death that awaits those too long immobilized by their illnesses. He could scarcely move his round, flabby arms, which hung in mountainous folds, drooping lifelessly like the branches of a tree severed from its trunk. It was difficult even to make out his eyes in that mass of human dissipation and sloth: his fat, puffy cheeks formed a mask so exotic and terrifying that he looked more like a dead Buddha than a living creature still capable of speech. His long, unwashed hair hung over his shoulders in two thick braids like forest lianas, swaying and twisting with the movements of the hammock like two gnarled roots spreading out from a trunk battered by the years. Even stranger, this spectacle of a body, which seemed to encapsulate every possible vice of inactivity, idleness, and neglect, had about it something of the sea, the slipping and sliding of invisible tempestuous waters rolling randomly over this amorphous mass, which shone with all the deathly, silent pallor of distant lunar wildernesses.

The bearers of this extraordinary cargo paused for a moment in the middle of the room, uncertain what to do next. Timóteo clapped his hands and prepared to be lowered to the ground. (It was, I believe, only when Timóteo hitched up his skirt and reached one bare, white foot toward the floor that Demétrio realized what was happening; from somewhere behind me, near where the Baron was sitting, came a deep, doleful roar as if someone had been mortally wounded. I spun around, convinced that someone had been stabbed. But I saw no one, nothing, apart from the hunched figure of Demétrio slumped against the table where the coffin lay. It was he who had cried out, of that there was no doubt—deathly pale, he was clutching his belly as if vainly trying not so much to staunch a gushing flow of blood threatening to drain his body dry and leave him lying defenseless on the table, as attempting to preserve, like some human dishcloth, his own mortal essence.)

I think, and I say this without any hesitation, that the situation would have been saved had Timóteo not gotten out of the hammock. His grand entrance was certainly extraordinary, but it might well have been taken merely as the act of a very sick man; however, by rising from the hammock dressed in one of those bizarre outfits of his, he insulted everyone in the room. Men will put up with a certain amount of the grotesque, but only as long as they do not themselves feel implicated in it. Standing before them, Timóteo was the very caricature of the world they represented—a comic character, at once both terrible and serene. He wore something that could not be called a dress exactly, but which had once been some sort of ball gown—goodness knows when or where—and which was now a faded mauve thing of shreds and patches, all ripped and hastily sewn back together. His wrists and neck were thickly circled with bracelets and necklaces—I had no idea where these had come from, but they were evidently the family jewels, no doubt secreted away in chests and drawers between layers of fine linens and foreign silks, gazed at by generations of covetous relatives, and yet there they were, resplendent and pure, adorning that vile, ignominious body. He looked slowly around at the crowd of shocked faces staring back at him. Nobody dared to move or say anything. As for me, I confess that my initial feelings, a mixture of extreme surprise and revulsion, gave way to a rising sense of pride, as yet undefined, but which thrust its roots down into the deepest corners of my being: for I sensed that Demétrio was the most severely affected by this little scene and would be the one to pay the highest price in the form of his downfall and shame. In my response I saw the old hatred that had always separated us, and which had its origins in my continual need to defend myself against his attempts to control and dominate us all. That hatred had always set us apart, our thoughts and opinions constantly at odds; a silent hatred, like two shadows pursuing each other. It was our mutual hatred that had finally exploded, and I could do nothing to stop it, for the irresistible impulse sweeping me along needed that violent eruption if I was to put back together the pieces of my own existence—both my old existence that I had now left behind, and my new existence, in which I had barely tried out my first steps. I confess that I was soon filled by a sense of euphoria, and a very strange euphoria at that. It was as if I had said to myself: "What do I care what happens, now that all of this means nothing to me, now that I've freed myself from the past, like someone abandoning an empty suitcase by the roadside?" Despite its strenuous efforts to smooth the rougher edges of events and turn genuine struggles and emotions into something safely mediocre, the day seemed now almost to be dissolving before me and, where death itself had failed to shock those poor, vain human beings, the apparition of that specter succeeded, a specter more powerful even than death because he was both alive and dead, bringing to the living a message from another world. No, I felt neither shocked nor afraid; unable to take my eyes off that extraordinary sight, I began to recognize in him—by what secret magic I do not know—the close physical presence of a family member, hidden from me until that moment by a mist of incomprehension, but who was entitled to a place at the Meneses table, and had come to claim it on the irrefutable grounds of its absolute physical resemblance, its warm consanguinity. And even more extraordinary, this vision of mine was not of a man, but of a grand old lady of the sort we had heard about without ever knowing precisely who she was, whose portrait we might one day find tucked away in the bottom of a drawer and sense, in a poetic flash of inspiration, that hers had been a mad, but transient spirit—a matron who had perhaps once been the tutelary deity of the family, but had been stripped of her mission and obliterated from memory by some fleeting drama of which only the scandalous echoes remained. And now here she was, reincarnated and timeless before our very eyes. As Timóteo swung his enormous, heavy, useless body to the floor, I suddenly saw the spirit of the lady who so ostentatiously moved within him: Maria Sinhá. The same Maria Sinhá who had provoked so much disapproval among previous generations of Meneses and whose portrait Demétrio had, out of family loyalty, ordered to be taken down from the wall and hidden in the basement—Maria Sinhá, who had rebelled against life's normal constraints and terrified the peaceful inhabitants of the surrounding countryside with her sorties on horseback dressed as a man, her gold-handled whip for punishing the slaves, her baths of perfumed milk, her brazen audacity. How could I not sense her living presence, like a palm tree standing in the desert, daring once again to defy and corrupt, her hand raised in a supreme gesture of insult by which she would annihilate once and for all her eternal, never-changing enemies?

Was I mistaken? Like the flag of a famous victory planted on some nondescript and nameless hill, I saw in him a Meneses—yes, a Meneses, with all the physical characteristics of a Meneses: his pale complexion, his prominent nose, his tendency to sloth and apathy, as ruthless in his aims as any other, as steadfast in his ideals, and as implacable and resentful as Demétrio himself. In short, a true Meneses.

More objectively, I noticed that he appeared dazzled. Accustomed to darkness, he suffered the myopia of all nocturnal creatures and, suddenly plucked from his usual habitat, he hesitated, blinking in the woundingly bright light. Then, steadying himself, he made straight for the coffin. He stretched out his arm and scattered a handful of violets over the body. It's hard to be entirely certain what happened next: I only know (because it made such an impression on me) that absolute silence reigned, as if we were all waiting for a sentence to be read out. Borne aloft by a mysterious power far greater than ourselves, we soared free and weightless, the shadows of our mortal flesh and bones projected onto a backdrop of supernatural occurrences, against which were being played out not the petty details of our own miserable adventures, but the grand finale of an intricate dance in which there twirled and pranced the ghostly projections of the angels and demons buried deep within us. Suddenly, Timóteo, who had stooped down over Nina's body as if to receive his orders, straightened up again, looked around one last time, and settled his gaze on the Baron. There, in all his baleful presence, sat the man who encapsulated all of Demétrio's dreams, ambitions, and respect, and he was holding a piece of crumbling pastry in his hand. I repeat: I don't know what happened next, nor what gesture of defiance or scandalous temerity Timóteo dared to commit—after all, insanity knows no limits. I noticed only that his eyes circled around the room and alighted on something, as if making a great discovery. Then he staggered, as if under the weight of an unexpected blow. I followed his gaze and saw, standing slightly apart from the group now huddled in the drawing room, my son, André. He was the person Timóteo was looking at, and Timóteo's eyes shone so intensely, so revealingly, that they seemed to be acknowledging an old acquaintance, rather than catching sight of a complete stranger for the first time. He had not, of course, ever met or even seen André, for I had never let the boy enter Timóteo's room. So the look of surprise on Timóteo's face made no sense at all, and was made even stranger by that inexplicable air of familiarity, as if they already knew each other. Finally, he looked away from the boy and, as if this were somehow an answer whose meaning no one could understand, I thought I saw him raise his hand and slap the corpse's face. Yes, he slapped the corpse. I have no idea why he did it, and even today the question still haunts me. Was it simply to demonstrate how little importance he attached to normal human behavior? Surely not, for on that score he had already crossed every possible boundary. Was it to challenge some occult force lurking in the dead woman's shadow? Possibly. But as I said, I was never able to fathom the meaning of that strange gesture.

Then, in what was the crowning moment of the grand ceremony unfolding before us, a hoarse, inhuman sound emerged from his lips, and before I could ascertain the reason, I saw him turn on his heels and fall to the floor, clearly having suffered a stroke. But, oddly, he did not sway and fall in the way a normal person would when suffering such an attack. Rather, he spun around for a second and with him all his jewels. It was as if a medieval tower, studded with precious stones and mosaics, were suddenly shaken to its foundations, to its very core, and its luxurious rubble shimmered with a thousand colors like a shattered stained-glass window: amethyst necklaces, sapphire and diamond bracelets, emerald brooches, gold and ruby earrings, pearls, beryls, opals, all setting the whole room glittering with their splendid eyes, which, briefly, blazed with life, and then with one final, furtive glimmer, fell limp and lifeless on his prostrate body.

Among the onlookers it was as if a spell had been broken. I heard cries and voices, while the more attentive among them rushed forward to help. Meanwhile, the others, as if the retreat had sounded, began prudently to leave.

54.
From Timóteo's Memoirs (ii)

I don't know if it's day or night, but it scarcely matters to me, since nothing in this world matters to me any more. A single force embraces and enthralls me, and my whole body throbs like a whirring dynamo. Yes, it's hot, so the sun must be beating down outside. As I climb into the hammock, I lean over and shout: "Quick!", and as the servants still seem to hesitate—is it the weight? the heat?—I again shout "Quick!" and beat my fists against the sides of the hammock. Their black skins gleam with sweat. (In the old days, when Anastácia used to carry me in her arms, I would ask her why her skin was so black, and she would reply: "Ah, master, that's because where I was born there ain't no day.") An intense brightness envelops me, and I think I might faint from the shock of entering this world of sharp lines and angles. There seems to me to be an excess of color and the air itself seems full of drifting, weaving currents of fire. At the end of the verandah, the foliage shimmers in the sunlight, and from the kitchen comes the shrill, monotonous cry of a caged parakeet. I could never have imagined that the day could be so cruel; my body, so used to darkness, is pierced by a thousand darts of light. I give the order once again: "Quick!" and my voice, imperious and commanding, is like a crystal shattering into pieces. And off we go at a steady pace, while I think to myself: "What if the Baron has already left? What if Betty told me too late?" And at the same time, as I proceed down the hallway, familiar objects, forgotten details from my childhood come flooding back. That blazing pane of red glass high above the verandah, for example. The buzzing of a bee, only it isn't a bee, it's a fixed point in my head, a single prolonged note drilling through me. I lean over and tap the gleaming back of the servant closest to me. "It's old Anastácia who runs the kitchen, and you'd never guess that she's over a hundred . . ." And while all these memories rush into my mind, I suddenly find myself at the open door of the drawing room. I hear the muffled rumble of water beating against its four walls; I see small groups of people and hear a rustle of whispers. The drawing room hasn't escaped the force of the searing sun outside, and in the sultry heat the visitors sweat and breathe with difficulty. From time to time, like an enormous mouth blowing in through the windows, a warm breeze crosses the room. The black servants stop and the voices stop: behold, my enemies stand before me. (Later on, sitting beside me and cooling my brow with a damp cloth, Betty will tell me: "Didn't you recognize her? That tall woman in a purple dress was Donana de Lara—don't you remember her? And the thin one dripping with jewels was the Baron de Santo Tirso's daughter. Very old, but stinking rich. Didn't you see Dona Mariana, from the Fundão plantation? And there were people from the town too. Senhor Aurélio from the pharmacy, Colonel Elídio Carmo, lots of them. I've never seen the house so full of people."

I don't know what impression I cause (and indeed I don't give it a moment's thought), but their stares reveal a degree of stupefaction. The hammock is still swaying, and I ask the servants to put me down. I sense I've gone a little too far, perhaps it's these old-fashioned clothes, or perhaps these jewels that no one knows about, the necklaces and bracelets I stole from my mother's jewelery box, or perhaps it's my hair, which I haven't washed or brushed in a long time. (Why would I? Who for? Life only has meaning when we want to reinforce the image of our idea of beauty in the eyes of another.) Standing there in all my lavish glory, I face down their stares as if I had just arrived from another world. At the far end of the room, almost against the wall, the dead woman lies stretched out, with a candle beside her. I go over to her, the bunch of violets in my hand. (Strangely, the space seems enormous and I walk with difficulty. Will they notice what's happening to me?) Perhaps at one time I would have hesitated, but there's no human force now that can hold me back. I move forward, and my eyes involuntarily, spontaneously, from deep within me, look for those brothers of mine who I haven't seen for years. There's Valdo standing over there; it must be him, as thin and erect as ever. Perhaps not exactly aged, but more angular. The other one, farther off, beside the table with the body, is Demétrio: yes, he has aged and not in a way that smoothes and softens, but as if a burning fire had been lit inside him, leaving a trail of destruction in its blackened wake. His eyes gleam, and I realize he is watching my every move. What does he find strangest about me: the manner of my appearance in front of all these people whom he so respects? Or the jewels that cover me and sparkle with a thousand colors every time I move? What must he be saying to himself? What must he think of this pantomime that he cannot truly understand, but which, with all the shallow haste of superficial people, he must by now have already classified and catalogued? As I approach, people draw back—you would think I was wearing not emeralds and topazes, but the mark of some dread disease, a leper to be avoided at all costs. (Tucked up in their beds, on a night that will become the saddest in their lives, they will find out the reason for their disgust. For they will discover, with no possibility of escape or hope of salvation, the fiery tattoo with which it brands its chosen ones. And before the break of day, they will invent colors, perfumes, and sweet names for this mark, hoping that it turns into a flower. But no, it will obstinately continue to plague them, searing them like a wound, until finally the light of their existence is extinguished.) All around me now is a stagnant lake of silence.

Finally, I see the sharp outline of the dead woman's face under the sheet, and suddenly the room no longer exists, nor do the people staring at me, nor does anything that has gone before, not even the dream of which we are the living embodiment. We are nothing but our foolish impulses, which float above truth and time like ethereal, inhuman breezes.

I dare to reach out my hand and draw back the sheet: Nina. Here she is, her hollow cheeks, her slightly aquiline nose. I see her again, alive, as she was that day I went to find her in the Pavilion. She seemed happy then and had that air about her of someone who is at ease with herself. Her voice, capable of such abrupt mutations, saying: "When I die, Timóteo, I want you to bring me some violets." Well, here they are, Nina. (At the moment I reach out my hand to place these violets in your coffin, just as I promised, just as you made me swear that day, I want there to be a brief moment of pure light and understanding between us. I never said as much to anyone, and I never would, if I didn't know that somewhere far from this world you were able to understand everything about this confused comedy of ours. I would never say it, Nina, because outrage was always my first response when confronted by love. Long before the music of passion breathed into me its golden notes of madness, I had already renounced any semblance of decency and had challenged men with the image of something which—ah, poor me!—I could not accept without despising myself. I'm one of those people who cannot live without exaltation: I consciously debased myself because I felt I was less worthy than the others and that it was through martyrdom that I would raise myself above them and become the greatest of them all. The day came, Nina, when martyrdom could take me no further, and the grotesque clothes I put on became less of a snub to the others than a suit of leaden, deadly armor.

I remember the early morning, when the birds would be singing in the trees in the garden outside my window. That was the only time I dared draw back the curtain a little and gaze with indescribable pleasure upon a world that seemed to me the only one that merited any attention at all, for it was touched by purity. The world of morning, with its flowers that had bloomed during the night and the first breezes coming down from the distant mountains. The world to which I bade farewell forever.

Well, it was at precisely one such moment that I saw him. My hand trembled and I hastily drew the curtain shut. I had seen him, and he was the only living soul out there among the flowers. It was a man, Nina, young and fair-haired like a delicate pagan god, intoxicated with life and with himself. Do you recognize him now, Nina? Can you find him in that far-off place of yours? Can you see him, Nina, just as afterward we so often had to reinvent him just to satisfy our thirst, our impatience, our longing for him? He was a man, and the same trembling hand that had closed the curtain pulled it open again, a-quiver with all the surprises this world can bring. Yes, a man. But he wasn't standing by my window and he wasn't looking at me. He was looking at something in the window next to mine—and that window was yours, Nina. I kept it a secret, and I'm revealing it now as an act of gratitude. For that discovery, the daily vision of that man, was the one thing that nourished me during my long exile shut up in that room. It was my only contact with the world, the only sad and solitary intrigue in which I participated, ever since I chose to sacrifice myself for the pity of others. How many times, as he disappeared from view and the curtain fell once more on my darkness, did I feel a little of that blond flash of morning sun still burning my retina, still lingering in my hands! But I wasn't fooled—it was your window, Nina, and every morning, in the sweetest and most spring-like of homages, he would carefully place a little bunch of violets on your windowsill. And then I, who had nothing but the vision of him for one moment each day and who lived only for the moment when I pulled back the corner of my curtain, I would wait until he had gone and, reaching out my arm—our windows were so close, Nina!—I would take the flowers for myself. It was like finally receiving in my hands a small fragment of the world, of his essence, of him. For now I know, Nina: youth smells of sweet violets. It's difficult to say precisely how long my little game went on for. I only know that I lived on it for days and days, or at least as long as the season for violets lasted. Then, when you left for the first time (it's strange, Nina, but one way or another you always seem to be leaving) and your window never opened again, how I suffered to watch him pass mournfully by that window where no one now lived! How inconsolably I suffered, the hours and hours I spent pacing restlessly around my room until the night outside fell upon me too, the sun darkened for the last time and he never again appeared because now there were no more mornings. And so I entered that natural death we call eternal night, all-embracing and all-encompassing, both inside and out.)

What a powerful thing the voice is: the echo of what she told me is more alive within me than the memory of her face. Was she beautiful? Yes, but the other Nina, not this one. The dead Nina is a creature reduced to her primitive, brute nature, her earthly matter. The Nina I knew, so restless, so fired by an inner flame that the others never managed either to locate or extinguish, no matter how they tried to hem her in or pin her down. It is a terrible truth, but we condemn everything that we love, first, to the slow death of our admiration, then to the insanity of our desires. In trying so hard to touch her fleeting spirit, we never succeeded in enslaving her (as was clearly our intention), but we were able to reduce her to this poor corpse lying here before me. Good, kind, amiable Nina? No, that's nonsense. But evil, cruel Nina? No, that's a lie too! For never had anyone so defied classification, so defied the petty strictures of human truth. Truth is not human, Nina. Do you remember the day . . .

There, I pay my secret debt. With a barely suppressed sob—that miserable body represents so many things to me—I scatter the flowers over her. Yes, Nina, there was a day, long ago now, when we scarcely dared to dream that victory would be ours. The alliance we later forged did not yet exist and we had not yet worked out the full extent of our plan. I was young and you were too—youth was the first thing that bound us together in this house of old people. I already had an inkling of it, though, on that other day, when, outside my window, I found a rose that had opened with the dawn. And so, standing before each another in that dawn, when my plan of vengeance was still in its infancy, I said: "The truth, Nina. Only the truth matters."

The truth was lying there before me. I bent slowly over the body and looked at her drawn, shrunken face, her black, hollow eye sockets. I remembered that when she was alive I had only ever met her in the darkness of my room—I had no clue how she would react to the light, nor how she smiled, nor how her eyes sparkled when she spoke to others. Dead, her face told me little; it was a cold, brutish thing, as if roughly molded from clay. And yet those tight lips were trying to say something—a word, an answer, who knows. I leaned closer, so that my face almost touched the sheet covering the body. And, the closer I got, the more I realized that the word, the answer, would come not just from her mouth, but from her whole body. I leaned still closer, almost lying on top of her, because the dead speak softly and their hidden language travels the entire length of their stiff bodies. In her resolute silence she represented the cold indifference of the earth, where one day I too would lie equally indifferent to those who gazed upon me. Then something, I don't know what, broke inside me and I stood up, my forehead dripping with sweat. I looked around me and saw that everyone was watching me. I scanned the room and what I saw made me tremble from head to foot: theirs was a petty, mean-spirited, suffering humanity, corralled like cattle within their own ineptitude and with no hope of escape. No breath of poetry, no touch of the supernatural would ever come to their rescue. They stood around the body awkwardly, expectantly, like vultures waiting for the opportune moment. I saw that this was the answer from those thin lips, closed now upon their own darkness. The path they showed me was the path to hell—a petty, human hell composed of all the infamies, foibles, and ordure of daily life. Suddenly a feeling came over me, a thirst for justice so strong that my eyes glazed over and my heart contracted as if in prayer. Oh, God! How I needed to believe in immortality! And yet, at the same time, I asked myself whether a Meneses could ever believe in immortality. My whole being was filled by such a strong need to transform and exalt mankind that I dared to open my lips and offer these words: "God, if you truly exist, then perform a miracle. Give me this miracle, O God in heaven, for I do not want to be merely the guardian of a corpse waiting to rot." I begged so earnestly that my whole body seemed to change, as if a scarlet wave of fire and hope washed over me. And it was then, Nina, that I opened my eyes and saw him, *him*, Nina—the young man with the violets. There he was standing slightly apart from the others, as fair-haired as he was all those years ago and still young, his head up, as if to confront that look of surprise on my face. He arose like an angel above the devastation of his suicide and hovered, immortal, before my eyes. Then I understood everything, Nina: how we had sinned and how wrong we had been. The answer was not to be found in the dark cavity of your mouth, nor in your poor body destined for the worms. It was there, Nina, in the miracle of that resurrection, in him, eternally young, as you had once been. God is like a bed of violets whose season never ends, Nina. Once again, I felt myself soaring above everything, and the eternity I had so forcefully demanded opened before me and I slid into an abyss of music. Love is immortal, Nina, only love is immortal. Not the love that is simply the desire for the body, the hands, the face, the eyes, all of which give rise to false and short-lived sensations, but, rather, the spirit that produces the love of these things and transforms them, creating them out of nothing when they no longer exist. I felt I had been saved, Nina, I who had lost my way through my own excessive shame—and I felt saved not because I had freed myself from that shame, but simply because by clinging to that vision of beauty, I planted within my feeble self a faith in something, and through that faith I knew another Faith would come. Because God is vast, Nina, and with him there is no end to understanding, forgiveness, and beauty.

So greatly did the light swell within me and fill me with the power of a sun arising from the depths, that I felt my sight fail me and I leaned heavily against the table.

There was doubtless a sudden, extravagant change in the air: our presence there, as though touched by some incantatory power, etched itself onto a space that was not ours and that lay beyond our understanding. I was seized by a kind of vertigo and, suddenly, indeed entirely unconsciously, I raised my hand and slapped the corpse's face. What impetus, what hidden will drove me? I wanted him to remember (if such a thing were possible) and to witness my repentance; I wanted him to know that I scorned his existence now that I had seen him and knew that he was still as beautiful as before. Nobody understood my gesture; perhaps they did not even see it. For some time, the soft, slack tissue of her cheek bore the dark mark left by my fingers. Make no mistake, Nina—it was our pact that I slapped. Yes, the truth. I had always sought the truth above all else. That had always been my defense, the august cloak in which I clothed my wretchedness. But what is truth when it is torn from its essence, and left naked and shameless? What is the untarnished truth, pure, dispassionate? No, that is not what interests us, Nina. I understood everything as I looked again at the people standing around me, *my* people, my worldly family, and then looking again at him, alive, the young man with the violets. No, it isn't truth, but charity that matters. Truth without charity is but blind, uncontrolled action, the voice of pride.

I don't know what happened to me then, but it was as if everything inside me came tumbling down, like an enormous building crashing to the ground. An icy wave rose up from my guts, engulfing my heart, stabbing it like a knife. I tried to cry out and raised my hands to my chest. Then I heard a shout bursting from my mouth. Everything around me went dark, I lost my balance and fell unconscious to the floor.

55.
Valdo's Statement (vi)

The sun had passed its highest point and was slowly beginning to set. In the drawing room, abandoned by all the curious onlookers, complete silence reigned. The inhabitants of the house were gathered around Timóteo, who had been carried to his room. The doctor, summoned urgently, had diagnosed a brain hemorrhage. Ana was there (taking the opportunity to fumigate the room), as were Betty, the old black servants, and even one or two neighbors who did not want to miss anything and, taking advantage of the general confusion, were observing the scenes with eyes full of malice.

Thus, as the sun's rays gradually lost their strength, the body lay alone, guarded only by the four candles, now nearly burnt out. I could not bring myself to leave her: for, at that moment more than at any other, it seemed to me that Nina needed someone by her side. Forgotten by everyone, she lay abandoned at the end of the drawing room, a white shape, neither a threat nor an attraction. Now that I was alone with her, I could finally gauge the distance between what she had been and what she was now. No, I wasn't being ungrateful—I simply felt that everyone had given up trying to grasp what lay behind that thin sheet and were clinging to the image of what she had once been, rather than what remained. It was as if they had completely lost touch with reality. I, on the other hand, knew very well that she was dead—truly dead—and this moved me even more. I sat down on a stool not far from where the body lay, paying close attention to the peculiar silence that death thrusts upon us: the silence of goodbyes, of letting things slip away like a mist heavy with nostalgia and remorse. But perhaps because of the hour and the soporific tranquility of late afternoon, I found my thoughts gradually turning to the future and of how I would leave that house and start a new life.

I believe it was at exactly that point that I saw a stranger enter the room. I say a stranger because, immersed as I was in my thoughts, I did not immediately recognize him or pick out any identifying features. He was a young man, almost a boy, reasonably tall, with fine features and fair hair. He moved gently, cautiously, as if he were afraid of waking someone sleeping nearby. There was something noble in the way he walked, and he carried himself with the grace and lightness of youth, an almost feline suppleness—yes, the person before me was, how can I put it, a young tiger, his body swaying in a nonchalant display of energy as yet unexpended. He had clearly waited for the room to empty before entering. He was wearing a pair of dark, rather old trousers and a light-colored sports shirt—from his clothes he could easily have been one of the servants, and I would indeed have taken him for one if there had been anything else in him to confirm that. In fact I'd go further: had it not been for the enquiring look he gave me, he would have escaped my notice entirely among all the many strangers who had passed through the house that day. It was not as if he were trying to work out who I was, nor that he was attempting to read my thoughts, no, but his cold, unfamiliar eyes pierced me, not so much as a means of establishing contact as of keeping me at a distance. Slowly, as if they had at last formulated a question, his eyes moved from me to the body in the coffin. Then once again he looked at me, with an expectant stare I could not even begin to understand. Was it an invitation, or was he simply asking permission? What did he mean by looking at me like that? Some inner impulse brought me to my feet: now it was my turn, and, without taking my eyes off him and without thinking that this would in any way diminish the distance between us, I went over to him, or, rather, to the corpse, which lay like a barrier between us. I took a few more steps and saw that his eyes were still following me. At that moment, I confess, I detected in them something familiar, something cunning and furtive that I had seen many times before, but so long ago that I could not identify who or what it reminded me of. It was nothing but a memory, if that's what one can call the physical sensation of an unidentifiable memory, and which awakened in me something familiar, something I had once been a part of, but which, along with so many other things decayed or scattered by time, lay buried like the remnants of a former self that had already had its day and disappeared into that continuous evolution of who we are, of what we do, and what we feel. But whether I knew him or not, that was the force propelling me forward until I was standing right beside the corpse.

Let me repeat, just to be clear, it was, by then, late afternoon. Shafts of thick, golden light filled with dancing particles of dust filtered through the yellow glass at the top of the windows. The heat was unrelenting, but an occasional breeze carried in from outside the hot breath of sun-scorched plants; a whole crackling, rust-red world seemed to impose itself on all things quiet and pleasant, creating an artificial atmosphere of harsh, restless shapes. More than anything else it was that feeling of disquiet—like a premonition inside me, beating its funereal drum—that made me lean forward and lift the sheet covering the dead woman's face. (As I did this, and as if drawn in by my gesture, the stranger also moved closer.) I wanted to say my final farewell. Before I left this place, before I abandoned her forever to the stagnant waters of memory, I wanted to see her one last time—for this was where her physical presence would end, and I wanted to take with me a final image of her, so that my eyes at last would close upon the sight of her flesh and then, if possible, transmute it into something merely perishable and meaningless.

I leaned over. (I sensed that, from the other side, the stranger also leaned over—what one saw, the other saw.) There was Nina, and I gazed at her for the last time. I don't think I have the strength to describe what lay before my eyes, nor the strange enchantment of the moment, created not so much by the absurdly brilliant light flooding the room as by the force of that unfamiliar gaze accompanying mine. No, it was Nina, just Nina, and this was where I would leave her, because I had no way now of fathoming the secret of her existence. What I saw neither shocked nor surprised me: on the contrary, combined with the sentiments welling up inside me, the sight of her assuaged the disbelief that was already taking hold of me. Only a muffled groan came from my lips, as if what should have been an expression of surprise had also become an expression of grief. I don't know if it was due to the stifling heat—the cicadas were screeching furiously—or the process of rapid decomposition produced by that particular type of disease, but the dead woman's appearance had changed completely. (I say "the dead woman" because I can no longer bear to say her name. We are poised on the frontier where human habits cease, and what I now have to relate is a vision of what takes place beyond the known world, rather than a demonstration of the shortcomings of this our terrestrial sphere.)

I wasn't struck only by how thin she had become, but by what you might call the slow obliteration of the firm lines of her face, a slackening of the nerves and the tension that had held her features in equilibrium. Everything familiar had gone, vanished, sucked in by some subcutaneous force, her skin, if you can call it that, was slowly falling into loose folds as if it no longer had the strength to sustain its human form. Behind this cascade of lava, not yet liquid, but impregnated with the oil of disintegrating tissue—all that was left of that fermenting, slowly dissolving matter—I could already see the outline of the only thing in her that was firm and unassailable by time, heat or disease: her bones. Her skeleton was already visible through the fragile fabric, and, in some places, was almost threatening to break through; it was clear that it would not be long before it emerged completely, free both of its enveloping flesh and of the pink, shifting light that had illuminated that flesh. Bumps, pockmarks, and black-lined cavities erupted here and there, like the carcass of a ship left high and dry in the sun by the retreating tide.

It was then, looking up, that I heard a voice and realized that the stranger opposite me was André. Yes, it was my son and I hadn't recognized him, neither his fair hair nor his manly bearing, his wary, feline gestures. As this information sank in, I felt disorientated and almost afraid of his presence, which I had completely forgotten about. Deeply troubled, I tried in vain to understand how such a thing could have happened and why he had seemed so different. Perhaps—and here I make my ultimate confession—perhaps it was because I had never really looked at him. I repeat: I had *never* really looked at him. This revelation stunned me and, like a trail of fire stretching back into my past, it made me realize the full extent of the havoc Nina had left in her wake. Ah, how I had loved that woman, even to the point of neglecting all my other duties . . .

"Listen," he said to me, and his voice was perfectly normal, as if what he was about to say was the most banal thing in the world: "Up until now, until this very moment, I have never in my whole life heard you say anything of any significance or that helped me in the slightest. Watching you, I've often asked myself what kind of empty nonsense fills your head. And yet there she is," and he pointed to the coffin, "there she lies. Before she died, she asked me if there was such a thing as life after death. Not just once, but several times, as if she were tormented by the idea. I replied categorically that there was no life after death, neither for her nor anyone else. I don't believe that Christ rose from the dead. Nor do I believe that he appeared on the road to Emmaus. But now," and he again pointed at the coffin, "I have such a horror of death and that disgusting smell, that now it's my turn to ask: is there such a thing as life after death?"

He fell silent for a moment, his hands resting on the edge of the coffin. Then he continued, speaking more quickly, almost breathlessly:

"So tell me, since you're the one who fathered me, and ought to be the one to teach me what I need to know. You are my father, aren't you? Aren't you meant to look after me, pay me some sort of attention? So tell me, then, is there such a thing as life after death? Do we rise from the dead someday, somewhere?"

Such strange things, uttered by someone who had previously barely spoken to me, left me in a state of shock, rendering me speechless. I had never been a believer, but nor had I ever dared to defy God. Despite everything, however, I sensed that at that moment I could not and should not lie. I have believed in many things, most of all in the power of good, the victory of morality over immorality, the necessity of religion, in short, everything in this world that is considered right. I have even believed in sin and its destructive power. But I could never believe in the resurrection of the flesh. How could I say that to someone so desperate? (Now I know that what was tearing him apart was his complete lack of hope. How we burn, dear God, as dry as a scorched cinder, simply because of the absence of hope! For it was God he did not believe in, and for a man as passionate as André such disbelief was dangerous, even deadly. He didn't want to know if there was life after death in order to fall on his knees and make his peace with God. No, he wanted to know so that he could then confront and insult God directly. It was Creation itself he couldn't forgive—God's invention of man, man's existence, and subsequent banishment.

"Tell me," he implored, almost in a whisper. "Tell me something, because everything you say is important. I don't trust invisible signs any more, and I want some kind of tangible, worldly proof. I am your son because I was conceived from your flesh, and it is you who must tell me, yes or no: is there such a thing as life after death?"

He stood there, waiting for my answer, and I merely bowed my head and stepped back, as if I no longer had the strength to look at what lay in the coffin. Taking this as a refusal to speak, he exclaimed with a force that literally made me shudder:

"Ah, I knew it. I don't believe we will be reborn, and I never have. There is no eternity. She's dead, utterly dead, so dead that it's impossible even to think about her, or only as a piece of rubbish, a pile of rotting flesh, a heap of animal dung you might step in. Is that what we are, God? Is your image, in which they teach us we are made, is it nothing more than a mask to conceal the underlying putrefaction? Are we doomed to fade into nothingness? Ah, the injustice of it! There's no mercy, and without mercy how can we imagine God or have any respect for him? Well, God, here you are: here's what I think of *your* creation."

And with that he leaned forward over the dead woman's body and spat on it. He spat not once, twice, or even three times, but over and over again until he had no more saliva left. He was exhausted, and the sweat ran down his forehead.

"There's one thing I want you to know," he said to me. "I don't love you and I have never loved you as a son should love his father. I don't even think of you as my father, just as I don't think it's my mother who's lying dead in this coffin. In fact, I don't feel anything at all toward my family. I don't love any human being. And do you want to know why? Well, listen carefully, because if it wasn't true, then I might well love you as my father, and respect the other members of the family, and acknowledge this corpse as my mother. But none of that will happen, *because Christ is nothing but a lie.*"

After uttering these fateful words, he stared at me so intensely that he seemed almost to want to pierce my very thoughts. Then he sighed wearily and left the room. The corpse lay between us, and I shouted after him:

"André!"

He stopped and slowly turned to face me.

"André!" I shouted again, and this time there was a new conciliatory tone in my voice.

Then something incredible happened: as if I were threatening him, he turned again and began to run, literally began to run, through the drawing room and onto the verandah where one or two latecomers still lingered. Sensing that I was about to lose him forever, I called out his name and started to run after him, because with him went something that was absolutely precious to me and irreplaceable. One of the people on the verandah tried to hold me back, asking if I needed something. I pushed him to one side and rushed down the steps after André. He was still running, and had now almost reached the pond. I continued after him, calling out his name again and again, but he did not turn around—it was as if I were precisely the thing he wanted to avoid. However, the chase could not last long: he was younger and faster than me, and his motive for fleeing the house was, quite possibly, stronger and more powerful than the motive impelling me to follow him. I stopped and wiped the sweat from my forehead—I had lost the race. With André gone, the last knot binding me to the past was undone.

(I could still see him—and I will never forget. The searing, late afternoon sun was bathing the garden in the golden light of one of its final days of splendor, but not even that could hold him back. I knew he was not even aware of the garden, just as he could no longer hear my voice. He was still running, and the last image I have of him is of his hair flying behind him in the wind as he raced toward the Chácara's main gate, running faster and faster until, when he reached the gate, he flung himself out into the road like a bird escaping its cage. I'll finish with that image. Needless to say, I never saw him again.)

Looking around me, I suddenly found myself alone, completely alone in the garden. I heard the gate creak open again and saw the hearse driving up the main avenue. It was an entirely unremarkable vehicle, painted black and decorated only by a few dull golden tassels. Its wheels squeaked ponderously over the sandy path and, when it passed in front of me, I saw that it was driven by Senhor Quincas, the Vila Velha carpenter who made the coffins, also drove the hearse, and, in the absence of the official gravedigger, sometimes buried the dead. Senhor Quincas, old and ruddy-faced from too much rum, stared at me as he drove by, and with such a look of surprise that, for a second, I felt I was in the wrong place, somehow a stranger, an intruder. A small group was gathering on the verandah, getting ready to carry the coffin.

I leaned blindly against a tree, watching that clumsy vehicle, so at odds with the splendor of the afternoon, and I whispered softly, several times, not the name André (which, in any event, was not the name I knew him by), but Nina, and I let the sweet sound of that name mingle freely with my salty tears.

56.
Postscript in a Letter from Father Justino

Yes, I have decided to respond to that man's request. I don't know him and I can't think why he's collecting such information, but he seems to have an urgent interest in the matter. Moreover, I believe that whatever the reason for his urgency, it must have God's blessing, for the last thing the Almighty would deny his consent to is the revelation of the truth. I don't know what this person is looking for, but in the way he asked me for my statement, I sense a thirst for justice. And if I am now finally—and fully—agreeing to his request, it is not so much out of a desire to recollect past events (for so many things are lost with the passage of time), as in the vague hope of restoring some respect for the memory of a creature who paid so dearly in this world, and for failings that were not entirely her own.

I can still remember the last time I saw her, when we were halfway through the terrible epidemic that ravaged our town. The Meneses house was one of the last to fall, although it had already been thoroughly ransacked by the infamous Chico Herrera gang. I can still see the house now, its massive stone foundations rising up as simply and majestically as an ancient monument in the wilderness of the garden. Almost all the rendering had flaked off the walls, the windows had come loose from their frames, and the garden and even the worm-eaten steps were completely overgrown—and yet, for anyone who knew the history of Vila Velha, life still seeped out through the cracked walls, exposed joists, and fallen roof tiles of its abandoned skeleton, which continued to ring with the echo of recent events.

When the main house threatened to collapse, Ana (the person I am writing about), went to live in an old gazebo at the bottom of the garden. It could not have been a less appropriate or less salubrious choice of accommodation. As soon as I entered, led by a black servant who seemed perfectly familiar with the place, I heard someone coughing in one of the farthest rooms. I asked the servant if it was Dona Ana, and he nodded. In my priestly vocation—following in the ways of the Lord as one might say—I have been summoned to attend the dying in many strange places. However, I have seen none as sad and forsaken as that hovel. In other places there was an energy that throbbed until the very last second, a warmth that clung to the surrounding objects no matter how wretched, but there, in that tiny cellar that seemed more like a suffocating prison cell, the air was stale and heavy with the stench of sweat, and the departing soul was leaving this life surrounded by utter indifference and desolation. I had never seen a sadder sight, nor one so abandoned by the Grace of God.

She was lying on a pallet bed made of planks from a packing crate, covered with a straw mattress that was full of holes. I could not, at first, see her face, but I could hear her labored breathing. The cramped space was filled with the tepid, nauseating smell of someone who has been suffering from a prolonged illness and been unable to attend to her personal hygiene. For a moment, I thought I was in one of those adobe shacks that serve as shelter for the lowliest of peasants, not by the bedside of the last known heiress of the proud Meneses family. It would be impossible not to reflect upon the transience of worldly glory and, while the servant struggled to open a jammed window to give us some light, I unconsciously began to say a few prayers. In the corners, like shadows waiting in ambush, I sensed some breathing, shapeless thing, something like the spirit of evil.

Finally, a thin, watery light entered the room. There she lay, half sitting up, her eyes shining, her face gaunt.

"Ah, Father Justino," she murmured. "I thought you would never come."

I sat down beside her, trying to hide my feelings. Whichever way I turned, though, I felt her eyes following me. Her insistent gaze rather irritated me—it was almost as if she were waiting for me to say something to soothe her troubled soul. And what could I, a poor, miserable priest, say? What words, what consolation, could I say to her beyond what I had already tried to tell her on other occasions, and which had proved so entirely useless in the face of her desperate will to oppose me and to resist? She sensed my hesitation and, removing one trembling, still strangely youthful hand from beneath the tattered bedspread, she grabbed hold of one of my hands and pressed it to her soft, feverish lips, covering it with the drool of a toothless kiss. A slow dribble of saliva dripped between my fingers; she stared at me with pleading eyes.

"Speak, my child. That is what I am here for." With my other hand (for she was still holding on to me, as if fearing I might flee), I stroked her hair, by now almost entirely white.

"Only one thing matters, Father. There is only one thing I want to know."

Perhaps it is our intimate knowledge of the dying that tells us they will only give their last (and most painful) confession at the moment when it can no longer be postponed. Or perhaps, who knows, as we sit by the bedside, we have a sixth sense that allows us to anticipate what is about to happen. I don't know. The truth is that, with my eyes attentively closed, I could tell almost exactly what wounds she was about to re-open. That desperate, lost soul had been struggling her whole life with a problem she would never manage to resolve on her own, and which even after all this time still kept her there, her life perhaps hanging by a thread, and waiting for someone—possibly me—to come and tell her the one thing she wanted to hear, but which, out of honesty or simple pity, was precisely the thing neither I nor anyone else could ever say. Because clearly present in her shriveled body was a voice ceaselessly asking what is goodness, does heaven exist, do we have a right to be happy, is there life after death? Or is there any justice in the face of death and (for such is our blindness) does anything survive of our pathetic, futile human passions?

The most extraordinary thing is that the conversation flowed as if it were simply the continuation of something that had already gone before. She had not changed one iota since the last time we saw each other, neither the course of her life, nor the way she lived it. What I saw (and for this I did not even need to look at her), was that she was entirely part of that proud, obstinate family who followed their destiny as if swept along by a current to their inevitable fate. The torrent was now rushing to its end, and what could she possibly want but to afford me another glimpse of what had constituted her life or her mistake, if you like, but which had been her sole motivation, the reason for her battle with the others?

"Father . . . I don't know if you remember . . . the last time . . ."

Of course I remembered, and I can set it down here, for it wasn't a formal confession, nor on that or any other occasion, did she ask me to keep it secret. I remembered—and with such clarity—how several years previously she had asked me what sin was. What could I say in response—me, a poor priest—other than what I had learned in books and embraced through my faith in God? And yet, I think I did add something that derived more from my own experience than from the teachings of the catechism. I told her not what was laid down in law, but what accorded with the things, the people and the house I saw around me. (Such is the true law of God: it can take on the appearance and color of the moment in which it is called upon. Is that mere flabby ambiguity or compromise? No, truth must encompass all aspects of human contingency. What does truth bring us when it embraces only one single aspect or shows one single face, which often hide the true essence of the facts? I repeat: God's law is mutable and various, precisely because it has the candor, the austerity, and the fluidity of liquid: it penetrates and refreshes, it brings life and fertility to land that, before, produced nothing but the dry thorns of death.) Ah, this clamorous, nebulous thing we call sin, this victory of the strong which is yet so characteristic of the weak and indecisive, of the monsters and tyrants, who, throughout the centuries, have used its banner in order to massacre and oppress! The dark shadow of the Jesuits who, in its name, raised bonfires and lit infernos—how then can sin be set in a context of understanding and justice? Ah, the bed of the weak, the resting place of the sad and effeminate! And how much greater is the sin of not risking the supreme sin, of being human and alone, and gazing upon the one resplendent face of God, that beacon of light and forgiveness shining in the abyss? What can we say to those melancholy guardians of fruitless virtue, to those aesthetes of goodness, to those warriors without stomach or courage or imagination for the fight?

However, I felt another peril beginning to circle around me, and only then did I perceive its true nature. It was error—the false eagerness of the predestined, the cravings of troubled souls whose only support is their own reason. Reason. At least that was what I understood as I listened to her recount a series of atrocities with an effort that seemed to transfigure her. I repeat: none of this was told to me in the form of a confession; on the contrary, she herself asked me to disclose the facts so that this stain—for stain there was—should weigh less heavily upon her tomb. If I have kept silent until now, it is because I considered it unnecessary, as you may judge from what follows, to return to the subject. But since an opportunity now presents itself to establish the true facts, what prevents me from saying now what I heard, and thereby trying to raise from its shadows the massacred ruins of that house laid low by fear? (There lay the house, as if devoured by an evil nurtured in its very own entrails. In the midst of that luxuriant, untrammeled landscape, it maintained a strange reserve, as if turning in upon its own ruins and blindly meditating upon the void within and unravelling the harsh, lonely memory of days long gone . . .)

"It was years ago, Father," she began, "when my sister-in-law left for the first time. I can hardly say how the whole madness began. All I know is that one evening, I was hiding in the bushes outside this Pavilion, and I watched Nina saying goodbye to Alberto. And then, as soon as she had disappeared, and as if driven by something stronger than myself, I called out to him: 'Alberto!'"

For what was, I confess, the first time, I looked her straight in the eye. The black servant had succeeded in opening the window, and a remnant of dull, greenish twilight reached us now along with an occasional breeze. Her eyes slowly turned toward that sliver of light as if in remembrance of something that happened long, long ago, and which drifted in on a breath of wind and vibrated in unison with some final, dying chord of her soul. Of course, I already knew the story of that passion, which like all human passions had been a delusion, but I couldn't help but shudder to see her eyes searching endlessly for the last few, broken pieces of that moment when she had truly lived, her miserable, half-dead body still trembling when she said his name. The enslavement of the flesh—what other name can we give to the soul's long submission to the body? For the memory belonged less to her tormented soul than to the senses: a single, combined memory of pleasure, knowledge and death, one single shining moment in her entire existence, like a firework that shoots into the air and disintegrates, leaving behind it an even deeper darkness. Ah, but perhaps it would be better for us all if I spare the reader my own emotions and continue faithfully retelling what I heard that evening long ago.

She went on talking, telling me how he whirled around in alarm when she said his name, for he clearly thought that, up until then, his affair with Nina had gone unnoticed. "What do you want? What do you want from me?" he exclaimed as soon as he saw Ana. She was standing motionless beside a bush, and her face must have eloquently expressed the suffering that consumed her. And Alberto, despite his rough manners, could not fail to understand what was going on. "There's no point," he said with a look of evident disgust. She didn't say a word and moved closer. She touched him with her hand, lightly on his forearm, then sliding her hand up to his elbow, then to his chest. Suddenly, like someone in the grip of a sudden madness, she flung her arms around him and, sobbing and crying, clasped him to her. Alberto tried to push her away, afraid that someone might see them, even though it was already dark. But Ana would not let go and stood there with her eyes shut tight, as if every sign of life had drained from her body. He tried in vain to free himself from her embrace, but that embrace was not so much an impulse of life as a spasm of death. Then the inevitable happened: the night, the scent of the roses, and, above all, Alberto's youth, all played their part. But more than all those things combined was the part played by Nina's recent presence, and the heat she always left pulsating though his veins. Finally, he returned Ana's embrace and kissed her, and Ana gave herself to him right there, on the grass, as if it were the first time a man had ever possessed her.

From that point onward, as far as I recall, her account became somewhat confused, perhaps because she no longer had a clear recollection of what had happened, or perhaps because, having reached such a climax, what came afterward was not as interesting. The fact is that what happened next was plunged in obscurity, one of those pauses that exists to reinvigorate our life, and perhaps—who knows?—lead it on to greater challenges. All Ana remembered was that, at a certain point, she realized she was pregnant. And pregnancy was certainly a pressing matter, particularly since it was the first time any such signs had manifested themselves even after all those years of marriage. How would she explain the situation to her husband? What could she tell him? Such were the questions ceaselessly occupying her mind. It was around this time, more or less, that the troubles between Valdo and Nina became more acute. The goings-on at the Pavilion were no longer such a secret, and Nina, under the pressure of circumstances, was threatening to leave the house. (I believe, my friend, that we are now reaching the crux of the whole story. No matter how far ahead we look, no matter how divergent the paths we follow, we will always find ourselves returning to the events of that period—they are the foundations of the building, the keystone of the arch, the mainspring on which everything depends.) To add to an already difficult situation, Nina also pronounced herself to be pregnant, and the prospects of this future Meneses heir became the subject of keen discussion among the entire family. Are you following closely the plot of our little story? Two women, both pregnant, one of them the center of attention and the subject of daily conversation within their little world, whilst the other one is alone with her secret, feeling, minute by minute, a new life growing and pulsating within her. Ana took to following her sister-in-law like a shadow: she drank in the other woman's every gesture, every move, every thought as if it were a life-giving tonic. It was instinct that guided her, with that sixth sense that only women possess (and only certain women at that), knowing that it was from there that salvation would come. However, Nina needed freedom to live; she was like a bird, and blithely unaware of the evil of her ways. (And at this point, gripping my hand tightly, Ana asked: "Can such a woman be aware of right and wrong, Father? A woman who burns her own clothes because she thinks they're infected with the disease devouring her? Is it possible? And other things, countless other things too.") The truth is that Nina was sick to death of the suffocating atmosphere of the Chácara and was talking of leaving and yet, if the scandal had not broken, she would have stayed forever. I believe it was Demétrio who threw her out—he could forgive her for sleeping with her husband, but only because he believed she didn't love Valdo. But with the other one, the one he came across one day kneeling at her feet . . . (Ana recalled these things reluctantly, wearily.) Before leaving the Chácara for good, there was one last period of relative peace when even Ana thought everything had been sorted out. The affair with the gardener had not yet been discovered, and Nina, on the pretext that it was summer, had moved into the Pavilion—the very Pavilion in which I now sat listening to the dying woman's confession. Summer was not the only motive: Valdo, convalescing after his failed suicide attempt, maintained that he would be able to rest better in the Pavilion. Even she could no longer remember how long the truce lasted—two or possibly three months? Until Demétrio, who had never really accepted the move to the Pavilion, revealed the scandal and practically forced Nina to leave. As if the air had suddenly grown thinner, Ana felt a void opening up around her. Emptiness, total emptiness. She would spend all day sleepwalking through that house of sleepwalkers. Then, terrified her secret would be discovered at any moment, she had an idea, an idea that would be the greatest lie of all. She could not even say how long the thought had lingered at the back of her mind; she simply felt that she could not wait another day and that now was exactly the right moment to try to save herself, if indeed she wanted to be saved. And so, one morning while sitting in bed brushing her hair—a habit she had learned from Nina—she said to her husband: "Demétrio, I know that, despite everything, you'd like Nina to come back. Well, I know how to bring her back." (He was suffering as he never had before. Despite having made her leave, he had never loved her more or been so much in need of her presence, drifting aimlessly around the house like a rudderless ship.) Demétrio stared at her, pale and surprised—although perhaps less surprised than he should have been at such a proposal. (And yet, who knows what Ana herself thought at that moment? Watching his troubled face, full of subterranean fears that, despite his best efforts, revealed the secret that had been torturing him for so many months, had she perhaps finally understood the reason for her husband's remoteness and disdain for their marriage?

Had she perhaps found a justification, however fleeting, for her own acts of madness and adultery? Now, I'm not trying to downplay any of these events—I am merely, as I said earlier, seeking to restore some respect for the memory of a creature who paid so dearly in this world for failings that were not entirely her own.) "Demétrio, I know how to bring Nina back," she repeated. He did not believe her, but seeing a new determination on her face, as if nothing mattered more to her than her sister-in-law's return, he asked: "How?" Ana lay down beside him and, such is men's blindness, he did not for one moment feel suspicious of that gesture of studied resignation. "We talked about it once," said Ana, forcing herself to contain her own emotions, "and she hinted that if I were to go and fetch her, then she might perhaps come back." "*You?*" asked Demétrio, astonished. "Go to Rio? To find her?" "Yes, why not?" "To *Rio*?" he repeated. "But you know nothing about Rio!" Ana smiled: "No, I don't, but so what? I only need to ask." Now there was a look of distrust in her husband's eyes. Then he thought for a few moments about his wife's proposal. Ah, but it was easy enough to read his thoughts! He was probably thinking: "They never got on before; they always avoided each other like the plague, like enemies. Why this sudden closeness?" But then his old-fashioned reasoning, so easy and accommodating, quickly followed: "Well, they're women. What do I know of these things? Women understand each other." He looked again at Ana: "If that's how things are, then I agree. But you must, of course, speak to Valdo first." She'd had her suspicions before, but had never been sure. She had seen only vacant stares, a certain distance, unexplained silences when she entered a room—but what was an absence or a silence in a house so full of silences? Now, as she looked at the man lying in bed beside her, his eyes closed, she not only understood everything, but even guessed the precise details of the drama: his sleepless nights thinking about the woman lying so near and yet so far, in the arms of another; the times he had gotten up and tiptoed into the hallway to listen at the other door to the sounds of a pleasure that eluded him;

the moments of unrelenting lucidity when she noticed him looking at that magnificent young woman, and saw him run his hand through his white hair, saw his cold, mean-spirited face; and countless other such incidents that were now confirmed by his present reaction; and she gazed at him almost triumphantly.

Valdo showed little interest in her plan. Firstly, because he knew Nina well, and secondly, because he was far too immersed in his own sorrows to give the necessary attention to such an unlikely proposal. He simply shrugged, and Ana concluded that she had won.

It was not difficult to imagine what she was going to do in the capital. After studying minutely the details of the journey, she said her goodbyes and left the Chácara, taking up rooms in an obscure boarding house in Flamengo. From there she began to write a series of letters intended to deceive her husband and Valdo (for Ana was quite convinced her sister-in-law would never under any circumstances return to Vila Velha, and so there was no need to try and find her), saying that she had found the fugitive, but that she was sick and needed to be looked after, and that they could not, therefore, return until Nina was completely cured. So as to avoid any awkward questions, she added that Nina's illness appeared to consist of nervous instability and physical exhaustion, and other more or less obscure symptoms of some non-existent disease. Demétrio replied once or twice to her letters, sending her money and telling her to take her time. And so Ana stayed, while the real motive for her visit, her pregnancy, advanced toward its conclusion. As for Nina, Ana did not at first go to see her, but she did find out where she lived, both in order to salve her conscience and because she knew that sooner or later she would be obliged to go and find her. At this time, Nina was living in a luxury hotel, or so it seemed to Ana's inexpert eye. On certain afternoons, walking slowly on account of her condition, she went as far as the door of the hotel and spoke to the doorman and to the other staff, trying to piece together the details of her sister-in-law's new life. Ah yes, Nina was living well, on her own, whiling away her hours in that bourgeois hotel. She had always had the gift of being able to choose luxury and idleness over anything else. Then, when Ana sensed the birth was approaching, she took herself off to a hospital. A few days later, she returned with a son in her arms. And only then did she decide to go and find Nina. Only then was she ready to appear before her. Nina was still in bed and took fright when she saw Ana, dressed entirely in black, standing motionless in the doorway. At first, neither of them spoke, but merely scrutinized each other cruelly. Finally, Ana stepped forward and spoke. She had come to fetch her. Valdo wanted her to come home. Nina laughed: she would never go back. That was her final answer. Still standing, Ana stared at her coldly, for it could scarcely be said that she had expected any other answer. And when Nina scornfully showed her the new clothes and jewelry she owned, adding that she would never give them up for the bland, insipid life of the Chácara, Ana asked calmly where the child was, the Meneses' heir. It was Nina's turn to stop in her tracks then and stare at her in astonishment: the child? How could Ana be so naïve as to think that she, Nina, would keep the offspring of that despicable clan? She had no idea where he was; she had left him at the hospital where he was born, with one of the nurses. She had made a point of abandoning him. (Nina was certainly capable of such a thing. She was certainly cruel enough to do that, her flaws were what made her the person she was. Cold? Indifferent? But perhaps she should not be judged on that one action.) Ana merely said: "I'll go and find him." And although Nina did not reply, she was nevertheless sure that Ana really would go and find him. Why? Simply because that was how it should be, and in stating that she would never return to the Chácara, she was probably only telling half the truth. She knew vaguely that she would return one day. When? Well it scarcely mattered. But when the moment came, she would need an alibi, a reason to confront the hostile gaze of the Meneses again. And so Ana left. And then she confessed to me, her eyes fixed on mine, that she had never gone to the hospital and had never tried to find any of the nurses. The boy she had brought back to the Chácara as Nina's son was not Valdo's heir and he wasn't a Meneses either; he was the fruit of her own passion for the gardener. Valdo had not asked any questions and had not even shown the slightest sign of gratitude for the news she had brought him. It was as if during all the time she had been away only one day had passed at the Chácara; one long, heavy day filled with silence, shadows, and resentment.

In that stifling room in the Pavilion, the dying woman tried to grab my hands. Her voice was almost inaudible after her long account of events, but even so, freed of the weight that burdened her, she seemed to gain a final burst of energy.

"That is what I did, Father. André was my son, not hers."

There was a pause.

"But, my child, during all that time, did you not even once, just once, think of him as your son and treat him as such?"

"*My* son!" Her voice rang out almost angrily. "What did it matter to me if he was my son? He was alive. He had everything he could possibly need. How could I accept him or consider him a son of mine when everything within me froze at the mere idea of it, at the thought of my husband's reaction and my punishment. Ah, Father, no one enters the Meneses family with impunity!"

"But not even for one single day, not even for a single minute . . ."

She seemed to remember something:

"Yes, there was one day. A long time ago. She told me that his eyes and mouth reminded her of Alberto. So I went into his room and tried to force him . . . But Father, why remember such things now?"

It was clearly pointless for me to insist; she would not understand then, just as she had never understood.

"But," I asked, "didn't Nina ever realize the truth?"

Ana heaved herself up on her elbows. I could see her eyes shining again:

"That is something I have always suspected, Father. Nina must have known André was not her son. On one occasion"—and even I trembled at what she said—"I came across her crying in the little storeroom off the hallway. It was the same place where they had laid Valdo on a couch after his attempted suicide. Nina was sitting on the couch with a crumpled piece of paper in her hands, probably a letter. Seeing her so distressed, I sensed (although I don't know why) that my moment of triumph had arrived: that piece of paper, that letter, must be the proof of some misdemeanor, a crime perhaps, which, when revealed, would destroy her forever in the eyes of everyone. What mad, unbounded hope seized me at that moment! I threw myself upon her and tried to snatch the document from her. She did her best to stop me and then, when she saw that she could not fend me off, she cried out just one word, a man's name: 'Glael!' I froze, and at the same time I had the feeling that she had just named someone sacred, someone I did not know and who was probably her real son, conceived of her own flesh. Had she lied to me? Had she, in fact, not abandoned him anonymously to the tender mercies of a nurse? I don't know, because that woman was contradiction personified, and there was a side to her entirely plunged in darkness. I didn't have the courage to persist and so I left her. It was time to go, and, in any case, I could already see Valdo coming down the hallway."

Noting my silence, Ana touched my arm:

"And during all that time, Father, she allowed André to think he was committing the most heinous of sins."

"Is that possible?" I could not hold back a groan. I was almost struggling for air.

"Compared to all the rest, Father, isn't that the worst, the most wicked, of crimes? Driving that boy to such despair, to such remorse, for something he did not do?"

I could not contain myself and stood up. She followed me with her gaze:

"Perhaps you'll say, Father, that by taking on the weight of a sin she did not commit, or that was not at least as grave as it appeared, she possessed a greatness that none of us . . ."

At that moment a sob, a deep, genuine sob, burst from her lips:

"That's what it is, Father. How does one weigh guilt? I think that is what has forever hardened my heart."

And then, possibly sensing the condemnation that lay in that strange substitution of which she was only now realizing the full implications—Nina taking the blame for something she had not done, while she, Ana, had hidden her own grievous fault out of fear of the Meneses—her voice suddenly exploded, filling the tiny room:

"And I, Father, am I not to be saved too? Did I not sin like the others? Did I not exist?"

What could I say, how could I reply now that the final moment had come? I believe this was the only time I came to regret my priestly vocation—for what rose in my chest was regret, rather than a cry of deep, inconsolable sorrow at the irredeemable blindness of the human condition, its helpless incomprehension. Of all people, why come to me? Me, a sick old man, an uneducated, rather unintelligent priest whose one goal in life has been to serve and fear God, not to disentangle these intricate human problems? We country priests are nothing but doleful beasts of burden, plodding horses of only moderate utility, as blind and confused as any other men and distinguished only by our constant, anxious desire never to stray from the paths of righteousness. But how do we discern the paths of righteousness among so many others? How do we render justice and dictate God's will? I drew back and, as she implored me with a mixture of incoherent words and tears, I stood by the barred window and looked up at the darkening sky. A great void opened up in my soul as if there were nothing inside me, neither the fear nor the remembrance of God. A refusal, a rejection. A searing, bitter taste rose suddenly into my mouth.

No, there was nothing I could say. Once, certainly, I had said something about such matters, but it was so long ago that I could no longer remember. And no doubt it was this that burdened her. What good would it do to repeat words that had once had real meaning, but which now seemed so strange and paradoxical, as if they had been spoken not by me but by others in my place? The house of the Meneses no longer existed. Its last redoubt, that cellar, which had once sheltered love and hope, would also soon fall into ruin. It was this place that Ana had chosen as her refuge, just as creatures fleeing a flood seek shelter on the highest point of the roof. At that precise moment, the house of Meneses was disappearing forever. A last glimmer of its existence still flickered in the form of that dying woman. I knew what I could say: "My child, what you said is perfectly valid. We are not to blame for the way things are, but it's still valid. So many of us confuse God with the idea of goodness. Or we reduce Him to a simple notion of evil that must be avoided. Goodness, however, is an earthly, human measure. How can we use it to measure that infinite thing that is God?" But those words, those precise words, did not come to my lips because she would not have understood them and would have continued to plead with me, not in the name of God (whom she did not know), but in the name of the sin that had always tormented her. And so her soul would have to endure, alone, until the very end, the consequences of her errors. Perhaps I am mistaken, but it scarcely matters. Absolution from a priest who has lost sight of good sense scarcely matters either. The crime whose origin I could not reveal to her was not that she had concealed the fruit of her love, nor that she silently acquiesced to another woman's sin. No, what I reproached her for was not having understood and accepted her own errors, and having shrouded in anonymity her one cry for salvation. The Meneses had taken her back, and the struggle that ensued had become merely a struggle between Meneses, with no profound consequences and without ever—ever!—losing sight of that human measure of goodness which they had chosen as the supreme standard of their existence. But, alas for us, God often takes on the appearance of evil. God is almost always everything that shatters the hard, tangible surface of our everyday existence—for He is not sin, but Grace. Even more than this, God is action and revelation. How can we think of Him as something static, a thing of inertia and stillness? His law is the law of the storm, not the calm.

I turned back to her, prepared to grant her forgiveness, but in the name of precisely that evil that stood in opposition to her rudimentary notions of morality, an evil which I would offer to her as a supreme indulgence to the dying. Then evil, clothed at last in the form of the divine Grace she had so forcefully denied, could assuage her pain and give her the certainty that she and her mortal essence had lived and suffered right up until the very last. But then, standing in that almost pitch-black cellar, I realized that Ana Meneses was no more. I leaned over to close her eyelids and, while I cannot be sure, I do not think I saw in her face any sign of the peace we associate with the dead.

Lúcio Cardoso (1912-1968) is one of the leading Brazilian writers of the period between 1930 and 1960. As well as authoring dozens of novels and short stories, he was also active as a playwright, poet, journalist, filmmaker, and painter. Within the history of Brazilian literature, his oeuvre pioneered subjective scrutiny of the modern self, bringing to the fore the personal dramas and dilemmas that underlie perceptions of collective existence.

Margaret Jull Costa is one of the most acclaimed translators of modern times. She has translated dozens of works from both Spanish and Portuguese, including the works of Javier Marías, José Saramago, Eça de Queiroz, and Fernando Pessoa, among many others. Her translations have received numerous awards, including the International IMPAC Dublin Literary Award, the Oxford-Weidenfeld Translation Prize on three occasions, and the Portuguese Translation Prize. In 2014 she was made an Officer of the Order of the British Empire.

Robin Patterson was mentored by Margaret Jull Costa, and has translated *Our Musseque* by José Luandino Vieira.

Benjamin Moser is a writer, editor, critic, and translator, as well as the new books columnist for *Harper's Magazine* and a frequent contributor to the *New York Review of Books*. He has published translations into English from the Dutch, French, Spanish, and Portuguese, and is the author of *Why This World: A Biography of Clarice Lispector*. He currently resides in the Netherlands.

Inga Ābele (Latvia)
High Tide
Naja Marie Aidt (Denmark)
Rock, Paper, Scissors
Esther Allen et al. (ed.) (World)
The Man Between: Michael Henry Heim & a Life in Translation
Bae Suah (South Korea)
A Greater Music
Svetislav Basara (Serbia)
The Cyclist Conspiracy
Can Xue (China)
Frontier
Vertical Motion
Lúcio Cardoso (Brazil)
Chronicle of the Murdered House
Sergio Chejfec (Argentina)
The Dark
My Two Worlds
The Planets
Eduardo Chirinos (Peru)
The Smoke of Distant Fires
Marguerite Duras (France)
Abahn Sabana David
L'Amour
The Sailor from Gibraltar
Mathias Énard (France)
Street of Thieves
Zone
Macedonio Fernández (Argentina)
The Museum of Eterna's Novel
Rubem Fonseca (Brazil)
The Taker & Other Stories
Juan Gelman (Argentina)
Dark Times Filled with Light
Georgi Gospodinov (Bulgaria)
The Physics of Sorrow
Arnon Grunberg (Netherlands)
Tirza
Hubert Haddad (France)
Rochester Knockings: A Novel of the Fox Sisters
Gail Hareven (Israel)
Lies, First Person
Angel Igov (Bulgaria)
A Short Tale of Shame
Ilya Ilf & Evgeny Petrov (Russia)
The Golden Calf
Zachary Karabashliev (Bulgaria)
18% Gray
Jan Kjærstad (Norway)
The Conqueror
The Discoverer
Josefine Klougart (Denmark)
One of Us Is Sleeping
Carlos Labbé (Chile)
Loquela
Navidad & Matanza
Jakov Lind (Austria)
Ergo
Landscape in Concrete
Andreas Maier (Germany)
Klausen
Lucio Mariani (Italy)
Traces of Time
Amanda Michalopoulou (Greece)
Why I Killed My Best Friend
Valerie Miles (World)
A Thousand Forests in One Acorn: An Anthology of Spanish-Language Fiction
Iben Mondrup (Denmark)
Justine
Quim Monzó (Catalonia)
Gasoline
Guadalajara
A Thousand Morons

WWW.OPENLETTERBOOKS.ORG

Elsa Morante (Italy)
Aracoeli
Giulio Mozzi (Italy)
This Is the Garden
Andrés Neuman (Spain)
The Things We Don't Do
Henrik Nordbrandt (Denmark)
When We Leave Each Other
Bragi Ólafsson (Iceland)
The Ambassador
The Pets
Kristín Ómarsdóttir (Iceland)
Children in Reindeer Woods
Diego Trelles Paz (ed.) (World)
The Future Is Not Ours
Ilja Leonard Pfeijffer (Netherlands)
Rupert: A Confession
Jerzy Pilch (Poland)
The Mighty Angel
My First Suicide
A Thousand Peaceful Cities
Rein Raud (Estonia)
The Brother
Mercè Rodoreda (Catalonia)
Death in Spring
The Selected Stories of Mercè Rodoreda
War, So Much War
Milen Ruskov (Bulgaria)
Thrown into Nature
Guillermo Saccomanno (Argentina)
Gesell Dome
Juan José Saer (Argentina)
The Clouds
La Grande
The One Before
Scars
The Sixty-Five Years of Washington
Olga Sedakova (Russia)
In Praise of Poetry
Mikhail Shishkin (Russia)
Maidenhair
Sölvi Björn Sigurðsson (Iceland)
The Last Days of My Mother
Andrzej Sosnowski (Poland)
Lodgings
Albena Stambolova (Bulgaria)
Everything Happens as It Does
Benjamin Stein (Germany)
The Canvas
Georgi Tenev (Bulgaria)
Party Headquarters
Dubravka Ugresic (Europe)
Europe in Sepia
Karaoke Culture
Nobody's Home
Ludvík Vaculík (Czech Republic)
The Guinea Pigs
Jorge Volpi (Mexico)
Season of Ash
Antoine Volodine (France)
Bardo or Not Bardo
Post-Exoticism in Ten Lessons, Lesson Eleven
Radiant Terminus
Eliot Weinberger (ed.) (World)
Elsewhere
Ingrid Winterbach (South Africa)
The Book of Happenstance
The Elusive Moth
To Hell with Cronjé
Ror Wolf (Germany)
Two or Three Years Later
Words Without Borders (ed.) (World)
The Wall in My Head
Alejandro Zambra (Chile)
The Private Lives of Trees

CPSIA information can be obtained
at www.ICGtesting.com
Printed in the USA
JSHW021821060922
30096JS00003B/4

9 781940 953502